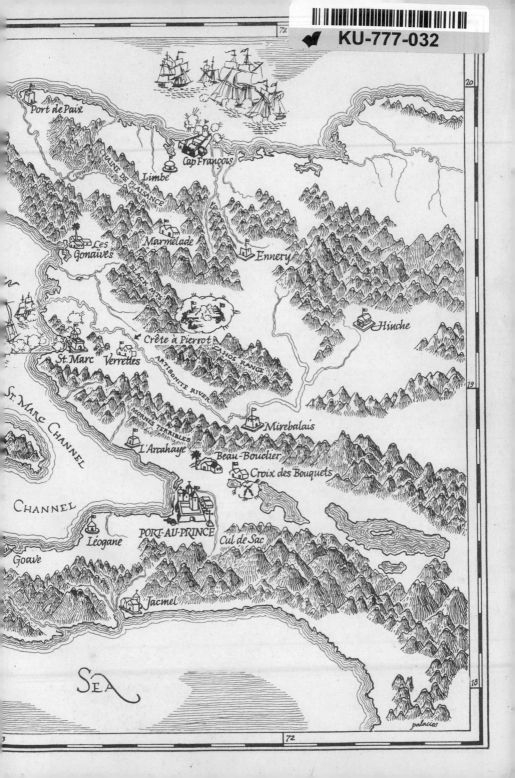

LYDIA BAILEY

LYDIA BAILEY

by

KENNETH ROBERTS

COLLINS
14 ST. JAMES'S PLACE LONDON
1947

COPYRIGHT
PRINTED IN GREAT BRITAIN
COLLINS CLEAR-TYPE PRESS : LONDON AND GLASGOW
1947

To Ben Ames Williams
in gratitude for patient assistance
in a struggle
that long seemed hopeless

ACKNOWLEDGMENTS

For their generous and unfailing help, the author is profoundly grateful to Major A. Hamilton Gibbs, Middleboro, Mass.; Mrs. Elizabeth C. Moore, New York City ; Major John Houston Craige, Philadelphia ; Clara Claasen, Doubleday & Co.; Marjorie Mosser, Kennebunkport, Maine ; P. M. Hamer, National Archives, Washington ; Robert C. Gooch, Elsie Rackstraw, Colonel Lawrence Martin and Harold W. Glidden, Library of Congress ; Lt. Com. M. V. Brewington, Office of Naval Records & Library, Washington ; Milton Lord and John J. Connolly, Boston Public Library ; Clarence S. Brigham and Clifford K. Shipton, American Antiquarian Society ; E. N. Brandt, *Saturday Evening Post*; Coert Du Bois, Ruth B. Shipley and E. Wilder Spaulding, Department of State ; Sylvester Vigilante, New York Public Library ; R. W. G. Vail and Dorothy Barck, New York Historical Society ; Charles K. Bolton, Shirley, Mass.; Edwin J. Hipkiss, Boston Art Museum ; John Oliver LaGorce, National Geographic Society ; Rupert Hughes, Los Angeles ; Dean Harry J. Carman, Columbia University ; Grace Trappan and Mrs. George Merriam, Portland Public Library ; Charles Wellington Furlong, Cohasset, Mass.; Everett E. Edwards, Department of Agriculture ; Charles S. O'Connor, Clerk, Supreme Judicial Court, Boston ; Mrs. Alexander Burr, Kennebunk, Maine ; Newman F. McGirr, Columbia Historical Society, Washington ; Elinor Gregory Metcalf, Boston Athenæum ; Florence M. Osborne, Essex Institute, Salem ; Atty.-Gen. Frank I. Cowan, Portland, Maine ; Professor William Thomson, Harvard University ; George Graves, Massachusetts Horticultural Society ; B. Y. Morrison and S. F. Sherwood, Bureau of Plant Industry, Beltsville, Md.; James S. Allen, Clerk, U.S. District Court, Boston ; Bruce Chapman, New York City ; Walter G. Davis, Maine Historical Society ; W. J. Eckert, Navy Department, Washington; Robert Hale, House of Representatives ; Philip G. Hodge, U.S. Information Service ; Senator Wallace H. White.

FOREWORD

I'M NOT over-enthusiastic about books that teach or preach, but I may as well admit in the beginning that my primary reason for writing this book was to teach as many as possible of those who come after me how much hell and ruin are inevitably brought on innocent people and innocent countries by men who make a virtue of consistency.

All the great villains and small villains whom I met so frequently in the events I'm about to set down were consistent men—unimaginative men who consistently believed in war as a means of settling disputes between nations ; equally misguided men who consistently believed that war must be avoided at all hazards, no matter what the provocation ; narrow men who consistently upheld the beliefs and acts of one political party and saw no good in any other ; short-sighted men who consistently refused to see that the welfare of their own nation was dependent upon the welfare of every other nation ; ignorant men who consistently thought that the policies of their own government should be supported and followed, whether those policies were right or wrong ; dangerous men who consistently thought that all people with black skins are inferior to those with white skins ; intolerant men who consistently believed that all people with white skins should be forced to accept all people with black skins as equals. And I know that any nation that cannot or will not avoid the dreadful pitfalls of consistency will be one with the dead empires whose crumbling monuments studded our battlegrounds in Haiti and in Africa.

My first great lesson in the perils of consistency came from my uncle, who was Colonel William Tyng of Falmouth in the Province of Maine—the town whose name was later changed to Portland.

He was a lawyer and shipowner, patron and erector of St. Paul's Church, First Master of the Falmouth Lodge of Free Masons, Sheriff of Cumberland County, and colonel by virtue of a commission from Governor Gage. Prior to the Revolution, he had taken repeated oaths of allegiance to the King and Government of Great Britain, and, since he had a low opinion of men who refused to fulfil their obligations or their oaths of allegiance, he remained loyal to the King when the Revolution broke out in 1775. As a result he was branded as a Tory, his home was plundered of its plate and valuables, and he and his family—with the exception of his mother-in-law—took refuge with the English in New York.

His family consisted of his wife, his wife's sister (who was my mother), and my father, Albion Hamlin, for whom I was named. My father was Colonel Tyng's cousin, and had gone to sea as a cabin boy in one of the colonel's ships, had captained that same ship at the age of nineteen, and

9

had then been put in charge of all my uncle's shipping interests, not only the building of the ships, but planning their voyages and cargoes. After he moved to New York he became an officer in DeLancey's Third Battalion, a Loyalist regiment, and I always think of him as dressed in that uniform of green faced with orange, smart-looking in spite of being patched, darned, and faded from innumerable marches and battles.

All my uncle's property was confiscated by the Portland rebels, of course ; but since he had befriended many Portland men during his life in New York—among other things effecting the release of Edward Preble from the Jersey prison ship—he held the affection and regard of those in high places. Consequently his lands were sold for a nominal sum to his mother-in-law, Madam Ross, who continued to live undisturbed on the family farm in Gorham. They even allowed Madam Ross to buy my uncle's three slaves as well ; for in spite of all their consistent preaching about Liberty, Freedom, and Equality, the rebels thought slavery was a good thing under certain circumstances for certain sorts of people.

At the end of the Revolution, when Loyalists by the thousand left New York and New England to take refuge in New Brunswick, Nova Scotia, and Canada, my uncle went with them ; and my father, my mother, and I went too, in the transport *Martha*, which carried the officers, men, and families of DeLancey's Third Battalion and Maryland Loyalists. On the voyage the *Martha* struck an uncharted rock off the southern tip of Nova Scotia ; and, since there were only enough boats for the women and children, the two regiments were drawn up in company formation on the deck of the sinking vessel while the women and children were handed into the boats. All but three of the men were drowned. I think of those regiments whenever those who consistently call themselves Liberal speak contemptuously—as they consistently do—of Tories.

I was ten years old at the time, but I can see my father now, on the deck of the *Martha* in his old green-and-orange uniform, walking up and down along the front of his company. We were lying off in a long-boat, and the *Martha* was rammed high up on the sunken rock with her stern sinking deeper and deeper into the water. We could see him talking to his men, holding them steady, I suppose ; and when the ship slipped off the rock like a vessel sliding down the ways, a sort of shining image of him and his men stood there on the empty sea. That's how I always see him when things look dark—a figure in shining green, walking steadily in the face of danger and sharing his courage with his friends.

So my father died ; and a few weeks later, as a result of shock and exposure, my mother died too, and I was left in my uncle's care.

In return for his sacrifices for the Crown, my uncle was given a grant of land in Queen's County, New Brunswick, and made Chief Justice of the province. He also acted as mediator between the Loyalists and the Home Government in arranging the settlement of wild lands ; and people all up and down the river regarded the big square house he built at White's Cove as a sort of royal palace.

I had the run of my uncle's small but excellent library, ranging from the works of the historian Josephus to the *Travels* of William Bartram, and instruction in French from an impoverished Frenchwoman who had been driven from Nova Scotia when the French residents of that unhappy country had been scattered to all parts of the world by Boston troops. Thanks to her I was able, by the time I was fourteen, to earn my keep by working in my uncle's office, writing his letters, keeping his letter-book up to date, entering in his day-book the troubles and the complaints of the Loyalists who were perpetually at him for advice and help, and recording the exaggerated claims of the French Canadians, whose chief object in life seemed to be to get the better of Loyalists by fair means or foul—preferably foul.

On winter nights, to help the entire family with the French tongue so necessary to a resident of Canada, my uncle had me read aloud from the only decent French book to be had in New Brunswick—a French biography of Christopher Columbus ; and before I'd finished the story of that amazing navigator, I could roll up a French verb in the back of my throat and blow it out through my nose as boldly as though I'd eaten frogs from infancy.

Now the Loyalists who forsook the United States for New Brunswick at the end of the Revolution were fine people, who had elected to be loyal at a time when loyalty was visited by persecution, certain ruin, and probable death ; and in partial recognition of their loyalty the British Government promised to help establish them in their new homes. The promises, unhappily, weren't kept. The necessary food, seed, tools, never arrived on time or in sufficient quantities, so that the situation of the Loyalists was often desperate.

Since my uncle was a man of integrity, he resented England's failure to fulfil her obligations to the Loyalists, and his resentment grew with every passing year. In 1793, when I was twenty years old, one of the towns on the St. John—a town half logs and half canvas—burned to the ground at the beginning of winter, and ship after ship came out from England without supplies for those poor people, or tools to enable them to build new dwellings. That was more than my uncle could stand, and he sent an ultimatum to the Colonial Office.

Every person in that town (he wrote with an angry hand and a sputtering pen) has fought for the King, frozen for the King, starved for the King, worked his fingers to the bone for the King. They're starving, they're dying of exposure while His Majesty's ministers and clerks roast their fat buttocks before glowing fires, and froust so late between feather mattresses that they can't find time to help better and more deserving people. For years I have humbled myself to His Majesty's Government, begging the bare necessities of life for people who sacrificed everything to keep the British Empire together ; but all I've been able to get them are idle promises, forgotten as soon as

made. Any scarecrow would be as efficient a Chief Justice as I, and
accomplish as much for the deluded people whose loyalty, I now strongly
suspect, was grossly misplaced. It becomes my unpleasant duty to
demand that all supplies listed in my past five letters be dispatched
immediately. Failing this, have the kindness to replace me immediately
as Chief Justice of this province and as Mediator for Wild Lands, for
my resignation from both offices will be automatic.

The supplies didn't come ; so after my uncle had stayed through the
winter and done everything he could for those unhappy people, he
distributed all his possessions on the St. John to neighbours up and down
the river, and with his wife and me sailed straight back to Portland, where
he was made welcome and the title to all his lands returned to him : the
farm in Gorham, on the outskirts of the city, and even the enormously
valuable strip of land across the middle of Portland Neck, from the harbour
to Back River.

My uncle was welcomed, on his return to Portland, because of the
politics of the time, which were violent and bitter.

In 1775 he had been driven from the city for being loyal to the
government he had sworn to uphold. In 1794 he was received with open
arms because he had been loyal to England in 1775 ; for Portland was a
Federalist stronghold, and the Federalists, fearing that the ideas of the
French Revolution might become popular in America and so cost them
their newly acquired wealth, had fallen in love with everything English
because England was at war with France—which shows how political
principles for which men die in a given year are relegated to the attic the
following year, along with childhood playthings, old fashioned dresses,
broken furniture, and dusty love-letters.

Like everybody else in Portland, my uncle considered himself a
Federalist when he first came back from New Brunswick. He certainly
considered himself so while Washington was still President ; and at first,
after John Adams became President, Colonel Tyng was willing to agree
with the Portland people who were forever telling each other that those
men were America's greatest sons, patient, wise, tolerant, well worth
following in everything : that John Adams was a great President, a
bulwark against Jacobinism. He was willing to agree, too—at first—with
all the Portland people who were everlastingly damning Thomas Jefferson's hellishness and the frightfulness of Thomas Jefferson's Republican
party. Jefferson was a Jacobin, the Portlanders said, because he sympathised with France and the successful effort of the French people to rid
themselves of the aristocrats.

New England's fear of Jacobins was beyond belief. The section was
full of merchants, shipowners, manufacturers, landowners, who had
amassed fortunes since the Revolution. They mistakenly thought that
their wealth made them aristocrats, so they were in constant agony

lest the violence of the French Revolution should spread to America, and all aristocrats be guillotined, as in France—or at least deprived of their homes, their fortunes, and their high positions.

The worst of all epithets, to their way of thinking, was "Jacobin"; and we soon found that anybody who opposed a wealthy New Englander, any admirer of Thomas Jefferson, anybody who refused to do as the Federalists wished him to do, anybody who voted against a Federalist, anybody that New Englanders disliked, was a Jacobin, an outcast; a dirty, ignorant, worthless, dangerous, bloody Jacobin.

My uncle had no quarrel with that argument—not at first. As for me, I didn't care. I knew one thing and I was determined to be consistent about it at all hazards : my father, my mother, and my uncle had originally been driven from their homes and their country for political reasons, and as a result my parents had died. Politicians had murdered them, and I had no use whatever for politics or politicians, no matter who they were. This dislike was so profound that it even led me to view the entire legal profession with a jaundiced eye. It was painfully evident that most politicians were lawyers, and I never worked on a case without fearing that the hair-splitting forced on every lawyer might some day make me willing to split hairs in matters that had nothing to do with the law.

I didn't care, even, when Congress passed the Alien and Sedition Law and my uncle began to rage at the Federalists' iniquities. "What in God's name are they thinking of?" he'd shout in the privacy of our law office. "Why, damn these damned, ruthless, self-seeking——"

His tirades wearied me, and I closed my ears to them.

It made no difference to me that President Adams was determined to keep himself and his pet politicians in office at all costs. The truth was that I wasn't much interested in any one but myself at just that time—a state of affairs that may have been partly due to believing that my heart was broken, something that almost any young man can understand if he will send his mind back to the period when he used to go calling on Sunday afternoons.

I didn't want to hear about petty politics, governmental waste and extravagance, or the willingness of Portland Federalists to condone such things ; so I was overjoyed when my uncle, in disgust over man's stupidity, decided to retire to his five-hundred-acre farm in Gorham and take me with him to do the actual farming of his acres. All I wanted, I thought, was freedom from politics, space in which to escape those who discussed political matters.

Farming, I thought, was simple and easy, and any one could be a good farmer. This was what I thought at first, in my youthful ingorance. But when I went to neighbouring farmers for advice on ploughing, planting, fertilising, milking, and all the multifarious activities of a farm, I found their ignorance as bad as mine, and in its consistency, even more appalling. That was how I came to make the acquaintance of Jared Eliot's *Essays upon Field Husbandry in New England,* Samuel Deans's *New England Farmer,* James Anderson's great *Essays on Agriculture,* Lord Kames's masterly *Gentleman Farmer,* and Arthur Young's monumental *Course of Experimental Agriculture.* Those books gave me a heightened appreciation of the true worth of land and the magic that results when it is properly treated. They taught me the dreadful consequences of ploughing up and down hills, so that the soil is washed away ; the need of ploughing at right angles to every slope, to prevent erosion and to increase the size of crops ; the benefits of using lime lavishly and often ; the need of fertiliser ; the necessity of repeatedly ditching fields so that water can never stand upon them ; the reasons why crops should be planted in rotation ; the benefits to be gained by restricting cattle to small sections of meadows and moving them frequently ; the absurdity of the superstitions that attach, in farmer's minds, to every phase of farming ; and a thousand other things of which city dwellers never have the slightest inkling. Best of all, those books taught me the value of experimenting.

My first year was one of mistakes, mishaps, and discouragement ; but from then on I was perpetually amazed at the endless wealth that rewarded our industry and study. The shelves of our rock-walled cellar came to be stacked with jars of preserves, crocks of butter, and boxes of maple sugar ; bottles of ketchup, maple syrup, and cucumber relish ; bags of beans and field-peas ; ducks and chickens in kegs of lard. We made an ice-house, with ice-cakes set solid between the outer walls, and in it we hung saddles and legs of lamb and mutton, succulent hams, shoulders and back-bacon from corn-fed pigs, beef that melted in the mouth, smoked geese and turkeys, smoked salmon from the Kennebec, fat bear-haunches for mince meat.

My aunt was a great hand to work, and from the flax we raised she wove endless yards of linen for shirts and sheets and tablecloths.

When in the third year, I really began to get the hang of farming, I was happier than I had ever been before and thankful that I had given up the law and no longer had to plead the cases of contentious clients before sleepy judges. My uncle made me a present of half the farm: I was dependent on nobody, and no day was sufficiently long to let me do the things I wished to do. As a result of my following the advice of Kames, Young, and Anderson, all our fields took on a lushness that seemed miraculous, for their lushness held during droughts. And, best of all, I was my own master and free of politicians.

At last, I said to myself, I was doing something that was worth while, something I wanted ardently to do—and if I lived to be a million years old, I wouldn't move an inch or lift a hand toward anything that would embroil me with politics or politicians.

I was going to be consistent, and that was all there was to it—consistent, like the farmer who ploughs up and down hill because it's easier ; like the farmer who burns the dry grass on his fields because the burning makes them greener than unburned fields, though it ruins them in the end ; like the farmer who continues to take crops from the soil without putting anything back. I realised that the stupid consistency of those farmers was wrecking their land and wasting their substance ; but I couldn't see beyond farming—I couldn't see that my own consistency was just as ruinous and stupid as theirs.

CHAPTER I

On AN autumn evening in 1800, the four of us—my uncle, Colonel William Tyng ; his wife, my Aunt Emmy ; my aunt's mother, Madam Ross ; and I—were sitting around the big table in the sitting-room of our Gorham farm when we heard a horse's hoofs rustling in the drifts of maple leaves on our driveway. Aunt Emmy looked at me and asked, " Who's that, Albion ? " as if she suspected me of having second sight.

When I went to the door to find out, a bow-legged man swung himself groaningly from the saddle, felt tenderly of his back, and said he wanted to see Judge Tyng. He added that he was Hopestill Hicks of Boston, employed by the *Independent Argus*, and that he had an important message for Judge Tyng from Thomas Bailey. As he spoke, he drew a paper from his pocket and wagged it in my face ; but when I made as if to take it from him, he hastily snatched it back.

" You ain't Judge Tyng ! " he said.

" I'm his nephew, Albion Hamlin," I said.

" I don't give a damn if you're the Prophet Ezekiel," he said. " This goes into the hands of Judge Tyng and nobody else, and Thomas Bailey told me to stick to the Judge till he writes an answer to it."

I knew Thomas Bailey, from hearing Portland Federalists talk about him, as editor and owner of the *Independent Argus*, a paper forever doing its utmost to stir up trouble by publishing diatribes excessively offensive to Federalists and the Federalist Party, and by declaring flatly that the Federalist Party did not, as it claimed to do, contain all the rich, wise, and good men in the country.

" Tie your horse to the hitching post," I said. " I'll get my uncle."

Hicks spat copiously and contemptuously. " Hitching post be damned ! The Judge'll be all night figuring out his answer to this-here message, whether he wants to or not. Where's the barn ? My horse goes in a stall along with a peck of oats and a mess of clover ! "

My Aunt Emmy brought Hopestill Hicks a pitcher of milk, a plate of cornbread, a pat of sweet butter, and four cold pigs' feet, and he sat beside the fire chewing noisely while my uncle read us the letter from Thomas Bailey.

" Honoured Sir (it ran) : You don't know me, but I know of you from my friends General Henry Dearborn of Maine and John Langdon of new Hampshire, whose political views, unless I have been misinformed, are the same as yours and the same as mine. I know that you were a Loyalist during the Revolution, that you were robbed of your property in Portland for your Loyalist leanings, that you took your family to

New Brunswick after the Revolution and were made Chief Justice of
that Province. I know why you resigned as Chief Justice and returned to
Portland. I know you were made welcome there, and your property
restored, because of your English sympathies, now so entrancing to
those very Federalists who hated England so violently during the
Revolution. I even know, Judge Tyng, why you gave up your law
practice in Portland and retired to your farm in Gorham.

"Of all men in this country, you have best learned how reason and
truth vanish when men grow mob-minded. You are well aware that the
Federalist legislature of Massachusetts has placed politics above
patriotism by refusing to declare the Sedition Law oppressive and
unconstitutional, which means that reason and truth are once more
being obliterated in this country.

"That law will never be repealed until the Federalist Party is
thrown out of office and the Republican Party of Thomas Jefferson put
in power. Until then, no man and no newspaper can print the truth
without persecution and abuse. While it exists, a free press is impossible
in America, and Federalist waste, extravagance, and wrongheadedness
will daily become more strongly entrenched. I believe you must agree
with me that the Sedition Law is a greater threat to the liberty of free
men than the British King and all his ministers could ever have been,
for it makes us slaves to the Federalist Party.

"Sir, I implore your help. You have been a great Chief Justice, a
steadfast guardian of all men's rights, regardless of party. You are
my only hope, for in all New England not one fair-minded jurist
remains upon the bench. My own strength, owing to a lung complaint,
has failed me when I need it most. Give me, sir, an outspoken opinion
of the Sedition Law, pointing out that it is neither right, reasonable,
necessary, nor constitutional, so that those of us who still cling to
our freedom may be furnished with the ammunition of your thoughts
and words. Because I know the vindictiveness of the Massachusetts
Federalists, you may depend upon me not to reveal your identity. I
have sent you a dependable man who will accurately take down your
comments, and your identity will be kept a secret. Do not fail me, sir.
Only a free press can maintain the majesty of a people.

"Believe me to be, sir, your obedient, admiring and desperately
urgent servant,

"THOMAS BAILEY."

My uncle, when he had finished reading, got up from his chair
stiffly, as though his joints and muscles pained him, glanced fretfully
from me to Aunt Emmy and Madam Ross, then went to stand in front
of the fire. That stiff movement of his was a characteristic one, and I
didn't like it.

"I hope you spotted the weakness in that letter, Uncle Will," I said.
"He says he'll keep your identity secret, but of course he can't."

" Why can't he ? " my uncle demanded.

" Because such information always leaks out. Hicks tells some woman friend——"

" Me ? " Hicks asked. " I ain't got any—not any regular ones, that is."

" Another thing," I said.   " If he keeps your identity a secret, the opinion's no good ; it might as well be written by any sailor or brewer, or by Bailey himself. Well, why not let Bailey write it ? "

" The man's a whiner," Aunt Emmy put in. " He says he's sick, but he's well enough to write a letter as long as a snake's tail."

" Silence ! " my uncle roared. " Order ! " He glared at her, then turned to me. " You know as well as I do why Bailey can't write it or get anybody but me to do it. Bailey doesn't know enough about constitutional law ; and, as he says himself, there isn't a judge in Massachusetts whose brain and judgment haven't been ground into pulp and sawdust by that damned Alien and Sedition Act ! "

He turned irascibly to Hicks. " Why didn't he say how long he wanted it ? How do I know how long an opinion he can use ? Constitutional ? Of *course* the Sedition Law isn't constitutional ! Why, good God, I could write an entire book on its damnable injustices—oh the narrow-minded, contemptible, shortsighted, treacherous, cowardly, idiotic asses who wrote such twaddle and called it legal ! "

Hopestill Hicks took a pig-bone from his mouth and tapped it on the table to emphasise his words. " You tell me what to say, and we'll do the worrying. If you want eight columns, take eight columns."

" Eight ! " my uncle shouted. " I can't say what I want to say about the Sedition Law in eight columns—no, nor in eighty ! Why, that law permits the arrest of honest men for daring to speak up when Congress does something wrong ! But when did Congress ever do anything right ? It'll never do anything right. Congressmen never do anything that won't get votes for themselves. They no sooner get into Congress than they have to lie, hedge, and trim so they can be re-elected ! Look at the men in this Congress ! Look at the men in the President's Cabinet ! Perjurers ! Petty thieves ! Liars ! Dastards——"

" Oh, Colonel Tyng ! " Aunt Emmy protested.

Hopestill Hicks, in the middle of a draft of milk, rapped sharp knuckles on the table and swallowed convulsively, like a turkey downing a giant grasshopper. " *That's* the stuff ! " he cried. " Dastards ! That's practically the exact word for 'em ! Only one letter wrong ! Dastards ! That's what Bailey wants ! We'll run it on the front page—two solid columns : we'll set it pica ! " He smacked his lips.

" Pah ! " my uncle said. " Two columns ! "

" You can say a lot in two columns," Hicks reminded him. " I never stuck type on the Bible, but I figure that the whole story of the Flood, from gopher-wood ark to dry ground, was just about two columns."

My uncle glared at him, then at his wife, mother-in-law, and me, as was his custom when his mind was furiously at work. I saw that he actually intended to give Hicks the opinion for which Bailey asked ; and, recalling the physical and mental misery my uncle, my aunt, and my own parents had suffered for years for daring to defy openly the opinion of the majority, I made one more effort to stop him.

"If you give Bailey an unbiased opinion," I said, "and he prints it, he'll be jailed. Then you'll feel obligated to go to Boston to defend him, and before you know it you'll be in a mess up to your ears."

"By the Lord Harry," my uncle shouted, "you talk like a wet-nurse ! If the Sedition Law had ever touched you directly, you'd feel a damned sight different ! "

"I propose to take good care it *doesn't* touch me," I said ; "but it's going to touch you if you do what you're figuring to do."

"You're worrying about your own security," my uncle said. "You're afraid something'll break in on your peace and comfort here on the farm. So's Emmy. So's Madam Ross."

"Yes," I said, "and why not ? You gave up your law practice in Portland and moved out here to this farm because you couldn't listen to your Federalist friends in silence, didn't you ? Of course you did ! You knew that if you spoke your mind, your friends would in all likelihood become enemies overnight, and you and your family would certainly suffer ! Why in God's name should you mix in politics ? I've heard you say repeatedly that when peoples and nations go mad, any sensible man will keep his own counsel, buy a farm, and live in peace and plenty. What's wrong with taking a little thought about our security ? "

"Because there's *no* security except in a tranquil mind," my uncle said. "Because any man who, by so much as the blink of an eye, permits himself to condone injustice, has forever lost all hope of tranquillity—and Bang ! goes his security with it."

"I don't see it," I said.

My uncle nodded. "No, I guess you don't. Not now you don't ; but you will ! "

"But why should you consider yourself to be the one man ordained by Providence to speak out ? " Aunt Emmy asked. "Seems to me you're attaching undue importance to your own ideas ! "

Hicks, who had produced a travelling pen-case and a package of paper from an inner pocket, cleared his throat, rattled his pen against his inkwell, and said, as if in time to the words he was writing on the sheet, "Noted Jurist Calls Sedition Law Unconstitutional ! "

"Exactly ! " my uncle said. He glared at Aunt Emmy and then, before our eyes, changed from an irate husband to a sober judge, eyed Hicks threateningly, and embarked on his opinion in the same measured tones I'd heard so often in New Brunswick.

"The Constitution of the United States expressly commands the Congress to make no law abridging freedom of speech or of the press. In violation of this express command, Congress has passed the Sedition Law ;

and the Sedition Law does exactly what the Constitution forbids. It abridges freedom of speech and of the press. Consequently this law is not constitutional and is void——No objection to that, is there, Albion ? "

"I think you're deliberately asking for trouble," I said.

"Pish ! " my uncle said. "(Don't put that in, Hicks.) Now, then : when Massachusetts ratified the Constitution, she plainly asserted that liberty of conscience and freedom of the press could *not* be cancelled, abridged, modified, or restrained by the United States. Yet the United States, in the Sedition Law *has* abridged, modified, restrained, and cancelled liberty of conscience and freedom of the press, and the Massachusetts Legislature has assented to it."

"I suggest leaving in the ' Pish,' " I interrupted.

"Look here, Albion," my uncle said. "When I want your opinion, I'll ask for it."

"If you don't listen to some of our opinions, you may find yourself in no position to ask us for them."

"That's my look-out," my uncle said.

"I'm not at all sure of that," I said. "Aunt Emmy and Madam Ross and I think it may prove to be *our* look-out before you're finished."

My uncle started to say something, caught himself, and turned to Hicks. "Put down that the Federalist Party and the Massachusetts Legislature have thus authorised and condoned the very injustices that the authors of the Constitution sought to prevent. The Federalist Party is at the height of its prosperity and power, both in Massachusetts and in the nation. It controls the Senate. It controls the House. Yet it is inevitable that any party which thus uses its power and prosperity to force injustices upon the people must perish."

"Don't forget to put in about the dastards in the Federalist Party," Hicks said. "You take Timothy Pickering. *There's* a first-class dastard ! A failure at everything, and everybody knows it—a failure as a farmer, as a lawyer, as a merchant. Hell, he was even a failure at teaching the violin ! So he's Secretary of State, and working his brain to the bone to get us into a war with France ! That's how you can tell the President's a real dyed-in-the-wool dastard ! He picks dastards to advise him and act for him, and only a dastard can stand dastards around him."

"There you go, Uncle William," I said. "You're willing to have your opinions interpreted by an intemperate man."

"Intemperate ! " Hicks cried. "Who wants to be temperate about those dastards ! "

"Colonel Tyng," Aunt Emmy said, " I appeal to your better nature ! "

"Ladies," my uncle said desperately, " you'll do me the kindness to retire. You know nothing about the Alien and Sedition Law, and yet you have the presumption to attempt to influence me in my attitude toward it ! That's a woman for you ! There's nothing on earth she isn't willing to deliver an opinion on ! "

Aunt Emmy and Madam Ross silently left the room, their backs eloquent of impotent resentment.

Hicks turned on me furiously. " What's intemperate about telling how Oliver Wolcott never did anything in his life but live on public money ? He spends his days being a dastard, and his nights figuring out ways to get this country to fight France, so he's Secretary of the Treasury ! What's intemperate about saying James McHenry got to be Secretary of War because of being the outstanding mediocrity of all time ? That ain't intemperate ! That's cold fact ! "

" Well, what of it ? " I asked. " You can't stop 'em from being dastards by calling 'em so ! I say it's damned nonsense to howl and yell about something you can't remedy."

" By God, Albion," my uncle said, " if I hadn't brought you up to have your own opinions and act on your own judgment, I'd speak pretty plainly to you. Why don't you go to bed where you belong ? "

" For the same reason I don't leave a sheep to freeze in a snowstorm," I said. I knew his temper was near the breaking point, and there was just a bare chance of so distracting him that he'd stop his dictating and perhaps—in a day or two—change his mind.

He only glared at me, however, turned back to Hicks and calmly resumed dictating. " Let us examine the Sedition Act and the reason for its passage. What is the Sedition Act ? It is an act providing for a fine of no more than two thousand dollars and imprisonment for no more than two years for the writing, printing, uttering, or publishing of any false, scandalous, or malicious writing or writings against the Government of the United States, or against the President, or against any members of his Cabinet, or against any member of the Senate or the House of Representatives, or against any of the government's policies or lack of policies in regard to anything."

" Oh, for God's sake," I said, " what if it is ! A law that's no good is bound to be repealed or ignored eventually. You can't change it by rushing into print with all this twaddle."

" ' Twaddle ? ' " my uncle cried. " ' Twaddle ' that the Federalists of New England conceived the Alien and Sedition Law, and enacted it, because they consider themselves chosen by God to regulate the affairs of the nation and of the entire world ? (Put down that pen, Hicks !) Twaddle that the Federalist Party numbers among its members practically all New England shipowners, manufacturers, merchants, and landowners who have grown rich since the Revolution ? (I'm not talking to you, Hicks !) Twaddle that these windbags consider they hold a monopoly on the wisdom and goodness of America ? Twaddle that they think they're the aristocracy of America and are trying to perpetuate themselves by law ? "

" Well, isn't it twaddle ? " I asked. " Do you think for a moment that these nincompoops can perpetuate themselves ? Why, hell and damnation, they'll be dead and forgotten in four years' time, and it takes four years to build an asparagus bed ! "

" What's an asparagus bed got to do with it ? " my uncle shouted. " No : don't tell me ! Shut up ! Put this down, Hicks. In passing the Sedition Act, the Federalist Party had only one object in view—to stifle all criticism of the Federalist Party. It wished to destroy the Jacobins, the Jeffersonians, the radicals, and the democratic foundations of the United States with one deadly blow ; and so crushing and so comprehensive is the Sedition Act that it virtually abolishes the Bill of Rights, those first ten amendments to the Constitution which specify that Congress shall make no law abridging freedom of speech or of the press, which secure the people against unreasonable searches and seizures, which safeguard life, liberty, and property, which entitle accused persons to trial by an impartial jury."

" Now see here," I said, " you're scaring yourself half to death with an imaginary bogey ! Nobody's going to abolish the Constitution with just one act ! "

" Damn it, Albion," my uncle shouted, " they *have* abolished it ! You just don't know a damned thing about the cases that have been tried under the Sedition Act ! I *knew* you weren't listening to me when I told you about 'em ! "

" I never made any secret of it," I said. " Nobody'll read this long-winded stuff you're giving Hicks, either."

" By God," my uncle said, " they'd better, and *you'd* better ! We've had a regular reign of terror under the Sedition Act. Matthew Lyon of Vermont was prosecuted for writing that he couldn't support President Adams and his party . . . (All right, Hicks ∙ write this down and I'll make it a speech.) . . . because under Adams every consideration of the public welfare was swallowed up by a continual grasp for power, by an unbounded thirst for ridiculous pomp, foolish adulation, and selfish avarice—all of which was true. He was prosecuted for saying that men of real merit were daily turned out of office for daring to think independently —which was evident to every man in possession of his senses. He was pilloried for saying the Federalist Party was doing its utmost to promote hate and persecution among mankind—which was an understatement. The indictment against Lyon charged him with stirring up sedition. He had *not* stirred up sedition : he had merely committed lèse majesté by criticising the President. Yet Lyon was convicted, fined one thousand dollars, and sentenced to four months in jail. There, by God ! (No, no, Hicks ! That's an aside !) I suppose *that's* long-winded, Albion ! "

" So far as I'm concerned," I said, " it is. Lyon was probably an ass who deserved all he got."

My uncle hopped with rage. " Open your mind, you stubborn pup ! Look at Anthony Haswell, editor of the *Vermont Gazette*, tried for daring to print an advertisement saying that Lyon was being badly treated in prison ! They called his advertisement seditious, if you can believe it, and he was fined two hundred dollars and thrown in jail for two months ! I suppose *he* was an ass ! Thomas Cooper, editor of a Pennsylvania newspaper, criticised President Adams for political ineptitude, and *that*, by God, was lèse majesté ! They fined him three hundred dollars—no, come to remember, it was four hundred—and gave him something like six months in jail. Was *he* an ass ? Can't you see, you young fool, that since the Sedition Act is a direct attack on our civil liberties and the Bill of Rights, it must inevitably destroy the democratic features of the Constitution ? Can't you see that the right of free speech is basic to all other democratic rights ? Can't you see that where free opinion ceases, tyranny begins ? "

" Free opinion isn't going to cease in this country for any length of time," I said. " There couldn't be any free opinion during the Revolution —except on the rebel side—but it reappeared afterward."

My uncle shook his fist at me. " All over the United States men have been jailed, fined, and persecuted by Federalists for daring to express their opinions freely ! (Put this in, Hicks, by James !) If you can't get mad over that, I'm ashamed of you ! If it's permitted to continue, if Federalists are permitted to remain in office, are permitted to destroy the principles for which the American Revolution was fought, then republicanism in America is dead, freedom in America is dead, and the United States is nothing but a despotic oligarchy ! That's as simple as A-B-C, and anybody not a damned fool will admit it ! "

I was afraid he was right, but I didn't want to think about it. In fact, I was determined not to think about it ; I wanted peace and security too much to think about it. So there was nothing for me to do but bow as dignifiedly as possible and march upstairs to bed, leaving the two of them rumbling at each other far into the night.

CHAPTER II

THERE was no doubt whatever in my mind that if my uncle hadn't written that opinion for the *Independent Argus,* Bailey himself would have written a similar one, or got somebody else to do it, and would have been arrested just as promptly. My uncle certainly wasn't to blame for his arrest, as I saw it ; but I couldn't make my uncle see it that way. The moment he heard Bailey had been arrested for publishing the opinion, he told my aunt to pack his bag : he was going to Boston to act as Bailey's lawyer.

" Colonel Tyng," my aunt said—which was how she always addressed him, extremely formal, as though they weren't too well acquainted, " Colonel Tyng, it's folly for you to do any such thing—folly pure and simple ! You know as well as I do that your kidneys couldn't stand any such coach trip ! "

The Colonel gave her a frosty look. "Emmy," he said, "I'll thank you to leave my kidneys out of this ! As for a coach trip, you're the only one talking about any such thing. I'll go up to Boston in style in the captain's cabin of Tom Oxnard's brig, and I guess the Atlantic Ocean's big enough to take up any slack in my kidneys ! "

"Albion," my aunt said, "don't stand there like a bump on a log ! Speak to your uncle ! "

"I certainly will," I said. "Uncle Will, you're under no obligation whatever to rush to Bailey's defence. I've heard you say a hundred times that you'd never run after your own hat when it blows off, because somebody else'll always pick it up and bring it back."

"Look here, Albion," my uncle said, "I don't like your attitude in all this ! I'm doing what I think is right, and nobody worth his salt lets a mere kidney stand in the way of doing what he considers right ! "

He went stamping off, and to Boston he certainly would have gone if —in lumbering down the front stairs with an armful of law books he proposed to take with him—he hadn't missed his footing, and pitched all the way to the bottom, putting his knee out of joint, spraining his ankle, and coming within an inch of apoplexy. His groans were agonising to hear, and I was glad that I could get away from them by pelting off for the nearest doctor ; but my anxiety was tempered by profound relief that his accident would definitely put an end to his determination to defend Thomas Bailey.

But I had forgotten how indomitable my uncle could be. The doctor and I got back to find he had dragged himself, with my aunt's help, all the way upstairs and into bed ; and the doctor had no sooner got an opium pill into him and snapped his knee back into place than my uncle asked when he could go to Boston.

"Boston ! " the doctor cried. "Good grief, man, why make so much trouble over a little thing like suicide ? If you're determined to kill yourself, do it quietly with a pistol ! Or, when I'm not looking, help yourself to some laudanum out of my bag ! Boston ! Good God ! "

"I'm going to Boston," my uncle said.

The doctor put down the bandage he was winding around my uncle's ankle. "We'll settle this right now, Judge ! You won't move out of this bed for a month ! You'll give me your word to that effect, or I'll tie you down with ropes and put two men in this room to see you don't come untied ! I swear to God I'll have you wrapped in a wet sheet and committed ! Do I make myself clear ? "

My uncle grunted and closed his eyes. The doctor glared at him ; then picked up the bandage and went on with his winding. As he left, I heard him shouting to Aunt Emmy to hide my uncle's clothes—lock his bedroom door and nail down the windows—take any steps necessary to keep him in bed.

My uncle groaned, opened his eyes, kicked at the bedclothes with his good leg ; then raised himself on an elbow to look at me. "Lock up my clothes, eh ? " he said. " Just try it if you want to see me knocking at the neighbour's doors, stark naked ! Albion, get me some clothes ! Somebody, by God, has got to go to Boston, and that means me."

I just laughed, but I laughed too soon ; for he instantly threw back the bedclothes and laboriously swung one leg over the side of the bed. Seeing what was in his mind, I picked up his clothes, threw them into the hall, and changed the door-key from the inner to the outer side.

" You lock that door," my uncle said, " and I'll break the glass in the window and crawl out if I have to cut my ass to ribbons ! Somebody, by the Lord Harry, has got to defend Thomas Bailey ! "

That violent and determined old man never called on the Lord Harry except in moments of dire need. He meant what he said : no doubt of that.

" All right," I said. " All right ! Let's discuss this whole business like two reasonable human beings."

" Well," my uncle said grimly, " don't do too much discussing ! I got to get started for Boston." He drew the bedclothes over his legs once more, groaned, and then said, " Oh, by the way : did I tell you that Bailey was to be tried before Justice Chase of the Supreme Court ? "

" Yes, you did, and he could be tried before Lord Chancellor Bloody Assizes Jeffreys for all I care ! That's no occasion for you—or for me either, because you needn't think I don't see what you're driving at— to get mixed up in this case."

" Driving at ? "

" Yes, driving at ! You think you're going to talk me into going to Boston in your place, and taking on Bailey's defence, just because I won a few cases before Judge Pettigrew. Well, I may have been a lawyer then, but I'm a farmer now, and I'm staying a farmer ! "

My uncle groaned again. " Chase," he said, " is a strange character. Frightening ! Lawyers are afraid of him, and for excellent reasons."

" What's more," I said, waving aside his attempt to cloud the issue, " we've got seven acres of land to plough, stump, lime, and harrow before the ground freezes, and it'll never be done unless I'm here to do it."

My uncle seemed not to hear me. " Chase was as violent a rebel, during the Revolution, as ever lived. There's just one word to describe him, and that's ' tumultuous.' He can smell a tumult a month in advance ; and when it arrives, there's Chase in the centre of it."

" To hell with Chase ! " I said.

" Just be quiet a minute, Albion. I want you to visualise this skunk Chase. He made his own father take a compulsory oath of allegiance to the rebel government ! He carted a batch of Philadelphia Quakers three hundred miles to a prisoners' camp in the dead of winter because they growled a little at the rebels' new order of things. A delegate to the first Continental Congress he was, and always in a fight ! He went to Canada with Benjamin Franklin and Charles Carroll of Carrollton to try to swing Canada to the rebel side in the Revolution—though all they did was pretty near destroy the rebel army. He was a signer of the Declaration of Independence."

" He's got nothing to do with me," I insisted. " I don't care if he signed the Ten Commandments ! "

My uncle snorted. " You don't, eh ? Well, you'd care if the Chases of this world should get their way ! This great rebel Chase changed his mind overnight, and began to hate all revolutions. Since Jefferson sympathises with the French Revolutionaries, Chase hates Jefferson. Since I admire Jefferson and despise everything John Adams stands for, Chase hates me too. He'll hate every one that stands up for Bailey or argues against the Alien and Sedition Law. He's even left the bench to make speeches against Jefferson ! A Supreme Court Judge leaving the bench, for God Almighty's sake, to make political speeches ! There's *nothing* he won't do to keep Federalists in power, and that's why he'll tear Bailey's counsel to pieces ! That's why a man's got to be a fighter to get anywhere with him."

" Now listen," I said. " These meadows have got to be limed this fall, and you well know that if I'm not here to do it, you'll never be able to persuade Eddie and Owen to put on half enough lime. What's more, low spots on this farm must be drained, or the hay'll winter-kill."

" Oh, be-helled and be-damned to your lime, for God's sake," my uncle shouted. " To hell with your low spots ! To hell with your drains and your winter-kill and your bloody hay ! What do you want to do, anyway ? End up squeezing a cow's teats and squawking ' Heh ! Heh ! Heh ! Ninety-nine years old, b'gosh, and still able to shovel manure with the boys ! ' What's cow food when a man's freedom's at stake ! "

" Don't ' freedom ' me," I said. " That damned fool Bailey wouldn't have any freedom anywhere in the world, except to make trouble for others. Look at the way freedom's used around here ! If I go to Boston, the hired men will feel free to talk you into ploughing instead of harrowing, and you'll feel free to wreck a root-crop it's taken me three years to build up ! "

" I believe, by Heaven," my uncle cried, " that you're scared to go to Boston ! I believe you haven't got the gumption to stand up before that old scoundrel Chase ! " He sighed and his voice quavered. " You remember your father, don't you, my boy ? "

" Leave my father out of it," I said. " I'm not a half-witted Suffolk County jury, that goes all starry-eyed when you pour somebody's aged father or grey-haired mother into its ears."

" Is that so ! " my uncle shouted. " I've only got your word for it that you're not half-witted, and that's not evidence ! I'm talking about something that's important to you, or ought to be, but you can't get away from hay and manure and pigpens ! A farmer can be a gentleman part of the time, at least ; but you, by the Lord Harry, you're helled and limed and harrowed and manured the whole damned time ! Well, go ahead and stick your head into your lime and manure ! I'm going to Boston if I have to be carried there on a stretcher and without a damned thing on me but Emmy's lace pants—which you'll soon be wearing yourself if you don't stop talking like an old woman ! "

I studied for a time. My uncle had made me really angry, no doubt of that. " Well," I said finally, " I came pretty close to losing my temper just then. I guess we'd better stop arguing because, if I had really lost it, hell nor high water couldn't have got me to Boston ! "

" You intended to go all the time, didn't you ? " my uncle asked.

" Oh, I suppose so," I said slowly. " Though I don't relish the idea of being put to a lot of trouble by a man I don't give a damn about."

" Listen, Albion," my uncle said. " I'm afraid I went a little too far myself when I said that about hay and manure and pigpens. I didn't mean a word of it. You've made a fine farm out of this place—and, since I know what it takes to do that, I can tell you something that's as certain as death and taxes : you may think you don't give a damn about Bailey ; but you will when you talk to him. An injustice to one man is an injustice to you and to the whole world."

CHAPTER III

THOMAS BAILEY lived in a three-storey brick house on Hanover Street. The name on the doorplate read FAULKNER, and it was Harriet Faulkner, mistress of the house and Thomas Bailey's cousin, who admitted me.

Mrs. Faulkner was a thoughtful-looking, dark-haired, dark-eyed woman perhaps a year older than I. When I first saw her, I thought her thin and austere, even scrawny. Her cheeks were hollow, and she had a long neck, and I told myself that there was something about Boston that put ice-water instead of blood into the veins of everyone in the whole frosty town.

When I said I wanted to see Mr. Bailey, she looked at me so coldly and asked my business so sharply that I disliked her manner even more than I disliked her looks ; and when I gave her what I considered a sufficiently complete answer, she studied me impassively and kept on asking questions : What was my age, was I married, who were my associates in Portland ? How had I come to know Mr. Bailey ? What were my politics ?

When she found me evasive, she told me abruptly that Mr. Bailey was ill—too ill to receive callers ; and I think that if I hadn't been firm with her she'd have contrived to shut the door in my face, making it look as though the door had closed of its own accord.

When she saw I was determined to come in, she turned on me a smouldering, smokey look that suggested she might possibly be less austere than I'd thought. As she preceded me up the stairs to the top floor, I saw she wasn't as thin as I'd thought, either. She had a willowy way of bending over, almost as though she hadn't a bone in her body ; there was

a pungent, powdery perfume about her when she moved, the odour of
orris-root ; and a dry swishing sound came from her skirts ; so that a
man's senses, unless he were blind, deaf, and noseless, were acutely
conscious of her.

I could see with half an eye that Harriet Faulkner took good care of
her lodger ; for when I got to the third floor I was shown into a sitting-
room that was neat as a pin, and strikingly furnished with oriental
objects—wall-hangings embroidered in gold and silver, a rug as beautiful
as a painting, a statue of a many-armed goddess wearing a crown set with
bluish stones across each of which moved a band of light, so that the statue
seemed to be watching me from a score of eyes. The windows, which were
spotless, looked across Boston harbour and the mouth of the Charles
River to Bunker Hill and the Mystic marshes. Beyond the sitting-room
was a bedroom. Harriet Faulkner opened the door, walked in, and gave
a twitch to the bed-clothes.

" Here's a man to see you about the trial, Cousin Thomas," she said.
She gave me a curiously penetrating look. " Mr. Hamlin wouldn't take
No for an answer, but I want to make it clear that he's not to tire you out
and get you to coughing."

. She stared me straight in the eyes and threw back her shoulders
defiantly. I saw then that her throat was as smooth and white as a child's,
and that her breasts were small and round instead of drooping, as I'd first
thought. There was something sleek about her, and restive, so that I had
an inclination to stroke her arm, as one might stroke an uneasy animal.

Most emphatically I'd been mistaken in Harriet Faulkner's thinness ;
but there was no chance for such an error about Thomas Bailey, for his
body, beneath the bedclothes, was like a bundle of long bones. His bushy
jet-black hair had receded from his forehead to the top of his head, to
form a sort of black halo. It was hard to tell his age, for his hollow cheeks
were flushed and his lips scarlet, as if he were all afire inside. He had been
scribbling on a pad of paper, laced together with shoestring, and the floor
near the bed was littered with sheets covered with sprawling writing.

When I told him I was Colonel Tyng's nephew and had come to
Boston at the colonel's expense to help defend him, he gave me a clammy
hand, motioned to the chair beside the bed, and spoke in a remote
whisper, as if his mind as well as his body moved on tiptoe.

" Very kind of you, my boy. Very kind of you and Colonel Tyng, too.
Most encouraging thing about the whole business is people's kindness.
Even some of the Federalists have been kind—a most interesting sign,
Mr. Hamlin. More and more people are finding out what we've found
out. They won't stand it much longer. No : not much longer ! But the
fact remains that they still *are* standing it ! They still can't understand
they've got to fight Federalist persecution ! They still can't understand
they'll never be free so long as all their judges are Federalists first and
judges afterwards." He started to cough, changed his mind, and held
his breath until his face was crimson.

Harriet Faulkner looked pleadingly at me, and I now realised to my amazement that she was almost beautiful.

" Wouldn't it be better if you didn't talk ? " I asked Bailey. " Wouldn't it be better if I put questions to you and you wrote the answers ? "

He shook his head emphatically. " No, I want to talk ! They're bound to kill me before they're through with me, so I'll have my say while I can. What is it you want to know ? "

When I looked doubtfully toward Harriet Faulkner, who had gone to stand at the window and seemingly intended to stay there, Bailey made a gesture of protest. " Don't hesitate to speak before Cousin Hattie," he whispered. " Cares for me like a sister. Say anything you like before Hattie."

Harriet turned from the window and fixed me with a level glance. " Cousin Thomas depends upon me, Mr. Hamlin. If anything happened to him and I shouldn't be here, I'd never forgive myself ! Never ! " She came to the side of the bed, picked up the scattered papers from the floor, pushed deftly at the sick man's pillows so that they were miraculously raised beneath his head, and made me so painfully conscious of her kindness and my own lack of perception that I got to my feet and moved to the head of the bed, so as to be out of her way.

Then for the first time I saw, hanging on the wall opposite the bed, a small portrait of a young girl, her hair black, parted in the middle, and gathered up in a little crown of curls, as if to let her pretty ear peep out, her eyes—which she might have just raised to meet my own—as blue as a far-off mountain on a summer evening, her shoulders sloping like those of a child, and her round arms a pearly pink against the purple velvet of her gown. Held lightly in her slender fingers was a miniature of a girl, even younger than she.

I make no pretence of knowing the whys and the wherefores of that peculiar mental state which leads a man to be fascinated by one woman to the exclusion of all others. With some men, apparently, it's due to their own inflamed imagination ; with others, a matter of persistent and ruthless action on the woman's part. In some cases, probably, the man is temporarily sick. I'm reasonably sure of only one thing : that there's no possible way to explain why a seemingly rational and sensible person should arrive at the inflexible conclusion that a given woman, often witless, sometimes misshapen, usually wholly helpless, is a paragon of all the virtues, a unique and veritable angel accidentally dropped out of Paradise. So I can't explain why I was affected by that portrait. I only know I felt a sudden desire to have it for my own.

To me there was something heartbreakingly gay about the almost smiling lips and the sidelong glance of the girl in the picture—something intimate and personal that caught so unexpectedly at my throat that when I tried to ask, " Who's that ? " I had to cough and try again.

" That *was* my niece, Lydia," Thomas Bailey said. " Lydia Bailey. She died last year in Haiti."

There was just a hint of Harriet Faulkner in the portrait, but there was also a quality of unquenchable youth that Harriet Faulkner certainly had never possessed. Even if the girl in the portrait had lived to be a hundred, she would have remained always young in mind and spirit ; whereas Harriet Faulkner had, I suspected, even as a child, been as old in wisdom and seriousness as the Cumæan Sibyl. Consequently, while the portrait faintly resembled Harriet, it wasn't *like* her at all. Harriet, when I had first seen her, had given me the impression of cold austerity, but the girl in the portrait couldn't ever have given any one that impression.

" What a pity ! " I said. " What a shame ! When—where did she—"

Harriet Faulkner, in the act of tucking in the sheets on the opposite side of the bed, raised reproving eyes to mine.

" Yellow fever in San Domingo—or Haiti, rather," she said. " We don't speak about it. It was a great blow to Cousin Thomas."

" I can well believe it," I said. " Yes, I can well believe it. She——"

Harriet shook her head warningly, came around the bed and placed her hand upon my arm. I could feel its warmth burning through my sleeve, and it had a weight and a clinging quality that were surprising in a woman I had thought angular and austere.

When I nodded apologetically and sat down again in my chair with my back to the portrait, Harriet put her hand on mine as if to thank me. Her hand fastened so strongly on my fingers that my eyes went quickly to her face. Since she seemed unconscious of my gaze, however, and left the room impassively, I told myself that I had been right in the beginning : she *did* have ice-water in her veins, after all.

I continued to be as conscious of that picture as though I were facing it. I could feel its smiling eyes silently urging me to look around ; silently begging me to understand the meaning of that sidelong glance. The impact of those eyes upon me was as physical a thing as the pressure of Harriet Faulkner's hand had been, and the pressure seemed to be upon my heart.

Thomas Bailey was speaking, but so disturbing was the influence of the portrait behind me that I couldn't concentrate on what he said until I turned my chair so that I could meet those pictured eyes.

" Briefly," Thomas Bailey said, " your defence should be based on the injustices already perpetrated under the Alien and Sedition Law. In my office you'll find a complete account of the Matthew Lyon case in Vermont—how the Federalists in that state persecuted and tortured Lyon for telling the simple truth about the ridiculous pomp and selfish avarice of President Adams."

Matthew Lyon ! That was the man of whom my uncle had spoken ! Persecuted and tortured ! My uncle hadn't made it clear, but it was clear to me now—though I'm not sure what made it clear : Thomas Bailey, or Harriet Faulkner's personality, or my unexplainable interest in that dead girl's picture. Whichever it was, I suddenly felt a hot indignation that

Thomas Bailey should have suffered from the workings of a law so indefensible, so barbarous as the Alien and Sedition Act—the law that until yesterday I had considered merely injudicious.

"Matthew Lyon," I repeated, entering the name in my case-book. Bailey sighed. " Make your blood run cold, the Matthew Lyon case will, but I doubt if you'll be allowed to mention it—not before a Federalist judge who'll do his utmost to protect that other Federalist judge who found Matthew Lyon guilty of telling the truth about politicians."

" I can try," I said. " No judge on earth can stop me from trying ! "

" I hope not," Bailey said. " I wish you could bring out how the Reverend John Ogden of Vermont was jailed because he dared to carry a petition to Congress in behalf of Matthew Lyon. I wish you could tell how a packed jury in Windsor, Vermont, sent Anthony Haswell to jail for two months because he said certain Federalist officials were worthless. I wish you could tell how Judge Chase imposed a year-and-a-half jail sentence and a four-hundred-dollar fine on an undefended man who dared to say a good word for Thomas Jefferson."

" I'll tell all of 'em," I returned. " Why shouldn't I ? "

" Well, they're court records, of course, witnessed and sworn to ; but if you try to get them before a jury with Chase on the bench, you may be put in jail."

" I'll do the worrying about that," I said, and I meant it. I could see that Bailey was a good man, deeply loved by Harriet Faulkner. I couldn't disappoint Bailey, or Harriet Faulkner, or that girl in the picture. No hardship, it suddenly seemed to me, would seem excessive if by undergoing it I could make people more aware of the enormities that Federalists were inflicting on them !

Bailey nodded, coughed, then rolled over on his left side to ease the violence of his coughing. He coughed and he coughed—great racking coughs that doubled him up. Fumblingly he brought out a handkerchief and pressed it to his lips. As if by magic the linen was splashed with scarlet, and he sank exhausted against the pillows.

" My God, Mr. Bailey," I said, " you can't stand trial ! What in God's name are these Federalist butchers trying to do to this country, anyway ! " Distressed by his condition, I got up to walk the floor.

" Wait," he whispered. " Always feel better after a little bleeding. Don't like to be left alone. Makes me depressed. Talk about something. Tell me about Portland—about anything that interests you. Old newspaper man like me finds it restful."

" I'll talk about you," I replied. " It's sheer wanton brutality to bring you to trial."

" Yes," Bailey murmured, " sheer wanton brutality. That's politics. Always consistent, politicians are—always descend to sheer wanton brutality, flavoured with idiocy, when they're threatened with loss of position or loss of power. Try to ruin everybody who's against 'em ! This wouldn't be a bad world if it weren't for the people in it."

He looked up at the little portrait of his niece. " Strange how things come about. Two years ago, you'd have thought nothing could happen to either of us. Now she's gone, and I soon will be."

" That's not true," I said. " Those who fight for what's right are never gone. They're always with us. Look at that picture ! She's not gone ! Why, she's on the verge of speaking."

" I know," Bailey said. " That's why I keep her in front of me all the time. Striking face, hasn't she ? "

" Yes," I said, " she has. I'll never forget her." It was true, though it didn't lessen my desire to have the portrait for my own, so that I could constantly refresh my memory of it. " But we'd better discuss the Matthew Lyon case," I said. " Was he——"

" No, no ! " Bailey said. " Does me good to talk about Lydia to someone who likes her picture. Looks a little like Hattie—just enough to upset her. Not that she'd ever show it. Too kind-hearted, Hattie is, to bear malice."

" I can see that," I said. " How did your niece happen to go to San Domingo in the first place ? "

" Well, she was teaching school in Philadelphia—a school that my brother David had started. He'd have liked me to help him, but I was a rolling stone—an irresponsible fool forever hunting romance in strange places. I went to India to publish a newspaper, and it took me five years to realise that there's mighty little difference between a newspaper office in India and one in Boston : merely hotter and dirtier, and a lot worse-smelling, and the typesetters don't wear anything but underdrawers and diapers—grown men, too. When I came back, David was dead and Lydia was alone in the world. Meanwhile she'd grown up into that——" He raised a listless hand toward the portrait.

" I wanted her to come to Boston and keep house for me, but Hattie thought it might make talk, and probably it would have. You know how people are about a girl as pretty as that ! Anyway, I always wanted to do something for her—felt uncomfortable because I couldn't do more. Had her on my mind a lot. The picture shows why, somehow."

" It does indeed ! "

" Yes," Bailey went on. " Well, a sea captain came to the office one day to put an advertisement in the paper. Friend of his in San Domingo —rich French planter—titled family—wanted a teacher and companion for his two little boys—big pay—fine opportunity. I said to him, ' Got just the one for you, and you won't have to pay for an advertisement.' So I sent word to Lydia and arranged her passage to San Domingo. That's how I happened to have that picture : she wouldn't let me pay for her passage unless I took the picture. It's not a bad painting, Mr. Hamlin. It was done by Gilbert Stuart, the Philadelphia painter, to pay for a relative's schooling—smaller than he usually painted, but that does it no harm. That miniature she's holding is Stuart's relative, who was greatly attached to her. Never knew anybody who *wasn't* attached to her, except——" He hesitated, started to cough again, but choked it down in a few seconds.

" You'll have to stop," I said.

He shook his head. " I'd rather talk. I should have done more for her before she went. I had some jewels—Indian rajah gave them to me because he liked something I wrote about him—two cat's-eyes, size of partridge eggs ; and ten rubies, one for each finger and two big ones for the thumbs. I didn't need 'em, and she might have used 'em. Don't know why I didn't give 'em to her, since she'd have inherited 'em in the end, anyway.

" Same thing's true of my twenty shares in the Barque *Kingfisher*. The damned French seized her in the West Indies when we wouldn't come to their help against the British, as we'd promised to do, and I'll never get a penny out of 'em. But there was Lydia right on the spot ; and if the shares had been hers, it wouldn't have surprised me at all if she'd got some sort of settlement out of the French. Able, Lydia was. If you were on the wrong side of an argument, she could make you feel pretty uncomfortable just by looking at you."

" What were the twenty shares worth ? "

" About sixteen thousand dollars. There were something like a hundred puncheons of rum in the cargo, and a lot of indigo."

" That would be quite a windfall," I said. " I suppose your Cousin Harriet inherits, now that your niece is dead."

" Yes," Bailey said. " Hattie'll get everything. She's been mighty kind to me ! A fine woman, always cheerful in the face of adversity."

" Where's her husband ? "

" Lost at sea," he replied. " They were on a voyage together, and he went overboard when they were crossing the bar at the mouth of the Mississippi. He never had a chance."

Bailey rolled over on his side and again burst into racking, wrenching coughs that splattered his handkerchief with bright blood.

I ran to the door, called Harriet Faulkner, and stood watching her as she hurried up the stairs and into the room, slipped the pillows from under Thomas Bailey's head, bathed his face and forehead, and murmured soothingly to him. She seemed an angel of mercy in very truth. When she looked up at me, she put her finger to her lips ; then held out her hand and clutched mine almost fiercely.

" It's not your fault ! " she said. " Don't think I blame you, Mr. Hamlin ! But abrupt visits are too difficult—too exciting. You must come to this house, Mr. Hamlin—make it your home ! Then he'll be used to you—it won't excite him so ! "

Even before I had a chance to protest, which I had no thought of doing, she again pressed my hand in a manner that forever put an end to any notion that she had even a thimbleful of ice-water in her veins.

B

That was the beginning of Harriet Faulkner's fascination for me, and of my attachment to her interests—an attachment that I can't exactly say I was to come to regret, since any sort of experience, no matter how unpleasant, is bound to be of value to any man capable of putting pen to paper.

CHAPTER IV

NOTHING was too much for Harriet Falkner to do for me in the days before the trial of Thomas Bailey. I had heard Aunt Emmy say that any woman of moderate intelligence, no matter how unprepossessing she may seem, can make a conquest of any man she wants, old or young, rich or poor, married or single, provided she wants him hard enough. If this *is* true, then I think that the principal weapons of such a woman are an eager responsiveness, a ready smile, an unfailing willingness to be of help, and openly expressed sympathy. Certainly Harriet Faulkner had all those qualities to a degree that I had never before experienced, and I was grateful for them—stirred by them, too.

After my uncle's return to Portland from New Brunswick, I had become (as I thought) engaged to a Portland young lady. Engagements are apt to be long in Portland, for some reason unknown to me ; and frequently they end by the engaged ladies' unexpectedly marrying sea captains or naval officers just back from long voyages. This is what had happened to me : the lady of my choice, who had been subject to occasional fits of the sulks and was admittedly averse to the dullness of farm life, had suddenly married one of the Shailer boys, just home from his first voyage to Spain. I wasn't heartbroken, but I was certainly discouraged by the traits the lady had shown.

Thus Harriet Faulkner's constant cheeriness, her watchfulness over my own comfort as well as over her cousin's needs, made Boston almost endurable. My only worry now was the Bailey case. For Aunt Emmy had written to say that Eddie and Owen had changed their attitude since my departure, and had been heard to speak disparagingly of farmers who doubted the efficacy of lime ; that my uncle had taken to hobbling to the barn three times a day, and had laid plans for clearing the alders from the long swamp and turning it into a five-acre fish pond—a piece of news that seemed to interest Harriet as much as it pleased me. No matter how early I might rise of a morning to work on Bailey's case, she was always up, always warmly cheerful, always ready with scrambled eggs as soft as curds, tinker mackerel broiled two minutes over glowing coals, doughnuts that melted in the mouth, and coffee with thick cream in cups that held a pint.

For another thing she came to me for advice, which is something that awakens any man to a woman's helplessness and to her finer qualities. It was her habit to wait until I'd finished work at night, and then to bring in a pot of steaming coffee and wedges of mince pie, juicy and redolent of rum. Over these welcome midnight suppers she told me with affecting frankness of her late husband, who had been an unperceptive man if ever there was one ; of her finances, which might have been worse ; and of her expectations when her cousin died—as of course he was sure to do, and soon.

"I'll be frank with you, Mr. Hamlin," she said. " My husband and I were unsuited to each other. He was a cold man, interested only in making money. He'd go on long vayages and leave me alone for months at a time, and when he returned he'd be as silent and distant as a stone post."

I thought he must have been a fool, and said so.

"No, he wasn't a fool." She hesitated for a moment. " He was an extremely smart man, Mr. Hamlin. I know he was actually far wealthier than seemed to be the case after his unfortunate death. He was lost at sea, you know."

"Yes, your cousin told me."

She sighed. " When his estate was settled, there wasn't the fifth part of what I'd expected. Not the fifth part ! In my opinion he had been carrying on with another woman in one of the ports he visited."

When I tried to express my sympathy, she stopped me. " I'm not complaining, Mr. Hamlin. It's not my nature to complain. I only mention such personal matters because I want your advice. Among my cousin's belongings are twenty shares in the Barque *Kingfisher*. The French seized her without reason——"

"I know all about that," I said. " My uncle and I were consulted on several French Spoliation Claims, three years ago."

"I knew it ! " she cried. " I said to myself last night, ' I *know* Mr. Hamlin can help me,' and how right I was—and how fortunate ! Mr. Hamlin, those shares had a value, my cousin believes, of sixteen thousand dollars. Is there any possibility of recovering that amount or any part of it in case I should inherit the shares ? "

"Yes," I said, " there'd be a possibility. Not a strong possibility ; but if a good lawyer worked hard on the case and saw the proper people in Washington, I think he'd get somewhere eventually."

Harriet leaned forward and spoke pleadingly. " Mr. Hamlin, I told you my unfortunate husband's estate was only one fifth of what I'd expected and hoped it would be. Even so, I'm comparatively fortunate. If I could add the value of the *Kingfisher* shares to my present capital, my path would be greatly smoothed. If my poor cousin should die, would you try to recover it for me ? Would you ? "

When I hesitated—not because I wasn't willing to accept her suggestion, but because lawyers are never supposed to show eagerness—she lowered her voice to a whisper. " I'd be forever grateful, Mr. Hamlin. Of course, I'd expect you to have the tenth part of the value of the shares if you were fortunate enough to collect anything. I'd expect to bear all expenses, too—and I'm sure you'd never have cause to regret your efforts to help me."

Her eyes widened as they gazed into mine, and I found it impossible to mistake her meaning or to look with disfavour upon it.

" You wouldn't want me to take it on a contingent-fee basis, would you ? " I asked, and I wasn't speaking seriously. " Some people think that's not ethical."

I was surprised at the glance she gave me. If I hadn't known her so well, I'd have sworn it was contemptuous. As it was, I felt it must be merely one of disappointment.

" I don't mean to say I won't take the case," I hastened to say ; and I added, though I hardly knew why, " If I *should* take it, would you let me have the little portrait of Lydia Bailey as my fee ? "

She looked at me oddly. " Why do you want it ? "

" Why ? " I repeated. " Why, because I—because it looks like you. Because it'll remind me of you."

Harriet shrugged. " *I* don't think it looks like me—not really. It's such a vapid face, always half-smiling at us behind our backs."

" That may be," I said, " but there's something about it that brings you to mind. If you'll let me have it, I'll take the *Kingfisher* case."

" Very well," Harriet said. " You may have it—and more too—after the trial."

I have no intention of inflicting on anyone a full account of that humiliating trial. I have often wished that I myself could forget every detail of the experience—the dusty damp smell of the court-room, which undoubtedly arose in part from the jurors' and spectators' habit of spitting on the dirty floor ; the stony stares with which the jurors watched poor Bailey, who lacked the strength to sit up straight and wasn't even allowed to have Harriet beside him ; the bitter rage of Nelson, the prosecuting attorney ; the almost murderous rapidity with which Chase slammed in our faces any door to justice for our client.

Only one thing made the proceedings endurable, and that was Harriet's presence. She was always in an aisle seat, as close to Bailey as she could get ; and her concern over her cousin was touching ; her eager attention to me irresistible. She had all that was needed, I thought, to make a man supremely happy, and I may have betrayed how I felt.

Chase was a giant of a man with so huge a backside that he seemed wedged permanently in his chair. He was bland-appearing, with pursed lips that looked as though they were mumbling cardamom seeds. Since he was heavy-eyed, with thin, bristly hair and a thin, bristly suggestion of a beard, he reminded me a little of Henry VIII. When he leaned forward to deliver an opinion—always an opinion that did rank injustice to Bailey or to me or to my two colleagues, Henry Grafton and Edwin Nicholas—his lips drew away from his yellow teeth, and his eyes popped wide open, so that I was reminded of Henry VIII gnawing a bone and dripping gravy on his doublet.

Just a little of the trial should be enough to show what confronted us. When the jurors were called, we proposed to challenge any man who had read the article in the *Independent Argus*, and formed or expressed an opinion on it.

But Grafton had no sooner put the question to the first juror than Chase was at Grafton with bared teeth. " That question," Chase said, " is improper and you shall not ask it ! The whole state has read the case and very probably formed an opinion. If I indulge you in putting the question, men would be misled by your ingenuity, and the traverser might never be tried."

We did our best to find a way to exclude at least a few violent Federalists from that jury ; but Chase gnawed and snapped at us until we were helpless with fury before this violent politician who protected himself from attack by shouting that our every challenge was inspired only by politics. In the end we had no choice but to accept a jury who had long ago tried and convicted Thomas Bailey in their minds.

On the very first day, Grafton retired from the case. Nicholas lasted two days longer—until Chase refused to admit our best piece of evidence : a letter written by John Adams at the beginning of the Revolution, inveighing against any encroachment on the freedom of the press. " It is improper," Chase said in overruling our motion to read this paper, " to submit to a jury speculative productions, written at a period of disorder and commotion, however respectable and illustrious the author from whom they emanated."

That finished Nicholas. He put away his papers and sat in stony silence, unwilling to defer longer to such a judge.

Chase's greatest spleen was reserved for me, perhaps because of my youth ; perhaps because Grafton and Nicholas had chosen to conduct the case in their own way and to ignore most of my suggestions—an attitude not calculated to add to my stature in the eyes of anybody, particularly a judge of Chase's calibre ; perhaps because he knew my uncle had been Chief Justice of New Brunswick ; most of all, perhaps, because I didn't look at him when I rose to sum up.

The truth was, I didn't dare look at him. I hated him and his injustice so profoundly that I couldn't have looked him in the eyes without showing my feelings and thus spurring him on to greater injustices. It seemed to me, during that summing-up, that I would never live through it without exploding with rage.

" Your honour and gentlemen," I said, when I rose to face the jury, " our defence of Thomas Bailey has been more than the defence of an individual. It has been a defence of the people of the United States of America against encroachments on their liberty."

Judge Chase threw himself back in his chair and cast his eyes upward, as if asking Heaven to witness his martyrdom.

" The men responsible for the liberation of this country from England's
rule," I went on, " were never quite able to live up to their own high
standards. They argued that men must have freedom to think as they
wish, and to speak as they think. Without that freedom, said this country's
leaders, political truth could be neither discovered nor disseminated. They
held that a country can't be happy unless it has liberty, and can't have
liberty unless it has courage. They held public discussion to be a political
duty, and an inert people to be the greatest menace to a country's freedom.

" That was what they preached, but not at all what they practised.
The leaders of the Revolution practised the suppression of all opinion that
ran contrary to their own. They encouraged the imprisonment, the tarring
and feathering, the banishing, yes, even the killing of men who dared to
say they saw no adequate reason for fighting England—although at this
very moment, only twenty-five years later, there are men of wealth, men
of high position, throughout New England who are ready to persecute,
to imprison, to banish, or in any other convenient manner to silence those
who dare to say that this country has no adequate reason for fighting a
war in behalf of England. Thus, in the space of a quarter-century, has
public discussion been encouraged and liberty protected ! "

Judge Chase picked up his gavel and tapped it on his desk. " This
court cannot permit a political harangue in the guise of a summing-up.
May I remind you, young gentleman, that this court is not the hustings,
and that you are not soliciting the votes of the jury for the position of
Public Executioner on the Jacobin ticket ? "

" Your honour," I said, and I kept my eyes on his hairy fat hands so
I wouldn't have to see his scowling face, " I'm interested in no man's
vote, except to see that he has a right to cast it without interference ;
and my only interest in any political party is my interest in seeing that it
is willing to protect the people's liberties."

" Your intention, sir, is clear," Judge Chase said. " You are maligning
the Chief Executive of the United States and the government itself. Your
government, sir, must not be subjected to the attacks of small, ignorant,
and uninformed men. Your duty, sir, is to have faith in your government.
Yet you deliberately imply that it is acting without proper reason, without
a knowledge of the country's present necessities and future needs. I warn
you : this is sedition ! I shall permit no such partisan attack in this
court, no such treasonable utterances ! "

I opened my mouth to protest against this *petitio petendi*, this arguing
in a circle, for the very case itself challenged the assumption that free
criticism constitutes sedition ; but I closed my mouth when I saw the
faces of the jurymen. Nearly all those men were Federalists, as I had good
reason to know because of our vain efforts to get a few non-Federalists
on it ; and yet every one of them was staring at the floor, embarrassed
by this travesty of a judge, or gazing contemplatively at his boots, or
eyeing the ceiling. I realised that further protest would be futile, so I
merely bowed to Judge Chase. " With your honour's leave," I said.

The judge gave me a contemptuous wave of his hand. " You may proceed, Mr. Hamlin. But remember this : I've been patient so far, even when you have mocked slyly at the properly constituted authorities who are conducting the affairs of this country with wisdom and justice. Such underhanded attacks, sir, are not to be countenanced by honourable men. They are stabs in the back, sir, from one who has, by implication, stabbed his own country in the back on another occasion. I refer to the fact that your family were Tories when every decent man in America was a Patriot."

The court-room was so still that a single bluebottle fly, frenziedly thumping and buzzing against a window pane, sounded as noisy as a child's drum. Every face—barring Harriet Faulkner's—looked either blank or actually hostile. Harriet's hands were clasped together, her eyes bright with anger ; but, so far as I could tell, she was the only person in the room besides myself who was desperate with rage at the judge. By now I realised that I'd lost my case, and I made up my mind that I might as well be hanged for a sheep as for a lamb.

I turned to the jury. " Gentlemen, it is commonly said that your fathers fought for liberty. Not only did they fight for it—they gained it ; and in gaining it they won the perpetual right, according to the Declaration of Independence, to life, liberty, and the pursuit of happiness. That liberty, gentlemen, is now in dire peril, and unless you arouse yourselves you will surely lose it.

" Thomas Bailey has already lost it. He has been denied the liberty of saying what he wishes to say in his newspaper. He is fighting here in this court to regain that liberty. I pray you, gentlemen, to remember that liberty, once lost, is almost impossible to regain. Remember that no matter how much you may want liberty, you can't win it *or keep it* without fighting for it. If you're afraid to fight for it ; if you lack the public spirit to exert yourselves in behalf of it ; if you're too careless or too indolent to realise when you're losing it ; if, gentlemen, you let yourselves be cheated of your liberty by clever tricks or laws ; if for a moment you relax your hold on liberty because of discouragement, because of panic, because of a persuasive leader, even when that leader is the President of the United States——"

Judge Chase half rose from his chair to bang his desk with his gavel and cry, " That will do, young gentleman ! "

" If for a moment you relax," I repeated—and I had to shout to make myself clearly heard above the thumping of Judge Chase's gavel—" if for a moment you can be coaxed, forced, bribed, or cheated into trusting your liberties to that one leader, then you are unfit for liberty ! "

Judge Chase was standing, and so were all the lawyers within the bar and all the spectators outside it. " I fine you four hundred dollars for contempt of court," the judge thundered.

The court-room was a babel of confused shouting, of cries of encouragement, of angry denunciations, and I raised my voice.

"As an American, I've been guaranteed by the Constitution of the United States the freedom to express my mind, just as Thomas Bailey, by that same Constitution, is guaranteed freedom to express his. For God's sake, gentlemen, look around you ! Courts everywhere are silencing and jailing Jeffersonians, suppressing free speech, striking down the liberty of the press——"

Judge Chase's voice cracked with rage. "Bailiffs ! Arrest this man ! "

Two uniformed officers with staves were pushing through the excited people, and as I took a firm hold on the rail of the jury box I noticed tears on Harriet Faulkner's cheeks.

"The fundamental law of America is outraged by this judge and by the laws he's enforcing," I shouted. "Those laws were passed as an experiment on the American mind—an experiment to find out whether you'll suffer in silence an avowed violation of the Constitution ! If you don't reject——"

The bailiffs had me by the shoulders, pulling at me, but I held fast to the rail. "If you don't rise against it," I went on, "if you don't repudiate it and its authors, you'll see immediately another Act of Congress declaring that the President shall continue in office for life ! "

I felt my coat rip in the bailiff's hands. Then the rail gave way ; my hands slipped from it and I was dragged ignominiously through the crowd and out of court.

CHAPTER V

I HADN'T been wrong when I was sure I had lost Bailey's case. From my cell on the second floor of the Suffolk County Jail I heard the poor man brought in, coughing and coughing ; heard him taken upstairs and along a corridor opposite the one my cell was on. As I listened to the key rattling in the lock, the coughing went on and on, interrupted only by the breathless silences that meant horrible bursts of spattering bright blood.

The sound of that coughing beat upon my brain like hot hammers, and my inability to do anything to help Bailey drove me into a frenzy. I shouted for a prison guard ; listened in vain for a reply ; shouted again at the top of my lungs. Then I rattled my cell door and bawled and bellowed until the inmates of the other cells set up an opposition roaring of their own, telling me hoarsely to shut up, wanting to know if Mama's boy had hurt his finger, and calling affectedly, "Guard, guard ! Please come in and sing me to sleep."

I waited until they'd stopped their hooting ; then I got as close to my cell door as I could and spoke to them earnestly.

"Listen ! " I said. "Listen carefully and you'll hear the coughing of a dying man, sent to this prison by a rotten judge for doing nothing whatever except trying to tell the people the truth about rotten politicians and their rotten politics. I'm that man's lawyer, and I'm here because I tried to protect him in court before that same rotten judge. I'm sorry to interrupt your meditations, or your naps, or any games you may be playing ; but I want all of you to know that I'll do my best to tear this damned jail to pieces if they don't let me go to that client of mine and do what I can to ease his last hours. I wasn't making that racket just out of cussedness ! "

When nobody said anything, I went to the standing bed-place in the corner of my cell, threw the straw mattress on the floor, and contrived to kick off the side-board from its supports. Using this as a flail, I beat the cell door with it, all the time bellowing for the guard, so that the uproar was deafening.

That did the trick and two guards instead of one came running up from the floor below. " Here, here, for Jesus' sake ! " one of them shouted. " Any more of that and you'll get yourself rolled in a stays'l and have a bucket of slops jammed down over your head ! "

" Now look," I said. " Do you know who I am and why I'm in here ? "

" Contempta court," said the same guard. " Using disgusting language to a Soo-preme Court judge. Also four hundred dollars' fine."

" Yes," I said, " that's near enough to show you that I'm not a menace to society."

" I dunno about that," the guard said cautiously. " Fellers can't go sassing judges in court without making other people think that maybe everybody can sass judges. Then where'd we be ? "

" Listen," I said firmly. " Chase put me in here because he's determined to destroy free speech in this country and to punish every man who insists on using it. Are you in favour of free speech ? "

" I dunno whether I am or not," the guard replied ; " but by God if you go to busting up these beds, I'll put you in a strait-jacket. Those beds cost money, by God."

" But," I told him, " all I want is to be allowed to leave this cell long enough to help my client, Thomas Bailey—the man you can hear coughing himself to death."

" The doctor's with him," the guard said. " There ain't nothing you can do for him."

" That's not the point. The point is that he's my client and I'm not a criminal. He needs me, and there's no reason he shouldn't have my help. Will you be an honest man, a merciful man, and let me go to see him ? "

" How in hell can I do any such thing ? " the guard demanded angrily. " You're in jail ; and when you're in jail you're in jail ! You can't go running around like a damned goat ! You're a prisoner, and it ain't for me to let you stop being one."

" I see," I said. " If you had the authority, you'd probably do what I ask ; but since you haven't the authority, you aren't willing to do something that might get you into trouble."

" That's about it."

"Then get the sheriff for me," I said. "The sheriff can do anything he wants in this jail."

The guard snorted. "Who, me? Me bother John Riley? Goddle-mighty, John Riley's too big a man to bother with little stuff like this!"

Not all the talk in the world, I realised, would get me anywhere with this pig-headed man, and I suspected that if I weren't careful I'd find myself in solitary confinement, where I'd be of no use to Bailey or anyone else.

"It's not so little as you think," I said. "I don't believe all these other men around me think it's so little, either. I think I could persuade them to do me the favour, of saying so. Maybe if they started kicking their doors and shouting for the sheriff, he might decide to take a hand in it himself."

My words had an instantaneous effect. From every cell came thunderous bangings and demoniacal howlings which sent the two guards running from door to door, threatening the inmates with dire punishment.

Thus freed from scrutiny, I took pencil and paper from my pocket, scrawled Harriet's name and address at the top and wrote:

> Give the bearer five dollars when this is delivered. Your cousin is dying. Get somebody capable of standing in front of the jail and raising public hell with the sheriff himself.

I knotted a silver dollar in one end of my handkerchief and tied the other end around the note. Then I picked up the side-board from the bed-place and with it smashed a hole in the high barred window of my cell. I heard the guards behind me bawling angry warnings, heard the key rattling in the door; but by the grace of God I contrived to hang the handkerchief over the edge of the board, push it through the broken window and disengage it before the guards could get their hands on me.

I spent that night in solitary confinement in a black and windowless cell to which no sound could penetrate.

The same two guards took me out the next morning, and I could tell from the look on their faces that something had happened.

"Are you going to let me see Bailey?" I asked.

"It was like I told you," the spokesman said. "You couldn't 'a' done a thing for him. He died last night."

Not another word did they say as they took me back to the cell from which they'd hauled me on the day before. The window was broken still, but the bed had been fixed. I gathered that the guards regretted the harshness with which they had treated me, for when, half an hour later, a tumultuous shouting and thumping arose from the street outside, the spokesman brought me a high-seated chair from which I could peer through the broken pane and see a part of what was going on in the street below.

The cause of the turmoil was a raffish-looking old man with stringy grey hair, angry eyes, wrinkled stockings, a soiled snuff-brown suit, and a long black cane. At his elbow stood Harriet Faulkner, and on both sides of them were onlookers, all listening with obvious respect to his angry voice.

"What I have to say," he shouted, "is going to be said to you, John Riley, and in public!" He shook his black cane at the jail entrance. "Open that door like a man, Riley, or I'll stand here till every citizen of Boston is packed into this street! Then I'll tell what I know about all the things that have happened since you've been High Sheriff of Suffolk County." He stamped forward and beat upon the jail door with his cane until the whole outer world seemed a-clatter.

I heard the double clank of the bolt; then the creaking of hinges, followed by a mellow voice, the voice of an orator-politician. "Now then, sir, nobody in Boston wants any trouble with Sam Adams, so just you be off quietly, sir, and save me the trouble of using force."

So that was Samuel Adams! That was the man who, single-handed, had kept alive the spirit of rebellion in the American colonies, and by his persistent demagoguery had brought on a war that resulted in the deaths of untold thousands and the banishment of other thousands. He looked as if he hadn't had a decent meal for a week, a clean shirt for a month, or a moment's happiness in a decade.

"Force!" Adams cried. "You try to use force on me and I'll blazon it to high heaven from every street corner in this town! Try to force me to conform to your ideas of right and wrong, John Riley, and I'll raise such a dust in all New England that you and your jail and your judges will be blown to Hell, Hull, and Halifax!"

He thumped his cane upon the cobblestones. The crowds on either side shuffled their feet and stared unwinkingly at the jail door.

"What I've got to say," Adams went on, "I can say in a few words. In this jail you've been holding two men who deserve the gratitude of every citizen of this country, and I want you and your jailers and the whole world to know exactly what I think about it! Those two men were deprived of their liberty because they did their best to save liberty for all of us—for you as well as for me! They were thrown into this jail because a bad law and an unjust judge dared to say that none of us have the intelligence or the right to question the decisions or the acts of the few men who accidentally govern this country. When you consent to hold those men in your jail, you're as much as saying that a chosen few are justified in forcing the whole world to do as they see fit. Are you one of the chosen few, John Riley? Do you for one moment imagine your position gives you the right to impose your will on me or anyone else?"

Sheriff Riley spoke up quickly. "All I can do is obey orders, Mr. Adams! When a man's committed for contempt—when a man's properly convicted by a jury and sentenced by a judge, what's a sheriff to do?"

"What's he to do?" Adams cried. "Good God, Riley, you have no business being sheriff of Suffolk County if you don't know what's to be done in a case like this ! If you think there was good reason for jailing these men when they'd done nothing but try to preserve our liberties, you're not fit to be an inspector of privies in this town, let alone High Sheriff of a county ! And if you knew, as I damned well suspect you did, that they were improperly convicted and unjustly jailed, then it was your privilege and prerogative to treat them as honoured guests. If either one was ill, you could have seen he had the best of care. If he was ill enough, it was your duty to insist that he be released in order to have proper treatment. But he died alone in your damned jail when he should have been in his own home, tenderly nursed by those for whose freedom he fought ! "

"He'd have died anyway," Riley said sullenly.

Adams raised his cane furiously. "That's no defence, you fool ! If you've got the spine of an eel, pick up your hat and get to Judge Chase as fast as your legs'll carry you ! Tell him every word I've said, Riley ! Tell him there are *some* of us who haven't forgotten why we fought the Revolution, even if he has—as the Adamses of Quincey have, and the Wolcotts and the Pickerings and the McHenrys have ! Tell him he'd better authorise you to let your political prisoners out of this jail if he doesn't want to step into a hornet's nest that'll make every joint in his body and his brain ache for the rest of his life ! And don't shut that door, Sheriff ! This lady and I want to see Albion Hamlin, that other prisoner of yours—unless you've killed *him* too ! "

I'd been brought up to hate Sam Adams as the one man responsible for all the tribulations of the Loyalists ; yet when the jailer opened the door of my cell and Harriet walked in with Sam Adams at her heels, I found that I felt no trace of rancour toward him. He looked sulky and embittered, and—what was worse—he was unmistakably slovenly and dirty ; but I've seldom felt more gratification than when that dishevelled, angry-looking man took my hand and shook it.

"I've been sick, Mr. Hamlin, or I'd have come here sooner. Maybe I'd still be sick if Mrs. Faulkner hadn't routed me out. You've done well, Mr. Hamlin. No doubt what you've done will be forgotten in five years, because these Alien and Sedition Laws are things people will want to forget as soon as they can ; but you'll always have the pleasure of remembering that you came out openly for what you knew to be right. Even if the whole world says you were wrong, you'll still know you were right."

When I fumbled for words to thank him, he made a grumbling sound, looked fiercely from me to Harriet, and added, " This young woman is smart. She's a good friend of yours, and she's got a quick brain. In my opinion, you can act on any idea of hers without creating any trouble either for her or for yourself."

He glared at me sharply, as if to imply that I should ponder well his words. Then he said, " Good-day to you both," turned on his heel, and stalked stiffly out, almost as if offended.

We could hear his cane tapping on the floor of the corridor, so that I thought of Samuel Adams as an angry woodpecker, flapping away to drill holes in the wooden heads of men willing to sacrifice their country's liberty to their own selfishness.

Sam Adams's back was no sooner turned than Harriet Faulkner was in my arms. Her many kindnesses during the days and nights that I'd spent at her house, her unfailing attendance at the trial, and her open espousal of her cousin's cause and mine, Chase's cruel treatment of her cousin, and Bailey's death, and now her instant and effective response to the note I'd sent her—all these left no doubt in my mind that she was the one woman in the world for me. The black veil and other mourning that she now wore, the weight of her slender body against mine, and the indescribable sweetness of her lips filled me with a melting tenderness. I'd have done anything for her—anything.

I remember only vaguely what she said to me and I to her. I was in a sort of weak and helpless daze, with no thought except to engulf her in myself—to draw her so close that she became a part of me.

" I·lay awake all night and thought," she said. " Beautiful dear thoughts, my darling ! "

When I tried to answer, she passed a black-gloved finger across my lips. " I thought of everything," she went on. " I thought of our future—yes, and of what that terrible judge might do if ever you tried to pay him back for what he did to poor Cousin Thomas and to you and me. You *have* considered doing that, haven't you, darling ? "

" Considered it ? " I laughed.

" That's what I suspected," Harriet said. " I told Mr. Adams I feared you'd have that on your mind, and he said you mustn't. He said Chase has so much power that there's only one way he can be attacked, and that's through impeachment proceedings. He said the one sure way to get back at Judge Chase would be to escape from this jail."

" But you don't walk in and out of jail as you do a court-house ! "

" Wait," Harriet said. " Kiss me, Albion. Kiss me hard."

Indistinctly I heard the guard's voice. Harriet turned her face from mine and spoke over her shoulder. " Five minutes more," she said softly. I felt her passing something to the guard through the bars : heard the guard say gruffly, " Only ten minutes more, Ma'am ! "

He moved away, leaving the door-gratings clear, and Harriet stood with her back against the gratings. " I told Mr. Adams what I'd planned," she whispered. " He said it couldn't fail—that the sheriff's frightened—that Riley *wants* you to escape. If you leave Boston at once, they'll do nothing."

From beneath her long cape she miraculously produced a bundle—a black dress, a black cape, a black veil, and a widow's cap exactly like her own. " Quick, Albion ! " she whispered. " Put on the skirt, then stand close to me and I'll fix the cloak and cap and veil."

" I can't do this," I protested. " What'll happen to you ? "

" Nothing," she said. " Nothing at all. They won't know anything about it for three hours, anyhow, because I'll be in your bed with the sheet over my face. You heard what Mr. Adams said ; it's really his idea. When I'm ready, I'll send word to Riley, and you can be sure he'll get me out of here without any fuss. And I've every reason to be inside this jail, haven't I ? There's nobody else to take care of poor Cousin Thomas. Now put on the skirt, Albion."

I pulled on the sheath of black stuff, so long that it concealed even my shoes, and Harriet pinned it tight around my waist. She'd thought of everything—even the handkerchief with the black border which she pressed into my hand. " Now kneel down," she said. She put the cape around my shoulders and fastened it in front ; put the snug widow's cap on my head, tying the black ribbons beneath my chin. To the top of the cap she fastened a black veil that hung almost to my waist ; it had the same dry and dusty perfume of her own veil. She pulled me to my feet, turned me so that my back was to the door, placed her fingers against my lips, and whispered, " Don't move "—then slipped over to my cot, took off her own cap and veil, and in a moment was between the blankets.

" Come and kneel beside me, Albion ! Kiss me good-bye ! "

I raised my veil for a long and breathless moment.

" Yes," she whispered, as if in answer to a question. " Yes ! Yes ! Now listen ! All the *Kingfisher* papers are in your room, underneath the picture you think looks like me. There's money there, and a false beard. The money'll last you until you reach Washington or wherever you have to go, and there'll be more. I'm depending on you, Albion, to get me what I need from the *Kingfisher*. Here's the key of the house : I'll put it in your pocket, dear. When you've used it, hide it under the front step, the bottom door step ; put it on the left side—nobody looks under the left side. Take the picture and the papers and the money, and be sure you're gone from Boston within two hours. Will you promise ? Quick, Albion, say you'll promise ! "

She kissed me again, kissed me hard, and I'd have promised anything. There was something about those kisses that reached deep down inside me and robbed me of everything but eagerness. " Now," she said, " you'll never be able to forget me, Albion ! "

" Never as long as I live," I told her ; and I never have—though not for the reasons a man usually has for never forgetting a woman.

When the jailer rattled his key in the lock and threw the door open, he stood aside respectfully for me to pass out, and I, holding the black-bordered handkerchief to my eyes, went with bent head along the corridor, down the stairs, and out through the steel-barred doors ; and I must have played my part of grief-stricken relative better than I had thought possible, for no man ventured to intrude upon my grief.

CHAPTER VI

MANY and many a time, during the ensuing months, I wished with all my heart that I had never heard of French Spoliation Claims, had never gone to Washington to attempt to wrench Harriet Faulkner's sixteen thousand dollars from a reluctant Congress, and had never been caught in that endless waiting in the outer offices of Congressmen and departmental whipper-snappers which is the unhappy lot of every man who wishes reimbursement for losses for which the government is responsible.

I hated everything about Washington—that raw, mud-smeared, newly created city. I hated its blazing, steamy heat in spring, summer, and autumn ; its moist and biting cold in winter ; the vast, be-puddled, churned-up distances between its buildings ; the determined ignorance of a large part of the duly elected and appointed representatives of the people; the universal gossiping and backbiting among those who considered themselves socially superior ; the unwarranted importance arrogated to themselves by public men whose mental attainments and value to the world were noticeably inferior to those of any competent journeyman carpenter.

There were a number of things that kept me from giving up in disgust : my own unwillingness, after my loss of the Bailey case, to be again defeated in a task to which I'd set my hand ; the encouraging letters my uncle and Aunt Emmy wrote me almost weekly in reply to my own discouraged ones ; and above all my indignation at a government that so blithely taxed its citizens in order to toss their money away unwisely, yet at the same time refused to pay its just debts. That resentment was fanned at this particular time, too, by the insolent demands made upon the United States Government by the robber states of Barbary. Not only were they continually threatening to take toll of American ships unless bribed with frequent costly gifts—a ship, a score of cannon, a hundred thousand dollars, five thousand stands of arms—but our government was cravenly dispensing these unnecessary bribes, even while refusing to listen to my attempts to obtain simple justice for my clients.

Never a day passed that I didn't long to get out of Washington and go back to Harriet and to the farm in Gorham ; but, like many another man, I'd embarked on an enterprise without realising how many facets it possessed. I was like a man from the city who longs for the bucolic pleasures of owning a few cows and a farm, and is then amazed to learn that he cannot properly enjoy them unless he builds barns and dairies, fences, innumerable acres, enters the hay-and-grain business, studies cow diseases and their remedies, takes up cheese-making, maintains large numbers of pigs to eat up his surplus milk, and devotes all his days to multifarious activities that are as unpleasant as they are unavoidable— as wearying as they are unanticipated.

By great good fortune I found a small room—more of a closet than a room—at Conrad's Boarding-House on the south side of Capitol Hill, looking down on the winding Tiber and the miserable plain that stretched from the Capitol to the Potomac—miserable because of the way the inhabitants had girdled and hacked down for firewood the magnificent tulip-trees that until recently had made that now desolate plain into a series of parks and groves.

The star boarder at Conrad's was Thomas Jefferson himself, whom I had never expected to see, much less to meet, when I set off for Washington ; but he was as unpretentious as the least of Conrad's many boarders : just a tall, angular, red-headed, benevolent-looking man, who sat unobtrusively on one side of Conrad's long table, apologetically asking for the butter and obligingly passing the salt.

To me the most important man at that table was Samuel Harrison Smith, owner and editor of the *National Intelligencer*. He was one of those men who speak to everyone they see, as a matter of course ; and the very first night of my long stay at Conrad's he tapped on the open door of my hall bedroom—a tall, thin man, stooped a little at the waist. He smiled at me bashfully with an air of being willing to believe anything and trust anybody ; but when he stepped into my narrow quarters and saw the little painting of Lydia Bailey that I had propped up between my books, his look changed to one of keen inquiry.

" Why," he said, " I know that lady ! I knew her in Philadelphia ! Isn't that David Bailey's daughter ? "

" Yes," I said, " that's who is was. She's dead."

" Dear, dear," Smith said, " that's unfortunate ! I remember her well. How did it happen—and, if you'll pardon me for asking, how do you happen to have her portrait ? "

At that I told him all about my uncle and myself and the Thomas Bailey case, and about Harriet Faulkner and the French Spoliation Claims, and of how I carried Lydia's portrait with me because of the resemblance it bore to Harriet. Smith had a way of nodding his head appreciatively while listening, with the effect of commenting favourably and at length on everything, even when he hadn't uttered a word.

I couldn't have met a more helpful man than Samuel Harrison Smith. He had been a newspaper editor in Philadelphia before a number of influential Washingtonians had persuaded him to come to Washington to start its first newspaper. His wife had been a Bayard of Delaware, which is something like being a Preble or a Wordsworth in Maine, only more boastfully so ; and the two of them together knew everything there was to know about Washington, Washington politics, Washington society, and Washington scandal.

Smith even knew about the Bailey case, and seemed more than amiably disposed toward me because of my part in it, and it was he who told me which senators to see, which representatives to see, whom to ask for in the State Department, how to delve into the State Department records. It was he who directed me to that strange and unexplainable man Tobias Lear, and in the end suggested the association with William Bartram that had so violent an influence upon my life.

When I first came to Washington I had only Harriet's inherited shares in the *Kingfisher* claim to occupy my attention ; but in a month's time, thanks to my uncle's efforts in Maine and Mr. Smith's representations in Philadelphia, I had a dozen offers from Maine and Philadelphia ship-owners whose vessels had been summarily boarded and seized, unjustly condemned, and high-handedly sold three years before by the French in the West Indies. To name a few of them, there was the ship *Three Brothers* of Portland, Captain Lendal Smith ; the *William* of Portland, Captain Colin Campbell ; the sloop *George* belonging to Wise & Grant of Kennebunk ; the ship *Louisa* of Bath, Captain John Clark ; the ship *Fame* owned by Hall & McClintock of Portsmouth ; the brigantine *Philantrophist* of Portsmouth, Captain Hodgdon ; the brigantine *Friendship* of Salem, owned by Nichols & Hodges ; the brigantine *Six Brothers* of Salem, Captain Needham ; and the brig *Franklin* of Philadelphia, Captain Peck.

This seems as good a place as any to explain the French Spoliation Claims, which are simple enough to understand, though not creditable to this country and therefore not understood.

To my way of thinking, all those claims resulted from an unparalleled piece of national ingratitude on the part of the United States. When the cause of the American rebels during the Revolution was almost hopeless, Benjamin Franklin was sent to France to persuade the French to grant the rebels money, arms, clothes, artillery, ammunition, and recognition. Only France was in a postion to help the struggling rebel government ; and, lacking that help, the rebels would have had to lay down their arms. To make a long story short, the French provided everything for which Franklin asked, and in return Franklin signed a treaty with the French guaranteeing that the United States would, in return, protect any French possession in the West Indies that might be threatened by any other nation. This treaty was ratified by Congress—the first treaty entered into by the United States.

Later, when England went to war against Revolutionary France, the English set out to gobble up, one by one, all the French islands in the West Indies. On that, France invoked the treaty, and asked that the United States come to her help as agreed. Congress, however, refused to live up to the treaty, saying that this country was determined to be neutral. Thus the United States disgracefully dishonoured the treaty to which she owed her national existence.

The French Government, naturally resenting such flagrant ingratitude, ordered that American ships and cargoes in the West Indies be seized on any pretext whatever, taken into French ports, and condemned and sold. French cruisers, French privateers, the French Government, and French courts, working in collusion, seized, sold, or destroyed eight hundred and ninety-eight American vessels.

Congress undertook to straighten out the claims of the American shipowners whose vessels and cargoes had been seized by the French. The American Government, of course, argued that France was responsible and should therefore pay the claims. France replied that the United States Congress, in refusing to live up to its treaty, had shown itself to be made up of treaty-breakers, ingrates, shirkers of responsibility, ignorers of obligations. If Congress had lived up to its treaty, the French said, the vessels would never have been seized : and thus Congress and Congress alone was responsible for their seizure.

My task, therefore, was to find a way to persuade someone to introduce in Congress a bill calling for the payment of my clients' claims ; and there were times when the Labours of Hercules seemed, by comparison, like an afternoon's diversion.

Of all the claims, the *Kingfisher* claim was worst, for the *Kingfisher* had been stopped at night off the coast of Porto Rico by a French privateer. Although the *Kingfisher's* papers were all in order, the French captain ordered her captain, mates, and crew into her three boats and set them adrift. They finally made land at Curaçao, were marooned there penniless for several months, and were then brought back to the United States through the kindness of the captain of another American merchant ship. Thus the captain of the *Kingfisher* had no knowledge of the name of the French privateer that had captured him, or the port into which the *Kingfisher* had been sent, or the reasons advanced for her condemnation and sale. And all I had was the affidavits of the captain, the first and second mates, and the crew, together with those of the owners and of the firm that had put the cargo aboard.

The ignorance of the senators and representatives to whom I went daily to state my case was beyond belief. Nearly all were lawyers, the petty, quibbling type of lawyer who is against everything on general principles ; and I came back to Conrad's Boarding-House every night almost too tired and discouraged to eat ; but every night I'd sit down in front of that little portrait of Lydia Bailey and pour out my discouragement in a letter to Harriet Faulkner.

I even came to have a sort of feeling, in time, that it was the portrait that was alive, and Lydia to whom I was writing ; that Harriet was the faint and pictured likeness of somebody I had known only slightly, and long ago. I can't explain this as I'd like to ; but after a few weeks of staring for hours on end at the almost smiling lips, the sidelong glance of the girl in the portrait, I was even uncertain how Harriet Faulkner had really looked, while Lydia Bailey's image came instantly to my mind a thousand times a day.

What disturbed me most about my Washington experiences, I think, was the attitude of the gentlemen in the State and Treasury Departments, who were so afraid of hurting somebody's feelings that they seemed wholly unable to do or say anything definite. A Congressman, for example, was unwilling to sponsor a bill asking for the payment of a just claim against the government unless the Treasury Department and the State Department were willing to recommend it ; but the gentlemen in the Treasury and State Departments were so afraid of committing a diplomatic blunder in recommending to Congress anything that might hint at a slur against France or a slur against Congress or a slur against itself, that to get an answer out of anyone was more difficult than making a sow out of a silk purse.

Smith only laughed when, in the privacy of my room, I cursed the State and Treasury Departments and the cautious and cat-footed little nobodies who lowered their eyelids and raised their eyebrows whenever I entered their offices. " Maybe," he said, " you'll get somewhere when the administration changes."

" Yes," I retorted, " and maybe I won't ! They'll put in a new Secretary of State, yes ; but we'll only be allowed to look at him every Fourth of July ! All the little pinfeathered tea-drinkers will stay in office, frightened of France, frightened of England, frightened of Congress, frightened of each other, frightened of the voters, frightened of opening their mouths, frightened of having the truth known about them and their ineptitude."

" Perhaps things might be worse," Smith said with a twinkle.

" Like hell they might ! " I told him. " I went to the French Ambassador and asked him to let me see the official statement made by the French Government in reply to our suggestion that the French pay for the vessels they'd seized. He gave it to me fast enough, and I saw that the French hadn't been afraid of hurting *our* feelings ! It came right out and accused Congress and the State Department and everyone in the government of being no better than petty thieves ! Why can't our own government talk that way when it has occasion to ? Look how the State Department and Congress and everybody else in the government has acted about the Barbary pirates ! Bribing the Dey of Algiers with ships, naval stores, hogsheads of American dollars, trunkfuls of Portuguese gold, and gifts for his wives and his generals and his admirals, for God's sake—and all to persuade him to keep his hands off American ships ! And does he do it ? He does not ! Why talk soft to people who don't understand softness ? "

" Wait till after election," Smith said. " Jefferson's going to be elected, and everything'll be all right then."

It was next to impossible to transact any sort of business in Washington during that entire winter of 1800-1801, when Congressmen fought and wrangled and cut each other's throats in their effort to decide whether Thomas Jefferson or Aaron Burr should become President. Jefferson and Burr, by a strange political freak, had received the same number of votes

in the November election, and the burden of deciding between them lay
in the hands of Congress.

Tedious and costly though a journey to Washington then was, people
hastened there by hundreds. Hotels, lodging-houses, boarding-houses, all
were crowded. In one house, fifty men slept on the floors, with no beds
but blankets and no coverings but their greatcoats.

Day after day, during February, the members of the House of
Representatives balloted to decide whether Jefferson should be President,
or Burr ; and in their voting they revealed how invariably a consistent
politician, in order to defeat a political enemy, will sacrifice all the best
interests of his country.

Burr was a man beneath contempt. Jefferson, on the contrary, was a
great man whose election was desired by three-fifths of the people who had
sent their representatives to Congress. Yet the representatives from the
New England states and South Carolina, hating Jefferson, voted almost
solidly for the unspeakable Burr.

Not until the thirty-sixth ballot did the Federalists give way and allow
Jefferson to be elected.

With the installation of Jefferson as President I lost my pessimism and
began to think that, as Smith had assured me, my troubles would shortly
be over. Throughout Washington and everywhere else in America, there
had never been seen such an exhibition of heartfelt joy as on the day John
Adams went out and Jefferson came in. Everywhere there was bell-
ringing and cannonading : no business, no labour, was anywhere done.

Jefferson's inaugural speech confirmed me in my hope that all would
now be well : for he said freely that it was time to put away animosity,
heartburning, and strife, and bring back that harmony and affection
without which liberty and even life itself are but dreary things. He
condemned political intolerance as being as bad as religious intolerance,
which, he insisted, had been driven from our shores.

Knowing how people in the Province of Maine felt about the Papist
French, and how those in Newport felt about the Jews, I had some doubts
about this last statement ; but I heartily agreed with him when he went
on to point out that political intolerance was as bad, as wicked, as capable
of bitter persecution and bloody deeds as was religious intolerance. A
minority, he argued should have the same rights as the majority. He
called for universal acceptance of the principles of good government ;
then—and this, it seemed to me, shouldn't have been necessary—he
explained what he meant by good government : equal and exact justice
to all men ; peace, commerce, and an honest friendship with all nations,
but entangling alliances with none ; states' rights, majority rule, honest
elections, a well-regulated militia, economy in the expenditure of public
money, payment of the debt, diffusion of knowledge, freedom of the press,
freedom of the person, and freedom of religious belief.

Jefferson may have been foolishly optimistic in that speech of his ;
but I was even more foolishly so than he, for I—like an idiot—thought

that he had good government sufficiently at heart to pick public officials who would think as he thought and act as he acted.

One of my troubles, before Jefferson took office, had been an epidemic of record-burning in the Treasury Department, in the War Department, even in the State Department. How these burnings came about, nobody seemed to know ; but if any Army officer, say, had been court-martialled and perhaps found guilty, all the papers in his case had a queer way of getting destroyed in an unexplainable holocaust. Or if a battle had been lost through somebody's carelessness, or something discreditable had appeared in the records of high officers, those papers, too, had a way of going up in flames.

One of the more interesting fires had taken place in the Treasury Department during the secretaryship of Oliver Wolcott of Massachusetts —and though that fire took place at dusk, when the workers in the building had departed, it just happened that a number of carts were standing in the vicinty of the building, and were able to cart away several dozen of Mr. Wolcott's private boxes, bundles, and trunks. Among the documents consumed were a number that would have required the payment of money by the government—among them several shipowners' claims. As a consequence, the Treasury Department staff were confused over just which papers had been lost. Naturally they were unable to trace any papers at all until they could recover from that confusion ; and, since they (as has been the case since the beginning of time) found a confused existence easier and pleasanter than an ordered one, they never did recover from it.

When, therefore, Mr. Jefferson didn't immediately replace Mr. Wolcott with another Secretary of the Treasury, and the confusion persisted, I was still baulked in my efforts to get from that department any of the papers in the *Kingfisher* case.

Early in the summer, however, Smith offered me a ray of hope, bringing me the information that a man by the name of Tobias Lear had come to be recognised by Mr. Jefferson as an authority on the West Indies.

" What you'd better do," Smith told me, " is to see Lear as soon as possible and get in his good graces. He can probably do more for you than anybody in the Treasury Department or the State Department. You shouldn't have any trouble doing this, because he comes from your part of the country—Portsmouth, New Hampshire—and he used to be George Washington's secretary."

I didn't like the sound of it. " If he was Washington's secretary," I told Smith, " he must have been a Federalist, because Washington was a Federalist. Why should Jefferson pick a Federalist as one of his advisers ? And why should any Federalist have any use at all for me after my opposition to the Alien and Sedition Law ? "

" Don't ask me," Smith said. " I don't understand politics. I only write about 'em."

" Well," I said, " how does Lear happen to be an authority on the West Indies ? Has he lived there ? "

" No," Smith said, " he hasn't ; but he's President of the Potomac Canal Company, so that he has a good deal to do with boats and West Indian trade and such matters."

I looked hard at Smith to see whether he was serious. He was. " Boats ! " I said. " That means canal boats. I don't believe I could get anywhere with a canal-boat expert."

" You've got to," Smith said. " You're dealing with French Spoliation Claims, and all your cases have to do with ships that the French seized in the West Indies. But no department of the government will do anything about such cases without first consulting Lear. That's the way things are done in Washington. The most influential men in Washington aren't elected. They come in by the back door. Lear got in by the back door, and he has a passion for diplomacy. You know he married a niece of General Washington." He coughed. " It's an interesting thing, too : he's kept possession of all Washington's papers—all his correspondence."

He looked complacent, as if he'd made everything clear.

" What's that got to do with it ? " I asked, and I must have spoken sharply ; for the things Smith had partly revealed, coupled with the dry manner in which he had spoken, had infected me with something like aversion toward Mr. Lear.

" I don't know that it has *anything* to do with it," Smith said. " But Lear's a peculiar man. I know that when Washington toured the New England states at the end of his administration, Lear went everywhere with him. When Washington entered a town, it was his custom to get out of his carriage and ride into the town on horseback, leaving Lear in the presidential carriage. In many places the crowds made the mistake of thinking that Lear was Washington, and they cheered him to the echo. I have a feeling that Lear came to consider himself as great a man as Washington—if not greater."

" What if he did ? " I asked. " That doesn't make him a greater man, as I see it. It just makes him a damned fool."

" You may be right," Smith said. " All I know for sure is that Lear has all of Washington's correspondence in his possession, that he is ambitious and has an excellent opinion of himself, and that a great many men, high in public life, wrote letters to General Washington in the heat of political strife that might be damaging to them to-day—if they should be made public or put in the records where they could be examined." He shot a quick look at me. " If there should be any delay in burning 'em, they might prove *most* embarrassing."

" All right," I said, " I'll see Lear, but I'll tell you this much : when these cases are settled, I'm through with law and Washington for life. I'll stick to farming, where a man can keep his self-respect."

Colonel Tobias Lear—colonel by virtue of his peacetime service in

General Washington's household—was not an easy man to see ; but see him I did, eventually.

He had a neat little office at the head of Lear's Wharf, from which he could watch the goings and comings of the canal boats, sloops, and schooners that entered the very shadow of Capitol Hill from the Potomac ; and it seemed to me, when I was finally ushered into that snug little office, that Colonel Lear affected the appearance of his great friend and benefactor General Washington, for his air was one of high dignity and he had a way of staring impassively from the window so that his profile was presented to me. Also, he kept his lips tightly pressed together, as if considering important matters ; and his hair was prematurely white, so that he made himself look more than a little like the Gilbert Stuart portrait of Washington. He had the calculating winsomeness of a man who is spoiled by the ladies, so I knew he'd insist on doing things his own way or not at all.

As rapidly as possible I put my case before him : I was a resident of his part of New England, a lawyer and farmer by profession, with several clients who had claims against the government for losses incurred through the action of the French in seizing American ships illegally, and selling both ships and cargoes in West Indian ports. In proof of my statements I laid upon his desk a list of my clients and their ships, pointing out that the ship *Fame* had been owned by Hall & McClintock of Portsmouth, his own home town.

When I had finished, Colonel Lear gave me a sweet smile and delicately touched the sheet I had placed before him. He put me in mind of a dignified white tom-cat lackadaisically extending a paw toward a kitten's plaything.

" I hardly see why you should do me the honour of calling on me about these matters, Mr. Hamlin," he said. His utterance of my name seemed to strike a chord in his memory. " Hamlin ? Hamlin ? Are you by any chance related to the Hamlin who defended Thomas Bailey ? "

" I *am* the Hamlin who defended Bailey," I said. " My uncle had intended to do so, but he fell ill and I took his place."

" Very interesting," Lear said, and his eyes were veiled. " Most unpleasant experience, but laudable—oh, laudable. Yes ! Ah—tell me, Mr. Hamlin, how did you happen to come to me ? "

" Well, Colonel," I said, and I steeled myself to using soft soap because Smith had warned me that Lear had to have it, " there's nobody in New England who isn't proud of your connection with General Washington, and who doesn't know that your friendship would be the greatest asset he could have in this city. No other New Englander knows so much about public affairs ; so, being a New Englander myself, I presumed on that fact."

" I see," Colonel Lear said. He examined the list of ships. Then he shook his head and looked unhappy. " You know, Mr. Hamlin," he said, " most of the ships seized by the French were sold in Haiti, and

things are in a dreadful state in Haiti—or should I say San Domingo ? "
He smiled patronisingly. " Haiti is how the Negroes themselves refer to
San Domingo, Mr. Hamlin. Yes—ah—well, Mr. Hamlin, the Negroes
have seized power down there and driven out most of the Frenchmen
who formerly held office. Philadelphia, New York, Savannah—all those
cities are full of French officials."

" So I've heard," I said, " but that has nothing to do with the justness
of these Spoliation Claims."

" I'm afraid," Lear said, " that it has a great deal more to do with it
than you suspect. With all the French officials absent from their posts,
there's no way to authenticate the justice of these claims."

" But there is," I replied. " Every one of these ships was seized by the
French—and seized unjustly. We have the affidavits of the officers and
the crews to prove it."

" That may be so," Lear said, " but you haven't the French documents. For example, in the case of the Barque Kingfisher, on what grounds
did the French court condemn her ? "

" I don't know, Colonel Lear," I said, " and that knowledge, it seems
to me isn't necessary. She was seized by the French, and her value was
twenty-five thousand dollars as attested by the builders, Lord & Dutton
of Ipswich. Her cargo was valued at forty-two thousand dollars, to which
the loaders, Burbank & Towne of Boston, have sworn."

Lear was patient with me. " I understand all that, Mr. Hamlin, but
there may have been some action on the part of the Kingfisher's captain—
some failure on his part—that caused the French to take action against her.
Now, for example, what was the name of the French ship that seized the
Kingfisher ? "

" We don't know," I said ; " but that has nothing to do with the
justness of this claim."

" Oh, yes," Lear said. " Nobody can make such a demand on the
United States unless all the evidence is complete and in order."

" But it is complete," I said. " The Kingfisher was seized in retaliation
for the failure of the Government of the United States to carry out the
terms of its treaty. That government was responsible for breaking the
treaty and it is therefore, responsible for the losses suffered by those whose
property was taken from them."

Lear looked regretful. " Of course, Mr. Hamlin, I can only give you
an opinion on such a matter as this. You really overestimate my importance and my influence, but I feel quite sure I am on safe ground when I
say that you can never collect these claims until you have the additional
evidence I mentioned."

I wondered what in God's name was in the man's mind. He looked
like a sensible, amiable, educated man, and yet it seemed to me that he
was quibbling like an old woman. At the same time, I saw clearly that I
could argue forever without changing his stubborn refusal to admit the
obvious.

I got to my feet. " Well, Colonel," I said, " I appreciate your advice, and I'll make every effort to get the additional proof. May I assume that if I'm successful you'll say a good word in my behalf ? "

" Oh, my dear Mr. Hamlin," Colonel Lear said, " I'll do everything in my power ! Everything ! But let me assure you again, you over-estimate my influence."

He got up from his chair slowly and cautiously, as a cat might have risen. In fact, I've never since that day been able to see a cat without thinking of Tobias Lear.

When I told Smith about Lear's insistence that my evidence was incomplete, he looked thoughtful. " Now that's an odd thing," he said. " All those ships were lost, as you say, and lost because of Congress's sullen refusal to help the French against the English. What does Lear care about the intricate little details of their loss ? He must have a reason for it ! You don't do things like that just because you want to keep on being a damned fool."

" I'm not so sure of that," I said. " Lear's one of those consciously winsome men—wavy white hair, lovely profile, elegant manners. A man like that often can't help making a damned fool of himself."

" That's possible," Smith said, " but I don't believe it. He's a planner, a plotter. Look at his persistence in hanging on to all of Washington's correspondence. He doesn't do that because he's a damned fool : he does it for a good reason. How many American ships did you say the French seized ? "

" As far as I'm able to make out, there were eight hundred and ninety-eight of them, with a total value of something in excess of five million dollars."

" Five million dollars, eh," Smith said. " Well, well, well ! That's a lot of money, isn't it ! If it's not an impertinence, how would you expect your clients to reimburse you if you should be successful in collecting their claims ? "

" I haven't given it much thought," I said, " but I think probably it ought to be on a percentage basis—say five per cent or seven per cent of the amount recovered."

" Exactly," Smith said. " You'd be in a splendid situation, wouldn't you, if you had so much influence—so much knowledge of happenings in the West Indies—that you'd be able to collect a great many claims : say two or three million dollars' worth of them. You'd be one of the richest men in the United States, wouldn't you ? And you certainly wouldn't want some unknown upstart to cut the ground from under your feet by offhandedly collecting a lot of Spoliation Claims before you'd done anything about them yourself."

I stared at Smith, and gradually his meaning dawned upon me. Lear had influence : Lear knew the West Indies ! And certainly I was unknown.

"I see," I said, "I see. That hadn't occurred to me before. It wouldn't surprise me at all if you were right ! "

"No," Smith said, " it wouldn't surprise me, either. If he got the proof himself, there wouldn't be much question about his being able to collect, would there ? "

"Damn it," I said, " he doesn't *need* any more proof."

"No, but it wouldn't hurt him to have it, would it ? " Smith asked.

"No," I admitted. " It wouldn't hurt him. It wouldn't hurt him a bit. In fact, a lot of people would be impressed by his having it."

"In that case," Smith said, " do you know what I'd do if I were you ? I'd go where I could get that proof. I'd go to Philadelphia and see some of those refugees that the Negroes drove out of San Domingo. You'll find 'em out at Bartram's Gardens across the Schuylkill. Bartram's a naturalist and a kind man, and he's encouraged them to use his Gardens as a meeting place where they can sponge on their friends."

"Is that William Bartram ? " I asked.

Smith seemed surprised that I knew of him, and I explained that Bartram's *Travels* had been a sort of Bible to me ever since I came across it in my uncle's library.

"Well," Smith said, " you'll find every Frenchman in Philadelphia hanging around Bartram's Gardens every day of the week, and Bartram can give you the history of every last one of them."

Smith's words excited me. The prospect of getting out of this filthy hole of a city, of being closer to Harriet, of somehow obtaining enough evidence to circumvent Lear, to whom I had taken a profound dislike, filled me with more enthusiasm than I had felt for months.

CHAPTER VII

EVEN before I hunted a place to live in Philadelphia, I set off for Bartram's Gardens, carrying my carpet bag and the little portrait of Lydia in its wooden box, and I'm bound to say that those gardens, known and celebrated in every great university in Europe, were something of a disappointment. They were on the banks of the Schuylkill some three miles below Philadelphia and in size were less than half as large as our farm in Gorham. No effort at all had been made toward formality, so far as I could see ; the whole area was something of a tangle, badly in need of brush-hooking. At the upper end of the gardens there was a long rambling house, and paths wandered irregularly through and around thickets. Along the paths were benches, with miniature garden-plots here and there—experimental vegetable beds, I took them to be.

It was early afternoon when my coach stopped at the gate handiest to these tangled gardens ; and I had no sooner gone to the gate to get the lie of the land than I saw a barefooted farm labourer, dressed in leather breeches and leather vest, hoeing a bed of earth from which stubble protruded. He didn't look like a helpful farm labourer, either, for his movements seemed doddery and ineffectual. When I looked more closely, I saw he was hoeing salt into the soil.

" Is that an asparagus bed ? " I asked.

He straightened up to look at me, making hard work of it, as a man does when he's been using a hoe too assiduously ; but his eyes were wiser than any I had ever seen on a farm labourer. " Asparagus," he said. " Yes. Still producing well, too, in spite of being fifteen years old last spring."

" Well," I said, " I hope you won't be offended if I say I think you might get better results with lime than with salt."

He hobbled to a nearby bench and sat down, patting the wood beside him by way of invitation. " What makes you think so ? "

Feeling a little sorry for the barefooted old codger, I sat down.

" Well," I replied, " it was largely an accident, using lime on our own bed. People down our way always use brine out of their pickle barrels on asparagus, claiming it helps 'em ; but all the beds keep running out just the same. Smaller and smaller shoots every year, and tasting more and more of straw. You know how it is."

" Yes," the old man said, " I'll agree salt doesn't do much to asparagus except keep out weeds. I guess I'll start another bed."

" It doesn't even keep out weeds down our way," I said. " You won't need a new bed if you lime and mulch."

" I take it you're from the South," the old man said.

" No, I'm from Maine."

" But you said ' down,' " he protested. " Twice you said ' down our way.' Maine is north, and north is up, isn't it ? "

" Not in England," I told him. " If you live in Boston and set out to go to Maine, you always go on a southwest wind ; that's our prevailing wind. So you go down wind from Boston to Portland—' down to Maine.' And when you return you go ' up ' to Boston."

" Well, I declare," he exclaimed. " I don't know but what you do ! You're a farmer, or you wouldn't know about lime ; but you must be something else, too. You wouldn't be a mariner, would you ? "

" No," I said. " I'm a farmer by inclination, but a lawyer by necessity."

Then, since he seemed really interested, I went on to tell him my name, and I described our farm in Gorham and told him how our horse Blue Belle had stepped on a hornets' nest one April morning and over-turned a load of lime on the end of our asparagus bed, and how we'd trampled the lime into the mud in our efforts to free Blue Belle from the harness before she hurt herself.

" There was nothing to be done about it," I told him. " The lime was so mixed with the bed that we couldn't pick it up without hurting the crowns. But two months later the asparagus in that section was twice as big and more than twice as heavy as that on the rest of the bed."

" Did you figure the amount of lime to the acre ? " he asked.

" Yes," I said, " I figured about six tons. The next year I divided the rest of the bed into sections and limed the strips with varying amounts. The strips that had one and two tons to the acre didn't show any results ; the one with three tons was better ; the one with four tons did fairly well ; but those with five and six beat anything you ever saw."

" Don't you use any salt to keep down the weeds ? " he asked.

" No," I said, " we throw spoiled hay on the beds and never have any trouble with weeds at all. In the fall we harrow it in."

" Who's we ? "

" Well," I said, hoping I wasn't treading on his toes, " we have two hands on the farm, but sometimes I think I'd be better off without 'em. I've never tried anything yet that they haven't objected to."

His answering smile seemed a little weary, and I, suspecting I was wasting both his time and my own, got up to go. " Do you know where I'd be apt to find Mr. Bartram at this time of day ? " I asked.

" That's one of the few things I'm sure of," he said. " That's me. I'm William Bartram."

I sat down in a hurry. " Bartram ! " I cried. " Good God ! Me making suggestions to William Bartram ! No wonder you smiled ! "

" Oh," Bartram said, " I was only smiling because there never was a man who experimented on a farm who didn't have to fight everybody who worked for him. You ought to read Marshall's experiments."

" I have, sir," I said. " I've read all of Marshall and all of Anderson— and Jared Eliot and Lord Kames. I wouldn't be without 'em, but I'd give up all of 'em rather than give up William Bartram's *Travels*."

I was a little embarrassed by my own plain speaking, and Bartram seemed embarrassed too, for he wriggled his bare toes on the gravel walk. " Where are you living in Philadelphia ? " he asked.

" Nowhere, sir," I said. " I've just come here from Washington, and for the express purpose of seeing you."

Seeing that he still looked encouraging, I told him about my effort to collect French Spoliation Claims for my clients, and my desire to see and talk with some of the French refugees who I had been told frequented his garden.

" Bless my soul ! " Bartram said. " You've come to the right place for French refugees. They're here from dawn to dark, talking, trading, making love, manufacturing little articles for sale, gambling. We have all kinds here : prime ministers, authors, poets, generals, captains, rakes, priests, scientists, judges, advocates, planters, academicians, ambassadors, senators. Which kind would you like to see ? "

" Well," I said, " most of all I'd like to see somebody who was connected with the Marine in San Domingo around 1797. Most of my clients' ships are supposed to have been taken into San Domingan ports

and sold there. Another valuable person for me to see would be a judge
—such a judge as might have condemned American ships captured by
the French."

"Nothing could be simpler," Bartram said. "I can direct you to the
exact men. M. Camille Laboulaye was Chief of the Marine for the
Department of the North of San Domingo with headquarters at Cap
François, and M. Faure was a member of the Tribunal of Commerce
at Cap François. You'll see both of them this very day."

When I started to thank him, he stopped me. "The shoe's on the
other foot, Mr. Hamlin. You've experimented with soils and lime and
such-like things, and you needn't think you're going to get away from me
by just saying ' thank you.' You can talk to a million Frenchmen, for all
of me ; but since you're going to do it in these gardens, you're going to
do it with a pruning knife in your hands or a hoe, or something that'll
make it easier for them to talk to you—and at the same time you'll be
helping both of us. How's that for an idea ? "

"Excellent," I said. "I'd consider it a pleasure and an honour."

"I wouldn't look at it that way," Bartram returned dryly. "I'm
going to get a lot of work out of you, and in return I'm going to give you
a room with a good view of the Schuylkill and a mattress stuffed with the
plumage of *Anser Canadensis.* We'll feed you on *meleagris americanus, tetrao
tympanus, salvelinus fontinalis, arum esculentum,* and garden fruits in season."

That was how I came to set up the little portrait of Lydia Bailey in
the home of William Bartram, and to interview Frenchmen who had
fled to America to escape the vengeance of the blacks who had refused to
concur in the French idea that liberty, equality, and fraternity were all
right for Frenchmen but bad for negroes.

CHAPTER VIII

How these French refugees in America contrived to exist, I never understood. There was a bookstore in Philadelphia that had been started by
the celebrated Moreau de St. Méry, the man who wrote the monumental
book on the Negroes of the French part of San Domingo—the part known
to the Negroes as Haiti ; and wealthy Philadelphians often went to his
shop to leave donations of clothes and hats and shoes and money, together
with such things as bags of beans and potatoes and field-peas, and in cold
weather sides of beef and pork, barrels of corned beef, and such-like. The
person in charge of the shop would put these where anybody who wanted
them could have them, so that the bookshop's flavour was rather of
groceries than of books ; and the French, being an unduly proud people,
not nearly so logical as generally supposed, would wait until nobody was
looking ; then help themselves to whatever they needed.

They all seemed to have a profound aversion to any sort of manual labour and to spend their days and nights in futile talk, most of it directed against the black rascals who had driven them from their homes. These same black rascals, if I understood correctly, had freely offered to allow any property owner to return to Haiti and resume possession of his property. But the Frenchmen were hesitant about accepting ; the blacks, they insisted, couldn't be trusted. So the refugees stayed on in Philadelphia, half starved, threadbare, cantankerous, idle, and the most garrulous lot of human beings who ever wore trousers.

M. Laboulaye, when I met him, proved to be kindness and affability itself. His recollection of the *Kingfisher* case, and of the other cases I mentioned, was at first hazy. He had, he said, undergone a great deal of mental distress at the hands of the villainous blacks who had seized power in San Domingo and replaced white men of ability and distinction (I'm quoting M. Laboulaye) with scoundrels of every shade externally, but universally black within. Thus his memory was apt to be at fault— an unhappy state of affairs that was complicated by his inability to afford cigars, which had always proved stimulating.

When I produced a cigar from my scanty stock, he was effusive with his thanks, but suggested that whenever I had occasion to buy cigars in the future I should let him know, inasmuch as he was acquainted with a man who knew a man who had access to certain vintage cigars from the Vuelta Abajo fields.

Rum, too, stimulated his memory. When I set out my bottle of Medford rum for him and he had taken a sip of it, he asked me earnestly if I'd ever sampled a true rum from Jérémie or Jacmel. Those, he said, were the finest rums in all the world, and if ever I had occasion to buy more rum, he strongly urged that I allow him to act as entrepreneur, since he knew a man who knew a man who had lived in Jacmel and would be happy to favour him with as much rum as I might need.

There was no question that his memory was favourably affected by the cigar and the rum, because little things about the *Kingfisher* case began to come back to his mind—how she had been captured by the French privateer *Voltigeur*, Captain Lombard, fitted out and owned at Curaçao. The papers relative to the vessel and her cargo had been secretly dispatched to Cap François and there placed before a Court of Commerce composed of three men of colour, as Negroes with an ad-mixture of white blood are always called in Haiti. M. Laboulaye had been particularly impressed by the case on account of the condemnation pretext. Usually American vessels captured by French naval vessels or French privateers were condemned because the seals on their clearance-papers were oval instead of square, or because it was alleged that the captain had failed to provide himself with a proper list of Seamen—an improper list, in French eyes, being one in which not all the names were fully spelled out. That was what had happened to the *Catherine*, owned by Anthony & Moses Davenport of Newburyport. But the *Kingfisher* had been condemned because her captors claimed to have found, among her papers, a letter in

" hieroglyphic or other characters." The key to the hieroglyphics had fortunately turned up at the same time, and it had been proved to the satisfaction of the three coloured gentlemen that the hieroglyphics were in some way dangerous.

" In what way were they dangerous ? " I asked M. Laboulaye.

" In the same way that the simplest things are consistently held to be dangerous in time of war. The hieroglyphics were meaningless ; therefore they were dangerous—dangerous and secret ! One could not speak of them, even ! No, no ! They were hurried into our archives, where nobody will find them, ever ! And so the ship was ordered sold."

" Did you protest ? " I asked.

He looked at me wide-eyed. " Protest ? I ? My friend, you see me here, alive ! Would I be alive if I had protested to a court composed of men of colour ? Aha ! Figure to yourself ! Protest ? Never of the life ! "

By following all of M. Laboulaye's suggestions, and allowing him to get me the Vuelta Abajo cigars and the Jacmel rum, I found there was almost nothing he couldn't recollect. Whenever his own memory failed, he went to acquaintances among the émigrés until he found someone who had kept a journal ; and out of these journals he picked up many an addition to my store of knowledge on Spoliation Claims. Often he brought the owner of the diary back to call upon me, so that the diarist's memory could also be refreshed with a little rum and a cigar.

All in all, I was immeasurably content during that spring and summer and autumn that I spent with William Bartram, for I was getting the evidence I needed, I was learning many new methods of farming and soil treatment from working with Bartram, and I was able to be of considerable help to him as well, which is always a satisfaction. What I couldn't understand was why I could sit night after night before Lydia's portrait and write letter after letter to Harriet Faulkner, without having more than a faint desire to leave Philadelphia.

One evening M. Laboulaye came to see me with a M. de Busigny, who had succeeded to the task of operating M. Moreau de St. Méry's bookshop, now that the latter gentleman had returned to France ; and the moment that M. de Busigny entered the room and saw the portrait of Lydia, he burst into a torrent of French and waved his arms excitedly at M. Laboulaye.

" My God, it is she ! She that had the imagination, the verve ! "

I thought the man an odd fish, but his excitement excited me.

M. de Busigny rapped M. Laboulaye upon the chest with his fingertips. " Hah, but there was a forceful one, forever urging upon us that we should help ourselves. I can hear her speaking to me now ! ' Why does nobody translate that book of M. Moreau de St. Méry's ? ' she would demand. ' There never was such a book written about the Negroes of any country, and now look at all your countrymen, who speak English, yet sit here and talk and eat and make no move toward translating that

book ! What is the matter with your countrymen, Monsieur ? ' she used
to ask. ' Do they care nothing for fame ? Do they not appreciate the
honour of translating a great book ? ' "

Busigny turned to me suddenly. " She's your friend, Monsieur ?
Your sister, perhaps ? Your wife ? For two years we have seen nothing
whatever of her. She vanished—we never knew why, though she'd brought
us gifts from time to time and practised her French upon us. Where is she,
Monsieur ? "

" I'm sorry to say she's dead."

" Ah," M. de Busigny cried, " the poor little ! So young ! Look what
happens ! How this is life ! Look at us, the best that Haiti has to offer,
driven out, ejected, spewed forth ! And now this poor little ! She is
dead ! " He struck his forehead. " My God, but how the life is unfair !
How did she die ? "

" Yellow fever," I said. " She went to Haiti to be a governess—for
whom I don't know—and she died of it there."

M. de Busigny made commiserative clicking sounds with his tongue ;
and thereafter, whenever M. Laboulaye or any of his friends came to see
me, they referred to Lydia's portrait as " the poor little," and reminded
each other of kind things she had done in the days of M. Moreau de
St. Méry, and how she had held her end up of a conversation with the
great Talleyrand when he too was an habitué of Bartram's Gardens and
of M. Moreau de St. Méry's bookshop.

Repeatedly I found myself on the verge of passing on to Harriet the
pleasant things all these Frenchmen had to say about Lydia, and repeatedly
I stopped myself when I recalled what Thomas Bailey had said—something to the effect that Harriet had never liked Lydia's portrait because
it reminded people of Harriet, and in a way not entirely flattering to
Harriet.

This, then, was my situation in December of 1801, when M. Laboulaye
came to see me, accompanied by an American sea captain, George Lee, of
Philadelphia, who had been present in Cap François when the ship
Three Brothers had been condemned and sold.

Captain Lee, M. Laboulaye had told me, made frequent trips to
Haiti, doing little personal errands for Frenchmen who were unable to
return to the island themselves.

Lee was a bluff, burly, hearty-looking man in a short blue jacket. A
blue cap was perched rakishly on the side of his head, and I think I would
have picked him out as a mariner at any distance or in any sort of crowd,
not only because of the ruddiness of his face and the nautical cut of his
clothes, but because of his swaggering, wide-legged gait.

He even brought a sort of harbourside flavour into the room with him
—a musty, tarry scent of soggy dock piling, sour mud, stale tobacco, rum
dregs, and bilge. Mingled with these familiar odours was an elusive yet
pungent trace of feminine perfume that came and went among those other
coarser odours as a mouse might run between grain bags.

As he seized my hand and shook it, his eyes went over my shoulder to Lydia's portrait. " Ho," he said, " there's a surprise ! Who'd ever have thought I'd come across *that* face again so soon ! "

I couldn't believe my ears. " Soon ! " I cried. " What do you mean ! You don't mean *that* face ! "

" Oh, I don't, don't I ? " he said. " Well, mister, it beats hell the way things happen ! I left Cap François only two weeks ago, and I saw that very girl the day before I sailed."

My heart began to thump so that I could hardly speak. " That's impossible," I said. " She's dead."

He looked scornful. " Dead ? Dead, hell ! I don't make mistakes about faces—not women's faces. I saw that same face fourteen—no, fifteen . . . What day of the week is this, anyway ? "

" Wednesday."

" Then it was sixteen days ago that I saw her, sitting at a sidewalk café in the Cap François Plaza. Having a cup of coffee, she was."

" Alone ? "

" Hell, no ! She had two little bastard boys with her, one on each side of her, stickying themselves up with sirop and water."

" She's alive," I whispered. " Alive ! " I could neither grasp it nor believe it. " You're sure ? Did you hear her speak ? "

" Of course I heard her speak. Damn it, I hung around that table for half an hour hoping she'd look up and say howdy-do."

" They were speaking English ? "

" Of course they were speaking English ! Why should I waste time listening to a girl who couldn't speak anything but French ? "

" Did you learn anything about her—where she lived or with whom ? "

Lee gave me a rueful look. " No, I didn't ! I tried, but she wasn't a sociable sort. They'd come some distance, though. They all had on riding clothes."

I did my best to think coherently. This man Lee didn't look good to me ; everything he said betrayed trickiness and unreliability. Yet I felt confident that he was telling the truth. He *had* seen Lydia Bailey ; Lydia Bailey *was* alive. And if so, then Thomas Bailey had been mistaken in thinking her dead. I wondered how this could have happened. How could Thomas Bailey have been mistaken about his own niece ? If she was alive, she would have continued to write to him, and he'd have known she wasn't dead.

" By God," I thought, " Lydia would have been Bailey's heir if she hadn't died ! And she didn't die ! Harriet made up her mind that she wanted to be Bailey's heir, and there was only one way for her to do it ! Harriet's to blame ! "

I went to the closet and with shaking hands took from my portmanteau the little case in which I carried Lydia's picture.

M. Laboulaye protested. " I believe Captain Lee has information that will be valuable to you in the *Three Brothers* case."

"Good," I said. "I'll take it down."

I went back to the cupboard for my remaining cigars and my last bottle of Jacmel rum. "Accept, my dear M. Laboulaye, these small tokens of my gratitude and affection. Thanks to you, all my Spoliation Claims are as complete as it's possible to make them. I'll give you a list of the ships, and if you discover anything else about them, I'll be grateful if you'll write to my uncle, Colonel William Tyng of Portland, in whose hands I'm leaving all the cases. You'll find he'll be grateful—as I'll be when I return from Haiti."

"From Haiti!" Laboulaye exclaimed. "But you cannot go to Haiti! To travel about there is dangerous!"

"Then it's equally dangerous for that lady in the portrait to be there!" I reminded him. "In any case, I've just learned something about her that makes it necessary for me to see her." I turned to Lee. "You're sure it was the one in the portrait that you saw?"

Lee laughed. "You can't fool George Lee on a pretty woman's face! One look and I can give you the exact measurements, all over!"

"And would you be willing to sail me to Boston and Portland first; then to Haiti?"

"Why not?" Lee asked. "Make it twenty dollars extra and I'll take you to Halifax! Just name your sailing date and I'm at your service."

"Dawn," I said. "We'll sail for Boston at dawn to-morrow."

Bartram, when he heard my news was as excited as I. "If only I were younger," he kept repeating, "I'd go myself! There's nothing like it! Unknown places—unknown people—unknown customs—unknown birds and shrubs and flowers! Ah!" He sighed ecstatically.

"These Frenchmen," I said, "say that no white man can travel in Haiti without being in danger."

"Pah!" Bartram cried. "That's what every stay-at-home thinks. You can travel anywhere on earth in perfect safety if you keep a smile on your face and act like a decent human being!"

When I undertook to tell him some of the other discouraging things M. Laboulaye had said about travelling in Haiti, he wouldn't listen. "All those Frenchmen," he said, "are lazy, shiftless, helpless, ruined by slavery. They've never been anywhere or seen anything. That's why they're here, why they were driven from their homes—because they and their kind were unable to understand what was happening around them." He held to the lapel of my coat and spoke earnestly. "Some years ago I had occasion to make a trip through the Indian sections of the Carolinas and Eastern Florida. When my friends heard my plans, they distressed. They'd never seen a Cherokee, but they knew! Oh, yes: they *knew*! If I tried to cross the mountains among which the Cherokees lived, I'd die of starvation and exposure! The Cherokees were savage and warlike, and I'd be tortured, scalped, and killed before I'd been gone a week ! Horrible ! When I went right ahead with my preparations, they were sure I was crazy."

He patted my arm. " Be friendly, and everyone you meet will be friendly. There's too much suspicion in this world—too many people who have never learned how to smile and understand other men."

When I tried to thank him for all he'd done, he was impatient. " You'll need funds to make such a trip. Do you have enough ? "

I said I thought so.

" You've got to know," Bartram said. " You've got to have enough to buy presents to take along."

" What sort of presents ? "

" Anything at all—anything to give you confidence—anything that'll please simple people."

" Well," I said, " I don't know about that. I haven't much time. I can't waste any of it buying presents."

Bartram looked exasperated, then lumbered from the room. When he returned he brought with him four small circular packages, small cartwheels fifteen inches in diameter.

He handed me one of the cartwheels. " I'd been wondering what to do with these. I got 'em years ago, thinking I'd use 'em to travel among the Indians of Mexico. The very best French gold braid, Albion, and an Indian or a Negro would sell his soul for a yard of it. Take it, my boy, and pay me back by finding some new seeds for the Garden. You'll find Haiti full of 'em ! "

He wouldn't take no for an answer—and I've often thought that if the rulers and presidents and governors of this world could have half of William Bartram's understanding, his desire to improve his own surroundings at no cost to others, his knowledge of the fundamental decency of the small people of every land, his eagerness to learn, there'd be an end to hatred between nations—and an end to wars.

CHAPTER IX

EVEN in the very moment when I walked up the front steps of Harriet Faulkner's house, I hadn't made up my mind what I would do or what I should say. There was no question in my mind that Lydia Bailey was alive and in Haiti, and that Harriet was the only person who had wanted Thomas Bailey to think of Lydia as dead. Harriet was the only person with sufficient motive to do such a thing, and the only person in a position to keep Bailey from receiving letters from Lydia when she wrote him, as she must have.

All I knew was that from the first moment I saw Lydia's picture I had been in love with her ; that I had been attracted to Harriet because she vaguely looked like Lydia ; and that Harriet must be stopped from appropriating whatever property was rightly Lydia's.

I had long known that Harriet was firm and determined ; but not until I'd learned that Lydia was alive had I realised that her firmness must be an adamantine hardness, conceivably impervious to assault unless that assault was made carefully.

I rang the bell, and it was Harriet herself who came to the door, as on that far-off day when I had reluctantly come to Boston to defend Thomas Bailey. At sight of me she screamed, threw up her hands in astonishment ; then flattened herself against me and clung as if she intended never to let me go.

That settled the matter : I'd have to approach the subject of Lydia after Harriet's own fashion.

It seemed to me that the time to mention Lydia would never come ; for when Harriet had me sitting on that well-remembered couch on which we'd spent so many evenings before the Bailey trial, I couldn't seem to struggle out from beneath her questions any more than I could escape her embraces. How had I happened to come back to Boston without giving her a warning ? Why, only yesterday she'd had a letter from me, telling about the experiments in developing new strains of potatoes. When was I going back to Washington ? What did Mr. Jefferson look like ? Why hadn't I seen Mr. Jefferson about the *Kingfisher* case ? Had I any information as to when there might be a settlement of the *Kingfisher* claim ? What were the women like in Washington ? What were they wearing ? She had heard they wore nothing beneath their evening gowns, which were often transparent ; was that true ? Why hadn't I told her about the ladies I'd met in Washington ? I talked about everything except other ladies—and my letters were cold.

" They weren't meant to be cold—they were just letters," I said ; and then I tried to change over to my real interest. " I can never thank you enough for giving me the little picture. I used to look at it every night when I wrote you. Do you know where Lydia's buried, Harriet ? "

She didn't move, but I sensed a sudden stillness in her as she lay against me—a stillness in which there was a barely perceptible withdrawal. " What a strange question ! " she murmured. " No, I have no idea where she's buried. Why do you ask ? "

" I don't know," I said, trying to keep my voice indifferent. " I was wondering the other day whether they buried yellow-fever victims in lime pits, or how. The body wasn't sent home, was it ? "

" Certainly not," she said. " What's got into you, Albion ? "

" Nothing's got into me," I said. " It's only that you can't help being curious about a person if you see her picture every day for a year or so. Probably she was buried on the plantation where she worked. Where was that, by the way, and what was the name of the planter ? "

Harriet straightened up on the sofa and moved a little from me. " I don't know. I have an extremely bad memory for foreign names, and she lived in a place that was deep in the country—not in a town at all."

" But letters that were written to her had to be written to some town or other ! They couldn't just be directed to a piece of property some-where in San Domingo or Haiti, whichever you want to call it."

" I know that as well as you do," Harriet said, " but it just happens that whenever I wrote her I gave my letter to Cousin Thomas, and he enclosed it in his."

" I see. . . . Couldn't you find some of the letters she wrote your cousin, they might mention the name of her employer and his address."

" All such papers were destroyed as soon as Thomas died," Harriet said. " As you know, she died a year ago last June, and even before then she never wrote Thomas."

" Isn't that a little peculiar ? " I asked. " Your cousin told me that he got her the position in San Domingo, and even paid her passage. That's why she insisted he take the portrait."

" What's strange about it ? " Harriet asked. " She was just ungrateful, like almost everybody in this world."

I thought of the sensitive lips, the shy smile of Lydia's portrait. *That* was no picture of an ingrate ; for if it had been, an artist of Gilbert Stuart's ability couldn't possibly have kept the truth from appearing.

Harriet seemed suddenly to melt once more. She flung herself against me and threw her arms around my neck. " Albion," she cried, " you silly, silly boy ! I do believe you've got some idea in that foolish head of yours that Lydia isn't dead at all."

" Yes," I said, " that's it. I think she isn't dead. I think she's alive this very minute—and that you've known it all the time."

Harriet's lips were against my cheek. " Silly, silly boy," she whispered. " Why, we had *proof* that she was dead ! "

" Do you still have that proof ? "

" Of course ! " She jumped to her feet, and ran from the room.

When she came back, she handed me a letter. It seemed a little the worse for wear, as though it had been purposely crumpled, folded, and refolded. The wax seal was gone ; only a faint pink mark showed where it had been. However, it was addressed clearly enough to Thomas Bailey, Esquire, Boston Mass. I opened it and found it dated simply " At sea, June 20th, 1800."

Dear Sir (the letter read) : I write this at the request of the employer of Lydia Bailey, spinster, teacher of English to her employer's two children. By the greatest misfortune, an epidemic of yellow fever has swept San Domingo during the weeks just past, and it was the unhappy fate of Miss Bailey to contract this disease. She was stricken while attending to her duties as a teacher, and after she had suffered for three days the black vomit appeared and she died almost immedi-ately. Owing to the infectious nature of the disease, she was buried at once and all her personal belongings were buried with her. The wages due to Miss Bailey at the time of her death, plus the money found in her belongings, came to one hundred and twenty gourdes, or twenty-four dollars. On my advice her employer is sending you, by me, the equivalent of this sum, one half in coffee and one half in rum, inasmuch as these commodities will have a far higher value in America.

Regretting the need of conveying these dismal tidings to you, I remain, sir,

Your obedient and humble servant,

ALEXANDER BEAN.

I studied the letter, front and back. " Who's Alexander Bean ? "

" Dear me," she said lightly, " I don't know who he was. I know he was all right, though, and telling the truth, because we got the coffee and the rum, just as he said in his letter. I think you'll admit nobody's going to send three hundred dollars' worth of coffee and rum to somebody he doesn't know, just for fun. That's how much it was worth here : three hundred dollars ; and that proves the letter was no joke ! "

" I don't think for a moment it was a joke," I said. " There are some odd things about it, though. For example, Mr. Bean doesn't mention the name of Lydia's employer, the town in which her employer lived, or his plantation. He was as forgetful as you are."

She shrugged. " What's so strange about that ? "

" If you don't see what's strange about it, no words of mine could make you understand."

" I don't like your tone," Harriet said. " You're implying that I somehow had a hand in deceiving my cousin. I haven't the slightest idea what you've heard, but I won't be talked to in any such way—not even by a person I regarded as more than a friend. I've had enough, Albion, and I'll ask you to leave this house."

" I can't do that," I said ; " not until I take the steps I consider necessary. I am not—as you said—' implying ' that you somehow had a hand in deceiving your cousin : I'm stating it as a fact."

" That's an absolute lie," Harriet said.

" I'm saying," I went on, " that this letter from Alexander Bean is a forgery, probably written by yourself."

" How dare you ! "

" I'm saying that when you tell me your Cousin Thomas never heard from Lydia, you're telling a deliberate falsehood to account for the destruction of the letters he certainly received regularly from her."

" You must be crazy ! "

" I'll go further : the proof that Bailey got letters from Lydia must have been in the diary I saw him keeping while I lived here. I know I'll never see that diary. You've destroyed it to protect yourself."

" Everything you say is a wicked lie ! " Harriet cried. " You're accusing an innocent women of an atrocious wrong, without a scrap of proof."

" Oh, no, I'm not. There's all the proof in the world, though it's mostly negative. Do you think any jury on earth would believe that though you lived in the same house with your cousin you can't remember where his much-loved niece went to live, can't remember whom she worked for, can't produce even one letter or diary of Bailey's that might reveal her whereabouts, can't account for the letters she wrote him during all the time he was led to believe her dead ? "

" She *was* dead ! " Harriet insisted hysterically. " She *was* dead ! "

" Listen," I said. " She's alive ! An American sea captain saw her with two children in Cap François less than three weeks ago."

" He was lying ! "

" No, he wasn't ! He was telling the cold truth, and you're caught— because when I see her, as I shall, I'll learn that she has written regularly to her uncle in spite of not hearing from him. Then I'll have proof that you've been destroying all her letters, since nobody but you had either the opportunity or the motive."

" You haven't a shred of proof of anything you say ! " Harriet protested. " My cousin made a will leaving all his property to me. That property is mine, and it'll stay so in spite of your lying accusations ! "

I stared at her, marvelling at the horrible things women will do for money and security—shuddering, too, at my narrow escape.

" Harriet," I said, " you don't realise that every word you say confirms my charges. If I go before the Judge of Probate in this city, with Lydia Bailey as my client, and state the facts in your case, he'll have that will declared null and void. What's more, if we want to press the matter, you'd probably spend the next few years in jail, convicted on the charge of obtaining money under false pretences."

She said nothing—just sat silent and sullen.

" So I have only this to say," I went on. " If from this moment you sell, use, or destroy anything that came to you through the last will and testament of Thomas Bailey, I'll make it my business to see that you *are* put in jail, because when I come back from San Domingo, either I'll bring Lydia with me, or I'll bring incontrovertible proof that the ' Alexander Bean ' letter was a forgery that enabled you to steal a fortune from a young and defenceless girl."

I picked up my hat and met Harriet Faulkner's hard, defiant stare for what I hoped was the last time—and if looks could have killed, I would never have lived to reach the street, let alone Haiti.

I went to Portland to spend two days with my uncle, Aunt Emmy, and Madam Ross. When I'd shown them Lydia's picture and told them about Harriet Faulkner, they made me feel sorry for those benighted souls who talk about New Englanders' frosty lack of feeling.

My uncle licked his lips over my documents on Spoliation Claims ; and Aunt Emmy and Madam Ross summoned three needlewomen to stitch new shirts for me. Even Eddie and Owen, who had reluctantly done my bidding when I was directing farming, proudly bragged of doing the very things that once they'd been so averse to doing. The hay,

they boasted, would run two tons to the acre, first crop, and one ton the
second crop—though, when I'd made them use a ton of lime to the acre
for that very purpose two years before, they'd told all the other farmers
in town that I was crazy.

When my uncle, Madam Ross, and Aunt Emmy drove me to the
wharves, they overwhelmed me with advice. " I've put a flannel belly-
band in your bag," Aunt Emmy said. " I found it," my uncle added,
" and wrapped it around those pistols *I* put in. You bring her back here
for Christmas, Albion, and bring some of that old San Domingo rum
with you. We'll mix it with brandy and just a little peach cordial, and
make her sorry for all the time she wasted in San Domingo ! "

We were two weeks making that voyage between two worlds—that
almost unbelievable miracle which changed the ice, cold, and bleakness
of New England to the searing sunlight, the deep blue water, the drifting
golden gulfweed, the skittering flying-fish, the billowing clouds, and the
palm-fringed islands of the Caribbean.

Captain Lee called off the names of the islands as we passed as readily
as I'd have called the names of Portland streets—Eleuthera, Abaco, Hole-
in- the-Wall, Berry Islands, Little Isaac, Great Isaac. . . .

These must have been the very islands that Columbus saw, according
to that ancient French book that I had first read to my aunt and uncle
on those far-off winter nights in New Brunswick. I had found a copy of
it in Moreau de St. Méry's bookstore in Philadelphia, and now, as I
re-read its pages, I reflected that Columbus must have seen those islands
through emerald-tinted spectacles ; for to me the islands looked like hot
and dusty pancakes on the ocean's rim, their colours sadly faded, their
greens all grey, their blues smudged.

Yet my excitement grew as we rounded the blunt nose of Cuba and
turned southward in the path Columbus followed, and although I still
thought he'd misrepresented those Sugar Islands in his account to his
credulous countrymen, I found something thrilling about the things he
said he saw. I read aloud to Captain Lee the account of Columbus's
first glimpse of San Domingo—or Hispaniola, as he called it.

" It was lofty and mountainous," said Columbus, " with green
savannahs and spacious plains, grown thickly to trees of enormous size,
all of which bore fruit so sweet and so beautiful as to be the product of
a true rather than a terrestrial paradise."

Captain Lee nodded. " Wait till you see the women," he said.
" Creamy, like thick cream, but flexible as snakes—unless you prefer 'em
black. Some do. They're solider."

He stretched out his arm. " There it is," he said, " high up, high
up."

Hung high in the hot, transparent pure air, was a blue, blue blade,
a vast point unreal in its sharpness, unreal in that it was bluer than a
sky already so deeply blue as to seem bluer than anything on heaven or

earth. It was a mountain peak : one lone blue peak, I thought at first ;
and then I saw others and others and still others, towering pointed things,
cocked at incredible and impossible angles, just as Columbus had
said.

That night we saw lights gleaming at the foot of the mountains, and
at dawn the scent of the island came out to us—a poignant perfume, soft
and languorous, all-enveloping and heart-stirring.

When morning came I saw exactly what Columbus had seen and
faithfully described : tumbled purple mountains ; misty blue peaks
stabbing up out of rich forests ; velvety plantations draped opulently
over green savannahs ; lush valleys slashed as if by giant axes through
cliffs carved by Cyclopean chisels into battlements and castles.

San Domingo—Hispaniola—Haiti ! Columbus had been no liar ;
and I wondered whether the rest of it was true, too : whether there was
something accursed about this fantastic, unreal island : something that
would cast a spell around me, just as it had cast one around Columbus,
involving him in countless perplexities for the remainder of his life,
dooming him to an infinity of woes and disappointments, and darkening
all his days with undeserved humiliations.

CHAPTER X

HAITI, the French part of San Domingo, is like the back of a man's right
hand when he holds it before his face, forefinger and little finger extended
to the left, the two middle fingers folded against the palm, and the thumb
pressed out of sight against the hidden fingers. The knuckles are the
dividing-line between the French part of the island and the Spanish part.
The space between the two fingers is the seventy-mile-wide, pale green,
pale blue Bight of Léogane. The extended little finger, almost touching
the outstretched nose of Cuba, is the Great North Plain, with the capital
city of Cap François at the upper edge of the large joint. The depression
between the down-folded middle fingers is the valley of the Artibonite,
walled by mountain chains whose names are as fantastic as their shapes.
At the base of the index finger, where it joins the down-folded second
finger, is Port-au-Prince, a hundred miles south of Cap François across
a stormy sea of mountains. And between the knuckle and the first joint
of the outstretched index finger are the rich sugar, rum, and coffee sections
of Léogane, Jacmel, and the Cul de Sac.

We made port at Cap François—the very harbour into which Columbus
had sailed to establish his first settlement in the New World ; and I felt
that I knew it from Columbus's own description :

" The high and rocky mountains on either side of the harbour rose
from among noble forests and swept down into luxuriant plains and
cultivated fields, and the rich smiling valley between the two mountains

ran far into the interior. The air was mild as in April, and the sailors were enraptured with the beauty of the country, which surpassed, as they said, even the luxuriant plains of Cordova."

I was excited, too, by the crumpled mountains that seemed to be suspended from the clouds, like a vast theatre curtain painted by an artist with a liking for violent colours ; by the city of blue, pink, and white houses grouped around a shining white Plaza on the waterfront ; by the fleet of American brigs and schooners that lay at anchor in the cup-shaped harbour, their bows headed into a hot south-west wind perfumed with flower odours. Somewhere beyond those purple mountains I knew I'd find Lydia Bailey. Harriet Faulkner could insist that Lydia was dead as often as she liked, but she was so alive that I could almost hear her calling to me from beyond those mountain-walls.

As we glided through the fleet of American vessels, Lee gave me the lie of the land. " That white Plaza at the edge of the harbour," he said, " is all white stone, and so are the roads for miles into the country. The long white building high on the left, that's Christophe's palace. He's the black general that keeps order in these parts." He looked at me oddly. " Don't get the idea that black generals are anything like white generals. They ain't exactly human when they get excited.

" Those stone buildings at the edge of the Plaza, they're warehouses and government offices built by the French before the blacks drove 'em out. That's where the stores and taverns are, too : the Plaza." He sighed ecstatically. " Wait till you see that Plaza filled to the scuppers with niggers ! " He lowered his voice. " And full of women ! By God, Hamlin, you can talk about women, but you don't know anything about 'em till you've had coloured ones ! "

His face as he described the more delectable points of those women, grew red and sweaty, he constantly licked his upper lip by protruding the lower, as if feeling for an imaginary moustache ; his eyes roamed from the shore to my face and back again as if hopeful of discovering in me an excitement equal to his own.

" You can have any shade you want," he said, leaning close to me so that I was conscious of his breath, which wasn't pleasant. " Some like 'em pure black, and God knows there's enough black ones. But take my word for it, the best of the lot are the sacatras. They're about three shades lighter than the mulattoes—seven-eighths French and one-eighth nigger ; keep their carriages just like regular ladies, and buy their perfume straight from Paris. By God, Hamlin, there ain't anything like 'em anywhere in the world ! "

He gazed at me complacently, as though he had been the first to discover the women he described. Not having a ready answer, I raised my eyebrows and made sounds of amazement.

" I'll tell you what," he resumed. " Wait till I've got my papers in order. Then I'll go ashore with you and make you acquainted with a piece of yellow goods you'd be a week finding."

"Oh," I said, "I won't put you to all that trouble, Captain. You know I've got business to attend to——"

"Let it wait," Lee said. "That's what everyone does in San Domingo. Women and rum come ahead of everything."

"My business won't wait," I said. "Don't worry about me, Captain. I'm figuring on living ashore, anyway."

Lee looked irritated. "This girl's clean, if that's what's worrying you," he said. "You'd better trust my judgment. If you depend on your own, you'll go home with a fine case of yaws."

He seemed almost insulted because I wouldn't follow his suggestion, and I was hard put to it to explain to him that I had nothing whatever against his choice of women.

It never occurred to me, when I bade Lee good-bye and set off for shore with my carpet bag and my neatly corded bundle of gold braid, that my path and his might cross again ; but I know now that we'd all get on better in this world if we assumed that we'll be sure to have further dealings with everyone we meet.

I truly believe there never was a city anywhere in the world as strange or as odd-smelling as Cap François in that January of 1802. What Paris looked like, I didn't then know ; but it seemed to me that Cap François was a Paris such as one might see in a nightmare—a Paris with one side open to the blue and emerald waters of a palm-fringed harbour ; a Paris filled with black, brown, and yellow Parisians chattering a hardly understandable French ; a Paris filled with generals straight out of a delirium : generals as black as the underside of a stove-lid, wearing swords twice as long as swords should be, muffled to the throat in long-skirted military jackets of colours far from military—pinks, light blues, pale purples—and crowned with chapeaux so overwhelming that the black faces beneath them seemed dwarfed and wizened, like those of apes with their heads in bushel baskets.

When the *Hope*'s longboat nosed its way through the scores of lighters and ships' boats packed against the front of the quay that ran the full length of the Plaza, I felt I might be smothered ; for a score of jet-black porters struggled for possession of my carpet bag and my bundle of gold braid. One of them, by persistent use of a hoarse voice and threatening gestures, took possession of them and of me at the same time, shepherding me up the steps of the quay and on to the white-paved Plaza, where it seemed to me that all the Negroes in the world were congregated.

There were Negroes of every gradation of colour, and in every imaginable form of dress and undress : Negro roustabouts ; Negro grandees ; jet-black men, shoeless, tattered, with flattened noses and enormous banana-shaped lips ; pale-brown elegants with aquiline features, little crinkly whiskers such as Frenchmen wear, and garments grotesquely exaggerated in style and cut.

There were fat Negresses in brown dresses like nightgowns, carrying baskets filled with short lengths of sugar cane, which sold for an infinitesimal copper coin and in such numbers that the whole Plaza seemed to be covered with the chewed fragments ; skinny old witch-like Negresses, in shapeless gunny-sacking, selling charms, philters, and powders from wicker trays hung by cords from their scrawny shoulders ; buxom black prostitutes, in waists and dresses slit to show enormous breasts and thighs ; and—most noticeable of all—innumerable slender, coffee-creamy-coloured mulatto women, every last one richly if not startlingly dressed, all of them in carriages, all carrying scarlet parasols, all freely and openly making advances to the pale-brown elegants, to American sea captains, even to all the American sailors scattered through the crowd.

Around and among these gaudily dressed black, brown, and yellow people ran naked little boys and girls, their dark skins glistening with perspiration, screaming as if all hell were after them, bumping into passers-by, diving beneath horses, rolling in the chewed sugar cane that littered the white paving stones.

The smells of the place were unexpected and startling : odours seemed to lie upon the Plaza in thick, undulating layers. Most powerful of all was the scent of coffee and of sugar, sticky-sweet and reminiscent of my boyhood days in Portland, when I'd lean down into the sugar barrel to filch a scoopful. Blended with the coffee-sugary odours was a musky, animal smell that I took to come from the dark-skinned thousands all about me. Weaving through those odours came the stench of human excrement from open sewers that ran across the white Plaza to empty themselves into the harbour ; the smell of decaying fish ; and, whenever one of the slender, coffee-creamy Negresses or one of the pale-brown elegants came near, a scent of perfume so violent as to smother every other smell, even the foulest.

My squatty porter went surging on before, bellowing hoarsely and making useful play with my bundle of gold braid against the rumps of idlers who obstructed his progress. In thick Creole he bawled for permission to make road for a Blanc—which is how all Negroes in Haiti invariably address a white man. " Bon jour, Blanc," they say. " How do you do, White."

This obstreperous guide led me to the heavy stone arcades that formed three sides of the garish, hot, odorous Plaza. Beneath the arcades were shops selling jewellery, lace nothings, boots, wines, bonnets—fripperies for men and women, but fripperies more elegant and costly than anything New York or Philadelphia had to offer.

I think my guide would have ignored me if I'd tried to divert him from his purpose, for seemingly he was determined that there was only one place in Cap François that an American could go ; and so I found myself in the foyer of the Hôtel de la République—a hotel so magnificent, so glittering, and so much more sumptuous than anything I had ever before seen that I could hardly believe my eyes.

The lobby was crowded with important-looking black men, some in those same fantastically coloured uniforms I had seen on the Plaza ; others dressed with almost startling elegance—skin-tight pantaloons, long-tailed satin coats, ruffled shirts, flowered waistcoats, enormous cocked hats, and beribboned canes as tall as their shoulders.

There was a porters' room off the main lobby, and when my porter led me there to leave my bag and bundle, I thought I'd stumbled into a school ; for the room was crowded with small black boys on benches, each boy clutching a package or two. From the chief porter I learned that these were the private package-carriers of the generals and the dark-skinned elegants in the lobby, all of whom were waiting for the doors of the dining-room to be opened.

I think the thing that impressed me most about all the black men in the lobby, next to the dazzling colours of their garments, was their show of politeness. There was a perpetual hand-shaking, bowing, chapeau-flourishing, a constant calling of titles, such as Mon Général, Mon Amiral, Mon Cher Commissaire, Mon Cher Ministre. Yet, when the doors of the dining-room were thrown open, this mass of black men moved so suddenly forward that I expected to see some of the smaller ones trampled to death.

They surged into the long dining-room like a brightly-coloured wave, treading on each other's heels and calling out, " After you, mon Général." " Pray do me the honour to precede me, M. le Ministre."

There were a dozen long tables in the room, laden with platters of bread, bowls of pickles, jars of honey, legs of lamb, and enormous fish resting magnificently on long wooden platters. The floor was sanded, perhaps to give diners a better foothold when they ran for their seats.

Those black men threw themselves on the food like a horde of giant locusts, all conversation ceased, and the room was clamorous with the clanking of knives and forks against plates and the noisy champing of all those black jaws.

I paid off my porter, found an official of the hotel at a desk, explained that I wished to dine, and was waved into the dining-room, where I speedily found there was still plenty to eat upon the tables in spite of the ravenous inroads already made upon the heaped platters ; then gave a little more attention to my surroundings.

Beneath the generous platters, the tablecloths were sadly soiled and covered with sketches, hen-tracks, and diagrams of fortifications evidently made with anything handy, from knives to cigar-ash. Crawling on every-thing—tablecloth, platters of food, the diners' knives and forks, even on their hands and faces—were flies by the countless thousands : big, noisy flies with shiny blue bellies. Other thousands hovered dartingly around the chandaliers, or crawled meditatively upon the ceiling.

I couldn't take my eyes from the dazzling uniforms all around me, and it was more than I could do to keep from being an eavesdropper to the magniloquent speeches that came fragmentarily to my ears.

Sitting near me were two black generals. One wore a purple uniform encrusted with gold braid, its folded collar high around his ears, so that to turn his head he was forced to turn his upper body. The front edges of that bedizened collar were thick with grease where his lips had rubbed when he turned his head incautiously. His companion wore a uniform coat of black velvet frogged with silver. His breeches were bright yellow leather, mostly concealed by shiny black jackboots whose tops reached a foot above his knees.

The smaller general, in a crow's voice, was holding forth impressively to his companion on the subject of a review of troops in which he had that morning taken part. "Ah, mon Général, it was magnificent ! The appearance of those troops was without parallel ! Never do my troops appear upon the field without causing me an indescribable sensation." He struck himself upon the chest, coughed chokingly, and seemed about to strangle.

The taller general sympathetically reached inside his coat and brought out two pale, thin cigars. The two generals lit them and draped their arms across the backs of their chairs with an air of profound importance and worldliness.

" I also have that feeling, mon Général," the taller general said. " When I lead my troops upon the field, thoughts pass through my head with such rapidity that I could weep. I think of their loyalty, their bravery, their love for this great land of ours, and I know that no troops in all the world could stand for a moment against our army."

The smaller one puffed pale cigar smoke whose odour resembled that of lightly salted hake—that powerful effluvium, which poisons the air of Maine in the autumn. " Your thought is understandable, mon Général," he rejoined. " The tenue, the discipline of these brave men reflects the spirit of their officers. They have never been conquered, nor can they ever be conquered. The English have tried it without success. The Spaniards have tried it without success. No other soldiers in the world have the magnificent qualities of our soldiers none ! Not for a moment would I hesitate to engage any army in the world ! "

The tall general raised a simian eyebrow. " Most certainly not, mon Général ! I have thought often and often that I shall soon take a regiment of these brave men of ours to Paris and arrange for a demonstration. It is possible that I may go next month."

The smaller general looked doubtful. " I had planned to go to Paris next month myself, mon Général, but only to display my horses. The expense of transporting a regiment—that would be épatant ! "

The taller general shrugged his shoulder . " If the Treasury should prove unwilling, I would arrange the matter myself. I, too, have horses, as you know, mon Général. You had planned to display your horses in France ? "

" Only to review the troops, mon Général, and to let Bonaparte see that a general of Haiti is the equal of any officer in Europe—that there is nothing Europe can do that we cannot do better."

The taller general nodded understandingly. " An excellent idea, mon Général. It was my plan to race my horses in a few of the great races.

No other horses in the world are as fast as those horses of mine, mon
Général—except perhaps your own."

"That is true, mon Général." The smaller one leaned his elbows on
the table as if considering whether he, too, should enter his horses against
the finest products of Europe's stables.

I shot a quick look round the table to see whether others had heard
this modest exchange ; but those near me were busy with their own
important conversations. So far as I could see, everyone at the table
was on the verge of exploding with importance, barring two ununiformed
black men at the far end. One—short, grey-haired, partly bald, and wholly
worried-looking, who wore a simple suit of wrinkled white linen—was
fixedly regarding the ceiling with a sort of melancholy detachment. His
companion, a hulk of a man, also in white linen, had a velvety black face
and shoulders so broad that his bullet-head seemed strangely dwarfed.
He was biting into a leg of lamb, and so huge was the bite that his own
eyes were closed by the distention of his jaws.

As the big man completed his colossal bite, his eyes opened and looked
straight into mine, almost as though he'd been waiting to catch my
attention. I had an uncomfortable feeling that he'd watched me listening
to the conversation of the two generals, and had read my thoughts, which
had been neither sympathetic nor complimentary. I even felt that he
was about to come around the table to speak to me. If this had been his
intention, however, he was distracted from it.

A few seats removed from him sat a young and gaudily clad Negro
general hunched over a plate on which were piled slices of bread covered
with honey which he was shovelling into himself in dripping gouts and
gobbets. Suddenly he stopped, clapped both hands to his mouth and
shrieked horribly, as if stung by a thousand hornets. He leaped to his
feet, moaning and swallowing convulsively, and looked wildly about him ;
then ran to the big black man who had been watching me. From the
anguished expression of the sufferer, I knew what had happened : he had
a bad tooth and the honey had been too excruciatingly much for it.

The big Negro peered inquiringly into the other's mouth, nodded his
understanding, and examined his own fingers doubtfully ; then he leaned
over and rubbed them on the sanded floor, obviously to remove the juices
of the leg of lamb. Then he gripped the sufferer's hair with one hand,
thrust the sanded thumb and forefinger of the other hand into the mouth,
looked ruminatively at the ceiling—and twisted, as one twists a key in a
lock. The sufferer howled again and started back convulsively. The big
man's thumb and forefinger emerged, as from a cavern, holding a tooth
the size of a small carrot.

I wondered how in God's name any man could possess such strength
in his fingers ; and while I wondered, the big man dropped the tooth
on the floor, wiped his fingers on the tablecloth, picked up his leg of
lamb, and raised it to his lips. Again his eyes met mine—and again I
became acutely aware that I was too openly betraying my thoughts.

As I left the table to get my little portrait of Lydia from my bag, I told myself that I must be more guarded in this singular country if I wished to keep out of trouble.

I wanted a quiet place in which to sit alone and plan what to say to the American Consul when I should go to him about Lydia, as I knew I must. I thought I'd found that quiet place around the corner from the Hôtel de la République. On a comparatively cool and quiet side street, a few doors from the Plaza, I saw tables and chairs on the side-walk, all of them empty, and had the thought that here was a haven where I could sit peacefully over coffee and rum and lay my plans.

There was nobody inside the café except a languid, light-coloured mulatto waiter whose skin had a sort of greenish-yellow cast. So far as I could see, he was doing nothing but study himself in a mirror, first profile, then full face, throwing back his head proudly and moving his lips in silent speech. He paid no attention to me until, after waiting an unconscionable time, I called to him that if he weren't too busy I'd like coffee and rum.

On this he favoured me with a glance so offensively contemptuous that I wondered what ailed him. He came reluctantly to the door and looked down his nose at me ; then, in an almost hating voice, he asked in Creole what sort of coffee I wanted.

It seemed to me he was deliberately trying to make me feel ill at ease, so in my best French I said curtly that I naturally wanted the best.

He told me superciliously that in Haiti one should do as others of importance do : name the sort of best desired.

In the midst of his mumblings, a procession of Negro boys came out of the Plaza towards us. There were seven of them, eight or nine years old, dressed in short cotton pants over which hung striped cotton shirts. The larger boys carried bundles on their heads, the smaller ones had lesser parcels, and all the parcels put together wouldn't have made the tenth part of a load for a sick donkey. They passed us single file, flat black feet slapping the pavement and eyes rolling whitely. The last boy, who was also the littlest, had two packages which seemed to be causing him trouble, for he shifted them constantly from one hand to the other, and his saucer-like eyes looked worried.

As the last boy passed, the sulky waiter spat at him and kicked his ankle, as if to take out on him the spleen he had begun to vent on me. The boy tripped and fell, his parcels flying among the chairs and tables. A lightning-quick flick of the waiter's shoe sent one of the parcels spinning into an opening in the outer wall of the restaurant—a sort of drainage pipe. Then the waiter shouted indignantly at the boy and kicked him again.

CHAPTER XI

I GOT to my feet and reached for the miserable creature ; but another more competent than I was before me—a veritable giant of a black man, who materialised as suddenly and magically as though he'd popped from the ground like the Slave of the Lamp. It was the same enormous tooth-extractor who had watched me so amusedly in the hotel dining-room. He put his hand on my shoulder in an apologetic way, and I sank back into my chair as though pressed down by something elemental and irresistible. " With your permission," he said, in a breathless small voice, " I wipe this man so he stay wiped. No sense white men hunting trouble in this place. They too much trouble without asking."

He moved past me, gathered the slack of the waiter's jacket in a ham-like hand, and lifted him a foot from the sidewalk. " My goo'ness me my," this mountain of a man said in a faint, lackadaisical voice. " Luckiest nigra in whole world, that what *you* are ! Anybody but me catch you kicking his wife's nigra boy, you get your skull knocked outside in with cocomacaque. Me, I give you one little wipe."

He set the waiter down on his heels with a jarring thump, removed a broad-brimmed hat of woven straw from his head, and tossed it on a table together with an enormous walking-stick ; then, with a black forefinger the size of a cucumber, he delicately turned the waiter's head to one side. The waiter, haughtily contemptuous, pushed petulantly at the black finger, whereupon the huge Negro's upper body rolled a little to the left and his right fist came up against the waiter's jaw almost gently, I thought. The waiter's head jerked upward, his body leaned sharply like a sapling in a gale, and his feet performed an awkward backward-moving dance that carried him through the door of the café as if projected from a gun. From the dark interior came the sound of a heavy fall—breaking glass—then silence.

The wiper stooped over, lifted the little black boy from the side-walk, gave him a slap on his rump, and made a commanding gesture with his hand—a fluttering, revolving gesture which said more plainly than words that the little boy was to pursue his six companions and bring them back to wait further orders.

He gave me a bashful smile, picked up his huge white hat, and adjusted it carefully on his head, which looked oddly small for his body, as a coconut might look if perched on the stump of a pine. " She's not my habit to wipe folks," he said, " but I very dark-minded about folks cruelling little pickity boys. I think very barbarous. Also not my habit to interfere without being invited, but I know from how you start to wipe that you no Frenchman. This no time to altercate in Haiti. I hope you pardon my intrusion."

" It never occurred to me you were intruding," I said. " In fact, it

was a great relief to see how neatly you—ah—wiped him. He certainly
deserved wiping ; and I'm grateful to you for taking it off my hands."

It dawned upon me suddenly that this huge black man had been
talking an elegant sort of American language. " Why," I said, " I believe
you're an American, too. You don't belong here—not with that manner
of speech."

He seemed immeasurably pleased : his head drooped on his shoulder
and he giggled. " I King Dick," he said. " General King Dick."

" King ? " I asked. " General ? Are those names, or titles ? "

Instead of answering, he looked down at the little black boy, who
seemingly hadn't moved since he'd been picked up and slapped on the
rump. The boy's face was contorted with despair and fear.

" What matter you, Alciatore ? " King Dick asked. " I give odors
you bring back those others."

The boy, speechless, held up one package and burst into tears.

King Dick's eyes rolled whitely. " My, my ! Oh, my goo'ness me my !
One gone ! That one very uncomfortable one, Alciatore. That my pearls ! "
He looked stricken. " You mean you look and look and they no sign
of it ? " He stooped over to peer under all the tables.

I went to the drain into which the waiter had kicked the package.
There it was, elbow-deep in the opening ; so I fumbled for it and handed
it to King Dick.

At the sight of it, the boy leaped in the air, made a squealing sound,
then went bounding down the street like a small black monkey. King
Dick subsided weakly into a chair, took from his pocket a green handkerchief the size of a pillow-slip, and mopped his brow.

" My goo'ness me my," he exclaimed. " That a lesson to me ! What I
care about not being stylish ! You know what in that package ? Pearls !
Nobody supposed carry his own bundles in Haiti, not even pearls ; but
not amusing when boys drop pearls in drain pipes. I rather carry my
own bundles and stop being fashionable ! "

" I don't know what I'm expected to believe," I said ; " but isn't it
unusual to go shopping for pearls in Haiti, and aren't kings something
new in this part of the world ? "

He looked at me intently ; then went to the door of the café and
stood there, shouting for coffee and rum in a sort of hog-French—an
Anglicised French, slurred thickly into a soup-like speech that was
scarcely recognisable. He was a surprising figure of a man, a good six
and a half feet tall, with tremendous shoulders. There seemed to be
substance to the blackness of his face, as though it would come off if
rubbed. His mouth was as large as his head was small ; and when he
smiled, there seemed to be the fearful possibility that his face might
be permanently separated into two parts by an expanse of innumerable
glistening teeth. Against the blackness of his skin his eyeballs were so
white and round that his usual look was one of innocent and benevolent
surprise ; whereas, when he smiled, his eyes were so narrowed by his

all-embracing grin that he looked featureless—except for that vast exposure of teeth.

His clothes, as I have said, were of simple white linen, but the stick he carried was peculiar : a five-foot length of bamboo ending in a warty knob the size of a summer squash, which made it too unweildy to be regarded as a cane. Yet, being bamboo, it must necessarily be too fragile for a weapon.

When he came back to the table, his manner toward me was off-hand. I'd seen lawyers similarly off-hand when trying to trap witnesses.

" That Alciatore very unfortunate if you not here," he said. " If those pearls be lost, that unfortunate for me, too. My, my ! Yes ! Very costive."

" That's possible," I said, " if you think you wouldn't have looked in the drain yourself—and are sure they're real pearls."

He took the little parcel from his pocket, opened it and lifted a pad of black velvet. On a similar pad lay four shimmering globes of concentrated moonbeams, two the size of sparrow eggs, the other two the size of humming bird eggs. He picked up one of the larger globes and turned it back and forth before my eyes. The colours in it put me in mind of a still ocean and the distant pale blue of the Maine coast on a hazy August morning.

" Beautiful ! " I said. " Those pearls must be worth a great deal."

" I seen worse," he said. " Pearls been cheap since French revoluted. Necks to wear 'em on been a litto scarce." He held the glowing sphere close to his flat nose and stared at it with eyes that seemed about to pop from his head. " Ordinary times, pearl like this bring four thousand. Cost me two and a half."

" Two and a half thousand ! " I cried. " Two and a half thousand *dollars* ? "

He nodded. " How much reward you think proper ? "

" Reward ? " I laughed. " I don't want a reward ! The box was there, and I picked it up. Sooner or later you'd have looked in the pipe yourself, even if I hadn't been there."

He put the pearls back into the box, tied it up and thrust it into his pocket, and stared at me impassively, much as a judge stares at a witness when making up his mind about his reliability.

The waiter, his skin several shades greener than when I'd first seen him, came cringing to the table and placed upon it a pot of coffee and a squatty black bottle labelled " Meil de Jacmel."

King Dick eyed him severely. " You been very malice," he said in horrible French. " Imagine me to be Christophe, I would pull out your arms by the roots, take out your eyes with a spoon. Good thing I'm me, not Christophe ! Remember that, case I ever need help." He picked up his club and with its squash-like head dabbed at a fly on the table. It must, I thought, be feather-light, for so accurately did he wield it that the fly was audibly mashed.

The waiter backed away.

The seven little black boys, I saw, had returned and were standing round-eyed across the street, watching us. King Dick made a peremptory circling motion with his odd club, and all seven turned and faced the wall. He put the club on the table and gave me the portentous nod with which a man of large affairs expresses satisfaction at one of his own successful endeavours. " They trained young, where I live," he said. " Around my place, they do what I say, and quick."

I picked up his club, and almost dropped it, for it was as heavy as a bar of iron. " Why, what's this ? " I asked. " I thought it was bamboo."

" That cocomacque," he said. " Male bamboo. Everybody in Haiti got a cocomacque, but nobody got one like mine."

His gaze wandered off across the Plaza to the oily blue water of the harbour. " Been some time," he said absent-mindedly, " since I run into anyone who didn't want something, even when she hadn't done nothing. My goo'ness me, they not *anything* you want ? "

" Well," I said, " if you happen to know the American Consul here, you might say a word to him for me. Do you know him ? "

" Yarse." I thought he eyed me furtively. " That Colonel Lear."

" Lear ! " I cried. " Not *Tobias* Lear ! Is he a white-haired man who walks like a cat, softly, as if he walked on egg-shells ? "

" Yarse."

" How long has he been here ? "

" Sick-sem months," King Dick said.

" Well, by George," I said, more to myself than to King Dick. " I believe Smith was right ! I believe Lear had himself appointed to this place for a damned good reason, just as Smith suspected."

" You already know that Colonel Lear ? " King Dick asked.

" In a way," I said. " I've met him, and I don't like him, but I've got to see him because he's the American Consul and the lady I'm hunting is an American."

King Dick looked interested. " You hunting a lady ? My goo'ness me my ! That always pleasant work. Tell me some more ; then we go see Colonel Lear."

I told him my name and how I had been forced against my will to turn from farming to the law ; how I had discovered the portrait of Lydia Bailey and been told she was dead, only to learn that the report of her death had been spread by an unscrupulous woman who wanted Lydia's property.

King Dick's eyes, while I was speaking, flicked across my face from time to time. When I had finished, he asked how long ago I had seen this lady. I replied I had seen only her portrait—never the lady herself.

He said cryptically that if I felt as I did about somebody I had never seen, I would probably feel considerably worse after I had seen her. Where he wanted to know, did she live ?

When I said that her enemy in the United States had destroyed all papers that might have indicated where she could be found, King Dick said softly, " My goo'ness me my ! I guess you going to want more help than you thought you would ! That Colonel Lear very polite, very educated, but not very experienced about black folks."

He picked up the bottle the waiter had brought us, filled our glasses and ceremoniously raised his own to me. The golden liquor was pure nectar, and I said as much.

" They no ' Nectar Brand ' rum made here," King Dick said. " This ' Honey of Jacmel,' it not poison, but it not real good. They three real good rums—from Cayes, Jérémie, and Anse-à-Veau ! Oh, my goo'ness me my ! Make this rum taste like slumgullion."

Smacking his thick lips with the sound of a horse pulling a hoof from mud, he changed the subject abruptly. " What you do if that lady lives Jacmel or way south ? "

" Go to Jacmel, of course. Wherever she lives, I'll go."

" You got plenty money to travel with ? " he asked solicitously. " Travel pretty costly in Haiti."

" I hope to have," I said. " If I am obliged to travel far, I hope to finance myself by selling this." I drew a length of gold braid from my pocket and showed it to him.

His eyes, as he stared at it, looked like teal-eggs. " My, my ! " he whispered. " That better than Voodoo."

" I don't know what you're talking about," I said.

King Dick smiled weakly and made a fluttering movement with a huge hand. " How much gold braid you got ? "

" Six hundred feet," I said. " I'm hoping to dispose of it at about three dollars a foot."

His enormous mouth widened in a grin that seemed to split his head in two. " That very, very nice braid," he said. " Enough for two hundred generals. That five dollars a foot."

" No," I said, " that's too high. I couldn't get that much for it."

" Oh, my goo'ness, you got it already. That braid all mine ! "

Ignoring my protests that my profit on the transaction would be too large, he poured himself another glass of rum, sipped it lingeringly ; then rapped smartly on the table for the waiter, who hurried toward us, green-faced. With him he brought coloured beans in a saucer to show the amount we owed. King Dick picked up the saucer and poured the beans into the palm of his hand. He passed his other hand lightly over the palm, and closed his enormous fist on the beans. Then he blew on the fist, held it before the waiter, and opened it. The hand was empty. The beans had vanished. The waiter stepped backward and fell over a chair.

" No beans, no pay," King Dick said coldly. He took me by the elbow and turned me toward the crowded Plaza. As we entered that congested square, he drew a green silk handkerchief from the breast pocket of his coat. With it came a shower of coloured beans. " My, my ! " King Dick said in a faint whisper. " I better be careful where I carry that handkerchief."

CHAPTER XII

He was now, King Dick told me as we slowly made our way through the crowded streets, a " Général de Place." Before that he had been a regular general in the Negro army of Toussaint L'Ouverture when the mulattoes of the south had revolted in 1799 because they objected to the freeing of Negro slaves, and to being ruled by Negroes.

" Everybody always revolting till Toussaint came along," King Dick said. " Negroes always revolting against Blancs and burning everything and everybody. Blancs always revolting against Negroes and killing everyone. Mulattoes always revolting against Blancs and Negroes and tearing everyone to pieces." Undisciplined Negroes and mulattoes, he observed darkly, were the killingest people, outside of Blancs.

Toussaint, King Dick said, had put an end to most of this slaughtering in 1795 by organising the Negroes into an army ; and in 1798 he had driven out the English, who with " English boggetedness " had wasted a hundred thousand men trying to capture the island, and had " sweppup " all the French ; following which Toussaint set up his black government, and declared a general amnesty to all enemies, whether black, white, or mulatto, and even though they had helped the English.

" That's interesting," I said. " He must be a great man. I'd like to see him. Is he hard to see ? "

" Hard ? Oh, my goo'ness no ! " King Dick said. " He that little grey-headed man in white sat beside me at dinner. He built that hotel. He stop in there whenever he come to Cap François : take any seat, any tablo ; talk to anybody unless they talk big. That something Toussaint can't stand : big talk."

As if in proof of this, King Dick went on to say that when the last war was over, Toussaint urged all plantation-owners, even though they'd opposed him, to return to their plantations. If plantation-owners had been massacred, or had fled Haiti and were afraid to return, Toussaint turned over the management of their plantations to high officers in his army, and every plantation-manager became a general—a Général de Place. All blacks who had been freed by the Revolution were ordered back to the plantations for five years on a profit-sharing basis. The workmen got a quarter of the profits, the government a quarter, and the remainder went to the owner or the Général de Place appointed by Toussaint.

" Very good profits I realise last year," King Dick said. " Two hundred sixteen thousand dollars. Workmen divide fifty-four thousand ; government take same amount." He eyed me pensively. " That leaves me a hundred eight thousand. That not bad, my my no ! "

I found it hard to believe the things he told me so carelessly in that faintly lackadaisical voice of his ; and when I asked him how he had happened to become a black general in the first place, I found it even harder. I didn't know then, as I do now, that there are some persons to whom things always happen, so that their lives are as eventful as those of most persons are uneventful. I thought King Dick must be drawing the long bow : that no one person could have so many things happen to him. But we live and learn : I know better now.

He was born, he said, in the Sudan, where his father was a king who was unlike most African kings in that he urged agricultural pursuits on his people instead of inflicting war on them. When he was eighteen years old his father had sent him to purchase jewellery for his wives from a trader who had travelled all the way from Alexandria. King Dick smiled enormously when he spoke of this trader and wagged his head as if in delight at fond memories. The trader was a gentleman from Vienna, he said, who knew everything and had been everything—a soldier, a sailor, a Frenchman, an Italian, an Arab, a doctor, a dervish, a Marabout, an engineer, a monk, an actor, a Prince of Trebizond. King Dick had taken to me when he first saw me in the hotel dining-room, he said, because I reminded him of this trader. His head-wagging and chuckling continued as long as he spoke of him, as at a thousand amusing recollections.

The trader's name was Eugene Leitensdorfer, and by some chance that name clung in my memory and kept recurring to my mind for no reason whatever ; so that I have come to believe, as do the Arabs, that certain things are ordained, and that some of us, at any mention of that which is ordained, ring feebly deep within, as if a toy tuning fork were vibrating in a closed chamber of the mind.

It was Leitensdorfer who had taught King Dick about pearls : how to tell real ones from imitations, and how to distinguish between those that were good and those that were not so good. In teaching him about pearls, he said, Eugene Leitensdorfer had taught him many other things as well : how to move three nut-shells over a pearl in such a way that nobody on earth could tell correctly under which shell the pearl rested. Also he had taught King Dick how to make money vanish into thin air, and other similar tricks which he had found extremely valuable in business as well as in war, since the vanishing-pearl trick is based on nothing but deception and tricking people into watching the wrong thing, which— according to King Dick—is almost all there is to business and to war.

In all likelihood, he said, Leitensdorfer had saved his life ; for on his return to the Sudan he had fallen into an ambush, been captured by another king and sold to Arab traders, who hustled him off to Timbuktu, the great caravan centre and slave market.

Because of King Dick's size and powers of endurance, he said, he would probably have been sent to the salt mines and died there ; but the tricks that Leitensdorfer had taught him made people laugh— especially a rich date merchant from the oasis of Jalo, who had paid high for him so that he could learn the pearl trick. The date merchant had taken him on the long road to Jalo, kept him there for a few months, and then taken him to Derna where he had presented him to a friend, an English naval captain, who wanted him because he was big enough and strong enough to work a pivot-gun by himself. It was the naval officer who had taught him English and given him the name King Dick.

When the English naval captain retired and went to Spain to make his fortune in the sherry business, he had taken King Dick along—first to Xeres ; then to Surinam to sell sherry to rich Surinam planters ; then to New Orleans, where the English captain gave him his freedom and set him up in business for himself.

Thus he knew all about wine, guns, and countless other things, such as all the caravan routes in North Africa, the quality of the various oases— of which Jalo seemed to him infinitely the best—and cities, of which Derna was the most beautiful ; the methods of making couscous among the innumerable different tribes of Arabs and Moors, the method of baking beans peculiar to the Jews of North Africa, the odd habits of Arab Marabouts, the ways of African witch doctors, the fighting qualities of the different people among whom he had sojourned—the best, he thought, being the Negro Rangers of Surinam and the black Arabs of Jalo.

It was his wine business in New Orleans that had brought him into contact with the Spanish governor of New Orleans, who in turn had used him as a confidential agent. It was this work, he said, which had led him to become General Wilkinson's secretary.

He rolled his eyes at me. " You know General Wilkinson ? "

I said I didn't.

" Hoy ! " he said. " You don't know General James Wilkinson, big- gest general in America ? Biggest round ! Biggest everything ! My goo'ness ! "

" Well, I never heard of him," I said. " What was he general of ? "

" Everything," King Dick said promptly. " He was general of every- thing on the Mississippi River and everywhere else he ever heard about ; and if you named a new place to him, he'd be general of it that same day, as soon as he got opened."

" I beg your pardon," I said. " Did you say ' opened ? ' "

King Dick nodded.

I shook my head. " But how did you become associated with this General Wilkinson ? "

" Commercial business," King Dick said. " First time sick thousand dollars : second time sem thousand dollars. That what he get."

" From whom and for what, for God's sake ? "

King Dick spoke carelessly. " Favours for the Spanish governor."

" An American general did favours for a Spanish governor ? Do you realise what you're saying ? That would make him a traitor ! "

King Dick said nothing—just strode ponderously along beside me, making dainty dabs at flies with the knob of his cocomacaque as if it were fragile as a lady's fan.

" It's all beyond me," I said. " What you tell me doesn't explain how you got to be Wilkinson's secretary, or how that made you a general in San Domingo."

He began to explain patiently. When he carried the second package of money from the Spanish governor to Wilkinson, he said, Wilkinson had seemed unwilling to let him go back to New Orleans, and had offered him a position of trust. Wilkinson was a great hand with the botto (which I interpreted as " bottle ") and with what King Dick called " litto open pills that made him feel nice." (" Open " after more puzzlement, I then translated as " opium.") Thus Wilkinson needed near him someone who could pick him up and carry him home when overcome by open pills or the botto—who could also be trusted to take messages to the Spanish governor when more money was needed.

I looked hard at King Dick to see whether he was serious. Apparently he was.

" But what brought you to Haiti ? " I asked.

His head drooped on his shoulder and he tittered. I almost expected to see him put a bashful finger to his lips. Wilkinson, he explained, had a strong leaning toward new and elaborate uniforms, and although he was—as King Dick put it—a boopety, short man, he had an enormously corpulent upper body. Thus his upper garments weren't a bad fit for King Dick, and the King frequently tried on the general's uniform coats and waistcoats and practised military gestures and movements before a mirror. Unhappily for him, the general surprised him at this pastime one afternoon when King Dick thought him in bed and unconscious from over-indulgence in open pills and whisky. Not being quite himself, the general had reached for his pistols with the obvious intention of wiping out what he regarded as a stain upon his honour ; so King Dick had left him at top speed.

Because of Wilkinson's influence everywhere along the Mississippi, King Dick hadn't even stopped at New Orleans, but had taken informal passage in the hold of a ship bound for parts unknown. Unfortunately the vessel was a privateer, and King Dick had chosen for his resting-place the housing of a Long Tom which had been concealed in the hold. When the crew came to the hold to sway up the gun, he had been discovered. The captain, a Frenchman, had promptly taken advantage of King Dick's strength and knowledge of pivot-guns, and given him the freedom of the ship—which made it possible for him to fall overboard at the first port : Cap François. He made for the nearest wharf, arrived still wearing the general's coat and waistcoat, both badly strained at the seams, and created a profound impression even in the act of wading ashore. He was at once taken before Toussaint, who asked him a few questions and promptly the next day made him a real general for three reasons : King Dick could read and write ; his association with General Wilkinson, when the latter was

sober, had taught him how to behave like a general even though he knew
nothing of the prescribed military science of generalling ; and, third, he
explained to Toussaint some ideas he had of teaching other strong
Negroes how to operate artillery, even when reluctant to do so.

King Dick talked and talked. He told me that he preferred white
Englishmen and white Americans to people of his own colour, though he
was hard put to it to explain why. I gathered that he trusted them more,
and the good ones gave him a feeling of mental satisfaction that he couldn't
get from those with darker skins. In his opinion, the best army officers were
those who were intelligent and lazy ; the second best were those who were
intelligent and industrious ; the third best were those who were lazy and
thick-witted ; while the lowest and most dangerous were those who were
both industrious and thick-witted—and a soldier should instantly rid
himself of such men. I gathered further that he was suspicious of any man,
white or black, who was always doing and saying things designed to
further his own interests.

Before we'd come to the end of our walk, it seemed to me that I knew
King Dick about as well as I knew anybody in the world.

The Consulate General of the United States of America was housed
in three high-ceilinged rooms above a bank on the corner opposite the
Cap François opera house. When I walked into its outer office, with
King Dick looming behind me like a black cloud, I found three American
sea captains already there, restlessly fingering their caps and, as they
talked, staring from the dusty windows at the fleet of American ships in
the harbour.

They glanced up at us as we came in. At sight of King Dick, one, who
was sallow-faced and lank-haired, pointedly turned his back and said to
the other two in a querulous southern voice, " What I say is, they ain't
got any right to make a white man eat with niggers ; and the way things
are now, you got to eat with niggers if you want to eat at all. Either that,
or put your food in a basket and go out and eat it on the sidewalk."

" I'll tell you one thing," another of the three said. " You got to be
mighty careful how you do your complaining, or Lear'll pretend not to
understand what you're talking about. He's one of those damned New
Englanders."

" No, he ain't," the first one said. " He had the bad luck to be born
there, but he married a Custis and lived around slaves all his life. He
knows just as well as we do that no decent white man ought to be expected
to eat with 'em."

" He may know it," the third one said ; " but I'll bet you anything he
won't try to argue that little black Toussaint bastard into letting white
men have a dining-room to themselves."

" Listen "—this was the first one again ; " what do you think would
happen to him if I went home and told my senator that a respectable
American sea captain had refused to complain because white men had

been made to eat with niggers? Why, he'd get up in the Senate and tear that Toussaint limb from limb."

The word " limb " seemed to distract him from the subject in hand. " Say, that one I was with last night, I learned something from her I never knew before." He cast a glance over his shoulder at King Dick and me, then lowered his voice to a hoarse whisper. " I've been paying her two dollars a night, every time I make port, and that runs into money. Well, you know what she'd rather have than all the two-dollar bills in the world? One of those Chinese bone sewing sets that sell for seven dollars in New York! I asked her, ' If I bring you one of those next time I make port, how many nights is that good for? ' She said, ' Every night for five years.' Yes, sir, that's what she said, and she's high-class stuff, like all the rest of 'em at No. 16. There ain't one of 'em that ain't been kept by a rich Frenchman, one time or another, and there ain't one of 'em that's darker than octoroon."

The second captain made a clucking sound. " Last time Captain Jennings of the Barkentine *Jupiter* came back from Canton," he said, " he sold fifty of those boxes for five dollars. I could 'a' saved some money if I'd bought half a dozen ! "

The first nodded. " I figure I spent over a hundred and eighty dollars on that yellow wench when I could 'a' had her for less'n twenty."

I looked at King Dick. There was no expression at all on his black face, and I wondered what he thought of white men who couldn't sit at the same table with coloured people, but went out of their way to sleep with them and have children by them. I didn't wonder long, for he gave me an odd, blank look and said faintly, " My, my ! Some folks, they born to see everything wrong-end-to."

" ' Blind guides,' the Bible calls 'em." I reminded him. " ' Blind guides, which strain at a gnat and swallow a camel.' "

I hadn't lived long enough to know that men seldom have the good fortune to follow a guide who isn't blind.

When the door of the inner office at last opened, revealing the imposing figure of Colonel Lear bidding farewell to the caller with whom he had been closeted, King Dick got suddenly to his feet, gave me a peremptory nod, smiled engagingly at the three American sea captains who had risen to take advantage of that open door, and walked straight past Lear and his departing caller.

I thought for a moment that the three sea captains and Lear, too, were about to protest ; but seemingly all four of them thought better of it, and when Lear closed the door on his caller and turned to greet us he was affability itself. " My dear Hamlin," he said, " I have wondered whether French Spoliation Claims might not bring you here."

He turned to King Dick. " My dear good friend," he said, " this is indeed a pleasure ! Sit down, gentlemen. Sit down ! "

" I'm afraid," he went on to me, " that you're going to be disappointed in finding documents to support your claims. Things are very much upset in all government offices—papers misplaced, you know."

" Have you been looking for some of them ? " I asked.

" Oh no, no," Lear said hastily. " My reference was to documents in general. I've found it extremely difficult to locate anything."

" Well," I said, " don't worry about my Spoliation Claims, because that isn't what brought me here." I unfastened the catch on the case that held Lydia's portrait and set it on Lear's desk.

" *That's* why I'm in Haiti," I told him. " Have you ever seen that lady, by any chance ? Her name's Lydia Bailey and she's a governess for the children of a French planter somewhere on this island."

" No," Lear said, " I haven't. It's not a face you'd forget, once you'd seen it. What's the planter's name ? "

" I don't know. The documents in her case have been lost. All we know is that she's here. Captain George Lee of Philadelphia saw her in this city late in November. She was with two young boys, her charges, and all three were in riding dress."

Lear studied the portrait carefully. " No," he said, " no. I'm very sorry to say I don't know." He looked up at me quickly. " Is she by any chance one of the clients that had a Spoliation Claim ? "

" Well," I said, " I never thought of it in exactly that way, but as a matter of fact she is. At least, she's the rightful claimant to a number of shares in a ship that was captured and sold here."

" Well," Lear said heartily, " we must see what we can do about the lady. Now let me think. If her plantation was in this part of the island, or anywhere near it, I'm sure I'd know her. Since I don't, she must be in the south. Yes—she *must* be in the south. If I were you, I'd take a boat and go by sea to St. Marc. That's where wealthy planters often go for sea bathing and amusement."

" Used to," King Dick put in abruptly.

Lear looked puzzled. " Used to ? "

" Dessalines live there now," King Dick said.

" Oh, yes, I see what you mean," Lear said. " Still, St. Marc seems to me the most likely place for Mr. Hamlin to start his hunt."

" I'll need a passport, won't I ? " I asked.

" Oh, yes," Lear said ; " I'll make out one for you immediately ! Immediately ! " He rose from his desk and went to an inner office where I heard him speaking to a clerk.

King Dick's eyes slid around and fastened on mine. " That kind, nice gentleman, he very anxious to help you go somewhere else, just as far away from here as you can get."

" Who's Dessalines ? " I asked.

" Big general," King Dick said. " Big, big general." He rolled his eyes in such a way that I got the impression of something enormous, frightening, overwhelming. " Don't like Blancs," King Dick added.

" Do you think Lear's advice is good ? " I whispered.

King Dick snorted. " Good for *him*," he said. " That Colonel Lear, he very nice man. Nice to himself. Don't you worry, though. To-morrow we go to my house and I show you things Colonel Lear don't know and don't believe."

In no time at all Colonel Lear, all smiles and amiability, was back with my passport. " I wish you the very best of luck, Mr. Hamlin," he said, handing it to me. " You may be sure I'll spare no efforts to find your charming client. Now let me see, what shall I do in case I come across information you should have ? "

" Send it to Mirafleur," King Dick said. " I get it to him."

" But you won't know where he is, will you ? " Lear asked.

" Oh, yes," King Dick said. " I see with drums."

To me he sounded in earnest, but Lear apparently didn't think so ; for he laughed heartily and wagged a sly finger at my black friend.

It seemed to me, as we left, that Lear might easily have shown more hospitality—though I admitted to myself that I wouldn't have accepted it ; and I took considerable satisfaction in having King Dick murmur to me, as we emerged again on the white pavement of the garish Plaza, that Colonel Lear was so kind and good that he always believed the wrong things, and usually at the wrong time.

CHAPTER XIII

EARLY the next morning we left the stinks of Cap François behind us and set out on horseback across the flat green plain that stretched off and off to distant blue mountains. Behind us, gabbling endlessly, trotted a horde of Negro boys with all our bundles and boxes.

The plain was like a funnel, for there were hulking green mountains on both sides of us—mountains whose close-packed tropical forests steamed as though fires smouldered beneath them. Not only the moun-tains steamed, but also the road we travelled, and the whole plain through which we rode. I had the feeling of gasping and stifling in a vapour bath ; but King Dick and the half-naked black boys who ran and squealed behind us seemed almost cool beneath that broiling sun.

On either side, extending from the roadsides to the foothills of the mountains, were plantations of sugar cane ; and the plantation houses set down amid palms on little hillocks throughout that vast plain were something extraordinary. The porticos and pillars that surrounded them made them look large enough to house a dozen families each ; and the sheds, mills, warehouses, and outbuildings that stretched out from them were like compact towns.

All the plantations, King Dick told me, and thousands of others like them in every part of the island had, until recently, belonged to French-men and mulattoes who had become fabulously wealthy by forcing hundreds of thousands of black slaves to work in the fields until they dropped from exhaustion. It was those black slaves, he said, who but five short years ago had risen against the brutality of their masters and turned the richest island of the Indies into a shambles of death and destruction.

" Then how did these plantations escape ? " I asked.

" Some didn't," he said. " Mostly didn't." He waved his hand toward the plantations near us. " Four years ago these rackoned and ruined, all of 'em. No slaves cut cane, no slaves clean coffee bushes : no cane cut, no coffee picked."

" But look at them ! " I protested. " I never dreamed plantations could be so rich ! "

King Dick wagged his head. " That because of Toussaint. They only one Toussaint. He do what he say he do. Everybody else don't know what to do or where to go. But that Toussaint, he say everybody on this island going to be free and equal, and he meant it. Not like free and equal in America, where nobody mean it. Toussaint kill and drive out everybody who say black men can't be free, plantation-owners mostly dead or hiding somewhere. They no crops because of weeds ; they no black men working, because of figuring they free and don't have to." He chuckled. " Toussaint stop all that, quick. Now all back and better. Reason why ? Share profits. All working, all free, all equal, all good, long as Toussaint make behave. Stop Toussaint—*boum !* She all gone ! Stop Toussaint, all nothing ! "

Toward dusk we turned off from the hard white road that split the green plain like a white ribbon, and rode toward the mountains that hung at our shoulders like gigantic curtains of purple velvet propped into peaks by invisible poles. Cool drifts of air came down from those white-dark mountains, and an odour of flowers that brought piercingly to my memory the scent of Maine meadows beneath an August moon.

With the gathering dark, far-off throbbings came from the mountain slopes, dim throbbings that became louder, that became the sound of far-off drums, drums that came closer and closer, that took on character and personality, that became distinguishable as big, hoarse drums ; as smaller, quicker drums whose thuddings were broken by unexpected catches and stumblings ; as little, hurried, high-pitched drums, whisperingly babbling and jabbering, like adolescent girls exchanging secrets in the dark.

If there was a place in Haiti where a man could close his ears, from dusk to dawn, to the rumbling and booming, the throbbing and thudding, the rattling and tattling of the drums, I never found it. I don't believe such a place existed—and a good thing for me it didn't.

The plantation house of King Dick, which bore the name of Mirafleur, was at the foot of the mountains, high enough above the plain so that the cane fields seemed like an inland sea of green beneath its broad verandas ;

and beyond the waves of cane, framed between the purple mountains, was the Caribbean, violently blue and streaked like watered silk with breeze-lanes.

Behind the house, extending up and up the slope, were the coffee plantations growing beneath sheltering groves of trees that looked like New England elms and maples ; and the bright orange of the coffee berries sprinkled everywhere against the dark green of the shrubs were like flickering fireflies miraculously visible in full daylight.

Thus, in spite of the daytime heat, the green of the plantations and the blue of the sea gave an illusion of coolness ; and in the evening the night breeze, flowing down the mountain slopes to pluck at the jalousies and curtains of Mirafleur with flower and coffee-scented fingers, was truly cool.

As King Dick and I rode up the slope to the steps of the veranda, I was conscious of Negroes, hundreds on hundreds of them, among the pepper-trees that edged the roadway. They seemed to be in constant furtive and excited movement ; and we dismounted at the foot of the veranda stairs to the tune of the tremulous thrumming of three drums held between the knees of black drummers.

Light flooded from the door at the head of the stairs, and outlined against the light was a slender woman with a towering head-dress and a gown so long that she carried the train thrown over her arm.

" That my English-speaking wife," King Dick said. " When I speak Creole I sweat, so Cloryphène do my talking."

He addressed her formally as " Madame Cloryphène " ; and when she came down the stairs with a languid, slinky sort of walk, he said to her, " This my friend, the great M'sieu Hamlin."

The lady looked up at me droopingly. Her face was dusted with a bluish powder, like the faces of the cream-coloured women who rode around the White Plaza of Cap François, and she seemed almost too lackadaisical to speak, though she contrived to murmur, " M'sieu."

King Dick clapped his big hands before her face. " Things too slow around here," he said sharply. " To-night we dance—big dance—big, big dance. We got to see into next week ; far away as Jacmel and Léogane ; got to find a white lady from America, teaching two white boys." He turned to me. " That what Mr. White-lace Colonel Lear don't believe. He say you can't see into next week with Voodoo." He turned back to Madame Cloryphène. " Tell Atténaire get me every Gangan, Hungan, Mambu, Bocur anywhere around, and let 'em have all goats, roosters, and rum they need. Tell 'em start dancing quick. Along about midnight we be out ; see how they get along ; find out what we want to know."

Cloryphène ceased to droop and went briskly away, doing a little dance-step at intervals. King Dick led me up the veranda stairs and into a room more like an assembly hall than a room in a private dwelling. It extended the width of the house, so that a breeze was bound to pass through it if there was one, and the furnishings were a mixture of tawdriness and elegance, of cheapness and luxury. There was French furniture, its upholstry worn and spotted ; and scattered among the French fauteuils and divans were kitchen chairs. In a corner was a rosewood spinet, beautifully inlaid, and before it a bench that looked to me like a shoe-shining box covered with carpet. Hanging from the ceiling was a chandalier with innumerable glass danglers, curlicues, and supporting cables. It had sockets for two dozen candles, but held only six guttering stubs. Between the heavily barred shutters stood elaborate French mirrors reaching from floor to ceiling, and pinned to one wall was a gaudy woodcut of the young Bonaparte brooding over a battlefield on which scores of heavily moustached and admiring soldiers lay dying.

There were cobwebs in corners and around the glass festoons of the chandalier ; and, in spite of the breeze that drifted through the jalousies, the place had a musty, mouldy odour.

Before the revolution, King Dick told me, the plantation had belonged to a wealthy Frenchman named Lejeune who had used cowhide whips on his slaves to such good effect that his yield of coffee, sugar, and rum had been almost twice that of his neighbours. He had nearly died from a mysterious ailment, and had suspected his slaves of making an image of him and sticking pins into it to bring about his death. In an attempt to wring confessions from his slaves, he had thrust candle ends beneath the skin of their buttocks and set fire to their own fat. He had pushed shark-hooks beneath their back-bones and hoisted them from their feet. He had triced them up by their thumbs, tied cords tight around their scrotums, and fastened the ends of the cords to active young pigs. Under this treatment several slaves had died so openly and noisily that French magistrates had been obliged to go through the formality of trying him for murder. Although he was clearly guilty, French logic and realism freed him on the ground that the punishment of a wealthy white would make the blacks lose respect for their white masters.

When the revolution started, M. Lejeune's slaves had followed their own negroid ideas of logic and realism by seizing him, removing his clothes, and pegging him to an ant hill, leaving his legs free so that their thrashings would irritate the ants and divert his former victims. So suddenly had M. Lejeune's punishment come upon him that he had saved nothing—life, money, house-furnishings, or family. Thus, King Dick concluded with a deprecatory chuckle, M. Lejeune's wife and daughters were ravished, his mulatto mistresses given to his former slaves, and the furnishings were those that I now saw around me.

The place was crawling with black servants, most of them pop-eyed little boys who seemed to me wholly useless except to get under foot. King Dick found them irritating too, for he shooed them away as one brushes flies from a sugar bowl. " These not mine," he told me apologetically. " They my wifeses'. When I away a day, all they little boys come nosing around, trying find out where I been, who I bring back."

I thought I hadn't heard correctly. " All these servants belong to Madame Cloryphène ? "

He looked startled. " Oh me my, no ! My wifeses ! Amétiste, Claircine, Roséïde, Aspodelle, Floréal, Marméline——" He hesitated ; then muttered the names to himself and checked them off on his black banana fingers. " Cloryphène, Amétiste, Claircine, Roséïde, Aspodelle, Floréal, Marméline." He shook his head, baffled. " My, my ! That only seven ! " Then memory triumphed. " And some Atténaire's. That make eight ! My goo'ness me, I getting old, forgetting wifeses' name ! "

I could hardly believe my ears. " You've got eight wives ! "

" Eight in Haiti," King Dick said carelessly. " I got——" He caught himself as Cloryphène came into the room. " Cloryphène," he said sharply, " I wish to repast, and I want all ladies come right here. Everybody get best-dressed and best-perfumed, so M'sieu Hamlin see everything, smell everything. He my best friend, Cloryphène, my very best friend ! "

CHAPTER XIV

AT KING DICK's table that night, I had my first experience of bachamelle, which is salted codfish cooked in the Haitian manner—boned and stewed with potatoes, pimentos, oil, garlic, and butter, and the whole thickened with manioc flour, which is like oatmeal. Every Haitian, man, woman, and child, King Dick said, would eat bachamelle or some similar preparation of salt codfish for breakfast, dinner, and supper every day in the week, if given the chance. I thought at first he was exaggerating, but I know different now ; and I never see or smell a salt codfish that all Haiti doesn't rise before me, and quick memories of black faces, endless green forests, heaps of dead black men and women, glaring blue skies, and the warty black toad-face of the part-devil, part-soldier whom I hated more than any man, bar two, that I have ever known.

We washed down our bachamelle with rum and coconut milk, which moved King Dick to explain to me his matrimonial situation.

" I not permanent married to Cloryphène or Aspodelle or Amétiste or those others," he said. " They just here on trial for good reasons, mostly helpful ones."

He flapped a hand at the swarms of flies that had seemingly been attracted from every part of Haiti by the pungent odour of the bachamelle ; then checked his wives' names upon his fingers.

" Amétiste, she play spinet ; Roséïde, she stomach-dance, very excetticating ; Cloryphène, she got nice legs ; Marméline, she make dress just like Paris ; Claircine, she expert at loving ; Atténaire, she know Voodoo ; Floréal and Aspodelle, they just extra, in case of visitors."

D

Again I thought he was exaggerating ; but when after dinner, we went back into the big central room, I found he'd been understating.

The room, empty and barn-like when we left it, now vibrated with life and colour, for eight women had entered it, attended by numerous small, barefooted black boys.

These women ranged in complexion from pale yellow to darkest stove-lid ; and their satin gowns, heavily puffed at the shoulder and extremely low both back and front, also differed widely in colour—red, blue, green, yellow, orange, violet, grey, and white. The black boys who stared pop-eyed from behind the ladies' skirts wore long coats made of the same material as the gowns of their mistresses.

Those dark-skinned women had shown almost a genius for selecting inappropriate colours. The blackest of them, whom I guessed to be Amétiste, since she sat on the spinet-bench looking dreamily into space and tinkling the keys, had a swollen rotundity that made me wonder how she could seat herself without splitting her gown at seat and breast. Her dress was white ; her massive arms and bosom, emerging from the gleaming satin, were a glistening black, as solid-looking as polished ebony.

The others were younger, and their figures in satin gowns that clung to them like sheaths of wet silk, were beautiful. Their flesh-tones, however —doubtless because the colours of their gowns were badly chosen— seemed tinged with bluish green, as though they hovered on the verge of seasickness.

Two, as we entered, were contending for the same chair. One, clad in yellow, bunted with her buttocks at one in blue. The bunt brought the blue girl to her knees, but only for a moment. She rose screaming, hurled herself at her yellow-clad rival, and made a partly successful attempt to tear the yellow satin from her upper body. There was a babel of squealing, and both women fell to the floor and thrashed around, on which the little black boys squalled too, and the room became a maelstrom of turbulent sound and colour.

" Hoy, hoy ! " King Dick shouted. " Don't I tell you no fighting ? "

Bearing down upon the battle, he separated the combatants with a double sweep of a long arm. They slid across the floor, one bringing up against a leg of the spinet with a crash, the other sliding head-first into the wall with such force that her towering head-dress was pressed down around her ears.

They got to their feet, rearranging their gowns with those downward-pushing gestures common to Pharaoh's daughters and to all women since ; and at once they and all the others were languid and elegant, as though no excitement had ever entered their lives.

King Dick, in a rage, burst into an oration directed partly at his wives and partly at me. " Eight wives and can't get nothing done right ! Ask pork for supper, what I get ! I get coubouyon ! Ask peace and quiet, what I get ? I get bellering and yellering ! Now listen what I say ! Don't fight around where I taking my ledger ! If you got to fight,

fight outside and keep on till somebody wins permanent ! Next time two of you gets fighting in here, I wipe everybody ! Everybody get wiped— Marméline, Cloryphène, Amétiste, Roséïde, Claircine, Aspodelle, Floréal, Atténaire—all get wiped good ! Now get along out before I wipe someone just for luck."

The eight ladies moved from the room droopingly but rapidly.

King Dick threw himself into a chair beside a table on which rested three bottles of rum and a pitcher of cloudy coconut milk. " They like all women," he said gloomily. " When I want 'em to look nice and elegant, so you can pick out a good one for yourself, they fight. You got one picked ? "

" Well," I said, " to tell you the truth——"

King Dick made an airy gesture. " Take one blind, why don't you ? They all good, except maybe Amétiste. Amétiste, she a Nangola, and Nangolas got pretty strong smell, even to me."

I told him I appreciated his generosity, but felt I should start at once on the task before me.

He drained his glass and instantly refilled it. " You don't like 'em," he said, and I thought he spoke accusingly.

" I've implied nothing of the sort," I said. " I—I think your wives are charming. Possibly New Englanders are not so free—that is to say, our upbringing—I mean our ideas of hospitality——"

King Dick filled his glass for the third time. " That all right," he said. " I'm sick of 'em myself. I had too much of their myze."

I found the word baffling, and said so.

" 'MI, 'mI," King Dick explained patiently. " They pretty near 'mI me to death : where 'mI going, who 'mI going with, how long 'mI going to stay, when 'mI coming home, what 'mI going to do when I get there ! My goo'ness me, no ! Can't stand asky-nasky women, always asking-nasking ! "

He held up a rum bottle. Finding it empty, he lifted the lid of the spinet, dropped the bottle on the strings ; then got to his feet and walked out on to the broad verandah with the silent smoothness of a big cat. He was an imposing figure, outlined against the night sky and the far-off lights of Cap François, cocking his ear to the throbbing of the drums.

" Little drum, medium drum, big drum," he said. " Hoy ! Time we go Humfort and see what those Gangans finding out."

CHAPTER XV

WE set off for the Humfort or Voodoo temple preceded by two black boys with torches ; and in the wavering light of those torches King Dick's eyes glistened and rolled whitely as he told me about Voodoo. It was a religion, he said, practised in Dahomey and various other parts of Guinea —and by Guinea he seemed to mean all of Africa. The religion had been brought to Haiti from Africa by slaves who had been Hungans, Mambus, and Gangans in the Old Country—a Hungan being a Voodoo priest, a Mambu a Voodoo priestess, and a Gangan an extra special Hungan, extremely high-priced, and almost invariably successful in the making of drogues, gardes, and arrêtes.

Personally, he insisted, he found Voodoo useful but distasteful. For one thing, the chief god of the Voodoo people was Damballa, who was always represented by a serpent, and if Damballa had any snake in him, it stood to reason he couldn't be much good, for experience had taught King Dick there never was a snake worth worshipping—or worth eating, for that matter. Some people like them, he said ; but for him they tasted too snaky. Aside from his own experience, too, the Bible blamed all the troubles of the world on snakes and women, which was probably right, but no high recommendation for either.

For another thing, King Dick said, Voodo Hungans and Mambus pretended to be able to foretell the future, once they were possessed by certain gods known in Voodoo circles as *Loa*, by examining the insides of dead roosters ; but roosters' insides, in his opinion, contained little of value ; and roosters' insides, he was positive, were no different from the insides of turkeys, or ducks, or even crows.

He objected to Voodoo worship, too, because those who practised it couldn't seem to do so without drinking rum and dancing all night ; and he, as a Général de Place in charge of a plantation, objected to all-night drinking and all-night dancing, whether done in the name of religion or in the name of pleasure, since the dancers and drinkers were invariably unable to work efficiently the next day.

He also had minor objections to Voodoo.

According to him, the predictions of Voodoo priests in military matters could be painfully inaccurate, and he instanced black generals in the last war who had based the strategy of their battles on the advice of Hungans and Gangans who had been possessed by Ogun Badagri, one of several Voodoo gods of war. The results forced Toussaint to shoot both generals and Hungans, if they could be found.

Voodoo physicians, too, left much to be desired ; for although they professed to be able to cure anybody of almost anything, from love to a broken neck, King Dick said he had never known one to cure a single case of the yaws, which was the most popular of Haiti's many diseases, especially among men who associated promiscuously with females of slight virtue. He added, with dark laughter, that they were unable even to cure their own splitting headaches after dancing and drinking all night.

" Now you've confused me," I said. " You told me in the beginning that there's something to Voodoo and you expect some sort of help from it tonight ; but from what you tell me now, a man's a fool to trust Voodoo. Where's the sense to it—if there *is* any ? "

King Dick's tone was philosophical. " You and me, we think like Americans, but nigras think like nigras. They believe everything. They not *anything* they not believe. If nigra hear he die next Tuesday, three o'clock afternoon, he do it. If sick nigra hear he not sick, first thing you know, he not sick. Now then, suppose nigra wish to go Cap François. Right away he pay a call on Hungan and ask him what day look best. Hungan kill a white rooster for Papa God ; then he and nigra eat what Papa God leave, drink rum, dance all night, and Hungan tell him Papa God say go Cap François Monday. If somebody don't tell nigra Monday be good, nigra afraid go *any* day. See ? "

I said I didn't.

" Now look," King Dick said. " In Haiti we got Azeto. Azeto very malice. Howl in trees after dark and maybe suck blood of night travellers. Hungans and Mambus, they construct gardes carrefour against Azeto. If you have garde carrefour in your pocket, you not afraid of Azeto. So you start at midnight for Port-au-Prince : not wait for dawn, because Azeto helpless against gardes carrefour."

I laughed.

" Nothing to laugh about," King Dick said. " Maybe you think no such thing as Azeto. Guinea people know better. They know from boy-hood days that the world full of Azeto ; also full of Bakuba Baka. They all sorts of Bakas, but Bakuba Baka is biggest Baka."

" What in God's name is a Baka ? " I asked.

" Very bad thing," King Dick said. " Move around in night : push people down mountains, drop rocks on 'em, freeze 'em to death with cold wind. If you see a grey pig in night-time, be careful if on foot or horseback. Grey pigs contain Bakuba Bakas."

" Aren't all pigs grey at night ? "

" Yes," King Dick said, " but Hungans can give you instruction so you don't fear Bakas—not even Bakuba Baka."

" What would the instruction be ? "

" Ride a mule," King Dick said. " A mule know a Baka a mile away, and tell the rider. Any mule, she's revulted by a Baka."

" Nonsense," I said. " A mule's sure-footed, that's all ! He's safer and wiser than a horse. There isn't a man strong enough to drag a mule across a weak bridge."

" That what I telling you," King Dick said. " Voodoo makes you do what you might not do unless you believe in Voodoo. Best Voodoo remedy against any kind of accident is a drogue. You know what a drogue is ? "

I said I didn't.

" A drogue," King Dick said, " is something made by big, big Hungan. If you have a drogue, you never be frightened in war, because you can't be killed. That a helpful feeling for a soldier, especially if he have to lead troops into heavy gunfire. Best general we had, last war, for riding into enemy guns was Hyacinthe. His drogue was an ox-tail from a litto ox. He carry it in his left hand and never let it go."

" Never ? " I asked.

" Very near never," King Dick said. " Anyway, he never get killed. He just die."

" I see," I said. " What sort of drogue got you safely through the war ? "

" I had two," King Dick said. " Still have 'em. Very useful. One a six-barrel pistol I borrow from General Wilkinson. The other my cocomacaque with knob on end—biggest cocomacaque on this island. I got an ox-tail, too. When I go somewhere, I tie her on behind me, where tail belongs, so feels natural to ox-tail, so she likes me, keeps me safe."

I began to have a vague understanding of the benefits of Voodoo.

" Some ways," King Dick went on placidly, " Voodoo helpful to me. That why I learn how to make things disappear, like those beans. When I make things disappear, everybody know I big Hungan. That why I walk on fire sometimes. Only very big Hungan able to walk on fire."

" Do you mean it ? " I asked. " Are you really able to walk on fire ? "

" My goo'ness me my, yes ! " he said. " That important ! I also pick up hot coals in fingers. When I do that, black people afraid of me. If I can walk on fire, I can do anything. That what black people say."

" I'll believe it when I see it," I said.

" I merely explaining why I like Voodoo and still *don't* like it," King Dick said. " Walking on fire not hard to do when you know how. Nothing hard when you know how. You get four-five things from chemist —quicksilver, hamitalis, camphire, storax—paint it on feet. Then you walk on fire. Wash on hands and you can pick up coals."

" I see," I said.

" Yarse," King Dick said. " Anyone who walks on fire is big Gangan —big, big Gangan ! He can call for drums and find out anything anybody knows. That one thing very nice about Voodoo."

We had moved through dark groves of coffee trees to the sound of rumbling, throbbing drums—a sound so penetrating and all-pervasive that it seemed to be pounding inside my head, like the roaring that comes with fever.

The planation changed to jungle : the path narrowed, so that the light from the torches flickered through the snake-like lianas and gigantic leaves—and suddenly the Humfort stood before us in a clearing, a low building like a New England hen-house.

Only in height did the Humfort resemble a hen-house, for against its glowing red interior a throng of Negroes swayed, leaped, whirled ; and the whole place throbbed with drummings and howling.

At the entrance stood two Negroes, almost as tall as King Dick. They saluted us respectfully and we went into a close-packed mob of howling black men and women.

Two hundred Negroes were crowded into the Humfort, and the place had a rank odour like an uncleaned rabbit hutch. At the far end was a sort of altar, covered with a checkered cloth. The wall behind it was decorated with crude paintings of a snake standing on its tail. Fastened to the front of the altar were religious prints in glaring colours, such as I used to see in French kitchens in New Brunswick.

On the altar were loaves of bread, platters of cake, dishes of roasted meat, bottles of every shape and size, battered drinking-vessels. On the earth floor in front of the altar blazed a fire whose smoke partly escaped through a hole in the roof. On one side of the fire sat three wizened black men with drums clutched between their knees—drums which they kneaded and bumped with the heels of their hands, and with such earnestness that their faces dripped perspiration.

When we came in, the motions and howlings seemed as meaningless as the yowling of black cats fighting in a barrel ; then I saw there was more to it than that.

There was rhythm in the drum beats ; rhythm in the wailing song that the dancers sang as they hopped jerkily in a slow-moving circle. It made me think of dropped stitches, of speech broken by hiccups, of a stutterer hurriedly gasping the phrase on which his tongue is caught. A bar of the song would start smoothly enough, then without warning break into hurried repetitions, unexpected hesitancies. This breathless rhythm seemed to enter into the legs of the dancers, into their stomachs, arms, heads, backs. Their stomach-muscles twitched, their buttocks wagged, their arms flapped, their heads rolled on their shoulders as if on swivels.

I could make nothing of their singing at first ; but after a time I caught the name " Papa Legba " endlessly repeated. I gathered they were urging Papa Legba to open a gateway for them so they could pass through. It was Papa Legba, they sang, who sits on the gate. Oh yes, he sits on the gate on the gate and gives us the right to pass.

From a door behind the altar came an old Negro in a sort of white nightgown. His hair was a crinkly white halo that ran from ear to ear around the back of his head, and on his wrinkled face was an expression of helpless worry. There were two little black boys with him, each similarly dressed in a white nightgown. One carried a white rooster in his arms ; the other led a black goat dressed in a blue calico petticoat. When the goat rose on his hind legs to nibble at a loaf of bread on the

altar, the old Negro reached inside his nightgown, whisked out a two-foot
knife, and slapped the goat with the blade.

King Dick nudged me. " Uncle Bogay," he whispered. " Best Gangan
north of the mountains."

It seemed to me Uncle Bogay's appearance was against him, but he
had produced the knife from under his nightgown with surprising celerity.
And for such a helpless-looking old man he was effective ; for when
he held out his hands toward the dancers, the howling stopped and the
only sounds inside the Humfort were the dry rustling of the dancers' feet
on the hard earth floor, the throbbing of the drums, the crackling of the
fire.

There was something about the dancers, about the tawdry furnishings
of the Humfort, that depressed me, and I wondered whether they weren't
a painful caricature of man's trumpery efforts to achieve great things with
hopelessly inadequate tools and trappings. The old bottles and battered
cups on the altar, the fly-specked prints, the gobbets of food for the
nourishment of strange black gods, the glazed eyes of the dancers, the
shuffle of their bare feet on the dirt floor, the red handkerchiefs tied
around the heads of these self-appointed priests and priestesses—what
were all these things but a burlesque of Greater Gangans in lands that
posed as civilised—greater, paler Gangans who led their followers in
dances no more profitable !

The greatest Gangan north of the mountains rolled up his eyes. " I
call Papa Legba," he bawled, and thanks to my weeks of study in Philadelphia I was able to understand him. " I call Papa Damballa ! Meat
is sweet and awaits you, Papa Legba, Papa Damballa ! What is life
without meat without meat without meat ? I call Papa Gede, I call
Papa Agasu, I call Ogun Badagri, I call Ogun Ferraille, I call Erzilie
Freda ! Meat is sweet. Oh meat is sweet, sweet, sweet, is sweet ! Gods
and men must live by meat, sweet meat, sweet meat. I call Damballa
Wedo, I call Aida Wedo ! I call Papa Legba——"

Out from the circle of dancers staggered a corpulent Negro, barefooted, naked above the waist, a fillet of red handkerchiefs around his
head, and a similar girdle for a belt. He lurched to the fire before the
altar, stepped into the bed of glowing coals, and did a shuffling dance
upon the red embers. With each scuff of his feet the coals were momentarily blackened, only to glow again when his feet moved forward. On
each foot the great toe stuck out sideways at a right angle to his other
toes, and as his feet pressed down upon the fiery surface, the coals, forced
upward by those prehensile great toes, sent up little tongues of flame as
they rolled upon the upper part of his feet. The dancers ecstatically
chanted, " Papa Legba ! Papa Legba ! "

The Gangan came out from behind the altar, took the dancer by
the arm and led him back to his original place, where he went on dancing
and howling as if nothing had happened to his feet—and, so far as I could
see, nothing had.

Uncle Bogay's two little black attendants came to him, one carrying the white rooster, the other a bowl. Uncle Bogay picked up the rooster, clutching both wings in one claw-like hand, and swung it back and forth over the head of the man who had danced upon the coals. The little boy with the bowl held it before Uncle Bogay, who flicked his long knife at the rooster's outstretched head. The head fell to the floor ; the rooster's body flopped in the Gangan's grasp ; a jet of blood poured into the bowl as from a pump.

A Negress, her hair gathered into crinkly black points fastened with string, howled and leaped upward to grasp one of the poles that held up the roof of the Humfort, and clung there like a black baboon. She had, I gathered, been possessed by Papa Damballa.

The Gangan pulled at her until she fell to the floor. The little black boy stepped forward with a fresh rooster. The Gangan's knife flicked again, and again a jet of blood poured into the bowl.

With increasing rapidity the dancers were possessed, some falling to the floor in convulsions, others leaping like jumping-jacks, still others climbing into the rafters and hanging there, bat-like. The Gangan pulled them from the rafters, quieted leapers, somehow restrained those who writhed upon the floor. Each of the possessed ones had a rooster slaughtered for him, and was then dragged from the Humfort and laid out on the ground, his feet to a common centre, so that all of them together looked like the spokes of a giant wheel.

The Gangan led the goat out from behind the altar, took it by the muzzle, pulled up its head, slit its throat and held it motionless until the blood stopped draining into the bowl already half-full of chicken blood. The three drums throbbed and rumbled ; the diminished circle of dancers chanted a song in which I could catch the words, " With the help of the blood I look in the bowl and see."

King Dick gave me the merest faint hint of a wink as he murmured, " If we find out anything, we find out now."

The Gangan was surrounded by women, who already were picking the roosters, tossing the feathers into the fire, skinning the goat. There was something ludicrously professional about him : he had the air of a grotesque tavern-keeper out of a bad dream, supervising the preparation of a devil's banquet in a nightmare kitchen ; his air of proprietorship was almost insufferable when he turned from the women and signalled to the rest of us to go out into the night. With wrinkled black neck protruding buzzard-like from his white nightgown, pipe-stem black legs sticking out beneath voluminous shirt tails, he herded drummers, dancers, attendants, and spectators from the Humfort.

Hunkering in the centre of the ring of prostrate bodies, he held the bowl of blood to the lips of each in turn. Then he drank himself, wiped his lips on the back of a black hand, and wiped the hand on his leg. There was no sound from the circle of bodies ; none from any of the rest of us who stood looking down at the old Gangan with his bowl of blood ; none from the three drummers squatting against the side of the Humfort, their drums between their knees.

Far away other drums thudded and thudded, slow, fast, slow again. They put me in mind of the drumming of partridges in the spring of the year, that strange and unexplainable drumming that seems miles away when it may be only a stone's throw, and that makes itself heard far, far off, even against a wind that drowns a shout at twenty paces.

The prostrate bodies were like dead men. The Gangan stared into his bowl of blood ; the distant drums throbbed and rumbled. The fat Negro with the red handkerchief girdle—the one who had been possessed by Papa Legba—got to his knees, crawled to the bowl of blood and peered into it. The others did the same. All of them, kneeling in a cricle around Uncle Bogay and his bowl, had the look of black crows around a piece of broken mirror.

When the kneeling figures stopped their mumbling, they got to their feet and just stood there, scratching themselves. The Gangan knelt beside his blood bowl and looked up at King Dick like a preoccupied ape.

" The Gods do not like," he said in hoarse Creole. " Everywhere there is trouble," he went on. " Where you going, you need protection from every God, especially Maît' Carrefour and Ogun Badagri. You need protection from danger on the highroad, from war, from the loup-garou. I have counted ; you will need fifteen gardes and wangas. This will be expensive—oh, very ! "

" That's too much ! " King Dick said, and he, too, spoke in Creole.

" No," the Gangan said. " You need fifteen wangas. We saw soldiers in the blood—many of them : marching and marching, all with guns."

" That nothing," King Dick said lightly. " For ten years this island been full of soldiers. Won't hurt me."

" The soldiers we saw in the blood are not that kind of soldier," the Gangan said. " They are white soldiers, wearing white coats."

" You see too much," King Dick told him. " Nobody asked you to see white soldiers—only one white woman. Where soldiers coming from ? Out of mapou trees like Ogun Badagri ? And when they coming ? In a hundred years ? In a hundred years anything can happen ! "

The old man scratched his armpit. " The blood said nothing about how they would get here, or when ; but we could see them everywhere —on the plains, in the mountains, in the cities, and soon. They are as good as here already, or they wouldn't be in the blood. You cannot travel without fifteen wangas. The price of the wangas, fifteen for you and fifteen for your friend, will be fifteen hundred and twelve gourdes. Also you must give each of us one meter of gold braid."

" Do you think I'm made of money ? " King Dick asked. " And what reason for fifteen hundred and twelve gourdes ? Why not just fifteen hundred ? Why twelve extra ? "

The Gangan looked dignified. " Because that the price."

" That no good reason," King Dick said. " You add twelve to fifteen hundred gourdes because you know fifteen hundred gourdes too much to ask for anything. It not real—not sound real."

The Gagan scratched his head.

" If you look carefully into bowl of blood," King Dick said, " you see me refuse to pay fifteen hundred for thirty wangas. You see I give gold braid, but only pay twenty gourdes for each wanga. That six hundred gourdes. Hoy ! Big price ! "

"Not as big fifteen hundred and twelve," the Gangan said. "But if you say we'd have seen six hundred gourdes in the blood, then we must accept it ; for the blood always speaks truly."

" We tell that better when we find her we seek," King Dick said. " Where is she ? "

The Gangan looked stubborn. " You must promise to pay before you go hunting for her."

" That not necessary," King Dick said. " You not afraid, perhaps, your wangas don't protect us and lady not be where you say ? "

" You have far to go," the Gangan said, " and we make better wangas if paid beforehand."

King Dick looked at him coldly. " We pay when wangas finished, but they must be finished within an hour. If we have far to go, we start tonight. Where is the place ? "

The Gangan picked up a twig and made marks on the hard-packed earth beside him. " You cross high mountains at Dondon ; then bear westward to Marmelade, five leagues along the lower slopes of the mountains, then come back the same distance to St. Miguel in Valley of Goave. From there the road goes straight south to Mirebalais, across Black Mountains. You pass through Mirebalais and continue onward, on the road to Croix des Bouquets and Port-au-Prince. One league outside of Mirebalais is a mapou tree, and under that mapou tree will be a Hungan from Mirebalais—a wise Hungan who knows all Gods of Cul de Sac. He take you to the one you seek."

King Dick turned to me triumphantly. " I make him say it more slow. You write on paper where he tell us to go for that lady—then you understand how much good that white-lace Colonel Lear do you when he advise you to go to St. Marc. In St. Marc you find no lady at all—only Dessalines."

I knew nothing about Dessalines, but I felt I had learned more than a little about Colonel Lear, none of it in any way pleasing to me.

CHAPTER XVI

To make our wangas those black Hungans and Mambus worked as though driven by an overseer with whips. Seemingly the ingredients of their charms were rigidly specified and not to be changed—bits of earth from the four corners of crossroads ; scrapings from cemeteries ; thunder-stones left embedded in trees after lightning had struck ; freshly made rum called clairin, colourless as water ; red candles, a new piece of soap, sulphur, garlic, rusty iron nails, brown shoemaker's thread, small seeds stitched to a piece of calico in the form of a cross, bright-coloured feathers from tropical humming-birds, bees' wings, cakes of wax made from honey-comb, an evil-smelling liquid called Baigne de Mambu.

Now I know mighty little about Voodoo, but there's no question that a Voodoo drummer can send a message the length and breadth of Haiti in an hour, and get an answer in another hour. I have next to no faith in the protective wangas of Mambus and Hungans, and yet there's this about them : I was glad to have those little bundles of earth, knotted string, feathers and garlic, some of them no larger than a fisherman's salmon-fly ; and I tied them together and tucked them away as carefully as though I really needed them to protect me from thunder, from perils by river and by sea, from the living dead known to Haitians as Zombis, from evil spirits who live in trees and in caverns, from death by knife, gun or cocomacaque.

Did I believe that Voodoo spirits had told the Gangan where Lydia was ? He had learned beforehand from King Dick that I was seeking an American lady who had charge of two French children ; and up and down the island, and back and forth, night and day, the drums talked across hill and valley to one another, asking questions, carrying messages, as I've heard they do up and down the long stretches of the African rivers. So the Gangan could have drummed forth an inquiry and had his answer —and yet I was glad that the Voodoo spirits had told him what I wanted to know.

Yes, such is the human mind ! I would no more have left those wangas behind than would King Dick—who sometimes said he didn't believe in Voodoo. And I had another wanga even more potent : Lydia's little portrait, which I'd removed from the frame and stretcher and rolled up inside a bored-out bamboo riding crop.

A map of Haiti—the French or western part of San Domingo, as distinguished from the Spanish or eastern part—looks like an irregular horseshoe with the open end pointing to the west. The upper arm is the Great North Plain. The rounded end is the vast valley called the Artibonite because the Artibonite River flows through it. The lower arm is known simply enough as the South.

Those three mountain-rimmed districts, cut off from each other by tumbled ranges, constitute—thanks to the fertility of the soil, the stiffling steaminess of the climate, the dependability of the rains, and the avarice of the plantation-owners, whether white, mulatto, or Negro—the most valuable colonial possession in the world ; and as I rode with King Dick up the slopes of the mountains that rim the Great North Plain, I saw why plantation-owners could become fabulously wealthy in three years or less.

The lower slopes were covered with coffee plantations ; and so thick and matted were the coffee shrubs on badly tended plantations that the houses were choked and buried by them. They broke in green masses over slave quarters and outbuildings, engulfed boundary walls, surged on to verandahs, and curled over verandah roofs, just as the green water of a spring-tide floods up and over the wharves and beaches of the Maine coast.

On well-tended plantations, armies of black men hacked at the tangles of coffee shurbs with machetes ; and the masses of shoots and branches that they'd dragged from their cuttings were many times larger than the shrubs they had left.

Higher up the slopes of the mountains were forests of logwood and mahogany—sources of untold wealth if means could be found to get the timber to the sea. And everywhere on the lower slopes and in the valleys, in places so inaccessible that everything in them must have been brought in on mule and donkey back, were plantation houses, splendid great places triple the size of the largest houses in Portland.

I thanked God a hundred times that I had King Dick to guide me over those seventy-five miles to Mirebalais, for Haitian miles aren't like miles anywhere else. To go forward a mile across those helter-skelter, tortured ranges, we climbed paths that twisted like snakes up the mountain shoulders. They ascended from steamy hot valleys into pine forests where the keen winds smelled of snow ; then dropped down and down into cañons and gorges where we rode through a perpetual green twilight beneath arches of tree-ferns the size of Philadelphia horse-chestnuts.

Thus for every mile we went forward, we went upward, downward and sideways another two miles—or so it seemed to me. Never again do I expect to see any such tangled mass of mountains as those into which we climbed from the Great North Plain. They were like waves pitched up in a choppy sea. Off to our right stretched chain on chain, all scrambled together as if kicked into confusion by some drunken Vulcan : the Marmelade Chain, the Plaisance Chain, the Cahors Chain, the Mountains of the Northwest. Straight ahead, across a twenty-mile savannah, was a barricade of domes and peaks so steep that I felt we'd be forever finding a way through them. They were the Black Mountains, and their very names were forbidding— Mount Devil, Mount Take-Care, Mount Misfortune, Mount Hell.

Yet King Dick clambered up rocky gorges of those Black Mountains, found paths over knife-sharp hogbacks, booted his mule across mountain torrents and through steamy, stifling swamps. He pressed forward by night and by day, as tireless as a black panther. How I kept up with him —how our mules contrived to keep going with the quarter-hour rest they were allowed every two hours—I cannot say. All I knew then was that I had to keep up. I had to know about Lydia ; and whatever a man has to do, he can do.

In any case, I did keep up, and on the morning of our third day of riding he led me through a notch in the mountains and gave me a complacent grin. Below us, a velvety green bowl of tropical lushness, was the Valley of Artibonite, with the broad brown ribbon of the Artibonite River winding snake-like through it from end to end. Across the valley, not fifteen miles away, were more mountains, veritable devils of mountains, between whose peaks shone the milky blue-green water of the Bight of Léogane.

At mid-afternoon of that day we came into the town of Mirebalais, that sleepy place so hidden in verdure that it looked as though nothing had happened there, ever, and as though nobody lived in the town except a few people half asleep.

As we went out of Mirebalais on the road to Port-au-Prince, the mountains toward which we rode seemed to reach out to us like surging waves. They were darkly purple with the sun at their back—the Terrible Mountains, King Dick said ; and the highest of them, Mount Terrible, was pockmarked with caves as though a titanic cannon had blasted holes in its rock ledges while they were still soft. High along its sides were white bands, as though the Creator had built this mountain in layers, using white cement to bind His work together, but had gone away to work on something less forbidding. The white bands, King Dick insisted, were beaches made ages ago when the ocean covered all these jungles.

They could have been vanilla frosting for all I cared ; for as he spoke we turned a bend in the road, and there, beneath a mapou tree, stropping a machete on the palm of his hand, was a small half-naked black man with a fibre ring worked into his wool so that it stood up from his head like an inverted coffeepot without a bottom. Over his shoulder he wore a sash of red cloth edged with blackened silver lace, and his blue-and-white-striped trousers were supported by a leather belt that held a pistol and a machete-sling.

" My my ! My goo'ness me ! " King Dick said faintly. " She gros Nègre ! Grossest one I ever run into in the back part of nowhere ! " He took off his hat, bowed politely to the small black man, and gave him an amiable greeting in Creole.

The little man stared up at us wide-eyed, so that I thought of him as childish—as a player at soldier with his red sash and his openly displayed machete. " I am Ti-Bobo," he said to King Dick in Creole. He looked at me. " Is this the 'ti Blanc spoken of by drums ? One who wishes to find a woman ? "

" Who else ? " King Dick asked. " Where is the woman ? "

" Drums spoke of gold braid," Ti-Bobo said. " I have spent much time on this affair. It was necessary to make charms. You can pay me with gold braid : also three hundred gourdes for charms."

" She might not be the right woman," King Dick protested.

Ti-Bobo gave him an impatient answer. " I know her—a soft spoken Blanc, polite to black men. She been to my plantation in Mirebalais with two small children. They ride on mules, without servants, carrying food in bags that hang from their shoulders."

I wondered why in God's name a white woman should go to the plantation of a half-naked black man with a coffeepot head-dress.

As if he read my thoughts Ti-Bobo added, " She comes to learn songs we sing to *loa*. I have many *loa*—more than any in the valley of Mirebalais or Arcahaye—Genenibo, Erzilie Freda, Erzilie Gé Rouge ; 'Ti Kita Demembré ; Simbi en Deux Eaux ; Bumba Trois Iles ; Legba ; St. Jacques ; Ogun Ferraille, Ogun Balandjo, Ogun Ashade ; Lemba ; Aizan Keleké, Aizan Wedo, Aida Wedo, Damballa Wedo ; Baron Cimitière, Baron Samedi, Bosu Trois Cornes ; Congo Wangol, Maît' Mapou ; Agasu ; Agwe, Agweto Woyo ; Kadia-Bosu ; Sobo Gran' ; l'Afrique Guinée."

He reeled off this long list proudly, tilted back his head and eyed us across a nose as broad as it was flat.

King Dick looked unimpressed. " You want your money now ? "

Ti-Bobo left no doubt in our minds that he did.

" Oh, oh," King Dick said, " what you so impatient about ? You go with us, I hope."

Ti-Bobo scraped the ball of his thumb on the edge of his machete. " Don't you hear drums all last night and this morning ? "

" I hear," King Dick said. " When don't I hear drums in Haiti ? "

" Maybe you don't read those drums," Ti-Bobo retorted. " Yesterday an army of black ships begin to arrive off Cape Samana, full of Blancs in uniform. Now those ships move all together, like one ship."

King Dick stared at him, his eyes like bantam eggs. " Move where ? "

" Toward Cap François, the drums say. The drums say Blancs in those ships, they are all French. They say when they come ashore, all of us will be slaves to Blancs once more. You know what happens to every-one when Blancs come among us ? That is why I wish to waste no time. I wish to be back with my own people if Blancs come."

King Dick fumbled in his pockets, producing from one a length of gold braid, and from another a handful of gold coins. The gold vanished into Ti-Bobo's pockets as if it were dross, but he cupped the gold braid in his black hands and peered at it between his thumbs.

" He see whether it sweats," King Dick told me. " That how they tell a thunderstone. If it sweat, it got a *loa*—a Papa God. If not, it just another stone."

Ti-Bobo opened his hand and looked up at us exultantly. The surface of the gold braid was dulled by a thin fog of moisture, such as forms on any piece of metal when held between two hot, damp paws.

" My, my," King Dick said faintly, " now you safe from Blancs and everything else." He gathered up his reins. " Catch hold my stirrup," he told Ti-Bobo. " We do a little sweating ourselves."

I doubt whether there have ever been country houses as magnificent as those that looked down from the shoulders of the Terrible Mountains to the Bight of Léogane and the beautiful plain known as the Cul de Sac.

As soon as we topped the pass in the mountains, we could see them far below us, on mountain promontories, on savannahs between hills, on symmetrical islands of pale green in settings of darker green.

It seemed impossible that men could have built, in places so remote, such monumental and complete fortresses in which to house themselves and their belongings. When the houses stood on steep slopes, vast masonry walls rose up out of the earth to make artificial plains, and on each man-made plain were terraces and towers amid alleys of palms, coffee shrubs, and chinaberry trees ; fountains playing in formal pools ; guest houses and workmen's quarters ; smithies and store-houses ; kitchens and stables. These enormous plantations seemed to me as permanent as anything man could build—and so, perhaps, they would have been, except for the human jealousies and cupidities that result in war and slavery, which ruin everything.

At the narrowest part of the road, Ti-Bobo stopped us and jerked a thumb at two twin hills that seemed to be crowding the road into a deep cañon. " Beau-Bouclier," he said. " It is the place."

We went up the rough path between the two small peaks, and as we topped the rim we saw before and below us a circular valley sheltered on all sides by a rim of hills. From the centre of the valley rose a rocky knob or boss ; and on this central elevation was a round, white-columned stone house. Symmetrically arranged around it were lesser buildings of the plantation—sugar houses, storehouses, a distillery, stables, workmen's houses, and the like, all circular and all with white pillars, miniatures of the big house upon the central knoll. Thus the house with its outbuildings was like the carved boss in the middle of a vast green shield—which accounted, of course, for its name : Beau-Bouclier—Beautiful Shield ; Beautiful Buckler.

I stared down at it in an agony of anticipation. It seemed to me I had been struggling forever to reach this place ; and now I was conscious of a violent trembling within me : a sort of horror at the thought of what might happen to me if Lydia weren't there.

King Dick had no such fears. " You go down, Albion," he said. " You tell that lady this no place for her. You tell her she better leave this place fast and go away to America quick. It no place for us, either, and I think I send Ti-Bobo to Port-au-Prince right now to make sure they be a boat waiting to take us back to Cap François. They going be trouble, Albion, so don't you waste time ! "

As I rode down into the circular valley I heard King Dick's voice issuing orders to Ti-Bobo, and somehow it had changed. There was authority in it, and sharpness, and an urgency that made me curse the stubborn caution of all mules, in particular the mule that carried me and refused to run down hill, no matter how hard I raked him with my spurs.

CHAPTER XVII

FROM all around, as I crossed the bottom of that gigantic green cup, rose the sound of drums, to whose thumpings innumerable Negroes hacked with machetes at the weeds and creepers around the coffee shrubs ; and the thumping of my own heart seemed to keep time to the throbbing of the drums.

Close under the veranda two little Negroes in green shirts and white pantaloons ran out and held to my bridle and stirrups.

When I climbed from my mule, I caught sight of a white dress on the veranda above—a white dress and a pretty elbow, and shining black hair like a cap of laquer that half concealed a little ear ; and at the sight I was all clumsiness, my fingers all thumbs, my legs like stumps. As I stumbled up the stairs she showed no sign of hearing me, and to me her back seemed eloquent of disapproval, so that I cleared my throat and coughed in embarrassment.

On that she turned to face me, and to my relief she wasn't the girl of the portrait at all, but a pale woman with fishy eyes and a look of secret defiance, as if she took pleasure in being contrary.

Doing my best to control my breathlessness, I spoke to her in French, introducing myself and asking for a lady named Bailey.

She took forever to answer, and I was conscious of nothing but a shaking in my knees and a vague desire to slap such a damnably slow woman. At last she rose reluctantly and went to the door of the house, where she screamed affectedly and offensively for someone named Gabriel, all the while poking and pushing at her hair with one hand and eyeing me from under her elbow—which I now saw to be pointed and slightly yellowed.

I wasn't alone in finding her offensive ; for a gentleman in white linen burst from the house, thumping clenched fists against his eyebrows as if to beat back his disapproval.

" My God, Eloïse," he cried in French, " how many times have I told you there must be no screaming at this hour ? "

The lady looked haughty. " You needn't shout at me, Gabriel ! For one thing, I was not screaming ; but even if I had been screaming, it wouldn't have been the sort of screaming about which you told me. That was screaming at servants. In this case I only called you because of this American gentleman here. You can see he's an American. He has asked for a lady named Bailey."

" A lady named Bailey," I thought. " She's not here ! This fool of a woman doesn't know her ! "

" Ah, Mon Dieu," the gentleman said, rolling exasperated eyes to heaven, " I say you were screaming ! You always scream ! Even when you whisper, it is a screamed whisper ! "

The lady laughed whinnyingly and probed with questing fingers at her back hair. " No matter what I do to help in this house, I can do nothing right ! One would think I'd never been a mother myself ! Never, in all the times that we visited the Choiseuls, were we expected to inconvenience ourselves for their children—and if ever there were more beautiful little gentlemen than the children of the Duc de Choiseul, I have never seen them."

The gentleman seemed to control himself with an effort. Coming towards me, he gave a pale smile, as though he had an unpleasant taste in his mouth.

" It is unfortunate that you should arrive here at such a moment," he said. " This is the hour when my sons read in English, and we made a rule long ago that nothing must interfere with this reading, ever. Pray be seated, M'sieu. Possibly a small glass of rum will make the time seem short. I am Gabriel d'Autremont, and this lady is my sister-in-law, Madame Serpinard."

Two sons, and they read English ! Hope revived so suddenly within me that my knees shook.

" I'm looking for a lady named Bailey," I said, and my voice shook too. " Lydia Bailey. Is she here ? "

Autremont raised his eyebrows. " But of course, M'sieu. She is governess to my sons."

I could only say, " She is ? " and stare at him like a fool.

" But certainly, M'sieu ! Ah, we would find it impossible to exist without Mademoiselle Bailey ! My sons adore her ! Such élan ! Such unending cheerfulness ! Such——"

I regained enough of my senses and my power of speech to interrupt him. " Will you let me see her at once, please ? I've just had unexpected news—extremely disturbing——"

Autremont raised his eyebrows. " Dear me," he said, " I think all American men must be in a hurry, always. Everything is intensely important to them, is it not, and to waste a moment might be disastrous ! " He smiled, as at a petulant child. " In Haiti, M'sieu, we find that haste makes waste, and we seldom have unexpected news. Pray compose yourself, M'sieu, and explain to whom I am indebted for this pleasure ? How have you arrived at Beau-Bouclier ? In what manner did you receive this unexpected news ? "

I found his amused condescension infuriating. "It's a long story," I said. "If you'll let me explain to Miss Bailey——"

He raised a protesting hand. "Now, now, M'sieu! I have told you the rule I have made, and in all fairness I am entitled to hear this unexpected news."

"Well," I said, "I'm a lawyer employed by Miss Bailey's uncle, who died recently. I came to Cap François to hunt for her, and by great good fortune I learned her whereabouts. When I left Cap François four days ago there was talk of a war ; and at Mirebalais——"

Again he raised his hand. "Talk of war? Who made such talk?"

"Hungans," I said.

He shrugged his shoulders. Madame Serpinard rolled up her eyes and said, "Zut alors!"

"Look here, sir, I ask you to take my word that this is important. When we reached Mirebalais yesterday we learned a French fleet had been sighted off the end of the island, headed towards Cap François."

"A French fleet!" he cried. "No! How did you learn?"

"A Hungan named Ti-Bobo heard the drums say it."

He laughed delightedly. "Marvellous, M'sieu! We've heard for months that Bonaparte might send an army to restore order, but we'd come to believe that he must have forgotten us! Ah, Heaven! How I hope your Hungan is right, M'sieu! Think if we could have a government of white men again instead of all these niggers! But sit down, sit down, M'sieu! You have come far! We'll have a thimbleful of rum, eh, and then we'll dine at our leisure and you can speak to Mademoiselle Bailey."

I saw he had no intention of letting me see Lydia until he was ready to do so.

I went to the balcony rail. King Dick was there, silently waiting. I called to him that I needed help.

He came up the stairs softly and quickly, grinning from ear to ear, ducked his head politely to Autremont, stared blankly at Madame Serpinard, and turned abruptly to me. "Where that lady?"

"She's in the house," I said, "and M. d'Autremont won't call her. I don't want to do anything illegal, and I'd like your advice."

"Mm, mm," King Dick said in a hushed voice. "What Toussaint say, if we not back in Cap François when he need me? I rather be illegal than that!" He spoke sharply to our host. "You call that lady to come out, please."

Autremont looked as stubborn as my own mule. "I've already explained to this gentleman that Mademoiselle Bailey——"

"Talk, talk, talk," King Dick said sharply. "Surest way to get into trouble, time of war ; talk!" Brushing Autremont aside, he went lightly to the door, stepped into the hallway, and thunderously beat upon the floor with his cocomacque.

In an instant the house seemed to erupt black servants ; but I had eyes for none of them when I saw Lydia come into the hallway from an inner room, with Autremont's two sons pressed close to her side.

When I stood staring at her and she at me, King Dick came out, took me by the arm and pushed me inside the house ; I heard Autremont protesting ; but in spite of his protests, King Dick closed the door and left me with Lydia and the two children in the cool dimness of the jalousied hallway.

Every man, I suppose, makes a fool of himself at one time or another over the woman he loves ; and the most propitious time, I suspect, is the moment when he first sees her after long months of anticipation. I was no sooner alone with Lydia than I seemed to lose the power of coherent thought. So long and so ardently had I thought of her that I forgot I was a complete stranger to her.

" Why," I said, " you're smaller than your portrait ! No, that's impossible, of course ! The portrait is small. I've always seen you differently ! Perhaps it's because your hair is covered." She had an orange handkerchief knotted tight around her hair.

She shook her head. " You've seen me differently ? I don't think I understand—have I ever had——" She stopped. " Oh ! You saw my portrait ! That means you saw it at my uncle's ! "

" Yes," I said. " It's mine now. I was his lawyer."

" You were his lawyer ? " she asked slowly, and immediately repeated her words. " You *were* his lawyer ! *Were !* . . . Is my uncle dead ? "

" Yes," I said, " he's dead."

I brought her a chair, and as she sank into it she thanked me with a look so exactly like her picture that my heart turned over. Her hand moved flutteringly to a small green stone that hung on a chain at her throat " I thought something must be wrong," she said, " when Cousin Harriet wrote all his letters." She touched her fingers to her forehead.

The smaller of the two boys pressed his cheek against her shoulder. She put her arm around him and drew him to her. " No, no, darling," she said. " I am not unhappy. The gentleman has been a kind friend, and I am glad because my uncle can no longer suffer." She smiled at me across the boy's brown hair, and when the boy threw his arms around her and kissed her I realised she was everything I had ever imagined and a thousand times more. Had I ever had a doubt lest I was making a fool of myself over a portrait, the doubt was dead now. The impact of her presence was like a flame, burning away everything except the one single conviction that the world would be no world for me unless she was a part of it.

She took the smaller boy on her lap and put her arm around the other. " Will you shake hands with Paul and Raymond ? " she asked me. " They are Frenchmen and their home is in Cette, near the Camargue in France, where there are herdsmen—cowboys—who ride better than anyone else in the world."

I shook hands with them and told them my name was Albion Hamlin, that I spoke French but lived in America, in the town of Portland, that I had two horses, one named Blue Boy and the other named Blue Belle, and that I would like to see the herdsmen of the Camargue.

She looked at me over the top of Raymond's head. " They have cowboy clothes," she said. To the boys she added, " Mr. Hamlin would like to see them, I think."

" Yes," I said, " I would. I didn't know there were cowboys in France."

" They carry lariats and ficheirouns," Raymond said.

" Darling had them made for us," Paul said.

The smaller boy slid off her lap, and the two of them went hopping and skipping from the room.

Lydia watched them go ; then turned back to me. " When did my uncle die ? " she asked. " Why did he die ? It's only a week ago that I wrote him—only a month ago that I had a letter from him, written by Cousin Harriet."

" He died over a year ago," I said, " in the same jail that I was in . . . I've carried your portrait with me ever since he died. It's with me now, rolled up in my riding crop. Even before he died he thought you were dead, but you never seemed so to me. I wrote letters to you—that is, they weren't to you, but in my heart—I mean, you seemed more real to me——"

She nodded. " I think I partly understand. You needn't explain."

" I want to explain," I said. " I can't find the words."

" Then don't try just now," she said gently. " Tell me how it happened—how he came to give you my picture. I think perhaps he was fond of you."

" Yes," I said. " It was damned persecution, that's what it was ! Let's see : it's hard for me to tell it straight. Your face—I mean, seeing you in the flesh, so exactly like—well—— My own uncle was a judge in Portland. When your uncle wanted to publish an opinion on the Sedition Law—an opinion that would show it to be unconstitutional and an outrage against free men—he asked my uncle to write the opinion. When the opinion was published, your uncle was arrested and tried for sedition. Since my uncle felt partly responsible, he wished to defend your uncle ; but he was too ill to do so, so he persuaded me to do it for him. That's how I came to be your uncle's lawyer. If I hadn't, I'd never have seen your portrait. It was the first thing I ever saw that I *had* to have. You'll never know such a feeling—emptiness, I mean——"

She shook her head in kindly warning.

" I can't help it," I said. " For over a year I've thought of nothing— well, it seems as though I'd known you always. That's why I—well, the judge in the case was a bad judge—a politician who wouldn't admit evidence. As a result he put me in jail for contempt of court, and made such a one-sided charge to the jury that your uncle was found guilty

and also sent to jail. He died there of consumption. Just after he died
Harriet gave me your portrait. I never understood before why Harriet
disliked it, but I understand now."

Lydia sighed. " He thought I was dead."

" Yes. That was Harriet Faulkner's doing. She made your uncle
believe it ! She swore you were dead, and I believed her, of course. I
carried your portrait for over a year before I learned from a man in
Philadelphia that he'd seen you in Cap François. Even then she insisted
you were dead. She had a letter that proved it—a letter that said you
died of yellow fever a year ago last June."

" I think perhaps I'd rather not hear about it," she said.

" You've got to ! When I went to Harriet and accused her, she stuck
to her story. You were dead : you'd written no letters : those you had
written had been destroyed : she'd forgotten the name of the plantation
to which you'd gone. Since she'd hoodwinked your uncle, she thought
she could pull the wool over my eyes too. She even thought she could
make me think you'd never written your uncle—never shown any sign
of gratitude. I knew she lied, because I had your portrait. It disproved
everything she said."

She looked at me in such a way that a giant vice seemed to close
upon my whole inner breast.

" Ever since I've been here I've written him every two weeks."

" Of course," I said. " I was sure of it ! I was sure, too, that Harriet
wanted your uncle's belongings, and the jewels he'd brought home from
India, and whatever she might be able to get in French Spoliation Claims
from his shares in the barque *Kingfisher*. She must have hoped you would
never come back from San Domingo. She must have hoped you'd never
know your uncle had made you his heir. Perhaps she even thought you
might be so helpless you wouldn't know how to fight for your
rights."

Lydia nodded. " Poor woman ! She seemed so sweet from her letters."
She dismissed Harriet with a small gesture, and looked at me questioningly.
" And how was it you finally found me, Mr. Hamlin ? "

" Why," I said, " I met King Dick, that big black man who pounded
on the floor. It's because of him that we've got to return at once to Cap
François. Toussaint trusts him, and King Dick can't fail him if there's to
be trouble. He took a fancy to me and got some men to send messages
with drums."

" Now I'm beginning to understand," Lydia said. " You want me to
go back to America and claim my uncle's estate."

" Yes," I said, " I do."

She shook her head. " You've been very kind, Mr. Hamlin, and I
appreciate all you did for my uncle and all you're trying to do for me.
And I'll talk to M. d'Autremont. But I want to be honest with you : it
may be difficult to do as you suggest."

" Why should it be difficult ? It was easy enough for you to come from Boston to Haiti, and why should there be any difficulty in going back again ? All you have to do is let us help you go."

She shook her head again. " It isn't as easy as all that, Mr. Hamlin. Naturally I should be glad to have whatever my uncle has left me, but I came here to attend to the education of M. d'Autremont's children ; and if you knew Haiti as I do, you'd know I can't abandon them at a moment's notice."

" I'm not asking you to abandon them," I said. " I'm only asking you to start for America with somebody who can help you, and before there's trouble."

She leaned forward. " Trouble ? Are the French coming ? We've heard repeatedly—I didn't believe it—I hoped it wasn't true ! "

As rapidly as I could I gave her the information Ti-Bobo had picked up from the drums. When I'd finished, she sat staring down at her folded hands.

" I never believed the things I heard," she said. " They seemed too fantastic ! But of course it was inevitable. I see it now ! It was bad enough for Toussaint to take this island from the French, but what Bonaparte couldn't forgive was that the deed should have been done by a black man called the Black Napoleon. ' A slave in revolt against France,' Bonaparte called him. ' A black upstart ! ' ' An outrage to the national honour of France ! ' I should have known the day would come when he'd put Toussaint in his place, no matter what the cost." She looked up quickly. " What does your black friend think will happen ? "

" He says it means fighting—the worst sort of killing, of whites by blacks, of blacks by men of colour. He's so sure of it that he's sent a man to Port-au-Prince to arrange for a schooner to take us back to Cap François to-night. He says that the French can't come ashore without wanting to control everything, and that if they control everything they'll surely make slaves of the Negroes again."

She sat silent and, I thought, dubious.

" You've got to believe me," I said. " You mustn't think King Dick and Ti-Bobo are unrealiable just because they're black. I've never known a white man more worthy of trust than King Dick. He's been a good friend ; and, if I'm any judge, he's told me the exact truth about everything. If he says there's going to be trouble, there'll be trouble ; and when he says you should leave this place and start back to America, he means it."

She leaned forward and brushed my fingers with her own. " Some day I'll explain to you why it's impossible for me to leave Paul and Raymond. They need me and love me, as you've seen. I can't abandon them if trouble is coming ; and I don't believe, Mr. Hamlin, you'd want me to abandon them *after* they're in trouble ! " She gave me that side-long glance that seemed to reach down into my heart.

" That's how I feel about you," I said desperately.

" Then you know how I feel," she said. " I believe your friend is right in thinking you must return at once to Cap François. I believe he's right when he says that the French wish to take this island from the Negroes and make them slaves once more. And I believe equally that I cannot leave this family so suddenly, when I'm most needed."

" Listen," I said, " I won't give you up now that I've found you. You have no idea what it has been like—waiting and hoping——"

She interrupted me. " I won't run away and I have something important to tell you : something I'm sure your friend doesn't know. But you and every other American ought to know it. It's something I didn't believe until just now ; but now that the French are coming in force, I know it's true."

She lowered her voice. " During my stay here I have heard many private conversations among influential Frenchmen. They have freely discussed the probability of Napoleon's sending a French fleet and army here ; and they weren't boasting. But there was something else they discussed in whispers. Listen : Do you know who owns Louisiana—New Orleans ? "

I thought of King Dick's little boopety General Wilkinson, and his traitorous dealings with the Spanish governor of Louisiana. " Certainly," I said. " Spain owns it."

She shook her head. " No. That's what the world thinks, but influential Frenchmen know that it belongs to France."

" Impossible ! "

" All highly placed Frenchmen," she went on, ignoring my protest, " know that Spain signed a treaty with France a year ago—a treaty that allowed France to buy all of Louisiana. The treaty has been kept secret, but Bonaparte to-day owns Louisiana and New Orleans."

" My God," I said, " such a thing *couldn't* have been kept secret ! "

" That's what I thought," she said, " but it *has* ! " Then she seemed to change the subject. " Did you know that there have never been, in any country, so many foreigners, as there are French in America ? There are thousands in Philadelphia alone, thousands in——"

" Yes, I met M. de Busigny and the others, and I know *that's* true. But I can hardly believe the other. . . ."

She leaned closer. " All those whispering Frenchmen know that Bonaparte has a plan—a plan so daring and vast that many of the French who once hated him as an upstart and a murderer are beginning to think of him as a saviour who will make of France a more glorious empire than the world has ever known. It's a plan to overwhelm and retake this island overnight ; then to hurry his victorious army to New Orleans and seize all of America for himself."

I laughed.

She put her hand upon my sleeve. " Don't laugh ! I laughed, too, once, but not now ! Those Frenchmen were whispering state secrets—they *knew* ! Anything—everything—is possible to a madman like Bonaparte ! He's the personification of audacity, and nothing succeeds in war like audacity ! Thousands of those Frenchmen in America—great soldiers, some of them : great statesmen—have sent back word to France that the country is helpless—unarmed—without artillery—without a navy worthy of the name—without a general capable of defending the strongest fort in the world against a handful of determined men."

She pressed my arm by way of emphasis. " Do you know what those whispering Frenchmen said ? They said that if a well-trained army of fifty thousand men could be launched against the United States from Haiti, every city in America could be captured in a year's time, and Bonaparte would be the master of America and the world ! All that's necessary is to take Haiti without a struggle, and the whispering Frenchmen insisted that arrangements have been made to do so. Arrangements : do you understand ? "

" Yes, I understand—but I don't believe a word of it ! "

" Why not ? Those whisperers predicted an invasion, and here is is ! Why should a great fleet be needed to bring this island into submission ? Why should a great army be necessary to defeat untrained Negroes ? You'll find that the army is commanded by Bonaparte's most trusted generals. You *must* believe me ! You must do what you can to help stop this invasion."

Suddenly I believed her. To launch an attack on America would seem wholly feasible to a man whose armies had overrun Egypt and Italy. Her words had sounded fantastic because I'd thought of America as too far from France to be invaded ; but after all, England had invaded America : a British Army under Burgoyne had come within a hair's-breadth of crushing New England : another British Army under Cornwallis had slashed hundreds of miles through the South like a knife through lard. If the British could do it against a warned and prepared America, the French could do it against an America without an army, a navy, or generals. I'd been a fool to laugh. . . .

" What can I do ? " I asked. " I believe you now, but there's nothing I can do except tell King Dick."

" That's better than nothing," she said. " He can tell Toussaint, and when Toussaint knows that ' arrangements ' have been made to let the French land without opposition, he'll know that some of his own men can't be trusted, and he'll be on the lookout for them. I know those whispering Frenchmen were wrong about Toussaint L'Ouverture. I know he won't make arrangements with anyone, or willingly let the Negroes be enslaved again. I know he can't be bribed or frightened. He's a great man : one of the greatest, I truly believe, who ever lived. The French don't know him or understand him or appreciate him ! They can't see beyond the colour of his skin. They can't recognise what a great governor he's been, and they can't understand his passionate determination to be free."

I tried to think, but had only confused thoughts. " Lydia," I said, " if the French *don't* take the island without trouble, I'm coming back to make sure you're safe."

She stood up quickly. "Yes," she said. "I want you to come back, but not unless it's safe." A sudden thought seemed to strike her, and she touched the little green stone at her throat. "This is a thunderstone, a great wanga. A powerful Hungan in Mirebalais swore that nothing could harm any person who wore it." She slipped it from her neck and handed it to me. "This is to show you I'm grateful, and that I'm more concerned for your safety than for my own."

I caught at her hands, and she looked up into my eyes, a straight clear look that drove every thought from my head—that almost kept me from realising that Paul and Raymond had come back into the room. They were wearing wide-brimmed hats, short jackets, and long leather pantaloons with the seat removed, and carrying rods tipped with small metal tridents.

She freed her hands from mine and went to kneel between the two boys. "Would you like to ride with my kind friend to the notch?" she asked. "You can show him how they ride in Carmargue, and how you say good-bye in English."

They hugged her ecstatically and went whooping from the room.

She got to her feet, hesitated a moment before me, pressed my hand lightly; then went past me on to the veranda; and there was something about the pressure of her hand and her slight hesitation that was like a burst of song in my heart.

CHAPTER XVIII

M. d'Autremont's lean face, when we bade him good-bye, made it plain that everything had turned out to his satisfaction. Lydia, he could see, had no intention of accompanying us; and with each passing moment he had become more and more certain that the coming of the French would be an unmixed blessing, so far as he was concerned, rather than the catastrophe that King Dick and I feared.

"I've tried to persuade your friend," he said to me, "that there's no need for all this hurry. Dine with us, my dear M'sieu Hamlin: rest here to-morrow; then on the following day you can set off comfortably for Cap François on your mules instead of travelling miserably on a wretched fishing-vessel. It's all nonsense to think the French will cause trouble when they land!"

King Dick closed his eyes and chuckled. "Maybe they not the only ones to cause trouble," he said faintly.

"Oh, come now," M. d'Autremont said. "What chance would Negro troops have against a French army? Do you think any of these Negroes in gold lace and glass beads would dare to match wits with Bonaparte's generals?"

Since I didn't want him to hate me I refused to discuss the matter, and merely said, " We have no choice in the matter, sir. King Dick has duties in Cap François, and we've arranged passage. Perhaps I'll have the pleasure of accepting your hospitality some other day."

How soon that was to be, and under what circumstances, I wouldn't have believed even if I'd been told—and that was my first lesson in the futility of making predictions about a war. Nobody ever makes them correctly, though after the war is over almost everyone claims to have done so.

Paul and Raymond, on their ponies, accompanied us up the green slope to the notch in the lip of that giant cup, brandishing their tridents and making cheerful whooping sounds. As we rode out of the notch and on to the Port-au-Prince road, they shouted after us the words Lydia had taught them : " Farewell, friends, and a safe journey ! " Great though my disappointment was, I knew Lydia was right. She couldn't abandon them—not at such a time as this.

As we rode towards Port-au-Prince I told King Dick what Lydia had told me, but what he thought about it I couldn't tell. He growled and grumbled, partly to himself and partly to me, and from his grumblings I gathered that he was chiefly concerned over his inability to determine whom besides Toussaint he could trust with the information.

He'd tell Toussaint, yes : but whom else, he wanted to know, could he tell ? In all Haiti only Toussaint valued a man for what was inside his head : only Toussaint wholly disregarded a man's colour. Everybody else thought perpetually in terms of colour. Why, he wanted to know, should every woman of colour long for children lighter than herself ? Why were black and mulatto generals for ever changing sides in a war ? Why should black soldiers be willing to fight for freedom one day : then freely follow leaders into the camp of those who were fighting against freedom ? Why did every black man except Toussaint hate mulattoes ? Why did mulattoes hate blacks ? Why should both of them hate whites ? Why did light-coloured Negroes consider themselves superior to darker-coloured Negroes ? Why should black men trust white priests more than dark ones, and at the same time never tell the truth to any white man ?

He accepted without question everything that Lydia had told me, but he didn't know what to do about it any more than I did.

The little schooner that waited for us in the harbour of Port-au-Prince was small and bug-infested, and stunk of long-dead fish, rotted sponges, and Port-au-Prince sewage, which is powerful beyond belief.

Thanks to a thick-witted Negro captain and a somnolent Negro crew, we were three sweltering days making that journey out of the Bight of Léogane and along the northern coast.

The French ships of which the drums had warned us were constantly in our minds ; and King Dick was anxious to avoid them. " Those French," he said, " they worse than blacks when they preparing trouble for others. They believe nothing and nobody, not even themselves. When we see French ships, we run ashore and ride mules rest of way. If we don't see French ships, we run into Limbé, around corner from Cap François, and ride to Le Cap in two hours."

He was right about the troublesomeness of the French, but he under-estimated their ingenuity as trouble-makers. Not a French ship had we seen when we reached the beautiful deep harbour of Limbé, and we thought we were safe when the captain of our little schooner, at King Dick's direction, made for the harbour entrance. When we were at its narrowest part, an eight-oared patrol boat with a swivel-gun in her bow came out from behind a point of land and started for us like an overgrown eight-legged water bug.

"My, my! My goo'ness me!" King Dick cried. "That French boat!"

He ran to the tiller, where the captain stood as if frozen, his thick lips slack and his eyes crossed with befuddlement. So violently did King Dick throw over the tiller that the quarter-deck jerked as if kicked. When the longboat increased its speed by stepping a mast and setting a lugsail, King Dick gave up, dropped the tiller, stretched himself, and yawned cavernously.

Our schooner came up into the hot breeze and hung there, her sails slapping and slatting. The longboat rounded-to under our lee amid a thumping of oars and shouting of orders; and an officer, sweating pro-fusely in blue jacket, gold braid, and cocked hat, came up over the stern, followed by two seamen in striped trousers and shirts.

"Who is captain of this vessel?" he asked in French.

The captain pawed at the deck with one foot and made ducking motions with his head.

"What is your cargo and why do you come to Limbé instead of Cap François?" the officer demanded.

When the captain found his tongue, the officer professed to be wholly baffled by the thickness of his Creole accent. "Never mind, my friend. Whatever you have, we will purchase—even the mules. But you have no business in Limbé. Bring your schooner to Cap François and tie up a cable-length from the flagship. No vessel can enter or leave port without permission."

He turned a speculative eye on us.

"Sir," I said, "I'm an American, in Haiti on a matter connected with the law. Would there be any possible objection to my going ashore here and now?"

"A very great objection," he said politely. "It should be evident that nobody from any vessel can be allowed to land until our entire fleet receives permission to land. Thus we avoid confusion."

"But," I protested, "I'll cause no confusion by going ashore."

"Ah, M'sieu, but you would," the officer said sadly. "Look you: the French fleet is in Cap François on a peaceful mission. Therefore, we have no authority to say that anyone can enter or leave a port. If we gave you permission to proceed, we would be exceeding our authority. Already the general has sent a letter to the Commander of Cap François announcing his intentions, and we expect the reply soon. You will be good enough to follow me to Cap François ! "

He saluted us with a great show of politeness, but the sailor in the bow of the patrol boat moved the swivel-gun in our direction and blew hopefully at the end of his lighted match.

I wanted to question the officer further ; but I remembered how my uncle used to insist that an army is a breeding ground for stupidities, and that civilians who question or oppose those stupidities invariably end by being insulted, forcibly silenced, or shot.

We followed the patrol boat the few remaining miles to Cap François, and as we rounded the headland and the harbour opened before our eyes, we were confronted by the biggest and blackest ships in the world—more warships than I had believed existed. They were all at anchor, and in a moment almost we were in among those towering black-sided monsters, whose open-mouthed guns stared out at us from triced-up ports. Their ratlins and yards were covered with ant-like human figures, their bulwarks topped by countless heads.

We tacked in and out among the ships, eventually coming to anchor a cable-length in the lee of the biggest and blackest ship of all. And there we sat with the hot January sun beating down upon us, staring at the endless activities of the thousands of men who swarmed like bees upon the vessels of that far-spread fleet. We felt helpless and exasperated, as I suppose all men feel when they find themselves confronted by so much as a hint of a war they haven't foreseen, don't want, and have no desire to enter.

While we were silent, cogitating, a Baltimore schooner came slipping through the anchored warships that lay between us and the town. So trim and clean were her lines that she seemed to skim the water rather than cut through it. There were six men on her quarter-deck, one of them all a-glitter in a French uniform, so I took the vessel for a government despatch boat.

But when she drew nearer, I saw that Colonel Tobias Lear was one of those upon her quarter-deck ; and by the lettering on her transom stern I saw she was the *Nelly* of Havre de Grace, Maryland.

" There's a piece of luck, first crack out of the box," I said to King Dick. " If I can get word to Lear about the French plans, he might be able to do something."

The *Nelly* was bound for the flagship, and when she turned on her heel and moved up into the wind alongside us, a tall man at her tiller saluted us with an upraised hand and shouted, " Ahoy, Admiral ! " He had a cheery, mocking smile, curly black hair, little crinkly side whiskers, and an upper arm so thick that it looked to be nearly as wide as his chest was deep. In spite of his height and solidity, he had spring and bounce, perhaps from his manner of standing on his toes, which gave him a pigeon-toed look.

King Dick removed his hat and made this gentleman a deep bow, then grinned expansively and called, " How you, Admiral ? "

When I looked at him inquiringly, he said. " That Captain Rodgers. He captain in American Navy once. Now they no American Navy, so he get rich buying rum, coffee, logwood."

" If he's a captain, why do you call him Admiral ? "

King Dick looked baffled and said he didn't know : if a person met with his approval, he called him either Admiral or General, and almost inevitably the persons thus addressed became either admirals or generals, or attained correspondingly high positions in life.

" Thank God he's a good friend of yours," I said. " If Lear doesn't believe me, maybe your friend will, so let's get aboard that schooner without any loss of time."

Three minutes later we were in the schooner's dinghy, pulling hard for the *Nelly*.

Those six men on the *Nelly's* quarter-deck—the French officer, Tobias Lear, Captain Rodgers, the Negro mayor of Cap François, and two merchants—were a singularly diverse company.

Rodgers, to whom I took an instant liking, was the only one who seemed unaffected by the military and naval tumult all about us ; and he greeted King Dick with as much concentrated attention as though the *Nelly* were tied up at the dullest dock at Havre de Grace. How, Rodgers wanted to know, had King Dick come to be on a schooner, and where had he been, and why ? King Dick's manner of talking seemed to give Rodgers enormous pleasure, and he watched King Dick's lips when he spoke, as if impatient for the words to emerge.

When King Dick told him how we had gone together to Beau-Bouclier, he turned the same concentrated attention on me, as if deeply interested in my affairs—and I truly think Rodgers was genuinely con-cerned over the affairs of those he liked, just as he always had the most profound contempt for men and measures of which he disapproved.

I excused myself to Rodgers as soon as I decently could, and went to Lear, who was talking to the young French officer.

" Ah, Mr. Hamlin," Lear said affably, " I trust your trip was success-ful." He presented me to the French officer, a handsome and polite young man, Captain Lebrun.

To Lear I said, " Yes, Colonel, it was successful in a way. If you could spare a moment, there are things about it I'd like to tell you."

Lear didn't look enthusiastic, but Captain Lebrun immediately moved away, so that Lear had no option except to hear me.

" Colonel," I said, " I picked up some information at the plantation house I visited. I didn't believe it at first, but now I think it's true. In the first place, Spain sold Louisiana and New Orleans to France almost a year ago."

" You don't know what you're talking about ! "

" Yes, I do," I countered, " it was a secret treaty."

" Now look here, Mr. Hamlin," Lear said, " I haven't time to listen to any such nonsense. We're already in a dangerous situation, and if Captain Lebrun should overhear a few words of what you're saying, I might be in trouble."

He'd have turned from me if I hadn't moved around in front of him. " Wait," I told him. " How many men on these ships ? Who are the generals in command ? "

" There are twelve thousand men," Lear answered coldly. " I'm not sure of all the generals, but I know they're Bonaparte's best—Leclerc, Rochambeau, Hardy, Boudet, Baron Delacroix."

" That's what I was told," I said. " That Bonaparte would send his best. Do you know what he's planning ? He's planning an attack on the United States."

This time Lear didn't even grant me the courtesy of an answer, but just brushed me out of his way and went straight to Captain Lebrun again. Of course I couldn't persist in talking before Lebrun, so there was nothing for me to do but go back to Rodgers and King Dick.

" I think you'll be interested to know, Mr. Hamlin," Rodgers said, " that the French officer you just met, Captain Lebrun, was sent to Christophe yesterday by Leclerc, the French general. Leclerc wanted Christophe's permission for the French army to land."

" What Christophe say ? " King Dick asked quickly.

Rodger's reply was careless. " Oh, he said he couldn't answer until he saw Toussaint, and unfortunately he couldn't locate Toussaint."

King Dick's eyes rolled expressively.

" The captain had a nice time, though," Rodger's went on. " Stayed at the palace, and had his dinner all alone in the state dining-room, off gold plates and all that. Then he was allowed to spend the evening in his room by himself, so he'd have plenty of time to think things over."

" My, my ! " King Dick said. " That Christophe not afraid of nobody ! "

" That's how it looks," Rodgers said. " We hear that Christophe won't give Leclerc permission to come ashore ; that if Leclerc insists on landing, Christophe intends to burn the city. That's why Colonel Lear's out here, with that Deputation from Cap François. They're going to try to persuade Leclerc not to land till Toussaint can be found."

He went to the taffrail. The *Nelly's* longboat lay alongside, manned by an officer and four men, as smart as a Navy boat crew.

Rodgers turned and signalled to Captain Lebrun, who, after a deal of heel-clicking and bowing, went over the side and into the longboat and was rowed to the flagship in solitary grandeur.

" Less embarrassing that way," Rodgers whispered to me. " Those black men in the Deputation are so scared they'd have fallen all over his feet, and probably upset the boat into the bargain."

He told us of the excitement that had swept Cap François at the sight of the French fleet. "Every white plantation-owner is in a delirium at the thought of French rule," he said. "They think it means bigger profits and the return of slavery. The mulattoes and octoroons and métifs and sacatras are just as excited. They figure the French'll grant 'em all the rights and privileges of Frenchmen."

He shook his head dubiously. "But the blacks : that's different. Most of 'em don't do much thinking. They say white men's promises aren't reliable—that if they want to keep their freedom, they've got to keep away from French generals. They say that if they let the French come ashore, they'll lose their two chairs and their extra pair of pants."

He lowered his voice. "See that black man at the rail ? He's one of the Deputation to Leclerc. He's mayor of Cap François—a free Negro. He's scared to death Christophe'll resist. He might lose his position. His house might be burned down. He figures slavery'd be better than losing his property ! "

"Captain," I said, " while I was in the mountains back of Port-au-Prince I picked up some pretty important information about this expedition. I tried to tell Lear just now, but he wouldn't listen. It'll be a sorry day for the United States as well as for the Negroes if the French take Haiti without a fight. If this Deputation is half-hearted about resistance, I'd like mighty well to hear what's said. What's more, I think you ought to hear it too."

Rodgers eyed me intently. Seeming to make up his mind suddenly, he shouted brusquely to Colonel Lear, who came carefully towards us, as if expecting the deck to shift beneath him.

"Colonel," Rodgers said, " I've been thinking about this Deputation of yours. If you don't mind, I suggest that you also take King Dick, Mr. Hamlin, and me aboard the flagship with you."

Lear shook his head. "That's not necessary, Captain. The four of us are amply sufficient to state our case."

"No doubt about it, Colonel," Captain Rogers said ; "but to tell you the God's truth, three of the Deputation are shaking in their boots at the thought of facing Leclerc. As for you, you'll be so busy talking you won't have time to see what's going on. On the other hand, I haven't anything on my mind, and I've had plenty of experience with Frenchmen when I was captain of the *Maryland* in West Indian waters. I've learned to keep my eyes open when I'm around 'em ; and if you take me with you, it's just possible I might see something that the rest of you would overlook. As for Mr. Hamlin, he's a lawyer, trained in the weighing of men's words ; and all of us know King Dick takes a disinterested view of everything he sees. Whenever you can get disinterested views, Colonel, you're lucky. I wouldn't give two bits for the opinion of a man who has an axe to grind."

Colonel Lear spoke coldly : " I wouldn't care to take the responsibility, Captain."

" I wouldn't ask you to," Rodgers said. " *I'll* take it."

There was nothing for Lear to do but yield, but he didn't yield grace-fully. I knew he was a man who wanted to do things his own way or not at all ; but I didn't know he was one of those strange men who will persist in doing things their own way, even though they bring disaster on the rest of the world by their persistence.

CHAPTER XIX

WHEN we climbed the towering, cliff-like side of that huge black ship, I could hardly believe that I really saw what I did see upon its quarter-deck, for the spectacle belonged on a theatre stage rather than on a man-of-war.

Over the entire deck was stretched a striped silk awning, raised tent-like in the middle by a spar extending from the mizzenmast to the top of the stern lantern, all glass and gilded iron, that rose from the peak of the carved and gaily painted stern.

On the windward side of the deck was spread a broad carpet ; and on the carpet, on couches and upholstered benches, was an amazing assem-blage of ladies in silks and officers in satin, all bejewelled, bedizened, bepainted like actors in a play.

In the centre of this gathering, talking to Captain Lebrun, was a lady I knew must be Bonaparte's sister, General Leclerc's wife. She couldn't have been more than eighteen years old ; her voice was shrill ; her face as round, as regular, as vapidly pretty as that of an angel in a Raphael painting. She had only one defect—one might call it a deformity. Her ears, though not large, were two flat pieces of white cartilage, carefully covered by an elaborate dressing of her hair : but a quarter-deck can be breezy, and as we approached, the wind lifted the waved tresses on the left side of her head, so that I had a glimpse of her unfortunate defect, though with a beautiful small hand she swiftly restored the dislodged tress to its place.

Her body couldn't have been more effectively displayed if she'd been naked, and I'm bound to say it was a marked improvement on any feminine figure that Raphael ever put on canvas.

How her dress held to the upper part of her body was beyond my comprehesion. It was supported by a filmy strap over each shoulder, but it had neither sleeves nor back. Her uncovered breasts rested in two silken cups that were supported God knows how ; and below those cups the flowered white silk of her dress clung so closely to her that only a blind man could fail to see she wore nothing whatever beneath the dress except pink stockings held up by blue garters with rosebuds on them. I hope I'm not a prude, but it seemed to me there was something shockingly indecent

E

about this lady, her squeals of laughter, her voluptuous turnings and posturings, as well as about the way the officers crowded around her and ran their eyes over her, and I found the sight of her downright embarrassing.

When Captain Lebrun saw us, he left Madame Leclerc and came to us, escorting another officer so affected, so fussy, so artificial, so ineffectual-seeming, so undersized, so needlessly stern and disdainful in his manner that he seemed unreal, like an actor. In spite of the heat of that January afternoon, he wore white silk stockings, little black pumps, white satin breeches, a yellow vest, and a heavy blue coat stiff with padding. Its collar came almost to his ears, but—unlike the uniforms of all the other officers— the coat was severely plain, like those worn by Bonaparte in all his pictures.

When this little man, who hardly came up to our shoulders, thrust his fingers between the buttons of his coat and stood looking up at us imperiously, I realised that he was indeed an actor : that he was dressed to look like Bonaparte, that he thought he looked like Bonaparte, and that he was doing his best to act like Bonaparte.

His hands, with which he made great play, touching a lace handkerchief to his lips and flicking imaginary nothings from himself, were like a woman's. The top of his head came barely to King Dick's shoulder, and in all his movements there was a quick petulance.

" These are the gentlemen, General," Lebrun said. " Messieurs, this is Captain-General Leclerc, Commander-in-Chief of this expedition and brother-in-law of the First Consul." He spoke magniloquently, as if to impress us, and certainly he impressed me, though not in the way he intended. I was amazed, even, that this sallow little shrimp of a man, who couldn't have been a day over thirty, should be Bonaparte's favourite general, favoured with the hand of Bonaparte's adored sister—who was a baggage of the first water, if rumour and her own appearance could be believed. I was deeply impressed, too, by my own good fortune in not being under his military jurisdiction.

Before the Deputation had ceased bowing and scraping, Leclerc gave them a tongue-lashing as violent as it was contemptuous. His spittingly hissed words put me in mind of an angry cat.

" I tell you this, gentlemen," he cried, " you're wasting my time and your own, coming here to implore me for favours ! Am I the one to grant favours ? Bah ! I send my representative, Captain Lebrun, to General Christophe, asking him to prepare a suitable reception for me, for my wife, for the personal representatives of Bonaparte himself ! And what happens ? General Christophe insults my representative. He demands his credentials ! He insults France, he insults Captain Lebrun, he insults me by sending me a message that he can do nothing I ask until he has communicated with Toussaint L'Ouverture.

" Do you think I'm a child, gentlemen ? Don't you suppose I know, just as you know, that Christophe could get a message to Toussaint in six hours' time, even if Toussaint were hiding in the darkest corner of Haiti ? It is my opinion that Toussaint was lurking at Christophe's elbow at the very moment when Christophe framed his insulting message ! How dare you come here asking favours when the one to whom you should go is Christophe ? "

" Sir," Lear said, " may I say a word ? "

Leclerc looked at him coldly. " What word can alter the fact that this black general has insulted France ! Whom do you represent, sir ? "

" I am Tobias Lear, sir ; Consul General and Commercial Agent of the United States of America."

Leclerc sniffed. " America ! Well, say your word, Monsieur."

" All these gentlemen ask," Lear said, " is forty-eight hours. Give us forty-eight hours, sir, to inform Toussaint of your arrival——"

" Forty-eight hours ! " Leclerc cried. " Forty-eight thunders ! Forty-eight hells ! We've been coasting along this island for the past two days ! In that time a thousand messengers must have informed Toussaint of this fleet ! He must know I'm here, and he must have been in communication with Christophe ! Don't you suppose I know what Toussaint and Christophe are up to ? They want forty-eight hours' delay so they can more strongly resist my landing ! "

Lear raised a protesting hand. " But, sir——"

Leclerc stamped angrily. " But nothing, M. le Consul Général ! All that can be said has been said in the message I sent to Christophe by Captain Lebrun—a message written by Bonaparte himself."

From an inner pocket of his plain blue coat he drew a paper which he slapped with his fingers and shook in the faces of the Deputation.

" Here ! " he shouted. " Here is the answer to every question that Toussaint or Christophe could raise. Listen to it, Messieurs ! Listen to Bonaparte's own words ! "

With shaking hands he held the paper close to his eyes and read :

" Whatever your origin and your colour, you are all Frenchmen ; you are all free and all equal before God and before man.

" France, like San Domingo, has been a prey to factions and has been torn by civil war and by foreign war. But all is changed ; all nations have sworn peace and friendship toward them ; all Frenchmen likewise have embraced each other, and have sworn to be friends and brothers. Embrace the French, and rejoice at again beholding your brethren and your friends from Europe. The government sends to you the Captain General Leclerc ; he brings with him large forces to protect you against your enemies and against the enemies of the Republic. If you are told, ' Those forces are destined to rob you of liberty,' reply, ' The Republic will not allow that liberty shall be taken from us.' . . . Rally round the Captain General ; he brings you abundance and peace ; rally round him. Whoever shall dare to separate himself from the Captain General will be an enemy to his country, and the wrath of the Republic will devour him as the fire devours your dried sugar canes."

Leclerc looked up at us. " Signed ' BONAPARTE,' Messieurs ! "

He folded the paper and thrust it inside his coat. " That is all, gentle-men. Return to Cap François. Return to Christophe and say to him that no other terms are possible. To-morrow I land ! "

" But, sir," Lear said, " General Christophe says that if you insist on landing before he has had an opportunity to consult Toussaint, he'll burn the town. At best, Cap François leaves much to be desired ; but if the town is burned, thousands will be homeless ! Millions of dollars' worth of property will be destroyed ! There'll be looting—and if the blacks come in from the hills, there'll be worse. I beg of you, sir, for the sake of your wife——"

Leclerc wagged a forefinger at Lear. " Look around you, M. le Consul Général ! Count these frigates : count these troop-ships : count these sloops of war, these merchant vessels loaded with supplies ! Upon their decks you see veterans of the campaigns that have made Bonaparte feared in Europe ! You see generals who have defeated great armies sent against him. You see his own sister : his own brother Jérome : the two sons of Toussaint returning from their school in France ! Never has one of Bonaparte's campaigns been more carefully planned ! Everything has been foreseen ; everything is here, ready to be used, down to the last spool of thread, the last nail, the last bandage ! We have prepared for every contingency that might arise ! How do you dare urge me, M. le Consul Général, to allow all these plans, all these eighty-three vessels, all these guns, ammunition, men, supplies, to be jeopardised by the whim of one black man ? Bah ! Such urgings are idiotic ! Go urge Christophe not to be an idiot !

" That is all I have to say, gentlemen—except for this one thing : I'll wait half an hour after you have set foot on land. If, within that time, Christophe sends me a satisfactory message, I will take it under considera-tion. If not, my final plans are made, my final orders will be instantly issued, and thereafter nothing can change them."

He turned from us, but Lear didn't give up—and I'll say this for Lear : in spite of the many things I eventually held against him, he was always persistent.

" Sir," Lear told Leclerc, " unless we have that statement in writing, Christophe might easily question our authority. And—if I could have the favour of a few words alone with you, sir—a matter of grave importance to France and America . . ."

Leclerc looked exasperated, but motioned Lear to follow him into the great cabin.

As we stood at the head of the sea-ladder, waiting for Lear to come back, we could hear Captain Lebrun describing to Madame Leclerc the beauties of Cap François and of Christophe's palace—the magnificence of the rooms, the gold plate on the table, the rich uniforms of the black servants, the exotic fruits growing outside the windows, the beautiful women, the glittering shops, the huge opera house. His words were punctuated by Madame Leclerc's affected screams, her poutings and gesturings, her fan-flourishings, the flaunting of her charms as she turned from one to another of her admirers.

Whatever the Deputation might think about Christophe's threat to burn the city if Leclerc dared to land without permission, it was clearly evident that Lebrun didn't expect it to be burned. As for Madame Leclerc, she already saw herself installed in Christophe's palace as Queen of Haiti—another glittering star in that constellation of Bonapartes appointed by Napoleon to rule his conquests.

Already, with shrill bursts of girlish laughter, she was promising apartments in the palace to such officers as were quickest to sense her wishes and obey them. Rooms must be thrown together, so that every night there could be a ball ! Her own furniture was to replace that of General Christophe—in particular her huge bed ; never, she squealed, would she sleep in a bed in which a black man had slept.

She wriggled her hips and rolled her eyes, and all the officers about her ogled and smirked until Rodgers laughed in my ear and said she reminded him of the coquetries and struttings of a poultry yard.

At least he had been able to get one concession from Leclerc, Lear told us, when we had boarded the *Nelly* and set off into the harbour towards the city. Leclerc had promised he'd do everything possible to insure the safety of Americans in case there was trouble when the French troops landed. He'd regard all the American ships in the harbour as American soil, and agreed that all Americans in Cap François would be allowed to take refuge on those ships.

" What about those who aren't Americans ? " Rodgers asked. " What about the French ? "

" I thought of that," Lear said ; " but when I asked Leclerc whether we could take the French aboard our ships, he said No. I think he figures that Christophe won't dare burn the town if the French are made to stay in it."

" I don't doubt it," Rodgers said. " Well, you're a good friend of mine, Colonel Lear, but you might as well understand now as later that if there's trouble ashore and I find a lot of helpless French caught between Leclerc's army and Christophe's blacks, I'll put them on the nearest American vessel I can find."

" That wouldn't be wise, Captain," Lear protested. " I trust you'll do nothing to make either Leclerc or Christophe angry at the United States Government or its representatives. I've recently had an example of unguarded speech that might, if overheard, make every American *persona non grata* in Haiti." He eyed me meaningly.

" Unless I'm greatly mistaken, Colonel Lear," I said, " Leclerc is already contemptuous of the United States Government and its repre-sentatives. In view of what the French plan to do, don't you think that any attempt to conciliate them would be a mistake ? "

" I think," Lear said, " that I prefer not to be seen in conversation with you."

" Oh, come, come ! " Rodgers said. " It can't be as bad as all that ! What is this information that Colonel Lear finds so distressing ? "

" That the French have bought Louisiana from Spain——"

" Poppycock ! " Rodgers interrupted. " But I wouldn't let it disturb me if I were you, Colonel."

" It's not poppycock," I put in. " The purchase was made a year ago, and kept secret while Bonaparte perfected his plans."

" Don't you suppose the State Department would have told me if there were any truth in this fairy tale ? " Lear asked.

" Not if the State Department hadn't learned of it—and it hasn't."

Lear threw up his hands and turned away, but Rodgers caught his sleeve. " Let's hear the rest of this, Colonel. What Hamlin tells us might just possibly be true. There's no limit to Bonaparte's ambition—and he's sent a pretty big army and some pretty important generals to Haiti if his only purpose is to take back half of one small island. His brother Jérome is in the fleet, as well as Pauline. I think you'd better listen to Mr. Hamlin."

Lear said something that sounded like " Faugh ! "

" I'll tell you why he sent this big army and his best generals, as well as his sister and his brother," I said. " He expects to land in Haiti without opposition. Then he plans to pour in reinforcements until he's got as many men as he needs. Then he plans to send that army to New Orleans —a few days' sail with the proper wind—and conquer the United States."

" That's a madman's dream ! " Lear exclaimed.

" I don't know about that," Rodgers said slowly. " What have we got in America to halt such an army ? We've got no army of our own. We've got no navy worthy of the name. Our generals are nincompoops—or worse ; you've heard of Wilkinson, haven't you ? If you want to know what I think, Colonel, I think you'd better send this information to Washington with all possible speed."

Lear snorted. " And be withdrawn within a month ! " This time he stalked away from us, as disgusted a man as ever I saw.

Rodgers eyed me covertly. " You're sure of your information ? "

" Sure enough to do anything I can to persuade you or anybody else to my way of thinking."

" Well," Rodgers said, " the world's full of people like that. You can tell 'em a million times what'll happen to 'em if they're unprepared, but they'll never believe you till it's too late."

We were a silent and gloomy group as we rowed ashore and climbed again to the white-flagged Plaza of Cap François.

It was just as I had left it ten days before—the same stinks, the same gusts of perfume, the same throngs of blacks and mulattoes, the same innumerable light ladies of colour driving around and around in their own carriages, the same glittering shops, the same cafés smelling of coffee, the same tattered sugar-cane sellers smelling of everything. Where would they be to-morrow, I wondered, as we set off for Christophe's palace as fast as we could go.

I was like everyone else on the eve of war : I couldn't have imagined the thousandth part of it ; and if I could have, I wouldn't have trusted my imagination. I truly believe that the most ignorant of all people are those who dare to express opinions on war when they've never had a hand in the fighting.

CHAPTER XX

I'M SURE no black man had ever before built a palace so sumptuous and at the same time so tawdry as that of General Henri Christophe, Governor of the City and Province of Cap François. It stood on a hill above the town, a dazzling white building with roof-high columns all along its length ; and as Rodgers, King Dick, and I followed Lear and the Deputation up the white paved road, Rodgers told me about the strange man who built it.

There seemed to be nothing about Haiti that Rodgers didn't know ; and this, I found, was due to his own observations during the two years he'd been a naval officer in the West Indies, as well as to the frequent visits he made to the sea captain under whom he'd first sailed—a Captain Folger, who, for his services in carrying dispatches between France and America during the Revolution, had been rewarded with the post of Consul in the little Haitian town of Aux Cayes.

" This Christophe," Rodgers said, " came from the English island of Saint Kitts. That's how he got his name, and how he happens to speak English as well as French. ' Saint Kitts ' is Saint Christopher, so Christophe helped himself to the saint's name. He's been helping himself to things ever since.

" When he was twelve years old he ran away from Saint Kitts on a French brig, and the French sea captain sold him to a naval officer in Estaing's fleet to be button-polisher, bootblack, waiter, handy-boy. Estaing recruited five thousand San Domingan Negroes to go to Savannah to help Washington's army whip the British. They never even went ashore in Savannah, Estaing being what he was ; but Christophe must have heard considerable talk about freedom, liberty, and equality while lying in Savannah harbour, because he certainly believes in all of 'em, especially for himself."

" Who doesn't ? " King Dick asked. " Only Toussaint believes in 'em for everybody."

Rodgers seemed about to protest, but thought better of it and went on with his story. " When Estaing's fleet came back to Cap François, the French naval officer sold Christophe to the proprietor of the Crown

Hotel, a stone's-throw from here. He was a stable-boy for a while ; then
he got to be billiard marker and waiter. What he saw around stables
and 'hotels seemed to sour him on Blancs. He saved up enough money to
buy his freedom, and when Toussaint organised an army to fight the
people who wanted to work black men sixteen hours a day, and starve
'em and cut 'em to ribbons into the bargain, Christophe joined him."

When I commented that Christophe sounded unpleasant, Rodgers
gave me an odd look. "Unpleasant? There never was a good soldier
that wasn't unpleasant. White ones are bad enough, but black ones have
more occasion to be unpleasant. Christophe'll fight on anybody's side to
get what he wants, which is freedom from white men ; and when he
starts to fight he stops at nothing. He never waits to be attacked, either :
he always attacks ! If he sets out to kill, somebody always gets killed and
stays killed. He's never sentimental about an enemy, either before or
after fighting him. Soldiers shouldn't be soft-hearted, and Christophe's
heart is as soft as the knob on an anchor. Give him time, and he'll cut
the throat of every man who kicked him or whipped him when he was a
slave. That's the sort of general an army needs to win a fight nowadays—
especially with Bonaparte ! "

The palace lay at the end of an avenue flanked with alternate palms
and pepper trees ; and as we neared it, I found it hard to believe that a
Negro who had been slave, bootblack, stable-boy, and tavern waiter
could have created this imposing building, placed so artfully against a
background of purple mountain. From its portico Cap François was
spread beneath us like a rug all blue and green and white ; and the
French battleships, on the outer edge of the harbour, looked like insects
upon its cerulean rim.

The palace door was guarded by two Negro sentries, magnificent in
red and purple uniforms embellished with gold chains, tassels, and braid.
When they presented arms, they slapped musket-butts with white-gloved
hands, and stamped with their right heels, extremely military. Hanging
at their hips were torches made of bunches of tow bound to the ends of
faggots.

At the sound of musket-slapping, a black officer popped out from a
small doorway beside the palace entrance. In place of a sword he wore a
machete and at his hip hung a torch twice as big as those on the sentries.
He gave Rodgers a queer half-salute, half-obeisance, making play with his
right hand, sweeping it up to his forehead and bringing it down against
his thigh with a resounding slap.

Another attendant, gaudy with jingling chains and brass buttons, led
us along a corridor walled with red and gold brocade, and rapped upon a
door. It opened an inch, and we were inspected by an eyeball that seemed
to have streaks of chicken-fat across its white. To that jaundiced eye our
guide spoke importantly, addressing it as Lord High Admiral—which
seemed strange, since Haiti had no navy.

The Lord High Admiral admitted us to a room in which eight or ten generals, one a mulatto and all the others black, were seated at a long table in the middle of the room. There was something unreal about them, perhaps because their uniforms were every imaginable colour—pink, violet, pale green—and covered with gold braid, gold frogs, gold aiguillettes, gold danglers, gold chains, and jewelled decorations. Two of the most gorgeous were mere boys. All but one, King Dick whispered, were good soldiers and rich ; all, he murmured, lived in houses that cost millions.

I didn't need to be told which one was Christophe, for he was dressed in a spotless white uniform, with a scarlet sash around his middle, and he towered above all the other Negroes in the room. He was black, but his features were as regular as a white man's, with a straight nose and thin lips. In fact, he suggested a black John Adams, except for being two feet taller : he had the same thick hips, buttocks, and stomach, and the same upper body tapering to narrow shoulders. In spite of his great height he contrived not only to look like John Adams, but to resemble an animated overdressed pear on legs.

Close behind him sat two secretaries, eager, pleasant-looking young black men in uniforms as glittering and gaudy as the generals'. Each had a portable desk open on his knees and held a pen poised above a writing-tablet.

Christophe singled out the black mayor of Cap François and spoke to him fretfully. " Of course you have been unsuccessful, Télémaque ! I told you you'd be unsuccessful ! Well, what did you learn and what did he say ? And before you tell me, you might explain how it happens that your Deputation has grown so much larger."

Christophe's voice had a peculiar flat tone—a cold absence of expression that sounded downright malevolent.

" I'm responsible, General," Rodgers said quickly. " I knew that Mr. Lear and the mayor and the rest of your Deputation would be busy listening to General Leclerc ; so when I found General King Dick and Mr. Hamlin just arrived from Port-au-Prince and tied up to the flagship on a captured schooner, I persuaded Mr. Lear to let the three of us come along to see what we could see. I can explain everything to your satisfaction, sir, but it's important that you read the note General Leclerc sent to you by Mr. Lear."

" And why is it important ? " Christophe asked.

" Because if he doesn't receive a satisfactory answer within half an hour after the time we landed, he'll order troops ashore tomorrow."

" But I've made my answer," Christophe said. " How could I make any other ? " He held out his hand. " Let me have the letter, Mr. Lear."

Lear gave it to him, and Christophe examined it, front and back ; then handed it to one of his secretaries, who read it aloud.

" I learn with indignation, Citizen General, that you refuse to receive the squadron of the French army which I command, under the

pretext that you have no order from the Governor General. France
has made peace with England, and its government sends to San
Domingo forces able to subdue rebels, if rebels are to be found in
San Domingo. As to you, Citizen General, I avow it would give me
pain to count you among rebels. I warn you that if this very day you
do not put into my possession the Forts of Piccolet and Belair, and all
the batteries of the coast, to-morrow at dawn 15,000 will be disembarked. I hold you responsible for whatever may happen.

"LECLERC."

When the reading was done, a squatty little general in a dark pink
uniform threw back his head and burst into a hyena-like laugh, which
seemed only natural, since his wizened face and a shock of white wool
made him look like something out of a jungle.

"That La Plume," King Dick whispered. "Old incompetent!"

Christophe's clenched fist thundered upon the table. "One at a
time!" He pointed a finger at Lear. "M. le Consul Général, if you
have something to say, say it!"

"With all due respect, General," Lear said, "I beg you not to be
angry at the general's letter. I believe that if you make him a friendly
answer, he will be more reasonable in his demands. Meaning no offence,
General, I think your cavalier refusal to let him land has hurt his pride.
After all, he respresents Bonaparte and France, and you and Toussaint
L'Ouverture are admittedly the agents of France in Haiti. Naturally he
is distressed by your lack of co-operation."

The generals and the Deputation nodded their heads in assent.

"What's more," Lear went on, "General Leclerc thinks that if you
want to communicate with Toussaint, you can do so almost immediately.
In fact, General Leclerc is convinced that Toussaint is here in Cap
François at this moment. He thinks you're pretending he's elsewhere so
that you can gain time to defend yourself."

Christophe's voice was icy. "How can I make a friendly reply to this
French general? Is he friendly? He is not! Neither are his intentions.
He wishes us nothing but harm; he'll do us nothing but harm. If I'm
friendly, he'll take advantage of me—he'll take advantage of all of us!
I have my orders from Toussaint. Those orders are to refuse entry to the
French fleet at all ports. Toussaint is certainly within his rights in
issuing this order. Years ago the French civil commissioners of this island
made a law forbidding any armed force to land in this colony without
authorisation. That law has never been repealed."

"But sir," Lear protested, "that law was intended to apply to English
or Spanish armed forces."

"It doesn't say so!" Christophe told him. "It says *any armed force*.
What's more, Toussaint is Governor General of this colony: why didn't
the French Government do him the courtesy of notifying him that an
army was being sent here? Toussaint believes it's because Leclerc's

army isn't on a peaceful mission. If he's wrong—if Leclerc's mission *is* peaceful—then Leclerc should have informed Toussaint. If it isn't peaceful, he'll attempt to land without notifying Toussaint, and will thus be the first to commit an act of violence. Kindly inform me, Mr. Lear, in what way Toussaint's reasoning is at fault."

" There's nothing wrong with his reasoning," Lear said ; " but I think you're unduly stubborn when you persistently refuse to accept Leclerc's assurances that this is a peaceful expedition : that the free population of this island will continue to be free."

There were murmurings and noddings of assent from Christophe's generals. Christophe eyed them coldly, then turned to Rodgers. " You and your friends are silent, Captain. Am I to understand that you agree with Mr. Lear that the French are here on a peaceful mission, as Leclerc insists : that if Leclerc and his troops come ashore, the free population of this island will continue to be free ? "

Rodgers snorted. " You're to understand nothing of the sort ! Leclerc's assurances were put into his mouth by Bonaparte. Bonaparte is making himself master of Europe ; and if he can, he'll make himself master of the world. His promises are as worthless as those of any man determined to climb politically or militarily. Such men always break their promises."

Christophe's generals stared glumly at Rodgers. Christophe pointed a long black forefinger at me. " And your opinion, M. l'Avocat ? "

" Well, sir," I said, " Leclerc made one admission that ought to be considered. He told us Bonaparte had never planned a campaign more carefully than this one—not even his Egyptian campaign ; that Bonaparte himself had attended to everything, foreseen everything, decided everything ; had included in his expedition the élite of the French army, veterans of all his successful campaigns. If Bonaparte was so careful about these details, he'd be equally careful to give Leclerc detailed instructions on how to act. Of course, I have no way of knowing what those instructions would be, but from all I've heard of Bonaparte, I suspect they'd be heavy-handed against those who've—well, who've dared to usurp Bonaparte's prerogatives in the past."

Christophe leaned forward. " Let me be sure I understand you, M'sieu. Please speak more plainly."

I was silent for a moment, trying to recall the exact words Lydia had used when she told me about Bonaparte's determination to punish Toussaint. Christophe tapped the table impatiently.

" Well, sir," I said, " I hope you'll understand I don't want to hurt anyone's feelings, but—well, it's known that Bonaparte has long been bitter because black men are successfully governing a colony that once was French. It's common knowledge that he hates Toussaint because he's called the Black Napoleon—common knowledge that Bonaparte regards Toussaint as a slave in revolt against France ; an outrage to the national honour of France ; a black upstart."

Christophe studied his hands, pressed so tightly against the table-top that his fingernails were blue. " Continue, M'sieu."

" If all these things are true," I went on, " if Leclerc has detailed instructions from Bonaparte, if Bonaparte is angry because Negroes have taken the world's richest colonial possession out of his hands, then Leclerc's instruction would—well, they would certainly deal with the—with the future of Negroes in Haiti." I stopped, reluctant to speak the thoughts that came to me.

Christophe gave me a thin-lipped smile. " Suppose you let us hear what you imagine those instructions would be."

" I think, sir, you're the one to do that. You're a military man—I have no wish to presume——"

Christophe broke in on me. " I must insist on hearing how Bonaparte would treat us, according to your views. You have thought about these matters to better effect than have some of us."

I looked desperately at Rodgers, at King Dick, hoping for encouragement. They were staring at the floor, at the ceiling, as if embarrassed by my embarrassment.

" Well, sir," I said, " if I'd been Bonaparte, sending a fine army to regain control of this island, I'd have told Leclerc to promise any Negro anything—anything at all—in order to get quick and easy possession of all strategic points. I'd have told him to assure Toussaint that nobody would be disturbed in position, in rank, in property. I'd have told Leclerc not to be too hard, at first, on rebellious Negroes : told him to leave them unmolested in the hills, bribe them, disarm them when possible. Then, when Leclerc's officers and men had so established themselves that resistance would be impossible——"

Rodgers made an impatient movement and interrupted me. " You'd have told him to strike ! "

Rodger's words gave me confidence. " That's what I certainly would have told Leclerc if I'd been Bonaparte, determined to revenge myself on men I regarded as slaves in revolt against me, the Great Bonaparte : against me, the Master of Europe—the Master of the World. I'd have instructed Leclerc to speak softly and be gentle until he was safe from successful opposition ; then to arrest every Negro in San Domingo who held a position of importance : to arrest every general, every colonel, every major in Toussaint's armies : to arrest every General of Place, every black deputy, even every Hungan and Mambu with enough influence to own property—yes, and to arrest the drummers and destroy their drums. I'd have told him to put every last one of those black generals and colonels and majors and Mambus and Hungans and drummers aboard that fleet of transports out there in the harbour and send them all to France—and you can be mighty sure that if I were Bonaparte, not one would ever come back to Haiti ! "

" You don't know what you're saying ! " Lear cried. " General Christophe, I protest ! Mr. Hamlin has no standing here ! He has no right to imply that an officer and a gentleman would be guilty of such cruelties."

" Don't interrupt M. Hamlin," Christophe said sharply. " He hasn't finished."

" I'd do even more than that if I were Bonaparte," I said. " I'd instruct Leclerc that if any man in this island, black or coloured, undertook to utter one word in defence of blacks who have spilled so much French blood in the past, he should instantly be arrested on any pretext, thrown aboard a transport, and sent to France for the rest of his life."

" You haven't a shred of evidence for all this ! " Lear cried. " There's no proof that Leclerc has anything but the kindest feelings for any Negro in Haiti."

" No evidence ? " I retorted. " Just before we left the flagship, Madame Leclerc spoke freely in our hearing of her plans. She was greatly pleased by what Captain Lebrun told her about this palace, except for the room she intends to take for her own bedroom, and the lack of a ballroom. Since she means to use this palace as her own, she proposes to make several small rooms into one large ballroom ; and she plans to refurnish the bedrooms with her own personal belongings, since she finds it distasteful to think of using the personal belongings of its previous occupants. That's evidence enough for me—evidence that she and her husband intend to seize the property of persons for whom they have nothing but contempt : persons who can expect no justice."

" Mr. Hamlin," Lear said, " you're deliberately encouraging race hatred—you're cold-bloodedly instigating war ! Do you know what that means ? Do you know the history of this island ? It will mean suffering and death for hundreds—for thousands—of innocent persons ! Anything is preferable to war, sir ! Even if you're right, which I deny—even if Leclerc intends to make slaves again out of these people—it's better to maintain peace."

" I deny everything you say," I said, speaking as much to Christophe as to Lear. " You're arguing that if the Haitians themselves abstain from destruction, there won't be any destruction. The exact opposite is true. People who make war in order to escape slavery may possibly win. The Haitians will certainly win if they refuse to fight in the way the French want them to fight—if instead they fight from behind rocks and in the mountains. This will doubtless mean death and suffering for thousands, as you imply. But people who tamely allow slavery to be imposed on them without resorting to a defensive war are inevitably doomed to years of death and suffering—and far more of each than any war would bring to them."

No mere worm could have drawn from Lear the glance he gave me ; but before Lear could do more than look his hatred, Christophe held up a slender black hand and spoke over his shoulder to one of his secretaries. " These gentlemen want an answer to Leclerc. Write it. Say to General Leclerc that if he tries to enter this city without my permission, he'll do so only after it has been reduced to ashes—and I'll fight him across the ashes ! "

From every general at the table, from Lear, from the three coloured members of the Deputation, burst a babel of protest. They shouted, " No, no ! " " Not necessary ! " " You can't destroy warehouses full of sugar ! " " There'll be looting ! " " What calamity ! " " What horror ! " " I pray you, my General ! " " No, no, no ! "

The little general in the dark pink uniform bounced up and down like a jumping-jack on a stick, his mouth, his nose, even his ears, working in anguish.

Christophe's reply was violent. " I say Yes ! Can't you remember what slavery means ? I'll burn every house, raze every plantation, and destroy the last mouthful of food on this island rather than be a slave again ! "

Lear, as pale as chalk, made one final effort. " Sir, the French have artillery that outranges anything of yours. They have the best of muskets —unlimited ammunition—more and better-trained troops, veterans of Bonaparte's greatest battles. Your soldiers wouldn't have a chance against those French regiments. You'll be annihilated if you try to fight Leclerc ! "

" Annihilated ? " Christophe asked politely. " Annihilated in our own country, among mountains and swamps known to us from childhood ? No, no, M. le Consul Général ! The army doesn't exist that can annihilate men in their own land—not if they love it sufficiently."

He got up from the table and looked darkly at those around him. " That's my decision, and you could talk here for ever without changing it. You gentlemen are to go at once to your commands outside the city. If you hear three guns, the French are landing. Whatever you hear, let no white men pass out of Cap François until we know our friends from our enemies."

When Rodgers, King Dick, and I started to leave the room with that galaxy of generals in pink, blue, cerise and lavender uniforms, Christophe came out from behind his table and stopped the three of us. " One moment, gentlemen, if you will be so kind," he said. " I'd like a word with you alone."

Colonel Lear must have had the ears of a fox and the eyes of a crow, for he stopped short as if expecting Christophe to ask him to return also. Instead of that, Christophe closed the door in his face—a bit of rudeness that did nothing, I knew, to lessen Lear's dislike of me.

" You gentlemen have served me better than you realise," Christophe said, " and I wanted you to know that your help is fully appreciated." He went to a small door near the table at which he had sat among his generals, opened it and said, " Now they are gone, mon Général."

Immediately there came to the door the same wrinkled little black man I had found so unimpressive when I first saw him sitting beside

King Dick in the dining-room of the Hôtel de la République. Now, however, he was a figure so gaudy that he almost pained the eye. He wore a tight blue jacket and over it a flowing red cape that hung to the top of his high black boots. The cape was thrown back over his epaulettes, which were gold and the size of bread-boards. His coat sleeves had elbow-high red cuffs ringed with eight stripes of gold lace. His waistcoat was scarlet ; his pantaloons were white ; his hat was a little round one with a red feather sticking straight up from it. Clutched against his breast was a sword too large for him.

He was ugly in a benevolent sort of way : bandy-legged, and so stooped as to seem almost humpbacked. His voice, when he spoke, was a rasping croak. Yet the sum of these defects was more than pleasing. That hoarse voice was warmly sympathetic : the wrinkled black face solicitous and benign.

He sat himself down in the nearest chair, nursing his oversize sword between his knees, removed his little red hat and wiped the perspiration from his forehead with a white cotton glove, and beamed upon us. " That was helpful, what you said," he told us confidentially. " Some of these generals of mine, they believe anything a white man promises." He poked at the chairs near him with the scabbard of his sword. " Sit down ! Sit down, gentlemen ! "

He gave me a kindly nod. " That was good," he said, " that about slavery ; but what was more important to them was what you said about Leclerc's arresting every Negro who holds a position of importance. That woke them up ! When they heard that, I could hear their minds fluttering. Even through the door I could hear their brains chattering and saying that perhaps old Toussaint is right." He eyed me sharply. " In a short time, M. Hamlin, you have learned an extraordinary amount about Haiti and the intentions of the French."

" I had unusual sources of information," I said.

" And a fortunate thing for many of us that you did ! "

" If I've helped you, General, I'd like the credit to go where it belongs. There's a lady near Port-au-Prince—an American—whom I tried to persuade to go home, but she won't abandon her friends. I think she'll need help—more than I can give her."

" I'll make sure she gets it," Toussaint said. " Perhaps I can send you to Port-au-Prince in a ship. Just at the moment, of course, the French are allowing no ships to move out ; and if they should insist on landing, I'd be better pleased to see all the Americans in this town placed aboard ships. They'd be safer there than anywhere else." He looked suddenly at Rodgers. " What would you say, Captain, if I put you in charge of placing all Americans aboard those vessels ? "

Rodgers spoke quickly. " I'd make sure they got there, General."

Toussaint stood up, clutching his long sword against his breast, and I got up too, as did Christophe, Rodgers, and King Dick. There was something profoundly impressive about that bandy-legged little black man—something that made me instinctively respect and trust him.

"Start making your arrangements at once, Captain," he told Rodgers. "I'm afraid there's no time to waste." To me, almost severely, he said, "Don't think of trying to go back to Port-au-Prince alone. You'll never get there alive. I'm grateful, and you can depend upon it that I'll send word to you how to go, and when. I'll take King Dick with me until then, and he will bring you your instructions. Is that clear?"

When I said it was, and thanked him, he nodded abruptly, clapped his little red hat on his head, beckoned to King Dick, and popped back through the doorway from which he'd emerged, a grotesque figure, but a great man—a greater man, in my opinion, than most of those who bulk largest on the pages of history.

CHAPTER XXI

SPURRED on by Toussaint's warning that we had no time to waste, and by the thought of the flames that soon might sweep the city, Rodgers and I sat ourselves down at a table before the Hôtel de la République and hurriedly made out a list of American ships and captains.

In the bright light of the garish Plaza, surrounded by its vivid odours of rum, sugar, perfume, sweat, sewage, and the indescribable rank scent of a tropical night, the flames that I imagined were small and inoffensive ones, burning palely in a silent city . . . Perhaps it is this very failure in imagination that leads men and nations to embark on wars so blithely and so unprepared.

When we had finished, Rodgers tore the list in two and handed me one of the halves. "I'll work eastward from the hotel," he said, "and you work westward. Meet me here when you've finished. Speak to every captain you see. Tell each one he'll probably have to take aboard as many refugees as his ship will hold. If one of 'em admits he can accommodate twenty, don't accept it. Tell him he's got to take forty. If he agrees too quickly, raise it to fifty. Find out what his cargo is, and how it's stowed. Refugees can sleep on deck, or on top of barrels, or even on the ballast. If a man can't save his life any other way, he's glad enough to sleep on rocks and in mud."

Almost the first American captain I encountered was Captain George Lee, that hearty, ruddy mariner whose amiability had lightened my voyage to Haiti. His companion was a slender, rounded thing, the pale colour of molasses taffy; and she was twisted across his lap and draped around his shoulder as though she didn't have a bone in her body. Her skirts were up around her hips, and even her golden legs looked flexible as flax.

"Hallo there, Hamlin!" Lee shouted as I stopped at his table. "I wondered what had become of you. Sit down and have a tot of rum."

He gave the taffy-coloured girl a resounding slap on her bare thigh, went through the motions of biting a segment from her golden shoulder, and sat her upright on her chair. "What do you think of this little piece of yellow satin, Hamlin? Plenty more where she came from, my boy! Sit down and I'll send her to get one for you."

"I don't want to disturb you," I said. "I only want to tell you what's been decided in case the French try to force their way ashore."

"Hah, that's the hell of it!" Lee cried. "Let the damned French get ashore and they'll fill these girls so full of sores and sickness that it'll be as much as our life's worth to touch 'em! Sit down, sit down, Hamlin! This is your last chance before the French spoil everything. We'll split a bottle of rum and make a night of it."

I showed him my list of captains. "I've got to see all these men to-night," I said. "If the French try to come ashore, the town's to be set afire, and all the Americans here must be put aboard ships for safety. How many can you take in case the town's burned?"

"Burned!" Lee said. "This town?" His look of incredulity slowly changed to one of speculation, and his eyes slid from me to the golden girl beside him.

"You'll have to stick to Americans," I went on. "It'll be a tight squeeze to find places for our own people. How many Americans can you take on the *Hope*?"

"How many can I take?" Lee asked. "Why, I can't take any! We've got just enough food for our own needs! Who'd supply 'em, and who'd pay? Not the French—they never pay for a damned thing!"

"I'll put you down for ten," I said; "but you'd better give it some thought to-night and see how many you could stow away if you really had to. The signal for burning is three guns, and the meeting place for all American captains is in front of the Hôtel de la République. Get your longboat to the foot of the steps nearest the hotel as soon as you hear the three guns."

"Ten!" Lee cried. "Are you crazy, Hamlin? Here, sit down, sit down and cool yourself with a little rum! Nothing like rum and a piece of yellow satin to give you a good night's rest."

I left him talking and went on to a table where three other American captains were drinking a mixture of black rum and limewater. When I gave them Rodgers's instructions, they—like Lee—seemed to think I was mad; and even when I left, I knew they only half-credited my information.

When my work was done and I rejoined Rodgers, I found him as discouraged as I. "They won't believe they're in danger, damn 'em," he said. "What's worse, they won't listen when they're told what to do in case of trouble. Well . . ."

He looked at the figures I'd put down. " That's not bad ! " he said. " Let's see, Oxnard says he can take care of forty-two, does he ? Oxnard's an optimist. If he takes more than thirty aboard, he'll sleep on deck himself. Well, that's all right : if he says forty-two, we'll hold him to it. And Eli Bagley says he can take care of six, eh ? He'll take fifteen, that's how many he'll take ! And God help 'em ! They'll either starve on Bagley's food or choke on the stink of his bilge ! "

He added five to every other figure on my list. " That's what they'll have to do," he said. " When the trouble starts, we'll give every captain a smell of a pistol if he makes any objections. That's one of the nicest things about a war : you take whatever you want at the point of a gun, and call it military necessity."

We heard the three guns late in the afternoon.

" There'd been a hot, flat calm all day long ; even the oily surface of the harbour had seemed to smoke with heat ; the sharp purple peaks behind Cap François and the steamy sugar plantations of the Great North plain had reflected the sun's rays back at us ; and the white Plaza and the massive arcades fronting it had wavered and quivered as if seen through the vapour from boiling water.

Towards twilight a breeze sprang up to ruffle the pale harbour slicks into crinkled streaks of darker blue. It strengthened and strengthened, until every lazing vessel came smartly into the wind, heading towards the open sea. The breeze went on towards the town, dispelling the twilight heat haze that dimmed Christophe's long palace, the garish opera house, the churches, the arsenal, the stone buildings built by the French, the innumerable shops beneath the arcades.

And on the heels of that twilight breeze came the three guns.

On all the ships in the harbour, captains stood up and shouted to their look-outs. Seamen ran forward to climb into forechains and foremast ratlins. Look-outs hung over foretop nettings to cry in distant muted voices that a French corvette had got under way and was running in towards the forts.

As the breeze had blown away the heat haze, so did the thud of those three guns put an end to the drowsiness of Cap François.

Hard on the heels of the three explosions came a burst of cannonading from all the forts at the harbour's mouth. We could see the cannon-flashes dart from the dusky headlands. Then, at one end of Christophe's long white palace, appeared a splash of yellow flame, a flower of fire, bright as a star against the darkling mountains. It wavered, flickered, faded, crawled slowly upward like a far-off fiery serpent, writhed and twisted, puffing out a billowing gout of lurid smoke.

In the beginning, that night seemed a series of fiery tableaux.

Off the long quay abreast of the Hôtel de la République, the long-boats of the American ships were clustered as thick as bananas on a stalk ; and the brigs and schooner that had been tied to the piers at either end of the quay were warping out into the harbour.

Half of Christophe's palace was ablaze, a geyser of sparks whirling upwards from it. Above the city's skyline rose fiery pyramids, and the windows of the opera house glared redly from the flames within.

I had the passing thought that the crews of the merchantmen, pulling hard at their oars to warp their vessels to a safer anchorage, were more fortunate than Charon's passengers—but alas, that was because I didn't know how bad a man-made hell could be.

The Plaza was thronged with Negroes, mulattoes, and whites, all unfrightened : all pleasantly stimulated ; flame-drunk ; garrulous and animated by the mounting flames, the glowing sky, the incessant chattering and squealing.

The American captains were grouped near the entrance to the Hôtel de la République. One of its windows had been stripped of glass and sash, and at a table in the window sat a young man from the Consulate, on either side of him an American flag and ship's lantern. All around me were American captains—Fernald, Oxnard, Cammett, Lee, Minot, Thurlo, Motley, Bagley, Lowther, Codman.

Rodgers shouted orders to the man from the Consulate—orders intended as much for the captains around him as for the young man himself. The latter had to lean far forward to hear because of the yells and squeals of the throng on the Plaza, and the rushing crackle that filled the air above and around us, momentarily growing louder.

" You'll have to use discretion," Rodgers shouted. " Some of the whites that look to you for help won't be Americans. If they're deserving, and you think they can't get away unless we help 'em, we'll have to make room for 'em somehow. Understand ? "

The young man wiped the palms of his hands on his sweat-soaked shirt and nodded.

" Don't let 'em take furniture," Rodgers shouted. " Don't argue with 'em till you get 'em down to the quay. Then make 'em pile it in a heap and leave it. Understand ? If they won't leave it, take it from 'em and throw it in the harbour. Is that clear ? "

Again the young man nodded. Sweat stood in beads on his hands and ran in rivulets down his cheeks. The heat was almost unbearable.

A wild-eyed man burst from the crowd, trundling a wheelbarrow loaded high with odds and ends that repeatedly slipped off. Beside him ran his wife, dragging a five-year-old child by the hand. Whenever anything fell from the barrow, she scrambled for it ; the child stumbled and was jerked to its feet ; the mother replaced the retrieved treasure on the barrow—and instantly something else slipped to the ground. All the while the mother kept up an agonised shrill crying : " Jenny ! Willy ! Willy ! Jenny ! "

" Arsenault gets these people," Rodgers shouted. " Captain Arsenault

—you're first on the list ! Take 'em to your boat and come back here for the two missing children. Be sure you get Willy and Jenny ! "

A gust of acrid smoke swirled down upon us. When it lifted, the sky was filled with sparks like blazing snowflakes.

That fiery canopy changed everything. I got a picture of countless staring eyeballs, of glistening faces alarmingly tinged with red, of panic movements. There had been laughter when we came up on the Plaza ; but now there was only a high-pitched wailing.

A fifteen-year-old girl, her dress ripped from her shoulder, slipped out of the crowd as a water-melon seed pops from a man's fingers. She fell on hands and knees and crawled to the wall of the hotel, where she sat beneath the two American flags, plucking at her torn dress. The cloth was gone, but she pulled and strained at the ragged edge, trying to draw it over her bare shoulder.

The Plaza glared in the light of flames we couldn't see because we were so close to the hotel. It seemed to me that all the black faces in the world were congregated between us and the harbour ; and in the red glare of the fires those black faces were tinged with blue, purple, amethyst, green. By that garish light I could see the shrouds and ratlins on far-off vessels—see men in the rigging, holding to the yards like toy sailors hung on ship-models.

There were more black men in the Plaza than there had been. . . . Smoke gusts came down again and set me coughing. All the captains coughed and coughed ; their eyes ran, and their noses. Rodgers, between coughs, was questioning the kneeling girl.

A moment before, I'd been surrounded by American captains. How it happened, I couldn't have said, but in that moment a herd of panic-stricken whites rushed upon us, clutched at us, dragged at our arms and coats. Their eyes were staring, their mouths contorted, their words hardly distinguishable.

A lanky man, whom I took to be a storekeeper from some southern city like Charleston or Savannah, pulled at me and chittered like a woodchuck corned beneath a wall. I couldn't understand him, perhaps because I couldn't get my eyes off a carriage that was making slow progress across the crowded Plaza. It was such a carriage as those in which languid light ladies rode on the day I first came ashore. The five women in this one may have been light, but they weren't languid. They were octoroons, and in the glare of the flames their faces were darkly ashen.

" My wife—my daughter—I couldn't get in—black soldiers——" the lanky man stuttered. " Help ! Need help ! "

The carriage had stopped. A score of black hands reached for the horse's head and stretched up towards the women, who were on their feet, huddled together.

Other black hands grasped the driver. He half-rose to his feet, then toppled from the carriage and vanished. One of the women snatched the whip and lashed the horse, which reared on its hind legs and fell on its side. Above the roar of the flames and the tumult of the crowd I heard the women screaming. Black hands pulled at them. One woman's dress came clean off, leaving her naked. Then all five seemed to lose their balance and they plunged downward into the crowd as into dark water, and there was no further sign of them save an eddying in the crowd, little whirlpools in that mass of black humanity.

Rodgers, beside me, had a pair of splitting-wedges—axe-like affairs, fine for splitting logs or breaking down a door. God knows how he'd got them. He pushed one of the wedges into my hands.

The lanky man shoved between us, panting out his story about the black men who had barred him from his home—from his daughter and his wife.

" All right, all right," Rodgers told him. " Show us where you live ! We'll get 'em ! We'll get 'em all ! "

When we moved out from the shelter of the shops and government buildings that walled the Plaza, the heat struck against us like a blast from a thousand smithies. The flames were everywhere, as thick as candles on a devil's birthday cake. In places the fires had flowed together ; elsewhere they were single conflagrations ; but all were horrible in their violence.

In the beginning the wind had been master, the fires moving as it directed, away from the water-front and towards the mountains. But in this short time the flames had taken possession of the wind, scorching and twisting it into hot hurricanes that filled the dark skies with unearthly yowlings.

We turned into the first side street leading off the Plaza, the heat pouring against us as from a funnel. Houses were blazing on one side of the street, and as we walked, the flames leaped across to the other side as though belched from cannons.

The lanky man's house was faced with dirty pink stucco, like most of the Cap François houses ; and the man, pointing it out to us, shook and was speechless. I took his lantern from him and entered. In the hallway the smell of charred wood was strong, but nothing was afire except a smouldering heap of bed-linen.

" They'd be in the cellar," Rodgers called to me. " Go down and see what you find. I'll stay up here—this man's worse than useless ! "

After some fumbling I found the cellar stairs. Not a sound could I hear when I opened the door and listened. When I shouted, nobody answered.

I lowered the lantern by its lanyard, then stooped quickly and looked into the dimly lit, musty-smelling cavern. At the foot of the stairs lay an elderly woman. She looked like a sack of old clothes, and her head was bent under her shoulder, as if a melon had been pushed there. I went down and rolled her over : she was a mulatto woman, and her neck was broken. I raised the lantern and looked around. On a pile of boxes in a far corner was the body of a girl. She was naked, and her clothes lay on the floor, every which way. There was blood on her, and her throat looked as though a dog had worried it.

" That must be his daughter," I thought. I found myself saying the same words over and over. " That must be his daughter ! That must be his daughter ! "

When I held the lantern close to her, I saw she was what King Dick called a griffe—almost white, but not quite. I didn't need to put my hand on her to know she was dead. But she certainly wasn't the lanky man's daughter—she was too old for that ; and she was too young to be his wife, even if he'd married a woman of colour, which wasn't likely.

Rodgers called from upstairs, " Anything wrong ? Want any help ? " I said I didn't know.

" Hurry up ! " he shouted.

I wondered where two women could conceal themselves. As cellars went, this one was free from clutter : there were no heaps of sacking, no accumulation of barrels, no bags of provisions. There wasn't a place where anyone could hide—except beneath the pile of boxes on which lay the body of this murdered girl.

" If there's no place but the boxes," I told myself, " then they're under the boxes."

I took the dead girl by the ankles and pulled her on to the floor.

Hiding beneath the boxes were a grey-haired woman and a girl with long black pig-tails. The woman was unconscious, but before she'd fainted she had crammed cloth into the girl's mouth so that she couldn't speak or scream, wound a skirt around her eyes and ears, and wrapped her arms so tightly about the girl's head that it was God's wonder she hadn't suffocated.

For the first time in my life, as I tore the gag from the girl's mouth and slapped her mother back to consciousness, I knew the meaning of the word " frantic." I was in an unreasoning frenzy at the whole world— at that fool Autremont, who had told me there was no need for hurry : at those two worthless brats of children who had held Lydia in Beau- Bouclier ; at myself for not knocking Lydia on the head and taking her away willy-nilly ; at Bonaparte, for bringing all this hell on helpless people ; at Leclerc ; at Christophe ; at the flames and the heat and the black beasts who had mauled and murdered in this stinking cellar ; at the women and the girl whose miserable needs were keeping me from Lydia. I half-dragged, half-kicked the two women to the cellar stairs and up. I'd got to get to Lydia !

CHAPTER XXII

THAT lurid night of flames, sweat, and blood was a never-ending nightmare in which we laboured furiously at tasks beyond our powers. Smoke filled our lungs ; sparks stung our flesh and burned our clothes ; jets of flame roared· at us from overhead, searing, singeing, baking, until we smarted from the perspiration that turned to salt upon us.

There were times when I was sure my lungs were ablaze and I'd never breathe again ; times when I wondered whether the things I did, unwilling and unthinking, were done only because the blistering heat had set my blood a-boil and my brain a-simmer.

The burning sugar sent up an all-enveloping sticky soot that transformed us into black men, except as the smoke brought tears streaming from our eyes to cut white furrows down our cheeks.

That burning sugar was a devil's broth. It burned with a sickening sweet acridness ; and part of it, in the burning, turned to boiling syrup that ran in sluggish rivers from the glowing ruins of the sugar-houses. Every street became the bed of a black and sticky stream. Pools of molten sugar, cooling, lay all about, sugar traps that blistered and fouled the feet of those who walked on them and broke through the crust—and no tongue can tell the dirty discomfort of shoes caked with sugar syrup.

There was no way of escaping that dreadful stickiness. It was in our hair, our ears ; it covered our hands, our faces. It crawled up our sleeves and down our necks ; through every opening in our clothes. Whatever we touched, we stuck to. Whenever we brought a handful of panic-stricken people to the quay-side, we tried to clean ourselves by climbing down into the harbour water, which stunk of burnt sugar and was hot. But wash ourselves as we would, that horrid stickiness was everywhere upon us as soon as we exposed ourselves again to the scorching heat and were dry once more.

That same cloying stickiness, I think, must have crept into the brains of the white families left in Cap François. Certainly panic couldn't have held so many of them motionless in their homes when houses burned all around them and black men hunted everyone lighter than themselves as hounds hunt foxes.

Yet every time we returned to the meeting place before the hotel, hoping to be told that everybody was safe, there were always some who hadn't been found ; always more families to be searched for. Even when we were assured that all had been rounded up, Rodgers kept going back again and again into the blazing streets, hunting for anyone who needed help. I never saw a man so tireless or so fearless.

By midnight the hotel was ablaze, and the young man from the Consulate had been driven down from his window. Each time we saw him thereafter he was farther and farther out in the square, doing his best to stay near his post, but driven off by the heat. Somebody had brought him six sugar hogsheads ; boards were laid across four of them ; and on the platform thus made, the two other hogsheads held an overturned sugar-copper. Sheltered from sparks beneath this huge kettle, he worked on and on. He was as sticky as we, because each time he raised his hand, papers clung to it and had to be picked off ; each time he put down his pencil, he had to shake it from his fingers ; when he got up to ease his tired legs, his chair stuck to the seat of his trousers and rose with him.

Rodgers and I thanked God for one thing : as more and more of the city caught fire, and as the blacks more and more openly showed their hatred of whites and mulattoes, panic became more widespread, and the roads to the hills were crowded with refugees, many of them white but most of them people of colour : griffes and mulattoes, quadroons and octoroons, sacatras and marabous, métifs and mameloucs.

Thus, after midnight, the throng on the Plaza had dwindled and we no longer had to force our way through throngs half-crazed by the loss of their homes, by the roaring flames, by apprehension of what might happen to them if they fell victim to one of the roaming bands of black men that prowled everywhere on the lookout for loot and revenge. Yet those throngs of blacks grew steadily larger and more threatening ; and oftener and oftener we found ourselves in trouble.

Twice, indeed, I thought we were gone—once when we tried to save a South Carolina warehouse owner who didn't want to be saved, and later, at dawn, when we got wind of a family of Americans who had been cut off from reaching the water-front by a throng of blacks, and had started for the hills.

When we found the South Carolinian's house, the top part of it was already afire, and the doors and shutters were locked.

Rodgers put his ear against the door and looked around at me. Nobody could have heard anything through that door, what with the roaring of the wind and the crackling and hissing of the flames ; yet we both sensed suddenly that there was somebody inside.

" Swing first," Rodgers told me.

I drove the blade of my splitting axe into the wood above the lock, and—when Rodgers had driven his own wedge into the crack I'd made, and I'd pried out my wedge and swung it again at the widening opening— the whole door buckled and we hammered it apart.

Inside we found a wild-eyed man leaning against a closed inner door and threatening us with a pistol.

" Put that pistol down ! " Rodgers shouted. " We're your friends."

" You keep away from me," the man said, and I saw he was wholly demented. " I can't afford to take risks ! I've got 'em in here in this room, and here they'll stay, where I can be sure of 'em ! "

" You damned fool," Rodgers told him, " open that door ! Don't you want to save 'em ? "

" Oh, yes," the man said. " Naturally. But it's my wife and her sister, and my two sons, one five and one twelve. You can see what would happen. If we went outside and the blacks started for one of us, we'd get separated. Here we're together and safe."

Unseen hands pounded the door behind him. He put his free hand against the door and called to his family, " It's no use. You just don't understand. I'd rather shoot you myself than have you go out among those blacks." Then he turned and wagged his pistol in our faces. " And I'll shoot you, too, if you try to make me let 'em out."

" Your roof's afire," Rodgers told him. " If you stay here five minutes longer you'll be burned to death. You don't want your wife and children burned, do you ? "

" It's a bright death," the man said. " Better than a black death ! Better than parting with everything you own ! Better than falling into the hands of those blacks ! Stand back ! "

" Now listen," Rodgers said. He walked to the man, slapped down the hand holding the pistol, caught him suddenly in his arms, and threw him face-down on the floor.

We tied his hands behind his back and hobbled his legs so he couldn't take long steps. As we dragged him out of the house he was cursing and shouting meaningless words and phrases. Then we hustled the others out into the street.

From the wife's sister we learned that her brother-in-law had packed all his valuables into a pillow-case, hours earlier, and they had started towards the quay. In the very moment of their setting out, a group of Negroes had run past, loaded with loot, and one had snatched at the pillow-case. The brother-in-law had contrived to hold on to his belongings and to push his family back into the house. The Negro had rushed in after them, struck the brother-in-law on the head with a club, wrenched the pillow-case from him, and run off with it. The brother-in-law had thereupon barricaded himself inside the house and sworn to kill the first who tried to escape.

By this time we were making our way along the flame-lit street. The man made no effort to resist when we pushed him towards the waterfront ; but the hobbles on his legs forced us to go slowly. When we reached the Plaza and started across it, the blacks pushed up around us so threateningly and in such large numbers that Rodgers told me to cut the rope on the man's legs.

I was still on my knees, and Rodgers was ordering the women to get on as fast as they could, when the South Carolinian, freed of his bonds, leaped over my head like a deer and vanished in the direction from which we'd come.

I got to my feet and ran after him as hard as I could, and so did Rodgers. When we turned again into the street on which he lived, we caught a glimpse of him, far ahead—a capering demon outlined against the crimson smoke of burning sugar.

When we reached his house, the whole upper floor was blazing, and as we pushed open the door a part of the ceiling gave way, pouring a cataract of blazing embers into the dining-room. Against the light from that burning room the South Carolinian was struggling with three Negro looters who'd contrived to scrape together bundles of clothes and food and house furnishings. When he saw us come through the doorway he turned and ran into the flaming dining-room.

Rodgers pushed the black men out of his way and ran for the dining-room. One of them had a two-foot cane-knife in his hand. He swung it at Rodgers' knees, but my splitting-wedge hit the small of his back and he seemed to break in two. Then Rodgers' splitting-wedge came down on a second black head and sank into it as into a melon. As the third Negro ran for the outer door, our two wedges hit him at the same time, and that was the end of him.

When we turned back into the blazing room, the South Carolinian had stopped screaming. You could tell he was a man, but his clothes were mostly burned off and his flesh was swelling, like a broiling beefsteak.

There came a time, after endless hours of sweat and labour, when the high black peaks above the glowing coals of Christophe's palace were outlined against a rosy glow. I looked dully at that rosy glow, unable to conceive of it as anything but another burning city, somewhere beyond the mountains. So drugged was I by heat and weariness that I couldn't imagine an ending to that dreadful night.

" Daybreak ! " Rodgers said. " Now we can get back to the ship."

The rosy glow, as Rodgers spoke, turned warmly yellow ; and with a sort of shock I realised that Rodgers was right. Here it was, a new day, and I'd got to find Toussaint and get his permission to sail to Port-au-Prince. I'd got to reach Lydia ! In the growing light I stared desperately around me, wondering what had become of Toussaint, of Christophe, of King Dick.

The Plaza was by now almost empty. Here and there we saw the wrecks of carriages, wheels broken and spokes missing—probably taken by blacks who lacked weapons. Dead men lay in gutters and corners, like heaps of cast-off clothing.

At the far edge of the vast flame-lit square, near the quay steps, a knot of dark figures still struggled, and on the ground near them were other dark figures, motionless. I saw fists and clubs rising and falling, and heard the inhuman yapping that men make when they're at each other's throats.

I looked for the Consul on his sugar hogsheads. The hogsheads were scattered and broken ; the sugar-copper that had sheltered him from sparks was on its side.

" I can't go back to the ship," I told Rodgers. " You go back. I'll stay here."

Rodgers caught me by the arm. " Oh no ! You'll come with me ! Look yonder : there's one more fight you've got to help me stop."

I forced my tired legs to run towards the dark figures ; heard Rodgers shout at them ; saw him swing his splitting-wedge—and that was almost the last thing I did see.

There came a blinding yellow flash like a score of bursting suns— a flash that lit up the figure of Rodgers flying headlong towards the harbour as if dragged by his splitting-wedge ; the outermost ships in the harbour ; struggling Negroes, who, incredibly, were sprawled in the air, like ungainly wingless birds. I myself seemed to be rising endlessly in a hot turbulence that pounded at my eyes and ears, that seemed to be ripping the flesh from my bones.

I came back to consciousness with my brain floating on a sea of irritating words that stabbed and stabbed at my aching head like rusty nails. The words meant nothing, but the manner in which they were spoken struck me as offensive and painful. There were two speakers, and I could have killed both with pleasure if that would have let me go back to sleep again. My eyelids were like lead ; and when I finally got my eyes open I thought they'd burst from the pain of the light.

It was broad day, and I was lying across the knees of King Dick, who sat on the edge of the quay, shouting down to someone beneath him. His voice, which I had thought once pleasing, rasped in my ears like a saw biting through a knot. My brain cleared a little, and those painful rasping sounds began to make sense. King Dick was telling someone to go on out to his ship : that I couldn't go too because I had to be kept ashore.

I wondered to whom he was speaking. When I sat up to see, my head throbbed, my eyes blurred. When they cleared I saw Rodgers lying in the stern of his boat, a few yards off-shore. He looked like a half-dead convict, his hair singed to a stubble ; his face, streaked with grime, was a travesty of the one I remembered ; his trousers were dripping wet and dotted with cinder-holes through which his skin showed ; his once-white shirt, plastered to his torso, was a singular blend of black and crimson from soot and blood.

Scattered around us were a dozen bodies. I couldn't tell whether some moved feebly, or whether my own blurred eyes made them seem to move. Beyond the Plaza a cloud of smoke rolled upward from a nightmare of desolation and emptiness. Where, only yesterday, had stood Christophe's palace, the opera house, the admiralty, all the shops and warehouses and barracks, all the smudgy pink, pale blue, and dirty yellow houses, there now was nothing but crumbling walls and smoking embers. The few unburned buildings resembled fangs in an old man's mouth.

" What happened ? " I asked King Dick. " Who hit me ? "

" Arsenal blew up," King Dick said faintly. " Two thousand tons of powder all blow up, my goo'ness me my my ! Pow ! Blow you into the harbour ! "

He put his hand against my back and pushed me to my feet. I felt for my riding-crop ; it was still thrust into my boot. When he took his hand away, I'd have fallen if he hadn't caught me.

He shook me. " You got to stand up, Albion ! "

" I can't. My bones feel bent."

" Unbend 'em ! We go find that lady of yours. We go through mountains again."

" No," I protested, " not those mountains ! I can't walk. We've got to go by ship. I'm going to take her back to America in a ship. Toussaint said he'd give me permission to sail. I'm going to Toussaint ! "

" See now, Albion," King Dick said. " They no ships to go in. Any ship sail from here, French blow her out of water. Any ship sail into Port-au-Prince, French blow her too."

I moved my head stiffly, suddenly recalling how my uncle used to do the same thing when he encountered cruelty or injustice.

" You hear me, Albion ? " King Dick persisted. " French landed five miles away, so to come down on this place from behind. They gone to Port-au-Prince too. Toussaint say so."

I stood there swaying, trying by force of will to get some strength into my knees.

King Dick slapped my face hard, and a thousand pinwheels went whirling in my head with a roaring sound. " If we going get that lady of yours before French cut us off," he shouted, " we got to hurry ! Toussaint said it ! Go quick, he said. Hurry ! "

" All right," I said. " We've got to hurry." I essayed the motion of running, but my knees buckled and I fell. This time I got up myself.

" Did you say they've landed in Port-au-Prince ? "

" Port-au-Prince," he said in a hushed voice. " Toussaint say Dessalines somewhere around Port-au-Prince, and he very unfriendly man to French." He rolled his eyes suggestively. " Toussaint say maybe it be worse in Port-au-Prince than here ! Toussaint say we got to hurry —and that not mean lie down and think about it ! "

Worse in Port-au-Prince ? Worse than this scorched piece of hell ? I looked around at the blackened smoking ruins, at the dead bodies scattered all about us on the quay. The throbbing in my head turned into quick, stabbing pictures : a naked cream-coloured, screaming figure pitching from a carriage to vanish into a fluttering mass of outstretched black hands ; two unconscious women huddled under a box in a cellar ; a squealing man diving headlong into the flames of his home. . . .

Suddenly my knees no longer felt weak. I had no feeling at all except one of overwhelming fear for Lydia. I took my riding-crop from my boot and threw it to Rodgers. " Get that home for me," I said. " Send it to William Tyng, Portland. Give him my love ! "

When his blackened face nodded a clownish assent, I turned and stumbled across the cinder-strewn Plaza, King Dick at my side with a hand beneath my arm, our sugar-caked shoes crackling as we ran.

We hurried along the street that had led to Christophe's palace. The once-white pavement was black now : shining like ebony from the sooty burned sugar that had hardened upon it. Yesterday's handsome houses were now only the shells of buildings, among them a scant half-dozen that had miraculously escaped the flames and the explosion.

Out of one of those houses, as we passed, came two American sailors, each with a pail in his hand. My first thought was that they'd been helping to put out a fire. Then in the doorway I saw the back of another man, closing the door carefully behind him—a man whose swaggering, wide-legged way of standing was familiar to me.

" Why," I told King Dick, " I believe that's Lee ! It's Captain Lee ! "

Lee looked around at us, said something in a suppressed voice to the two sailors, and bolted into the house like a rabbit. The sailors hesitated, then started towards the house themselves. One of them stumbled, and from his pail spilled a cascade of shining coins.

King Dick moved towards them, but they reached the door before him. It opened to let them in and slammed shut in his face.

The coins that had spilled from the pail were silver dollars. The men must have been Lee's sailors, and they had certainly been taking money that wasn't theirs.

King Dick put the flat of his hand against a door panel. " You come out or I come in ! " he yelled. There was no answer. He drew back his arm. His left fist hit the door panel with the sound of a horse kicking a board out of a stall, and the panel burst wide open.

I took his arm and pulled at it. " To hell with Lee ! " I told him. " We've got more important business." I didn't care about anyone or anything except the one important thing in all the world—Lydia.

CHAPTER XXIII

FROM the hill-slopes, as we hurried towards King Dick's plantation, we had our first glimpse of the French—toy soldiers moving on a far-off pale-green rug. French ships, close to land, were still disembarking men, and their boats, like countless waterbugs, swam continually from ship to shore. Columns of white-clad troops moved along the main road towards Cap François, and parallel columns flowed through the cane-fields on either side. Flankers moved with beautiful precision beside the foremost troops, and a screen of light field-guns crawled at their head.

Groups of Negroes stared down across the cane-fields at the French ships and the laden boats crawling bug-like about them. When these black men saw us, they moved off into the bushes, vanishing as bears vanish in thick woods.

The air seemed charged with the far-off booming of drums. It throbbed ahead of us, behind us, in the valley below, on the mountains above ; we moved in the centre of a sphere of drumming. In my ears that booming urged me feverishly on. " Go, go, go ! " it seemed to say. " Go, go, *go* go, go *go* go go, go go *go* ! " I couldn't go fast enough ; and to stop, even for a moment, at King Dick's plantation, was exasperating.

To all my protests, King Dick was deaf. Toussaint, he said, had ordered it so. He had ordered him to find me in Cap François ; ordered him to take me first to Mirafleur ; ordered him to make all necessary preparations to abandon Mirafleur ; ordered him to see that I was darkened to a safer colour. Toussaint, he assured me, did nothing without good and sufficient reason.

As he went about his own preparations for our departure, he summoned two ancient black crones, who bustled about and made a sort of witches' broth out of bark, berries, and roots. Then they pulled off my clothes like two monkeys ; even removed Lydia's green stone that hung on a cord around my neck ; and they cackled with fiendish pleasure at my embarrassment.

Dipping sponges into the black brew, they rubbed it in my hair and ears ; dabbed it on my eyelids and pushed it up my nose ; scrubbed my back with it ; slapped their sponges against my buttocks with witch-like titterings. Fingers, toes, the soles of my feet—no part of me escaped them ; and when they were finished they stood me to dry on a sugar-bag, as naked as the day I was born.

From head to toe I was the colour of ancient mahogany ; and King Dick scanned me with approval. " That very neat job," he said. " Very gros nègre. What kind of uniform you want ? Admiral ? General ? "

I said I didn't want any uniform at all, and would like to wear as little as possible on account of the heat.

He nodded understandingly and said it was better to dress that way. Then there was no need of wearing a sword, and one could carry a cocomacaque. Swords, he said, were nice for military display, but there was nothing like a large cocomacaque for obliterating anybody who made himself offensive. Also the less one wore, the fewer rips one got from thorns—except in the skin.

Above his own waist he was naked except for two crossed belts for pistols, and an enormous humpbacked and gold-braided military hat that somehow put me in mind of a small gold-trimmed black camel. His belt, in back, passed through a slot in an abbreviated ox-tail, which swayed against his rump. " If anything happen to me," he told me lightly, as if he found the idea fantastic, " you make sure you get this ox-tail. That my wanga."

I reminded him that I already had a wanga, and that his own probably wouldn't help me if it had failed to protect him.

"Oh, my goo'ness me," he said. "This wanga not Voodoo! This wanga, she gets you what you need when Voodoo can't get it." He glanced hastily over his shoulder to make sure none of his wives were near ; then loosened his belt, stripped off the ox-tail, pried open its blunt end, and removed from it a slotted metal plug through which the belt had passed. He shook the ox-tail over his pink palm, and from it rolled a number of cloth-wrapped pellets. He unwrapped a few and lifted them out : they were pearls the size of white-oak acorns. When he moved his hand before my face the gems glowed softly, as if made of moonbeams smoothed by centuries of contact with rounded throats.

The very sight of them filled me with discomfort. "Put them away," I urged him. "We're wasting time. We've got to hurry ! "

King Dick shook his head and kept on playing with his pearls. "We got one more wanga to get before we start," he said. "That old Toussaint say not to travel till he give us one more thing. He be here soon, like a shadow."

I tried to sleep, but couldn't. I tried to rest, but found it impossible. I could only pace up and down the veranda, studying the roads that led towards the cloud of smudge hanging over Cap François and towards the far-off valleys whence rose columns of smoke from burning plantation houses. The thought of Lydia was a churning turmoil in my body and brain—a turmoil that wouldn't let me be at ease for a moment.

Towards mid-afternoon an undersized mouse-coloured pony came scuttling up the roadway with a little black man in the saddle. It was Toussaint ; and when he came up the steps and into the house, the ecstatic howlings of King Dick's black servants were enough to wake the dead. They fell to the floor, prostrating themselves, fainting with adoration.

When he was alone with us he gave King Dick a letter. "Go first to Beau-Bouclier," he said ; "then keep on with this letter until you meet Dessalines. The letter will be a protection for those with you. If you are in trouble, go to Crête à Pierrot in the Artibonite. That is a place the French may find difficult."

He wrinkled his forehead, looked around at the plantation house, then addressed me politely. "Your friend has done well with this plantation ; his men have worked well for him. But now it must be burned." He turned to King Dick. "Set fire to it. Send everybody of fighting age to me. Let the women and children take care of themselves. Do you want me to do anything about your wives ? "

King Dick shook his head. "No trouble getting unmarried, mon Général. She all had experience. Give her fifteen feet gold braid and she hide in hills till safe to come out and marry a colonel. Maybe fifteen feet even get her a general."

Toussaint nodded gravely. "Your philosophy pleases me, my friend ; you are honest with yourself. I am reluctant to send you with this American, but nobody else can be trusted. He is my friend as well as yours, because he wasn't afraid to speak out for us, so it's my earnest wish that he gets safely away with those he loves."

He bowed ceremoniously to me, saluted King Dick elegantly, and took himself off as unostentatiously as he had come.

King Dick shook his head and chuckled. " That old Toussaint," he said admiringly. " Now I divorce my wives and we start."

He picked up a box of gold braid from a table and shouted deafeningly for Amétiste, Claircine, Aspodelle, Floréal, Atténaire, Roséïde, Cloryphène, Marméline.

Unwilling to witness the casting-off of King Dick's wives, I left the house myself and waited on muleback at the foot of the veranda steps. There was a burst of female screaming, like young pigs impatiently squealing for their dinner. The din spread to the outbuildings and labourers' quarters, woeful beyond words ; and I suspected that King Dick was carrying out Toussaint's orders to burn the place. When he came out on the veranda, pulling his hat down on his head with both hands, a burst of white smoke puffed from the open door behind him. For an hour after we left we could see whirling sparks and billowing dark clouds that had been Mirafleur drifting down towards Cap François to join the smudged pall that still hung over that ruined city.

If it hadn't been for the fields of sugar-cane, the long rows of coffee shrubs on the lower hill-slopes, the far-off plantation houses half-obscured by the heat-haze, we might have thought all Haiti uninhabited. We saw never a Negro at work in the cane-fields : the coffee plantations were empty of toilers : even the rumble of the drums sounded less like man's work than like the all-pervasive humming of innumerable bees.

At our first resting-place, King Dick took from his sash the letter from Toussaint to Dessalines.

" That old Toussaint," he said affectionately. He thrust out an enormous tongue, placed the seal of the letter carefully upon it, breathed moistly upon the seal. No steam bath could have been more effective. The letter curled and became limp ; the seal softened ; King Dick picked gingerly at it and the letter fell open in his hand.

I read it over his shoulder.

Do not forget (it said to Dessalines), while waiting for the rainy season which will rid us of our foes, that we have no other resources than destruction and fire. Bear in mind that the soil bathed with our sweat must not furnish our enemies with the smallest sustenance. Tear up the roads with shot ; throw corpses and horses into all springs and wells ; burn and annihilate everything in order that those who have come to reduce us to slavery may have before their eyes the image of that hell which they deserve.

King Dick pressed the seal back in place and gave me a sidelong glance. " We got no time to rest," he said. " Less than I thought."

I was already untying my mule. My fingers seemed all thumbs. I found myself repeating those phrases : " Throw corpses and horses into springs and wells ; burn and annihilate everything." My mouth was dry ; my stomach-muscles fluttered ; I was afraid.

The unending booming of the drums was a throbbing accompaniment to the clatter of our mules' hoofs as we kicked them on and on across the Black Mountains into the Valley of the Artibonite, on and on through swamps, jungles, sinkholes, rocky river-beds, and the tortured paths to the Terrible Mountains. That threatening throbbing came to seem like something inside me, pressing me on, pulling me on, spurring me on through the frigid rain-squalls of the high mountains and the steamy heat of the deep valleys. I was sick with fear lest I might be too late.

The big green cup of Beau-Bouclier, when we reached it at sundown of the third day, was as peaceful and beautiful as on the day we'd first seen it, and I got myself off my mule and up the steps like a man in a dream, stumbling and fumbling on legs turned to jelly.

As I came up on the veranda, with King Dick close behind me, Madame Serpinard came from the house, followed by a fat twelve-year-old girl who was, as they say, the spit and image of her. At sight of me, Madame Serpinard screamed, and in a moment a score of black servants rushed from the door, followed by Gabriel d'Autremont, his two sons, and Lydia.

" Un Nèg' inconnu ! " Madame Serpinard cried.

" No," Lydia said, " it's Mr. Hamlin ! " She came to me and gave me her hand. I couldn't seem to let it go or take my eyes from her.

" Have you heard what has happened ? " I asked.

She nodded. " I was afraid for you. I'm glad you came to no harm. Oh, so glad ! " There was genuine relief in her voice.

" I told her there was nothing to fear," Autremont said. " I knew the French would protect all whites."

" Oh my ! " King Dick exclaimed. " Oh me my ! "

" Hark to me," I told Autremont. " When I left here before, I intended to come back in an American vessel and take you and your family to America."

He only smiled.

" At any rate," I went on, " that's out of the question now. The French are not letting any vessels sail from Cap François. But if you can escape from here, and if we can get back to Cap François, I have friends who may be able to do something for us."

" Escape from here ! Why *should* I escape ? You don't understand my position. My plantation will always be free from interference because my Negroes have always been treated fairly. Whatever happens, we won't be affected. If the French return permanently to the island, I'll still continue to treat my Negroes well. If Toussaint and Christophe remain in power, I'll be no worse off than I am to-day."

I tried hard to keep my temper with the stupid man. " M. d'Autremont, it's nearly sundown. The Negroes are on the move. They know just one thing, and that is, that if Frenchmen or mulattoes ever again control Haiti, all Negroes will be slaves."

"But that's beyond belief," he protested." All of them can't possibly——"

I couldn't hear him out. "Don't tell me what can't possibly happen in a war ! Anything can happen ! The French are ashore and marching. They're in Cap François. I had word from Toussaint that they're in Port-au-Prince. The Negroes know why, and there's nothing they won't do to stop it. Don't you know what Christophe did, for God's sake ? He burned his palace, the opera house, every government building, every tavern, shop, and private house in Cap François, so that white men shouldn't have them ! The blacks rushed in from miles around and looted the houses of the whites—and of the partly-whites too. They swarmed through the countryside in mobs, robbing plantations, killing white men, killing white wives, white children ! If you don't know what that means, I do ! "

Autremont remained scornful. "That can't happen here ! Our Negroes are faithful. They'd never hurt us. You don't think seriously I should abandon this plantation when nothing has happened—when there've been no threats against it—when there's no reason for anybody to make trouble for me ? "

"You talk too much," I told him. "You're leaving this place," I turned to Lydia. "He'll go. He's got to go ! They'll all go, and they'll go quick ! Get your things ! "

"You are a fool ! " Madame Serpinard cried. "I cannot travel ! I am too delicate to travel. What is this talk of ships ? I refuse to travel on a ship. When a storm rises and the ports are closed, I become ill — oh, dangerously ! It is the same with Simonette, but worse : she becomes green ! Do not speak to me of ships ! Are you a simpleton, Gabriel, that you permit these unknowns to dictate to you ? "

She seized her daughter's hand and went haughtily into the house, an offended and offensive woman.

Autremont continued to argue. "Even if you were correct in considering my household in danger, it would be impossible for us to leave here until the day after to-morrow. What you do not understand, my friend, is that such an establishment as this cannot be abandoned at a moment's notice."

"You're leaving here to-night—immediately ! "

"Under no circumstances ! "

"Go ahead and wipe him," I told King Dick.

King Dick put out a long arm, took Autremont by the elbow, turned him slightly, and almost caressingly tapped a huge fist against his chin. Autremont seemed almost to leave the ground ; his arms and legs flapped loosely, his elongated body bent as if his bones had softened, and he fell in a heap on the veranda with the sound of a bag of potatoes dropped from a height. King Dick seized his coat collar and stripped the coat half off, leaving him trussed like a turkey.

Then he turned to me. "Now you bring the women. Those drums getting excetticated, and we be better in bushes."

CHAPTER XXIV

Lydia, on her knees, was buckling canvas bags over Paul's and Raymond's shoulders.

"Where's that damned fool woman and her fat daughter?" I asked.

"Go through the house and across the garden," Lydia said. "Her house is part of the garden wall—the small stone house with the curved colonnades. She'll be reasonable when she knows we're really going."

"She'd better be," I said. "If you know where there's any money in the house, get it. Don't bother about whom it belongs to. Get it. What's in those bags?"

"Candles," she said; "medicines, tinder box, shoes, soap, combs——"

"Bring machetes, too, and a kettle and the old man's pistols," I told her as I started for the back of the house.

Once in the garden, I groped my way across it to the colonnade and found the door between two dimly lit windows. It was locked, but through the glass peep-hole I saw candles burning in the room beyond the hall. I pounded on the door, expecting to see the lady herself appear from the lighted room. When I saw nothing, heard nothing, I kicked the door and beat upon it with my fists.

It was heavy and solid, like teak. The windows beside it were barred, according to the Haitian custom, and I shook the bars : shouted and listened, trying to shut out the sound of drums. But the house remained as silent as a tomb.

With the heel of my shoe I broke the glass of one of the little windows, hoping I could reach through to the bolt or the key of the door. If not, I'd have to go back for an axe. Just as I'd got my hand between the bars, I saw something I hadn't noticed before. On the hall floor, huddled close against the door, I made out a bundle. It might be just a bundle of clothes—but it wasn't : it was a huddled body—the body of a small woman—the body of Madame Serpinard.

I could see blood on her. There were pools of it on the floor and splotches on the walls. She'd been hacked twice with a knife—no doubt a cane-knife—once in the upper arm, so that a slab of flesh hung by a shred from her elbow, and again in the head. Her skull was wide open, like a crushed egg. I could smell the heavy, flat, stale odour of blood, like the odour of grimy boys in a steamy room on a rainy day.

"Now wait," I told myself; "there's still that damned fat fool of a girl. You've got to find out about that fat fool of a girl."

I fumbled frantically, trying to reach the door key ; then stopped and thought. Madame Serpinard was lying against the door. Therefore she had been killed while trying to leave the house. But she never would have tried to leave the house alone if her daughter had been alive, or even inside the house. Therefore the fat girl had either been killed just before Madame Serpinard was killed, or been carried from the back door by one of the murderers.

Holding my breath, as a man does when he expects a blow from the dark, I ran on tiptoe back to the house. There was nothing in my head but a senseless refrain : " Damned fat fool ! Damned fat fool ! "

I found Lydia hooking a small kettle to the bottom of Paul's knapsack. Her eyes, as she looked up, searched beyond me for Madame Serpinard.

I picked up her canvas bag and put the strap over her shoulder. " Come along," I said. " Madame Serpinard isn't going."

" Oh, but she must ! She's the *last* one we can leave ! The Negroes hate her ! We'll have to carry her ! "

" It's too late ! It'll be too late for us, too, if you don't hurry ! Don't ask what happened ! " I caught her by the arm and lifted her to her feet. " If you don't want to see those boys chopped with cane-knives, bring 'em to the front door quick ! "

She put her hand to her throat and nodded.

I ran to the veranda. So rapidly had Autremont's world moved, so violently had it changed at the very moment when he was most certain of security, that even yet he was half-unconscious from King Dick's wiping. He was on the floor, resting against King Dick's knee, his coat still stripped back over his arms.

" Get him started," I told King Dick. " They climbed through a window in the rear and killed Madame Serpinard. I think they're coming around the house ! "

King Dick freed Autremont's arms, picked him up by the hair, thumped him down on his heels ; then slapped his face twice.

Autremont blinked, put his hand uncertainly to his chin, looked at his hand ; then stared at me. " Inexcusable ! " he muttered. " Odious ! "

I slapped him myself for good measure. " Don't make a sound or we'll all be killed ! Understand ? They've hacked your sister-in-law ! They're hunting the rest of us ! "

I felt Lydia behind me. " Shut the door," I told her, " so they won't see us against the light."

" Go ahead," King Dick whispered. " Leave the mules. They too noisy. Take these folks twenty paces down path, turn right twenty paces. Then wait. That clear, Albion ? "

I said it was, and fumbled for Lydia in the darkness.

" Take M. d'Autremont," she said. " He's not himself."

I got him by the back of his coat and pushed him towards the steps. When he swayed and stumbled, I turned him around, put my shoulder against his stomach, pulled him towards me, and hoisted him up. He was like a sack of grain, too heavy to carry far.

" Stay close," I told Lydia. " I can't see around him."

She took my hand, led me down the steps, and I made out, in the dimness, that Paul and Raymond were holding to her skirts. One of them snuffled, and she whispered, " Hush, darling ! "

I strained my ears for near-by movements. Far away—and not so far away, but ominously close—the drums boomed and bumbled ; and from amid their thuddings and rumblings came menacing throbbings, such as emerge from beneath a roaring waterfall.

At twenty paces we turned to the right, between the pepper trees, and came into coffee bushes whose whip-like shoots caught at our feet and knees. At the end of twenty paces we stopped. Through the branches of the coffee shrubs I saw a faint light in the windows of the house, but I heard nothing.

Autremont, draped over my shoulder, stirred and groaned. I lowered him to the ground and got him by the throat, ready to throttle him if he spoke.

He pulled at my wrist. " Won't do it again," he gasped.

I drew a deep breath of the warm, flower-scented tropical air. Perhaps I told myself, Madame Serpinard was killed only because she'd refused to regard Negroes as human beings. Perhaps we'd have been safe in the house, after all. Perhaps this hurried flight in the dark had been unnecessary.

I thought I saw a shadow pass a dimly lighted window. Then I saw another, and this time I was sure : the figure of a man had crossed that pale rectangle.

" Keep the boys quiet," I whispered to Lydia.

I could feel her drawing them close against her. We strained our ears for some sound other than the throbbing of the drums.

The sounds we finally heard seemed harmless enough. A man groaned, as if oppressed by dreams. Then there was a thump, such as I'd often heard at milking time on the farm when a milker dug his fist into a cow's flank to keep her from putting her foot in the pail. Close on that came a dull clatter ; then a thud and a slow gurgling, as of molasses running from a jug.

I turned my head this way and that, listening for sounds more sinister ; but again the whole world seemed silent except for the drums and the squeak of a night bird far overhead.

I felt rather than heard a movement behind me, but even as I turned to face it I knew it was King Dick. In a voice as faint as the rustling of a leaf he whispered, " All wiped ! Now we go."

" Did they come around to the front ? " I whispered. " Did you find out anything about that damned fat fool of a girl ? "

He said there had been four of them. They had come into the house with cane-knives ready to strike. He had silently wiped the first with his fist. The second and third he had wiped with his cocomacaque. But he had been obliged to use his knife in order to wipe the fourth successfully. " No use thinking about fat girl," he whispered breathlessly. " They finished with her."

He slipped past me and moved towards the western rim of the hills. The rest of us followed silently. So that was why they had been so slow coming around the house ! I tried not to think about the fat girl, but I couldn't help myself. They'd finished with her ! If the fat girl hadn't delayed them, they might have caught us unprepared—and that was something I refused to think about.

CHAPTER XXV

WHEN daylight came we found ourselves on the southern slope of a mountain that had seemed beautiful to me from a distance. From the veranda of Beau-Bouclier it had looked like an arrow-head, bent at the tip—hazy purple in the sunlight, the colour of a clouded amethyst ; but now that we were upon it, it was like all the rest of San Domingo—a jungle of colossal growths that had burst violently into being, and in the very bursting started to decay. All about us were mahogany trees festooned with loops, whorls, snarls of vines, waxy blossoms the size of cabbages, and hoorahs' nests of dead leaves from which sprang more rank tangles of leaves, blooms, and vines.

We were covered breast-high with black mud and green slime, for all night long we had stumbled repeatedly into pools of liquid as thick as syrup—pools that smelled as though all the barnyards, all the decaying matter, all the swamp mud in the world, had been boiled together for their making.

How Lydia contrived to look so lovely after such a night, and even when mud-stained, was beyond my understanding. She was dressed like a Negro woman, a blue cotton shirt open at the throat, a red handkerchief around her head, so knotted that the ends hung down over an ear, and a brown garment that was like a skirt and yet not a skirt, for it was only a length of printed cotton into which she wound herself, binding the ends with the folds so that they hung down front and back like sash-ends, handy to knot between her knees when the travelling was hard, or to tie over her head in rainstorms : a magic skirt, for she could unwind it, rinse it in water, wring it out, wrap it around her again, and look as fresh and sweet as a flower.

With the dawn we saw what King Dick had been hunting—yellow splotches high up the rugged mountain-slope, as though a giant had taken a brushful of yellow paint and slatted gouts of it in a line across the upper face of the mountain. These, King Dick again said, had been ocean beaches long æons ago, and waves pounding upon them had eaten caves into the mountain—caves that would shelter us until we decided what to do.

As we climbed up and up, we saw columns of smoke rising from every part of the plain and from the coffee plantations on the lower slopes of the mountains we'd left behind us.

" That small peak beside the lake," Paul said to Raymond, " that is the Rémusac plantation burning."

Raymond nodded. " And the next one to the left is the Chevignys', and the next one the Landrecines', both burning."

I turned to look at the plantations. They were all ablaze—plantation houses, storehouses, outbuildings.

" Then the next one is ours," Paul said thoughtfully.

I recognised the twin hills through which the roadway entered the green cup of Beau-Bouclier. From the centre of that green cup rose a dirty smudge of oily smoke.

" Not much time," King Dick said softly.

We turned our backs on those burning palaces and followed King Dick on and on, up and up through steamy forests, Autremont climbing haggardly close behind him ; Lydia herding the two boys before her, a tireless, patient shepherdess. I didn't mind the heat or the steam, or the mud-holes into which I stumbled, or the sweat that drenched me. For the first time I was wholly exultant and completely happy. Lydia was alive and so was I, and we were together. That, for me, would always be full measure of contentment.

Those yellow beaches were so high that when we reached them we saw a thunderstorm flashing far below us. From their appearance, the ocean might have pounded at them only yesterday, for their sands were soft as golden sugar and littered with seashells, among them oyster shells the size of pie-plates. The golden sands were partly roofed by arched caves, rudely suggestive of the arcades around the Cap François Plaza, but warped, lopsided, and of all sizes, as though Negro gods had carved them for practice and done badly at it.

The sand of those lofty beaches had never a footprint upon it—doubtless because rains washed them almost nightly—so that we might have been the first people to set foot upon them.

King Dick led us to a beach that jutted out from the others, protected on either side by flying buttresses, and from that golden platform we looked down on the whole southern quarter of Haiti as on an enormous coloured map, all greens and blues and purples. To our left were the towering peaks of the Morne de la Selle, backbone of the island's southern promontory, and far off to the right, lavender in the morning sun, were the mountain-mazes through which we had come from Cap François. Almost below us were the fertile central valleys : to the left the Cul de Sac, to the right the valley of the Artibonite. In both valleys plantation houses were burning.

King Dick, squatting before us, considered this vast landscape ; then drew a rough map in the sand, marking the towns with shells. " Port-au-Prince, that nearest," he said ; " nearest and worst. Only fifteen mile, but too much French. We keep away from Port-au-Prince. Beyond Port-au-Prince is Léogane, but that soon be French, if not now."

He swung his arm to the backbone of mountains that lay to our left and continued on and on to the westward, forming the southern promontory of the island. " Across those mountains, fifty mile straight south, they two towns, Jacmel and Les Cayes."

He swung his other arm off to the north-eastward, pointing to the green valley of the Artibonite and the distant coastline of the Bight of Léogane. " Up there, fifteen mile away, is L'Arcahaye ; twenty mile farther St. Marc. Which way we go, so we get back to Cap François easiest ? That is question to decide. I think you be safe here while I go down below to find out where is Dessalines."

Autremont was moaning plaintively. " You say we are to keep away from Port-au-Prince because the French are there ! Ai-yi ! What's the reason for that ? I am a Frenchman ; my children are Frenchmen ! All we need to do is to place ourselves under the protection of the French army, then wait until we're free to return to Beau-Bouclier."

King Dick rolled an eye at him. " That easy to say, but how you get to French army ? Toussaint let me come with Albion to help his friends get to safety—not to get to French army. No way to get to French army without mixing with nigra army, and that not safe. Anyway, no use saying we ought to do this, ought to do that, till we know more. Right now we don't know anything—except you got away safe from your plantation."

" You'd better go quickly," I told him. " If there's arguing to be done, we'll do it after you get back. What shall we do while you're away ? "

" Make everybody black," King Dick said. " Get water from dead bamboo stalks ; get bark from mahogany tree, chop it in little pieces and boil it ; then rub it on everybody, all over."

" On everybody ? "

" Everybody," King Dick repeated emphatically, " and all over."

Our brew of mahogany bark, when we took it from the fire, was as pallid as weak coffee and had a sour odour, highly offensive. It was, Autremont complained, underdone. He couldn't do anything without groaning and seemed on the verge of tears. " Ai-yi," he'd say, and wring his hands, unable to make up his mind.

But Lydia got to work promptly and cheerfully, rubbing Raymond's back with a piece of tow-cloth dipped in the weak-looking liquid. Then all of us sat around as solemn as a lot of owls, waiting for it to dry. I thought at first it wasn't going to work ; but ten minutes later Raymond's back was the colour of my old law-books.

Paul and Raymond used up the first kettleful, colouring each other and having their faces coloured by Lydia. Then they went for more bark and boiled it, and Autremont, groaning and protesting, submitted to being stained. Then he was unhappy because he considered his colouring imperfect, but he insisted that I re-stain him. Nothing suited him ; everything in the world was wrong.

I suppose we were like cooks who are never able to roast a goose properly until their third attempt. Our third brewing of mahogany bark looked like all the others, and we thought that when Lydia used it she would turn the same leathery shade as Paul and Raymond and Autremont. But when she came back, her arms and cheeks and throat were a velvety golden-brown ; and, owing to the transparency of her skin or to some peculiar property of the dye, there was a dusky flush beneath her golden throat and cheeks that made her radiant.

I never ceased to wonder at that quality in Lydia—that quality of being always more beautiful, in my eyes, every time I saw her : more beautiful in the dress of a Negress than in the finest muslin : more beautiful in rags then in velvets : more beautiful in the evening than in the day ; and yet, perplexingly, more beautiful the next morning : more beautiful when her skin was golden and velvety than when it was pearly white ; and yet, by a paradox, even more beautiful when the colour had faded and she was herself again.

She had the faculty, too, of making any place seem home-like so long as she herself was there, and the cave in which we slept that night turned into a home before we knew it. She had the boys cut palm cabbages and palm leaves with their machetes, and from the leaves they made bed-places on either side of the fire. She found protuberances on the cave-walls on which to hang her knapsack and the odds and ends we carried with us. And while the palm-cabbage was boiling in the kettle, the boys made a table from a flat rock and Lydia set two lighted candle-ends upon it. The truth of it was that no place, without Lydia, could ever again seem home to me.

It was perfect except for Autremont's mutterings—mutterings to the effect that he had been forced from Beau-Bouclier against his will ; that there was no need to abandon his plantation in the very moment when it would yield a fortune ; that life without Azilde was no life at all. Azilde's name recurred and recurred. The man seemed to have forgotten everything except Azilde, a name that meant nothing to me.

I only half-heard him, thanks to Lydia, who sat between the bed-places on the other side of the fire, reading to the two boys from a little book she'd taken from her knapsack.

Only two days ago I'd feared I'd never see her again, and now here I was within five feet of her, watching the play of the firelight on her cheeks and lips, the faint pulsing of blood beneath the golden velvet of her throat, the movements of her fingers as she turned the pages.

It was enough for me, almost, to be able to see her and to hear her voice, a beautiful voice that added immeasurably to the meaning of the words she read. She was reading from a thin little book of fables by Laboulaye, translating the French into English as she went along.

In time the boys' eyes grew heavy ; Autremont's groanings came to an end. Lydia placed her book on the table and sat looking down at the boys. Suddenly she raised her eyes to mine.

" You spoke ? "

" No," I said. " I mean Yes."

I got to my feet and went to the outer fringe of sand beyond the mouth of the cave. The velvety blackness of the scented void beneath me was dotted with the still-glowing embers of hundreds of plantation houses. I felt Lydia beside me.

" You'll never know how grateful we are," she said. " If it hadn't been for you and your persistence, we'd all be dead."

I reminded her that all of us are a hair's-breadth from death a dozen times a day.

" Yes," she said, and shivered. " But not that sort of death. I felt you were right when you first urged me to go, but the boys . . ."

I lowered myself to the sand and she sank to her knees beside me.

" I was afraid," she went on, " that you thought I didn't fully appreciate your kindness when you first came to Beau-Bouclier. It's true I told you I had a reason for not leaving, but you didn't even ask it."

" There wasn't time," I said. " What was it ? "

" Well, I was engaged to teach English and other things to M. d'Autremont's children. When I first arrived, I knew nothing about Haiti except what I'd read in Moreau de St. Méry, and very little indeed about people. Madame d'Autremont had died a few months before, and the two boys, Paul and Raymond, were being waited on from morning till night, hand and foot, by black slaves. Both were born here and are therefore Creoles."

" I thought Creoles were part Negro," I said.

" No: Creoles are white persons born in the Indies, and Creole children are all alike—all ! They're constantly surrounded by slaves. They're spoiled by their parents, spoiled by all the servants. They can't express a wish without having it immediately gratified. From their parents they learn that any lack of promptness, any lack of attention on the part of black servants, should be instantly and severely punished. To my knowledge there isn't a Creole child on any Haitian plantation who doesn't have the temper of the devil, the vanity of a peacock, the domineering instincts of a bully and a coward. They're little despots : little vile-tempered, foul-minded tyrants, thinking only of material goods and display ; caring nothing for things of the intellect, nothing for the improvement of their minds, nothing for religion."

" I can understand that," I said ; " and of course you can't change children brought up like that."

" Oh, but it's worth trying," she protested.

" I don't believe it ! You know what Dean Swift said : ' Give me a child to educate until he's five, and I don't care who has him after that.' "

" Yes," she said. " I think I'd have agreed with Swift in the beginning. Never an hour went by, during my first days here, that I didn't say to myself I couldn't bear to live among such people, and must go back home by the next ship. Then I began to get fond of Paul and Raymond, and to see things differently. I thought that if I could have a free hand I could save those two children from growing up to think that nothing is sacred except riches and profits."

" But they weren't worth it ! "

" Yes, they were," she said. " Teaching's my profession, and a teacher must save children, just as physicians must heal bodies. They must ! "

When I made no answer, she went on : " I told M. d'Autremont that if he'd give me complete authority over his sons, I'd do all I could for them ; but that if he interfered with my teachings in any way, or by so much as a droop of an eyelid encouraged his sons to resist them, I'd go back to America immediately."

" That must have made him groan."

" No," she said, " he wasn't like that in the beginning. He agreed to everything I said. He kept faithfully his part of the bargain ; so I had to keep mine. That would have been so even if I'd felt no particular affection for Paul and Raymond. But to me our arrangement came to more than a bargain. As the boys responded to my teachings, all traces of Creole in them vanished. All tne best of their French inheritance came to the surface—confidence, bravery, frankness, generosity. I found that I loved them almost as much as though they were my own. I couldn't leave them, because if I did I knew what would happen : they'd have slaves for companions, slaves for servants, slaves for attendants, and in a year's time they'd be Creoles again. Do you see now that I just can't leave them ? "

" No," I said, " I don't. You'll have to leave them eventually, and then they'll become Creoles again. You're just delaying the day."

" I don't believe it," she whispered. " I'm a teacher."

" All right," I said. " Have it your own way ! Maybe you're right. The fact remains that Gabriel d'Autremont can never go back to his plantation. He may not realise it yet, but he soon will. Then I'll make him take his children to America."

" Never ! " she said. " You don't know how profoundly some Frenchmen despise America and Americans. M. d'Autremont is one of them. He insists that Americans are hypocrites, sharp traders, for ever claiming to be neutral and secretly selling weapons to Negroes at exorbitant prices. He'll never go to America ! "

" If that's his only reason, I think I can talk him out of it."

" Ah," she said, " but it's not his only reason, poor man ! Like every other plantation owner in Haiti, he has a griffe who's his mistress. Other plantation owners have several, but M. d'Autremont has only one—the

Azilde he keeps talking about. Until he tires of her, he will love her as truly as any man can love a woman."

" Love ! " I said. " Tires of her ! You don't tire of a woman if you love her ! What's love got to do with it, anyway ? What's a griffe by comparison with you and the children ? Doesn't the idiot know that there's too much at stake to bother over a griffe, or to think of love ? "

At this she got quickly to her feet, and when I caught at her hand to keep her near me she turned abruptly and went back into the cave.

All right, I said to myself, let her go ! If she's offended at what I said about love, let her *be* offended !

I damned Autremont for a weak-spined, jelly-brained, deluded old fool, willing to sacrifice all of us to his infatuation for a mistress, and so lost to truth as to think that such an infatuation could be dignified by calling it love.

Then I began to wonder about love and about infatuation, and whether there is truly any difference between them, except in the minds of those who know nothing about either. I wondered about myself, and whether I might not behave even worse than Autremont if I were to be suddenly separated from Lydia. I wondered and I wondered, but the only conclusion I reached was that Autremont was an unreasonable old fool about Azilde, but that I'd be justified in doing anything at all to avoid being separated from Lydia.

CHAPTER XXVI

When King Dick came back at mid-morning the next day, he had a pack on his back, and in the pack a bag of rice, a bag of manioc flour, a dozen salted codfish, some avocados, and seasonings. He was starved, he said, and wanted some *féroce*. I wondered what sort of dish was violent enough to be labelled " ferocious," so I watched Lydia prepare it in her kettle. It was salt codfish pounded and fried with oil, pimento, garlic, and vinegar, then made into a glutinous paste with avocados and manioc flour ; and I marvelled that any human stomach, even an unpredictable black one, could demand such a mixture. But when it was done and I had a plate of it before me, I could have downed a pailful and called for more.

When we'd eaten, King Dick squatted before the map he'd drawn in the sand the day before, smoothed it over, and re-drew it. He laid down oyster shells to mark Aux Cayes and Jacmel, which we could see far away to the left ; Port-au-Prince, a little cluster of white dots straight ahead ; Léogane, nestled between the mountains and the sea twenty miles beyond Port-au-Prince ; and L'Arcahaye and St. Marc to the north along the Bight of Léogane.

We had those towns as clearly in our heads by now as though we'd visited them. We could even see the gap in the mountains and follow the windings of the watercourse that served as a road through the mountains to Jacmel. Below us we could see the roads to Port-au-Prince and Léogane, to L'Arcahaye and St. Marc.

The French under General Boudet, King Dick told us, had appeared off Port-au-Prince on the morning of the day we reached Beau-Bouclier, and demanded that Agé, the general in command, surrender the city to them. Agé, King Dick said, was a white Frenchman, a native of Haiti who had been put in command of Port-au-Prince by Toussaint because he had been Toussaint's Chief of Staff in the war against the southern mulattoes. Apparently, King Dick said, he wasn't so eager to fight the French as to fight mulattoes ; and when the French had asked him to surrender, he had been unable to say either Yes or No.

At this point one of his subordinates, Lamartinière, a great admirer of Toussaint, had reminded Agé of his duty by shoving a pistol against his ribs. Agé had then said No. It was a great pity, King Dick added, that Lamartinière hadn't pulled the trigger.

When Boudet was refused, he had landed anyway. So many mulattoes had gone over to the French that Lamartinière had been obliged to abandon Port-au-Prince and take to the hills with his garrison. With him he took as hostages all the whites he could find—men, women, and children, some six hundred in number. He had also tried to burn the town, but the French were so close that the fires were extinguished before they had fairly got started.

King Dick leaned over and with a black forefinger poked at the shells ranged before us in a rough semicircle.

" Nobody knows where Dessalines is," he said ; " but I think in St. Marc, waiting to see whether the French come ashore there. When they don't, he coming near Port-au-Prince to look and find what he can do. For that, only place would be Croix des Bouquets "—he tossed a small shell on to the map, close to the shell representing Port-au-Prince : then pointed to the sea of green far below us. We could see Croix des Bouquets —a mere X-shaped scar on the plain.

" That where I got to go to give Dessalines the letter from Toussaint," he went on slowly, " and what I think is, we all go there together. I think and I think ; and I think most surely that way the safest."

" How about a seaport ? " I asked, still hopeful of getting Lydia away from this hell-fired cauldron of an island.

King Dick shook his head. " Not Jacmel. That a mulatto garrison, in command of a mulatto. They only one road through the mountains to Jacmel, mostly river-bed. If that road full of mulattoes coming to join French, nobody better be on it. Léogane and Port-au-Prince, they not safe either. Lamartinière try burn those towns, same as I would."

" We could strike inland," Autremont said. " We could go to Le Cap the way you came from there, by way of Mirebalais and Dondon."

Again King Dick shook his head. " Those mountains full of maroons and cocos, burning and killing. Also Christophe, he come across those mountains pretty quick, maybe, to help Dessalines catch the French in Port-au-Prince, so they bad place for white people."

Autremont groaned. " I don't agree. We must try to reach the French. At least they're civilised."

" Nobody civilised in a war," King Dick said. " I think better we all go to Croix des Bouquets."

" King Dick is right," Lydia said. " Croix des Bouquets is best."

" But Dessalines ! " Autremont protested. " Anything might happen."

" Yes," Lydia agreed, " but a determined man with courage and the ability to speak his thoughts can accomplish miracles."

" I still refuse," Autremont said. " I cannot put myself and my children in a position where we'll have to take orders from black men ! "

" Consider this, M. d'Autremont," Lydia pleaded. " If we hadn't done as King Dick and Mr. Hamlin told us, we'd have been killed, just as Madame Serpinard and Simonette were killed. King Dick and Mr. Hamlin got us safely away from Beau-Bouclier, and we're still safe. These boys are in my care, and it's my dearest wish to keep them alive as long as possible. In my opinion, our best chance is to do as King Dick and Mr. Hamlin think we should."

" Ay-yi ! " Autremont complained. " Don't I know what's best for my own children ? "

King Dick rose suddenly from beside his map. " Ay-yi ! Ay-yi ! Ay-yi ! Talk ! Talk ! Talk ! That all some white people able to do. Albion think we better go to Croix des Bouquets. I think we better go. This lady think we better go. *You* say we better *not* go." He clenched his fist and eyed it darkly ; it looked as heavy and solid as a boulder. " Now," he added softly, " it time you begin to think instead of just Ay-yi-ing."

Autremont fingered his jaw and was silent. Half an hour later the six of us were on our way down the mountainside. For the sake of Lydia and the two boys I did my best to look confident and cheerful, but the truth is that I was neither.

As we travelled through the dust and heat towards Croix des Bouquets, I thought how fortunate it was for us we weren't trying to steal down into the cane fields and join the French.

At one moment the road would be wholly empty ; then a dozen barefooted Negro soldiers wearing draggled, tawdry uniforms but carrying new American muskets would pop out from the jungle to gather around us in a semicircle and nervously finger the triggers of their cocked guns.

" Anybody here seen Dessalines ? " King Dick would ask them. " I carry a message for Dessalines."

At the mention of Dessalines, they rolled white eyes at each other and went softly back into the jungle, and we would remain unmolested until we'd passed the next bend in the road. Then out would pop another band of Negroes to examine us and look covetously at our packs. If we'd been refugees, trying to pierce those hidden black lines, we couldn't have gone ten yards without being laid by the heels and—at the least —robbed of everything we possessed.

Croix des Bouquets was useful from a military standpoint because its crossroads intersected at the top of a gentle hill on which stood the ruins of a stone plantation house. From this house one looked for miles along the four roads : to the west to Port-au-Prince ; to the east into the high mountains whence we'd come ; to the south to the shark-toothed range behind which lay Jacmel ; to the north to St. Marc and the maze of high peaks that separated us from Cap François and its sanctuary of American ships.

There was a Negro army gathered around Croix des Bouquets—the one that had fled from Port-au-Prince under Lamartinière when the French landed. It was a strange army, both in appearance and in behaviour. Its soldiers, for the most part, were black, barefooted, bare-legged, without shirts ; their trousers were cotton, mostly patches and rips ; but they all had uniform coats, ragged, torn at the seams, and with buttons missing, but cherished as though they were powerful wangas, guaranteed to protect the wearers from infirmity and death.

Although the sun was furnace-hot upon us as we came up to that ruined plantation house at Croix des Bouquets, not one of those Negro soldiers had removed his coat. They had hats, too—garish imitations of French uniform-caps, blue cloth affairs with little vizors to which were stitched tarnished bits of gold braid—and they wore these perched on their heads in every position except the proper one : with vizors over the ears, over the backs of their necks, and even pointing straight up into the air.

From these travesties of soldiers, scattered everywhere on three sides of the ruined plantation house, came that familiar shrill Negro cacophony of squealing, empty laughter, and endless high-pitched gabbling. They lay in groups under untended coffee shrubs ; hunkered over gambling games played with beans in gourds ; chewed at sticks of sugar cane, from whose ends driblets trickled down to stain the fronts of their coats with a sort of pallid whitewash ; slept in impossible positions, their heads pillowed on rocks or logs.

On the fourth side of the plantation house, scores of apathetic sentries guarded a throng of white people, hundreds of them, all huddled together in the shade of a grove of coffee shrubs that had been left in the centre of what must have been a flourishing coffee plantation before most of the shrubs had been cut away to leave an avenue of fire for two field pieces in the direction of Port-au-Prince.

There must have been six hundred men, women, and children, all whites, in that throng huddled in the coffee grove, and they were quiet beyond belief. Even the children were quiet. We could see their eyes following us as we came up to the sentries before the plantation house, and there was a fearfulness in those rolling eyes, in the unnatural stillness of the children, and the very dogs, that made me uncomfortable.

If all our dealings could have been with Lamartinière, I'm sure we'd have escaped a deal of trouble ; for he was as kind and considerate as he was loyal and accomplished.

When King Dick had explained himself to the sentry, the sentry sent a message to the veranda of the plantation house, upon which we could see a group of officers ; and when the sentry delivered the message it was Lamartinière who detached himself from the group and ran down to the gate to greet King Dick.

In no possible way could I have told that he was a Negro, or had any faint trace of Negro blood ; for his complexion was as fair as my own normally was, or as that of my uncle or any of my friends in Portland—fairer by far than Autremont, even when Autremont had been unstained with mahogany dye.

Lamartinière wore a grey linen uniform with a collar as high as his ears, a black sword sash, and shiny black boots that covered his kneecaps. His wavy black hair was as glossy and thick as Lydia's, and in front of his ears were small black whiskers that gave him a look of dandyism. His movements were graceful, his gestures elaborate ; and his politeness to King Dick seemed too excessive to be genuine, though I soon found this to be Lamartinière's way with everyone.

He was ravished, he said, by King Dick's arrival : with his help, and through the services of all these brave men about us—and he gestured magnificently towards a black soldier lying beneath a bush, staring straight at the sun with a stick of sugar cane protruding like a lighthouse from his mouth—things must sooner or later go badly for the perfidious forces of Bonaparte.

King Dick indicated us with a wave of his huge hand and observed mildly that his first duty, after delivering a letter to Dessalines, was to get these Blancs to safety.

Lamartinière turned an amazed stare upon us. " Blancs ? "

" Oh, yes, Blancs," King Dick said, and, having explained our mahogany dye precautions, went on to tell how I had worked during the fire at Cap François, and how Toussaint had shown his gratitude by sending King Dick with me to warn the lady, who was also an American.

Lamartinière bowed low to her. " I'm happy, Mademoiselle, that you were warned in time."

" Not quite in time, Captain," Lydia said. " M. d'Autremont's sister-in-law was killed, and her daughter."

Lamartinière stared at Autremont's mahogany-coloured face. " So you are the unfortunate owner of Beau-Bouclier, Monsieur ! I have already heard that your house was burned."

Autremont groaned. " Isn't there any way, Captain, in which you could help me to return to Beau-Bouclier ? There was a lady—that is, I had a friend—I'd like to do something for her in case she should find herself homeless——"

Lamartinière shook his head. " Many such friends have been killed, Monsieur. Not by my men, you understand. Maroons came down from the mountains in great numbers when the French landed, and it was they who burned your house. They are everywhere, burning and robbing. You cannot go back to your plantation, M. d'Autremont."

Autremont sat himself heavily down, as a man does when he has reached the limit of endurance.

Lamartinière looked perplexedly at King Dick. " Everything is difficult beyond words. If I try to send these friends of yours to Port-au-Prince or Léogane, ten to one the maroons will kill them on the way and also any armed escort I could spare to send with them. If I let them go without escort and *my* men see you going towards the French—ah, it wouldn't do ! That leaves only the road to the north ; but what's happening to the north, I'm unable to say. I cannot even tell you where Dessalines is." His eye wavered. " I wouldn't recommend that you let your friends go to the north—not until General Dessalines joins us, which he's sure to do soon."

" What *would* you recommend, Captain ? " Lydia asked. " These two boys, the sons of M. d'Autremont, should be taken to a place of safety."

" Mademoiselle," Lamartinière said, " at this moment we know of no place of safety anywhere. We have heard that several of Toussaint's former generals came ashore at Port-au-Prince with the French—Petion, Rigaud, Villate. They are men of colour, and we don't know how many other men of colour will join them to fight for the French. We know that La Plume, the commander of Jacmel, has marched with his garrison, all men of colour, to Port-au-Prince and joined the French. How can I or anyone else say what will happen next ? How can I give you advice, Mademoiselle ? If you will remain here quietly, I'll do everything in my power——"

A confused shouting arose on the veranda of the ruined plantation house. Negro soldiers got up from under bushes and from beside the road, scratched themselves, yawned, and went with simian frowns to stand looking off towards the north.

A young Negro officer, gaudy in a red velvet coat and blue velvet breeches, clattered down from the veranda and gave Lamartinière a sweeping salute that stirred the air like the revolving arm of a windmill. " Troops coming, Captain," he said. " All black—perhaps Dessalines. You come and look, please."

" Yes, yes, yes," Lamartinière said. " Now we learn something." To King Dick he said, " Wait here with your friends, and when I learn what it is, I'll tell you at once." He hurried away.

The elder Autremont boy took Lydia's hand. " I think the captain is afraid of Dessalines," he said. " Why is he afraid of Dessalines ? "

" Don't try to guess what is in another person's mind, Paul," she said.

" It just wastes time. We'll read in the book, which is never a waste of time."

She unbuckled a strap of her bag, and in a moment she and the two boys were sitting by the side of the path, and she was reading to them from Laboulaye.

I went close behind her to listen, and King Dick came and squatted down beside me ; even Autremont looked less woebegone as he cocked an attentive ear.

But before the reading had well begun, all of us became aware at the same moment of something looming behind us, something dark and threatening—as when a massive cloud-bank, all in a moment, blots out the summer sun. Lydia turned to look behind her, and then we were all on our feet, Lydia with her arms around the two boys in a familiar shielding gesture ; King Dick with his hand frozen half-way to the hilt of his machete ; Autremont palely helpless.

Close to us, on a shaggy little nag, sat a Negro like a gigantic toad painted black and highly polished. He had thick, hunched shoulders ; long limber feet ; a face scarred with parallel knife cicatrices and mottled with warts ; an enormous mouth with lips drawn tight against his teeth in an angry grin. He wore a blue handkerchief bound around his head ; and pressed down upon the handkerchief was a chapeau like King Dick's— a double-ended, humpbacked affair that might have passed for a model of a Haitian mountain. His uniform coat, whose collar rose up to frame his toad-like head, was encrusted with arabesques of gold lace, and his knee breeches were of white plush, spotted and stained with horse-sweat.

His eyes were the ugliest part of him. The warty lids were half-lowered ; and the pupils, more like ebony than human eyes, were set in whites the colour and texture of blood-streaked goose-fat. Those eyes were never still. Although chiefly concerned with us, they were for ever darting away to examine the white prisoners, the ruined plantation house, the sky ; then swinging back to look us up and down.

When he spoke it was to King Dick, and in Creole as harsh and croaking as though his vocal cords, hardened from disuse, were being forced by main strength to do his will.

" Good-day to you, General," he said. " What do you here ? "

" A letter from Toussaint, General," King Dick said, and he unwrapped the letter from his sash and held it out.

So this was Dessalines ; Dessalines, who had been expected to come down from the north, but had come into Croix des Bouquets from the south as had we ; the great and terrible Dessalines, ex-slave, ruthless killer, bridegroom of less than a year, whose mulatto wife had been the mistress of a white planter.

Dessalines snatched the letter, ripped it open with a forefinger the colour of a rotten banana, eyed it suspiciously, and cast a black glance at King Dick. " Letter ! " he croaked. " Can't get the truth out of a letter ! You know what's in it ? "

"Yes, mon Général," King Dick said. "It's protection for my friends."

"Hah!" Dessalines said. "Protection! So they're Blancs! I thought so! That woman was speaking in English, and all of you were listening. Therefore they speak English and must be Blancs! What business do you have with Blancs?"

"Toussaint's business," King Dick said. "Toussaint's business is business of all of us, is it not—no matter how many forget to make it their business."

Dessalines climbed from his saddle and threw the reins angrily to the ground. "These Blancs have coloured themselves for their own purposes," he growled. "Very well, let them continue to be coloured! You know what I think of Blancs, General! See that these people stay black—smell black—behave black!"

His croakings brought a dozen officers, headed by Lamartinière, running to us. They swarmed around us, mon-généraling Dessalines. They had looked for him to come from the north, they said; they had sent men to meet him, not expecting him to come from the south.

"Sacred mother-in-law of God," Dessalines howled, "what do you expect me to do? Ride straight into anybody's trap? Holy aunt of Christ, am I expected to be a fool, not permitted to circle around and come in by the rear, to see what's happening? Where's Agé?"

"He stayed in Port-au-Prince, mon Général," Lamartinière said. "If I hadn't put a pistol against his ribs, I believe he'd have let Boudet walk into the town without opposition. When he felt my pistol tickling him, Agé at last mustered the courage to tell Boudet he could do nothing except by your orders, mon Général."

Dessalines squatted toad-like to glare at Lamartinière. "Bah! What then, in the name of Christ's sister-in-law?"

"Why, then," Lamartinière said, "I demanded powder for the garrison. The fool in charge of the powder-magazine wouldn't give up the keys, so I shot him. Then we fought Boudet as well as we could, but it was too late."

"Too late!" Dessalines screamed. "Jesus and Mary Christ! Too late for what? Why didn't you shoot that white snake Agé, too? Why didn't you shoot him when you had your pistol in his gizzard? What's a pistol for? How many houses did you burn?"

"We set fires," Lamartinière said. "We set fires by the score, but the French came in and put them out."

Dessalines made a rasping sound that seemed to come from the depths of his stomach. "Put them out! You stand there and tell me Port-au-Prince is no different to-day from what it was before the Blancs came? You tell me all sugar, all coffee, all guns, all ammunition, all rum—everything—fell into the hands of the French?"

"We set the fires, mon Général," Lamartinière said unhappily, "but we couldn't wait to make sure they burned, and we had no way to prevent the French from putting them out."

Dessalines snatched off his cocked hat and threw it on the ground. " Mother and father and all the brothers and sisters of Jesus," he screamed, " I've wasted my time all these years ! How often must I tell you there's only one way to make war ? Burn and kill ! Nothing else does any good. Now the Blancs are here to put you in chains again, to stuff gunpowder up inside you and blow you to pieces, the way they did before we freed ourselves—and what do you do ? Nothing ! You burn nothing ! You kill nobody ! " He leaped at his chapeau, stamped upon it, stooped and seized it, wrenched it apart, and hurled the dusty pieces from him.

" Sons of goats, fathers of pigs, brothers of cats ! " he howled. " If you'd burned the city, those Blancs would have had no place to live ! We'd have hacked them and hacked them ! You animals without milk ! You species of mules ! You—you——"

He tore open the collar of his gold-encrusted uniform. White froth stood at the corners of his mouth, and his dead-black eyes in their beds of yellow fat rolled upward.

Lamartinière had fallen silent, and so had the officers who had come down from the veranda, and all the poorly clad, barefoot black soldiers who had appeared from nowhere to stand listening at a respectful distance —so silent that the faint hushed plaint of a mourning dove, pessimistically picking in the dust of the crossroads, seemed loud.

Dessalines rubbed the froth from his lips with his black banana of a forefinger, eased his legs by pulling at the crotch of his stained plush breeches, and spoke almost kindly to Lamartinière. " But you were able to take away all the food you needed ? "

" Now it come," King Dick said softly. " Now he burning good inside, all red, without smoke."

" We took away all we could, mon Général," Lamartinière said ; " but the French came so rapidly that——"

Dessalines jerked a thumb towards the dusty enclosure where the sentries stood guard over the huddle of whites among the coffee shrubs. " They also took away food to feed themselves ? "

" No," Lamartinière said. " We feed them. They have a value. Later we can exchange them for our own men."

Dessalines shook his head. " They have no value ! In all Haiti there are no 'Ti Blancs worth anything to anyone. They work for the French, but the French hate them. Never do 'Ti Blancs consent to work for black men or men of colour. They have no value at all except to beget more mulattoes ! Mer-de-merde to more mulattoes ! There are too many mulattoes among our enemies. I refuse to let your men's food be wasted on them. Your men are my men, and all my men have work to do. Get rid of those Blancs ! "

" We're short of ammunition already," Lamartinière protested.

Dessalines spat. " Ammunition, Captain ? Merde ! Use machetes."

I couldn't believe I'd heard correctly. Dessalines' words, I told myself, must surely be some sort of black jest !

Lamartinière gave an order ; a drummer on the veranda of the plantation house picked up his drum, hung it over his shoulder, and thumped upon it. Black soldiers sprang up from nowhere and were herded by non-commissioned officers into a long line facing the mass of whites in their guarded enclosure. As another shouted order, this line of barefooted soldiers stacked their muskets and unhooked cane-knives from their belts.

I knew suddenly and horribly that Dessalines hadn't been jesting. I tried to speak, but couldn't ; tried again and found myself croaking, " Wait—wait—I appeal——"

King Dick took me by the arm and almost pulled it off. Dessalines turned and stared at me. His under jaw was thrust forward, his lower teeth bared. He looked like something scorched by hell-fire. He just stood there, showing his teeth and glaring.

" What is it, Blanc ? "

" Sir," I said, " give me a little time. These people can be more valuable to you alive than dead. If you send them back to Port-au-Prince, there'll be that much less food for the French to eat."

Dessalines turned from me and shouted at Lamartinière. The long line of soldiers broke from their ranks and started for the prisoners' enclosure in a dusty, thick silence—a hot, sweaty, cold, whirling, raging dead silence that set the sky to slipping sideways and the earth to lurching dizzingly beneath my feet.

King Dick shook me and shook me ; then slapped my face hard. The slipping sky steadied and I saw Lydia on her knees holding the two boys against her, trying to cover their eyes and ears. I took Paul from her, put him between my knees and folded my arms over his head.

Behind us the whole world broke into an uproar of screams and shouts, insane bellowings, animal-like howlings that stabbed the ears and scraped the scalp like jagged fragments of glass. I learned for the first time that screams of agony and terror are distinguishable, each from the other. Individual screams wove through all the other screams like writhing threads of flashing scarlet—threads that strangely enough were outside myself and at the same time squirmed and twisted through my own brain.

CHAPTER XXVII

IT's TRUE that Dessalines had the face and body of a giant toad ; but from what I've seen of toads, they're gentle creatures, never harmful to anyone or destructive to anything except pests that make unceasing trouble for mankind. So I think it's a gratuitous insult to toads to liken Dessalines to them. Yet he ought to be likened to something in the animal kingdom : for there was that about his thoughts and actions which was wholly unlike the thoughts and actions of those we call human beings.

To be accurate, he was more like a mink, which is unspeakably cruel, unpredictably vicious, possessed of amazing powers of endurance, wary in the highest degree, and capable of travelling vast distances and appearing where nobody would ever expect it to appear. It will go into a duck pond in broad daylight to gambol kitten-like before the fascinated gaze of a hundred ducks, only to return stealthily in the dark and cut the throats of all those ducks for the mere pleasure of killing—and, in a small way, this is just the sort of thing that seemed second nature to Dessalines.

We tried not to see those contorted bodies, piled in heaps, lying singly under bushes where they'd crawled to escape the hacking machetes, some wrapped in each other's arms, pitiful testimony to the ineffectiveness of love.

I tried to think calmly. Dessalines, Lamartinière, all the Negro officers, were no longer in sight. If they'd forgotten us, there was just a bare chance that we might get away from this accursed spot   provided we could plan fast enough and effectively enough ; but to think rapidly and clearly after what we had seen and heard, and with the knowledge that we were wholly helpless to defend ourselves, wasn't easy.

Autremont was possessed, even still, that we might find some sort of security by returning to Beau-Bouclier. Why not ? he demanded. Hadn't he lived in safety there for years ? There was no use reminding the dazed man that his house was burned ; that he was ruined. Like so many men of property in the hour of catastrophe, he couldn't believe that his former way of life had gone for ever.

King Dick scratched his head and said that if there was a way to cross the mountains in safety, so as to reach the valley of the Artibonite, we could get help from Ti-Bobo—but for the life of him he couldn't figure how Lydia could go safely.

Only Lydia insisted that we should stay where we were. " One of us dared speak his mind to Dessalines," she argued, " and Dessalines did nothing. When Dessalines decides to kill, he doesn't hesitate. Since he didn't kill us then, I don't believe he is going to. Therefore I think we're as safe here as anywhere."

It was a mistake to hope Dessalines had forgotten.

If we were going to stay where we were, King Dick said, we had to have food, and food wouldn't fly into our mouths ; we had to get it or arrange for somebody to bring it to us.

When he got to his feet to make those arrangements, a black soldier rose up from behind a bush and told him politely we were to stay until the general gave orders to the contrary.

At dusk one of Lamartinière's mulatto officers came down from the veranda and spoke to the sentry, saluted King Dick punctiliously, presented General Dessalines' compliments, and said the general was now ready to speak to us.

He and a dozen of his officers were in a half-wrecked room whose dirty windows overlooked the field in which lay those hundreds of hacked bodies. The room was full of flies and smelled horribly.

Dessalines was hunched over a table made from an old green shutter laid across two rum casks. His nose worked irritably, and he looked ready to spring at the first of us who displeased him.

He blinked at me. " You have been how long on this island, Citizen American ? " he asked abruptly.

" I landed at Cap François on the twenty-fifth of January," I said. I could hardly believe my own words. That was only fourteen days ago, so that the strange and dreadful events that made all my life hitherto seem so idle and so peaceful had happened within two weeks.

" It was your intention to return to America ? " Dessalines asked. I said it was.

He pointed his wrinkled black forefinger at Lydia. " With this lady ? " " Yes."

" You've been here only fourteen days," Dessalines said, " yet you speak Creole. I wish that explained."

I thought it wiser not to mention the French in Philadelphia. " My boyhood," I told him, " was spent in Canada, where two kinds of French are spoken—accurate French and careless French. I learned to speak both, and discovered that it wasn't difficult to change careless French into Creole by a twist of the tongue. I've done the same here : twisted— perhaps ' softened ' is better—careless French into Creole."

Dessalines made grunting sounds, glanced suspiciously at Lydia and Autremont ; then, dissatisfied, turned again to me. " Where are your sympathies ? " he asked abruptly.

" Where every decent man's are," I said. " With the weak—with those imposed upon and mistreated—those who have had to suffer injustices."

" You're against slavery ? "

" With all my heart."

Dessalines blinked. " That is good ! Citizen Général Toussaint sent you to find your friends, so it's my duty to keep you and your friends safe and sound until we meet him. For your own purposes you've darkened your skin and made yourself one of us ; therefore it's only right that I should treat you like one of us. I have use for a secretary. You will be my secretary. I make you a part of my army and you will remain near me at all times. It is a safe place during a war, for I am invulnerable. That is because I strike first and where I am not expected. See that you are always at hand. I am not patient."

" General," I said, " I know nothing about being a soldier——"

Dessalines cackled. "You will to-morrow, Citizen American. To-morrow you will be one of Dessalines' veterans."

" But I can't leave my friends," I said. " I was sent here—Toussaint himself ordered it—I was told to come for this lady and to arrange for her safety. Where's the safety if she marches with an army ? "

Dessalines lowered his head. " I said nothing about the lady marching ! What are you trying to do ? Give orders to Dessalines ? "

" No," I said, " but the lady's in my charge. I refuse to leave her ! "

" Merde ! " Dessalines shouted. " You refuse ? Christ and his fifteen black apostles ! You need reminding ! " He banged both fists on the table : then turned to the window and shouted hoarsely to a sentry outside. " Bring one of my prisoners—one of those 'Ti Blancs."

He sat glowering at me until the sentry returned, escorting one of the unfortunates who had been brought in by Dessalines' troops—a helpless-looking shopkeeper in a linen suit too tight for him.

" Get away from that prisoner ! " Dessalines shouted to the sentry. Almost in the same moment he dragged a cannon-like pistol from his belt and fired it from the window. The tight linen coat of the prisoner blossomed redly with glistening blood. The man stared down at that horrifying gush with a look of puzzled amazement, touched his hand to it, and immediately slumped to the ground like a wet towel.

Dessalines tossed the pistol to one of his officers, who reloaded it.

" Pay attention to what you see," Dessalines told me. " I care nothing for anybody ! I make my own plans ! Anyone who hinders me, I kill him ! You are coming with me, where you'll be safe. This lady and her children I shall send to my wife at St. Marc. There they too will be safe, unless——"

He reached over, snatched his newly-loaded pistol from the officer, peered into the muzzle, rapped it on the table to knock powder into the pan, and cocked it sharply.

"—unless you get in my way and I have to kill you."

I looked from the pistol to Lydia.

" M. Hamlin," she said quickly to Dessalines, " is as grateful as M. d'Autremont and I are."

Dessalines snorted. " He does well to be ! I've cut off the ears of men who seemed only half-grateful ! "

He turned to King Dick. " Mon Général, escort these people to my palace in St. Marc, and when you arrive there pile firewood in all public buildings. Send supplies to the Artibonite, where they'll be safe if we need them. If those French sons of mules ever try to take St. Marc, they're to get a mouthful of hot ashes and nothing else ! Understand ? "

King Dick gave Dessalines a sweeping salute, turned on his heel and pushed Lydia, the boys, and Autremont from the room.

That was how I came to be the henchman of the worst man in the world.

The creature was actually in need of a secretary. Like most of the black officers in Toussaint's army, he could neither read nor write. He had two other secretaries, both jet-black ; but they were so swollen by their own importance, that they couldn't move without posing, speak without bragging, or take dictation without elegantly elaborating the simplest sentences. At the end of my second day with Dessalines, he found he didn't need to dictate letters to me, but had only to give me the sense of what he wanted said. Thereafter he used his black secretaries as messengers, and all the letter-writing fell to me.

Not only was Dessalines a demon of energy, but he had the gift of instilling a corresponding vigour into all his lackadaisical black soldiers, who at first sight seemed to be hopelessly addicted to lolling under a bush and inflexibly determined to do nothing.

I've heard it said a thousand times that Negroes don't make good soldiers or good officers, but there never was a more mistaken idea. Any man makes a good soldier if he's properly trained, if he's led by good officers, and if he knows he's fighting in a good cause. In this respect black men are no different from white men. As to making good officers, those who read history can judge for themselves.

An hour after Dessalines had condemned me to be his secretary, he had rounded up his little army and was on the march. The noise of that marching was unbelievable, and I was sure that the French would promptly learn what was being so freely said by everyone in those shuffling, cackling black battalions : that we were going north to meet reinforce-ments—north to join Toussaint and Christophe—north to find a place where the French would have trouble finding us.

The French in Port-au-Prince could certainly see us, and there were times when I suspected they could even hear and smell us. We went openly along the dusty hot road towards the northern mountains, with Dessalines at the head of the column, surrounded by a score of black officers ; and behind him the long line of ragged black men wrangled in high-pitched voices, fired their guns at wheeling buzzards, and chewed unceasingly on sticks of sugar cane.

If this was the way Dessalines chose to move, I thought, he certainly was a poor leader. Not only was discipline non-existent in those straggling ranks, but Dessalines actually invited disaster by failing to send out advance scouts, flankers or a rearguard.

Towards sundown we passed through a notch in the foothills of the mountains. The blue water of the Bight of Léogane, long visible on our left, was now cut from our sight, as was far-off Port-au-Prince. Once through the notch, Dessalines halted that long and slovenly line of soldiers, and from that moment he was another man.

The halting-place was the side of a valley, so that the little black army was ranged on a slope, as in an amphitheatre. Dessalines climbed down from his horse and stood at the foot of the slope, a figure that would have been ludicrous but for its malevolence. He had a habit of putting his hands behind his back, lacing his fingers, and then squeezing and twisting his hands together as if in agony. When he spoke, his entire face—nose, forehead, cheeks, chin—writhed and worked in sympathy with his hands ; beads of sweat trickled from under the red bandanna that bound his head ; his voice rasped like sandpaper.

" Now then," he croaked, " you have diverted yourself long enough with sugar cane and laughter, and that is all ended. The Blancs who came into Port-au-Prince to send you back to the cane fields, they saw you eat your sugar cane and march off to the north, and they said to each other, ' Look at those black sons of goats ! What do they know about war ! They are good for nothing, fit only to be slaves ! We'll hurry after them and catch them in a pocket ! We'll smash them with guns, hack them with swords, and leave not one of them alive—not one ! ' " His laugh was fiendish.

" Well, my children, we will show those Blancs something unexpected ! While they are running after us, we'll skirt softly through the hills, beyond Croix des Bouquets, and strike the Blancs in the rear.

" Now listen to what I say. I'll break all the teeth of any man who laughs too loudly on this journey before us. I'll cut off the ears of any man who fires a gun. With my own sword I'll carve the legs from any man who struggles or stops for sugar cane. So take care ! Follow me quietly, each one, do not let yourself get sleepy, pay no attention to your stomach when it squeaks for food, and for ever afterward you can say to the whole world, ' Look at me ! Look ! In 1802 the Blancs sent all their great generals to make a slave of me again, but Dessalines and I made fools of them. Dessalines and I, we tricked them ! Dessalines and I stole past them like shadows ! Dessalines and I went without food, spoke in whispers, marched day and night on paths that would stop a goat ! Thus Dessalines and I, free men of Haiti, outwitted those who despised us : outwitted the great Boudet, who drove the English out of Guadaloupe ! Not even the armies of Bonaparte could make slaves of us again ! ' "

He turned away and called his officers around him. Lamartinière was given command of the advance scouts ; another was left in charge of a rearguard to watch the French and help messengers who might come hunting for Dessalines ; others were set to keep strict silence in the ranks. That straggling horde of ragamuffins suddenly and miraculously became an army shuffling silently off into the night like big black spiders.

There was little enough laughter in that army of Dessalines' after it turned and set off by a mountain path in the direction from which it had come. That path gave me a better understanding of why those black soldiers were so ragged. If they hadn't been barefoot, the mud-holes of the trail would have sucked the boots from their feet. Thorns and taloned vines reached from the roadside thickets to slash their pantaloons to ribbons. Roots tripped them, showers drenched them, the sour stench of sweat was heavy in their clothes, and the wonder was that they had any garments at all upon them.

By the grace of God I had a horse to ride, a stunted pony that groaned when it walked and constantly puffed out its belly in an effort to loosen up the cinch.

When daylight came we were far to the southward of Croix des Bouquets. The whole plain of the Cul de Sac lay before us, and the inland salt lake and marshes in which that valley ends. Port-au-Prince was far, far away, to our right, a pale blot on the rim of the hazy line of the Bight of Léogane.

We'd had no rest all night, except for brief halts to prevent straggling ; and Dessalines gave us no rest now. We went on down towards that stagnant salt lake, rimmed with salt marshes, and as we went he dictated letters to his wife—to Toussaint, to Christophe. From them I found out for the first time that we were bound for Léogane ; but from his own men Dessalines kept our destination a secret. When he told me the name of the town, he whispered it, rolling protuberant frog-eyes suspiciously at the officers near us.

We skirted the salt lake through marshes alive with birds. Some might have been transplanted straight from the marshes of Portland : yellow-legs, plover, curlew, green herons, night herons.

Hundreds upon hundreds of scarlet flamingos, taller than a man, flapped upward from the canebrakes and went drifting off across the lake in rosy clouds. We saw ibis, egrets, jacanas, grebes, coots that looked like hens, and untold millions of small shore birds that teetered their tails in unison, rose in unison, wheeled above us in unison and dimmed the sun like wisps of fog from off the sea. Far out in the shallow water lay crocodiles eyeing us malevolently, paddling sluggishly abreast of us with turned-up noses, as if disgusted at our failure to fall among them and be eaten.

The bottom of this shallow, evil-smelling lake was honeycombed with holes as large as my wrist, and the hurrying soldiers ran into the water, thrust their hands into those holes up to the shoulder, and triumphantly emerged clutching greenish fish the size and shape of small black bass. From these fish the black men squeezed the intestines ; then ate them as they'd have eaten bananas.

To hungry men, any food tastes good, and I found those fish as welcome as a St. John River salmon. Perhaps those particular fish had sweeter flesh than other raw fish ; certainly they were peculiar, for each one had in its mouth innumerable baby fish, half an inch in length.

Once beyond the lake and in the foothills of the mountains that guarded the southern side of the Cul de Sac, we turned westward. All that day and all that night we went on and on. The foothills through which we marched were forested with gigantic trees whose branches were hung with grey moss that looked like old men's beards.

Again the Bight of Léogane came into view, but the mere sight of those cool blue waters was our only refreshment. Dessalines wouldn't let us stop. I think there was something inside him that kept him from feeling fatigue, just as there was something inside him that made him merciless. The faces of his officers and men, black to begin with, had taken on a dusty haggardness, and they lurched and staggered in their walk. Yet Dessalines, when he turned to look at that lurching, wavering column, showed the same ferocity I'd seen in his face when he ordered the death of the white prisoners at Croix des Bouquets. He was pitiless and tireless, and I knew he'd stay so till the day he died.

By noon we were abreast of Port-au-Prince, by nightfall we had reached the headwaters of the long and winding Léogane River—the Grande Rivière du Léogane. There we rested while Dessalines reviewed his troops in the dusk, as if to make sure they were still with him.

I didn't dare sit down for fear I'd fall asleep and never wake up.

All night he drove us and drove us down that tortured river-bed, herding us on and on, threatening his men with a pistol the size of a cannon. " March on, march on ! " he croaked repeatedly. " Step-mother of Christ, do you want Bonaparte's Blancs to catch you ? Get on there, you horned animals ! Pick up your feet, you insects, or by the chamber pot of the Virgin I'll blow your backsides through your ears ! "

CHAPTER XXVIII

IF I WERE doomed to live in Haiti, I'd as soon live in Léogane as any-where. The town stands on a promontory with water on three sides of it, and from the shore it has something the look of a squatty medieval castle, set firmly on a rock and fronting upon a beautiful expanse—the whole sweep of the Bight of Léogane with the island of La Gonave swimming in the centre : to the left a huddled throng of mountains marching bluely off towards the far end of the southern peninsula : to the right and straight ahead that sea of peaks beyond which was Cap François and safety. Madame Beauharnais, mother-in-law of Joséphine Bonaparte, had a beautiful plantation in Léogane—until Dessalines burned it.

There's a mountain behind Léogane, lying between the river and the town, and Dessalines was across that mountain within an hour after daybreak, squinting down at the town, peering for signs of the French army along the road that ran out of Léogane towards Port-au-Prince.

Lamartinière and his advance guard were waiting there for Dessalines

—the first time I'd seen him since we'd started down out of the mountains for the salt lake on the preceding day—twenty-four hours that seemed like twenty-four years.

" No French," he reported to Dessalines. " No French anywhere." Dessalines' laugh was hyena-hoarse. " There soon will be," he said.

We slipped and slid down the mountain into a valley even richer than the Cul de Sac, the Artibonite or the Great North Plain. In places the sugar cane was twice as high as a man ; the plantation houses were closer together and airier ; every foot of the lowland was cultivated, and each plantation house had its own small distillery. In the hot morning sun the whole green valley steamed with richness, and from it rose a cloying sweet fragrance of rum and sugar.

Dessalines scrambled alongside his column with unbelievable rapidity. He hunched himself over his horse's neck, so that I somehow thought of him as moving on all-fours, like an angry black animal, barking at his soldiers, spurring them on, threatening them with dire retribution if they dared to straggle.

All those men were tired—not so tired as I, probably, for black men in a hot country have powers of endurance beyond the understanding of most white men. None the less, they were dog-tired, and certainly they were as hungry as they were tired. I doubt that anyone but Dessalines could have prevented them from breaking ranks and helping themselves to sugar cane, and I don't know whether it was the ferocity of Dessalines' manner that kept them from straggling, or the knowledge that he was driving and starving them for their own good.

He went jouncing up and down the line, a black djinn with rolling yellow eyes, elbows flapping like a bat's wings. Even now I can hear his hoarse hell's voice : " Get forward there, you one-legged dogs ! More speed, more speed ! Do you want to be castrated by Blancs ? "

How I hated that voice !

It wasn't out of kindness that he left me at the crossroads outside the town, with a score of sentries sent to guard his stores and ammunition, but because he didn't want to run the risk of losing the first competent secretary he'd ever had.

I hoped he would never come back when he led his column of eight hundred dilapidated, ragged, slack-lipped black ghosts on and on towards Léogane. I could see it winding like a snake through the cool green shadow of the sugar cane.

Then my heart sank at the thought of anything happening to him. I had to get back to Lydia ; and what would become of this black army if it were deprived of Dessalines' furious energy, I didn't like to think. Suddenly I began to hope with all my heart that he'd be safe, and for the first time knew how politicians feel when, for purely personal reasons, they support bad men and bad measures.

The serpentine black column vanished into sunlit Léogane on its promontory, dazzling white above the shimmering blue of the bight, a peaceful jewel against the lavender-and-violet setting of the far-off mountains to the north.

A hazy, wavering plume of smoke, grey against the distant purple mountains, rose from one of the houses. Dots that were people came out from the town and crawled about like disturbed ants.

Surprisingly, then, there were hurrying mulattoes close at hand, pelting towards high land on foot, with bundles in their arms ; mulattoes on muleback and donkeyback ; mulattoes in heavy-laden carts. Dogs barked in the plantation houses near us, and people shouted. There was a hurrying and scurrying all around us. Men, women, children darted from house to house, ran like fearful mice from one cane patch to another.

The wisps of smoke above Léogane became dark and thick, and flowered into a towering thunderhead—an ominous cloud that drifted slowly to the westward and was constantly replenished at its base by uprushes of blacker smoke.

The slowly boiling clouds of smoke surged and billowed, as if the heat within them were too violent to be restrained ; and then the smoke was rent apart by a burst of flame that mounted up and up above the town, a roaring volcanic jet of reds and yellows, rimmed with black as by a billion swarming, seething black bees.

I couldn't get the idea of swarming black bees out of my head. Fragments of that crawling flame-rim seemed almost to fly like smaller swarms to settle upon plantation houses outside the town, there to erect new cone-shaped clouds of smoke like beehives on which other swirling black nesses rose heavenward. East of the town, west of the town, all up and down the valley, those conical beehives of flame, of turbulent smoke, of swirling dark thunderheads, spread and came closer with all-pervasive buzzings and hummings such as might have come from countless angry, droning bees.

Black soldiers were around us again, twittering with excitement, laughing and chattering like hysterical women.

Then Dessalines too was there, as if he'd materialised from smoke. He glared at me, his thick lips working ; then stood in his stirrups to look westward along the road to Port-au-Prince. His eyebrows and eyelashes were singed, his once-white plush breeches were spattered with blood, smeared with soot, and had a hole the size of a teacup burned in them. He screamed hoarsely for Lamartinière.

When Lamartinière didn't appear, he drew his sword, thrust it between the legs of a passing soldier, and brought him to an ignominious halt. " Lamartinière ! " he croaked. " God's stepmother, can't you hear? Get Lamartinière ! " His arms twitched ; his eyes rolled ; he swung his big head from side to side as if possessed with a longing to hack someone to pieces.

Lamartinière rode up to him, his white skin cool and clean-looking among all the blacks.

" Take two hundred men," Dessalines shouted to him. " Go along the Port-au-Prince road to the mouth of the river ; burn every house between the mountain and the sea ; then join me where we left the river this morning. If there's a house left standing in this valley, Lamartinière, I'll hold you to blame ! Pour rum on everything and set it afire ! Kill some horses and throw 'em in the wells ! Leave nothing for Boudet ! Don't let your men get drunk, Lamartinière, because we've got to travel fast and far ! And don't let 'em kill any more Blancs ! Take 'em with you ! Use 'em to carry provisions ! I've thought of a better place to kill 'em ! "

He bared his teeth in ferocious amiability, and waved us on.

As we climbed the mountain behind Léogane, I could see the French moving out from Port-au-Prince, a long, long line of soldiers in white. At that great distance those white-clad veterans of Bonaparte's campaigns seemed slow, but a haze of dust hung above the guns that moved at the head of the line, so they were hurrying.

They were after us. They expected to catch Dessalines red-handed, and all the rest of us, too. Well, they wouldn't do it, not with Dessalines leading us. I found myself taking a sort of pride in that monster's ferocity : found myself admiring him because he'd outwitted the French ; because he'd left every plantation house in that valley an inferno, every distillery sending up blue flames from blazing rum, every cane field trampled and flattened, and every house in Léogane a smouldering pile of embers !

Long before the French reached that scene of desolation we were high up in the pine forests, so high that we were out of the tropics and the wind had the smell of approaching winter—a smell, almost, of New England's frost, wood-smoke, and evergreens.

CHAPTER XXIX

THAT was the beginning of a chase that must have been as maddening to Boudet and all those other veterans of Bonaparte's campaigns as it was wearisome to us. In his tireless marching, Dessalines was like a big black four-footed night hunter—a cougar, say, seen one night in a given spot, only to appear, the next night, threescore miles away. He taught me more about endurance than I had ever dreamed ; and while I naturally would never have chosen him as a teacher, yet I had him for a teacher willy-nilly ; and to give him his due, I suspect that if I hadn't had the benefit of his teachings in the ugly business of war, I wouldn't be alive to-day. They call war an art, but it isn't. It largely consists in outwitting people, robbing widows and orphans, and inflicting suffering on the helpless for one's own ends—and that's not art : that's business.

From him I learned that a soldier should never hesitate or delay, once a course of action has been decided on : should strike fast, pursue fast. I learned that war has much in common with hunting for the market, which consists in knowing where the game is, stealing up on it fast and silently, lying in wait without moving for hours if need be, intercepting it when it tries to escape, and killing everything in range. From him I learned, too, that a good soldier can starve his men and exhaust them in order to reach an objective ahead of an enemy, since success is worth more than food and drink, and prolonged rest ; learned that men will march better and fight better if told exactly where they're going and why.

What little food we had when we dodged away from Léogane we ate on the march, and it was always Negro food—salt codfish, rice, manioc flour, sugar cane, bananas, breadfruit, and custard-apples filled with a creamy substance like my aunt's sea-moss blanc-mange.

While we scrambled in and out of the ravines and over the hog-backs of the high mountains, Dessalines was for ever clambering up on a coign of vantage from which he could view the far-off town of Port-au-Prince. He hoped, I knew, for an opportunity to swoop down upon it and destroy it and all the Frenchmen in it ; and our only chances to rest were those he gave us when he lay behind a pinnacle of rock, a telescope glued to his eye, to study his chances of success. Even while he ate, he studied and squinted at the city : even while he studied and squinted he sent out spies and messengers, and dictated letters.

" I have made a fool of Boudet and burned Léogane," he wrote to Toussaint, " and am now hoping to burn Port-au-Prince. If Boudet is too careful, I'll circle back to Croix des Bouquets and let Boudet have another chance to catch me there, or perhaps in St. Marc."

He used strange people for messengers, having a special fancy for big-bottomed crones, who quivered as they took their orders from Dessalines ; then went, wagging their hips, down from the mountains and into Port-au-Prince, baskets of vegetables balanced on their heads, as imperturbably as if war and its consequences were a million miles away.

" I like 'em old and fat," he told me hoarsely. " Then they keep their minds on what they're doing, not always hoping for rape, rape, rape ! "

Next to fat women he favoured married couples who owned donkeys.

" No Frenchman going to stop a man riding on a donkey while his woman walks behind him with food on her head," he assured me. " Man riding that way, he looks too honest to be worth stopping."

When his messengers came back, they had the same tale to tell. Boudet had thrown a ring of sentries around the city and had no intention of being taken by surprise ; so Dessalines, grumbling and growling, stayed all night where he was. All around us the men slept as they had marched—in long, irregular lines, without fires, without blankets—the first night's rest we'd had ever since we'd set off from Croix des Bouquets. They relieved themselves openly, like animals, without moving more than a step from the spot on which they'd chosen to sleep. The night air sharpened the stench of their excrement and the acrid odour of their bodies—the sour, bitter, dirty-horse smell of stink-bush leaves after a September frost.

At dawn the next morning three French regiments came out from the town, marching straight towards the spot where Dessalines lay watching them.

This ended any possibility that Port-au-Prince could be surprised and burned ; so off we went again, up into, through, and out of the log-wood and mahogany forests : into that other higher world of towering pines and cold winds, where innumerable swallows wheeled and swooped, where turquoise, orange, and black butterflies the size of seagulls clustered on ferns as large as apple trees.

The French didn't follow us far, not that time ; for the route over which Dessalines led us would have killed men as weightily laden and as cumbersomely clothed as were those French soldiers.

Five days from the time when we had first set eyes on Croix des Bouquets we were back again at those miserable crossroads, and when we came in sight of the ruined plantation house, Dessalines told his men to be at ease. Instantly his army ceased to be an army and again became a mob—lighting fires all over the place ; cooking salt fish and rice in kettles with yams, bananas, pimentos, garlic ; firing off muskets at nothing ; gambling with their everlasting black and white beans ; filling the day and the night with yammering and high laughter.

The bodies in the field across from the plantation house were still unburied, and they stunk with a revolting sweet stench that rose up stranglingly about us to the sound of far-off humming like that of a distant stormy ocean—a persistent low murmuring that rose to angry roarings, then subsided only to rise again in a crescendo of buzzing. This was the sound of millions of flies feasting upon the heaps of dead.

Dessalines was as crafty as a black devil out of hell. All those camp fires he let his men light at Croix des Bouquets, all the chattering and shrill laughter, all the defenceless carelessness with which his soldiers slouched about the place, gambling, dozing, drinking, singing, chewing sugar cane, were for the purpose of misleading the French again.

What he was up to he wouldn't tell any of his officers ; but he told me, so that I could write to his wife—which was how I learned that he really loved her. That was a mighty strange thing about Dessalines : he was like an animal in that he helped himself freely and with a sort of open bestiality to any woman who caught his fancy ; and yet he was true to his wife in his own savage way. All other women were mere passing conveniences to him—and this was a piece of knowledge that proved of inestimable value to all of us.

I'll trap these Frenchmen (he had me write to his wife—and the

G

endearments he used to her were something astounding, his favourite being " Zoie " or goose). I'll not only trap them, my sweet goose ; I'll prove to you I'm right about them. All Frenchmen believe and say no people on earth are able to think as logically or reason as clearly as they ; but I say they're wrong. Most Frenchmen, 'ti Zoie, are ignorant, stubborn, and small-minded, for ever led by their strange obsession into trouble from which they extricate themselves—if at all—with the greatest difficulty.

Now this very Boudet, my little one, is the same Boudet who once captured Gaudaloupe. He's been honoured by the great Bonaparte ; he's practised French clarity of thought in Paris itself ; so he is sure that no black man could possibly outwit him. And, of course, being a fair soldier as soldiers go, he's determined to exterminate me at any cost.

Well, my soft-breasted goose, that very determination of his will destroy him and bring your Puss to you no later than the 22nd February, and this is what will happen.

Boudet, sitting angrily in Port-au-Prince, will learn that the great Dessalines is at Croix des Bouquets, resting after his long march to Léogane, and about to start for his home at St. Marc with his worthless black soldiers. Being a soldier, a Frenchman, and a master of logic, Boudet will at once understand that here is his great opportunity to catch your Puss between two jaws of a vice and squeeze him to death.

What will Boudet do ? I will tell you, my goose, and you will see that your black Puss thinks more clearly than that white Boudet ! Boudet will set out to catch your Puss front and rear. He will divide his forces. A part he will send by land, to catch me at St. Marc. The other part he will send by sea, so to fall upon me from the rear when I turn to fight. Then your Puss will chop him and hack him. Your Puss will blow his men from guns and impale his officers on bamboo. Your Puss will push coconuts up into their bellies and break the coconuts with cocomacaques !

He snatched the letter from me when it was finished, laboriously scratched a dozen crosses and an equal number of symbolic devices at the bottom, and with difficulty signed " Puss " to the whole.

Puss ! Good God—Puss ! And yet, why not ? " Puss," applied to Dessalines, was no more incongruous than " Honest John " or "statesman " applied to the thieves and mountebanks who blunderingly conduct the affairs of all the world.

We came straggling into St. Marc on the nineteenth of February, as sorry-looking an army as ever was. The men, barefoot to begin with, were still play-acting for the benefit of Boudet's spies, carrying their muskets every which way, wearing their ragged jackets unbuttoned, slouching helter-skelter without discipline, seemingly out of hand—a mere rabble of field hands pretending to be soldiers.

That town of St. Marc might have been created out of tinsel and painted canvas as a spectacle to amaze wayfarers. It lay at the bottom of the Bay of St. Marc, which was small and pouch-shaped, and the colour of a robin's egg ; and it was partly on a hill-slope, so that the houses ranged around the slope were like boxes in a theatre, fronting upon the beautiful small bay as on a stage.

All the houses were bright coloured—yellow, white, blue, pink—and framed in a billowing green foliage, from which they shone like jewels. For years, I learned, St. Marc had been a summer playground for wealthy French planters : then, when Toussaint's revolution had been successful and abandoned estates had been turned over to officers and ex-slaves, scores of black generals had hurried to St. Marc to buy or build themselves summer residences befitting their new stations in life.

Behind the town, like dark thunderheads, were the steep slopes of the Cahos Mountains, beyond which lay the valley of the Artibonite.

The central part of the town, close to the bay, was a miniature Cap François, its plaza stone-paved, its shops filled with jewels, dresses, and Parisian perfumes.

Dominating everything was Dessalines' palace on a headland at the southern point of the bay—a palace all white except for its roof and the tall fluted columns that held up the veranda, the roof black and the columns black with gold capitals and bases, extremely barbaric.

Behind the plaza, on the flat land at the foot of the hills, were the barracks of Dessalines' army, and waiting before the barracks, with a guard of honour—if two hundred shoeless black men in tattered trousers and ripped coats, unarmed except for clubs, could be called a guard of honour—were King Dick and several lesser officers.

While Dessalines' officers deployed their men in a long line before the barracks, Dessalines kicked his horse in the stomach and rode it up to King Dick, who saluted smartly. King Dick's two hundred men stood rigidly at attention, but the wide white eyes they rolled at Dessalines were like white butterflies in the dark.

" Any French anywhere ? " Dessalines asked.

King Dick said there weren't.

" This place ready to burn ? "

" Every place."

" Supplies ? " Dessalines asked.

" They've gone across the mountains to the Artibonite," King Dick said. " Four hundred cartloads to Verrettes."

Dessalines looked around at his ragged army, lined up in eight companies across the length of the drill-ground.

" Sir," I said, " If you haven't any immediate use of me——"

" Oh, Grandmother of Jesus Christ ! " Dessalines cried. " For ever thinking of women ! You'll stay with me——" He broke off glowering.

" No : go ahead ! Go to the palace and see that woman of yours ! " He stabbed his forefinger at King Dick. " Take him there, mon Général. Introduce him to my wife."

He leaned from his saddle to whisper hoarsely in my ear, " She'll give you dispatches from Toussaint and Christophe. Have them ready for me. And give my wife a letter. Write it as soon as you reach the palace. Sign it for me. I'll be there in an hour and I want to find her in bed ! "

He laughed, hyena-like, and pulled his horse's head around to face his long line of troops.

As King Dick and I kicked our horses out of the barracks yard I could hear Dessalines' wolfish voice, taking his army into his confidence. " I give you two days in which to rest, my children," I heard him shout. " Then you will go with me to teach the Blancs a lesson. My mind is made up, my children. There is only one way we can be free, and that is to rid ourselves of all Blancs for ever."

That was all I heard, but it was plenty.

" Well," I said to King Dick as we rode through the narrow streets of St. Marc towards the white, gold, and black palace on the headland, " thank God I'm free from that butcher, even for a few minutes ! What's the news ? How's Lydia ? "

" Lydia ? " King Dick asked vaguely. " She's all right, I guess. My goo'ness me my, oh yes."

" You *guess* ! " I said. " Don't you *know* ? Haven't you seen her ? Isn't she living at the palace ? "

" Now, Albion," King Dick protested, " no sense getting all excited. You wait till Madame Dessalines tell you everything."

" By God," I cried, " something *has* happened to her ! She's sick ! "

" No, no ! My goo'ness me no ! King Dick cried. " Everything all right ! You wait till we see Madame Dessalines and then you understand everything all right."

When I stormed at him, in a frenzy of apprehension, he only hunched up his shoulders and kicked his horse to a gallop, as if to escape my importunities.

Something, I knew, had gone wrong. What that something was, I couldn't even guess ; but after the manner of lovers at the merest faint hint of trouble, a score of tangled horrors whirled through my suddenly incoherent mind : she was dead ; she had fallen in love with another ; she had come to some terrible harm because her disguise had failed ; she had caught the smallpox, the yellow fever ; she was lost to me for ever. . . .

Show me a man supposed to be in love who isn't half insane, and I'll show you a man who's not in love.

CHAPTER XXX

Such was my mental turmoil, when we reached that gaudy palace, that I saw as in a trance the servants who let us through the gates ; the servants who ran beside us to the palace portico and held our horses ; the servants who pounded the knocker of the great front door ; the servants who waited to take our hats and usher us into a reception-room. How I contrived, with muscles quivering and mind a-churn, to write the letter that Dessalines had ordered me to write, I cannot say ; but write it I did, and other servants came from nowhere and took it from me to bear it off and up a marble staircase in search of Madame Dessalines.

I didn't even know how Madame Dessalines entered the room. All I knew was that suddenly she was there, looking up at me, and in those first moments I only saw that she was young.

My manners as well as my thoughts had left me, and I could only stare at her and repeat the one word, " Lydia."

" Your friend has told you ? " she asked, nodding at King Dick. She spoke in French, perfectly, like a Frenchwoman.

" Nothing," I said. " He's told me nothing ! She's ill—she's——"

" No, my dear M. Hamlin. By the greatest of good fortune we—your friend and I—were able to send her in safety to Cap François."

" Cap François ! " I said. " She's gone ! I—you had no right—she should have remained here—I'll never see her again ! "

Madame Dessalines took me by the elbow, as she might have taken a sick person, and turned me towards a chair. When I sank into it, she stood before me and spoke severely.

" Listen to yourself, M. Hamlin ! ' I,' you say ! ' I,' you think ! ' I'll never see her again ! ' ' I, I, I ! ' "

" Yes," I said. " That's true. But I—King Dick and I—we could have helped her. She could have depended on us. I'd have—that is, we could have——"

She smiled a twisted little smile and wagged a forefinger in my face. " My kind and good and love-sick young man, you must admit the truth to yourself. There are bad times like bad black storms coming in this country—even worse times than are already here. When they come, you can do nothing to help any person who is caught in those storms. Do you understand ? "

When I said nothing, she nodded at me wisely. " Now, M. Hamlin, I will tell you something I think you don't know. This Lydia of yours, she loves you. She is not wholly aware of it at this moment, but to me it is clear. Perhaps that will help you to be more of a philosopher about your great disappointment."

" She does ! " I said. " Are you sure ? How do you know ? "

From the depths of despair I rose as a drowning man rises into the sunlight from dark water, and for the first time I saw Madame Dessalines clearly.

Many men have tried to describe and explain the peculiar attraction of the coloured women of Haiti, but the truth seems to be that they are a race apart, developed by the fantastic quality of that island, and impossible to describe adequately to those who have never seen them.

Therefore I won't try to describe Marie-Jeanne Dessalines except to say she was slender, beautiful, graceful and golden-skinned. Her brown hair was bound by a pale blue turban, its fold fastened in front with a jet ornament from which rose a spray of fine white feathers ; and her dress, of yellow muslin with white figures stamped upon it, had short sleeves and was somehow gathered close beneath her breasts, so that it clung and swirled about her like the dress of a dancer.

" How do I know ? " Madame Dessalines asked. " I know because of the manner in which she looked at the letters you wrote for my husband ; because of the way she spoke of you ; because of her expression when she learned that we had found a fishing boat to take her to Cap François with that poor man M. d'Autremont, and his children." She stared at me wide-eyed. " You find this interesting, M. Hamlin ? "

" Oh my goo'ness me me my ! " King Dick murmured.

" Yes," I said. " I do. Are you implying that her expression was— that is, when you told her about the boat, was she——"

" In a way," Madame Dessalines said. " She has a great affection for those two children ; but in the moment after I told her to be ready to leave, I could see she had other thoughts. I could see she had been looking forward to your return. I could see that if her sense of responsibility for those children had not been great, she would have argued with me. I believe in my heart she would have preferred to stay here, dangerous though such a course would have been."

I stared at my hands, mahogany-coloured from the stain I'd put on them, and wondered how—and how soon—I could get to Cap François. My thoughts must have shown on my face ; for Madame Dessalines spoke up quickly.

" You cannot do it, my poor young man. For one thing, there is no other boat left in St. Marc."

When I looked at her despairingly, she shook her head. " No, M. Hamlin, you are wrong. You think she will be gone from Cap François before you get there. I promise you she will not. Of that I am sure. If M. d'Autremont wishes to go by boat to any place, he will be unable to do so, for the French have placed an embargo on all shipping. No vessels are allowed to sail. And if that poor half-crazed gentleman attempted to return to his plantation—and that fixed idea of his was one of the reasons that determined me to send him to Le Cap— he would be turned back by French sentries, no matter how hard he tried."

From outside came the sound of horses' hoofs and the shouting of orders. " Mon Dieu ! " Madame Dessalines cried. " He arrives ! "

From the bosom of her gown she drew a packet of dispatches, pressed them into my hand, and hurried to a wall-hanging which she drew aside to reveal a hidden door. She opened it ; then turned to me once more. " Compose yourself, unhappy lover. There is one other reason—the best reason of all—why your Lydia will remain in Cap François until you get there."

I waited eagerly to hear the reason, but she only smiled and let the wall-hanging fall behind her.

" One other reason," Madame Dessalines had said. " The best reason of all." I thought I knew what the reason was, and as I stared at the wall-hanging I must have had a fond and foolish smile upon my lips, for King Dick spoke to me sharply.

" Better read those messages—this no time for grinnying ! That Dessalines, he move pretty fast when he move, no matter what he do ! "

There were four dispatches from Toussaint and three from Christophe, and as I read them to King Dick, we saw what was happening to the north of us as clearly as though it were drawn upon a map.

On the fourteenth of February Leclerc had been reinforced by additional transports and battleships from France, so that he was now able to leave the captured coastal cities and set off into the mountains in pursuit of Christophe and Toussaint. Leclerc's available force, Toussaint wrote, was nine thousand veteran French and an unknown number of mulattoes and free Negroes who had hurried to join him. I didn't need to be told that if Leclerc's march should be successful, Toussaint and Christophe and their black regiments would have to fall back through the mountains and down into the coastal plain, where Boudet could strike from Port-au-Prince and destroy them.

King Dick stared at the ceiling when I had finished. " That bad," he said. " If Christophe and that old Toussaint get pushed across the mountains and something don't happen to Boudet, they only one place for me and you and Toussaint and Christophe and Dessalines to go ; right across into the Artibonite and live in bushes."

Inconsequently he added, " When you go back to United States, Albion, I go too. These black people, they almost too much for me, and I rather be in United States than here. Don't you try going anywhere alone, Albion : not without me. If they almost too much for me, they be altogether too much for you."

I thought he avoided my eyes.

" They're almost too much for you ? " I asked. " What are you hinting ? I don't like hinting ! If you know something, speak out ! "

King Dick shook his head. " All I know, they almost too much for me. Negroes hate mulattoes, mulattoes hate Negroes, big Negroes hate little Negroes, little Negroes hate big Negroes, poor mulattoes hate rich mulattoes for being rich, and hate other poor mulattoes for being poor, rich Negroes hate rich Negroes, Negroes don't hate mulatto women, Negro women rather sleep with white men than with Negroes, good Negroes hate bad Negroes, bad Negroes hate good Negroes, big Negroes hit little Negroes with cocomacaque, little Negroes let big Negroes hit 'em and cheat 'em, but won't let mulattoes or Blancs touch 'em . . ."

He shook his head, as if in despair at the peculiarities of all dark-skinned peoples.

" That's not new, is it ? " I asked. " It's never been almost too much for you before, has it ? What more have you found out ? "

" I not found out enough," King Dick said uneasily. " When I take those supplies to Verrettes, Ti-Bobo come from Mirebalais to see what happening. He say maroons in mountains, they stopped drumming."

" What are maroons ? " I asked.

" They black slaves who ran away to live in big forests, high up in mountains," he said. " They bad men, usually : oh, my goo'ness me my yes ! ' Maroon ' same as ' Cimarron,' and that what ' Cimarron ' mean —wild thing living on mountain-peak."

He seemed at a loss for words. " Ti-Bobo, he very thoughtful about those maroons. They very Voodoo. They drum, dance, drum all day, all night. Now they not drum. All together, all at one time, they not drum. Ti-Bobo say that means something he not like."

" And whatever it means, you don't like it either ? "

" Oh my goo'ness me my ! " King Dick said. " Very not ! That why I tell you not try go anywhere alone, in case you think it be nice to go Cap François or somewhere."

" I understand a part of what you're trying to tell me," I said, " but I don't understand all of it. You say maroons are runaway slaves— Negroes who've taken to the mountains to be free. You're implying that they're enemies ; but how can they be enemies to those who fight for freedom ? They insist on freedom for themselves, don't they ? If they were mulattoes, I could understand how they might be enemies ; but you say they're Negroes."

King Dick became more loquacious. " Oh my goo'ness me my Yes ! They very Nigra ! But they Voodoo, too. Dessalines, he not like Voodoo. He been very discouraging to Voodoo, because people who made Voodoo all night and listen to drum all day, they not work good. If workmen not work good, then plantations not make much money. If plantations not make much money, how you think Dessalines get this new palace— all this nice furniture out from Paris, France—all those uniforms—all those women—all those silver harnesses—all those three million francs in banks in Paris, France ? Oh my goo'ness No ! They no Voodoo allowed by Dessalines ! He put his foot down on it ! Put his foot down on Mambu and Hungan ! "

King Dick whipped up a black forefinger, levelled it dangerously, said " Boum ! Boum ! " and brusquely pushed the imaginary weapon back into his belt. I gathered that Dessalines' dislike of Voodoo had resulted in sudden death for many a maroon Hungan and Mambu.

" So you think that's how the minds of ignorant Negroes—bad Negroes—would work ? If Dessalines persecuted maroons because they were Voodoo-worshippers, they'd always want revenge ? That nothing else would matter ? That they'd think of nothing else ? "

" That what," King Dick said. " Big Negroes hate little Negroes, little Negroes hate big Negroes, poor Negroes hate rich Negroes——"

He broke off to listen to a distant commotion, a bumbling and rumbling that might have been the croaking of a giant frog far, far away. There was the sound of running feet : a knock on the door. It opened, and in the opening appeared a frightened black face. It gobbled Creole at us.

" Oh my goo'ness me my ! " King Dick said faintly. " That General Dessalines he very fast ! Already he said Howdy-do to his wife and got rested up ! Now he want those dispatches from Toussaint, and he want 'em quick ! "

CHAPTER XXXI

DESSALINES, in cocked hat, bejewelled coat, and white plush breeches, riding a shaggy steed through the mountains of Haiti, was an awesome spectacle ; but Dessalines striding bandy-legged around and around his wife's dressing-room in a dressing-gown of green brocade, decorated at sleeve and hem with triple rows of broad gold lace, was something out of an extravaganza. His enormous feet, shod in silver bedroom slippers, not only seemed loosely attached to his ankles, but stuck out as far behind as they did in front. Thus his heels looked prehensile, as though he could have hung from a branch by them if he had so desired.

I knew, the moment I saw him, that he was in an evil humour, for his under jaw was pushed forward so that his lower teeth were bared, and his sweaty black face glistened like a vanished squash.

" Christ's fifth cousin ! " he screamed, when I entered the room, " what kind of friend is this King Dick ? What do you think I'd have done to anyone who dared send away a woman of mine ? I'd have burned his legs off up to his hips ! "

Dessalines' attack took me by surprise, and I could only stand and stare at him, wondering why he should assail King Dick so suddenly and so furiously.

" My friend was only doing what he thought was best," I said. " I'm grateful to him, and to your wife, too, General."

There was a sort of satanic ferocity in Dessalines' voice. " You damned white fool ! What do you think'll happen to that woman if she ever gets to Cap François ? Don't you know the French'll tear off her clothes ; rape her ; rip her to pieces ? If you're a man, you'll find a way to go to Cap François yourself, through the mountains ! "

Now, why, I asked myself, should Dessalines advise the very thing that King Dick had warned against ? Why should he want me out of the way when, until an hour ago, I had been his trusted secretary ? Why was he resentful ? Resentful, that was it ! That shiny, warty face, the white foam at the corners of his lips, the flattened nose working like a rabbit's, those squinting eyes with the flecks of yellow upon the staring whites—everything about him was the epitome of resentment. Well, men resented a loss . . . or the possibility of a loss . . . and suddenly I knew what was passing through that dark and twisted brain. I knew beyond question that he had the mind of an Iago ; that he was raging at Lydia's escape because he himself had wanted her !

Hard on the heels of that realisation came another : of course Madame Dessalines had foreseen danger for Lydia if she remained in St. Marc ! The greatest danger of all was her own husband !

So the mind of Dessalines, Iago-like, was not only telling him that without Lydia I was of no further use to him : it was warning him that he'd better be rid of me on the chance that I might even prove somehow attractive to *his* woman.

Well, I might be wrong, of course ; but I was sure of one thing : the only way to get along with Dessalines was to pretend to agree with him. " I was going to suggest trying to reach Cap François," I said, " and I'm mighty grateful to you for being willing that I should do so. Since Toussaint sent King Dick here with me, perhaps you'll let him go with me, so that he can rejoin Toussaint."

" Yes, and perhaps I won't," Dessalines cried in a mincing voice that he doubtless considered an imitation of my own. " Don't you know we're trying to fight a war ? Christ's pastry-cook, what fools ! "

Croaking and grumbling, he flung himself on a sofa big enough for five people—a couch carved and encrusted with sphinxes' heads, lions' claws, griffins' wings, and brass inlay.

His thoughts seemed to leap about, as a monkey's does when he ceases searching himself for fleas and goes bounding off into a tree-top. " Read me those dispatches," he ordered.

" Before I read them," I said, " perhaps you'd better hear the information King Dick picked up at Verrettes."

" Merde ! " Dessalines cried. " Do as you're told ! I'm sick of people who try to regulate my acts and my thoughts. If I did what others want me to do, I wouldn't be Dessalines ! Read those dispatches ! "

During the reading he got to his feet and went prowling around the room, his silver slippers slapping like flails on the cream-coloured carpet. " Pah ! " he shouted when I had finished. " Let those Blancs come ! Let 'em come and find what Dessalines will leave for 'em ! I'll give 'em dead bodies to trip over ! I'll rot their guts with poisoned wells ! "

He put his hand inside his dressing-gown, scratched his stomach, and looked at King Dick. " What's that information you've got ? "

" Something for you to find out, mon Général," King Dick said. " Those maroons, they've stopped drumming."

" Mer de merde," Dessalines growled. " What else ? "

" How do I know, mon Général ? " King Dick said. " I've been carrying supplies to the Artibonite. All I do is guess."

" Well, for the love of Christ's gold-laced hat," Dessalines said, " go ahead and guess ! "

" I guess those maroons hunting a way to make trouble. I guess they don't forget how you burned their humforts with Gangans inside."

Dessalines spat noisily on the pale carpet. " Fimié pice ! Flea manure ! What do you think those cochon-maroons can do to me ? Why, there's not enough of 'em to bother a corporal's guard ! Christ's grandmother, mon Général ! If ten of my men should break wind at a given moment, they'd blow all the maroons in Haiti across the Cahos Mountains ! "

King Dick regarded Dessalines placidly. " How you *know* there not enough ? I not know how many they are, mon Général ; Ti-Bobo not. They been stealing women ten, twenty, thirty years ; not been using those women to bark up mapou trees ! You say they cochons-marrons, —wild pigs, yes ; and like wild pigs they been breeding. Find out more, mon Général ! "

" Kakamacaque ! " Dessalines snarled. " Monkey manure ! I have other things on my mind ! I think about armies and you talk to me about wild pigs ! I've got no time to waste on wild pigs, no men to waste on them, either ! " He leaned forward, frog-like. " Who told you all this kakacochon about maroons ? "

" Ti-Bobo of Mirebalais," King Dick said. " He came across the mountains to tell me."

" Fimié sec ! " Dessalines cried. With a wave of his hand he dismissed Ti-Bobo, in his estimation a piece of dry excrement. Then he eyed King Dick narrowly. " How many men did you set to guard those supplies at Verrettes ? "

" One hundred men, two small guns," King Dick said. " Also thirty more hidden in bushes to watch the hundred."

" Not enough," Dessalines said quickly. " If we lose those supplies, we lose everything. What were you thinking of to leave only a hundred and thirty to guard ? "

" Thinking of this town," King Dick said. " My judgment, it need guarding, so Blacks wouldn't rise against Blancs, and be no trouble."

" Merde ! " Dessalines cried. " Who cares what happens to the Blancs ? I'll take care of the Blancs ! You go back to Verrettes and take this friend of yours with you. Then you can hand him back to Toussaint with my compliments when that old fox comes running down from the mountains."

Dessalines threw himself on the sofa once more. " You understand your orders, mon Général ? "

King Dick said he did. " There one thing I should know, mon Général. How long before you reach Verrettes ? "

" Figure it for yourself," Dessalines said. " I fight Boudet until he becomes exhausted. Then I fall back and burn this town. Then I hide in the mountains, giving Boudet the privilege of entering St. Marc, battered and hungry, to find the place a heap of stinking ruins, without so much as one yam in it to eat ! Immediately my men and I run back through the high mountains and set fire to Port-au-Prince ! Then Boudet—that fimié sec, that mer' de mouton—will have no place to go : nothing to eat ! Then, by Christ's aunt, he'll be able to do damned little harm to Toussaint and Christophe, even if Leclerc should drive them over the mountains ! How long will that take ? You know as well as I ! "

" What do you intend to do about the whites when you burn the town ? " I asked.

Dessalines sprang up from the sofa, beating his breast with his fists. " Christ's mother and grandmother and all his female cousins ! " he bawled. " Must I account to someone whenever I belch ? I'll take care of the Blancs in the way that seems best to me ! You damned American sheep-faces, you're always thinking you know better how everyone should act ! Well, Blanc, Dessalines is one man who cares no more for Americans than he does for the smallest piece of fimié sec on a donkey's backside ! "

I had the momentary thought—and I suppose a similar thought has come to every man who has ever been a part of any army, subject to a bully or to an incompetent—that if ever I had a proper opportunity, an opportunity that would let me do it without harming anyone else, I'd blow this man's brains out through his ears with the most profound pleasure. And when I glanced helplessly at King Dick, there was something about his veiled eyes and his innocent expression that made me sure that his thoughts were no different from mine.

CHAPTER XXXII

IT WAS on the twentieth of February that Dessalines marched out of St. Marc to outwit Boudet ; and to me the thirty days that followed were worse than the endless tortured mental horrors of yellow fever. I can do no more than set down the bald facts of this nightmare ; to describe its details would be as impossible as to describe the dark and horrible shapes that come with yellow fever to slash at the eyes with bill-hooks, to tear at the entrails with poisoned claws, to gnaw with red-hot teeth at the brain, and to block with a smothering fiery darkness every thought, every movement, every effort to escape.

When Dessalines marched away on the twentieth, King Dick and I climbed up into the steep mountains behind St. Marc at the head of our two hundred soldiers and made our way down into the Valley of the Artibonite.

That brown river winds like a snake through the plantations of its broad valley ; and the roads to it and along it are gashes through an enormous steamy jungle, impenetrable walls of greenery that opened occasionally to give us glimpses of the river, of plantations, of rocky river-beds extending up into sharp hills, of towering mountain walls.

Everywhere along the road we saw traces of fleeing fugitives : smouldering embers of camp-fires, broken kettles, dead donkeys, fragments of food, bits of paper and cloth, smashed toys. They had been left, King Dick said, by plantation-owners and their families, hurrying to hide in the mountains.

At times I heard them in the roadside jungle, stumbling through thickets or wallowing in mud-holes ; calling fearfully to each other.

There's something about the terror of frightened people that does strange things to those about them. Perhaps it's for this reason that a hurt or helpless animal is often ferociously attacked by its fellows. Whatever the reason, I saw that the black men who marched close behind us were increasingly affected by the signs and the sounds of those miserable refugees. Their eyes rolled with a sort of ferocious irritability towards the distant fearful voices ; their ears seemed laid back against their heads, like those of animals about to spring.

I thought they'd lose that dangerous irritability when we reached Verrettes ; for at Verrettes the valley was wide, and the refugees shunned wide spaces and kept to mountain jungles. In Verrettes, however, things were worse. It was a dirty, hot town, and the supplies deposited in the main square by King Dick were guarded by tatterdemalion black soldiers under the command of a small but gorgeously uniformed Negro lieutenant with the elegant name of Rossignol de Marmelade. King

Dick called him " Lieutenant Ross." Rossignol de Marmelade said he had sent out scouts, and that there were thousands of refugees in the low mountains near Verrettes, all hungry. His eyes were apprehensive as he told us how easily all those hungry people could swoop down on the supplies if they took a notion to do so. He had, I saw, communicated his apprehension to his troops ; and officers and men alike were in favour of a wholesale slaughter of every white refugee who could be found in the neighbourhood.

" I, Rossignol de Marmelade, have watched these refugees," he said. " They are sweating with fear. With fifty good men, skilled at climbing among the rocks, I could kill five hundred in one day."

King Dick shook his head.

" But, mon Général," Rossignol protested, " that is what Dessalines would do."

" Yes, Lieutenant Ross," King Dick said. " You right ! That is what Dessalines do, but not what Toussaint do. Toussaint let whites alone and move supplies."

Rossignol raised his shoulders to the level of his ears, then let them drop. Clearly he thought—and so did his men—that the labour of moving the supplies would be far more trouble than merely killing a few hundred whites.

King Dick kicked his horse out from the shadow of the pile of supplies and looked around at the high mountains that ringed the valley. The broad brown river went winding off to our left through endless plantations of cane, and on the other side of the river small peaks were outlined against larger peaks, and the larger peaks had as a massive background the irregular flanks of towering mountain chains. King Dick pointed to one of the smaller peaks, rising from the centre of a tributary valley. " You see that long hill ? " he asked. " You know what it is ? "

" Crête à Pierrot," Rossignol de Marmelade said.

" Good ! That where we take these supplies. Across the river and up on Crête à Pierrot. Then no refugees bother us. You hunt up every horse, every mule, every donkey in Verrettes and we take them with us. Maybe for riding ; maybe for eating. Mm, mm ! They worse things to eat than donkey."

In later years I heard great stories about Crête à Pierrot—how Leclerc besieged it with twelve thousand men ; how its Negro defenders under Dessalines and Lamartinière fought off the French with a mere handful of defenders ; how the Negroes outwitted all the French generals, usually by jumping in a ditch at the crucial moment ; how Crête à Pierrot was the equal of any battle ever fought.

Unfortunately they were told by Negroes about their own heroes and weren't true. They were stories built on vanity, like the conversation of the two black generals who sat beside me on my first day in Cap François—those two generals who considered their troops the equal of any troops on earth, and their horses faster than any other horses ever seen anywhere ; who were going over to Paris to march their regiments in review before Bonaparte—when actually they would never travel ten miles outside of Haiti.

I don't know why so many Negroes lie so recklessly about their belongings and their abilities, but—barring Toussaint and King Dick— all the black generals I saw in Haiti could no more tell the truth than they could fly. Perhaps that peculiar habit of distortion is responsible for the frequency with which Negroes misjudge their own kind. Perhaps that's why Dessalines, who was a butcher, is a greater man in their minds than Toussaint L'Ouverture, who was more of a genius than any white man of his day. In any case, my story of Crête à Pierrot is stripped of all vanity and pride of race, and if Negroes don't like it, I can't help it. I have to tell about occurrences as they happened : not as somebody else would like to have had them happen.

In spite of the surliness of Rossignol de Marmelade, our three hundred and fifty black troopers moved that vast pile of supplies two miles down the Artibonite to one of the great humpbacked bends in the river—a bend so extreme that at its deepest point it was only a quarter-mile from the long ridge of Crête à Pierrot.

So far as we could see from that river bend, there was nothing on Crête à Pierrot except a Haitian jungle ; but when King Dick and I crossed the river and climbed the slope, we found the top of the ridge crowned with long walls, rising from an ancient moat. Moat and walls alike were choked with thorny tropical plants, with vines whose trunks were the size of my arm, with trees that would have taken two generations to grow in New England, but had probably sprung up here in less than a decade. Over all the walls grew a sort of red moss, which gave them the look of being painted with the mixture of red ochre and skimmed milk that we use on barns in New England. To us, standing on those walls, the Artibonite was a wandering ribbon of silver, half-hidden in the rank growth of the valley ; and the high and forbidding shoulders of Morne Rouge, the Red Mountain, towered behind us like a dark green thunderhead.

" What are these walls ? " I asked King Dick. " They're mighty little use as fortifications, and too big for any plantation house."

" What wrong with this for a fort ? " King Dick asked. " Just the place for supplies."

I looked behind us at the tree-clad slopes of Morne Rouge. " It's not the proper place for a fort," I said. " It couldn't be held five hours if the French put a few guns on that mountain."

King Dick was patient with me. " This fort not built against French," he said. " It built by plantation-owners in case of revolutions. When black slaves make revolutions they don't have cannon. This fort very convenient place for plantation-owners when in trouble with slaves. If slaves make trouble, plantation-owners come here from up river, from down river, from those two valleys behind. Then they safe until black men get good and go back to work."

Below us a long line of heavily-laden horses, mules, donkeys, and black soldiers trudged slowly up the slope. The men, in spite of their heavy loads, cackled and chattered like a flock of parrots. King Dick showed them where to pile their bags and bales ; then divided them into squads and set them to chopping and burning the tangled vines and shrubs that filled the fort.

Those hacking knives uncovered barracks at the foot of the walls, heavy guns in embrasures choked with foliage, cells for officers, a well, sally-ports, ancient but usable drawbridges for crossing the moat.

All through that hot evening and the long sticky night, Crête à Pierrot echoed to the hacking of the knives, the shouts of soldiers, the crackling of burning brush ; and by mid-morning of the next day the top of the long ridge was cleared of trees and jungle, and the entire length of abrupt, rusty-red walls was visible. Secure within those walls, snugly piled in embrasures, were all the salt fish, manioc flour, rice, and other supplies that Dessalines and his army would need when they fled into the mountains after having destroyed St. Marc, Port-au-Prince, and all the coastal towns on which the French depended for existence.

King Dick, stripped to the waist, stood on the ramparts and com-placently surveyed his well-performed task. " That good, Albion," he said. " We not lost a supply nor had a man killed. Everything right here where Dessalines can put his hand on it and run for mountains, whichever way it handiest to run. We done all we need to do for Dessa-lines, Albion, and when Dessalines get here and move on into mountains, we move too—only we move to Cap François and that lady."

CHAPTER XXXIII

IF I LIVE to be a thousand years old I'll never forget the arrival of Dessa-lines and his army at Verrettes.

We began to see his men late in the afternoon, straggling down out of the mountains on to the same river road we had travelled ; but instead of turning off that road at the spot where King Dick had placed sentries, they kept right on towards Verrettes.

" Oh, my goo'ness me my," King Dick said. " Either somebody killed all my sentries, or they something happening we don't know about ! "

He whistled shrilly for an orderly, demanded a pair of mules, and in the same breath issued instructions to Rossignol de Marmelade to be on the lookout for friend and foe alike ; to shoot anybody who couldn't satisfactorily account for himself, but to be particularly careful about shooting any soldiers who approached the rear of the fort, since they might belong to Toussaint, Christophe or even Dessalines.

" What would Dessalines' men be doing up to the north ? " I asked.

King Dick shrugged his shoulders. " They might be running," he said. " When black men start to run, they fast, fast ! " He made a swishing sound, murmured, " My goo'ness me," and added, " When they scared enough, they run three times around this island in time it take white men to walk across it ! "

When we had crossed the river and reached the Verrettes road, we found at once that King Dick had been correct in his suspicion that Dessalines' men had been running from something. The men who came out from the jungle on to the road to hurry along beside us were white-eyed and silent, constantly peering over their shoulders as if fearful of pursuit. Some of the soldiers drove whites before them, sometimes singly, sometimes in groups ; but so tattered were the garments of the whites, and so smeared were their faces and bodies with blood, mud, and sweat that we had no way of knowing whether they were 'ti Blancs or plantation-owners.

Just short of the central part of Verrettes the Artibonite bends in a loop that runs close against the foot of high cliffs known as Morne de la Tranquillité—the Mount of Peace. The loop is a plain that juts out from the mountains we had crossed in coming from St. Marc, and on that little plain we found Dessalines, Lamartinière, and all the rest of Dessalines' gold-bedecked staff. They were at the neck of the plain, which looked like an enormous stage with a back-drop of mountains. A thousand or more black troops were packed behind them, together with all their black wives and camp-followers ; and every last one was staring at the base of the cliffs that formed the rear of the plain.

Hundreds of whites were crowded together at the base of those cliffs, under the guard of Negro sentries. The sentries formed a semi-circle around them, so that there was no place for them to go except up the cliffs.

King Dick kicked his mule close to Dessalines. At the commotion we made, Dessalines gave us an impatient look, then turned away to stare at that close-packed throng of whites. When I looked more closely, I saw that many of the whites had already started up the cliffs. They were not easy to see, at first ; then the eye became adjusted to them and found them more easily, as one finds caterpillars on the undersides of leaves. Some were motionless, huddled on ledges and in depressions, half-hidden by shrubs, crouched behind pinnacles ; others crawled slowly upwards, fumbling from side to side, like ants feeling their way over an obstacle.

" All supplies moved to Crête à Pierrot, mon Général," King Dick reported.

Dessalines didn't look around. " I know that." He jerked his thumb over his shoulder. " Round up all our women and take them there too."

"We take the prisoners, too, mon Général?"

"Just the women, mon Général," Dessalines said softly.

The sentries guarding the prisoners were moving forward, driving more and more whites up the slope.

I suspected what was going to happen, and the very suspicion set me to quaking inside.

Lamartinière looked at me sharply, then rode his horse against me, so that King Dick and I were forced away from that group of watching officers.

"You had your orders," he said. "Obey them."

"For Christ's sake," I whispered, "you're not going to let this happen without a word, are you?"

"What do you suggest?" Lamartinière asked.

"Suggest!" I said. "How do I know what to suggest! Can't someone talk to him? Can't you? He'd listen to *someone*, wouldn't he?"

"Oh me my," King Dick said. "How you talk to a tiger when he made up his mind to jump?"

"Close your eyes and your ears," Lamartinière said. "This is unavoidable. When things of this sort begin to happen, they must continue. You will understand some day."

"Not if I live a million years."

"Then you'll never be a soldier," Lamartinière said. "Dessalines is a great soldier because he is always logical about war. War is fought to kill and destroy enemies, so he kills and destroys enemies."

There was a popping of musketry from behind us. I saw that all the whites were climbing among the rocks; that the sentries were firing at them, taking careful aim. From high up a figure fell, turning slowly, seeming to float downwards. Another fell, and another; then a clump of three. A man and a woman, their arms about each other, toppled outwards and fell with the same seeming slowness. I could hear a thin screaming, like the squealing of frightened rabbits. . . .

"If you were a soldier, with men under you," Lamartinière said, "you'd do the same."

The sentries climbed the ledges themselves, and their firing became more rapid. From the high rocks figures fell, jumped, rolled in increasing numbers, by tens, by scores. They came down as caterpillars fall from a nest in the crotch of a tree when touched by flame. A small girl rolled head over heels down a steep ledge, caught a shrub with both hands and hung there, her legs jerking as she felt for a foothold. She wore a single faded blue garment and long black stockings. I could see her open mouth, the whiteness of the thin thighs beneath her scanty dress. Her legs abruptly stopped their writhing: she fell like a wet rag, caught on a protruding rock, and lay motionless. . . .

I don't know what I said to Lamartinière.

"Yes, you would," he said, "or you'd do something you'd never believe yourself capable of doing."

From the cliffs, as bodies fell more and more rapidly, came a howling and squalling such as might be made by countless cats in the silence of the night, or by a myriad Brobdingnagian seagulls. There was something about the sound that forced me to look, though I was like jelly inside at the mere thought of what I'd see if I did look ; yet I couldn't turn my back : I had to see what happened.

I'd often heard the expression, "All's fair in love and war," but I never before realised how much love and war have in common. Just as men in love are half-mad, so too are men caught in a war. Certainly, on that brassy hot afternoon at Verrettes, everyone along that river—generals, soldiers, white refugees tumbling caterpillar-like from the cliffs, the hundreds who still sought the safety they could never reach—was half out of his senses from fear, rage, or eagerness to kill.

I couldn't get the thought of caterpillars out of my mind. Those helpless prisoners crawled on hands and knees to squirm beneath others who crawled helplessly, seeking cover where there was none.

After a little they ceased to seem human to me. They might have been lay figures among whom black soldiers moved, blowing holes in some with muskets, crushing heads with cocomacaques, hewing open stomachs, and lopping off arms with machetes. I found myself trying to count the bodies as I might have counted dead hake along a Maine beach. . . .

"How in Christ's name can you stand it ? " I asked Lamartinière.

"Look, my friend," he said, " there's nothing you can't stand when your own men have been slaughtered. You don't know what happened three days ago when he "—he jerked his head towards Dessalines, who sat hunched on his horse, staring frog-eyed at the slaughter—" sent a column to surprise Port-au-Prince."

"But a *man* doesn't do things like this—not if he's human," I said.

The sentries on the cliffs were stalking prisoners as they climbed fumblingly, like the dim figures of delirium, their black pursuers leaping at them like cats, and stabbing with bayonets. The bayonets went in easily enough ; but when the prisoners collapsed into shapeless heaps of old clothes, the bayonets stuck. . . .

Lamartinière waved aside my words. " You haven't seen enough of war. What would you do if you captured a town ; then saw your soldiers shot down, one by one, by enemies hidden in the houses ? "

"That has nothing to do with this."

"Yes, it has ! You would say to the people in the houses, ' Do not kill my men and you will be safe, but kill my men and I shall be forced to kill you.' Suppose that after you said that, your soldiers, who looked to you for protection, continued to fall into gutters, into piles of horse manure, their eyes shot out, their brains spattered in the dirt, their bellies slashed open, their intestines bulging through their clothes. What would you do then ? "

I couldn't answer. An old man was clinging to a tree-trunk on that grey mountain slope. Sentries were shooting at him. As the bullets struck, his head jerked, first to one side and then to the other ; but he didn't fall. He just hung there, his arms around the little tree. . . .

" I'll tell you what you'd do," Lamartinière said. " Whenever shots came from a house and killed your men, you'd send other men into that house to kill everyone in it. Everyone. You understand, M. Hamlin ? You'd kill them all. Men, women, children—all ! "

I tried to think dispassionately. Suppose King Dick were shot in such a way in my company. Perhaps Lamartinière was right.

" Look, M. Hamlin," Lamartinière said, " three days ago Dessalines, having fought Boudet to a standstill so that he and all his fine French troops were exhausted, ran around Boudet's flank and sent a thousand men to prepare the way for capturing Port-au-Prince. They were our best men under Jolivert, Moulet, and Dubuque. Half-way to Port-au-Prince they met unarmed black men on the road. Unarmed, you understand. Of course they thought those black men were friends, happy that Port-au-Prince was about to be freed from the French—happy because they could never be slaves again."

" Maroons ? " King Dick asked.

" Exactly ! " Lamartinière said. " Maroons ! They came down from the mountains, led by DeRance, and he joined the French ! "

The screams from the cliffs seemed farther and farther away—or perhaps the numbers of those left to scream were so few that they only seemed more remote. . . .

" They were with the French ? " I asked. " Why ? "

Lamartinière shrugged his shoulders. " They were maroons. Who would have suspected them of having joined the French ? There were no Frenchmen—only those black men, walking harmlessly along the road, squatting peacefully in the bushes, dangerous to no one. All in a moment's time they snatched up hidden muskets, pistols, and cane-knives—and became maroons, deadly enemies. In ten minutes' time there wasn't one left out of our thousand ! Not one—the maroons had killed them all ! So Dessalines didn't take Port-au-Prince, M. Hamlin ! No ; he was obliged to hurry across the mountains to this place and, as a matter of protection to himself and his remaining men, he rounded up all the whites he found along the road and in the mountains. All whites are our enemies, and we know now that our enemies will have no mercy upon us. That's why Dessalines has no mercy upon *his* enemies. This is a war we're fighting, M. Hamlin, and that's how things happen in wars—as you'll some day learn if you wish to stay alive while fighting a war."

If I wished to stay alive while fighting a war ! At last Lamartinière had said something that had a meaning. It meant that nobody who wasn't an idiot would have any part in a war if he could possibly help it, and I knew that if I could escape with my life from this one, nothing and nobody could ever coax or push me into another.

I think there must have been a thousand camp-followers with Dessalines' army. Among that motley throng of squealing, grumbling females we herded back across the great ox-bow of the Artibonite and up to Crête à Pierrot were pot-bellied black children with kinky hair tied in little points, full-breasted maidens, shrivelled old women, crotchety mothers-in-law, mothers heavy with child, little families of five or six wives, all sharing the same flea-bitten donkey, and even Madame Dessalines with two bags full of personal belongings slung on either side of a sleek young mule.

From the moment we climbed within the red ramparts of Crête à Pierrot, the place was a turmoil—a turmoil that increased when Dessalines rode in at dusk. He was in the best of humours, as if the killing of those hundreds of defenceless people had been a tonic ; and he came in shouting for fires. " Everybody have a hot meal," he bawled to his officers. " Kill enough cows and horses so everyone has meat ! "

He hailed King Dick with a sweeping salute. " Excellent, mon Général ! The French will hope for great things when they see our fires." His laugh was a hoarse squawk that echoed from the parapets.

" You expect the French soon ? " King Dick asked.

" They're near as a mule's ear, mon Général ! "

" This fort very bad against eighteen-pounders, mon Général ! " King Dick said. " If you light it up with fires, we get blown into that valley yonder." He jerked his head towards the dark wall of the Cahos.

" Fimié sec ! " Dessalines cried. " Build fires ! Cook everything we can't carry ! " He showed his teeth at King Dick. " You think I've become a child overnight ? You think I went out of my mind just because I had to destroy St. Marc ? Christ's undershirt, my friend ! I know a bad fort as well as the next man ! Light up the fires and let the French see we're here. Let them prepare to attack ! When they wake to-morrow, there'll be no fort here ! We'll level the walls and bury the guns in the ditch. We and all our supplies, they'll all be gone—gone into the Cahos, where no Frenchmen can ever reach us ! "

CHAPTER XXXIV

THERE never would have been a battle at Crête à Picrot if it hadn't been for Toussaint L'Ouverture, or if Toussaint hadn't materialised out of nowhere like an overdressed black ghost, just as Lydia had told me he was for ever doing.

Dessalines was in the very act of dividing the supplies and instructing all of us as to the mountain ravines where detachments of the army could hide to best advantage, when a pop-eyed sentry ran up to him and gasped something about the " Grand Général." Almost treading on his heels was Toussaint, dwarfish and outlandish in his long, red cape and his little red hat with the feather in it.

Dessalines bellowed like a bull at sight of him, and the two embraced and kissed—a tableau out of a dark harlequinade, but one that brought ecstatic howlings from myriads of onlookers, invisible in the darkness. " Glory ! " they screamed. " Thanks to God ! " " We shall be free ! " " Liberty ! " " Glory ! "

When Dessalines would have taken Toussaint to his own quarters, Toussaint worriedly seated himself on a bag of rice, hitched his cape out from between his legs, and removed his little red hat the better to scratch his head.

" I came here fast when I had your letter telling what the maroons had done to you. That was bad, mon Général ! "

Dessalines' voice shook. " Bad ? For every man of mine they killed, I'll kill a thousand ! " He eyed Toussaint defiantly.

" It was an act of God," Toussaint said, " but it changed my plans. I must have more time, or these French will overrun us. I cannot raise more troops unless I have more time."

Dessalines thumped his breast. " When we go into the mountains, mon Général, men will come from everywhere to join us. The French can never corner us in the mountains."

" Look, mon Général," Toussaint said. " I have a better plan than going into the mountains. I wish all your officers to hear this plan, so that I can persuade you that it's wise."

Dessalines crouched, hands on knees, to stare strickenly at Toussaint. " A better plan than going into the mountains ? If we go anywhere else, those white bastards will surround us ! In the mountains they can't find us, and we can jump out at them whenever we wish ! "

" That is only partly true," Toussaint said. " That is not my plan. My plan is to have them find you and corner you, here in this fort."

Dessalines looked incredulous. " This is no fort ! I tell you the guns are buried ! "

" Dig them up," Toussaint said.

214

" Name of a name of ten thousand Christs ! " Dessalines shouted. " Those French are moving in on us from three sides. Leclerc and Rochambeau are coming down from the north ; Boudet is coming in from the west ! If we aren't out of here to-morrow morning, they'll be all around us. And that Rochambeau, he can drag cannon from hell to the moon and back ! "

" Yes," Toussaint said. " That is true, if he has time ; but I have had information that Rochambeau is marching ahead of his heavy guns."

" That makes no differénce," Dessalines shouted. " He needs nothing but light guns to knock down this thing you call a fort ! I tell you if they should back a big mule up to these walls and kick him in the stomach so he breaks wind in the grand manner, the whole place would fall down ! "

Toussaint leaned forward and moved his ears, which somehow lent persuasiveness to his words. " Listen, mon Général ! You forget who you are. You are Dessalines ; Dessalines the tiger ; Dessalines who strikes at night like lightning, and is gone in the morning ! You have destroyed Léogane ; you have destroyed St. Marc ; you have trampled and burned the plantation houses ; you have come within an inch of destroying Port-au-Prince and leaving the great Boudet without food or shelter ! Until Leclerc is wholly safe from you, he is in perpetual danger. That is true, is it not ? "

" By God," Dessalines said, " because of what those maroons did to me and my men, I'll tear the heart out of that Leclerc, that bastard son of a female goat by a little grey monkey ! I'll fry it in coconut oil—yes, but I can't do it by staying behind these walls and letting off pop-guns ! I've got to get up into the mountains where I can pick off his men one by one ! Great-grandmother of Christ, I could build a privy out of clay and clam shells and have a better fort than this ! "

" I believe it," Toussaint said, " but you still do not understand your value to the French. Put yourself in the position of Leclerc, that great soldier, that trusted general of Bonaparte, that military genius whose triumphs extend from Africa to the highest snows of the Alps ! "

His face glistened with sweat. " Put yourself in Leclerc's place," he begged. " Consider yourself a Blanc of great importance, who has been annoyed by Dessalines. Dessalines has dared to oppose you, the great Leclerc, brother-in-law of Bonaparte ! What would you most desire to do to this most constant threat, this tiger of a Dessalines ? "

Dessalines shook his fist at Toussiant. " Destroy the piece of monkey-manure ! Shoot him in the back ! Chop off his privates ! Surround his army and feed it to the dogs ! "

" Exactly," Toussaint said. " Now look : I must have time to raise militia regiments in Ennery, in Limonade, in Dondon. They will not come to us of their own accord, as you think : I must talk to them, persuade them, pull them out of their holes. That takes time, and you must provide it for me. This you will do by staying here in this fort."

" But I tell you this fort isn't worth the droppings of a dung-beetle ! "
Dessalines cried. " Fifteen minutes of pounding from Rochambeau's
guns and there wouldn't be enough left of us to make a pot-pie for an
old woman with a bellyache and no teeth ! "

" Mon Général," Toussaint said, " I ask you to study the situation.
Here you are in this fort, with all your troops, all your generals, all your
colonels and majors and captains and sergeants, all your women—even
your own wife—all your children and horses and mules and supplies,
eh ? Bon ! Imagine that this information has been carried to Leclerc.
What then ? "

Dessalines thoughtfully scratched his crotch. " What then, eh ? Well,
mon Général, I can see it might be an opportunity."

" Truly an opportunity," Toussaint said. " Leclerc knows you are
here, preparing to defend yourself and your army in a fort that cannot
be defended. Instantly that great general seizes the opportunity to
capture you, your army, and your supplies. Do you think he'll wait
for Rochambeau's guns ? He, the great Leclerc ? Not he ! He has no
need of guns ! On the contrary : he sees clearly that if he were to use
guns, you would abandon the fort, and his great opportunity would be
lost. And why ? Because you'd escape into the high mountains beyond
his reach—vanish into the Cahos and thereafter continue to harry him
and hack him ! So he needs no guns—so he'll bring no guns ! "

Dessalines stared toadishly at the little black man in the red cape
as if wondering where all this was leading.

" That is the truth," Toussaint went on, " and it is why I tell you
that Crête à Pierrot must be defended and not destroyed. For Leclerc
thinks *you* have no guns—word has reached him that you have no artillery
of *any* sort. But you have—fifteen guns. Now bear in mind what I have
just said . that he will bring none. So you will be able to use those
fifteen guns effectively ; for this fort must be held until the last possible
moment."

Dessalines groaned. " Fifteen guns ! Fifteen dried pieces of manure
on a monkey's backside ! Those guns are a hundred years older than
God's grandmother ! "

"They'll hold together," Toussaint said, " and any gun that holds
together is useful at short range."

" Perhaps, if you have artillerymen," Dessalines said. " I have none.
If my men try to work those guns, they'll blow the fort itself to hell before
a Frenchman gets within a mile of us."

Toussaint dismissed his objections with a flip of his hand. " You
have Général King Dick, who knows everything about guns. He learned
from British and Americans, who are born knowing about guns. Also
his friend is an American, and therefore must know about them. They'll
teach your men how to handle your guns."

I wanted to shout that I'd have nothing to do with his rotten guns :
nothing to do with the defence of his miserable fort ; but I didn't. You

don't talk that way to generals in uniform. So, like every other man caught by an army, I just stood there, cold all over in spite of the oppressive, breathless heat of that stifling red fort.

Toussaint, his face wrinkled with anxiety, looked slowly around the circle of black officers that stared down at him. " I ask your agreement and help, my children ! For the glory of Haiti ! Glory awaits you here in Crête à Pierrot."

A knock-kneed colonel with a long heron-neck threw back his head and shouted " Glory ! " In a moment's time they were all shouting " Glory ! Glory ! " Dessalines had his arms around the little man, kissing his ear. Men wept and bellowed.

Still weeping, Toussaint tore himself from Dessalines' arms and went shuffling off towards the gate. Ecstatic black soldiers and camp-followers fell away before and closed in behind him until all I could see was the upright feather of his cap bobbing towards the sally port—and that bobbing bright feather was the last I ever saw of Toussaint L'Ouverture.

The shouts of black soldiers and their women followed him. " Glory ! Glory ! " " Liberty ! " " Papa Toussaint ! " " Glory to God ! " " Victory ! " They began to sing and to stamp about in the red dust. The whole interior of the fort seemed to vibrate with the song they sang, and the air to flutter as with the roaring of an enormous organ,

Allons, enfants de la patrie,
Le jour de gloire est arrivé !

Day of glory, indeed ! I almost wished that I could delude myself into thinking there was any glory for anyone in the prospect before us.

Much as I feared and hated Dessalines, I have to admit that he proved himself to be a better soldier in that war of the blacks of Haiti against the French and their mulatto allies than did all the great generals that Bonaparte had sent to recapture the island—Leclerc, Boudet, Rochambeau, Hardy, Bourck, Baron Delacroix. His judgment was better ; his audacity more indomitable ; his energy put that of all those Frenchmen to shame.

Toussaint had no sooner left than Dessalines started to harangue his officers hoarsely ; and half an hour later every soldier—barring the sentries who ringed the parapet—every officer, every woman and child within those ruddy walls, was stripped half-naked and hard at work on the inside of the fort, cleaning narrow casements, repairing officers' quarters, digging up the buried guns and chipping rust from them, emptying the well of its water to make certain it was usable, and re-stowing the mountain of supplies.

I hated the stench of the place and of the sweaty bodies all around me, the ferocious energy with which Dessalines prowled among us, the ominous silence of the hot and breathless darkness beyond those inade-

quate ramparts ; and a score of times that night I swore that to-morrow,
or to-morrow night, when sentries were fewer on the parapet, King Dick
and I would surely slip away into the rank jungle that covered the slopes
of Crête à Pierrot and take our chances in the mountains that looked
down so threateningly upon that death-trap of a fort.

We had a little rest at dawn—that sudden Haitian dawn that leaps
from the darkness like a burst of flame—but only enough of a rest to let
us eat a little.

While still my mouth was full of food, Dessalines was at me to write
out orders : orders for the regiment of Lamartinière to work with
machetes on the short slope between the fort and the Artibonite ; for
his own St. Marc's regiment, augmented by one half of Robillant's
regiment, to take their machetes to the mile-long slope between the fort
and the small town of Petite Rivière to the westward ; for the other
half of Robillant's regiment and all of Labadie's regiment to cut on the
north-east slope towards the roadway to the Lesser Cahos ; and for the
two regiments of Plontonerre and Granthonax to cut on the eastern
slope, commanding the valley roads leading to the main Cahos Range.

" Women, too ! " he said hoarsely, as he dictated to me. " Put that
in the orders ! All women, old and young, and all children able to walk,
to work with the regiments ! "

He breathed hard. I thought he was going to add that all unable to
work should be killed.

I forgot my weariness as I wrote, confident that if King Dick and
I could reach the thick growth of those slopes, nothing on earth could
stop us from slipping away unseen.

The slopes, Dessalines dictated in that rasping voice of his, were to
be cleaned as bare as the butt of a baboon. All brush felled was to
be heaped and burned at night—burned at the edge of the moat, in
equidistant piles that were to be kept burning from dark to dawn.

He wagged a finger at me. " I want those fires to burn bright enough
so that not even a rat could enter or leave this fort without being seen
by a dozen sentries ! Put that in too, so they'll know what they're doing !
Put it in orders that if these slopes are properly cleaned, there isn't a
French regiment on earth that can walk up any one of 'em—not while
we have powder and shot. I want not even a bush left within four
hundred paces of these walls ! "

Devil out of hell that the man was, he grinned at me now as though
he'd fathomed all my thoughts about escaping from the fort.

" One more thing," he said. " Ditches ! I want the slopes close to
the fort dug full of little ditches, ditches a foot deep, parallel to the moat.
They'll have to be dug with machetes. Send an order to the commander
of every regiment to detach one hundred men to dig short ditches parallel
to the moat. Draw pictures to go with the orders. Short flanking ditches
on each side of all four slopes. Understand ? "

" I'd understand better," I said, " if I knew whether they're to be
for men or for drainage."

" Drainage ? " he screamed. " Holy mother of Christ's mule ! I
swear by the under-garments of the Virgin Mary that white men are
stupid as headless hens ! White men ! Pah ! I'll show you what happens
to great white men ! Boo ! What results from all their greatness ?
Nothing but busted breeches ! "

He showed his teeth. " Drainage ! Those ditches are for men—our
men—to take shelter in when we blow the belt buckles of those white
species of monkey-manure out through their backsides ! Now do you
understand ? Now write your orders and draw the plans for those
ditches, and when you're finished help Général King Dick get those
guns ready for action. Understand ? "

I did. I understood that he'd shoot me rather than let me get away.

I truly believe there is no limit to men's endurance if the proper
incentive exists within their own minds, or if they are driven by a determined leader who knows exactly what he wants to do. I've heard it said
a thousand times that Negroes are lazy ; and probably they are. So
are most men, when left to their own devices. But inside and outside
Crête à Pierrot, before the French arrived, the Negroes worked as hard
as any humans ever worked.

Through the gun-embrasures, as King Dick and I toiled with the
raw gun crews picked at random by Lamartinière from the different
regiments, we watched those black men hacking at thorny, impenetrable
thickets all through the steamy, stifling hot day ; all through the sweaty,
oppressive night. They hacked and hacked interminably : then hunkered
down in long lines at the edges of the cleared land to gobble the food
that women and children cooked in pots over brush fires ; then got to
their feet again and hacked and hacked some more.

The brush accumulated behind them in ragged windrows, dark
green when first cut, but after an hour or two wilted to a sickly pallor
by the blazing heat of the sun. Among the windrows moved black
women and children, pulling and hauling at the shrubs, vines, and
branches, heaping them high or dragging them to the moat beneath the
walls to pile for the sentry-fires that Dessalines had ordered.

The soil uncovered by all this hacking and burning was a singular
dark red, the colour of dusty dried blood ; and as the earth dried in
the scorching sun, it rose in a reddish haze around the perspiration-
soaked Negroes swinging slow knives against the receding wall of jungle.
Their legs were coated with a film of red ; red dust clung to their woolly
hair, their ears, their backs. No matter how the hot breeze blew, it
brought a fog of red dust to cling to everything in the fort and everyone
near it, so that the whole place had the look of a hot and horrid hell.

Before the steady slow attack of all those seemingly unhurried
Negroes, the jungle shrank and vanished. When the cutting started,

woodcutters and trench-diggers were intermingled, close to the moat.
But as we made our slow circuit of the guns, scaling rusty iron from
each one with small charges of powder, clearing touch-holes, swabbing
out bores, repairing carriages, and instructing crew after crew in loading,
aiming, firing, and swabbing, the diggers of ditches were still close at
hand, but the cutters of jungle had moved off into the distance : their
high-pitched voices faded and became faint and far away. At sundown
the cutters were insect-like against a distant jungle wall ; between us
and them stretched dusty red slopes, dotted with circular black patches
where brush piles smouldered.

Fires burned all night, and long cane-knives flickered in the firelight ; and when morning came, the cutters on the south side had cut
all the way down to the Artibonite, so that for the first time we clearly
saw, from the embrasures, the brown waters and the curving bank of
the big bend. To the westward, where only yesterday had been nothing
but a mass of green, we could now distinguish the roofs of Petite Rivière,
a mile away. To the north and to the west as well the slopes were brush-
less, giving us at last a sight of the two passes into the high mountains,
and of the valley between the abrupt mornes on either side of Verrettes.
Upon all those slopes, tangled and impenetrable thickets when we had
first looked towards them, not so much as a squirrel could now have
moved without being instantly seen.

The inside of the fort was a sweaty, dark, foul-smelling purgatory
in which King Dick and I dragged ourselves wearily from gun to gun,
putting black crews through drills that steadily grew less clumsy, never
knowing when Dessalines' grinning black face would appear in the
embrasure behind which we worked. Black women brought us food in
buckets—a thick hot soup, full of salt codfish and manioc flour—which
I ate in a sort of daze, too tired to taste.

I was tired beyond the power of telling. My ears roared with weariness ; into the roarings came blank silences, the little silences of sleep.
Only fear of Dessalines, and of that grinning, shiny-black, yellow-eyed
face of his, kept me awake. Except for him, I'd have fallen in my tracks
and slept for ever.

Yet I learned that no matter how utterly weary a man may be, he
can get up and start all over again, a living corpse that somehow retains
the power of speech and thought and violent endeavour, even when
brain and muscles seem numb and useless.

We were in the midst of early morning turmoil—the squealing and
chattering of women pushing and crowding to draw water from the
well in the centre of the fort, the hee-hawing of donkeys, the clattering
of pots and spoons over the breakfast fires, the shouting of officers supervising the endless moving of supplies and ammunition, the shrill laughter
that seemed always to be a part of Negro crowds in the mornings and
at night—when King Dick came back from Dessalines' quarters, where

he'd been to get more needles for the women who were making powder-bags. He rolled his eyes at me, called one of the women to distribute the needles ; then squatted beside me in the red dust that covered everything.

" Look, Albion," he said. " We got to fight ! They no chance to get away." With his forefinger he sketched a small oblong in the dust, made an S-shaped wiggle along one side of it, and placed dots abreast of the other three sides—a representation of the fort and its approaches.

" When ? " I asked heavily. I had no desire to fight anybody.

" To-day," King Dick said. " Look, Albion : you remember what happened at Verrettes ? All those 'ti Blancs ? "

Did I remember ! Could I ever forget that girl in the blue dress, hanging from a rock, her white thighs shining above her black stockings : those couples embracing on the high cliffs, and toppling together, slowly turning as they fell : those heaps of bodies : the wailings and moanings that came faintly from the heights ?

" Same thing happened at Petite Rivière," King Dick said, tapping his forefinger on his sketch at the dot nearest to Crête à Pierrot. " Two Dessalines regiments came across the mountains by way of Petite Rivière with four hundred prisoners, all Blancs. They killed all those Blancs in a heap, same as at Verrettes."

" Why ? "

" Because the regiments got word what happened at Verrettes." He moistened his big red lips and rolled his eyes whitely at me. " Yesterday Boudet came across the mountains into the Artibonite with two thousand French troops. They got to Petite Rivière and right away they smelled those four hundred dead Blancs. You can smell 'em here if the wind turns west." In a hushed voice he murmured " Mm : mm ! " as if words failed him to describe the stench of all those murdered whites. Then he went on : " After they smelled 'em, they went and looked : then rounded up all nigras in Petite Rivière and killed 'em in big piles, same as the Blancs had been killed. Sem hundred ! "

Somehow this horrible story made next to no impression upon me ; I might have been hearing about the killing of four hundred chickens and seven hundred ducks.

" That old Toussaint," King Dick said, " he was right ! Those Boudet regiments got not one piece of artillery between 'em and they angry Frenchmen : oh my goo'ness me, yes ! They coming right along to this fort to-day : marching right up to it so to take it, same as that old Toussaint sent word to 'em they could, without artillery or nothing."

I clung desperately to a hope that we might get away before the fighting started. " How many men did you say Boudet has ? " I asked.

" Two thousand French, eight hundred mulatto troops from Jacmel under La Plume."

" That's not enough, is it ? Not enough for Boudet to surround this fort on four sides and still fight to-day. It'll take him three or four days to move his men through these jungles and place them properly, won't it ? "

" He not going to place 'em properly," King Dick said. " He going to march right up here : right up that big red slope. That old Toussaint, he had word taken to Boudet by deserters. Oh my, yes ! Those deserters told Boudet nobody couldn't make black men fight, not for anything ! Oh my goo'ness me my, no ! "

King Dick moved closer and spoke in a whisper, " Listen, Albion : do some thinking. Boudet going to attack all alone, to-day. Leclerc, he's in Port-au-Prince, waiting for Boudet to capture the fort. Rochambeau, he can't get here for six days if somebody attack him in back. Hardy, he can't get here for ten days if somebody attack him in back. Very good, Albion : what you do if you in Dessalines' place ? "

" Why," I said, " I suppose I'd do what I could to get around behind Rochambeau and Hardy, and attack 'em from the rear."

As we were talking I had become conscious of a confused to-do within the walls of the fort—shouting, running, the thumping of drums. Drummers climbed to the parapets, and the rattling and rumbling seemed to surge up out of the fort and spread over us like an invisible hot sunshade of sound. The confusion spread to the red slopes outside the fort, and those who had been hacking at the jungle and digging the ditches dropped their tools to straggle towards us up the slope, rust-coloured from their labours in the red earth.

" All right, Albion," King Dick whispered, " if you attacked 'em from the rear, would you do it yourself, or send somebody else to do it ? Think what you'd do if you same man as Dessalines."

Before I could answer, Dessalines popped out from the door of his quarters beneath the parapet, and behind him trooped generals, colonels, aides—the white skinned Lamartinière in a green uniform with gold facings ; fat black Plontonerre, wearing a naval officer's elaborate uniform and chapeau ; Granthonax in a pink uniform with a yellow cape ; Robillant, a huge black man all ears and knees and elbows, in a white linen uniform with black facings that somehow made him look like a gigantic skeleton. Dessalines wore nothing above his waist except a red handkerchief bound around his head and a bushel-sized chapeau pulled far down over it, pushing out his ears like the wings on Hermes' cap. His skin glistened with sweat, and he smelled rank, like a newly opened fox-den.

When he had climbed to the parapet, he plucked at the crotch of his breeches, as was his habit when about to speak ; then, hoarsely and affectionately bellowing " Mes braves ! " at the slack-lipped soldiers before him, he half-turned towards the interior of the fort, so that his words were directed also at all the black women and children crowded into the dusty parade.

" My braves," Dessalines shouted, " Blancs from the land of Liberty, Equality, and Fraternity have followed you into the Artibonite to kill you or make slaves of you and all your fellows ! They care no more for Liberty, Equality, and Fraternity than does my great-grandmother's pig ! Yesterday they arrived in Petite Rivière and found the bodies of our enemies. What did they do, those white offspring of goats and geese ? They killed seven hundred helpless men, women, and children for no reason at all except that they were black ! If they capture this fort and lay hands upon you, you too will be killed—all of you : all your helpless old mothers, all your innocent little sons and daughters ! Those who aren't killed will be slaves for ever, to be bought, sold, whipped, and raped."

I marvelled that Dessalines should be able to stir the emotions of his audience by a reference to helpless old mothers, when he must have known that all who listened to him were well aware that he would put a bullet through anybody's helpless old mother, including his own, if she were so unfortunate as to cause him inconvenience.

" Now, listen, my children," Dessalines went on. " You know me ! I am Dessalines ! Any Blanc who makes war on Dessalines is as good as dead before he starts ! These Blancs who are coming from Petite Rivière, their fate is certain. Some of them we shall kill ; the rest will die of the Siamese Sickness during the hot weather. Dessalines has never lied to you yet, my children, and he is telling you the truth to-day. These Blancs have brains like my grandfather's donkey. They think of nobody but themselves and they do nothing properly ! Never did my grandfather's donkey do what he should have done unless my grandfather first kicked his backsides half-way to his ears, and then stretched his neck three feet with a halter ! "

Hoarse and uproarious laughter burst from his audience. They slapped themselves, threw back their heads, stamped their feet ; and their guffaws were like the cawing of innumerable crows.

Dessalines rubbed a hand over his glistening face and shoulders, and wiped it on the seat of his breeches. " But to kill these Blancs, my children, I must have your help ! Listen carefully, now ! This fort is too crowded. There is not space inside for everyone. Therefore all of you are to make your camps on the slopes between the fort and the river, where you can see everything and be seen by all. There you will stay quietly until the Blancs appear at the foot of the hill. Then you will become actors and act a part for those intruders. They come here howling about Liberty, Equality, and Fraternity, do they ? Well, my children, the rear end of my body to them and their Liberty, Equality, and Fraternity ! They expect us to be struck dumb by their white military antics : to be a lot of helpless black fools and allow ourselves to be hoodwinked and killed ! But no, my friends, my children ! They call us macaques. Therefore we cover them with kakamacaque ! "

His audience were convulsed by his humour.

Dessalines, openly basking in this outburst of appreciative laughter, waited for the last raucous bellow to die away. " When the Blancs appear at the foot of the hill, you must pretend to be in a panic. You must run here and run there, as if overcome with terror. You must pick up your muskets : put them down ; snatch up your kettles : drop them. You must continue to do this until the Blancs come out on the slope and march towards you. When that happens, you must run. You must run up the hill towards the fort, but not too fast, and you must keep together as you run, in a long line."

He turned and snatched a smouldering match from the hands of a soldier who had brought a small mortar to the parapet.

" Listen well, my children ! Run to the vicinity of the moat here below me and all those ditches yonder : then run about, as if lost. I will be here, watching over you. When you hear this——"

He slapped the match against the breech of the mortar : its explosion pressed abrupt fingers against my eardrums, and from its muzzle a ring of white smoke went rolling and wavering upwards, like a lost halo scuttling back to heaven.

" When you hear that," Dessalines shouted, " leap into the moat or the nearest ditch. Leap in, lie flat, and don't move ! Don't raise your heads. Don't stir until I say you can. Then, by God, get up and chop those Blancs into little pieces ! If you don't, they'll rip out your guts and strangle you with 'em ! "

Dessalines buzzed around us like a big black bee while we loaded all the guns with langrage and musket balls ; and when he was satisfied and took himself off to supervise the placing of musketmen on the walls, I thought about him as King Dick had asked—thought as well as I was able, considering how I hated him for keeping me where I didn't want to be, for forcing me to do something I didn't want to do, and above all for preventing me from going to Lydia. At this last I was as nearly desperate as a man could be and still stay sane.

Yet I *did* think, and when King Dick asked me whether I had decided what I'd do if I were in Dessalines' place, I had an answer.

" Yes," I said, " I have. I'm Dessalines, whose chief strength is in attacking, not in being attacked. I've got twelve hundred men in this fort, which can never be defended against artillery. Until the French bring artillery against it, the fort can be defended by three hundred men as effectively as by twelve hundred. That's so, isn't it ? "

" That certainly so, Albion ! " King Dick said.

" All right then : I'm wasting nine hundred men by keeping them here. Lamartinière can direct the defences of this fort as well as I can ; therefore I'm going to let him do it. Me, Dessalines, I'm going to show myself to the French, all sweaty and noisy ; then sneak away and into the mountains, where I can attack Rochambeau and Hardy in the rear. Isn't that what you'd do ? "

" Why not ? " King Dick asked. " All I got to do is put men in trees and on cliffs and on sides of every ravine and gully. I could pick off those white-coats of Rochambeau's and Hardy's like shooting pigeons. When you think I better do it ? "

" Well, let's see : Me, Dessalines, I'll never get away if I wait till Rochambeau and Hardy and Leclerc move up close to this fort, because there'll be twelve thousand Frenchmen in a ring around us. Therefore I leave before they get here. Is that reasonable ? "

" That how I figure it, Albion. Way I figure it, that old Dessalines be a fool to stay here. He 'most everything that's bad except a fool."

" Very well then : I'm still Dessalines. If the French attack to-day, and my plans work out the way I expect, everyone's going to be excited inside the fort ; and as for the French, they won't know what hit 'em. They'll be stunned—confused. They'll probably not even send detachments to patrol the other sides of the fort. So if I want to get away without being seen by anyone inside or outside the fort, I probably ought to go to-night. Indeed, I certainly ought to go to-night, alone, to make sure of getting away. Then I can send back word for regiments to filter out to-morrow night and the night after."

King Dick examined his huge hands, opening and closing them experimentally, as though gauging their hitting power. " What you plan to do about Albion Hamlin and King Dick, Mister Dessalines ? "

" Kakamacaque ! " I said. " Fimié sec ! Let those fools of Americans fall on their faces in the manure of my grandmother's aunt's pig-pen ! I need them here to fight those guns ! "

" My, my," King Dick said admiringly, " That too much like him to laugh at ! That mean he going to-night and we better go with him. We got to ! " He clenched his left fist and eyed the knuckles doubtfully, as a woman might examine a new bonnet. " I wonder if he any harder to wipe than Autremont ? "

We had our first glimpse of the French at the hottest hour of that hot and breathless afternoon. Half a dozen officers in white uniforms rode out into the cleared land from the Petite Rivière road and stood together in a group, as if astounded by the red hill before them and the two hundred or more black soldiers camped part way up that shadeless, sun-baked slope. The group of officers separated, and out from the road behind them poured seemingly endless ranks of white-clad soldiers marching four abreast—ranks that turned sharply to the right on emerging from the road and continued on across the cleared land at the foot of the hill, until they formed a long low white wall against the higher dark-green wall of the jungle.

We could hear the faint rattle of the drums when that long white wall turned to face us. We could see the long line waver as it re-formed ; then, with hardly a moment's hesitation, it started up that long, long slope, straight towards us, moving with inexorable precision, as though marching in review before Bonaparte himself.

There was something painfully exciting in that advancing column

H

of white-clad men, in the far-off clatter of the drums, in the rapid running to and fro of the hundreds of black soldiers midway down the slope, in the confused hurrying and shouting within the fort as officers placed their men in position to fire on the approaching line, in the savage stamping, on the parapet above us, of Dessalines.

I think those blacks in Haiti were actors by nature, for they loved to strut in finery that struck white men as purely ludicrous : like Marie Camargo, they could dance for hours on end, dances that were theatrical performances in themselves ; not John Kemble himself could have out-done them in pretending to be possessed by strange gods ; nor could Garrick have taught ambitious thespians to better the performance of those black soldiers on the hill-slope, for they played to perfection the role of a regiment half-paralysed by fear. They milled about like cattle until the French line started up the hill. Then they broke and ran for the fort, darting from side to side as if crazed, arms and legs flapping. They ran until they reached the ditches and the moat, and there they stood, a strange sight, for they continued to go through the motions of running, convulsed at their own behaviour, their mouths wide open, and their yammering laughter was such that nobody within hearing could help laughing too.

Never, I think, did laughter vanish so quickly from the faces of so many as when Dessalines slapped a lighted match against the touch-hole of his little mortar.

With the roar of that gun, the whole world abruptly changed, as a sunlit forest changes when a black cloud obscures the sun. Within the blink of an eye all the capering black soldiers just beyond our gun embrasures plunged headlong into moat and ditches and were erased ; all their laughter was gone as though it had never been ; all the turmoil and confusion that had reigned within the fort had been replaced by a silence so thick that it pressed upon me like a blanket. All life, all sound, all movement seemed suspended everywhere except in that long line of white-uniformed Frenchmen marching towards us.

They were close—so close that I could see their features, their long moustaches, the buttons on their black gaiters, the stains on their white uniforms. They marched as if on parade, a six-foot space between each two companies. The captains at the left, the drummers behind the captains, the lieutenants on the rear flanks, and in the centre of the long line the division commander and his aides, all clean and glittering and cool-appearing, their wigs shining white beneath their black tricorns, their boots gleaming black through the red dust, their should-ered swords winking like ice in the brassy-hot glare of that Haitian afternoon.

The whole long line was businesslike and placid, as if there were no such things as war and killing and shattered bodies and the insane ambition of a small fat man in Paris.

King Dick, who had knelt to sight through the nearest gun-tube, got to his feet. " My, my ! " he said faintly. " Two French generals, right in the middle. Nobody going to——"

" Fire ! " Dessalines screamed.

The whole fort erupted smoke, concussion, tumult. The guns jerked back against their ropes, the crews shouted and ran with rammers, buckets, and powder bags, muskets rattled all along the front of the fort like innumerable giant hailstones pelting on a tin roof, and smoke drifted saltily thick into the gun-ports, obscuring our vision like a grey curtain that fluctuated, drifted, shredded and suddenly wasn't there.

What I saw with the lifting of that curtain now seems like something unreal : something too horrible to happen—and that was how it seemed to me even when the dreadful reality was before my eyes.

That long white line of placid men had, in a moment's time, been mangled beyond comprehension. They lay upon the ground, dirty and crumpled, ripped and writhing ; roaring, screaming, sobbing. The red dust hung above that torn and shredded windrow of bodies, and here and there a few dazed soldiers stumbled uncertainly through the red haze and the heaps of dead and wounded. I saw a headless body with blood gushing in a double jet from the raw neck ; a whole leg, torn off at the hip that moved and contracted itself in the moment I watched it : a man, his intestines slipping from a hole in his stomach, who fumblingly tried to stuff them back into himself, as one might try to push eels into too small a bag. Arms rose flailingly from the heap ; legs kicked in agony ; bodies contorted themselves, as if straining to be rid of their garments ; and unceasingly, from that miserable windrow, came an agonising wailing that wasn't human, that might have come from countless giant cats, yowling horribly in the dark.

I couldn't distinguish one from another : at first I couldn't find those central figures, those glittering and whitely gleaming officers who had marched midway of that long line. Then I saw a colonel tugging at a fallen man, and recognised the one at whom he tugged as one of the two generals, necessarily one of Bonaparte's great leaders. When the colonel got the general to his feet, his hat was gone, his white wig was twisted on his close-cropped head, his breeches were crimson from a wound. A second officer came from nowhere and supported the general while the colonel fumbled at the general's waist and took down his breeches. They carried him off that way, his breeches dragging around his ankles, his shirt-tail clinging wetly to his rear, his bloody under-drawers sagging between his knees like a red flag.

The French left their dead where they fell. If they hadn't done so, I believe that entire division of two thousand men would have ceased to exist, for Dessalines had no mercy on those who succoured the wounded or tried to carry off the dead. " Kill 'em," he kept shouting to the musketmen. " Kill 'em all ! They wanted this war, so let 'em have it ! Kill every last one of the bastards ! "

I had no sympathy whatever for the French, but I wished with all my heart that somebody would put a bullet through Dessalines' head.

There's something about military rank, in an army, that acts like a shield or a suit of armour for those who wear it. Generals and colonels, before they become generals or colonels, follow all sorts of trades and professions ; and in long wars butlers and shoemakers, school teachers and farmers, merchants and stage-coach drivers, doctors and cooks, rise surprisingly to high positions. In those high positions their word is not only law—it is a voice from the clouds, a final judgment, a clap of thunder from high Olympus that makes strong men cringe and leaves the bravest soldiers all a-tremble.

Why this should be I do not rightly know ; but the fact remains that when a butler or a butcher becomes a general, he is still a butler or a butcher when out of uniform ; but in uniform he is a potential dispenser of disgrace and degradation to every man of lesser rank, and therefore more feared than any deity or demon.

Thus when the two of us walked up to the door of Dessalines' quarters immediately after the changing of the guard that night, I had within me the same quaking feeling that comes to a young lawyer just before he rises to his feet to plead a case before a hanging judge.

What King Dick's feelings were I had no way of knowing, for he wore the same smile, half-abashed and half-friendly, that had been upon his face when I first saw him in the dining-room of the Hôtel de la République.

There was a single sentry outside the door of Dessalines' quarters ; a single flickering light in the lantern that hung beside the door.

When the sentry challenged, I stopped, as we had planned, and faced to the rear to guard against anyone's coming upon us.

King Dick, as we had also planned, stepped up to the sentry as if to give the password.

I heard a half-grunt, half-strangled squawk from the sentry ; then King Dick's voice saying, " All right, Albion." When I hurried to him, he had the sentry in his arms, hoisted up so that his own shoulder was wedged under the sentry's ribs ; and so great was the pressure on that poor black man that his eyes and tongue protruded.

I pulled at the latch of Dessalines' door. It rose easily and I went in. King Dick, carrying the unconscious sentry, crowded in behind me.

My first impression was one of innumerable packages, bales, and bundles crowded into one small cell. In the centre of the room, on the floor, was an enormous green handkerchief, and on the handkerchief were piled gowns, shoes, jewel-boxes, enough for a dozen women ; and before them knelt Madame Dessalines, eyeing them despairingly.

She looked up at us quickly, seemed puzzled by what she saw, then smiled pleasantly. " Why, it's M. Hamlin. I hadn't understood——" Her eyes went to the pistol in my hand and she stopped.

I saw Dessalines just in time. He had been kneeling on the floor, half in and half out of a trunk, and since he was naked to the waist, his black back had blended indistinguishably with the dark wall beyond.

At his wife's word he straightened up, whirled to face us and made a little movement to one side.

" No noise," I said. " No shouting or shooting ! "

I heard King Dick put the sentry on the floor, and out of the corner of my eye saw him apologetically take silk stockings from Madame Dessalines' pile of belongings. So I just stood there, watching Dessalines, while King Dick gagged and tied the sentry.

When at last King Dick came to stand beside me, Dessalines asked in a strangled voice, " What you want ? "

" Nothing but our rights," I said. " You forced us into your army against our wishes. If you intend to leave this fort, we intend to do the same, and do it safely."

" Well," Dessalines growled, " you don't have to come breaking into your commanding general's quarters with a pistol in your hands to tell me such a thing ! If that's all you want, just get out of here until I send word to you that we're going."

" We can't do that," I said. " We took a long chance coming in here like this. We wouldn't have done it if we hadn't been desperate, and if we hadn't been sure you were meaning to go off without giving us a chance to go ourselves."

Dessalines just looked at me, and I thanked God he didn't have a pistol in his hand. It seemed to me I could see that tortuous dark mind of his writhing and wriggling as it hunted for any sort of lie that would give him a momentary advantage over us. That was all he needed— just one small moment's advantage.

" We're not sure when you were planning to leave," I went on, " but we figured it ought to be around midnight. We think that's a little too late. We think you ought to leave in about an hour, and we'll wait right here until you start. Then we'll go with you—and it might be a good idea for us to take with us some of those packages of food I see out there."

Dessalines looked from me to King Dick and back again. King Dick's face wore that peculiarly blank look of his—a look that verged on complete idiocy.

" The trouble with you white folks," Dessalines said, " is you've got too many brains for your own good. Every damn one of you spends all his time imagining things. Whoever told you I was planning to leave here to-night told you a lie ! "

" Nobody told me anything," I said ; " but we know that Rochambeau and Hardy are closing in on you, and that mighty few people can escape from this fort once the French have got it surrounded. It looks to us as if you'd got to leave pretty quick if you're going to leave at all, and we know how your mind works. Whatever you do, you do without waiting. So we figure you'll be leaving to-night."

Madame Dessalines spoke rapidly to her husband, and he threw her a grimace that probably passed in his own mind for a smile. " Didn't you hear me say they could go when I went ? " he asked her. " These gentlemen are unduly suspicious."

He turned his attention to me. " You're not a real soldier," he said. " You're just a make-believe soldier. You come in here with a gun and point it at me—me, Dessalines ! " His throat fluttered and his voice took on a booming quality. " You come in here with one little pistol and point it at Dessalines, who has killed ten thousand men with his own hands, and think you can frighten him ! Mer-de-merde ! Why, you white fool ! If you were only half a soldier you'd know that a man like me can't be shot ! You couldn't even hit me."

He took a slow step towards me. " Look," he said, " you can't shoot ! You haven't the guts of a chicken ! "

He took another slow step ; then, with a rush, he wrenched the pistol from my hand. His wife jumped to her feet and screamed. Laughing like a hyena, he rammed the pistol against my stomach : I heard the click of the falling hammer ; saw the spark from the flint. When there was no explosion, Dessalines rapped the muzzle against the floor, again pushed it against my stomach and pulled the trigger.

" It's not loaded," I said. " We thought probably you might try something like that, and of course we didn't want any noise in here."

I think he tried to throw the pistol at me and shout at the same time, but before he could do either, King Dick's open left hand slapped him hard across the mouth, and his right fist crossed against his jaw with the sound of a plank hitting a horse's rump. Dessalines tripped and fell backward, and King Dick was on him like a big black cat, jerking him over on his face, wrenching his arms together and knotting a silk stocking around his wrists, all the time banging his head against the dirt floor. Then he pulled him over on his back and rammed silk stockings between those enormous thick lips. I thought he'd never stop. That mouth held as many stockings as my Aunt Emmy's rag-bag.

I have often said that a woman who marries a monster, or uncomplainingly lives for years with a bad man or a dolt, must carry concealed within herself all the evil qualities that are apparent in the man ; but Madame Dessalines seemed to be one of the exceptions to that rule. Unlike her husband and many other Negroes, she had nothing against any man because of his colour, and certainly she dared to be honest with Dessalines and to oppose him—a form of bravery dangerous for any wife even when she's young and beautiful and even if she is at the mercy of a far less violent man than Dessalines.

It was Madame Dessalines who made it easy for us to escape from Crête à Pierrot. The escape itself was nothing ; the truly terrible phase was our journey across the mountains to the north—a labour from which we couldn't for a moment rest because we knew the unspeakable tortures that awaited us if Dessalines ever caught up with us or if he succeeded in having us intercepted before we reached the safety of Cap François.

When King Dick got up from tying Dessalines, Madame Dessalines knelt beside him to wipe his warty forehead with a wisp of a handkerchief. " I had the feeling," she said, " that something was wrong when you told me yesterday that M. Hamlin could go with us."

He rolled his eyes and made a growling sound, wholly meaningless.

" I have told you and told you, Jean," she went on, " that I have known always when something has gone wrong. I have even told you how I know. It's because you try to look innocent, and you don't know how to look innocent ! " She sighed and made a brushing movement with her hand as if discouraging a fly. " But that is done now and I shall waste no further time discussing it. Now you must tell M. Hamlin how you propose to leave the fort."

Dessalines nodded and his eyes glittered in the candlelight.

She looked up at me. " If you take out the gag, he'll tell you."

" I'd as soon blow out my brains as take the gag from his mouth," I said. " He'd have Lamartinière at our throats in a minute—or else he'd tell us a lie that would get us killed."

" But he can't get away, gagged and tied like this," she said.

" He don't need his mouth to cross the Cahos," King Dick reminded her.

" He'll stay gagged," I said. " We'll let him use his legs when the time comes, but I've had enough of his lies and abuse. He must have told you something. Tell us what you know, and we'll guess the rest."

I think she had only been seeking an excuse to tell us what she knew ; and as a result of what she told us, we scraped the earth from a corner of the floor in that little room, found an iron door beneath it, and through the tunnel it concealed crawled safely to the bank of the river, well beyond the light of the fires that illuminated every angle and bastion of those blood-red walls.

As a final measure of precaution we bound Dessalines again when we were safely on the road to the Cahos Mountains, knotting his bonds in such a way that a woman would have been an hour untying them.

" Madame," I told his wife, " you've been my good friend, and I believe we're safe in your hands ; but I can't trust your husband. He's a great soldier, and there's nothing a great soldier won't do in order to destroy his enemies—nothing ! If he ever gets his hands on us, he'll show us no mercy ; so we've got to have half an hour's start of you. The one thing we don't know is where he plans to meet the men who certainly are going to join him. So from here we'll have to go alone. But we'll leave a knife stuck in a tree a hundred paces farther on, and you can cut your husband free with it. Remember—you'll find it when you've walked a hundred paces."

When I'd have thanked her for her kindness to Lydia, King Dick put a heavy hand upon my shoulder and turned me towards the pass into the Cahos.

"We got to get through that pass before morning," he said sharply, and pushed me before him into the black dark.

"That lady very sweet," he whispered when we were beyond earshot, "but it don't matter how sweet they are when you through with 'em. Tell 'em nothing : then they got nothing to tell. First thing we got to do is make sure we never lay eyes on that sweet lady again—or on that sweet Dessalines. Sweet ! Hoy ! "

CHAPTER XXXV

WE NEVER got through the pass. As soon as there was no possibility that Dessalines or his wife could hear us, King Dick bore off towards the steep slopes that lay on our right. " Best thing we can do," he told me, " is do the last thing Dessalines thinks we do : we stay right where we can watch everybody. When everyone busy with something else, we say good-bye to 'em."

We slept that night in the heart of a thorn thicket, and before we fell asleep we heard Dessalines and his wife making their slow way along the pass, his voice an angry croak, hers an occasional faint piping. I could imagine what he was saying about us, and I was absolutely sure I'd stop at nothing to keep from falling into his hands again.

At dawn we were on our way through the thorns, the tangled vines, the seemingly impenetrable green and dripping smother that clothed the steep sides of Morne Rouge, that towering dark mountain that frowned down upon Crête à Pierrot.

On its highest peak we hid the provisions we'd taken from Dessalines, along with our water-bottles, our meagre packs, and ourselves among the rock-fissures. At night we alternately froze and parboiled in the cold winds, the warm rains, the crashing thunderstorms that marched around that mountain in endless succession. From dawn to dark we took turns staring through King Dick's telescope at the far-off red fort on Crête à Pierrot—and what we saw made me wonder whether all mankind, if left to its own consistent stupidity, won't in the end destroy itself.

On the eleventh of March we saw columns of French troops fording the river near Verrettes—King Dick identified it as Boudet's division, hurrying from Port-au-Prince to relieve the troops that had first attacked us and in the attacking lost four hundred men. Leading Boudet's troops was a black regiment, with the black general Petion at its head—Petion being a Negro known to King Dick. He had fought for Toussaint in former wars, gone to France, and returned with Leclerc. I couldn't stomach the fact that Negroes should know so little or understand so little that they would consent to fight against other Negroes who were fighting to be free ; and when I tried to explain my feeling to King Dick, he nodded understandingly and said that Negroes were a good deal like whites, only more so.

We saw the French bivouac in the dusk, a huge square of regiments, with cavalry and cannon in the centre ; and when dawn came, that eager army had broken its square and had already reached the slopes of Crête à Pierrot—slopes covered with black regiments that slept or seemed to sleep.

Almost I could hear the logical French phrases falling logically from the lips of those great, those consistent French leaders—" Hah ! See those black fools, asleep and unprepared ! We have surprised them ! Come, then : let us advance upon those black miserables ! At one blow we take them all, eh ? Come, then, my children ! Come, fearless heroes of Italy and the Nile ! Let us overwhelm this black scum ! Onward for France and for glory ! "

Ah, yes ! They were consistent men, those Frenchmen : consistent in their contempt for black soldiers : consistent in their belief in their own invincibility and the superiority of their own logic to other sorts : consistent in their determination to take whatever they wanted from anyone too weak or too ignorant to resist—and for the consistency of a few, hundreds suffered, as must always be the case.

Up the slopes of Crête à Pierrot went those long white columns, and the same things happened that had happened on the day of the first attack. The black regiments streamed, ant-like, towards the fort, with the white-clad regiments in dignified pursuit.

Then, suddenly, there were no longer any scuttling black ants : there were only the long lines of white-uniformed Frenchmen. The red sides of the fort spouted a cottony cloud of smoke, and below us on the hot red hill-slope consistency and French logic had their reward. The long white lines fluttered and unravelled, twisted and frayed. The whole face of the slope was covered with Frenchmen who lay still, or wriggled like pallid half-crushed insects, or streamed in disorder down the hill. In that one charge another eight hundred Frenchmen were sacrificed on that slope to the consistent arrogance of Bonaparte and his generals. . . .

" One more French column left," King Dick said, " and that the worst. That Rochambeau with all his cannon, coming down from the north. When Rochambeau get through the mountains, everybody be gathered around Crête à Pierrot and maybe we get away safe."

So we huddled among the rocks on the summit of Morne Rouge and watched Boudet's army try to bury its dead : watched it join with the first troops that had attacked us : watched the two forces move around the base of Crête à Pierrot, setting up a besieging force.

We had been on that mountain top for ten interminable days when Rochambeau's army came out of the defiles to the north. and with all the incredible consistency peculiar to moths, ducks, gamblers, thieves, whores, and armies, advanced happily to their doom, just as moths rush to a flame, ducks to decoys, gamblers to inevitable loss, thieves to prison, whores to disease. They set off up the slopes of Crête à Pierrot, hopeful of surprising and capturing the Negroes who lounged and dozed in apparent helplessness. When those helpless Negroes jumped into the ditches, and the north wall of the fort belched smoke and flame, three hundred of Rochambeau's men dropped shattered, screaming, dying and dead in the red dust. Fifteen hundred men the French had lost, just as Toussaint had hoped they would.

" Now they do what they should have done long ago," King Dick said. " Now they knock down that old fort with guns, *Boum* ! When they do, they make so much noise that nobody have ears for us."

He was right. By the following noon the French had all their batteries in place, and the rumbling of those far-off guns was like the thumping of heavy-laden carts on cobbled streets. To the tune of that unending far thunder we made our way down the side of Morne Rouge and towards the swarthy slopes of the Cahos.

I'm not so sure that fear—the proper sort of fear, which perhaps should be called caution—isn't the sixth sense that helps men endure the unendurable. Certainly I was afraid of everything that stood between me and Lydia. I was afraid of those horrible black mountains ; afraid of what would befall us if we were captured by Negro troops and returned to Dessalines ; afraid of what would happen if we were taken by French troops who had heard, as all Frenchmen must have heard, of the heaps of bodies that Dessalines had left at St. Marc, Petite Rivière, and Verrettes; afraid of every man, woman, and child, whether black or partly black ; afraid of the dark, lest our bruised feet, on those mountains, would miss their holds and leave us as helpless as the miserable families who had clung to the cliffs above Verrettes and waited for Dessalines' men to shoot them down.

We clambered up those black mountains and crawled like goats along the northerly side, alternately seared by a sun that set red spots dancing before my eyes and frozen by rainstorms that slashed like icy whips. We went our crooked way through valleys, gorges, water-courses, mud-holes, first to the westward ; then to the eastward across jungles, plains, plantations, rivers ; then west again up into the cliffs and trees of the Marmelade chain; then east once more, across mountain spurs and through thorn forests, to Dondon.

There was a pass from Dondon across the mountains into the Great North Plain, but we didn't dare take it because we didn't know who held it. It seemed to me I'd been struggling and climbing for ever. A mountain range was no longer a mountain range to me—it was just another unending series of steps, with nothing to be considered but the next step.

I remember that last mountain chain as a racking torment of crawling, scrambling, wriggling : of watching and listening and crawling again : of padding my knees with fresh leaves : of readjusting the rags around my feet. Those rags were torn, black, bloody ; and every little while they slipped. Then they had to be rewrapped. They were tied with fibre from century plants—threads that constantly broke. I can't now recall the sharpness of the mountains, but I'll never forget the pain of those rags on my feet—the slashing pains when the hard and blackened parts of the rags cut into a raw spot ; the excruciating agony when fibre threads pressed against an inflamed tendon. The days were foggy welters of holding back lianas and thorns to let King Dick pass ; crawling through holes he similarly made for me ; hugging rocks ; peering through vines and leaves at the next rock ; watching, perpetually watching, for French-men who might shoot us : for Negroes who might hack us with machetes : for mulattoes who might betray us.

Yet all this pain and all this labour seemed, at the time, to have nothing in common with ordinary labour and pain ; they were a necessary part of life, of no account, provided I could accomplish what I had set out to do—keep alive and somehow get to Cap François and Lydia.

I'd been thinking that when we should have surmounted that last range of mountains—to see before us the plantations of the Great North Plain, the purple tropical sea beyond, and Cap François itself snug against its sheltering mountain—I'd feel a great elation : all weariness would leave me : I'd be strong again. But I was wrong.

The day came when the rocks, the twisted lianas, the thorny branches, the drooping great leaves before us took on an unaccustomed brightness. Instead of thick and gloomy forest darkness, we saw brilliance—a blue and golden radiance almost blinding after the jungle twilight through which we had so long struggled. Then, from a precipice, we saw our goal before us : the countless sugar plantations of the Great North Plain, framed on either side by purple mountains : at their far edge the tropical ultramarine sea, curving upward to the northern horizon, and limpet-like, upon the rim, the city of Cap François, a dirty grey smudge beside an infinitesimal harbour.

Never in my life had I wanted so such to be anywhere as I had wanted, since our departure from St. Marc, to be in Cap François. Never had I worked so hard to attain a goal. But now that the goal was almost won, I discovered what so many learn all too late : that the most perilous part of any man's endeavours comes at the moment when he nears his heart's desire.

It wasn't of Lydia that I thought, now that success was close upon us ; and I had no inclination to shout, as did Xenophon's men, " The sea ! The sea ! " I could only think confused thoughts about how we could cross the intervening miles without being laid by the heels : about whether the rags that served me for shoes would hold together long enough to let me limp across that endless plain. The elation I had dreamed of feeling was buried beneath a profound depression. I had no wish to leap with joy. Ah, no ! I had too much to do ! I could only concentrate on unwinding, for the thousandth time, those blackened, blood-caked rags, laying new leaves against sole, heel, and instep, and fastening them in such a way that I could remain upon my feet for one more day, for one more hour. . . .

God help the man who falls unwillingly into the clutches of an army, no matter where it's fighting or for what, and no matter how fine an army it is.

The French army had its hands on us before we were half-way across the Great North Plain, and there never was a better army, to begin with, than that French army that tried to capture Haiti.

At one moment we were walking along a dusty road that seemed as empty as an old snake-skin ; the next moment we were brought to a sudden halt by a shout of " Attention ! "

We turned to see a moustached soldier in a soiled white coat, standing in the middle of the road, pointing a musket at us. The musket ended in a bayonet the size—or so it seemed to me—of a cavalry sabre ; and before either of us had a chance to answer, the soldier brusquely motioned us, with that threatening bayonet, to the path from which he had popped out at us.

He took us to the charred ruins of a plantation house, where a more heavily moustached sergeant and a squad of listless soldiers were doing nothing and sweating at it—which was only reasonable, since they were dressed in heavy woollen uniforms more suitable for Maine snows than for a Haitian cane-field.

The sergeant seemed to take the same interest in us that a hunter might take in bagging two additional partridges ; for he asked us nothing, and only walked around us, eyeing my bandaged feet disparagingly and prodding appreciatively at King Dick's muscles. Then he went to a near-by shed, unfastened a bar from the door and shouted an order ; whereupon a dozen Negroes came out, scratching themselves, and stood staring slack-lipped at us or at their own bare feet.

Ten minutes later the lot of us were on our way to Cap François, with a corporal's guard marching on either side and in our rear.

When I asked King Dick what he thought they'd do to us, he shook his head. " Whatever they do, they not do long. They nothing a man can't get out of, one way or another." He pondered awhile, then added, " No matter what happen, we better keep quiet till I have a chance to use some of that one-way-or-another. Good thing for us I still have some of that one-way-or-another left ! " He was as near naked as a man can be and still be called clothed ; yet he had long ago discarded the little ox-tail in which he had carried his pearls. If he had any pearls concealed anywhere about him, it would be little short of a miracle—yet I'd already seen miracles in Haiti.

"Then I'm to tell no one, even a French officer, that I'm a white man and an American ? " I asked.

"Oh, my goo'ness Yes ! " King Dick said. " We can't talk, not till we know it safe to talk to who we're talking to. Suppose we tell the wrong man we Americans. First thing you know, he look at your feet and ask questions : Where you been, who you been with, what you been doing. What you do then ? If you lie, he catch you lying. If you tell truth, he not like it. White officers, they very afraid of people who tell truth. M'm, m'm ! That very dangerous ! That something people get put in jail for ; and French jail—hoy ! "

What they wanted us for we discovered all too soon. Long before we reached Cap François we saw, under construction on the elevation where Christophe's palace had stood, a tremendous building, as big as a dozen New England barns all joined together. Around and upon the structure crawled countless figures ; and as we drew nearer we overtook gangs of Negroes, guarded by French soldiers, hauling baulks of timber, or carrying planks, one plank to each two men, or dragging stones on wooden runners like the skid-sleds Maine men use for hauling cordwood in winter.

The corporal marched us up the long slope and around to the front of this enormous sprawling building, from which came a thunderous and unending hammering, banging, and clattering. The whole place, inside and out, was a-swarm with Negroes of every size and shade, working to their own singing, or the shouts of overseers, or the thumping of drums. They were lifting timbers and boards into place, driving spikes, hauling on ropes, passing chains of buckets from hand to hand.

We were taken to a little three-walled shed in which four white men were seated at tables working over drawing-boards. They were in shirt sleeves, but wore military boots and breeches, so they had to be soldiers. Outside the shed four half-uniformed mulatto messengers, each with a cocomacaque, stared at us contemptuously.

The chief of our guards halted, saluted smartly, and in a remote and military manner addressed one of the men as lieutenant and said he was reporting from Limonade with fourteen workmen. The lieutenant wagged a pencil at him by way of acknowledgment, ran a cold eye over us, drew a handful of francs from a table drawer and handed them to the corporal, who at once marched his men away.

When the young man snapped his fingers, one of the mulatto messengers got to his feet and said to us, in Creole, " You get twenty sous each day, and food like all the others. You must work hard, because this palace is for the lady of the captain-general. Each of you will wear a number around the neck ; and when you show the number, you will receive food and money and a place to sleep."

From a hook he took a handful of brass discs on chains, and handed one to each of us. Mine bore the number 7402. Seven thousand four hundred and two black men slaving for Pauline Bonaparte !

So here was I, who had planned a mutiny against Dessalines in order to reach Cap François, and had stumbled across the Cahos and the Black mountains and half of Haiti in order to get there—and now that I was in that greatly desired town I found myself as helpless as a baby or a black slave, and farther than ever from finding Lydia.

The lieutenant consulted his plans, then flirted a negligent hand at the messenger. " Take them to the fifth section," he said, " and turn them over to Duval." He eyed King Dick appraisingly. " You ! You speak French ? "

King Dick's lower lip drooped, his eyes were blank.

When the messenger shouted at him King Dick looked frightened. " Ask him what he did," the lieutenant told the messenger. " Was he ever in the army ? "

The messenger raised an imaginary musket to his shoulder, cried " Boom ! " and asked " Army ? Soldier ? "

King Dick rolled his eyes, a picture of stupidity.

" Pig ! " the mulatto shouted. " Answer, you black horse ! " He raised his cocomacaque and aimed a blow at King Dick's head. King Dick raised both arms, and almost accidentally the cocomacaque thwacked into one of his big pink palms. The mulatto wrenched at it. King Dick, as if to protect himself, stumbled backward, still clutching the coco-macaque ; then clumsily fell down, pulling the mulatto with him. He seemed to fall awkwardly, rolling over in mid-air and landing solidly upon the mulatto. He was equally clumsy in getting to his feet, for he pushed one huge hand against the mulatto's nose, dug a knee into his stomach, and lurched against the lieutenant's table, overturning it. The mulatto squealed ; the other officers jumped up from their tables, cursing ; the lieutenant bellowed angrily for the guard, and the whole place was in an uproar.

King Dick took me by the elbow. " This time," he whispered. " Now you talk, Albion. We got to see some bigger officer or we never get away from here."

The sentries ran to the open side of the shed and pointed their muskets at us.

" Throw that black fool into the guard-house," the lieutenant ordered. " He's spoiled a week's work. The good God help anyone who has to deal with these black savages ! "

" Sir," I said, " it's not this man's fault, and before he's put in the guard-house he's entitled to be heard. In addition to that, he's not in the army and is therefore not subject to army discipline."

" Not subject to discipline ! " the lieutenant cried. " I'll show you whether he is or not ! He's a cow, that's what he is ! A clumsy cow, with none of a cow's brains ! Sacred name of God, why didn't he——"

He broke off and eyed me incredulously. His brother officers, who were busying themselves righting the overturned table, straightened up and stared at me as well.

" Mon Dieu ! " the lieutenant cried. " French ! Real French instead of a mouthful of mush ! What's the meaning of this ? Where did a nigger ever learn to speak like that ? "

" With all due respect, sir," I said, " I'd like to protest your order sending my friend to the guard-house. He did nothing—nothing at all : merely tried to protect himself against an unwarranted attack. Surely any Frenchman of honour would agree that's no crime."

The lieutenant looked me up and down, from my bandaged feet to the sweat-stained handkerchief around my head. " Oh ho ! " he said. " A jungle lawyer ! "

He turned angrily to the mulatto who stood by the door, snuffling and wiping his swollen, bloody nose with the back of his wrist. " Well, what are you waiting for ? " he said. " Take those other twelve workmen to Duval, and don't use that club unless you're told to."

He watched the mulatto herd our twelve companions towards the sprawling structure behind us ; then motioned the two sentries away and turned to pick up the papers that had fallen to the floor, King Dick and I hastening to help him. Among them was an order directing that four additional rooms be added to the fifth section. It was signed " Lefèbvre, Chef d'Ing."—which I took to mean Chief of Engineers ; and certainly a Chief of Engineers in such an army as Leclerc's would have to be a general.

The lieutenant, his papers again in order, threw himself back in his chair and again looked me up and down.

" Now then," he said, " I'd like an answer to my questions."

" To tell you the truth, sir," I said, " I'm afraid to answer. From what you've said, I gather you're not well disposed towards blacks, and I long ago learned that it's a mistake to discuss private matters with an enemy."

The lieutenant looked as if he couldn't believe his ears. " Enemy," he whispered. " Sacré ! You black scum ! You filthy beggar out of the sewer ! I'll make you smart for this ! I'll——"

" I beg of you, sir," I said. " There's no occasion for such language. You're mistaken in almost everything you say. You know nothing whatever about me except that you don't find my clothes or my colour pleasing. I'm not being insolent : I'm only telling the truth—and since when has it been a sin to tell a Frenchman the simple truth ? "

The lieutenant's hands were shaking and so was his voice. " Don't you suppose I know insolence when I hear it ? You need to be put in your place, you black jackass ! "

" Let me remind you again, Lieutenant, that you know nothing about us. For all you know, we may be persons of importance. We *may* have some information that General Lefèbvre would urgently welcome."

The lieutenant burst into abrupt laughter, and as abruptly stopped.
" Do you think General Lefèbvre has time to waste on such as you ? "

" What makes you think his time would be wasted ? "

The lieutenant puffed out his cheeks as though he might burst.
" How could it be otherwise ! If you had anything worth saying, you'd
be willing to give me a hint of what it was."

" Not necessarily," I said. " I might have an important message for
him from General Boudet, and Boudet might have told me to deliver
it to nobody but General Lefèbvre. I might have some valuable information for him from General Leclerc. I might even have some important
proposal that General Dessalines had entrusted to me for General
Lefèbvre's ear alone."

The lieutenant shot a quick glance at his brother officers, who were
staring at the roof of the shed or contemplating their drawing-tables with
seeming absorption.

He raised his shoulders until they touched his ears. " Why didn't
you say so in the first place ? " he demanded. " You niggers are all
alike : squirm like eels till someone chokes the truth out of you ! I'll
take you to Lefèbvre myself, but God help you if you're lying ! "

CHAPTER XXXVI

KING DICK believed that all men in high political or military positions are
purchasable in one way or another. Young men, he said, are largely
honest ; but when men are bowed down with years and weighted with
honours, there isn't one in a thousand who can't be bribed with promises
of decorations, love, votes, social advancement, or financial rewards.

When the lieutenant led us past the sentries in front of General
Lefèbvre's tent, and the gaudily dressed aides who bustled in and out,
and I was confronted with the general himself and his fierce eyes and
enormous drooping moustache ; when I felt the hawk-like impatience
of his scrutiny—saw, too, the lieutenant's timidity in the presence of that
pouchy-eyed soldier—I was sure that King Dick was wrong.

" I apologise for this interruption, mon Général," the lieutenant
began stumblingly. " These men, they came in with a draft from
Limonade. They were as you see them here, unkempt and no different
from the others. Then one of them "—he indicated King Dick—" re-
sisted arrest ; and this one "—he flung out an expostulatory hand towards
me—" became insolent."

The general pulled at his swags of moustache. " A thousand
thunders ! " he said ferociously. " Haven't I told you not to bother me
with your petty annoyances ? You're in charge of workmen, and the
way to take charge of workmen is to take charge of them."

" Yes, mon Général," the lieutenant said hastily, " but this man was insolent in perfect French. What was more, he made an argument to which I, as a Frenchman, was forced to listen : it had logic. He refused to tell me his business and demanded to see you. What was more, he said that for all I knew he might have a message for you from General Boudet ; or "—he lowered his voice to a whisper—" or from Dessalines. Who am I to assume that this was untrue ? "

General Lefèbvre snorted and fixed me with a fishy glare. My eyes seemed to fascinate him, and he grumbled and snorted to himself. To the lieutenant he said, " Ah, well, it is possible. Anything is possible in this latrine of a country. Go back to your work, my brave, and I will attend to these two."

The lieutenant saluted smartly, turned on his heel, and marched out. General Lefèbvre snorted again, pulled at his moustache, eyed us suspiciously ; then rapped out a sharp order to his aides, who scuttled from the tent like startled chickens.

" Well," he said, " let's hear some of that perfect French. It ought to be amusing, coming from a blue-eyed Negro."

" Sir," I said, " I spoke to the lieutenant on behalf of my friend here. He has a mission to perform in Cap François."

The general raised his eyes to heaven and seemed to restrain himself with difficulty. " A mission ! Well, I have a mission, too ! This palace must be finished in one month's time, and I'm responsible ! What happens to me if workmen don't work ? "

He thrust his head forward and glared at us out of pouchy eyes. " If you've got anything to say, say it ! Don't hint at Boudet—Leclerc—Dessalines ! Say something intelligent, and say it quick, or I'll have both of you tied up and whipped within an inch of your life ! "

King Dick looked over his shoulder to make sure nobody was near the tent entrance. " With the general's permission," King Dick whispered in that atrocious Creole of his, " we, my friend and I, are afraid we might talk too much. As we look now, nobody will believe anything we say. We need gold lace, silk shirts, high boots, rings, and big hats, so that we may look respectable again."

General Lefèbvre's eyes seemed to search the air above King Dick and me. They wandered back and forth, occasionally stooping to our faces for a lightning moment. " Yes," he said at length, " there is something in what you say. Your appearance is not such as to inspire confidence. Wholly not ! But I do not think there is any place in this town where one would be able to get such things as you describe."

" If any one spends," King Dick whispered, " there is always everything, even boots and gold lace, where there seems to be nothing. For me, however, this would not be easy. I should be called nigger, and be stolen from. Of course, if I were in mon Général's position, I would have no difficulty. I would have less difficulty if mon Général should "

—he turned to me and threw out his big hands helplessly—" you see, my friend Albion, how I cannot express myself correctly."

" You're expressing yourself all right," I said. " Why don't you tell the general you have some valuable property you'd like to sell, but don't dare for fear it might be confiscated ? "

The general eyed me quizzically, and no wonder ; for if ever a person looked destitute of any sort of property, it was King Dick. " Property ? " the general asked. " What sort of property ? "

King Dick extended a huge black fist and opened it. There, nestling on his pink palm, were two pearls. As he moved his hand, they shimmered like globes carved from the heart of a New England dawn.

The general looked King Dick up and down, then rose from his chair to scrutinise him more closely and from all sides. He seemed puzzled by what he saw ; and when he seated himself again, he took the pearls from King Dick, put them on his desk, and examined them suspiciously. " Where did you get them ? " he asked.

" Raising coffee," King Dick said.

The general flapped an impatient hand. " No, no, where were you carrying them ? You are without garments, almost. I didn't see you get them out of your mouth or from any other place."

King Dick pretended not to understand him. " They are first-water pearls from St. Thomas." He poked them with a huge forefinger. " Only an expert would see that they are not perfectly matched : one is thirty-two grains and cost twelve thousand francs ; the other is not quite so good or so heavy—it cost eighty-five hundred francs. They are worth more, of course : perfect skin and fine orient."

The general picked them up, studied them carefully and nodded. " Yes, you have reason. I think I can understand how difficult it would be for . . ." His voice ran down to an unmelodious humming sound.

" These are very bad times," King Dick said ; " and, as in all bad times, people are looking for bargains. Now these two pearls—if I got five thousand francs for them, it would be enough to start me and my friend again."

" Five thousand francs apiece ? " Lefèbvre asked.

" No, mon Général," King Dick said ; " five thousand francs for the two. If you were able to get that for us, mon Général, it would be a kindness we shall never forget."

The general pushed back his chair and stared at the top of his tent-pole, where a black spider with red eyes was wrapping a moth in a tight grey web. " So far, so good," he said, " but certain questions still remain unanswered. This palace must be finished for the captain-general and his wife, and it's my duty to employ everybody who is able to work. If you are seen in the city, unemployed and unattached, every-one will ask, ' Why aren't these men working for Lefèbvre ? ' Now then, is there any reason why you shouldn't work on the palace, even if I do find it possible to dispose of these two pearls for you—for five thousand francs ? "

King Dick nodded at me and spoke quickly in English. " Now it time you tell everything, Albion."

" Ah ! Anglais ! " Lefèbvre said. " You are Anglais, eh ? "

" No," I said, " we are Americans. It's a long story——"

The general got to his feet excitedly, walked up and down his tent, pulling at his enormous moustache. " Ha, I spik Anglais vair' well. I have slip' wiz two-three Anglais gentilwooman—slipping dictionnaire, eh ? By two of zem I have children. Ha ! When I hear Anglais, I am excite ! You should see how I am success with Anglais gentilwooman ! Word of honour, there were times when I sink—sought—no Anglais—Anglish—gentilwooman could resiss me ! "

Suddenly abandoning his expansiveness, he threw himself into his chair again and lapsed once more into French. " It still is not sufficient ! I still have no good explanation for not putting you to work on the palace."

As rapidly as I could I sketched for him an account of my reason for being in Haiti, and of our experiences with Dessalines. " So there it is," I said. " If Dessalines ever finds out where we are, he'll have us killed. What's even more important : unless I can find the lady and help her get away from Cap François, I dread to think of what may happen to her. She has no resources of her own, and everybody knows what's going to happen to whites who stay here during the summer."

General Lefèbvre shook his head. " You jump about like a goat," he protested. " You leap from peak to peak, ignoring the valleys between ! This Dessalines, he is miles away among the mountains, defeated and helpless. How could he ever be in a position to molest you ? Also, what is it that ' might happen ' to the lady you mention if she were so unfortunate as to have to remain in Cap François during the summer, eh ? Already, you tell me, she has been here two years."

I hesitated, dubious as to the wisdom of telling this pouchy-eyed general what we really thought.

" Tell him," King Dick said.

" Well, sir," I said, " I don't know a great deal about Haiti, but my friend does. He thinks all the Negro leaders will soon stop fighting and join the French. When that happens, those leaders will come to Cap François to submit to General Leclerc. That's how Dessalines might find himself in a position to molest us, as you so delicately put it."

The general turned his head owlishly from me to King Dick and back again. " Now why should the Negro leaders decide to do such a thing?" he asked. " That Dessalines, that Toussaint, and that Christophe, they are like fleas. They go hop, hop in the hills, able to hide beneath a hair ! They could live in the hills for years."

" Yes, sir," I said, " that's how it seems to you and me, but we're not Negroes. My friend here says that Negroes are subject to sudden jealousies and wearinesses, and given to doing things with no more exertion than necessary. He says a great many officers in Toussaint's army are angry because so many other Negroes and mulattoes have joined the French— and by ' angry ' he means that they're jealous in a queer sort of way. For another thing, all the Negro officers, from Toussaint down, know that soon the quick malaria and the yellow fever will come, and when yellow fever or malaria strikes white troops, they're as good as gone. So my friend thinks Dessalines and Toussaint and all the rest of them will soon begin to ask, ' What's the use of running up and down all these mountains day after day and being blown to bits by French artillery, when all we need to do is join the French and wait till yellow fever kills them all ? ' ''

Lefèbvre pulled at his half-moon moustache. " And you think the lady you mention might also get yellow fever ? That's what you meant by saying that everybody knows what's likely to happen to her if she has to stay here during the summer ? ''

" Yes, sir.''

" Then you, too, think your friend is right ? You, too, think our troops will catch yellow fever, and we're as good as dead already ? ''

" Well, sir,'' I said, " I wouldn't have chosen to put the matter quite so bluntly, but I think that will prove to be the case.''

The general grunted. " Ah, well,'' he said, " perhaps now you have given me sufficient reason why you should not be put to work. If all of us are to be dead in three months' time, there will be nobody to complain about anything. Also, as a Frenchman, it is my duty to help a lady in distress. Finally, you have given me military information of some value, and a soldier of Napoleon must be grateful ! ''

He slapped his breast, looked at us fiercely as if defying us to question his logic ; then absentmindedly dropped the pearls into his pocket and got up from his desk. " You will sit in the shade behind this tent until I return,'' he said. " In case you are questioned, say merely that you are awaiting the orders of General Lefèbvre.''

He picked up an enormous chapeau, clapped it on his head, and strode from the tent without another glance at us, a perfect picture of a great French soldier, exuding honour and logic.

CHAPTER XXXVII

It was late afternoon when we left that monstrous half-finished palace, and never for a moment had the banging and hammering stopped : never for a moment had the sweating black thousands rested in their labours, or the overseers and sentries desisted from cursing and threatening the workers.

Not only had Lefèbvre brought back five thousand francs to King Dick (and I wondered how much of the actual selling-price he had pocketed for his trouble) ; he had more than fulfilled his part of the bargain by bringing us two clean though unironed linen suits to cover our nakedness, two woven straw hats, and two pairs of soft shoes.

When I tried to thank him, he looked at me coldly and twisted the ends of his moustache with delicate precision. " I'm no fool, M'sieu, and I do you the courtesy of looking beneath the colour of your skin and acknowledging you to be a man of intelligence in spite of the stain upon your face. What I have done, I have done in spite of my better judgment, and because of a sudden burst of sentiment within me. Now, however, that you have improved your appearance and will soon be recognisable as an American, I am free to say I do not wish your thanks. We have completed a business transaction, M'sieu, and there is nothing more to be said—unless you wish a little advice from me."

When I said that I did, he pointed a warning finger at me. " My advice to you, sir, is that if you wish to avoid trouble in Cap François, you admit to nobody that you are an American. There is no officer in the French army, from General Leclerc down, who doesn't regard Americans with contempt and hatred. They are known to be swindlers, sir ; thieves, men of low birth, without honour ! " He snorted.

" I have heard Americans say the same thing about the French," I said. " Perhaps, if we saw more of each other——"

Lefèbvre smiled sweetly. " Have no fear, M'sieu ! It is true that we lost eastern America to the *sales Anglais* through a series of misfortunes, and the Anglais lost it through their own stupidity ; but the day will come when Bonaparte will take back what is ours. Nothing can stop him, once this island is again in our hands, and that will be the end of your nation of swindlers, of men without honour ! "

I waited for him to continue, but he just glared at me out of those pouchy eyes of his.

" If there's nothing else, sir," I said," we'll be moving on."

That was the last we saw of General Lefèbvre. At the time I had a low opinion of him, but eventually I came to think of him as the kindest and best Frenchman of any I met in Haiti.

If ever there was a proper capital for a hell's island, it was Cap

François, a town of cinders, stinks, and soiled ruins—of crumbling sooty walls, black cellar-holes, and trash-filled streets. It steamed in the hot March sun, and the vapour that rose from it might have come from a cauldron of rotten fish or maggoty meat.

Everywhere we looked we saw French soldiers going through the motions of cleaning up the streets and the crumbling walls ; and as we came closer to the once-beautiful Plaza, now scorched and hideous, we saw tents by the score ; tents by the hundreds ; tents by the thousand ; and around and among them French soldiers parading, drilling, mounting guard, and engaging in every manner of housework, such as shaving, mending clothes, cooking stews in pots, emptying slops in the gutters, airing blankets.

All around us were signs designed to prevent all these military folk from losing their way : " To the Captain of the Port," " To the Commissary General," " To the Prison," " To the Commercial Wharf," " To the Admiral's Wharf."

Where there had been shops around the Plaza edge, there were now little stalls made of boards ; booths built of woven cane ; wine-shops made by lashing an umbrella or two to home-made tables ; and all these stalls and booths filled the entire space in front of the ruined arcades and gutted buildings. In these travesties of shops were Frenchmen and mulattoes and Negroes selling everything from silks to sugar cane. I truly believe that if all the buildings and all the cities in the world were to be ground into powder at a given moment, a million people would crawl from the ruins one moment later with food and clothing and worthless odds and ends to sell—yes, and find buyers, too.

There were even little restaurants under makeshift awnings ; and up and down the Plaza, now grotesque in its dirt and shoddiness, strolled innumerable light ladies of every colour, reeking of sweat and perfume, swinging their hips, laughing their shrill laughter, rolling their eyes at everyone whose garb suggested that he might have a franc or two in his pocket.

Every civilian—black, white, and cream-coloured—was packed into huts along that ruined waterfront ; and I knew that if Lydia was in Cap François, it was there that I'd surely find her—and it was there that I *did* find her, after peering into countless dens and rabbit-hutches that passed as homes for that homeless and penniless host.

Like every other lover before me, I imagined that I saw her a hundred times ; and when I actually did see her, I didn't believe it. She seemed like a dream—the foggy centre of a whirling throng of humans that buzzed and roared, though the buzzing and roaring may have been within my own head. I've never known what I said to her or she to me in those first moments of our meeting. All I know is that I held her close ; but, close though I held her, there was no way in which I could hold her close enough.

I was vaguely conscious that King Dick was pushing people away—

vaguely aware of staring faces, black, brown, white—vaguely aware of
a table covered with strings of coloured beads—and still in a foggy haze,
without knowing how I got there, I found myself inside a canvas shelter,
repeating Lydia's name over and over, as if to make her for ever a part
of myself, unable to keep my hands from touching her, fearful of losing
her if for a moment I let her slip from my grasp.

When my other senses slowly returned, I saw Gabriel d'Autremont
on a blanket in a corner, one of the two boys beside him, fanning him :
the other near-by, threading coloured beads on a string. Autremont
stared glassily at the canvas above him, as if I didn't exist.

" Never ! " I told Lydia. " Never again ! I'll never let you out of
my sight ever again ! "

There was no place to sit in that little hole of a tent, so I sat on the
floor and held her like a child. Autremont and the two boys might have
been three blocks of wood for all I cared.

When I told her how near I'd been to insanity a thousand times for
fear I'd find her gone when I got to Cap François, she clung close.

" I knew, Albion," she said. " Nothing could have made me leave
Cap François until I heard from you. I had a message from Madame
Dessalines that you'd escaped from Crête à Pierrot. She said that I
must tell you and King Dick to be careful—that you'd be in constant
danger until you were safely out of Haiti. She frightened me, Albion !
Do you still want to marry me ? "

" That's the first silly thing I ever heard you say. I've wanted nothing
else since the day I learned you weren't dead—no, long before that !
I think I knew from the very beginning that you weren't dead at all."

I got to my feet and went to the door of the tent. King Dick, I saw,
had already disposed of all the necklaces. " Come in here," I said to
him. " I want to get married, and I want you to do it."

He came into the tent, his eyes like china door-knobs, and handed
Lydia a handful of silver.

" Who, me ? " he asked. " That something I don't know about."

" Nonsense ! " I said. " You were Général de Place at Mirafleur,
and you had the right to officiate at wedding ceremonies in that district,
didn't you ? "

" Oh, my goo'ness," King Dick said, " marriages not officiated at,
not in Mirafleur or anywhere else in Haiti, not much. They just happen,
like breakfast or opening botto rum. Nobody officiates at breakfast :
just come and eat it."

" Well," I said, " we haven't any time to waste. Madame Dessalines
sent word to Lydia that we'd escaped from Crête à Pierrot and that
both of us had got to be careful—that we weren't safe until we got clear
of Haiti. So go ahead and marry us." I reached for Lydia's hand and
told her, " You start—you know the words."

Lydia nodded, and let her fingers lie along my wrist. " I, Lydia, take
thee, Albion," she said, and her eyes said even more than those all-

embracing words, " to have and to hold, for better for worse, for richer
for poorer, to love and to cherish, in sickness and in health, till death
us do part."

In a shaking voice I repeated the formula : " I, Albion, take thee,
Lydia, to have and to hold . . ." When I had finished, I looked at King
Dick.

" Man and wife," he said ; " just the way you've been feeling ever
since that night in the cave on the mountain."

Lydia blushed and laughed.

" Are you sure you'll feel married ? " I asked her.

She gave me the sidelong half-smile that Gilbert Stuart had caught
so marvellously in his portrait, and her eyes were radiant. " I *never* want
to feel married ! " she said.

The little ceremony over, the three of us fell to discussing our
immediate plans. Lydia had already made up her mind.

" Since I had no way of knowing when you'd come here," she said,
" I haven't tried to find out how we could get passage for Cette ; but
perhaps you and King Dick can ask about it."

" Cette ! " I cried. " What are you talking about ? Cette's in
southern France. Do you think I'm going to any such place as that, or
let you go there ? "

" Yes," Lydia answered, " I do. In the first place, M. d'Autremont——"

" Oh, to hell with Autremont ! " I said. " Let him get to Cette in
his own way. Or persuade him to do as he ought, and go to America
with us."

" My dear," Lydia said, " there's no way of going to America. The
French have allowed only one American vessel to sail from here in the
past two months, and that was Captain Rodger's *Nelly*."

" Rodgers ! I was counting on Rodgers to help us get away ! "

" I know," she said ; " but he's gone, and he's not coming back till
he has a load of supplies for the French army. So we'll have to turn
elsewhere." She went to a box in the corner of the tent, took a package
from it, and gave it to me. " This is all M. d'Autremont has—ten
thousand francs. He kept only a small reserve with his banker here in
Cap François ; and, because of the fire, this is all the banker could let
him have. With it there is also two thousand francs of my own."

" Damn it ! " I said. " You're not to spend your money on any such
crazy notion—I won't have it ! We can certainly find some way to get
us back to the United States, and I'll be damned if I'll countenance any
such folly as going all the way to France with that old fool. He looks
half-dead anyway. Well, let him stay here and die."

" Albion," she said, " he *will* die if he stays here, or if he goes to
the United States. Like most Frenchmen, he hates the United States.
Besides that, he's half out of his head because of his determination to get

back to Beau-Bouclier and hunt for Azilde. He can't seem to understand that Beau-Bouclier is really destroyed, or that if he goes alone into the country he'll be killed by the blacks. But if I can just get him over to Cette and among his own people, he'll recover, and the boys will be safe, and my conscience will be easy."

I made no comment. I was beginning to feel the force of her argument, but I still felt there must be some way we could get back home.

"I know what you're thinking," she told me ; "but you couldn't do it. Your own heart wouldn't let you. What's more, there isn't an American sea captain who'd dare to overstep the embargo, because if he did he could never again sail to the West Indies or to France. Not one of them would run the risk."

"Is this the reason you were in such a hurry to be married ? " I asked her. "So that you could twist me around your finger this way ? "

She laughed. "You don't really think I'm twisting you around my finger," she said ; then went on more seriously, "You know you'd regret it all the rest of your life if you abandoned M. d'Autremont and his two sons, or let me abandon them, at the very moment when they need me more than they've ever needed me before."

Since she was right, there was nothing more to be said, and King Dick and I went out into the steamy ruins of that ember-smudged city to buy or bribe our way to Cette.

CHAPTER XXXVIII

ORDINARILY I would never have gone to Tobias Lear again as long as I lived, so disgusted had I been at his eagerness to see Christophe surrender Haiti to the French without a fight, and so sure was I that he was primarily in Haiti to fatten his own pocket by interesting himself in French Spoliation Claims.

I say "ordinarily," because in ordinary times the French army wouldn't have been in control, and we could have gone to any one of fifteen or twenty French or Negro officials and got anything we wanted by bribery. But with the French army in control, there were a score of people who had to be seen and paid in order to get anything done at all, and we couldn't afford the time to see so many.

Ordinarily, too, I could have turned to Rodgers for help ; but now Rodgers was gone, and since Lear was the only American official we knew in Haiti, we were forced to consult him—just as all of us, every day of our lives, are forced willy-nilly to entrust our affairs and often our very lives to petty and unscrupulous business men, goverment officials, and politicians—to men whose every effort is devoted to furthering their own personal ends.

Lear, I knew, was that sort of man, and I hated to go near him : but

Lydia and the two boys, Autremont, King Dick and I had to get away from Haiti, and we had no time to lose ; so to Tobias Lear King Dick and I went, hoping that the leopard, for once, might have changed his spots.

The land on which the American Consulate had formerly stood, on the corner across from the Hôtel de la République, had by now been cleared of cinders and rubble, and a temporary Consulate had been knocked together out of rough lumber on the same spot.

I expected to find the place crowded with American captains ; but there wasn't one in sight—because, as I soon found, Leclerc had given orders that every American captain and seaman was to be confined to his vessel until the embargo was lifted. Consequently we had the good fortune to find Colonel Lear alone ; and the extreme cheerfulness and politeness of his greeting almost made me forget that he had twice caused me more distress than any other man except Mr. Justice Chase.

" Why," he cried, " it's Mr. Hamlin, isn't it ? With that brown skin I almost didn't recognise you—and maybe I wouldn't have, if you hadn't been with our old friend King Dick."

He laughed as if delighted to see us, and placed chairs for us. " I've been worried about the two of you vanishing into nowhere the way you did. Nobody's safe nowadays, even here, and I imagined the worst about both of you ! Tell me where you've been and what you've seen. I'm hoping against hope that I can get off a letter to Mr. Madison in a week or so, if only they'll lift this embargo. I got one off by your friend Captain Rodgers, but since then nothing."

I gave him, as rapidly as I could, a rough account of our escape from Beau-Bouclier, and of Dessalines' activities at Croix des Bouquets, Léogane, St. Marc, and Crête à Pierrot.

" There was only one way we could get away from Crête à Pierrot before the French brought up their heavy guns and blew it to pieces," I said ; " and that was to force Dessalines to take us out with him. King Dick and I had to be abrupt, and he naturally didn't like it. That's why we're here to see you. We must leave Haiti before he finds a way of getting at us ; and we must take my wife and M. d'Autremont too."

" Married, eh ? " Lear said, nodding and smiling, as if I'd done something that for the first time met with his whole hearted approval. " Well, well ! " Then he shook his head. " I may as well be frank with you, Mr. Hamlin : there isn't any possible way in which the French can be persuaded to allow an American captain or an American vessel to clear for any part of the United States ; and what's more, there isn't an American captain who would dare do it without official permission. He'd lose his master's licence, his standing, and his vessel."

" We don't want to sail for the United States," I told him. " My wife was employed as a governess here for the two children of M. Gabriel d'Autremont, whose French home is at Cette. He refuses to go to the United States, and my wife is sure he'll die if he stays here. What we want is to find some way of getting a vessel that'll take us to Cette."

"That's equally impossible," Lear said. "French merchant vessels are at least allowed to unload their cargoes, which American vessels cannot do ; but no merchant vessels, either French or American, are allowed to clear. They must wait. Leclerc is adamant about that. He won't let a merchant vessel leave port until his operations have been brought to a successful conclusion."

"I realise all that, Colonel," I said ; "but we all know the French. They're helpful when they're paid. Can't you direct us to someone who might help us ? M. d'Autremont has a generous amount to spend on his passage ; and King Dick can be helpful too."

Lear's head turned slowly towards King Dick, and his eyes widened, as well they might ; for in the centre of King Dick's broad pink palm lay two identical pearls, each half the size of a musket ball, shining with a peculiar silvery opalescence, as though each pearly sphere had been formed around a centre tinged with Negro blood.

"Are those genuine, by any chance ? " Lear asked.

"Very bestest," King Dick said. "From island of Margarita, off Venezuela."

Lear leaned forward, took one of them from King Dick's hand, placed it on his own palm, and stared at it fixedly. After a time he looked up at me.

"It has only just now occurred to me," he said slowly, "that there *is* one possibility—yes, a distinct possibility. In fact, if the necessary funds were to be forthcoming, I think I might almost call it a certainty."

King Dick only looked innocently puzzled, while I silently blessed him and his pearls.

"A most unfortunate thing happened on the morning after the fire," Lear went on. "An American sea captain by the name of Lee in some way found out that a French merchant named Guillandeux had hidden twenty-five hundred dollars in silver coin in his house. During the confusion and tumult of that morning, Lee came ashore with two of his sailors, went to Guillandeux's residence, took all the silver, and with it returned to his brig. My first knowledge of it was several days later, when his sailors lodged information against him. At first Lee denied everything : denied that he'd been ashore the morning after the fire : denied that he'd gone to Guillandeux's house : denied that he had taken any silver : denied that he'd hidden it aboard his vessel.

"I went repeatedly to his vessel with the French authorities and Guillandeux ; and—to make a long story short, Mr. Hamlin—we finally searched the brig and found six hundred dollars in silver. The other nineteen hundred dollars we couldn't find. Guillandeux insisted that the total amount stolen from his house had been twenty-five hundred dollars and that the six hundred dollars had been a part of it. Lee insisted that the six hundred was his own, and that he knew nothing whatever about the original twenty-five hundred dollars or the remaining nineteen hundred. Eventually I got a partial confession out of Lee, and turned over the six hundred dollars to Guillandeux. What became of the other nineteen hundred remains a mystery."

" It's no mystery to me," I said. " King Dick and I know all about it. When we were on our way out of the city on the morning after the fire, we saw Lee backing out of a house. With him were two sailors with two buckets filled with silver dollars. Each bucket would have held more than a thousand dollars. King Dick wanted to do something about it right then, but we didn't dare wait."

" That's interesting," Lear said. " Extremely interesting ! As you have doubtless guessed, Captain Lee is a thorn in my flesh, and threatens to be an even worse thorn in the flesh of the United States Government. What he has been doing will probably lead to all sorts of law suits and complications. And he's equally disturbing to the French, because they want to get Guillandeux's money back without any to-do ; yet they don't know how to institute proceedings against him in such a way as to assure the return of the money. I know they'd be glad to get rid of him, just as I'd be, because he's a bad and disruptive influence. The more I think about it, the more I think that if you were willing to restore the missing part of Guillandeux's twenty-five hundred dollars—along with any necessary charges—I might be able to persuade the French authorities to close their eyes and let Lee vanish. They'd never agree to let him go as George Lee, of course, any more than I could give him clearance papers. But if one of the two of you were to purchase the *Hope*, you'd be entitled to change her name ; then she could perhaps be cleared for a French port and no questions asked, especially if her owner were obviously French—as King Dick is."

I stared at King Dick, and King Dick impassively stared back. Although what Lear said sounded helpful and reasonable, actually it was neither. Lee, in looting, had been guilty of one of the worst of crimes, for which he should have been jailed, if not shot ; and he should just as surely have been forced to make restitution. Yet here was Lear proposing to make things easier for himself by arranging to let Lee go scot free, and to have somebody else make up Lee's theft ! And the French would be just as bad if, instead of making Lee pay for his crime, they should agree to save themselves a little trouble by shutting their eyes to Lee's criminal acts and letting an innocent third party make restitution.

" I'm not surprised that you hesitate," Lear remarked after a few moments. " I've dealt with Lee, and I know he's difficult and unreliable. Still, if you feel you must leave Haiti, that's the one way in which, according to my judgment, you can do it quickly and safely."

" Well," I said, " beggars can't be choosers. We're forewarned about Lee, and we ought to be able to protect ourselves against him. But I don't see how we can buy the *Hope* and be sure of still owning her when we want to return to the United States in her. Lee has no right to sell —he's only her master."

"The French," Lear suggested, "might be willing to condemn her. In that case her ownership could be transferred to King Dick."

King Dick placed the other pearl on the table before Colonel Lear. "We leave everything to you, Mr. Consul General," he said. "You had all these goings-on with Captain Lee, and he knows he better do what you say. I think better nobody see me change these pearls back into money; word might get around too soon. You go to St. Michel Rogun, jeweller, and you find this pair worth thirty-two thousand francs. Then you have that, and Albion's twelve thousand." He quickly added, "Albion and me, we got lots and lots to do if we to sail to-night—and that when we got to sail : to-night."

Colonel Lear, getting to his feet, had the bland and sleepy-eyed look of a big white tom-cat. "Knowing what I know about Captain Lee, gentlemen," he said, "I think you can depend upon it that he'll be ready to sail around two o'clock in the morning."

How Lear did it we didn't know, and we didn't care. All we knew was that he had the papers in our hands at dusk that very evening— papers stating that the *Cinq Frères* brig, out of Martinico, captain and owner Richard Roi, had cleared from Cap François on March 20, 1802. It was true—perhaps—that it had cost Lear all of the twelve thousand francs and both of the pearls to effect the transfer ; and it was certainly true that we sailed short-handed, since Lee's mate, cook, and two of his foremast hands had refused to sail with him. But we were a happy lot as the former *Hope* ghosted out of Cap François harbour in the wake of a French patrol boat, and even happier on the following day when, with two sailors painting out the name *Hope* on the stern, we watched the pearly mountains of Cuba rise from the indigo sea. King Dick planned to take on additional sailors and a cook in Santiago de Cuba, and to exchange his remaining pearls for a cargo of rum that would later repay all our expenditures.

Already the soft air, the heavenly blue of those tropic waters, the sight of shimmering flying-fish skittering out from under our bows, the golden clots of gulfweed swimming alongside, seemed to have cleared some of the black depression from Gabriel d'Autremont's mind ; his two boys raced each other up and down the ratlins like squirrels ; even Lee had so much the appearance of a bluff and honest mariner as he willingly took our orders that, if I hadn't known him, I'd have really thought him grateful.

Lydia sat beside me beneath an awning on the quarter-deck, writing to my uncle and Aunt Emmy in a hand as clear as copperplate ; and when she passed me the letters to read, the things she'd written made me laugh and made me uncomfortable, too. She had a knack of producing understatements so unexpectedly that every sentence was a delight, as well as a mirror of her own ever-changing charm. Kindness and gentleness gleamed in every line ; and if I hadn't already loved her to distraction, those letters of hers would have made me do so. How many times, how many, many times, I thanked my lucky stars that I had escaped from Harriet Faulkner ! I tried to say as much to my uncle when I wrote him what I thought he should do about getting Lydia's rightful property away from Harriet ; but I couldn't express myself : my gratitude was too profound : I had to give it up.

All I could tell him was that our passage to Cette would be, for me, the happiest that any man ever made.

CHAPTER XXXIX

No MAN could have been more in love with his wife than I with Lydia on the day I married her ; yet with each passing day, upon that voyage to Cette, I seemed to find more about her to love. Her constant care of Autremont and his two sons, her perpetual sunniness and good sense, her sweetness, her eagerness to be of help to all of us, made her the idol of the ship. As for me, as anyone who recalls his honeymoon will understand, the days and the nights slipped by on flashing bright wings.

She was profoundly concerned over those she liked ; and while she said little herself, she had a way of asking questions about matters in which others were absorbed, and then of listening so intently to what they said, that she gave the impression of being the most entrancing of conversationalists.

No cook, she said, could do his best unless encouraged, and her frequent visits to the galley evoked bursts of demoniac fond laughter from the black Jamaican she had found for us in Santiago to replace the cook who had deserted Lee in Cap François. Thus we were served savoury Creole foods made from salt codfish, rice, pimentos, yams ; with puddings and pies made fragrant with King Dick's special ancient rum ; and when, after dinner each night, we sat around the cleared table in the Great Cabin with the pewter lamps swaying and clinking in their gimbals, sipping at our glasses of that same rum, it was as good as being in a college to hear the useful information that she drew from each one in turn. I believe those nightly conversations did more to restore Autremont's health and make him forget his lost Azilde than all the medicines in the world could have done ; for when, at Lydia's persistent urgings, he described in greater and greater detail the method of wine-making peculiar to his home in Cette, the way in which King Dick would probably have to dispose of our rum cargo, the masterly riding prowess of the cowboys in the Camargue (near which Cette is located), or the remarkable cures effected by doctors at the neighbouring University of Montpellier, his eyes brightened, and for longer and longer periods his lethargy vanished.

King Dick, who, like every Negro I had ever known except Dessalines, was always smilingly silent in the presence of white men except when being questioned, under Lydia's questioning became a mine of information. Her probings into his past life followed curious patterns. They might start with the British Navy and the cantankerousness of British naval officers, due to enlargement of the liver resulting from restricted living quarters ; pass to the method of mounting and firing that most dangerous of all pieces of naval ordnance, the pivot-gun ; thence to the habit of friendly Arab horsemen of dashing headlong at each other and firing their guns into the sand at each other's feet ; thence to the incredible veneration with which the Arabs regard the wildest and most idiotic of Marabouts ; thence to Arab women and the custom by which their faces are screened from the eye of every beholder ; thence to Arab cookery and the mistaken idea that Arabs are averse to drinking alcoholic liquors. And no matter how the subjects under discussion leaped from one country to another, they always ended with Surinam, the place in which King Dick planned to spend his final days—and so wonderful a case did he make out for Surinam that even Lee, whose attitude towards almost everything King Dick said was too smilingly agreeable, seemed interested. As for Lydia and me, we knew that when our voyage to Cette had been completed and our cargo safely sold, we must see Surinam.

It was, King Dick said, the best of all possible places, with a climate ideal for the raising of products that were in demand everywhere in the world. It was perfect, he said, except for August and September ; and those were the months during which we could sell our products in Philadelphia or Boston or New York or even Portland. Then by taking the proceeds of the sales and investing them in rum from Jérémie or Anse-à-Veau, we could easily triple our profits each year and in ten years' time have plantations on which we could live in comfort all our lives.

According to his description the place was everywhere cut by deep canals full of the most delicious fish, and in the canals floated water-lilies the size of bushel baskets ; along the canal shores grew enormous mangoes, bananas, plantains, guavas, star apples, pineapples, avocados ; while back from the canals, in the plantations and the forests, could be found all sorts of partridges, wild turkeys, ducks, snipe, plover, teal and pigeon.

He spoke with a smacking of lips, too, of the vast quantities of shrimps and soft-shelled crabs that could be taken in a moment's time from any part of the canals, and described how everybody in the place made delicious curries and what he called foo-foos out of those succulent crustaceans.

And while he talked, Lydia scratched on the backs of old charts, sketching the plantation, the gardens, the stables, the boathouses, that we could build with the profits of our ventures.

Between times we studied navigation out of Bowditch, learning plane sailing, traverse sailing, parallel sailing, middle latitude sailing, and how to find the latitude and the time. I found it astonishingly easy to sweep for the stars, not through any fault of the grim New Englander who set down the instructions, but because I learned it by lying on the deck each night, Lydia's hair against my lips, staring up at a million pin-points opening into heaven itself.

I've never forgotten those stars and constellations—Aries or the Ram which bears 23 degrees east from the Pleiades or Seven Stars ; Aldebaran, 35 degrees east of Aries ; Pollux, 45 degrees east north-east of Aldebaran ; Regulus, 37½ degrees east by south, ½ south from Pollux, and so around the heavens to Pegasus, 44 degrees west of Aries ; and if I live to be as old as Methuselah, my heart will always thump within me at the memory of sweeping for the stars with Lydia.

The one thing wrong with our voyage was Captain Lee. I never liked him, and with each passing day I liked him less. I didn't like the way he looked at Lydia when he thought my back was turned : the way he contrived to let his hand touch hers when he passed her things at table. Neither did I like his attitude towards King Dick, who was ten times the man that Lee was.

I caught him watching King Dick from veiled and hooded eyes ; and late one night when King Dick had left us to stand watch, and Lee and I were alone in the cabin, he came out with it, like a man completely puzzled.

" I suppose, even if you go to live in Surinam, you'd figure on going back to Portland sooner or later, wouldn't you ? " he asked.

" Certainly. My only relatives live in Portland. Why do you ask ? "

" Well," Lee said, " I'm just wondering what you'll do in case this big black friend of yours goes home with you. Would you and your wife keep on having him for a friend, same as on this brig ? "

" Why not ? " I asked. " Nobody could have been a better friend to me than King Dick. What would you expect me to do ? Refuse to acknowledge him as a friend ? "

" I don't mean that exactly," Lee said. " I mean what would happen if your other Portland friends came to call on you and found King Dick in the house ? How about that ? "

" Well," I said, " how about it ? "

" Would you expect them to come in and meet him, or what ? "

" I don't ' expect ' anything of my friends," I said. " They do as they please. If they didn't like King Dick, they wouldn't have to meet him."

" I guess I don't make myself clear," Lee said. " What I'm getting at is, if you have a friend who's a nigger, what about all your white friends who don't want to have anything to do with niggers ? "

" What friends do you mean ? " I asked.

" Oh, you know what I mean," Lee said. " Take me, for instance : I just don't happen to like niggers, and nothing on earth could ever make me like 'em."

" Are you sure of that ? "

" Sure of it ? " Lee cried. " Of *course* I'm sure of it, and I'll bet you are, too ! Would you want your sister to marry a nigger ? Why, if a sister of mine wanted to marry a nigger I'd kill her."

" You're moving a little too rapidly for me. You say nothing on earth could ever make you like a Negro, but I don't believe you—not after the things I saw in Haiti. Suppose, for example, you'd been in my place : suppose you'd met a Negro who had more ability as a general and as a governor, and at inducing all ranks of society to live peaceably together, than any white man you ever knew. Do you mean to say you couldn't like such a man ? "

" Why don't you talk sense ! " Lee cried. " It wouldn't be possible to find a nigger who'd be a better general and governor than any good white man would be under similar conditions."

" It was possible in Haiti," I said. " Toussaint L'Ouverture is an unusual man, of course : one of the greatest I'll ever meet ; but I saw other Negroes in Haiti for whom I had profound respect. No man could have been a greater gentleman or a finer soldier than Lamartinière, Dessalines' second-in-command."

" You mean you met niggers you'd let your sister marry ? "

" Look, Captain," I said, " King Dick lacks some of the qualities that make Toussaint great, but not many. King Dick isn't ambitious, for one thing ; and like you and me, he's intolerant of the shortcomings of his own people. Apart from that, King Dick is a great man too."

" And you'd let him marry your sister ? " Lee persisted.

" I'll get to that in time," I said, " but for the moment let's stick to the original thesis. Suppose you found yourself in Haiti, as I did, and suppose you had the good fortune to meet King Dick. Suppose he befriended you, took you into his own home, helped you spiritually and financially, brought influence to bear on your behalf, went with you on long and arduous trips at considerable danger to himself, protected your interests at all times, in the end saved your life again and again by means of his wit, his knowledge, and his strength—and, to cap everything, placed all his resources at your disposal. Just suppose all that, will you ? How would you feel about such a man ? "

" All I know is," Lee said angrily, " I wouldn't have a nigger in my house. I wouldn't ask any of my friends to meet him."

" This friend of mine," I told Lee, " had worked for an American general before he went to Haiti. The general was an opium-eater, a liar, a braggart, a traitor. Which would you prefer to have in your

I

house : that white general, or the black man who'd befriended you ? "

Lee just sniffed, and I saw that nothing I could say, no argument I could produce, would have the slightest effect upon him.

" All right," I said, " I'll try to answer your question about my sister. I haven't a sister. If I had one, I'd expect her to choose a husband with whom she might expect to be moderately happy for the remainder of her life. Since she'd be the daughter of my father and mother, I'd naturally expect her to have good judgment—which would mean that she wouldn't marry a man thirty or forty years older than herself, or a prize-fighter, or a servant, or an hostler. I'd expect her to choose somebody of her own age ; somebody with whom she'd have tastes in common ; preferably somebody whose family she knew and liked. If I had a sister, it would never occur to her to marry King Dick, any more than it would occur to King Dick to marry my sister—if I had one. He's got too many brains to want to do such a thing."

" I know," Lee persisted ; " but suppose he *did*."

" Oh, for God's sake," I said, " I'm sick of that damned silly question ! It doesn't mean anything ! I'd be a fine specimen of humanity if I judged all my friends and acquaintances by my willingness to have them marry a sister I haven't got. That's a subject I've never considered, up to now ; but since you've brought it up, I don't mind thinking about it a little. And now that I *am* thinking of it, I can tell you off-hand I don't know of *anybody* I'd want to see married to my sister—though of course you've got to bear in mind that I haven't a sister. We're just supposing, Lee. You understand that, don't you ? "

He looked sulky.

" Most of the men I know around Portland," I told him, " are ignorant or contentious or dirty or penurious or crack-brained. All the farmers are determined to plough downhill, so that their top-soil goes to hell. They always scrimp on fertiliser, and they never cut their hay early enough. All the lawyers are afraid to take a stand against wrongheaded laws for fear of getting into hot water. Most of the sailors who claim to hate Negroes have yaws from sleeping with black women in Haiti. Most of the clergymen are sanctimonious old bores. All the politicians are so ignorant that it's agony to hear 'em uttering their platitudes on literature, finance, and government. If any one of 'em moved into the same house with my sister and me, I'd probably have to shoot him inside of a year, or move away permanently. Just suppose, Captain, that *you* married my sister. You'd be wanting me to defend you, wouldn't you, if you got into trouble in Haiti or some such place ? You'd be much more of a nuisance than King Dick would be. Since you press me, I'll be truthful : if my sister had to marry either of you, I'd rather see her marry King Dick."

Lee got to his feet and eyed me queerly. " By God," he said, " I never expected to live to see the day when a white man would come right out and admit he'd be willing to see his sister married to a nigger ! "

From that time on, there seemed to me to be something dangerously furtive about the way Lee eyed King Dick. Knowing only too well that Lee was bad at heart, I talked to Lydia about it, and together we speculated as to what harm, if he were so disposed, Lee could do to us. But none of us, alas—not even the most powerful of Hungans—are gifted with second sight.

We made Gibraltar fifty-four days after leaving Cap François—the fifty-four happiest days of my life up till then ; and since Lee reported that our water was running low, we put in there for more water. King Dick sent us all ashore to stretch our legs—Lydia, Lee, Autremont, the boys, and myself ; and off we went up Gibraltar's short and hilly shopping street.

We arranged with a local merchant for filling our casks ; then walked on to do as every visitor to Gibraltar invariably does—visit a perfume shop for perfume for Lydia. We left her there, went to an English haberdasher's for caps and shirts and suchlike ; then sat ourselves down in the cool of a wine-shop fronting on that narrow street and ordered ourselves a pitcher of creamy dark May-beer.

The order was scarcely out of my mouth when I heard a thick voice close by us saying gruffly, " Americans, I believe."

The man who stood somewhat unsteadily at my shoulder was, unquestionably, from his voice, an American ; and a seafaring man to judge from the brass buttons on his coat. When I told him we were, he said, " Pray do me the honour." He gestured towards a near-by booth and added, " Get mighty sick hanging around here with no Americans to talk to. Joseph Bounds of Newburyport, at your service. Captain. Brig *Gloria*."

" I'm waiting for my wife," I said. " Sit down here and have one with us. Albion Hamlin, Portland. Part owner of the *Cinq Frères*, bound for Cette with a cargo of rum. This is my sailing master, Captain Lee."

" Pleasure," Bounds said. " Cette, eh ? Well, hug the Spanish coast if you don't want one of those damned Tripolitans coming down on you."

" I don't believe they'll bother us much," I said. " The American Navy is in the Mediterranean, isn't it ? "

Captain Bounds snorted, gulped down a glass of May-beer, rubbed his lips with the back of a hairy hand, and looked cynically from me to Lee. " It certainly is," he said, " but it don't quite understand what's going on. You do as I tell you. Stay close to the Spanish coast ! "

" Don't think I want to abuse your hospitality, Captain," I said, " but isn't it overdoing things a little to expect me to put my trust in you rather than in the American Navy ? "

" Overdoing things," Bounds repeated. " Why, no, it ain't—not if you know who I am. The *Gloria*, she belongs to William Eaton—Consul William Eaton. William Eaton's the only man in the whole Mediter-

ranean, pretty near, that understands what's happening, or why, or how
to fix it. That's why I'm here in Gibraltar. Eaton sent me over here
from Tunis to tell the United States Navy what's going on."

" Well," I said, thinking to humour him, " if they've been told what's
going on, they can't be as ignorant as you make out."

Bounds was patient. " That's what I'm trying to tell you ! There's
the frigate *Constellation* out in the harbour, Captain Alexander Murray.
I go aboard and tell Murray what Eaton told me to tell him, and he
doesn't believe me. He says Eaton's crazy, and presses two of my crew
to boot ! "

" I didn't even know we were at war with Tripoli," I said. " How
did that happen ? "

" You'd be surprised," Bounds said. " We're at war with Tripoli
because Tripoli declared war on us—on the United States of America,
be-God ! That little dog-kennel of a country, full of bald-headed Turks
in velvet vests and satin pants, up and declared war on the United States
of America because we haven't paid 'em as much as they think they
can squeeze out of us to keep their hands off our ships ! So we're at war
with 'em, only we don't fight 'em the way we ought to. We're at war
with 'em, but we're going to keep right on paying 'em not to interfere
with our ships ! How's that sound to you ? "

" It sounds idiotic," I said.

" That's right," Bounds said. He threw up his hands in a despairing
gesture. " You'd never understand it or believe it until you've lived
with these Turks and Arabs and Moors for a while, so don't try it ! All
you got to do is hug the coast all the way in to Cette, and all the way
back to the Atlantic. You won't be bothered and it'll just be a nice
little summer sail for you. But do as I tell you and get in Cette and out
of the Mediterranean as fast as you can—if you don't want to see more
of the United States Navy than'll be good for you ! "

He pulled a scrap of paper and a pencil from his pocket. " Look,"
he told us, " here's the way those velvet-vested bastards from Tripoli
sail their courses." He drew a rough sketch of the north coast of Africa.
" They come out of Tripoli—here—in the night, go along the shore to
Zerbis, then run north to Susa, then skirt the shore until they reach the
Cape—that's Cape Bon, here. Then they run west to Algiers and make
a pass over towards the coast of Spain, looking for damn fools that stay
out in the middle of the Straits. Then they turn around and go back
the same way. So if you hug the shore, no Barbary pirate on land or
water'll ever see hide or hair of you—nor you of him. Just do as I tell
you : that's all. But, whatever you do, don't get out into the middle
of this damned minny-pond ! The stretch between Susa, Cape Bon, and
Sicily is bad—bad ! That's what I tried to tell Murray. If the United
States Navy would only patrol that stretch for just one summer, there
wouldn't be a cruiser from Tripoli, Tunis, or Algiers left on the whole
damned Mediterranean. But it don't ! There ain't that much brains

in the whole blasted Navy ! So keep away from open water : stick to
the north shore ! Even in the Gulf of Lions, get right up into it and
hug the coast. There's a breeze comes down off the hills at night,
understand, and you'll slide along as smooth as a kitty's ear."

I didn't know whether to believe him or not. " That doesn't sound
much like the American Navy," I said. " Who's in command out
here ? "

Bounds groaned. " We've had two," he said. " First it was Dale,
then it was Morris—both of 'em commodores. I wouldn't trust either
of 'em to get into my liquor chest without breaking the chest and the
key. Why, both together didn't have even half as much brains as the
Tripoli admiral. No, by God, they didn't have the brains of a billy-
goat ! "

I was sure, then, that I didn't believe Bounds. " You can't tell me
one of these Turks or Arabs can outsail an American naval captain,"
I said. " I've known two American captains, and known them well.
You can't find better naval officers anywhere."

" Who are they ? " Bounds asked.

" Edward Preble of Portland and John Rodgers of Havre de Grace."

Bounds nodded. " I've heard of 'em. They may be all you say, but
they ain't here. The ones that have been here are Dale and Morris, and
they ain't worth a zinc piastre. And that Tripoli admiral ain't a Turk
or an Arab, anyway—he's a Scot."

I laughed.

" There you go," Bounds said. He drank heartily and put down his
beer-mug with a bang. " Juss because you don't know a blasted thing
about the Mediterranean, you can't hear the truth about anything
without thinking it's a lie, juss like that damned fool Murray."

" How can a Scotsman be a Tripolitan admiral ? " I asked. " He'd
have to fight his own people."

" Oh, my God ! " Bounds cried. " Ain't the world full of folks juss
spoiling to fight their own people ? "

When I thought of the supreme pleasure every Federalist would take
in cutting the throat of every Jeffersonian, of the alacrity with which
the black maroons of Haiti had slaughtered Dessalines' black advanced
guard to the last man, I had to admit that there was something in what
Bounds said.

Lee cleared his throat. " How's this Scotch admiral call himself ? "

" He calls himself Murad Rais," Bounds said, " but his real name is
Peter Lyle. Wears a green turban and velvet pants."

" Is he a sailing admiral or a fish-pond admiral ? " Lee asked. " Do
you ever see him around ? "

" *Do* you ! " Bounds demanded. " Why, that red-headed bottle-
swallower keeps a score of little Tripoli skimming-dishes in damned near
every Mediterranean port, and every so often he comes round and calls
on 'em, regardless of who's anchored there. He's been ashore here at

night—right here in Gibraltar, and with an American frigate in port—just to buy himself a couple of cases of Scotch whisky ! "

At this moment I saw Lydia in the sunlit street outside, and went to get her and Autremont and the boys. While I was making them acquainted with Captain Bounds, and Bounds was bellowing commands for more liquid refreshment, Lee left us. Since I hadn't been conscious of his departure, and was always vaguely uneasy about him whenever he was out of my sight, I went to the door to see where he was going, but he had vanished.

"Lee's up to something," I told King Dick, after I'd given him the information we'd got from Bounds. "He had that queer defensive look in his eye that people have when they're thinking of turning against you. I may be wrong, but it's something we've got to think about. Now what could Lee do if he wanted to make trouble for us ? Could he possibly try to steal the brig from us ? "

"He wouldn't steal it," King Dick said, " unless he could get enough money to buy supplies. If I go ashore here and sell our cargo, I'd have the money and he wouldn't."

"Yes," I said, "there's something in that. What I'd like to do is put Autremont and his children ashore here and let them make their way to Cette by coach."

"I won't agree to that," Lydia said. "I promised him we'd take him to Cette, and a promise is a promise."

"Well," I said, " I don't trust Lee. If we put King Dick ashore here, and keep Lee aboard, one of us will have to watch him day and night. To be on the safe side, we ought to lock him in his cabin every night and heave the ship to. I don't like that idea. We'd lose time, and I still wouldn't feel sure about him."

"Put him ashore," King Dick suggested. "No use being embarracksed about him all time. Your lady, she can sail every bit as good as Lee."

Lydia nodded. "I believe I could sail her to Cette and back with no trouble. I've watched carefully, and Lee's done nothing that Albion and I couldn't do between us."

And that was the way we left it. A part of our plan was good, and a part was bad ; but I hate to think what would have happened to us if we'd made no plan at all.

When Lee returned to the brig towards midnight, King Dick and I were waiting for him at the head of the companion ladder. " Where've you been ? " I asked him.

"Well, for God's sake," Lee said, " why the welcoming committee and the personal questions ? It's just like being married again."

"I won't beat about the bush, Captain," I said. " I've had good reason to distrust you in the past, and I think we've got good reason

to distrust you now. Seems to me you were planning something against
us when you gave us the slip this afternoon."

"Nonsense! Nonsense! You're imagining things, Mr. Hamlin!
Why, I made a bargain with you gentlemen, didn't I? I sold you the
brig and agreed to sail her over here and back. You don't think I'd go
back on a bargain, do you?"

"Yes," I said, "I think you would."

Lee roared with reassuring laughter. "No, no, my boy! What do
you expect me to do? Sit around Gibraltar like a bump on a log after
fifty-four days at sea? I suppose you'd have liked me to blart it right out
to your lady that I was going up the street to get myself a little female
companionship. That's what I done and that's what I got. I suppose
you think I ought to got a speaking trumpet and hollered that all over
Gibraltar! What's more, I suppose you think fifteen or twenty minutes
is enough to devote to feminine companionship."

"So that was it, was it?"

"That was it, my boy! That's all it was! Just a simple case of one
of those ladies in every port that every sailor always has."

"And I had absolutely no reason to be suspicious of you?" I said.

"None. None whatever, my boy!"

"In that case you'll have no objection to going ashore here in Gibraltar, and letting us pick you up on our way back from Cette."

"Going ashore?" Lee cried. "I certainly would have objections!
What do you know about navigating a vessel! Why, good God, man,
if you ran into a bad blow, you'd pile her up on the rocks, sure as
shooting!"

"Even if we did," I reminded him, "you'd lose nothing by it. You
haven't forgotten that she's ours, have you?"

Lee eyed me warily. "I was thinking in terms of getting back to
America."

"That apt to be engroppling," King Dick said. "Ought to be pretty
embarracksing, going back to America, considering you sold us a ship
you not own."

"Well, you know what I meant," Lee said. "I meant Surinam, or
wherever it was you were planning to sail."

"Well, you needn't worry," I said. "When we come back from
Cette we'll pick you up and take you to Surinam with us. As for being
able to sail this brig, I think we've learned enough in the past eight weeks
to be able to get from here to Cette and back without any great trouble—
unless the trouble should be caused by you."

Lee eyed me blankly, as if he found my words hard to comprehend.
Then he burst into his familiar hearty guffaw. "Trouble?" he shouted.
"Now what trouble would old George Lee want to make for two good
friends of his—what trouble could he make!"

"He could make plenty if he got the chance," I said; "but I hope
he'll never get it."

In the confusion of unloading, during the next few days, we lost track of Lee, and found that most of his belongings were gone from his cabin. We gathered that he had gone ashore to solace himself with more female companionship ; but we didn't worry about him, for Gibraltar is a small place, little larger than a village, and I was sure that King Dick could put his finger on him whenever he desired.

On the sixth day after our arrival in Gibraltar we sailed for Cette, bearing north-eastward into the Mediterranean over a sea flat as a sheet of pale-blue watered silk.

I had an awning rigged for Lydia beside the lee rail, and I might truly have been voyaging towards the Happy Isles, with her sitting in her canvas arm-chair, busy with her mending or reading bits out of Bowditch, with the ragged lavender mountain slopes of Spain towering up at our left, and off to our right the endless misty blue mountain wall of Africa marching off into mysterious infinity.

CHAPTER XL

BY FOLLOWING Captain Bounds's advice to the letter we came easily and safely to Mount St. Claire, that solitary high pyramid rising from flat salt marshes and lagoons, as if on guard above the rich and delightful city of Cette and its sheltered network of canals and basins.

When the officials of the port learned that we had as passengers M. d'Autremont and his two sons, there was as much excitement and running about as though we carried royalty itself.

Frenchmen with beards and long moustaches went screaming up and down the docks like women, while elegantly dressed but smelly soldiers and policemen climbed into our rigging to howl directions to which nobody seemed to listen. In the end, however, we found ourselves tied up within a stone's-throw of the Hôtel de Ville.

In the course of a few hours, scores of Autremonts began to arrive on horseback and in chaises and coaches ; and the brig became a bedlam of Frenchmen and Frenchwomen, all shrieking and weeping and shaking their bunched fingers in each other's faces, or kissing each other and the Autremonts and us too.

Gabriel d'Autremont, to whom the sights and the noises and the smells of Cette seemed the most potent of medicines, refused to listen to us when we protested that we must sail at once. He screamed at us, clutched his head with his hands, protested that we had saved his life—as indeed we had—and refused to let us go until we had endured, as he put it, his hospitality. He screamed at his relatives, and they in turn screamed at us and wept.

When we said we had no one to guard the vessel in our absence,

Autremont produced a gentleman with a moustache the size and shape of two full-sized powder horns, a former mayor of Cette, a man honoured —said the Autremonts—by all France. He himself would guard the brig ; and for us to refuse the offer—they insisted—would be a stain upon his honour and upon the honour of the Autremont line. So there was nothing for it except to go.

We drove northward from the town amid a cavalcade of Autremonts ; and at frequent intervals we halted while little Autremonts ran from carriage to carriage with bottles of wine that was like nectar, and plates of Roquefort cheese so fresh and juicy that the bread within it had not yet turned to mould.

Both Lydia and I readily understood Autremont's determination to return to this part of France ; for when we got into the high land above the canals and endless lagoons that stretched in either direction as far as we could see, every inch of soil was beautifully cultivated with vines and olive trees and all sorts of crops : beans, artichokes, tomatoes, melons, and in occasional fields a sort of clover that beat anything I ever saw for richness and thickness.

A plateau, with the walls and towers of Montpellier upon its crest, lay before us, and beyond Montpellier to the north-east and the north-west were tumbling mountain ranges, a beautiful spectacle. Even the farmhouses were beautiful, most of them being of stone with round towers or pointed square towers, and avenues of fruit or olive trees leading up to their doors.

Gabriel d'Autremont's home was such a place, with two square towers and a regiment of outbuildings grouped around a courtyard, all the outbuildings covered with grape vines and stained with brilliant yellows and blues by the spray used on the vines.

I truly think all those Autremonts would have made us welcome in their home for the remainder of our lives. The womenfolk couldn't keep their hands off Lydia, and were perpetually stroking her and fondling her hands, or walking with their arms around her waist. The men soon found that I was interested in their work : their methods of planting and pruning grape vines, the types of soils that were best for different sorts of grapes, their way of making and storing wine—to say nothing of how they pruned olive trees, pressed out the oil, and riped cheese beneath manure in caves. I wanted to know, too, about their other crops. They marched me all over the place from field to field, from terrace to terrace, from grove to grove, till I seemed to be moving in a sort of revolving whirlwind of Autremonts—a whirlwind that frequently came to rest while wine was being decanted from a keg on a donkey's back, so that all of us could fortify ourselves against fatigue.

I found that numberless vineyards around the Autremont's produced almost all the *vin ordinaire* drunk in France : that from the grapes and the grape vines came various by-products—spirits, fertilisers, verdigris, cream of tartar ; that proper vine culture depended on a plentiful supply

of seasonal labour ; that there were only two slack months in vine-tending
—December and January, the months in which olives are picked and
pressed.

With Surinam and William Bartram in mind, I sat myself down
beneath an olive tree, with a semi-circle of Autremonts before me and
the donkey with the wine-keg on its back anchored close at hand, and let
them tell me exactly what they did and when. In my mind's eye I still
see those irregular pencil scratches—irregular from the piece of board on
which my paper rested, I'll always insist, rather than from the tumblers
of wine. " *February*, hoe, plant, manure, disinfect ; *March*, debud, prune ;
April, spray, powder ; *May*, spray ; *June*, spray, hoe, deleaf ; *July* and
August, maintain property, scour vats and presses, prepare for harvest ;
September, pick grapes ; *October*, press wine and distil ; *November*, prune."
And how little I guessed how and where I should later put that knowledge
to use. . . .

The delight of the Autremonts was boundless when I asked why so
many vines were planted on soil that certainly was stony and apparently
infertile. " Oho ! " they shouted. " Infertile ! This one knows his
onions ! " " He should learn how we manage ! " " No—let him stay
here and do it himself ! " " Oho ! "

Whether Gabriel d'Autremont had had this thought in his head for
some time, or whether the cries of his relatives put it there, I cannot say ;
but almost immediately after that shout was raised, he took me by the
hand and pressed it.

" Look, my dear M. Hamlin : What they say is true ! They are trying
to tell you something that is known to few people, something I didn't know
myself when I went to Haiti. They are aware that you saved my life, that
you brought me back to my home at great inconvenience to yourself, so
they find you sympathetic. Good ! Now what they want you to know
about this part of the country—what they hope will lead you to consider
remaining here—is that it is a wonderful country for a man of your natural
interests. No other place on earth, except possibly the north coast of
Africa, can raise grapes like our grapes. And what is remarkable ; our
grapes are produced on soil that is, as you have just noticed, stony and
infertile—that is, practically useless for other crops. We can grow vines in
sand, and on hill-slopes where nothing ever grew before except the *macchi*
—rosemary and broom ! My people can show you where you can get as
fine a vineyard as there is in all the Midi, and for next to nothing ! We
will find you a small chateau : not too old, not too new—some little place
built for a shooting-lodge years ago. Does the idea please you, M.
Hamlin ? "

I looked at him, not knowing what to answer. Then I looked out over
the country around me : the long line of shimmering lagoons between us
and the sapphire Mediterranean beyond ; in the opposite direction the
blue-green peaks of the Cevennes to the north ; and far, far to the south-
west the high saw-toothed Pyrenees. Closer at hand stood the solid,

ancient opulent stone buildings that were the heart of the Autremont vineyards ; and everywhere, on terraces, under olive trees, the close-packed ranks of grape vines, each fastened with twists of broom to trellises of crossed canes. The whole countryside, beneath the sunlight of the Midi, was tinged with warm gold ; and that golden warmth seemed to flow into me, through me, to fill me with eagerness to turn this sunlight into purple wine like that in my glass.

" Why," I said to Autremont, " I must confess the idea never occurred to me until this moment. We *had* planned, as you know, to go to Surinam to settle. I don't see . . ."

" Pah ! Surinam ! " he cried. " Rubber and indigo ! Big things, wet things, hot things ! Here you have small, beautiful things ; small, beautiful houses ; small vines ; small glasses of wine gleaming like rubies ; small cheeses of a flavour indescribable ! " He rolled up his eyes and kissed his finger-tips.

" Wait ! " I told him. " Don't say any more now. I must ask my wife —I want her to hear everything you have to tell us about this astonishing idea."

" Ha, ha " " the Autremonts cried. " He is willing ! " " Let us drink to Madame ! " " Let us drink to the Chateau 'Amlin ! " " The wine— the wine ! "

Singing and shouting, they escorted me back to the terrace between the two pointed towers of the chateau ; and there, spurred on by their womenfolk, they did their best to explain the situation to Lydia. When they had quieted down at last, she looked at me.

" What do you yourself think about it ? " she asked.

Before I could summon words to formulate my first startled thoughts, Autremont broke in. " Look—look around you ! Have you ever seen anything more beautiful ? " He swept his arm towards the west. " Yonder, only a few miles into the hills, is Carcassonne, the most beautiful fortress in all the world. We will go there to drink wine and marvel at the men who built those walls and towers ! "

He swept his arm eastward. " There, on the ridge, you see the houses of Montpellier, which has the finest hospitals and physicians in all France, and a great university, and fairs all through the year. A little farther on are Nîmes, Arles, Avignon—all ancient : all interesting."

A female Autremont, a pretty young thing, seized Lydia's hand. " Oh, you *must* come here to live ! Nîmes is exciting, but Arles is entrancing ! The Arlésiennes—so beautiful in their white fichus and black velvet head-dresses ! And the markets and the fairs are wonderful ! Do stay with us ! "

Lydia seemed to be infected by the general enthusiasm, but she still looked perplexed. " With all these wonderful things so near at hand," she said to Autremont, " I'm surprised you could bring yourself to leave them for Haiti."

He shrugged his shoulders. " Always the grass is greener on the other side of the fence, Madame. In any case, the Haitian plantation had belonged to my grandfather, and somebody had to manage it ; otherwise those who remained here in Cette couldn't have done so well with the wine as they have done."

Lydia's eyes met mine, and what she saw there seemed to satisfy her. To Autremont she said, " Everything you tell us is something to take into consideration. But we have a friend, you know, and we can do nothing without consulting him. Suppose, for example, that he wanted to come here with us. What do you think all these good friends of yours would say when they found he had a black skin ? "

" But we have all colours in France, Madame," Autremont said. " Here we look at what a man *is* ; if he has ability, we care nothing about his colour or his appearance ; if he is without ability, we avoid him. As for your friend, King Dick, he would be welcome because he is your friend, even if he were not the man of character and ability I know him to be."

When Lydia and I, with hearts full of gratitude, assured all these hospitable people that we would urge King Dick to return with us to Cette, the delight of the Autremonts was something beyond the experience of the New Englanders, who are prone to express delight with little more than wintry smiles.

When we left Cette to lay our changed plans before King Dick in Gibraltar, we were laden with gifts ; and a horde of Autremonts, headed by Paul and Raymond, ran alongside our carriage a good mile, waving to us and shouting things that brought a thickness to my throat, and put me almost as much in need of a handkerchief as was Lydia of mine.

On the following morning two boatloads of shouting Frenchmen towed us from the bustling canal and the dock-lined outer basin of Cette ; and as our sails filled with a milk-warm breeze from the African coast, and we bore off to the south-westward with the golden Mediterranean sun at our back, I knew beyond any doubt that I was the happiest and most fortunate man in the world. There wasn't a cloud in our sky ; not even a faint trace of a threat to the inexpressible joy that Lydia had brought me. If I'd been on a farm, I'd have remembered that such cloudlessness is a weather-breeder, the forerunner of howling north-easters and hurricanes and floods. But I wasn't on a farm : I was in Heaven.

CHAPTER XLI

WE NEVER had a chance. Sixty miles from Cette the mountain barrier between France and Spain juts out into the sea to form a series of craggy capes—Cape Béar, Cape Cerbère, Cape Creus—with small sheltered bays between ; and they must have been watching for us from the high shoulder of one of those capes.

The vessels came sliding out from behind a headland, driven both by sails and by oars ; and the moment we saw her singular xebec rig, lateen on her main and mizzen, square on her foremast, we knew she was heading for us, and suspected the dreadful truth.

Lydia got up from her chair and came to stand beside me at the wheel. " It may not be what you think," she said.

My heart was like a granite hitching-block. " Maybe not," I said. " Anyway, we're helpless. She can sail two knots to our one. We can't even try to fight. There's a traversing-piece in her bow ; and if we so much as fired a pistol, she'd blow us to pieces."

I gave Lydia the wheel and went down on the main deck, where our small crew, white-eyed, were watching the xebec's approach.

" You may as well know the situation now as later," I told them. " In all likelihood she's a cruiser out of Tripoli, and since Tripoli has declared war on the United States, we're a fair prize. In all likelihood, too, Captain Lee's mixed up in this. I just want to warn you not to make any resistance when they take us prisoner, as they're bound to. Do as you're told, and do it quickly and cheerfully, even if they beat you or spit on you. And I advise those of you who have a little hard money in your sea-chests to swallow as much of it as you can. Put on the best clothes you've got—but don't try to fight if you're stripped of 'em. Keep up your spirits, and sooner or later the Navy'll get us out of this."

Since there was nothing more to say or do, I went back to the quarter-deck and took the wheel again, my brain a welter of tangled agonies and impotent rage. Lee, of course, had to be the answer to everything. It must have been planned, and only Lee could have planned it : he must have found a way to escape from Gibraltar and make a trade with some-body. I didn't blame myself for buying Lee's vessel and shipping him as sailing master : in no other way could we have escaped from Cap François and Dessalines and yellow fever, and saved Autremont and his sons into the bargain. But I'd known Lee for what he was from the very first day I'd met him ; and in spite of knowing him, in spite of suspecting that he was planning something hurtful to us, I had utterly failed to anticipate that something. If only I had treated him as such men deserve to be treated—if only I'd shot him, or let King Dick break his arms or his legs, or tied him up and thrown him overboard . . .

Lydia shook her head, as if she could read my thoughts—as indeed I think she always could. " There was nothing you or any of us could have done, Albion. You couldn't have murdered him in cold blood. You couldn't have done more than you did, not until you found out what he was planning. And as long as he was alive, he'd have found a way to get at us. Men like that can always find a way."

" That's why he asked Bounds about that damned Scottish admiral," I said. " He was planning it even then ! Ten to one he'd got word to one of those Tripoli skimming-dishes that Bounds spoke about—yes, and before we decided to protect ourselves from him, too ! "

Lydia stroked my arm.

Strangely enough, I was even angrier at Tobias Lear, who at bottom was more to blame for all this than was Lee, and at myself who had gone to Lear for help, in spite of knowing that Lear was one of those consistent men who can't do anything right.

" Whatever happens," Lydia said, " remember that it was I who insisted that we go to Cette. It was all my fault ! But we had to go ; if we'd abandoned the Autremonts we'd have come to hate each other."

" It was nobody's fault," I told her. " Everything'll come out all right if we don't let ourselves lose our tempers." I laughed at the thought of Lydia losing her temper, though a moment before I'd have sworn that I'd never laugh again. " And always remember that the American Navy's in the Mediterranean. Get word to someone—that's all we need to do. Remember that if you write with lime juice, the writing's invisible until it's held over a flame. If anything should happen to me, try to get word to King Dick in Gibraltar, or to Captain Bounds, or to that consul, William Eaton, that Bounds told us about. Bounds said he's the only man in the Mediterranean who knows how to fix everything. A man like Lee can't do us any harm—not for long."

I wasn't just talking to keep up Lydia's courage ; I really meant it —which shows that even then I had failed to realise the depths to which a man can sink when cursed with consistency, as was that man Lee.

The xebec's commander was a good navigator, for without any alteration of her course she crossed our wake a hundred yards astern, hauled her wind and came up alongside us, not half a pistol-shot away. The gun-crews of the two traversing-pieces in her bow were at their stations, and she was crowded amidships with a strange-looking lot of brown-skinned sailors wearing canvas skirts, little short jackets, and peculiar floppy red hats reminiscent of red flannel under-drawers. Every last one of them had long curved moustaches that looked as rigid as teapot handles. On her quarter-deck were five men wearing green turbans and voluminous trousers of various colours, like people bound for a masquerade ball ; but of Lee's blue peajacket and dilapidated old cap there wasn't a sign.

One of the five men swung himself into the mizzen ratlins and hailed us in good English, which seemed curious, since he was clad in bright yellow balloons of trousers that fluttered in the breeze and were confined at the waist by a broad pink sash. " Come into the wind and back your tops'l," he bawled. " I'm sending a boat."

I did as he told me, and the xebec followed our movements like a dog on the heels of a woodchuck. All too quickly her longboat, filled with sailors, ran up beneath our counter ; and its occupants, led by one of the green-turbaned men from the xebec's quarter-deck, swarmed up our companion-ladder to form a half-circle around Lydia and me.

The words of the green-turbaned man meant nothing to us ; but his intention was clear, and was made even clearer by renewed shouting from the xebec. " Get your people over the side and back to this vessel," the yellow-trousered man bellowed. " No dunnage—come as you are and be quick about it—all of you ! Lady and all ! "

Sweating with apprehension and helplessness, I helped Lydia over the side into the waiting boat, rounded up the crew and sent them after her, then climbed down the ladder myself, hoping against hope that we'd be allowed to return for our belongings ; but we were no sooner in the boat than our brig payed off to the south-east, so that I knew we had nothing to our names but the clothes upon our backs.

When I followed Lydia up the xebec's companion-ladder and mounted to the quarter-deck from the waist, I saw that our suspicions had been correct to the last detail ; for one of the remaining four men in green turbans and voluminous trousers was red-faced, defiant-eyed, swaggering George Lee.

I tried not to see him as I faced the freckle-faced man in yellow trousers and pink sash—the same one who had hailed us, and who now snapped out an order to one of his green-turbaned associates. A boatswain's whistle twittered from the waist, one of the green-turbaned men put the helm hard over, and the xebec fell off into the wake of the already distant brig.

The freckle-faced man moved over to the weather rail and beckoned us to him, at which Lee and the other men in green turbans hurriedly moved to the lee rail.

The freckle-faced man favoured us with a bleak but not unkindly smile. " From what I hear, Mr. Hamlin," he said, " you're a man of some intelligence, and I have no doubt "—*nae doot* was the way he said it —" you've been able to put two and two taegither."

" I recognise Lee, if that's what you mean," I said, marvelling—in spite of my churning emotions—at this odd combination of Moslem garb and thick Scots speech, which I won't try to reproduce hereafter.

" That's what I mean, and it saves some explaining, Mr. Hamlin. I'll say at the go-off that your crew'll be housed in the foc'sle, and you and your lady'll have officers' quarters till we get ashore. I'm Murad Rais, in case you don't know, of His Highness's Navy."

" Yes, sir."

" Now you've probably heard all sorts of silly tales about Tripoli and about His Highness the Bashaw and about the good people who serve under him ; but you can take my word for it, Mr. Hamlin, 'tisna so, most of it.''

" I'm glad to hear it," I said.

" F'rexample, Mr. Hamlin,'' Murad Rais went on, " you take this war His Highness was forced to declare on the Americans. 'Twoulda been wholly unnecessary if only your country had lived up to its agreements and conventions, d'you see ? But when it deliberately went back on its given word, Mr. Hamlin—when it failed to pay the stipulated sums and send the stipulated presents to His Highness at the stipulated times— there was nothing for His Highness to do but protect his honour by a declaration of war.''

" Yes, sir," I said. " But surely a gentleman of His Highness's high sense of honour doesn't make war on women and on civilians.''

Murad Rais pursed his lips. " Such a remark is designed to cloud the issue, Mr. Hamlin. The issue is this : your country contracted in a duly signed and executed treaty to supply to His Highness, in return for the free and peaceful privileges of these waters, certain sums of money and certain naval stores. These have not been supplied, Mr. Hamlin. It therefore becomes our duty to reimburse His Highness from the sale of such property as we may seize under the rules of war. Thanks to Captain Lee, who is now one of us, we have been able to seize the *Cinq Frères* brig, which is actually American, though sailing with papers obtained by bribery and corruption. In view of this, Mr. Hamlin, it ill behoves you to speak so loosely of making war on women and civilians.''

" If it's a matter of money, sir," I said, " I think we could raise enough to make it worth His Highness's while—if you'd allow us to get in touch with some of our friends.''

" Ah," Murad Rais said regretfully, " I feared you wouldna understand how very, very delicate the situation is. Here's the way of it, Mr. Hamlin : Captain Lee enters into an arrangement with you in Cap François ; and in return for his kindness you practically take his vessel from him and put him under the command of persons with no nautical knowledge, so that the safety of his vessel's endangered. Then you openly insult him, remove him from the command of his own ship, and set him ashore in Gibraltar, where he'll be helpless if abandoned.''

" Sir," I said, " Captain Lee has misrepresented things. He was in serious difficulties in Cap François, with both the French and the American authorities. He'd been caught looting. The French didn't want him in Cap François, but couldn't give him clearance papers unless they gave them also to other more deserving American captains—which they refused to do because there was an embargo on all vessels in Cap François. The American authorities wanted to get rid of Lee, too, so that he wouldn't cause further trouble between French and Americans ; so they closed their eyes when we made arrangements—private arrangements— with the French. In return for those arrangements, Lee sold us his brig.

We kept him on as captain, because that was the only way we could escape the embargo. The reason he was put ashore in Gibraltar was that we suspected him——"

" Hmph," Murad Rais broke in, " I'm not interested in all the moot points of the story. You know yourself, Mr. Hamlin, that when people get to arguing about the rights and wrongs of military and naval matters, they can argle-bargle for ever without getting at the truth. What's clear is that Lee was captain of the *Cinq Frères*, exactly as he says. He was sailing a voyage in your employ, and you put him ashore at Gibraltar. That's true, isn't it ? "

" I can't answer yes or no to that, sir," I said, " unless you let me present the rest of my evidence."

" 'Twould be a waste of time," Murad Rais said. " Captain Lee's thrown in his lot with us, and we've taken his vessel back. She's an American vessel, no matter how she's registered ; so she's a fair prize. You were aboard her, so you're a prisoner of war, just as is the crew. That's the state of affairs, and all the evidence in the world won't change it. What makes it delicate and difficult is the fact that you're so ill disposed towards Captain Lee. He says this is the case, and your own statements about him are proof that he's correct."

I began to see what he was getting at, and such a feeling of strangled, choked fury swept over me that if I could have got my hands on Lee, I'd have killed him even if I were killed doing it.

" You see," Murad Rais went on, " the moment we agree to let you try to get yourself ransomed—say through a foreign consul now residing in Tripoli, or through consular agencies in Gibraltar, or through other agencies elsewhere—you're bound to make things extremely difficult for Captain Lee. Since the full story's not known, and since your word would be taken as to the reasons for Captain Lee's joining us, his reputation as well as his family would suffer. Consequently it was a part of my bargain with Captain Lee that the question of ransom shouldna be allowed to be raised in your case."

" That's inhuman, sir," I said. " You can't——"

" No, no, no," Murad Rais interrupted. " It's ordinary self-protection ! This is war, Mr. Hamlin ! Surely you must know that any country fighting a war not only can but must protect itself from trouble that might arise from poorly guarded prisoners. I well remember hearing the tale of Burgoyne's army in your revolution. According to the terms under which Burgoyne surrendered, the Americans agreed to send his army back to England immediately on the signing of the convention. Instead of that, they broke all their promises and kept Burgoyne's army in miserable prison camps for four long years. We'll no be as inhuman as all that, Mr. Hamlin—no' unless you force us to."

He looked suddenly at Lydia. " I'll have a chair brought for you, Ma'am."

" I'd rather stand," Lydia said.

"Well," Murad Rais said, "I want to be clear and aboveboard in everything I do, and I don't want you to be in doubt any longer than necessary. The Arabs have a saying that two of the greatest comforts in life are success and despair, and they seem to regard doubt as the greatest of all discomforts. Now, according to what Captain Lee tells me, your lady has been a teacher—a governess—and you've been a farmer as well as a lawyer. That's a fact, is it not? "

"Yes," I said. "That's a fact."

Murad Rais grinned contentedly. "Aye ! That's what I thought. Well, the way we ordinarily handle prisoners is this : they're taken before His Highness, who's privileged to take such of them as he needs for his own use. The remainder are either held as possessions of the State, to be used in dealing with the enemy, or sold and the proceeds of their sale deposited in the Royal Treasury. Is that clear ? "

With a heart as heavy as lead I said that it was.

"Well, then," Murad Rais said, "this is where the delicate part of it comes in. His Highness's brother, with whom His Highness has had considerable difficulty for some years, is in exile ; but his three little sons remain in the palace. For a long time now His Highness has wished that they might be properly instructed as befits their station in life. Also, I have a country place in the Pianura, eastward of Tripoli, with gardens and palms and all that—a bonny place, Mr. Hamlin. My vegetables, especially my melons, are excellent, though no so good as they should be, thanks to the stupidity of my Arab workmen. So you see, Mr. Hamlin, there are two ready-made posts in Tripoli, exactly suited to the talents of you and your wife—and I may say, Mr. Hamlin, that Captain Lee has spoken very highly of those talents."

I couldn't trust myself to say anything.

"Now then, Mr. Hamlin," Murad Rais went on, "those posts are yours on one easy condition. Just give me your word of honour—your solemn oath—that you will make no attempt to communicate with any agency either inside or outside of Tripoli in order to secure assistance or ransom money or any other relief."

"We can't bind ourselves to anything like that," I protested.

"Don't say that, Mr. Hamlin," Murad Rais said. "Take my advice and don't say it ! Can't you see that my bargain with Captain Lee leaves me no choice ? Unless you take your oath to do as I suggest, you'll have to be sold, and your wife, to the highest bidders when the first caravan comes through Tripoli. God only knows who'd buy you. God only knows who'd buy your wife."

"You'd sell us separately ? " I asked.

Murad Rais looked surprised. "But of course, Mr. Hamlin ! For security reasons alone you'd have to be sold separately. And here's another thing I'd want you to understand clearly : if the two of you take your oath with no mental reservations, each one of you will be held to blame if the other fails. Is that plain ? "

"It's all plain," Lydia said quickly. "Put it in writing and we'll sign it."

I couldn't believe that the whole thing wasn't a dark and evil dream. Barely an hour ago we had coasted blithely below the pale and sunny slopes of Cape Cerbère, believing ourselves the happiest people in the world ; and although Cape Cerbère was still in sight, blue and amethyst in the morning sun, these men in nightmare garb, these horrible men whose manner of thought was as strange and as antiquated as their dress, had wholly destroyed our happiness and our freedom. For us, Cape Cerbère, called after the three-headed guardian of Hell who dwelt in Stygian caves forlorn, was aptly named !

CHAPTER XLII

I THOUGHT nothing could have brought me closer to Lydia than the happy weeks we'd had together since we sailed from Cap François ; but common disappointments and despair, I found, can unite people more completely than any amount of that indefinable condition known as happiness.

Murad Rais took Lydia at her word ; and the two of us sat for an hour in the cabin of the xebec while Lee and Murad Rais between them framed the terms of the Convention, as they called it, that condemned us to unprotesting slavery.

They were cheerful about it, as all scoundrels are when they have the whip hand over somebody ; and the utter detachment with which they spoke of Lydia and me made me hope with all my heart that Lydia didn't understand what I understood about it—that they were closing every avenue by which we might obtain relief. But whenever, at the end of a passage between these two genial blackguards, I stole a quick glance at her, her eyes instantly met mine and with such high courage that I soon knew she understood as well as I, and with a far braver heart.

"There's one thing you've got to be specific about," Lee said. "You've got to be specific about that nigger friend of his—that King Dick that got put ashore at Gibraltar. The first thing Hamlin would do if he could, is to send some kind of word to him, and he'd make trouble. He's a born trouble-maker, even if he is a nigger."

"Aye," Murad Rais said. "I'll make a point of it. No attempt to obtain help by means of letters, signs, signals, or the spoken word from anybody of any nationality or colour, race or creed."

"Why not name him ? " Lee asked. "I tell you I don't like that black bastard, or trust him."

"Oh, aye, I understand," Murad Rais said ; "but if we name this King Dick or the Danish Consul or anybody specific like that, it'll imply that Hamlin's free to break his word and get help from some person other than those we name."

"I don't see it that way," Lee said sourly.

"Well, I do," Murad Rais said, "and I've had more experience with this sort of thing than you have, Captain Lee. Anyway, it's all covered by the opening clause, which specifies that the signers of this Convention are signing it under oath, and agreeing to all the clauses in it without any mental reservations. What more do you want?"

Lee grumbled under his breath, and I couldn't blame him for grumbling ; for if I'd done to somebody what he'd done to Lydia and me, I'd never have felt safe while that somebody was alive. "I'll tell you one thing I want," Lee said. "I want it fixed so they don't get to see each other alone between now and the time we get to Tripoli. You let 'em get their heads together in a corner, or spend the nights together, and they'll find some way to cook up something."

At this I didn't even dare to steal a glance at Lydia, but just sat there with as expressionless a face as I could command, knowing that any word of protest would only make our case worse—if that was possible.

"Well now," Murad Rais said, "they're agreeing to this Convention without any mental reservations, and unless you insist——"

"Well, I do insist," Lee said. "The woman's smart, and so is he, for all his talk of ploughing and manure and hay, and how people ought to use more lime and plant more larches—enough to make you sick !"

"'Neither of the signers of this Convention,'" Murad Rais read from the paper he held, 'shall take advantage of appeal to the Bashaw, seeking sanctuary with a Marabout or in any other holy place, or otherwise avail himself of the customs of the country, without the other signer's forfeiting all rights under this Convention and being instantly sold by private or public sale, as shall be decided by the properly constituted authorities.' I tell you I've got everything covered here, Captain Lee." He looked up at me. "You wouldn't go so far as to argue, Mr. Hamlin, would you, that you and the lady were being forced to sign this document, and that signatures obtained by force are invalid?"

"Well, sir," I said, "it is a fact that signatures obtained in such a way can be proved worthless."

"Oh," Murad Rais said, "then we'll have to cover that one. We'll have to put in a clause that says this is done of your own free will, and in return for treatment more favourable than could be expected by any ordinary prisoner of war."

There wasn't a thing to be said to those two men. They were above the law, like victorious army generals in a conquered country, or unscrupulous business men, or corrupt politicians in high places.

Murad Rais read over the finished paper to us, and we signed it, and Murad Rais tucked it away inside his pink sash, beaming amiably upon us. "You've done the right and the wise thing," he said, "and the way you've done it bears out Captain Lee's statements about your good sense. You'll eat at my table while you're aboard this xebec, but you'll keep to your own rooms at all times when you're not here in this cabin with Captain Lee or myself, or on deck with him or me."

So profound was my helplessness, so overwhelming my fear for Lydia, that I seemed deprived of the power of coherent thought. All I could do was conceal my inner turmoil from Murad Rais and repeat endlessly to myself, " Patience, patience ! Wait, wait ! Patience, patience ! " Although I said them so often that they presently ceased to have meaning for me, I seemed to get a little comfort from them.

For ten days we sailed east and south, and they were bitter long days of heart-sick rage. I had to conceal my loathing for Lee : I couldn't show my furious resentment against Murad Rais : I didn't dare reveal any part of my own despair. Worst of all, I couldn't be alone with Lydia ; and there's almost no mental agony so great as to be with a person you love in a time of dire tribulation, yet be unable to comfort her, and in the comforting alleviate your own consuming hopelessness.

To give Murad Rais his due, he was polite enough. He even seemed to me to be a kindly sort of person, so that I had vague hopes that in the end he might do something that would help Lydia and me. He talked volubly during our dinners in his fly-filled cabin, and the whisky bottle passed frequently between Lee and him. Like so many persons of importance, he could speak only of food, and he'd spend hours telling us about the different sorts of cous-cous he had eaten in North Africa and comparing the merits of cous-cous made from sheep's heads, cous-cous made from strips of lamb, cous-cous made from chicken and red peppers, cous-cous made from goat, and cous-cous covered with plain tomato sauce or with tomato sauce mixed with sheep cheese or goat cheese or mare's cheese. He had eaten cous-cous made from old camels, long dead ; had eaten it in Gabès, in Sfax, in Kairouan, in Tripoli, Tunis, and Bengazi. Ah, yes, Murad Rais was polite enough in his way ; all of which, in the end, led me to wonder whether the persons who most pride themselves on their politeness aren't at heart the most inhuman.

Murad Rais sailed past the eastern tip of Minorca and made a straight run for the African coast, striking it at Cape Bougaroni. Then we coasted along the luminous ramparts of the Majerda and Aures high on the right : the Gibraltar-like mountain behind Bizerta : the Gulf of Tunis out of which long, long ago poured the galleys of the Carthaginians : past Cape Bon : then out of sight of land and across a sea like blue silk until we raised the island of Lampedusa ; and with a heavy heart I knew that the next land we'd see would be the coast of Tripoli—and so it was. By a coincidence that came to seem ironic we sighted the palms and minarets of that miserable place on the Fourth of July.

I've heard Tripoli called romantic, and maybe it is. It's a flattish place, bristling with palms like feather dusters ; its houses are flat and square, gleaming white against a background of two low hills, with here and there domes and minarets rising from the feather dusters. I know this, though : no matter how romantic a city or a village or a house may seem, you'll find some mighty unromantic things if you take the trouble to look beneath the surface.

We rounded a sort of fort on a point of land, and entered a long, long harbour dotted with ketches and lateen-rigged vessels of every sort. The city lay at the bottom of the harbour like a coloured illustration out of a book of travels. There was a huge pile of a Castle at the left, blue where the shadows lay on its white wall. From its base sprouted a mole, and within the shelter of the basin formed by the mole was a dockyard with a half-built vessel on the ways. The rest of the city swept around to the right—little flat-roofed white buildings with domes and minarets protruding from them, like something built for small girls who play with dolls. Close to the water was an ancient arch, forlorn, out of place—a sort of forgotten plaything.

Murad Rais and Captain Lee had their heads together as we made our way into the long harbour ; and the first thing I knew, he had summoned four armed men to the quarter-deck and given them some instructions. Then, as carelessly as though he were wishing us the time of day, he ordered us to our cabins. " Honeymoon's over, Mr. Hamlin," he said. " I'm putting two guards at each of your doors. You're not to communicate with anybody till you're instructed to do so."

We anchored at the bottom of the harbour, perhaps a half-mile from the blue-shadowed Castle that rose like a headland at the eastern end of the town, and from the little windows of our cabins we had our first confused glimpse of the life of Tripoli, tremblingly seen through waves of heat.

The men on shore were swathed in white robes, in grey robes, in bright colours. I made out a string of camels lurching along the waterfront and vanishing behind the walls of the Castle, to reappear against the palm trees that stretched off and off, away from the town, away from the Castle, towards hills and what looked like the beaches of the Maine coast.

Boats were rowed out from the Castle—galleys propelled by a dozen Negro rowers, and under canopies at the stern were men in turbans and muslin trousers, in yellow slippers, in gold cloth and silver cloth, in purple velvet and crimson satin, in orange damask ; men with white shawls thrown over their shoulders, with gold and silver sashes, with curved swords and moustaches like a black duck's wings.

I could hear movement on the deck above me, shufflings and tramplings, the rattling of cordage. From the small boats clustered about us came a perpetual yelling and screaming of which I couldn't understand a word. The white, hot sky changed to an orange and then to a lemon-green ; the screaming and the shouting gradually lessened and gave way to what by comparison was silence.

One by one the galleys pushed away from the xebec's side, towards the greenish-dimness of the shore. The heat and stillness of the little cabin was torture. I didn't want food any more than a sick man wants food ; and my lack of knowledge of Lydia, of what she was thinking, my inability to see her or speak to her, my utter helplessness, was in truth an illness, one that parched my lips and made my eyeballs ache and filled me with a frenzied desire to beat on the locked door, to tear at the port-hole, even though I could scarcely get my head through it, let alone my shoulders. I was a sick man indeed, with just enough sense to know that the only possible way in which I could be of value to Lydia or myself was by being patient, by waiting, by showing nothing whatever of my furious resentment that such things could happen to persons who had harmed no one.

The whole harbour was a phosphorescent green, and Tripoli a black and white fringe, pin-pointed with lights, against an olive-green sky in which swam a polished moon, when the outer bolt was shot on my door and it was thrown open by one of Murad Rais's lieutenants, who motioned me on deck.

Lee and Murad Rais were at the companionway, handing Lydia down into a longboat. I saw Lee go over the side after her ; and then I was in the boat myself on an afterthwart, and still as far removed from Lydia as though a wall were between us.

Murad Rais, following close behind me, rapped out an order ; and the boat's oars thumped and creaked.

I can smell that harbour now, and its fishy, warm dankness, layered like a cake with odours of musk, garbage, sweat, and dirty dry animals. I can almost feel again the weak, cold sickness that kept my hands tremblingly wiping the perspiration from my eyes and upper lip as we came closer and closer to the bulk of that Castle whose flat-topped towers leaned out blackly against the green sky.

The Castle rose straight up from the rocks at the edge of the harbour. There were guards on the rocks where we landed, and an open door at the foot of that towering wall of masonry. The door led into a passage-way dripping with water and lighted by sentries with tin lanterns. There were slippery steps that turned at sharp angles ; less slippery steps ; long passageways, smelling of ammonia, that led us into an open square within the Castle, a sort of village green in miniature, with stone arches which supported balconies that seemed to be porches for small elevated houses with latticed windows.

Above one of the arches there was a swinging lamp, and on either side trousered men with flopping red caps and drawn swords. The passageway inside was lighted by other lamps on chains ; and the walls were tiled. It led us into a sort of hallway, empty except for three tired-looking boys sitting close together on a bench beside a curtained door.

Murad Rais drew aside the curtain, threw open the door, and ushered us into a glittering reception hall in which three men were sitting on a raised platform. The hall, the platform, the men had a sort of tawdriness and unreality, like a scene in a theatre.

The platform was covered with crimson velvet fringed with gold cloth and studded with jewels or pieces of glass. Scattered over the marble floor were soft-toned rugs ; and the walls were made of many-coloured tiles on which were depicted trees and animals and birds.

Of the three men upon the platform, one was a Negro in a yellow turban and yellow satin trousers ; another was a white-beared old man who looked half asleep ; and the third, the one in the middle—certainly the Bashaw himself—was a majestic and benevolent-looking figure—as handsome a man as ever I saw. He wasn't over tall ; but his features— as much of them as could be seen above his glossy black beard—were regular and pleasantly olive-coloured. On his head was a white turban, laced with ribbons, and beneath a long robe of gold-embroidered blue silk he wore a jewelled belt in which were two gold-mounted pistols and a gold-hilted sabre.

Murad Rais stepped forward to the edge of the platform, saluted the Bashaw, bowed slightly to the Negro and the old man, then delivered himself of a brief speech in Arabic, which he followed by introducing Lee —who I'm bound to say made something of a figure in his green turban, baggy trousers, and broad sash.

When Murad Rais had finished, the Bashaw came down from the platform, patted Lee amiably on the shoulder, took a gold chain from around his neck and put it around Lee's. Then he came forward and examined Lydia and me, walking completely around us, nodding and smiling as if contemplating a gift that gave him profound pleasure. Then he spoke to Murad Rais, who turned to Lydia and said, " He wants you to tell him that you're doing this of your own free will."

" We both signed the paper," Lydia said, " and of course we stand by what was in the paper. By the terms of that paper I have agreed to teach his three nephews ; but that paper said that they are to be properly instructed. We can discuss the matter of proper instruction here and now."

" This is hardly the time for any such discussion as that," Murad Rais said.

" Why isn't it ? " Lydia asked. " Who are those three boys outside in the hall ? Are they the three to whom I'm to give proper instruction ? "

" That's a delicate subject," Murad Rais said. " Now just take my advice——"

" Why should we take your advice ? " I asked. " You stole our ship. You blackmailed us into signing your paper. We signed it, and we've got to abide by it ; but you've got to tell that man what my wife says. If she's going to teach children, she's got to teach them what they ought to know ; not what somebody else thinks they ought to know. You tell that man what she says."

The Bashaw, who had been watching me intently, spoke sharply to Murad Rais, who raised his shoulders helplessly and with obvious reluctance translated what Lydia had said.

When Murad Rais had finished, the Bashaw went to the door and called, whereupon the three boys—the eldest possibly fourteen and the youngest about nine, all three dressed like their elders in turbans and baggy trousers—walked into the room, clutching each other's hands, and stood there looking at the floor. They didn't seem frightened ; but, if I knew anything about children, they were.

The Bashaw again spoke to Murad Rais, who relayed his words to Lydia.

"These are the children," the Bashaw said. "The children of my brother Hamet."

"Your brother Hamet is dead ?"

"No, no, he is opposed to me. We are not in sympathy. Therefore he has gone away."

"Their mother has gone away too ?"

"No, their mother is here in the Castle."

"Then why aren't they with their mother ? Why were they sitting there in the hall when we came in ?"

"It was my wish that they sit in the hall," the Bashaw said. "Whenever we take prisoners, these boys are required to sit in the hall so as to see what happens to my enemies. Thus they learn not to be among my enemies."

"So," Lydia said, "these are the children you wish me to teach. What do you think they should be taught ?"

"I wish them taught English," the Bashaw said. "I wish them taught obedience—whatever young persons of position are taught in England."

"Of course," Lydia said, "it is obvious that, if you want me to teach the children these things, it is because you are unable to teach them yourself. Probably, too, if there were anybody else in Tripoli who could teach them, you wouldn't need me to do it."

The Bashaw nodded.

"Then it must also be equally evident," Lydia went on, "that since nobody else knows how to teach them, and you consider me capable of doing so, I must have complete control over all their actions. Otherwise my teachings can easily be made worthless."

"But I must know what they are taught," the Bashaw said, "so that I can tell whether or not you're teaching them the right things."

"If I'm to teach them," Lydia said, "I trust nobody but myself to understand what the right and the wrong things are. I have no intention of teaching them anything wrong. You, for example, must think that it's right to keep these boys sitting here late at night, watching helpless people dragged here and enslaved ; but if I'm to be their teacher, I can't allow such things."

"Nobody is allowed to say ' I cannot allow ' to me," the Bashaw said.

"Then I cannot be a teacher," Lydia said. "Make me a companion, or a hairdresser, or a dressmaker. A teacher must truly teach, or be no teacher at all. For example, if I say ' I must have certain books,' you——"

"You must not use the word 'must,'" the Bashaw said.

"Yes, I must," Lydia replied. "I must use it perpetually to myself. I must learn Arabic. I must keep my word. I must be true to my obligations. I must be patient. I must at all hazards do what I conceive to be right."

Her eyes turned to mine and clung ; but even if they hadn't, I'd have known that some of those words of hers were for me as well as for the Bashaw : "I must be patient—I must learn Arabic—I must be true to my obligations."

"Very well," the Bashaw said. "Since that is the English way, I will agree to the things you say." He went to the door of the room, and again shouted an order, on which a woman draped with veils, almost like a haystack covered with sheets and towels, appeared and beckoned to Lydia.

Lydia turned from her, came to me, put her arms around me and her lips against my ear. "There was nothing in the paper about sending a message," she whispered. "I'll find a way. Don't fear for me, ever." She released me abruptly, returned to the veiled woman, and with her and the three boys went silently from the room.

It seemed to me, when she was gone, that something had been taken from every part of me. It was as though a fog came between me and the gaudy colours of that garish room. My eyes were blurred ; my head seemed stuffed with cotton ; there was no feeling in my arms or legs ; the only sensation of which I was conscious was sick emptiness.

In the haze of that fever I heard Murad Rais discussing me with the Bashaw : saw the Bashaw summon a servant, who went away and returned with a red cap, a strip of muslin and two long pieces of brown cloth, each piece the shape of a blanket, and the two joined together by their upper corners.

"Now then," Murad Rais said, "you'll have no further use for coat or pantaloons around here—they'll only bring trouble to you. So off with them, and your shoes, too !"

I numbly did as I was told, and darkly saw the bearded Bashaw and his two attendants comment amusedly upon my appearance. Murad Rais clapped the red cap upon my head, wrapped it with the strip of muslin ; then draped the pieces of brown cloth around me, so that the fastened corners rested on my shoulders. He picked up one of the loose corners and threw it over the opposite shoulder.

"There," he said, "that's a barracan. You're safe in it as long as you keep your mouth shut, even though you *do* have blue eyes." Indulgently he added, "It's only for your own good. Without it you'd be called a dog and spat upon."

When Lee whispered to him, he nodded and held out his hand to me. "That green stone you're wearing : I'll take it."

When I protested, he was sharp with me. "It's too much of an identification. Hand it over."

When I took it off and gave it to him, he handed it to Lee.

"Come on, now," Murad Rais said. "Make a bow to His Highness and we'll be off."

Like a man in a dream, I had no feeling of resentment ; only an inarticulate and overwhelming sense of impotence, of fearfulness—fearfulness for Lydia, dread of what these phantasmagoric humans might do to her if I should even seem to cross their maggoty intentions and orders.

Darkly and endlessly the dream went on ; in it I bowed and scraped to that scented, velvet-clad Bashaw ; padded barefooted in the wake of Murad Rais, back through corridors into the Castle courtyard, and down to another courtyard thick with the ammonia stench of horses ; heard interminable shouting in unknown tongues ; struggled to mount a horse, hampered by those damnable brown blankets, which flapped disgustingly about my knees ; followed Murad Rais from the Castle into a narrow street and past a minaret that seemed to reach almost to the moon itself ; through a shadowed gate into alleyways of darkling shops reeking of smells such as I had never known : stinks of decay and ordure, worse than any of the stinks of Haiti, with occasional drifts and layers of pleasant scents—new tanned leather, musk, blacksmith's forges and tempering buckets, fresh-baked bread. Camels stared at me from the dark background of the dream—disdainful, unreal monsters, wishful to laugh at my plight but prevented by swollen, cracked lips. Palm trees were black against the moonlit sky, palm trees from whose leaves came dusty harsh hissings, titterings and cacklings which mocked me in a dry unceasing chorus, "Caught ! He's caught ! He's caught and helpless ! Helpless and caught ! "

CHAPTER XLIII

How many men, how many many men in every land, men in high positions, heavy laden with honours, seem honest, sympathetic, affectionate, even generous and gentle, but in reality are monsters—cruel, unperceptive, intellectually dishonest, ready to sacrifice anything or anybody for their personal gain or pleasure ! Murad Rais was such a man, though I have no doubt that he considered himself an enlightened, kindly gentleman : that he felt he was showing me special consideration when he made me his slave.

If I had been a free man, and could have had Lydia by my side, I could have been happy in Murad Rais's home ; for it stood in a garden dotted with orange and lemon trees, fig trees, and date palms, surrounded by sturdy high walls made of a sort of brick-clay ; and the land sloped a little towards the sea. Though the rear wall rose some thirty feet from the sand of the harbour beach, from inside the garden it was only breast-high ; so that over it one saw the whole harbour with its anchored polacres and xebecs, the crescent-shaped city, its minarets and domes and flat-topped houses, its crenellated Castle and Roman arch gleaming black and white in the moon's pale rays. I could even see, floating upon that flat and wine-dark African sea, the necklace of islands at the harbour's mouth—those islands that were to set up a chain of circumstances resulting so gloriously and so dishonourably for America.

The house itself, like all Moorish houses, was next to windowless and built around a courtyard. In front was a narrow garden planted with flowering shrubs, vines, and palms of various sorts, dimly seen in the steel-bright moonlight. Behind the house were dark gardens and a well and a water-wheel. On one side of the garden was a long stable : on the other side a row of small square houses, each one the size of a hen-house for a dozen hens.

Murad Rais went to the farthest of the houses, pushed open the door, took a sulphur spunk from a shelf just inside, and kindled a candle. "There," he said proudly, "you'll have the place all to yourself, as long as you behave and give satisfaction."

The room had a hard-packed dirt floor, a cot of boards raised a foot above it, and a single narrow window, barred. On the shelf beside the door were three earthenware bowls and a wooden pail. Beneath the bed was an iron pot. There was nothing else in the room.

Murad Rais sat himself cross-legged on the bare board bedstead, a strange-looking Scot in his green turban, yellow trousers, and pink sash, and generously motioned me to sit beside him.

"Now look here, Hamlin," he said, making diagrams of his words with a forefinger upon the palm of his hand, after the manner of Arabs, "I want to make sure there's no danger of your making a fool of yourself. Life's not easy in Tripoli for any Christian dog—unless he's got a pot of money ; and if you ever do anything to turn us against you or your lady, you'll regret it till the day you die. Understand ?"

I said I did.

"Make damned sure you do," Murad Rais said. "I know His Highness better than most men—know him well enough to call him Joe when I'm alone with him—Joseph being his name, Joseph Karamanli of the old Karamanli family." He coughed and dropped his Arab mannerisms to rub his nose with a knobbly knuckle. "Now you might think anybody named Joe would be a pretty easy-going man, and of course you saw for yourself how handsome and nice he is ; but if you let yourself get to thinking along those lines, you'll be making a dreadful mistake—just dreadful ! Why, Joe's eldest brother was Bashaw before him, and his other brother Hamet was next in line for the throne. There were two of 'em in Joe's way—fine men, both of 'em."

He looked at me sharply. "I'm being frank with you for your own good. I liked both of Joe's brothers—though, of course, it doesna make any difference to me who carries the Three Tails around this place, so long as I'm allowed to run the Navy. I'm no politician ; they're too canny for my gizzard—too canny altaegither.''

He winked at me and wagged his head portentously. " Well, there they were, in his way ; so he killed the eldest one and drove Hamet out of the city. He doesn't like people to get in his way. When anybody does, he takes steps—takes 'em quick, too. He went over to see his eldest brother one morning, hauled a pistol out of his sash, and shot him, *bang* ! Then went home to breakfast.''

I just stared at Murad Rais.

" Aye,'' he said, " that's Joe Karamanli for you. So you behave yourself, or you'll bring trouble on your lady, sure as there's a moon in the sky. Real trouble ! Understand ? ''

I nodded.

" Now look,'' he went on. " Farmers don't stand high in Arab circles. Lower than a snake's tail, they are. There's only two things lower : woodcutters and limeburners. That's why I've had such a hell of a time getting a good man to farm this place for me. The best I could do was Bedouins—the worst kind of Bedouins. And there isna anybody worse than a bad Bedouin, except a bad Maltese, or a bad Italian, or a bad Syrian, or a bad Jew, or any Egyptian—there are *no* good Gyps. My last Bedouins made such a mess o' things I had to shoot 'em.

" So I want you to do better for me. All you've got to do is tend strictly to business, raise the kind of crops this place is capable of raising, and take 'em to the bazaar outside the Castle and sell 'em. If you do that, you'll find I won't make trouble for you. You've got to be back in this garden every night at nine o'clock sharp, and you can tell when it's nine o'clock from the way the muezzins call. You're never to go into the city : never under *any* circumstances, unless you go in with me. But you can go into the bread bazaar and the vegetable bazaar or any other bazaars outside the walls.

" You'll have plenty to do and plenty to look at. I want you to keep your eye on the other gardens hereabouts and find out why my vegetables dinna thrive like theirs. You'll start working before sun-up each day ; take your fruits and vegetables to the market around nine o'clock and get a receipt from Abu Zirt ; then come right back and keep on working while there's enough light, so long as you're back inside these gates by nine o'clock. If ever you are not, the sentries know what to do about it. They'll notify the Castle, and the Bashaw'll take steps against your lady— take 'em quick ! Understand ? ''

I nodded again.

" All right,'' he said. " Repeat those orders.''

With a leaden heart I repeated them : I was to take charge of all crops in his garden, keep an eye on the other gardens, be working by sun-up, deliver produce to the proper dealer, be back in my quarters by nine o'clock each night, and never set foot inside the city walls of Tripoli.

" And,'' Murad Rais added severely, " you're in all respects to live up to the terms of the Convention you and your lady signed. You took your oath you'd never tell anybody you're an American ; you took your oath you'd never send a message to anyone anywhere asking for help. If you do—if in any other way you commit any act, overt or otherwise, contrary to your agreement, I take my oath that we'll at once proceed against your wife. Is that clear ? "

I tried to speak, but couldn't ; so I just nodded.

Murad Rais got to his feet, gave his pink sash a twist and pulled at his voluminous pantaloons, and glared around the room. " Hard work, neatness, order, and economy, Hamlin ! I insist on all of 'em ! "

He went to the door, blew out the candle with an explosive puff, and left me.

I was so whipped mentally that I lacked the willpower to stretch myself full length upon the boards of my unyielding bed. I just sat there in that hot and airless cubicle, vaguely conscious of the velvety feel of the packed earth beneath my bare feet, unable to think, unable to plan, merely existing, a sort of dead man in something little different from a grave. Even the pictures that passed through my numb brain were dim ones, though they were all of Lydia—Lydia kneeling to fasten knapsacks on Paul and Raymond d'Autremont, Lydia's picture smiling at me from the wall of Thomas Bailey's bedroom, Lydia in the golden sunlight on those golden beaches above the forests of Haiti, Lydia's eyes below mine in the candle-lit cabin of the brig *Hope*.

The brig *Hope* ! Hope ! That word sent a flicker of light through the darkened, dried-up recesses of my brain. There was a time when I had thought of Lydia as dead, but then the *Hope* had carried me to Haiti and to her. The *Hope* had saved us from falling into Dessalines' hands. If it hadn't been for Lydia and the *Hope*, I might have had my way and sought safety for ourselves by carrying Autremont to America instead of to Cette. Hope ! My mind was too confused, to battered, to find the meaning that I sought, but Hope had saved me before and it would have to save me again. Hope had brought me to Lydia ; Hope had brought me where I was ; perhaps in spite of Lee, in spite of Joseph Karamanli, in spite of Murad Rais, in spite of this living tomb that had engulfed me, Hope would somehow unravel the tangle of circumstances into which we had fallen.

I got my feet up on to the boards and slept.

CHAPTER XLIV

I LISTEN with a sceptical ear to tales of those who through some mischance or misfortune arc regarded as ruined and thus destitute. I'm sceptical because I'm sure that most of them have something : a razor, a few clothes, some books, a friend or two, or at least some charitable person to whom they can turn. But if ever there was anybody who was truly destitute, it was I during the first days of my captivity.

I had the barracan that Murad Rais had tossed me, and the pieces of muslin that bound the red cap on my head. But I knew not a word of Arabic ; and I had not an acquaintance to whom I could turn ; nothing to read, nothing to write with, nothing to write on ; no razor, no comb, no nothing ; just the odds and ends of information that I'd stored in my own head in the past twenty-nine years, and meagre enough they seemed in that grey July dawn. I regretted every moment that I hadn't put to better use when I had worked with William Bartram ; when I had scratched my head over the pages of Jared Eliot, William Marshall, Lord Kames, Arthur Young, James Anderson, and Samuel Dean.

I find it difficult to recapture my helplessness during the first months or the unutterable confusion in which I existed. Lydia, of course, was in my thoughts morning, noon, and night—how she was living, how she was being treated. And I was in a constant turmoil over our enslavement ; over my inability to express myself to anyone except by signs ; over the deadly slowness with which I learned.

For me there was no outside world—only the garden in which I worked and the shadowy bazaars outside the walls, peopled by spectres in pale burnooses and barracans, countless soiled ghosts whose screamings and shrill gibberish were as meaningless as the wailing of a multitude of sea gulls.

I think the women that I saw in the bazaars were my greatest cross in the beginning—though not because of their beauty, since all of them, except the lowest order of Bedouin women, were shapeless in cloaks and hoods and baggy trousers, with only a single eye peering expressionlessly from a slit in a veil, like the staring black eye of a hen. What infuriated me was the freedom with which these veiled women went everywhere—in and out of shops, out into the desert in the wake of caravans, in and out of mosques and up alleyways, and all without any man so much as turning a head to look at them. Recalling my escape from the Suffolk County Jail, I realised that if I could only be dressed like one of these shapeless and unapproachable women, I could go anywhere at all, unnoticed and unmolested. This burned in me like a fever through the long nights— this and the equal realisation that I was helpless to make any move without endangering Lydia.

In the first week of my imprisonment, I think I lived the equivalent of a year. As things about me became more familiar, however, each day merely seemed endless. Unable to sleep because of thinking of Lydia, longing for her, fearing for her, I'd go out into the garden and climb to the top of the wall and watch the night caravans go through, the enormous dubious shapes of soft-footed camels flowing beneath the palms like creatures out of a nightmare.

Where the caravans came from, where they went, I had no way of knowing. I had no way of learning Arabic, for I could only pick up a few words from people like caravan drivers or bazaar servants—words that had to do entirely with food, vegetables, and animals.

There was a scant seven acres in Murad Rais's garden—all of it shaded by date palms, as are all decent gardens in North Africa. The water-wheel was at the upper end of the garden, and a series of diversion ditches ran from it to all the beds. So far as I could see, the soil of the garden was nothing but sand ; yet the vegetables that grew in that sand, unsatisfactory though they may have seemed in Tripoli, were as good as anything I had ever seen in Bartram's Gardens, and better than anything I had ever raised in Gorham.

But as I watched what came out of adjoining gardens, it seemed even better than what this garden produced. And I began to suspect—as I followed the water along the ditches and dug into the wet sand—that one of the troubles here lay in the fact that Murad Rais's water supply didn't go deep enough and wasn't sufficiently large ; the water couldn't get down to the roots and stay there.

The only tool resembling a hoe that was to be found in this garden was a crooked piece of cedar, curved a little at the end ; and the neighbouring gardens seemed to have nothing better. As for ploughing, I gathered that it was commonly done with another crooked length of cedar tied to a rope ; the pointed end of the cedar was used to gouge a little furrow in the soil—though the stuff was more sand than soil.

My first task, therefore, was to improve the water supply and to obtain more efficient tools, so I waylaid Murad Rais and persuaded him to get me four of the knives that his sailors carried. Two of these, set to the hilt in a six-inch piece of wood attached to a four-foot handle, made a sort of sharp double-bladed hoe that could easily be driven into the ground with the sole of the foot, opening a hole that reached the roots of almost any plant. With two of these primitive but effective implements I made holes of varying depths beside each melon plant, each tomato plant, each head of lettuce, each cucumber vine ; and into each hole crammed anything I could find that was spongy or porous—pieces of date leaves, dead weeds, refuse of any sort, date stones, coffee grounds, all the leavings from Murad Rais's kitchen and the droppings and wet straw from his stables.

When the water from the irrigation ditches ran into these holes, the roots were moistened and the results were astounding. The vegetables seemed to leap forward—a growth more noticeable in the tomatoes than anything else. Those tomatoes swelled like red balloons ; side-shoots and blossoms popped from them : never one of the vines but bore a hundred fruits and more, and some of the ripe tomatoes, were eight inches in diameter.

Of course Murad Rais was gratified by all this, but he wasn't grateful. I saw him occasionally showing off his house and his garden to distinguished visitors : sometimes Europeans ; sometimes Arab dignitaries from desert tribes, beautiful, aristocratic-appearing gentlemen in snowy burnooses, or striped silken ones. But never did he say a word to me in the presence of any of these people. I might have been a pack animal as well as a slave for all the attention he gave me—and of course his guests never looked at me either.

It's difficult for me to recapture the bitterness of my thoughts during that period. I hated Murad Rais and George Lee as much as I had hated Judge Chase, as much as I had hated Tobias Lear, even more than I had hated Dessalines. And, of course, I hated Murad Rais's master, Joseph Karamanli, Bashaw of the Three Tails, that kinglet so contemptible as to make war on women, condone slavery, murder his own brother, trick another brother out of a throne, and live by blackmail and oppression.

The world would be a better place to live in if men of high position, men whose lives have been easy, could get the faintest inkling of the fury that boils and surges in the minds of those who are victims, or who even consider themselves victims, of injustice ! I can feel now the tightness in my stomach, the dryness in my throat, the rivulets of perspiration that trickled from me, as I lay at night upon the boards of my bed, staring up into the dark, raging at all the things that fear, resentment, impotence, desperation, brought into my mind.

In my bitterness I thought of the great men in Washington, supposed to know so much about Tripoli, the war with Tripoli, the things going on in the Mediterranean, the qualifications of those sent to the Mediterranean to conduct affairs there. Actually they knew less than I (who at this time knew practically nothing) about any of these things. Nor did they realise the helplessness of all peoples in all lands, doomed to be ruled, exploited, led by leaders who deserve no faith and no following. I reflected on the mistaken but widely held belief that men experienced in a trade or profession must necessarily be wise, and their way of doing things the right way—though any person of moderate intelligence should be able to see that most things in this world are done wrong. Most houses are badly built, most medicines ineffective, most garments ill-fitting, most farms badly run, most books badly written, most clergymen dull beyond relief, most civilisations extinct. I thought how hard it is to develop understanding in men's minds when schools so often refuse to let pupils advance at a rate faster than that set by the mediocre, the backward, the half-witted, the incompetent—or to encourage the promising ones to rise to a higher-than-average level. I raged at the idiocy of pleading for tolerance when actually the world has always needed intolerance : intolerance of mediocrity, of cruelty, of laziness, and stupidity and clumsiness, of knavery and trickery, intolerance of ignorance, of gluttony, of waste. I thought of the intellectual slavery in which so many men live, governed by nincompoops ; of the irony that so many black men, considered only fit for slavery, should be so much more emancipated than any white men ; of the hypocrites who prate about the desirability of equality, when really equality is impossible for any human beings anywhere. My mind turned then to the subject of religion : I considered Voodoo and Christianity, and how Christianity contains all the sillinesses and pretences of Voodoo.

I brooded on the helplessness of men, condemned for ever to endure the unendurable in war whenever rascally politicians choose to inflict war upon them ; on the overwhelming lack of understanding in the minds of those who make wars unavoidable ; on liberty, and how preposterous it was that Frenchmen should be howling about Liberty, Equality, and Fraternity at the very moment when they were doing their utmost to take all three away from Toussaint. And finally my thoughts came around to this Africa in which I found myself : dotted with the crumbling ruins of nations that had been reduced to heaps of rubble under leaders who were tolerant—tolerant of everything bad to such a point that they had brought destruction down on themselves and on the unhappy wretches they governed.

While I puttered around that palm-shaded garden overlooking Tripoli harbour, I looked like any other dirty, bare-shanked, barracan-clad Bedouin, as witless and thoughtless as any of the vegetables over which I worked ; but my brain was a soup of black and frantic resentment. Joseph Bounds in Gibraltar had said that the American Navy in the Mediterranean was led by fools and worse ; and I had been shocked and unbelieving. Yet there *were* American frigates in the Mediterranean : I had even seen one of them. The blackmailing, fratricidal Bashaw of this camel-dung town had got away with declaring war on the United States, and seizing American ships, without having one of those American frigates sail into Tripoli harbour and knock that urine-scented Castle of Joseph Karamanli into a cocked hat ! *Something* certainly was wrong with the United States Navy !

CHAPTER XLV

FOR FOUR MONTHS I existed in that accursed garden before I began to find out a little something about the world again—just barely began, like a child ; and the beginning, of course, was due to Lydia. Almost daily some woman from the Bashaw's palace came out from the city to walk in Murad Rais's garden with one of Murad's womenfolk ; and on a morning of my fourth month of slavery one of these swathed women came to the garden with a similarly swathed figure that I'd seen before and believed to be one of Murad Rais's wives. The two wandered through the garden, murmuring idly to each other. When they passed me, I was damming an irrigation ditch and was conscious of their perfume more than of anything else. It was mostly attar-of-rose, which wasn't strange, since every woman who had passed me in Tripoli had left a wake of either rose or musk behind her.

They stopped at a melon vine and peered among the leaves. I had hung the fruit in nets, so that none of it would bruise or rot ; and the woman I took for Murad Rais's wife signalled to me that she wanted one of the melons. As I was cutting it for her, the other cooed and murmured, fumbled somewhere in the recesses of her voluminous garments, pressed what I thought to be a coin into my hand, and instantly turned away.

It *was* a coin, but a single thin sheet of paper was wrapped around it— a paper that burned my fingers until those two women had finished their puttering and got themselves out of sight. Not until then did I dare look at it ; and then I found what I had hoped I'd find, a note from Lydia— a note written in tiny characters—a message that tore at my heart, so acutely did it bring into my mind her sweetness, her kindness, her unfailing gentleness and wisdom.

All the women of the Bashaw's harem, she wrote, were kind to her ; her pupils were obedient and willing, she was starting to learn Arabic— and so, she insisted, must I.

Remember (she wrote) that even an American workman needs only some 400 words to express his thoughts, and that Arabs need no more. Their way of living is so simple, and their speech so conventional and restricted to so few subjects, that when you have memorised the words I send you (turn over), you will find it easy to talk. Say you come from Afghanistan ; you will never meet an Arab who knows anything about geography. Use the words Allah and Prophet constantly. Mention Paradise and Hell and the Devil often, and run a string of beads through your fingers with devout mumblings. Don't worry if you forget a word or can't finish a sentence. Just mumble " Allah is the Greatest ! " or " Mohammed is the favourite of Allah ! " or " Allah confound all Christians ! "—any of these takes the place of a missing word or phrase.

Her next and final paragraph brought me the first solace I had known for weeks, with its tender words of love and its strong note of hopefulness. She ended by bidding me destroy the letter as soon as I had mastered its contents, lest it fall into other hands.

The other side of the sheet contained my first lesson in Arabic : the twenty-eight convoluted, spidery consonants, which can be written four ways, depending on whether they are unconnected with other letters, connected with the preceding letter only, connected on both sides, or connected with the following letter only ; the three signs which, placed above or below consonants, create short vowels ; the five silent letters that turn short vowels into long ones ; and the other five reading-signs that result in a guttural sound, or double or prolong a letter. Lydia knew that I was already acquainted with the fact that Arabic letters, words, and sentences are read from right to left.

I thought, as I studied that closely written sheet, that I'd have to live to be a thousand years old before I could learn any such strange-looking alphabet, let alone speak or read a sentence in it ; yet thanks to Lydia's encouragement, added to my own burning desire to emerge from this confused and meaningless world in which I lived, I found that before that night was over I had half of those Arabic letters firmly in my mind, and could pronounce and write them. In a week I had all the letters and all the signs by heart.

The year that followed was almost endurable, for I heard regularly from Lydia. Every week, without fail, she contrived to send me, through a Jewish merchant or some of the women in the Castle, another lesson in Arabic, together with a letter ; and I read and re-read those letters until each one was limp as a rag. In every letter, too, was something calculated to make my lot easier—a packet of small needles, or large needles ; a sailmaker's needle ; a packet of thread ; a piece of soap ; a razor ; a pair of scissors. But I presently recalled the danger she'd mentioned in her first message, and—much against my will—started destroying her letters ; retaining only an occasional bit that warmed my heart with its loving intimacy.

Soon her letters began to tell me about Hamet Karamanli, the father of the three boys whom she was teaching, and to hint at a great scheme concocted by the William Eaton of whom Captain Bounds had told us— a scheme to punish the reigning Bashaw, Joseph Karamanli, for making war on the United States and on American shipping, and to restore Hamet to the throne ; and I hoped as devoutly as she that something might come of it.

Once she wrote of learning that the plan had been approved by the United States Government and also by Commodore Dale before he had been replaced by Commodore Morris. Later she said that Eaton, in his efforts to help Hamet, had spent large sums, and that the American Navy had failed to reimburse him, so that he was in trouble with everyone —especially with Commodore Morris, who didn't approve of him or his schemes.

She spoke more and more critically of Commodore Morris, who evidently had made plans to attack and blockade Tripoli, only to go wandering off on futile expeditions. Americans, she said, were held in low esteem in the palace, partly owing to our naval officers and their habit of fighting duels whenever they went ashore, and partly because of the miserable quality of the consuls who represented the United States in such Mediterranean ports as Syracuse, Leghorn, and Naples. And she added that an old friend of ours, Tobias Lear, had come to Algiers as chief consul there. Perhaps, she added, it was just as well we'd given our word not to try to obtain the assistance of any American ; for if we hadn't and should ask Lear for help, he would probably do us more harm than good !

Her jesting words brought back, as clearly as though he stood before me, Tobias Lear's pale and beautiful face, his cat-like tread, his sleepy and contented eyes. I wondered what underhanded means he'd used to get himself sent to Algiers ; what unperceptive fool in Washington had let himself be bamboozled into putting Lear in a position where he'd bungle everything he touched. However, since Lear was where he could neither help nor hurt us, I presently forgot him.

Then Cette crept back into her letters, as if she actually thought there was a possibility we might some day be together in that lovely spot ; and I gathered that deep in her heart she was convinced there was something to all this fantastic talk about Eaton and Hamet and an American-financed expedition to put Hamet back on his throne.

Each week, too, she sent me a fresh list of words, a fresh list of sentences in Arabic, with the pronunciation and the translation beneath each word. I memorised every word, every sentence, through the long nights ; and to my untold elation I began to understand the shouts of the camel-drivers in the caravans, the gabbling of children, the bargaining in the bazaars—though it was with no elation whatever that I found myself understanding the converstaion of those about me when they talked of the terrible happening of October 31, 1803.

Every few minutes of every hour during the fifteen months and twenty-seven days I'd worked in Murad Rais's garden, I'd peered out at the harbour's mouth, hopeful of seeing an American frigate sailing past or standing off-and-on in token of the fleet that might some day reduce the place to ruins and liberate us. But all I ever saw were strangely rigged vessels—xebecs, polacres, ketches, Arab dhows, and goelettes able to pile a pyramid of sail on a few toothpicks of masts.

But on that miserable thirty-first of October, far out beyond the harbour's mouth, I heard the reports of heavy guns ; and when I ran to the wall and looked off to the eastward, I saw a tall black ship, her sails gleaming white in the noonday sun, running straight towards me, close-hauled on an offshore breeze, in pursuit of a smaller vessel that looked to me like the xebec on which Murad Rais had taken us to Tripoli. The black ship was a frigate, no doubt of that ; and to be firing on a Tripolitan vessel she had to be American.

Never, it seemed to me, had I seen such a beautiful picture. From her bows came jets of white smoke ; and the throbbing thump of her guns was sweeter in my ears than heavenly music.

The xebec ran closer and closer to the shore, and for half an hour the black frigate stood after her, firing and firing. Then, whether because the xebec was out of range, or because the water was shoaling too rapidly, she gave up the chase and payed off to the eastward, before the wind, out towards the open sea.

Not until then could I see how big she was. By comparison with all the other vessels in the harbour, she was a veritable leviathan, a solid great island of a ship : a heartening spectacle indeed to one who had prayed so ardently and so long for some symbol of America's might and majesty.

I suppose there's something weakening in endless waiting, in per-petually wishing to be free and never knowing freedom, in being kept, through no fault of your own, from the one you most love. Certainly a wave of weakness swept over me at the sight of that high-sided black frigate with her long rows of gun-ports and the gleaming striped flag that flew from her masthead ; and the weakness brought such a dimness to my eyes that the vessel blurred and wavered, and had the queer rigidity of a smudged painting of a vessel, immovable, askew, not quite right. Strange that a drop of moisture in a man's eyes should create the illusion of a motionless world !

I rubbed at my eyes to clear them, and saw that it wasn't the blur within my eyes that had made the frigate seem to stand still. She *was* still. With all sails set and drawing, she had stopped like a rock, abreast of the entrance to the harbour.

I couldn't believe it. I rubbed my eyes again ; then lined up the frigate with a projection on the garden wall. Thus sighted, there could be no mistake : the frigate didn't move so much as a hair. She had grounded on a reef : grounded hard and fast.

I felt I just couldn't be alone and watch that ship, that beautiful ship, lying helpless, almost within range of the guns of Tripoli. I couldn't share my feelings, of course ; but I must at least be near somebody—I couldn't go on watching it alone.

I ran from Murad Rais's garden and along the dusty road under the date palms, between the mud walls of the gardens—ran and ran, no different, in my brown barracan and lop-sided turban, from any of the scores of Arabs who were pelting towards the city walls and the open beach outside the walls.

God knows how the news could have flashed through the bazaars and out through the desert in such a short time ; but it must have, because white burnooses were thick along the beach and the rising ground behind. From them came a sound like the squalling of gulls, for all of them were chattering shrilly, as is the custom of Arabs.

The frigate was where I'd last seen her, but there had been changes. There was movement in her sails, as if she were drawing fluttering breaths —probably the crew was trying to back them in the hope that the breeze would turn her off the reef ; though I couldn't for the life of me see how that off-shore breeze could do anything but jam her more solidly aground, so long as her sails were drawing. There were splashes around her, tall splashes which must have been her bow guns being thrown overboard to lighten her.

Worst of all, there was movement in the harbour close to shore : a dozen xebecs and gun-ketches had raised anchors and sails, and were moving slowly towards the stranded frigate.

She lay there so steady and so unharmed that I *knew* she would slip backward off the reef. I knew it would happen at any moment—knew she'd suddenly start to move—knew she'd wear around and be enveloped in white smoke as she opened on the nearing xebecs. I knew it ! She had to get off ! It wasn't possible that she shouldn't get off !

Though even if she couldn't get off, I said to myself—ashamed to harbour such a thought—she was like a fort out there : a better fort than any Tripolitan fort could ever hope to be. She had to be armed with twenty-four-pounders, like every other American frigate ; with great store of small arms and powder ; shells, chain-shot, langrage ; cartridges by the million ; gun crews and gun pointers unequalled by those of any other navy in the world ; foretop and maintop men who could rifle a squirrel out of a tree at thirty paces or clip the head from a chicken at twenty. She would have a pike and cutlass for every man of her crew ; enough pistols to give each man two ; boarding nettings to hoist in case they tried to board her : everything essential—everything—to fight off for as long as necessary any attacking force that could be brought against her. And it couldn't be a long fight, for when the wind turned onshore, there'd be more water on the reef, so that she could easily get off and away.

But she *was* going to get off, of course ! I groaned and sweated and groaned again as the minutes went by and the xebecs moved closer and closer. She had to get off, but she wasn't getting off ! She was like a part of a glaring bright dream, in which everything is wrong : in which people change into other people ; in which legs and arms do the opposite of what they should ; in which there is neither rhyme nor reason, logic nor normal sequence. Here was this ship, all unhurt, erect upon a flat blue sea, her sails all misdirected . . . and now a boat was putting off from her bows, a boat that dropped anchor, so that those aboard must have been trying to haul her over the reef !

" Over, for God's sake ! " I shouted inwardly. " You can't haul a vessel *over* a reef ! Drop the anchor astern, you damned fools, and haul her off backward ! Or let her alone ! She'll free herself if you let her alone ! "

I sweated and I groaned and I didn't believe what I was seeing. It wasn't true ! Not a shot had been fired by anyone, yet her foremast swayed and slowly tilted over the side. Those damned fools had dismasted her ! Now she *was* helpless, even though they should get her off. Now she *couldn't* sail.

From the bows of the xebec nearest the frigate jetted white plumes of smoke ; and the thunder of the explosions was like hot cotton in my ears —hot cotton through which rasped the piercing shrill howls of the burnoosed throng all around me. They capered and they screamed, addressing themselves to the frigate. " Go in hell ! " " Ah, Jews ! " " Hogs ! " " Protestants ! " " Brutes ! " " Annihilate the children of whores ! "

There was an answering burst of white smoke from the stern of the frigate—one burst only : then a brief spatter of musketry fire. From the xebec, however, came repeated thunderings. Behind her the other xebecs came into the wind and lay silent, untrue to life, mirage-like.

That was how they lay all through the middle of that hot October afternoon : the xebec firing ; the other xebecs silent and waiting ; the frigate equally silent, just lying there.

And suddenly, for no apparent reason, the flag at the frigate's mast-head, that whipping bright banner, moved slowly downward, downward, to vanish behind the bulwarks. . . .

What was in the minds of the men aboard that ship I don't know, and probably never will know. Since any man can explain his behaviour to his own satisfaction, doubtless the officers of that frigate might be able to explain to someone's satisfaction the things they did that day. As for myself, I might have accepted ingenious explanations of their behaviour up to the time they hauled down the flag ; but not all the ingenuity in the world could invent a plausible justification of *that* !

The xebec had come no closer ; the supporting xebecs had neither moved nor fired a gun. Yet the flag had come down from the frigate's masthead. She'd surrendered without being boarded, without being cut to pieces. All her three hundred men, with all their muskets and cutlasses, their tons of powder and shot—all those Americans with stout bulwarks behind which to take shelter, with all those pikes and pistols and boarding nettings to hold off boarders—had given up without a fight !

Not even the xebecs, seemingly, could believe what they saw ; for they lay as they were, approaching no closer. They lay there and they lay there ; and in the end a boat put out from the stern of the frigate and rowed to the xebec—a boat that could have been sent for no other purpose than to tell the xebec's commander that the Americans, unbelievable though it was, had surrendered.

The tumult from the thousands of Arabs all around me and from the city itself was deafening. Men yowled and squalled, embracing each other, waving bunched fingers in neighbours' faces ; cannon roared from the Castle and the shore forts. The bad bright dream went on and on ; the xebec swept slowly up astern of the motionless frigate ; and in an hour's time, to a never-lessening accompaniment of triumphant screaming, caterwauling, and cannon-firing, the xebec moved in close to the Castle, and boatload after boatload of Americans, stripped to shirts and trousers, were being disembarked on the selfsame Castle steps up which Lydia and I had mounted fifteen months and twenty-seven days before.

CHAPTER XLVI

THE FRIGATE, as the whole city knew on the following day, was the *Philadelphia*, Captain Bainbridge. All the next day the celebration over the capture of the frigate continued, and the big half-dismasted vessel out beyond the harbour mouth was surrounded by a swarm of xebecs and lesser craft, even rafts and rowboats. Yesterday's wind had gone down during the night and late in the morning sprang up again as an on-shore wind.

I was already sick at heart over the capture, because I knew the Bashaw would now consider himself ordained by God to inflict further indignities on upstart America, that miserable country which had dared to invade his Mediterranean. With the rising of the breeze my sinking heart turned to lead ; for the frigate, instead of lying motionless, as she had lain since the preceding noon, began to move, to turn slowly, crippled though she was.

She was afloat ; she was free of the reef ! Surrounded by a flotilla of xebecs, dhows, polacres, rowboats, dugouts, and rafts, she moved into the outer harbour, into the inner harbour, a dishevelled floating island of a ship, and came to anchor so close to the Castle that we on shore could see the splinters where her stern windows had been hacked away on the previous afternoon to let her long-range guns run out.

God knows what the feelings of her officers and men must have been when they saw this beautiful ship floating free and clear under their very noses, manned—solely because of their own unspeakable folly—by enemies who had taken her without a fight. But at least I knew what my own feelings were. The surrender of that ship and the enslavement of her officers and crew meant that Tripoli and her pig-headed rulers who up to now had held America to be a nation of cowards, to be imposed upon at will, would henceforth hold her in complete contempt.

And certainly there was no mistaking how the people of Tripoli felt about it. There couldn't have been more joyful shouting, more boastful bellowings, more firing of cannon and muskets, if all America had surrendered to Tripoli—and indeed this is what most of them thought had happened.

The three hundred men from the crew of the *Philadelphia* had been put instantly to work in gangs, some of them dragging enormous blocks of stone to be used in harbour defences, some cleaning the streets ; so that wherever anyone turned, he saw a throng of half-naked American sailors toiling at all sorts of menial tasks beneath the eyes of moustachioed Turks who slashed at them with whips for any reason at all, sometimes for none.

Three hundred men are a lot of men ; and there were so many of these American work parties that I sometimes felt that a good part of America had been captured by Tripoli, just as it had often seemed to me in Philadelphia that all the Frenchmen in France and in Haiti had fled to America for refuge.

As soon as my morning work was done, on the day after the *Philadelphia* had been captured, I loaded ripe melons, tomatoes, peaches, lettuce, onions on my little cart, presented myself at the back door for inspection, and then set off for the bazaar.

The fruit and vegetable market occupied both sides of the street that led out of the Castle gate, and above the gate the wall of the Castle was stepped back so that it made a sort of parapet, with gun-ports. Some of the stones of the parapet were missing, others were all askew ; and on the parapet and on ladders at the front and at the foot of the wall were scores of newly captured sailors from the *Philadelphia*, hoisting rocks up to the parapet, pushing and tugging at the disarranged stones, while armed guards shrieked and lashed at them with long leather thongs attached to short-handled whips. Many of the Americans had bloody spots and lines on their shirts, where the whips had curled around them and bitten into their flesh.

While I watched, fuming at these slave-drivers, I saw the Bashaw himself come out on the parapet, accompanied by several Ministers in turbans and finery, as well as by his huge Negro brother-in-law, Ali Ben Zool, Murad Rais, and Captain Lee.

The Bashaw contemplated the toiling Americans with obvious satisfaction ; then, through Murad Rais, ordered that they stop their work, remove their caps, stand at attention, and answer the questions put to them—questions which the Bashaw gave Murad Rais, receiving the answers from Murad Rais in turn.

" What," Murad Rais shouted at them, " is your opinion of your captain ? Is he a traitor or merely a coward ? "

When the Americans were stonily silent, Murad Rais's tone became more reasonable. " Now, look here," he said, " His Highness wants to ask you a few simple questions, and he wants truthful answers. If he doesn't get 'em, you'll all suffer for it. Come now, what was it that made your captain surrender ? Was he a coward, or was he a traitor ? "

A solitary voice replied, " Neither."

" Oh, indeed ? " Murad Rais said. " But what captain of a forty-four-gun frigate with three hundred able-bodied seamen would strike his colours to a solitary gunboat without being either the one or the other ? "

" We were hung up on the reef," one of the Americans said, " and we'd thrown our guns overboard to try and get clear."

" You didn't throw them all overboard," Murad Rais said. " You kept some, because you fired them, but you couldn't figure out how to bring them to bear. If you don't want to call your captain either a coward or a traitor, maybe you'd prefer to call him a plain damned fool ? Come on now, speak up ! His Majesty wants to know why you struck your colours."

A lad who talked like a Down-Easter spoke up. " Sir," he said, " it's true there was only one gunboat, but there were others on the move, and the captain figured that when night came we'd be surrounded and cut to pieces. The captain thought we'd be given no quarter."

" He did, did he ? " Murad Rais asked. " What made him think so ? Damned if all sailors aren't alike, no matter what navy they belong to—believe any damned thing they hear, or any damned twaddle that anybody tells 'em ! Now look, I'll tell ye something in return for the questions you're going to answer for me. If your frigate hadn't struck, we'd never have boarded her. 'Twould have been too costly, we figured. We figured that all we had to do was chop up your top hamper ; then, when the wind changed in the morning and blew you off, you'd be sure to blow ashore, where you'd be helpless. That's the truth."

The men shifted their feet and glanced furtively at each other.

Murad Rais tried another tack. " You had no pilot aboard, eh ? " The men shook their heads.

" Yet your captain, though unacquainted with the harbour, ran close in-shore, where he'd no business to be."

" The lieutenant was at the wheel, sir," one of the men said. " Lieutenant Porter. He knew the harbour."

" Oh, aye," Murad Rais said. " He knew the harbour ! Have you not considered that the captain and the lieutenant might have been in cahoots ? You've discussed it among yourselves, haven't you ? You know, don't you, that a captain just doesn't give up his ship as easily as that, not unless he's wishful of turning traitor. If it wasn't that, he certainly lacked good judgment, which is a mighty queer thing for the captain of a frigate to lack ; and he was certainly afraid—afraid you'd be killed without any quarter being given : you said so yourselves. And for a frigate captain to be afraid—that's odd, too, isn't it ? Come now, don't tell me you've not discussed these things ! "

I had never seen men's backs so expressive of stubbornness as were those men's—they were determined not to answer Murad Rais's questions ; and I could tell, too, from the manner in which they avoided each other's eyes—just stared up with expressionless faces at Murad Rais—that they *had* discussed those very things.

Murad Rais shrugged his shoulders. " Did any of you hear mention, perhaps, of the number of American ships in the Mediterranean ? "

They answered that one quickly enough. A mealy southern voice said, "Thirty-eight frigates already in the Mediterranean and more expected next week."

"Oh, but that ain't so!" a shocked voice contradicted. "You must 'a' heard wrong. Them thirty-eight was bomb ketches. It was forty-two *frigates*."

"Ain't a fleet of gunboats expected to sail from Philadelphia this month?" another voice demanded.

"*Expected* to sail?" a bearded sailor protested. "They sailed two weeks ago! The Secretary of the Navy sent a letter to Gibraltar telling about it. Twenty-six gunboats, each carrying a forty-two-pounder."

"That's right," a man cried. "Jeddy's right! That's just exactly what it was : twenty-six gunboats all armed with forty-two-pounders."

Murad Rais snorted. "That'd be quite a sight, that! All those frigates and all those gunboats and all those bomb ketches, all running ashore because of being fearful of somebody that isn't there, and being navigated by captains that don't know their way around, and piling up on shore whenever there's enough breeze to get 'em there, and in the meantime lying out in the middle of nowhere so that nobody ever gets a sight of 'em! Very interesting, gentlemen : very interesting Navy, this powerful Navy of yours! This war's been going on a year and a half now, and just once we've caught sight of one of your ships. Right away she hauled down her flag ; so from now on she's our ship. Well, if you won't answer, you won't answer, but you can't expect any extra special treatment out of us—not unless you give us a little co-operation."

I was proud of these Americans for their refusal to talk about their officers, or to give even a faint hint about their real naval strength—though probably, like most sailors, they knew little about either. And for some reason I couldn't quite formulate, Murad Rais's insistence upon the treachery, cowardice, and lack of judgment of the *Philadelphia*'s officers was infuriating ; yet I had to admit to myself that the questions that had arisen in the minds of Murad Rais and the Bashaw were justified, and that no Navy at all would better serve America's interests than a Navy under officers like Morris and Bainbridge.

That very night Murad Rais and George Lee, both in gorgeous turbans, silks, satins, gold chains, baggy trousers, and orange slippers walked in the garden, puffing on cigars whose odour, as it blew downwind to me, made my mouth water.

When the two of them saw me working at the water-wheel, they paused to stare at me meditatively, their hands clasped behind their backs—and I'd seen enough of sea captains to know this meant trouble for somebody.

Then Murad Rais cleared his throat and addressed me. "Captain Lee called my attention to you this morning," he said, "when we were speaking to the Americans. Captain Lee seemed to think you were unduly interested in 'em."

" I won't deny I was interested in them," I said. " After all, they're my fellow countrymen."

" Ah, yes," Murad Rais said, " but they're ordinary seamen. You'd never be thrown with people of that type in America, would you ? "

I couldn't fathom what he was getting at. " I didn't give a thought to what sort of people they were," I said. " They were Americans, and they weren't being treated very well, and I was naturally interested."

" Ah, yes," Murad Rais said softly, " that's what Captain Lee was telling me. Now you take the officers of the *Philadelphia*. They don't have anything to do with the men in the crew. They're looking out for themselves. They have special food and special living quarters ; but they don't make nuisances of themselves, taking a lot of unnecessary interest in people who are unaccustomed to having interest taken in them. Now Lee tells me you've always been like that : you've always made a kind of nuisance of yourself about queer people—niggers, for example, and sailors, and suchlike."

" I see no reason why Captain Lee should exaggerate," I said. " I had a good friend who was a Negro, just as I had a good many friends who were white ; but I know a lot of white men I don't like, and a lot of Negroes too." I didn't dare to look at Lee. " Meaning no offence," I went on, " Captain Lee should be the last man to say any such thing about me. He's never made any secret about sleeping with black women ; and certainly nobody could be much blacker than the Bashaw's brother-in-law, Ali Ben Zool."

Lee thrust out an angry chin. " You dirty rat, Hamlin ! "

" Now just a moment," Murad Rais said to Lee. " Just a moment, Captain. Hamlin's a sensible man. He's done well here—behaved himself and raised good vegetables and improved the whole place, and I'm not going to have him badgered."

To me he said," You don't quite get the point, Hamlin. Captain Lee was watching you with considerable care this morning. In his opinion you showed in a number of small ways that you sympathised with the stubborn attitude of those Americans in refusing to answer simple questions—questions that you must have recognised as being justified. Everybody in Tripoli was watching the *Philadelphia* when she struck, and watching her for the next four hours, too. You've got eyes, and you must have known that all the questions I was asking were based on sound common sense."

" That may be so," I said, " but I wouldn't care to testify before anybody about what I thought might be in a man's mind. Those men were being asked to testify to something about which they knew nothing ; they had no way of knowing why you asked the questions ; they weren't represented by counsel. Under the circumstances it seems to me they did about what they ought to have done."

" Yes, that's what we thought," Murad Rais said. " Captain Lee was sure of his ground when he said you hoped they wouldn't tell us the truth and were glad when they didn't. Now any such attitude as that, with three hundred Americans scattered all over the place, is dangerous, in my opinion. Captain Lee thinks that if you're allowed to run loose in the streets, as heretofore, you'll find it almost impossible not to speak to these Americans, sooner or later ; and if you do, the cat will be out of the bag."

"But I signed an agreement," I said. "I'm bound by my word."

"I know, I know," Murad Rais said. "But Captain Lee is in such a delicate position that I'm inclined to agree with him. Hereafter you'll have to restrict your activities to these premises. From now on, Abu Zirt will come here each morning and pick up his vegetables and fruit, giving you a receipt. In no circumstances—none whatever—are you to leave these grounds. If you do so, you'll be shot. I've already given these orders to the sentries. And I need hardly say that any disposition we're forced to make of your wife, in case you *are* shot, will be of no interest whatever to you."

"Sir, I'd like to say a few words in my own behalf."

"I cannot listen," Murad Rais said. "I passed my word to Captain Lee, and so far as I'm concerned that's the end of it."

He took Lee by the elbow, and those two grotesque figures out of a street carnival went strolling off along the garden path, trailing fragrant wisps of smoke from their big cigars—men who didn't behave like men, or even look real, but who, alas, were real enough to condemn me to a limbo from which I could see no escape.

CHAPTER XLVII

I THINK the least of my distresses, which were many in those days, was my own discomfort ; and the greatest, I think, was worry over Lydia. She had, I knew, set her heart on the destruction of this robber kingdom through some sort of American attack ; and now here was our Navy apparently completely useless, and so many hostages in the Bashaw's hands that Eaton might never persuade the government to let him carry out his plans.

The next letter from her said nothing about her disappointment, but I noticed that she didn't mention Cette, either. She told me disturbing things she had learned about the *Philadelphia's* officers and crew—and I knew how unhappy such things would make her.

The treatment of the men from the *Philadelphia* (she wrote) is inhuman. They sleep in a dark powder magazine on a damp earth floor covered with sharp pebbles. All their clothes, except the shirts and trousers they stand in, have been stolen. For food they have small black barley loaves full of straws and chaff. They are made to do the

hardest sort of work, and those who hesitate because of unwillingness
or a failure to understand are brutally beaten. On the streets they are
frequently spat upon and stoned. The worst part of all this is that the
officers pay no attention to the men or their needs. The captain,
Bainbridge, pretends to be a compassionate man, and to have his
crew's interests at heart ; but I know that he has written a letter to
the Secretary of the Navy, asking that he and the other officers be
assisted by American funds, but saying that the crew needs no assistance,
since the Tripolitan Government will take care of them—which it
certainly will not do : not decently. The first lieutenant, David Porter,
is hard and hateful. It was he who ran the *Philadelphia* on the reef.
He despises every American who is so unfortunate as not to be an
officer, and ignores the men when they try to speak to him.

I have learned that Commodore Morris has been replaced by
Commodore Preble in the *Constitution*. I think he must be the Preble I
have heard you mention as coming from Portland. I hope—oh, how I
hope—that he's different from that awful Morris, this blundering
Bainbridge, this wretched Porter !

Preble in the Mediterranean ! That news was enough to offset all the
disheartening information in Lydia's letter. Preble wouldn't spend
fifteen months lying idly in port, allowing self-opinionated subordinates
to fight duels with everyone who didn't agree with their stupidities, as
Dale and Morris had done. I saw no way in which Preble could help
me ; but in the loneliness of that hated garden I prayed for some miracle
that would put an end to the Bashaw of Tripoli, his jackals Murad Rais
and George Lee, and our own slavery.

The miracle began with the appearance of Eugene Leitensdorfer
during the Bairam festival ending the month-long fast of Ramadan, which
in that year fell in January.

Murad Rais, who made much of this festival, entertained his personal
friends, as well as naval officers and government officials, at his country
place ; and all day long he and his guests applied themselves assiduously
to the bottle. Among the persons whom I saw roaming in and out of the
house and through the gardens was a swarthy, lively young man of about
my own height and build, and with sharp, wary, bold black eyes. His
complexion was a clear brown, and his beard a tight, spade-like affair
that gave him a dashing appearance, enhanced by his elegant Turkish
dress. He walked with a peculiar balanced springiness, and had the look
of being able—if he wished to exert himself—to leap over a ten-foot wall.
I took particular notice of him because whenever I saw him he was peering
and nosing into odd corners, examining the gardens, scrutinising everything—even me—as though hunting something he had lost, or suspected
of being there.

My report that the guests were given to drinking may sound curious.

in view of the widespread belief that Arabs are prohibited by their religion from using alcohol in any form. So they are—true ; but anybody who thinks that they consequently don't use it is bound to have some surprises —if he sees much of Arabs. All the Arabs who came to Murad Rais's house during Bairam, or at any other time, came as much for the rum he'd captured as for anything else ; and many a night I was wakened by the howlings, the shrill laughter and the blunderings-about of guests who had made too free with the bottle. Perhaps they were infected by the universal excitement over the capture of the *Philadelphia* and her crew. Whatever the reason, there was a vast deal of drinking at Murad Rais's house throughout the first day and night of Bairam, accompanied by salvos of cannon-fire from the Castle and the ships in the harbour, and by continuous shouts, musket-fire, and thudding of horses' hoofs from outside the walls.

Having seen similar parties in Washington while I was working on Spoliation Claims, I was not surprised when guests occasionally staggered from the house to stumble into bushes and fall down under the palms. Some of these I helped to pick up and put where servants could sort them out and take them home. I was, however, a little surprised one afternoon to see the dashing, spade-bearded young man come reeling from the house with his arm around Murad Rais's neck, and to hear Murad Rais call him " Murad Aga," and talk to him in English—or, rather, in Scots too broad to reproduce.

" I canna let you go back to the Castle in this condition," Murad Rais said. " You're full as a tick ; and God knows what you'll be trying to do if you go wamblin' up and doon the halls with all this rum in your nose. Why dinna you let me tuck you safely behind a sofa ? "

"'S my love for the open spaces, Murad old boy, God bless you," Murad Aga said. " I'll sit down here just a minute, just to clear my mind. Funny thing, Murad : when I have about this much, 'm only slightly affected, but see three things for every one I look at, 'n' have three thoughts about everything, too ! Now jus' lemme sit down beside those three bushes there, and soon's they turn into one bush I'll know I can rise and depart."

After a few mild protests from Murad Rais, and a few more drunken rejoinders on the part of Murad Aga, Murad Rais's attention was diverted by other noisy guests. The next time I looked, the swarthy young man was sitting, as he had threatened, beside the single bush that his eyes had seen as three. Then I forgot him and went away to tinker with a new water-wheel I'd built, damning all these idle, noisy, useless, overdressed, overperfumed barbarians.

When I'd tightened the lashings on the wheel, tested each bucket, and rubbed a little additional grease on the cogs, I turned towards the tool-shed —and there, beside the path, not ten feet from me, was Murad Aga. He sat cross-legged, in the Arab manner ; and from the contemplative look upon his face, I thought he must be feeling sorry for himself. When I made to step around him, he looked up at me so sharply that there was an almost physical impact in his glance.

" You're Hamlin, isn't it ? " he asked—and there was no more alcohol on his tongue or in his speech than there was in my own.

At his words my heart began to pound. If he knew my name and had come here hunting for me, it could only mean one thing. I nodded. That was all I could do : nod.

" I am Eugene Leitensdorfer," he said. " King Dick told you about me. He is my friend."

I glanced nervously over my shoulder, then went quickly around towards the front of the house to see whether we were overlooked ; but there wasn't a soul in sight.

" You do for me just one thing," Leitensdorfer went on, when I returned. " Walk to the place where you sleep and put your hand on the door ; then come back here to me."

I did as he asked.

" Now listen," Leitensdorfer said. " Have no fears about me. I go where I please and do as I please. I am an Arab, a Bedouin, a dervish, and many, many other things, so that I am safe wherever I am. At the moment I am known to be intoxicated ; helpless ; unable to speak or think clearly. Therefore I cannot be moved, even if I am found. Nobody can make me move, isn't it ? Until nightfall I shall rest under a bush, probably undiscovered. When it's dark, I'll come to your quarters and we will make plans."

He reached into his sash and took out a little book, got to his feet, staggered drunkenly, and staggering leaned against me and put the book in my hands. " A gift sent by King Dick from Grand Cairo," he said. " It'll help you pass the time till dark."

The book was treasure-trove indeed : Richardson's *Grammar in Arabic and English*, published in London in 1776. In King Dick's handwriting on the title-page were the words : " Be cheery. If we know everything, we find the way."

When I looked up, Leitensdorfer was staggering off. He reeled perilously along an irrigation ditch and suddenly sank from sight, as through a trap-door, behind the prickly foliage of a bed of artichokes.

To guard against intruders I stuffed my corn-husk pillow into the small window opening of my little kennel of a cabin ; and when Leitensdorfer crept silently out of the dusk of the garden and into the room, I closed the door behind him, jammed a wedge beneath it, and lighted a candle.

In the candle rays Leitensdorfer's black eyes gleamed like the jet buttons on my aunt's cape. " So," he began cheerfully, " this affair starts well ! In almost the first place I try, I find you and the lady. I think all the rest of it will go equally well." To frustrate the forces of evil, he knocked on the wood of my bed-place and made the sign of

the horns by extending the index and little fingers of one hand. " King
Dick——"

"Wait!" I said. "Before you go any further, do you know anything
about my wife ? "

"But of course, my dear Hamlin ! King Dick had predicted it might
be so, and naturally I hunted first for her, isn't it ? "

"How did she look ? Well ? "

"Ah, well indeed ! She is truly simpatico—oh, much ! What a *crise
des nerfs* to be separated from her, and yet be so near ! I was separated
from my last wife for six years, but she was a Copt and there is no risk
of a *crise* where a Copt is concerned. With you it must be different,
isn't it ? "

I had no time to waste on such a question. " Did she seem happy ? "

Leitensdorfer shrugged his shoulders and spread his hands. " How
can any man say whether a woman is happy, isn't it ? She looked
capable, oh most so ; and those three children, they adore her. When
I told her in a whisper that I had come from King Dick and asked
her where I could find you, she gave me such a look ! "

He sighed heavily ; then he caught my eye and went on hurriedly :
" She was alarmed, too, as I suspected there had been some mish-mash
on the part of that Joseph Karamanli—a pig out of hell if there ever
was one. When she whispered the name of Murad Rais, with whom
I once journeyed to Persia as a physician, I was happy indeed. Murad
Rais can refuse me nothing, because I owe him fifty dollars."

I must have shown my impatience, for he leaned forward and put
his hand upon my arm. " Do not be troubled because I do not tell you
everything in one breath, dear Hamlin. You have had a bad time : you
are bitter and ill at ease, frantic to be gone from this hell-hole ; and
for exactly these reasons I speak to you slowly, so that you will remain
calm and remember all I say. If I told it all in one gulp, as I can see
you wish, you might forget something important."

"You're right about the bitterness," I said. " I'd give anything to see
these people punished for what they've done. The reason Lydia was
careful was that she was afraid she'd do me a hurt. Your friend Murad
Rais made the two of us sign an agreement not to ask anyone for help.
It says that if either of us asks for help or tries to communicate with
anyone, the other'll be sold to a caravan."

"Ah, yes," Leitensdorfer said. " That Joseph Karamanli is a type.
That is the sort of thing he is for ever doing. Bashaw of Three Tails,
indeed ! Perhaps he is ! No doubt three privies are required to accommodate the outpourings of his three tails ! No, that thought is not
pleasing. I tell you the man is *all* tail ! Well, you have not asked me
for anything, so you have lived up to the letter of your agreement. The
lady did not ask anything of me, either, so she is equally blameless. She
wrote no letter to me ; you wrote none. If Murad Rais himself walked
into this room, he could have nothing against you ; nothing ! All you

have done is to pick me up, very drunk, isn't it, from underneath an artichoke, and give me shelter so that I would come to no harm in the damp night winds."

He hiccupped realistically and gave me a solemn wink. "Now I tell you everything from the beginning," he went on. "I have known your friend King Dick since these many years, when I travelled on the Nile, selling jewellery to kings and princes. He bought much from me, and paid well, and I felt an immediate affection for him, my dear Hamlin, even then. Now it is much stronger, when I see how he is a friend of yours ! There is nothing—nothing—at which he will stop in order to help you. He was sure that it was these Tripolines who had taken you and your wife, and he sits in black silences, yearning to meet them face to face and slowly separate them from their legs and arms with his bare hands.

"He waited and waited for you at Gibraltar. When you didn't return, he made a flank movement and went to Alexandria in the hope of finding me there. You see, my dear Hamlin, I have the entree ! Not only am I fearless, but I have the gift of knowing what to do at any given moment. I can shout as loudly from a minaret as a muezzin, using the same words, and in such a voice that I can be heard from Alexandria to Rosetta, almost. I have been in the Austrian army, the French army and the Italian army. I have been a theatrical manager, an actor, a restaurant owner, a Capuchin monk, and Chief Physician to the Pasha of Trebizond, whom I was fortunate enough to cure of an eye affliction by the judicious use of caustic lime. I am a better doctor than most, because I know a remedy that banishes the pain of gout. They make it from the seeds of autumn crocuses. I am also a Hadji, because I have travelled to Mecca three times, twice as a dervish and once as a Marabout—the most difficult journey that any white man can make. I have lived in the black tents of the Bedouins until no man can tell me from a Bedouin unless I wish him to ; and I'm able to speak Arabic, Persian, Turkish, German, French, Italian, and English—but I am disappointed in my English, even though it gets me where I desire to go."

While Leitensdorfer was speaking thus highly of himself, there seemed nothing boastful about his words : merely a detached and somehow engaging amazement at his own varied accomplishments.

"By the greatest good fortune," he resumed, "I returned to Alexandria two years ago, having spent six years abroad, the last of them as interpreter and companion to Lord Gordon on his travels to Nubia and Abyssinia ; so when your friend came to Alexandria, hoping to find me, there I was, Chief Engineer for the Viceroy of Egypt. This friend of yours, he has made a discovery ! He had it from a sea captain in Gibraltar, employed by the American Consul in Algiers. This American Consul, William Eaton, is a soldier who has become interested in the brother of Joseph Karamanli."

"I know about Eaton, and about the brother too," I said. "My wife told me."

"Hah, you know!" Leitensdorfer exclaimed, though he still kept his voice low. "Good! This brother Hamet I know well. He is on the Nile at this very moment, waiting for the American, Eaton. He is the exact opposite of the Bashaw; a good man, generous, far-seeing, peacefully inclined and wishful of furthering the welfare of everybody. What is more, he would be governing Tripoli to-day, and governing it well, if this hell's pig hadn't tricked him and driven him out. See how things happen, my dear Hamlin, isn't it? If the right brother instead of the wrong brother had been Bashaw of Tripoli, there would never have been any question of a war with the United States. American ships would be safe to come and go anywhere in the Mediterranean without interference from such pirates as Murad Rais. You and your wife would never have been molested; and if the two of you had landed in Tripoli, you would have been honoured guests instead of what you are—slaves to a lot of footpads."

There was something about his manner of speaking that made me boil with rage at Murad Rais and Joseph Karamanli, which I think was his intention.

"Now the word that King Dick brought from Gibraltar," Leitensdorfer went on, "was that this gentleman, William Eaton, has a plan to ally himself with Hamet, the rightful ruler, raise an army, using Alexandria or some such place as a base, and topple him from his throne."

"I know about it," I said. "I don't believe it'll work."

"But why?" Leitensdorfer asked.

"Because something'll happen," I said. "Eaton wouldn't be granted enough money. Those fools in Washington wouldn't *let* him succeed. Somebody'll be jealous of him and cut his throat."

"No, no!" Leitensdorfer said. "You do not understand the meaning of this great scheme! It means that there'd be an end to all this nonsense of great governments paying perpetual tribute to Tripoli and Tunis and Algiers, so that their vessels won't be captured. It means that a good and kind man will rule the richest province of North Africa. It means that with the proper sort of advice, a good ruler of Tripoli could unite all of North Africa—Morocco, Algiers, Tunisia, and Tripoli. How could your government fail to support him? Here would be the United States of North Africa, ruled by a man who would owe everything to an American! Any treaty that the United States of America wished to make with the United States of North Africa would be entered into without question. Do you see the possibilities in all this?"

"Of course I do," I said.

"Very good," Leitensdorfer whispered. "That, then, was the reason for my coming here to Tripoli. If such an expedition is being planned,

I must be able, as Chief Engineer of Egypt, to say whether or not it will be successful, isn't it ? If there were a prospect of its failing, Egypt could not, of course, afford to be in any way connected with it. But if it *can* succeed, if these governments of North Africa are to be changed by an American to rich and beneficent states, then it is important that Egypt should be in the good graces of her powerful neighbours. Therefore I secretly accepted King Dick's commission to find you. Publicly, I am here as the Chief Engineer of Egypt—a friendly tour of inspection, you understand—and I have decided that this plan of Eaton's and Hamet's will truly be successful ! "

" I can't believe it'll ever really come off," I said dubiously.

" But it must ! " Leitensdorfer cried. " These robber countries cannot go on for ever, making cowards out of all the great nations in the world, making slaves of their people ! Your country has been insulted, your citizens are held as slaves. This Three-tail Joseph Karamanli is taxing everyone to the limit, then seizing the money for his own personal use. Like all fools, he believes in trying to keep his people ignorant, because he thinks they will be easier to control. He has a contempt for agriculture, not realising that a country's wealth must come from the land : not from robbing his own people. Hamet is different : Hamet is a student. Hamet knows that the Arab people once produced great craftsmen, great mathematicians, great educators, great inventors, great architects, great military leaders, great and united armies. Men came from all over the world to attend the Arab universities in Cordova and Alexandria, and Hamet wishes to build such a university in Tripoli ! I tell you that the Arabs would unite behind a man like that, and fight for him as they did when they fought their way into Spain and up into France. This is the time to destroy the Joseph Karamanlis ! Your Eaton would be fighting for a good idea and in a good cause ; and what's more, he'd be fighting for the United States, too. He'd be fighting to release three hundred fellow Americans, and to make sure that such a thing can never happen again ! Do you mean to say your government couldn't understand such a state of affairs ? "

I sat there on that hard wooden bed, staring at the dirt floor, my brain a jumble of discouragement and longing. " If Eaton is just now leaving for the United States," I said, " it may be years before he comes back to raise an army and lead his expedition. Years ! "

" Look," Leitensdorfer said, " your good friend King Dick has no intention of leaving you here for years."

" There's no way out of it," I said. " We signed a paper, Lydia and I. If either of us tries to escape, or *does* escape, the other takes the blame and is sold into slavery. You tell King Dick not to make a move ! He can't help me without hurting Lydia ! "

" Now, now, my dear Hamlin," Leitensdorfer said, " give us credit for greater understanding ! You need have no worry about your lady ! Before I depart from Tripoli, I will find a way to explain everything to her—how, for example, she must never be alarmed if it is discovered some morning that you are dead."

"Dead!" I said. "If you mean what I think you mean, I'll never be allowed to be dead! Lee wouldn't allow it! One of the first things he does, whenever he comes ashore, is to make sure I'm still here. One of his greatest pleasures in life is to gloat over me—to see me condemned to everlasting slavery. If you think he'll ever believe I'm dead when I'm not, you're making a great mistake!"

"Hah!" Leitensdorfer said. "Lee! I heard about Lee from King Dick! He said he was sure that Lee was somehow connected with your disappearance."

"*Connected* with it!" I cried. "He was wholly responsible for it!" I told him how Lee had been aboard Murad Rais's xebec when we were captured, and how he had insisted that we be made to sign the agreement not to seek help.

Leitensdorfer listened intently; then studied the ceiling with lack-lustre eyes. After a while his eyes brightened. "I see it!" he whispered. "Is it for nothing that I am Chief Engineer? I tell you I have blown up a camel belonging to an enemy of the Pasha of Trebizond so skil-fully that nothing was left, not even a piece of split lip! Disturb yourself no longer about Lee! Think only of Eaton and Hamet, isn't it?"

He winked at me reassuringly, and God knows I wanted to be reassured. But I didn't know: I didn't know! I had to admit that everything he said about Eaton and Hamet was reasonable and right; but I remembered how many cowards held high offices in Washington, withholding help from those who most needed it, wasting untold wealth on useless ventures, and sending nincompoops to ruin the work of abler men. Therefore—I didn't *know*...

CHAPTER XLVIII

I THOUGHT I'd seen the last of Leitensdorfer: like all the rest of the turbaned, balloon-trousered Turks, Moors, and Arabs, he didn't seem real. Yet before the week was over I did see him again, in the company of Murad Rais and several of the officers from the *Philadelphia*. All of them had to listen to Murad Rais's boasting about his garden, and to be told how much larger his vegetables were than the Bashaw's own; and to hear this renegade Scot brag about *his* vegetables and *his* melons and *his* fruits, when I'd done all the work, was a trial indeed. I noticed, too, that when Murad Rais had me pack baskets of fruits and vegetables for these officers to take back to the ship, neither the officers nor Murad Rais so much as thanked me.

While I was packing the basket for Leitensdorfer, he came blundering in beside me with a melon, howling something at me in Arabic—so embarrassing the American officers and Murad Rais that they frowned at this strange creature who was being familiar with a servant. Apparently Leitensdorfer had known what would happen, for, while they were pointedly ignoring him, he drew a little package from his sash and dropped it where I could pick it up and conceal it beneath my barracan.

That package immeasurably lightened the weary hours of my hitherto endless nights ; for, in addition to a letter from Lydia and a roll of gold coins that Leitensdorfer had brought from King Dick, it contained a copy in Arabic of a dozen poetic essays—Assemblies, they're called—by Hariri, completely interlined by Lydia in English. These essays I was able to master in the solitude of my hut, thus gaining an understanding of Arabic and the Arabic manner of expression that I never otherwise would have had.

The letter itself, because of its implications and its outspoken promise that I might somehow have a hand in an attack on Tripoli, set a bright flame of hope to burning in my breast.

I have thought about the plan that Mr. Leitensdorfer brought, and think it is right in every detail. I know what you will say : that since we have not lived up to the agreement, I shall be sold into slavery ; but this is not so.

In the first place, both of us have lived up to our agreement in every detail. I have not asked anybody for anything, haven't spoken to anybody but you about the possibility of escape, and I shall never do so. Nor have you asked anybody for anything. Through no effort of yours, your whereabouts have been discovered by King Dick, as Lee has always feared ; and if King Dick makes it possible for you to get away, nobody will ever know, because you will still seem to be here, a mangled dead body. King Dick told Mr. Leitensdorfer, and Mr. Leitensdorfer has told me, that this will come about through Commodore Preble. How, I don't yet know ; all I know is that it is to come about through Commodore Preble.

When it *does* come about, you must go. What I want most of all, next to being with you again, is to see the inhuman people who rule this country on their knees suing for peace. Nothing can possibly happen to me, for nowhere is a woman safer than in this and every other Moslem country, where a veil is sacred. You can be of great help to those who march on Tripoli, because you can tell them what it's like ; you can tell them where to attack ; and, most important of all, only you will know, *when you receive messages from me*, that they are reliable.

Do not say that you refuse to go until I can go too. I myself have nothing to fear ; but knowing Lee and the miserable, bullying, heartless people who rule this country, I can never have a minute's peace while you are within their reach, and alone and helpless.

How anything that could benefit us was to come about through Commodore Preble I didn't understand. Nor did I dream that Preble would make himself felt so quickly in Tripoli. Yet exactly one week after Lydia had written those optimistic words he did more than had all the other American commodores and naval officers during all the preceding months of war.

It was just after midnight—this was in February—and I was toiling at my wonderful Arab grammar and dictionary, going over and over the first lines of Hariri, when I became aware of a far-off movement in the air, a sort of whispering.

I blew out my candle and went into the dark garden, heavy with the fragrance of almond blossoms. The whispering grew ; became a faint tumultuous cacophony ; grew louder. I could distinguish shouting ; then scattering gunshots, and shrill howls and screams. Against the thick black of the harbour a sudden glare of light lit up the yards and shrouds of the captive *Philadelphia*, lying at her anchorage off the Castle.

As I ran to the lower wall for a better view, the whole huge bulk of the vessel seemed to burst into flame. Fire licked upward from her main, fore, and mizzen hatches. Flames spouted from every gun-port along her side : flames that gave out explosions.

There was an offshore breeze, and clouds of pink and red smoke poured upward from the hatches and across the harbour. Against the background of those clouds I could see a ketch lying against the *Philadelphia's* side. Farther out in the harbour a gun brig, bright as a cameo in the light of the glowing smoke and the flames, stood slowly back and forth, and the flag at her peak was striped red and white.

Intrepid insects of figures moved along the bulwarks of the *Philadelphia*, and crawled ant-like down cables into the ketch ; while the *Philadelphia* herself, belching whirling sparks and clouds of smoke, drifted slowly towards the fort on the far side of the harbour.

The ketch, free of the blazing vessel, slipped slowly towards the brig, and from the two of them came the thundering of heavy guns and cottony bursts, pink in the light of the burning frigate.

I stayed at the garden wall, shivering as much from excitement as from the cold February wind. If Preble had ordered two vessels straight into Tripoli harbour to burn and sink the frigate so disgracefully abandoned, it must be that he, like Eaton, understood that such a robber state as Tripoli, governed by robbers, must never be bribed or argued into keeping the peace, but must be made to do so—by force, if necessary.

I watched there until dawn. The *Philadelphia*, aground on the rocks at the foot of the fort, was a careened and dismasted hulk, her bulwarks splintered, her guns dismounted—a fitting reminder to her captors that the spoils of war are seldom so profitable as they seem at first glance.

All Tripoli—except for the Jews, who hated Joseph Karamanli, and two-thirds of the Arabs, who had loved his brother Hamet—was in a fury at the loss of this floating fortress ; and (though I never learned any of their names) Jews of all ages appeared oftener and oftener inside Murad Rais's walls, all of them seemingly interested in nothing except selling jewellery, slippers, barracans, and other odds and ends to Murad Rais's household, but every last one of them adept at hunting me out and secretly giving me letters from Lydia. Sometimes these were rolled inside a length of bamboo, sometimes written on the flyleaf of a book, but always they were written in lime juice, so that nothing was to be seen on the paper until it was held over a candle-flame or a bed of coals, on which the writing popped into view, dark brown and as permanent as the most expensive of inks. These same Jews collected my own letters to Lydia, and never a one went astray.

How she found out the things she wrote me I could only guess. No doubt the Bashaw's agents in Malta, Sicily, and Gibraltar gave the information to Murad Rais's captains, who delivered it to Murad Rais, who in turn passed it on to his master the Bashaw, who probably told his wives—and they in turn doubtless told Lydia.

She was my eyes and my ears ; and although I couldn't go into Tripoli myself, through her I came to know it as well as though I had roamed its streets all my life—not only the Jewish quarters, which took up a third of the city, and the Maltese quarter, but the suks, the baths, the mosques, the Maltese bazaar, the beach at the far end of the city rimmed with coffee-houses, where sponge-boats were hauled up on the sand and white pottery vessels from Jerba were sold.

She taught me the customs of the Arabs, the Turks, the Moors, the Jews—the little things that no Arab would have thought to tell me : that Arabs are able to identify, from the adjustment of a man's barracan or burnoose, the part of Africa from which he comes ; that it is a mistake to consider an Arab woman a slave, since there are as many henpecked husbands among Arabs as anywhere else, and that nowhere do men defer so much to their wives' wishes and opinions ; that hospitality is almost a religion among the Arabs ; that every city in North Africa has a large Jewish population, because when the Jews had been expelled three or four hundred years ago from Italy, Holland, France, Spain, and Portugal, they took refuge in Africa ; that although Jews are universally despised and ill-treated, they can be depended on to help a Christian and hide him if he is in need of hiding, and pass him on from city to city or even across the Sahara ; that Arabs have been taught by Mohammed that they are better than any other people, just as Jews have been taught that they are God's Chosen ; that Arabs are the greatest liars in the world ; that the highest class of Arabs are those known as Sherifs, descendants of the Prophet, who are distinguished by having the title Sidi attached to their names ; that a Sherif may marry a Christian or a Jewess, regardless of whether or not she has been converted, and that their children will be Sherifs, but may not marry a Negress unless she has been converted ; that Sherifs have the delightful privilege of insulting anyone at all by cursing his father and grandfather, and need never fear that their own fathers and grandfathers will be similarly cursed in turn ; that religion, which is popularly supposed to be the salvation of a nation or a people, is the Arabs' greatest curse, since they occupy themselves with it to the exclusion of almost everything else, and are consequently as ignorant as they are bigoted ; that their word for God is always on the Arabs' lips, to such a degree that hundreds of them often sway their bodies to and fro and cry out " Allah ! " for hours on end ; that the phrase *Bism' Allah*—in the name of God—accompanies every Arab's every action, no matter how absurd, trifling, childish or evil : he says *Bism' Allah* when he gets out of bed, when he relieves himself, when he puts on his sandals, when he runs his fingers through his hair to comb it, when he perfumes his body, when he steps from his house into the street, when he kicks his donkey, when he slaps his wife's face, when he steals from a fellow traveller, when he cuts his father's throat, when he curses, when he dips a dirty hand into a bowl of cous-cous, when he spits upon an American captive ; that it is sinful to charge interest on a loan, but not sinful to stipulate that the loan be doubled when repaid ; that the favourite Arab curse for such disasters as losing a slipper, bruising a knuckle, slipping in a pile of camel dung, or burning one's fingers in a hot cous-cous—and particularly when hearing a donkey bray—is " God damn the Devil ; " that hashish or Indian hemp is a weed grown in every garden, which when dried and smoked in a pipe stifles thought, dulls pain, and occasions peculiar dreams and imaginings ; that Ramadan is a month of daytime fasting, during which no Moslem, under penalty of death, can eat, drink, smoke, take snuff, or have intercourse with women during the daytime, though after sunset any sort of gluttony and debauchery is permitted ; that there are exemptions from the law of fasting during Ramadan, so that madmen, invalids, travellers, old people, pregnant and suckling women, and children under thirteen years of age need not observe it ; that pilgrimages to Mecca are for ever being made from Tripoli and every other place in the Arab world, by sea, on foot, on camelback, on horseback, singly and in caravans of thousands, and that those who make the pilgrimage are entitled Hadji and are highly honoured ; that substitutes can be hired to make the pilgrimage to Mecca by proxy, so that anybody who wishes to do so can become a Hadji and acquire honour cheaply—for as little as a hundred dollars, provided he doesn't live too far from Mecca ; that anybody who wishes to pose as a Marabout can do so without fear of detection because of the senseless veneration in which such madmen are held ; that the higher an Arab's rank the more likely he is to marry a Negress ; that one of the best-guarded medical secrets of the Arabs (and I knew from whom she had got *this* piece of information) is their gout-cure, colchicine, which is made from crocus bulbs or seeds and is good for gout alone ; that most Arabs think rheumatism and dyspepsia can be helped by searing the back with red-hot irons—and that this treatment, for some reason, is frequently successful ; that the two best-known Arab remedies for wounds are rancid butter and cow dung, whichever is more accessible ; that the most successful preventives of accidents or hurts are amulets applied by a Marabout to the top of the head : that even the Bashaw protected himself by means of such amulets, and so was contemptuous of American attack—and that strangely enough these amulets are always successful when properly applied, because if a man is killed or wounded in spite of having an amulet on his person, it is only because the amulet has been improperly affixed.

Lydia taught me the five daily prayers that Arabs offer up in public in streets, gardens, or fields, at the top of their lungs and in a nasal howl, and the ablutions that precede them—the great washing, in which the body is washed all over ; the little washing, when only such parts are washed as can be reached without removing the clothes ; the washing-with-sand, which is used in the desert where no water can be had ; and the semblance-of-washing, when, in addition to having no water, the washer finds himself upon unclean ground.

Along with the prayers she taught me the seven positions for praying, and the phrases to be used with each position, and how the first finger of the right hand must move in a circle at certain times, and how the face must be turned first to the left and then to right at the beginning and the end. When I had learned these things by heart, and practised them in the quiet of my candle-lit hut, I was as good an Arab, so far as outward appearances went, as any of those who went swaying past Murad Rais's walls on the backs of supercilious camels.

She drew a map of the city—a map that seemed truly a miracle, for since it, too, was done in lime juice on four pieces of paper, and since lime juice is colourless, she could have only half-seen what she was drawing ; yet every quarter, every street, every little alleyway in the two huge Jewish sections was as neat and clear as could be. She even marked the guns on the walls—one hundred and fifteen of them ; and in the harbour she showed the entire Tripolitan Navy at moorings—nineteen gunboats, two galleys, two eight-gun schooners, one ten-gun brig—the Navy that never would have existed if Commodore Dale and Commodore Morris had had (as my aunt was given to saying) the gumption of a flea.

She marked Lee's house on the shore, not half a mile from Murad Rais's ; she marked the Bashaw's gardens, out beyond Murad Rais's. She marked the Marabout's Tomb and village, sanctuary for any criminal, out beyond the Bashaw's gardens. She marked all the bazaars and noted what was sold in them ; put dots all through the Jewish quarter, marking the houses of wealthy Jews who would do anything to put an end to the rule of Joseph Karamanli, and naming them in the margin.

The things she wrote me about the treatment the American seamen were getting made my flesh crawl.

After the burning of the *Philadelphia* the American sailors were put to work carrying powder and shot from the Castle magazine to all the batteries. In so doing they had to pass through the streets, where Turks crowded up around them with stones and clubs, beating them and stoning them until they streamed blood. I saw some of the poor men crawling on hands and knees, so battered they couldn't stand. They were like wounded dogs, silent, as if making a conscious effort not to see or hear or feel. Oh, Albion, I never truly knew what hate was until we fell into this man's hands—this man who lives by extortion, who is so lacking in understanding and decency that he thinks mere strength or high position or naval superiority gives him the right to torture us : to rob us of our happiness, of each other, of our right to live our own lives together as we see fit—to appropriate our bodies, our labour, our brains, our youth ! How is it possible that all these great nations with hundreds of great ships—England and France and Spain and Denmark and Italy—can agree to be blackmailed separately by this presumptuous and ignorant creature, when by uniting they could put an instantaneous end to his effrontery ?

And do you know what this despicable man is saying ? That he will never release the Americans unless the United States pays him two thousand dollars' ransom for each man—six hundred thousand dollars ! He boasts to everyone that he will make the Unites States pay this, and that in addition he will demand more for signing a peace treaty ; and on top of everything, the United States must go on paying him fifty thousand dollars each year for ever !

Oh, to be a man, and in a position to use powder and shot against this dreadful creature ! He is so lacking in understanding that he cannot conceive the extent and the strength of the outside world. The world, for him, is Tripoli ; and outside it there are only thinly peopled wastes, like the deserts outside his own city. Yet I think that, without knowing why, he must sense that he has overstepped the bounds. The burning of the *Philadelphia* frightened him somehow, though he continues to brag and pose and threaten. All the guards at all the gates are doubled. I hope—oh, how I hope !—that his fears will be more than justified—and soon.

CHAPTER XLIX

I'VE ALWAYS doubted that mere humans can sense the approach of disaster or of great events ; but all through the spring and early summer of 1804 I worked in a state of steadily growing excitement. Oftener and oftener I heard the throbbing of guns far out at sea ; more and more groups of wild-looking, tattered Arab horsemen came riding past the gates of Murad Rais's garden, sometimes on horses, more often on camels, looking as if robbery and murder were commonplaces to them. With each group was a Marabout, a holy man carrying a little striped flag on a stick, whose chief duty seemed to be to climb up on walls and hillocks, wave his little flag threateningly, and scream potent Arabic curses in the direction of the sea, where the enemies of Tripoli were lurking.

These Marabouts were peculiar people, usually filthy, dressed in all sorts of ways, sometimes practically naked, sometimes swathed in innumerable tattered rags and bags and towels and sheetings, almost certainly insane, but viewed with awe and veneration by all.

Late in March an American frigate came into the harbour under a flag of truce. What she wanted I never knew, because Lydia couldn't find out ; but she was American, and that mere fact was encouraging. What Lydia did find out, however, was that Preble was at Malta, doing everything he could to persuade the President, the Secretary of the Navy, and everybody else to whom he could write, to let him have more ships. He was buying small, shallow-draft gunboats all over the Mediterranean, Lydia said ; gunboats that could get close to shore, where a frigate couldn't go, and hammer enemy ships and batteries with one or two heavy guns.

Preble made no secret, Lydia wrote, of being enthusiastic about Eaton's plan to put Hamet back on the throne. He insisted that, with the help of the American Navy and a little American money, Hamet and Eaton could certainly march to Tripoli and take it ; had been heard to say publicly that if the President would only give him the ships, he would make the purchase of peace or the payment of tribute totally unnecessary in this Eastern world. " He's said equally openly," she wrote, " that such a country as Tripoli is must be beaten, and never again appeased. Oh, Albion, thank God for a man like Preble ! "

Towards the end of May I began to see American vessels manœuvring in sight of Tripoli—brigs, for the most part, towing gunboats. The American officers no longer walked past Murad Rais's house : they were confined to the Castle because of all the American activity at sea. But the poor seamen were constantly passing, hitched in teams to carts and hauling enormous burdens, while their guards lashed at them with whips, and the Arabs whom they passed spat upon them and belaboured them with anything on which they could get their hands—branches of trees, rocks, camel dung, dead dogs.

All through the heat of June and July there were American vessels in the offing. Murad Rais and Lee, when they came ashore, which was seldom, had no time to waste on farming, and they pretended a brisk preoccupation, which I delightedly interpreted to mean that they were uncertain of their position. I hoped I was right—with all my heart I hoped I was right !

With the increasing American activity, Lydia's letters became more and more encouraging. The Bashaw, she wrote, had built himself a bombproof room in the Castle. Surely that was a sign that he expected trouble of an unpleasant sort. There was more drinking in the town and in the Castle, she said, more smoking of opium and hashish, than had ever before been known—and this, too, I thought, was a good sign ; for people drink to drown their sorrows or to bolster up their courage. Because of the American ships, she said, food was harder to get, and a good half of the population of Tripoli would gladly have seen Joseph Karamanli's throat cut, and even taken a hand in the cutting without a qualm.

She said, too, that the Bashaw's pride was so insufferable that he couldn't bring himself to open negotiations with the Americans over his prisoners. Since they were the offenders, he insisted—their only offence being that they wished to sail wherever they pleased without interference—they must beg him on bended knee for an audience.

It was on August third that he had real cause for being annoyed at America and Americans. When I came out of my little hut on that calm and golden morning, I saw, far beyond the reefs that extended from the fort on the far side of the harbour, a long, long line of sails heading straight in for Tripoli.

As they came closer, I made them out—two bomb ketches and six gunboats in tow of five brigs and schooners, and towering over the rest a monster of a frigate which had to be Preble's flagship. When they were three miles away from the reefs at the harbour's entrance, they huddled together for a while—getting instructions, I supposed.

When a prisoner has waited hopefully but in vain for two years and a month to see his own country take firm steps against an enemy that richly deserves chastising, he has an excuse for wondering whether anything will ever come from any effort. Yet these ships were commanded by Preble, and it was Preble who had sent men in to burn the *Philadelphia*—and hadn't Lydia said that my escape from Tripoli would come about through Preble ?

I could see Tripolitan gunboats moving out from their anchorages, moving out through the openings in the ledges, so that they were outside the harbour. Those damnable ledges were so high that they hid things from me. When the Tripolitan gunboats passed outside, I could only

half see them ;   and even when I climbed to the top of the wall I couldn't
see much better.

I could neither stand still nor sit still with those American ships
lying motionless beyond the reefs. The whole town was breathless, or
so I thought. Certainly I had trouble getting my own breath, and the
whole city seemed to drowse in the August sun.

Not until noon did the line of American ships move again. They
moved straight in towards the reefs, as if they intended to run themselves ashore ; and the closer they came, the less I could see of the gunboats, for they sat low in the water, and the reefs hid their hulls. Behind
them the big frigate and the brigs and schooners, higher in the water,
turned a little, until they were broadside to the town. I couldn't understand why they didn't fire—I wanted them to fire until my stomach
hurt with the tenseness of waiting and wanting. Then a ball of white
smoke jetted from the side of the frigate, the brackish warmth of Tripoli
harbour pushed against my eyeballs ; and with that all the brigs and
schooners, all the half-hidden gunboats and bomb ketches, all the
batteries along the reefs and in the forts from which the reefs sprouted,
burst into a bellowing roar, a thunderous tumbling chorus of explosions
that beat against my face and eyes and ears with the force of padded
hammers.

I ran from one end of the garden wall to the opposite end, but I
couldn't see. I climbed to the roof of my little hut and down again to
run to the wall and peer into the curtain of white smoke that rose from
all those vessels, into the roaring bellowing booming that shook fragments
from the wall to which I clung. Still I couldn't see. The whole world
seemed to shiver and tremble. Green and brown lizards ran out from
chinks in the wall at the incessant thunder of those guns, and were
jarred from the face of the wall by the endless tumbling crashes ; but
the smoke billowed like thunderheads above and around the ships and
I couldn't see.

Near at hand, on the beach below the wall, people were streaming
out of Tripoli, white-burnoosed figures with their skirts kilted up above
their knees, a mixture of brown-clad, orange-clad, and blue-clad men
and women, afoot and on donkeys, running and running in a panic,
screaming, falling down, fleeing from the stupendous wall of sound that
rolled and thundered at their heels.

I caught a glimpse of gunboats emerging from that welter of sound
and smoke to crawl between the ledges, back to the safety of the harbour.
They seemed to jam in the openings, to cling together, with smoke jets
spurting upward from them, like jets of steam popping from kettle
spouts. I could see American flags on some of those boats, and knew
they'd come straight into the harbour with the Tripolitan boats, to
board them and capture them.

For two long hours that incessant cannonading continued, and then
it slackened. The cloud of smoke shredded and blew away. Some of

the Tripolitan gunboats were missing. Some were half-dismasted, some were on the rocks. Some were slowly moving away from the reefs, in tow of American gunboats, and the brigs and schooners were making fast to them and towing them away. All the Tripolitan boats were silent ; all the batteries on the reefs and in the fort were silent. We had beaten them ! We had beaten the Tripolitans !

The big frigate was moving slowly along among the brigs, schooners, and gunboats, and as they passed her and moved out to sea, this big black vessel squared off on another tack and let off a broadside whose bellowing roar was followed by a sound of smashing and crashing from the city, and by a brown dust that gushed upward to hang like a dirty haze among the minarets.

The black vessel came out from the smoke-cloud of her own making and tacked again, easy and graceful. Then she let off another broadside, a stentorian burst of thunder. The sound that followed it was a distant crunching, as of a score of wheels passing over clam-shells. One of the minarets came apart in its mid-section, and the top fell straight down, out of sight, leaving a splintered snag sticking up out of the city like the ruins of a lighthouse.

With that the big black vessel turned away almost contemptuously, and contemplatively moved off after her brood of brigs, schooners, and gunboats.

I wasn't conscious of having uttered a sound during those two hours of smoke and tumult, but my throat was so raw that I could hardly croak.

Three days later Preble came back again in the *Constitution*, accompanied by his brigs, schooners, gunboats, and bomb ketches, to give Murad Rais another bellyful. Again, to my disgust, I couldn't see what was happening, the American ships being hidden from me by the city. All I heard was the incessant thunderous banging and crashing for two hours during that hot afternoon of August eighth ; all I saw was a horde of becrazed Tripolitans running from the city along the beaches, frantically screaming with fright and dread of worse to come.

But on the morning following the second attack, when I went to the wall above the beach, hopeful of seeing the American ships once more standing in towards the town, I saw that a huge Marabout, clad all in black—black burnoose, black headdress, a black veil over his face—had pitched a tent on the beach just below Murad Rais's walls, and was engaged in the customary Marabout pastime of howling indistinguishable nothings at the top of his lungs.

I knew he was a Marabout because he held a little striped flag in his hand, and, as he leaped and howled, shook it threateningly at the wide expanse of sea. His back was towards me, but I could see that he was truly a holy and influential Marabout, for he had a blue-and-white-striped tent, and an entourage of followers, some twenty of them, all veiled like himself. They looked more impressive than any of the bands of Arabs I had seen on the beach and on the road, for their burnooses were pale grey, and they had horses and pack-mules tied to a picket-line.

His followers were busy, some at their morning ablutions and prayers ; some preparing a kettle of cous-cous, others getting out dates from a pile of baggage on the sand ; but, regardless of what they were doing, every one of those veiled Arabs had a short musket slung over his shoulder, quite unlike the antiquated eight-foot-long firelocks that most Arabs affected.

I was amused by the violence with which this gigantic Marabout leaped and screamed, his black robes flapping and ballooning around him, and by the serious mien of his followers, who accepted all this leaping and howling as being important and helpful.

Almost as though he'd felt my amusement, the Marabout turned suddenly, looked up at me, and raised his veil to see me better. The face was black ; and across it, when he saw me, spread a grin so wide that his face seemed almost split in two. To my inexpressible joy, my excited scepticism, the face was that of my old friend King Dick !

King Dick in Tripoli ! King Dick with a squad of cavalry under the walls of the very garden in which I worked ! I could scarcely believe it.

The rest of that day seemed interminable. Every few minutes I went to the beach wall to assure myself that King Dick hadn't been merely a figment of my imagination ; and each time there he was, sitting cross-legged on a rug before his tent, his face veiled, a row of amulets spread upon the rug before him.

As a result of the bombardment of the day before, the beach was covered with Arabs and their families, fleeing from the city that had twice suffered such savage attacks ; and they stopped frequently to stare at this holy man. Apparently they asked for help, for occasionally he picked up an amulet and handed it to his questioner, on which the questioner would drop a coin on the rug ; then resume his flight from the city.

Attendants brought him water-pipe after water-pipe, tamped them full of tobacco ; solicitously applied coals to the bowl ; brought him tea and dates. Occasionally he rose to leap again, scream curses, and wave his little striped flag ; then back again he would go to his rug to sit and sit, imperturbable, aloof, grave, holy-seeming : the complete picture of a black saint with nothing to do, not a thought in his head, no intention of going anywhere or doing anything—just a perfect saint.

I never moved from the rear wall after the sun went down. In the dusk I could see the grey-clad Arabs like spectres around the tent, puttering above a little fire ; and before I knew it, almost, I found that

L

I couldn't see the grey burnooses and the veiled faces so clearly, couldn't
follow their movements ; when I looked hard at one, I found that
sometimes I wasn't looking at a man at all, but at a dark spot on the
beach.

I could still hear them, though, scuffing in the sand. Then there
came from below me a faint rustling, a little grunt in the darkness ;
and, so suddenly that it was like magic, King Dick's head rose above
the wall. He came sliding over the top of it like a big black cat, caught
me by the shoulders, and landed lightly on his feet before me. At the
sight and the feel and the familiar sweaty smell of this true and faithful
friend, my throat contracted so that I was hard put to it to breathe,
and we just stood there like two fools, silently patting each other's
shoulders.

I took him by the arm and led him to my little hut ; and when he
had tucked his veil up under the band of his headcloth and in the yellow
light of my candle-end I could really see that enormous grin of his, I
recovered my breath, though my voice wasn't exactly steady.

" Well," I said, " I thought you'd never get here, and now that you
are here, I'm about as badly off as I was before."

" You mean because of *her* ? " King Dick said.

" Yes," I said, " because of Lydia. Even if you could help me get
away, I don't want to do it. If I went away from here, I'd be leaving
her."

"That not the way to look at it," King Dick said. " No matter what
happens, she be better off and we be better off if we stay together. Look,
·Albion : suppose this Bashaw gets tired of being banged at and thinks
he better run into the mountains. He'd take those three children, and
he'd take her, but he wouldn't take you. You'd stay right here. Then
you'd be separated. Then you wouldn't know where she was, and you
couldn't help her. You couldn't help anybody else, either—not by
staying here. I know her, Albion. She'd say just what I say."

Since she had already said it, I couldn't deny it.

" Who else," King Dick demanded, " can send us word about this
city, so we can believe what we hear ? Nobody ! That very important,
Albion. That make all the difference."

"I know it," I said. "I know you're right. But I think about it and
I think about it. If anything should go wrong . . ."

" Everything go wrong in a war," King Dick said. " Always ! No
matter what you do, things go wrong ! Best way to keep things from
going too wrong is to stay alive. Best way for you to stay alive, and her
too, is for you to do what I say."

" Well," I said, " we've got so much to talk about, I don't know where
to start. Who are these men with you ? "

" Black Arabs from Jalo," King Dick said. He shook his right arm,
and a knife with a twelve-inch blade dropped into his hand. With the
knife-point he scratched a serpentine line on the dirt floor and made

four little nicks along it, naming each nick : Tripoli, Bengazi, Derna, Cairo. Almost directly under the serpentine line he drew a straight line, and along that made three more nicks, naming them in turn Jofra, Jalo, Siwa. Then he slipped the knife neatly back into a leather sheath fastened to his forearm.

" Those three placcs," he said, " those pretty handy for finding out what happening anywhere. Caravans go through all the time. Jalo's the best : best people, best dates, best water. Remember I told you back in Cap François how I learned the shell-trick from Eugene Leitensdorfer, and how a date merchant from Jalo bought me from an Arab in Timbuktu and took me back to Jalo with him ? "

"Yes," I said, " I remember."

King Dick nodded. " Those black Arabs in Jalo, they know all caravan roads in all directions, so when Eugene Leitensdorfer found you here and told me, I went back to Jalo to see if my Jalo wife still alive, and let my friend Hadji ben Idriss help me raise some black cavalry. Those black Arabs very smart, Albion ; very pleased to go anywhere with me because I got French guns for them in Cairo, also grey burnooses. When we take Tripoli, they be rich—I promised."

" You say you had a wife in Jalo ? "

" Yarse," King Dick said. " Wherever I stay more than four days I get one wife to cook. Then I settle down and look around and get another for company. That one I left in Jalo, she pretty old now, but good cook." He murmured " Mm, mm ! " in a hushed voice : then said solicitously, " You look starved, Albion. You ever had sheep brains cooked in camel milk and eggs ? "

I told him I'd done well enough—that I'd had bread crusts and rice every day, and dates and vegetables from the garden.

" We fix you in Jalo," he said. " My company wifes do everything, so very easy living."

His talk of Jalo and company wives sounded fantastic and I only half believed him.

" Why do you and those men of yours wear black veils ? " I asked.

King Dick shrugged. " Some Marabouts wear veils so to be more holy. Very good thing to wear when doing anything at night. Very hard to see people all black and grey. Listen, Albion : that Captain Lee stole our boat. Maybe they nothing to do about it, but I like to try."

I went to the sunken box where I kept my books and Lydia's letters, and showed him Lydia's map.

" Mm, mm ! " he said admiringly. " This very good map. I think I use it a litto."

" You can't just sit here doing nothing, can you ? " I asked.

" Why not ? " King Dick asked. " Marabouts sit and do nothing. Some of 'em fifty years in one spot, mostly doing nothing. Anyway, I got to sit here until next bombardment, so I can unsit you ; then I got to wait a few days to be sure this Bashaw don't surrender—make sure everything all right—make sure he not discouraged and run away to the mountains."

" It's not safe," I protested. " To linger in the neighbourhood might make trouble for us—and for Lydia——"

King Dick shrugged his shoulders. " Nobody ever touches a Marabout except another Marabout, and my goo'ness, I can wipe any Marabout I've seen yet ! "

" If I leave here and go to Jalo with you," I said, " how long will it be before we'd be able to start back to Tripoli ? "

That, he said, he didn't know. When Leitensdorfer had returned to Cairo with news that Lydia and I were prisoners, he and Leitensdorfer had gone together to see Joseph Karamanli's brother Hamet, who had taken refuge among Arabs on the Nile. He had, he said, found him a fine man, but penniless, and eagerly awaiting Eaton's return from America, which he hoped would be soon.

Hamet, he said, reminded him of Lamartinière, that tireless and almost white Negro who had so impressed me in Haiti. Hamet's affection for Eaton, King Dick said, was extraordinary. King Dick had seen the letters that Eaton had written Hamet—letters in which Eaton planned a joint attack on Tripoli by sea and land ; and if Eaton kept his promises —if he was able to supply Hamet with the necessary artillery from the American fleet, a detachment of marines to spearhead his attack, and enough money to pay the way of a force of Arabs to march across the desert—and if the Navy did its part in landing food and ammunition at the proper points, Tripoli was already as good as in American hands. Eaton and Hamet would cut off the city from receiving any supplies in the rear ; the Navy could easily prevent them from getting any supplies by sea ; and nothing would be left for Joseph Karamanli to do but give up—surrender his American prisoners and relinquish all hope of trying to make America pay tribute.

Hamet, King Dick said, was as unlike his brother Joseph as day is different from night—and probably, he said, that was why Hamet had allowed himself to be robbed of his rightful position by his despicable younger brother. Joseph Karamanli believed in robbery, in slavery, in keeping people poor by extortionate taxes which he spent on himself. He hated America, France, England, and every other Christian nation, and was so convinced of his own superiority that he considered himself safe in making war on any or all of them—a policy that must inevitably ruin both him and his people.

Hamet, on the other hand, believed that since all of North Africa had once been a garden capable of supplying Rome, Greece, and France with wheat and vegetables, it could again be made a garden if those who lived in it were encouraged to stop fighting, were not robbed by taxation of all their earnings, and if some of the money now spent on war were to be spent instead on bringing teachers from America,

England, and France to show the Arabs how to get the best out of their country.

I was as stirred by King Dick's account of Hamet and Eaton as I had been by Preble's daring bravery, and with all my heart I wanted to do what I could to help them. I'd have felt that way even if I hadn't spent long months seeing Americans worked like beasts of burden, spat upon, stoned, clubbed within an inch of their lives ; even if Lydia and I hadn't endured a million torments at the insufferable Bashaw's hands.

" Look," I said, " suppose you're able to get me away from here without anyone being the wiser ? "

" Suppose ! " King Dick said. He smiled at me fondly and reassuringly, just as he had smiled before we walked in on Dessalines at Crête à Pierrot on the night of our escape. " That all planned, Albion."

" Planned for Lydia, too ? " I asked.

" Everything," King Dick said. " Look, Albion : these Jalo men travel faster than anybody else anywhere. Some Arabs at some oases never travel at all. Jalo men raise very fine camels, the fastest meharis, very fine dates. One Jalo man and one mehari—one fast camel—go from Cairo to Jalo in ten days. Jalo to Bengazi, four days. Jalo to Tripoli, nine days. When we leave here, I leave two Jalo men, my friends, always camped at the Marabout's Tomb in the Pianura."

He drew Lydia's map from under his burnoose, unrolled it, and showed me that sanctuary neatly labelled in Lydia's handwriting, not two pistol-shots from where we sat. " You write her quick, Albion. Tell her these two Jalo men always there. Every two weeks, after the next bombardment, she give one of those men a letter for you, telling everything : what the Bashaw doing, what the people doing, what everybody thinking. Nobody else in all Tripoli able to get such information for us. Then, wherever we go, that Jalo man find us, and as soon as one leave here, another come back from Jalo, carrying letter from you to her."

" How are you able to do all this ? " I asked.

" Listen, Albion," King Dick said. " Arabs very strange people. You find all sorts of Arabs, just like all sorts of Americans, only good Arabs are better than anybody you ever saw, bad Arabs worse than anybody you ever saw. Bedouins steal everything, lie always. Good Arabs rather die than let anything bad happen to a friend. Once a good Arab's your friend, he always your friend."

" As you are to me," I said.

King Dick brushed this aside with a flirt of his hand. " Hadji ben Idriss in Jalo, the one who bought me in Timbuktu, is both good and rich—rich in camels, horses, date palms. He like very much to see Hamet back on throne of Tripoli ; then his caravans be in no danger ever. So when he finds his old friend King Dick has friends who are in trouble, he provides him with house, helps him get wifes, lends him meharis, horses, black Arabs to ride them ; and, since he is a Sherif, he says he will curse any black Arab and his father and his grandfather who fail in any way to do everything I say. Also I am a great Marabout, can do some cursing of my own."

He leaned over to pat me on the shoulder. " Mustn't look as if I had done anything for you, Albion. Do you remember how you found my pearls in Cap François and took nothing for it ? You wanted nothing —only man in the world except Toussaint, who never expected something for doing good. Besides, we did well in Gibraltar, you and I. Our rum did well for us ! "

He went to the door of the hut, opened it a crack and peered out. There was a pink streak in the east, and through the crack in the door came the odours of a Tripolitan dawn : that peculiar blend of dusty walls, rank green vegetation, camel dung, and the flat fishy smell of the Mediterranean. " You write that lady," he said (as long as I knew him he never was able to call her by her name, though the time came when he ventured to call her Lilla, which is Arabic for " lady "), " you write that lady to find a good Jew to carry her letters, and be sure she never write except in lime juice. Everything going to come out good, Albion : remember how Arabs always say ' It is ordained.' "

He went quickly to the wall and peered over it at the dim beach below. What he saw seemed to satisfy him, for he slid cat-like over the top of the wall, grinned reassuringly at me as he pulled the veil down over his face, then vanished as effectually as any djinn assisted by thunderclaps and lamp-rubbing.

CHAPTER L

GOD KNOWS what gets into the minds of all governments at certain stages of their existence. It's easy to understand why Arab princes surround themselves with incompetents, eunuchs, dolts, and degenerates, for Arab princes consider themselves infallible : whatever they do must of necessity be right. Consequently they elevate childhood friends or toadying relatives to the most important posts in their kingdoms.

But only God knows why such things perpetually happen in countries regarded as politically enlightened, like England, France, America, supposedly governed by patriotic men. Yet they always have happened, and with horrifying frequency ; the pages of history are sprinkled with dolts, idiots, drunkards maintained in the highest offices—mediocrities whose stubbornness has sacrificed armies, whose blindness had destroyed navies, whose bad judgment has ruined their countries' prestige, starved helpless people by the million, wrecked cities, toppled arts, civilisation, learning, and understanding in the dust—and most of these fools' names hold unsullied place in the lying annals of their respective nations.

I'd thought often about these things during my long and lonely nights in Murad Rais's garden, but somehow I'd never expected to be affected personally by them. Yet the day after I'd followed King Dick's instructions and written Lydia about the men from Jalo who would carry her letters to me after the next bombardment, I had a letter from her that fairly turned my stomach.

The American officers are elated, because they have somehow heard that four additional frigates will probably arrive in the Mediterranean at any moment—may even be in the Mediterranean now ; but their rejoicing is as nothing by comparison with that of the Bashaw, because it's also known that your friend Commodore Preble is being relieved and recalled to the United States, and that the command of this new squadron will go to a much older officer, Commodore Barron.

The Bashaw has repeatedly said that Preble must be a madman to sail recklessly into the harbour, since only a madman could deal death and destruction while escaping all damage himself ; but he must know that if this is so, then all Preble's officers and crews are likewise madmen —those gallant sailors who ran their little boats into the middle of the Bashaw's fleet, regardless of their own safety, to capture vessels twice the size of their own, manned by triple their numbers !

What must be the feelings of Commodore Preble at being supplanted by an untried man at a moment when his leadership has won universal admiration ! Only a year ago all these pirate kingdoms felt only contempt for the American Navy. The French, the English, the Russians—they despised us, too, for our weak-kneed truckling ; and now that Preble has changed all that, he's to be sent home as a reward ! How can those awful men in Washington be so stupid ! When the new Commodore will get here and take command none of the American prisoners know, but they are sure that Preble will continue to attack until the last possible moment.

The Bashaw is afraid of this, and has offered to accept $150,000 as the price of peace and the release of the American prisoners ; but Preble said No ; he'd give him a hundred thousand dollars for the prisoners, but not a cent for peace and never another cent for tribute.

You'll never know what a weight will be lifted from my heart when I know you are safely away from this terrible city. The Bashaw threatens to do unspeakable things to the Americans, and I tremble to think of what might happen to you. King Dick is our only friend ; and the only true peace of mind I can know, until we are together again, will lie in being sure you are with him. You must go with him : you *must* ! Think what would have become of us if for a moment we had failed to trust and follow him on that dreadful night when we left Beau-Bouclier !

I wanted to think that Lydia was wrong, but I knew she wasn't. Preble, with the audacity of a great leader, had done what no other

American commodore in the Mediterranean had even thought of doing. As Lydia had said, he had not only filled all his officers with a single-hearted determination to batter this miserable despot to his knees, but he had made up for the timidity, the vacillation, the stupidity, the lack of daring of all preceding American commodores. He was a genius, a gleaming sword at the hearts of the enemies of America.

For a man imprisoned, or awaiting a decision that will profoundly affect his life, there's nothing so agonising as uncertainty. If my days in Murad Rais's garden had seemed endless when I had no hope of escape, now that escape seemed near at hand each day seemed an eternity and the laggard minutes were like hours. If I'd dared, I'd have spent all those days at the wall, just watching King Dick's black-veiled figure ; for the endless activity of his little camp was amazing.

His reputation as a Marabout must have grown and spread ; for Arabs of every station in life went to the beach to look at him, to marvel at his dexterity in making coins disappear, at the magical way a pearl on the rug before him would seemingly pass through three walnut shells with the speed of light. They bought his amulets ; prostrated themselves before him. Even the Bashaw and his suite came to consult him, which led me to wonder whether a Marabout in an Arab land is any worse than any successful charlatan in a more civilised country.

So far as I could see, King Dick never moved from his blue-and-white-striped tent and his rug, except at night, when two of his black Arabs stood upon each other's shoulders to let him mount into the garden to visit with me.

He rolled his eyes and shook his head when I told him the unhappy news about the replacing of Preble. "That bad," he said, " but Bashaw not safe yet and knows it." The Bashaw, he said, had demanded an amulet that would make him immune to American cannon-fire, so King Dick gave him one that was supposed to let him venture into the midst of the most violent bombardment without being so much as touched by cannon-ball, shell, bomb, or splinter.

" No matter what happen," King Dick said, " I be big, big Marabout ! If he go out and *not* get killed, my amulet did it. If he got out and *get* killed, look how much good I do how many people ! "

He talked constantly and enthusiastically of Leitensdorfer, who had remained in Alexandria to get news of Eaton, and he spoke of the oasis of Jalo with a sort of affectionate intimacy, a complete assurance that we'd get there, as my uncle, when living in Portland, might have spoken of the Gorham farm. " When we reach Jalo," he'd say ; or, " You're thin, Albion, you just wait till my wifes makes *meshwi* in Jalo ; " or, " Soon's we get to Jalo, we drill twice a day instead of once ; " or, " These vegetables of yours very good, Albion, but wait till you see what we raise in Jalo ! "

After the two years I'd spent in that accursed hut, that accursed

garden, I lacked his faith : considered his optimism almost dangerous.
For me, Jalo was as remote as a star. I couldn't believe that the day
would ever come when I would walk unhindered out of this garden,
a free man once more ; and I naturally kept at King Dick to find out
how he meant to work it. But he only looked at me wide-eyed and
innocent, and wouldn't tell me. Not until the grey dawn of August
twenty-eighth was I to learn of the simple sleight-of-hand trick by
which he would erase me completely, so far as Murad Rais and the
Bashaw were concerned.

At mid-afternoon on August twenty-seventh the American fleet
hove in sight like a far-off group of infant icebergs, heading in from
the eastward. By sundown they were a scant two miles away, straight
out in front of the Castle—three sturdy topsail schooners, three tall
black brigs, a frigate unknown to me, and the towering snowy-sailed
fortress of Preble's *Constitution* ; and towing behind each of the seven
larger vessels were smaller vessels, ten of them, either gunboats or bomb
ketches. Off the mouth of the harbour they executed a manœuvre as if
directed by a single hand. The brigs and the schooners rounded up into
the wind ; the gunboats and the ketches moved up between them, like
figures in a dance ; and there they lay at anchor, headed into the offshore
breeze, as harmless looking as a flock of gulls idly at rest upon a silken sea.

The consequent to-do, all up and down the beach and in the city,
was as violent as the American vessels were quiet. I saw what seemed
to be another general exodus from the city, both by beach and by road
as well as by fishing boat. From the city rose a continuous excited
shouting, and along the beach hurried Arabs, Berbers, Moors, Turks,
Jews, and Italians, fleeing to the safety of the desert : on camelback,
horseback, donkeyback, or afoot, laden with packs, or empty-handed,
or leading sheep, dogs, goats.

Around sunset the howling died down, since the American vessels
hadn't moved and apparently had no intention of moving until the
morrow. But as evening approached, King Dick and his troop of black
Arabs, who had been sitting around the tent watching the fleeing
Tripolitans, came suddenly to life. Behind the tent they dug a long
trench with their knives ; then the heap of packs and bundles was taken
down ; some were carried inside King Dick's tent, and others loaded
on pack-horses. Just before dark all but three of the burnoosed troopers
climbed into their saddles and went plodding off into the green dusk,
leading the pack-animals and five riderless saddle-horses, which left
none at all for King Dick and the other three.

Darkness had no sooner fallen than King Dick was up and over the
wall. " This is going to be it, Albion," he said, and so wide was his grin
that his face seemed all teeth. He took a rope from beneath his black
burnoose, seated himself on the top of the wall, and threw it down :
then tested it, as a fisherman tests a line. When he drew it up again,

a small keg was fastened to it. This he removed tenderly, like a fond father dandling a baby ; again lowered the rope, and this time brought up a compact bundle of clothes and sundry odds and ends.

" Now," he said, " nothing for you to do but take these bundles into your hut and wait a few hours more while I go back and tend to something. Just be patient, Albion, because you're getting to see something that old Bashaw won't like much, not even with my amulet stuck on his head." He beamed affectionately on me and added as an after-thought, " You can write a letter to that lady, and if you got anything you want to take away from here, Albion, get it wrapped up, because when I come back we might not have time to waste."

I think I only half-believed what he said ; and as I scratched at a long lime-juice letter to Lydia—the one I hoped would be the last I'd write from that miserable hut of Murad Rais's—I believed him less and less ; for hardly a sound came from the dark harbour.

But half-way between midnight and dawn I heard noises far out in the darkness : occasional thumps, dim cluckings and clackings that might have been made by sweeps, small rattlings that could have been capstans heaving up anchors.

I hastily finished my letter, rolled it into a segment of cane, and went to the garden wall to hear the better. I held my breath and turned my head from side to side ; raised and lowered myself in the hope of getting some clearer drift of sound. I'd been at this fruitless proceeding for God knows how long—long enough for my neck to ache and my eyes to be watery from staring—when a stab of flame leaped at my eyeballs, a level gash of orange lightning that spurted across the harbour to reveal a momentary tangle of masts and hulls, of ripples on jet-black water, of white walls and palm fronds. And as if that spurt or orange lightning had been a signal, a dozen other spurts flashed into being ; the little masts and hulls winked into sight and again vanished ; and out of that dark amphitheatre of harbour, as from the crater of a volcano, came the simultaneous and thundering crash of great guns.

When Preble's ships had bombarded Tripoli before, they had done so from the northward, beyond the ledges that extended from the far side of the harbour, so that I hadn't seen them well. But now, under cover of the darkness, they had come into the harbour itself, so that the flashing and the thundering were before my very eyes ; so close that it seemed to me that if I thrust my hand across the wall, it would strike against the cannonading as against something solid ; for its violence was such that it seemed as tangible as it was enormous.

Here was the thing I had prayed for during all these long months, but had never really believed could happen—had hardly dared even to dream of, because it hadn't seemed possible that any American ship could approach within range of all those hundreds of guns in the Castle and the harbour batteries without being blown to bits.

And when those guns in the Castle and the batteries *did* go into action, I didn't dare look—and yet I didn't dare not to. Not a hundred yards from Murad Rais's garden, a battery at the water's edge poured streams of flame in jets. The tall front of the Castle was honeycombed with guns, dozens upon dozens of them—one hundred and fifteen, Lydia had reported—and all these spurted fire into the harbour. In the incessant flashing, the black water twinkled and glimmered, and I could see, clear before my eyes, the American ships wreathed in smoke.

From the batteries and the fort on the far side of the harbour more scores of lightning-flashes converged upon those American vessels, so that they were lit constantly, caught at the centre of a spider-web of flashes and ear-splitting detonations.

The gunboats and the bomb ketches were close in, pounding and pounding at the score and more of Tripolitan cruisers lying at their moorings : pounding and pounding at the batteries that pounded back at them. They gave the strange effect of hiding behind a hedge of tall white poplars that bloomed and darkened in the never-ending flashes. Those poplars were the splashes from the Bashaw's cannon-shot, and how the gunboats stayed afloat behind that screen was more than I could understand.

Yet they miraculously did stay afloat and thunderously alive. They poured their shot into Tripolitan cruisers, houses, Castle ; and minutes stretched into a quarter-hour, a half-hour, an hour.

Out beyond the gunboats, the brigs and the schooners stood off-and-on, stationed there, I suppose, to tow off any gunboats that might be mortally wounded ; and they, too, moved behind waterspouts that rose and fell, poplar-like, around them as they sailed.

So fierce was my anxiety for the safety of those gunboats and the men upon them that, when King Dick's head came up again over the top of the wall, I so little expected him that I almost fell over backward. He rolled himself across the wall and stood beside me, breathing heavily. In his hand he held a rope-end.

" My goo'ness me my," he whispered, " that more noise than we made at Crête à Pierrot ! That Preble, he must have known exactly what we needed ! " He cast a quick look around the dark garden. " Everything all right, Albion ? "

I nodded, unable to take my eyes from those bellowing gunboats, firing from behind their fences of waterspouts.

" Give a hand here, Albion," he said. " This man just your size, but feels twice as heavy."

I laid hold of the rope with him. At the end was a dead weight—truly dead, for when we tugged it to the top of the wall and hoisted it inboard, I saw it to be the lifeless and naked body of a man.

" Who is he ? " I asked.

" Nobody much," King Dick said. " Been dead hours. We get him into your hut quick."

Inside the hut King Dick worked as smoothly and rapidly as he had worked on the guns at Crête à Pierrot. " First," he said, " we dress him in your clothes ; then you give yourself a black face off the bottom of that kettle."

I gladly shed my patched brown barracan and turban and helped King Dick put them on to that unknown man—now limp because rigor mortis had passed off. When, thus dressed, he was rolled over on to his face, I had the peculiar feeling that he was I : that I wasn't Albion Hamlin at all, but an unknown man standing there stripped of identity as well as clothes, staring at the husk of myself.

King Dick handed me the bundle he had brought up over the wall earlier in the evening, and when I unwrapped it I found a grey burnoose, a black turban with a veil in no way different from those worn by his black Arabs, a pair of long white underdrawers, and shoes of soft yellow leather.

I blacked my face and hands, and put on these new garments, a welcome relief from the miserable covering with which Murad Rais had supplied me ; and while I dressed, King Dick worked. With the point of his knife he pried a plug from the little keg, took a coil of fuse from the odds and ends that had been wrapped with the bundle of clothes, inserted one end in the hole, and wedged it in place with a sliver of wood. He put the keg on my three-legged stool, placed the dead man on my wooden bed, moved the bed close to the little keg, and carefully bent the limbs of the lifeless body so that it seemed to be reclining before the powder keg in rapt adoration.

" Everything now done, Albion ! " King Dick said. He cast a quick look around the room, placed the coil of fuse beside the door, and picked up the candle from the shelf.

" Go out to the wall quick," he said. He bent down and touched the flame of the candle to the end of the fuse, and a little red spark ran gnawing along it.

I pulled open the door and went into a tumult of cannonading, of flashing that so lit the sky that the palm fronds swayed and rustled against a flickering light. When I reached the wall, King Dick had his rope in his hand. " I don't need this," he said. " They come for me when they see you."

He knotted the rope under my arms, seemed to stumble against me, and, almost before I knew what had happened, I had been pushed over the top of the wall, had slid down its face, and felt the sand of the beach beneath my feet.

Two of King Dick's black Arabs, half invisible even in the flash of the cannonading, unknotted the rope from around my waist, pulled me towards the trench I had seen them digging earlier in the day, and pushed me into it. It was a shallow trench, so that I could see them go back to the wall, where one climbed on the shoulders of the other.

From somewhere above their heads came a shattering explosion, and a rain of clay and rocks rattled down around me. A minute later King Dick and his two Arabs were lying in the trench beside me.

" That very nice powder," King Dick said. " Couldn't have made nicer hole with twelve-inch mortar. Looks just as if made by shell-fire, and just enough left of you so not to make trouble when they dig hole to put you in."

He raised his head from the trench and looked out to the eastward. " Oh, my goo'ness me my," he said.

When I raised my head to look, too, I saw that a grey light had come into the east, so that we could at last see all those vessels clearly. The fire of the American gunboats had diminished, and the brigs and the schooners were moving towards them, apparently to take them in tow ; and close behind the advancing brigs and schooners towered the square sails of the *Constitution*, moving straight in as if she intended to sail on and on, straight against the front of Bashaw's Castle.

" Those litto boats," King Dick said, " they fired away all their powder ! Look good at this, Albion. This big ship, she's moving in so everyone fires at her, so let the litto ones get away."

It was a sight that made it hard for me to draw a deep breath. " That's Preble," I said. " He's from Portland ! "

I never saw anything so beautiful as that tall ship moving majestically among the smaller boats in the grey dawn light, steady as a rock. She was so close that we could see that the tompions were out of her bow guns, see the lighted matches flickering behind the guns ; and all her batteries were lighted up, as if she were sailing into a friendly port, proud to flaunt her strength and grace and beauty before the eyes of enemy and friend alike. We could hear the gunboat crews cheering and cheering as she moved among and past them.

And now the cannonading from the Bashaw's Castle and all the batteries rose to a hysterical crescendo. The surface of the harbour, all around the steadily advancing ship, was jetting up in spouts, foam-fountains as high as her main yard. We could see holes opening in her sails, see her running-rigging flying asunder, see ship's boats swung overside into that shot-lashed water to carry messages to the gunboats ; but she came on and on. Her two bow guns let off with a roar that stirred the sand before our trench. One of the shots struck the battery a scant hundred yards from where we lay, and up from it rose a cloud of smoke, dust, and debris. The other smashed into the front of the Bashaw's Castle, sending a brown burst of rocks and dust high in the air. She was so close in that her bowsprit seemed about to telescope itself against the Castle. Then, as effortlessly as though she moved in a regatta, her yards swung and she wore around parallel to the Castle.

King Dick shook his head, staring at me from protuberant white eyes. " Under the guns," he marvelled. " That Preble took her under the guns, so close they can't shoot down into her."

I found myself repeating over and over, " That's Edward Preble ! He comes from Portland ! Everybody in Portland knows him ! "

We could see the officers on her quarter-deck, watching the batteries through their glasses, watching the gun crews, and keeping tab on the sails, the signal flags, the brigs, and the schooners that were hauling the gunboats out of action. When she let off a broadside from her starboard battery, the whole town seemed to totter on its foundations. Our own gunboats moved steadily out behind their attendant brigs and schooners, but the Tripolitan cruisers fell suddenly into disarray and confusion. The masts of some hung overside, and they moved like crippled birds : others were ashore, canted at angles.

Those bellowing broadsides from the *Constitution* roared on and on, for half an hour, for an hour nearly. All the American gunboats had moved far out beyond the harbour mouth. The Tripolitan cruisers were silent, every last one of them. Not even from the Bashaw's Castle did a gun reply to the *Constitution's* final broadside. The forts, the batteries—every last one of them had been stilled, and the bright dawn lighted up a smoky harbour that had been torn and shattered by a handful of Americans in a small piece of America. The wind was freshening as the sun came up. The big ship, as if she had been waiting for the sun, payed off and moved towards that misty yellow disc—a sun-ship, sleek, shining, ageless, invulnerable, sailed by a man whose strength was such that he could have survived a thousand deaths.

CHAPTER LI

BY MID-MORNING there wasn't an American ship in sight, and those which had first put in saolton along the beaches the afternoon before were on their way back to the city again. King Dick's black Arabs, too, returned to the beach, staked out their picket-line, unloaded the pack-horses, and settled down as if for a long stay.

We were safe where we were, King Dick said, because no Arab, no Moor, no Bedouin dared interfere with a Marabout ; and he had to find out three things before leaving Tripoli : whether Murad Rais unquestioningly believed that I had been killed by a shell during the bombardment ; whether the Bashaw might not surrender his prisoners and abandon the war as a consequence of Preble's attack ; and whether there would be news of William Eaton in Lydia's final letter to me.

Two days later a little Jewish silversmith stood humbly before King Dick, laid a small silver coin on the rug in front of him, and sought information, as is the custom of those who visit Marabouts. " In what part of the land of dates will I find the best dates ? " he asked.

King Dick seemed to meditate ; then said, " Oasis of Jalo. Hadji ben Idriss."

The little Jew prostrated himself before this black-clad Marabout, and as he got to his feet to scuttle away he left a length of cane on the rug at King Dick's feet.

We went into the tent together, took the stopper from the end of the cane, removed the blank roll of paper within it, and held each sheet over a candle until Lydia's familiar writing came out brown upon it.

They suspect nothing. The Bashaw himself has had the insolence to offer me his sympathy because of your death. The sympathy of a murderer ! Hamet's wife comes to me a dozen times a day to weep with me in my sorrow, and I have to pretend to weep, too, though for the first time in all these long months I am at last truly happy—happy, that is to say, by comparison—because of knowing that you're beyond the reach of Murad Rais and Joseph Karamanli. There's no way of finding out when Eaton is coming back ; but the Bashaw's agents have been watching his brother Hamet, who is somewhere near Cairo. They tell him Hamet is restless, and sending messages here and there ; so the Bashaw thinks Eaton must be returning, and soon.

The Bashaw pretends to have no fear of Eaton. He says Preble won't attack again this autumn, because the weather will soon turn bad, and also because his ammunition has given out. Another thing he says is that Hamet will never dare attack Tripoli while his wife and children are hostages here in the Castle. If he does attack, the Bashaw threatens to kill all four—an empty threat, of course, because (as all the American officers know) the wife and children are quite safe, really ; for the Bashaw is enough of a soldier to realise that he must plan for defeat as well as for victory, and if he were to kill the hostages, and Eaton and Hamet defeated him, harder terms would be imposed than if he'd let them stay alive.

You will never know how happy I am to think that I can be of some help to Eaton and to Hamet when the expedition starts—that I can play even a small part in ridding the world of something evil. Hamet's wife says there are thousands of Jews in Tripoli who will carry messages for her if they think the messages will help replace Hamet on the throne and destroy the insufferable Joseph Karamanli. So you may be sure a message will go each week to one of the black Arabs at the Marabout's Tomb, and equally sure they will be carried with perfect safety.

I beg you never to forget that you are dead. Joseph Karamanli has agents everywhere, and because of that you must never, never let your identity be known—not until Joseph Karamanli and Murad Rais have been destroyed.

She added a paragraph whose opening words sent King Dick outside the tent, murmuring " My goo'ness me my ! " and that brought a flood of fond memories into my mind—memories of the long days and rapturous

nights on our happy voyage to Cette ; of our night together on the high
beaches of Mount Terrible ; of how she'd looked at me, after King Dick
had married us, and said she *never* wanted to feel married.

I read her letter again. Then I tore off the final paragraph and—
after carefully destroying the rest as usual—tucked the bit into the belt-
wallet King Dick had given me, to join all the other precious messages
she'd sent me earlier along with information I'd dared not retain. By
now, the bits of paper that had consoled so many lonely hours were limp
from countless re-readings, their lime-juice writing faded and rubbed
almost to nothingness. In their steady power of solace those bright words
had served me as usefully as had her lessons in Arabic, or the stream of
accurate information she had furnished.

For not once had Lydia ever been wrong—never once ! Thanks to
her, I saw everything clearly now. Whatever I could do to help shorten
the days of Joseph Karamanli, I must do—not merely because of my
love for Lydia, but because, with her, I wished to play some small part
in ridding the world of something evil.

CHAPTER LII

ON THE long, long ride to Jalo I learned many things, among them the
singular contentment that fills a man's mind in that enormous strange
world of emptiness and sky, of brilliant dullness and ever-changing
monotony ; of dusty grey shrubs and sparse grasses that send out delicious
odours ; of fiery noons, frigid nights, sunsets violent beyond all describing ;
of shifting sands, of sharp winds, that wash from the brain all doubts,
despondency, dark oppression, unhappiness.

There is something inexpressibly clean and magnificent about the
desert, something beyond the experience of those who know only oceans,
mountains, populated places ; and plodding on and on, across it, I
understood why the Bedouin, the nomad Arab, has a profound contempt
for the dirt, the restlessness, the stenches of cities ; why he regards
pityingly the pallid, harried people who dwell hideously and stupidly
in towns, and thinks of them as slaves, caught in a treadmill that holds
them in one spot, for ever moving yet for ever motionless.

King Dick, his twenty black Arabs, and I were stripped to the barest
essentials—burnoose and trousers, Arab slippers, a leather wallet, a bag
of dates, a bag of flour, a skin of water, a rug, a gun, powder, and ball.
We shared alike : one kettle, one goatskin of rancid butter for making
cous-cous. Our fare, by most men's standards, would have been considered wretched. Yet peace and contentment rode on that long journey
with me. I had no fear for Lydia's future or my own. I was confident
beyond any doubt that we were fated to be together again, and soon.
I not only looked like an Arab and acted like an Arab : I thought like

an Arab. What will be, will be ! Inshallah ! Allah will send the solution of the problem !

I learned the amazing hospitality of the desert. Whenever we overtook a caravan moving in our direction, or met one coming from some far-off place, food was always given us, for all desert travellers are brother nomads. Food, tea, and a rug by their brushwood fire were ours for as long as we wished to " fadhl " with them—" fadhl " meaning to sit down and talk.

King Dick's black Arabs had all looked alike to me when I first saw them, but now they became individuals and good companions. Abdul Rahim was the captain of the troop under King Dick, and his next in command, Moraja, was a sergeant with bow legs and a voice like the squawk of a startled great blue heron. Our cooking was done by Mohammed, the tallest of the troopers—probably because he was too tall to be bothered by the smoke of our camp fires ; and I even found his dishes savoury in spite of his use of clarified butter, which is a liquefied grease like that which rises to the top of baked beans cooked by an indifferent cook, but rancid.

We all ate with our right hands from the same kettle, squeezing the barley meal into greasy cakes that could be popped into the mouth without dribbling rancid butter on one's burnoose. Not only did we fare equally : we *were* equal. Each man unhesitatingly spoke his mind on any subject under discussion. But when Abdul Rahim gave the order to camp, and Moraja repeated the order in that blue-heron squawk of his, the neatness and rapidity with which the order was obeyed was almost miraculous. In five minutes' time horses would be hobbled, luggage piled in a semi-circle with its back to the wind, rifles stacked in three stacks, and all twelve tents would be off the pack-mules and erected.

I had had the idea—perhaps from seeing the miserable shooting of the Bashaw's gunners in Tripoli—that men who hampered their legs with burnooses must somehow be awkward on horseback and unskilled with rifles ; but King Dick's black Arabs shot as well as any New Englander who had been trained to stab at partridges in thick cover ; and King Dick was proud of them, as he had a right to be. For years, he said, these black Arabs, and their fathers and fathers' fathers before them, had followed the vocation of guarding and guiding caravans ; and every desert robber well knew that a caravan guarded by them was more difficult to attack and rob than a caravan guarded by ten times that number of white Arabs. This, he said, was why caravans guarded by black Arabs were almost never molested.

The desert, say the Arabs, is a sea, and Jalo its greatest port ; and, like many Arab sayings, it isn't far from the truth. Caravans come to it from the farthest confines of the desert—from Timbuktu, two months' travel to the south-west ; from Kufra, city of mystery in the heart of the desert ; from unnamed oases in that vast uncharted waste of sand. They bring to Jalo ostrich plumes, rare skins, ivory, wax, civet musk, incense, strange animals, slaves, and gold, exchanging these for treasures brought there by other caravans from Morocco, Tripoli, Bengazi, and Alexandria —for guns and pistols ; powder and shot ; Damascus blades and Birmingham daggers ; needles and pins ; Tripolitan burnooses ; Moroccan slippers, wallets, belts ; Jewish caps ; necklaces and brooches from Cairo and Paris ; brass trays and coffee-cups from Algiers ; dried fish, blue cotton, writing-paper, medicines, books, silks. . . .

The oasis of Jalo is S-shaped : a long snake-like twist of scattered palms growing sparsely from a sandy depression in the desert ; but when the traveller first passes from the desert and into the scanty shade of the palms, he sees no sign of village or town—just date palms and more date palms among the dunes of bright sand—until, rounding a dune with the expectation of seeing nothing but more palms and more dunes, he suddenly comes on Jalo, squatting on the top of a rise. He sees a long, fortress-like wall of buildings, bronze-coloured and solid, with little slits of windows, high up, like the gun-ports in a fort. And, in a sense, a fort is exactly what Jalo is ; for all its houses and courtyard walls are joined together, making one long wall. Thus all the houses on the rim of the town turn their backs on the desert and face in on twisting narrow streets, spanned by low arches and floored with hard-packed brown sand.

A traveller arriving at a desert town doesn't just walk in. He and his fellows must camp a mile or so outside the town gate to make themselves presentable ; and to them comes a deputation of sheiks and ekhwans, representatives of the town's governing body, to find out who they are, what they want, whence they're from and whither they're bound, what lodgings they need, and whether there is any dangerous illness among them.

Three men came out to meet us when we camped, and King Dick greeted them delightedly and made a speech to them about me, to whom he referred as Hamlin Bey from Afghanistan. The three new-comers were Hadji ben Idriss, a round, dark-brown little man in a snowy white burnoose, who many years before had rescued King Dick from slavery in Timbuktu ; Sheik Ibrahim Bishari, a great merchant whose caravans travelled from Wadai to Egypt and from Kufra to the inland sea of Africa ; and an ekhwan or wise man, Hamida Bey, whose bushy beard was dyed a pale lavender, which, with his green turban, gave him the look of an enormous inverted thistle.

After the three of them had fondled and kissed King Dick and greeted me approvingly, they gave us the news. The horses and troopers were to go to Hadji ben Idriss's camel farm for a week's rest, and there they would find fifteen more troopers who had been persuaded to join King Dick's troop. Ibrahim Bishari had invested in Wadai ivory for King Dick, ivory that would sell in Bengazi at a profit of fifty per cent. after all expenses were deducted.

They led us into the town, with its winding narrow streets paved with hard-packed sand, and escorted us to the house the town had set apart for King Dick when he first came to Jalo—a squatty building that was a labyrinth of passages, courts, and small rooms.

I never knew such hospitable people. They held our hands, patting them affectionately. " Be at home, by God ! " Hadji ben Idriss said. " I tell you I will return, we will all return. I will tell my wives ; and later, we will have a suckling camel boiled in sour milk, a dish worthy of Paradise as they cook it—a feast, by God, with date wine ! "

King Dick's wives—whom I never truly saw, since they were always veiled in my presence—brought us water for washing and snowy white burnooses to replace our travel-stained grey ones. The oldest wife, as near as I could tell, was fat and black, and from the wrinkles at the corners of her eyes I gathered that it was she whom I heard emitting fond and infectious squawks of laughter from the inner reaches of the house. The other two wives, in their voluminous trousers and wrappings, were so much alike that I could never tell them apart—which amazed King Dick, who insisted they smelled different, though to me the two of them had exactly the same sweetly oily odour. They waited on us hand and foot—a pleasant experience after my unending labour in Murad Rais's garden.

By the time we were washed and dressed, our three friends returned with servants bearing gifts—baskets of dates, a skinful of clarified butter, a bowl of camel's milk, two white hens, a live horned sheep, a skin of date wine, and baskets of bread, eggs, tea, and sugar slabs.

That was the beginning of a week of fadhling and feasting with a score and more of wealthy Jalo sheiks and merchants. King Dick, on the advice of Eugene Leitensdorfer—who had, of course, consulted with Lydia before advising King Dick—had spread the word in Jalo that I myself was an ekhwan in Afghanistan, a teacher of law and a great traveller, who had travelled even to America to inquire into universities, since in all likelihood Hamet, when he should regain his rightful position as Bashaw, would found a university in Tripoli like the ancient great Arab universities at Cordova, Cairo, Bagdad, and Granada, and would make me one of the chief ekhwans.

So while the sheiks and ekhwans fadhled and inquired and gabbled and drank gallons of our tea, mint-scented and strong enough to tan leather, I learned about Arabs—learned, too, to have a profound respect and affection for them, and to understand Arab customs.

Jalo, I learned, is the home of the Majabra tribe of Bedouins, the merchant princes of Libya whose ancestors for centuries have managed caravans almost like sea captains, altering their courses in mid-desert when they learn of unexpected market conditions.

I learned that Arabs might look idle, but weren't. Hadji ben Idriss, for example, seemed content to do nothing but fadhl and drink little cups of mint-scented tea, but actually he was as busy as he was rich. He controlled a matter of ten thousand date trees, which produced rosily golden dates, seedless and juicy, celebrated in Arab song and story for hundreds of years and in demand all along the North African coast. Among his palm groves he had gardens in which he raised fruit and vegetables of all sorts. He had agents and correspondents in a score of cities and oases, and was constantly dispatching couriers to them by horseback and camelback. He was also inordinately proud of the horses, camels, and sheep he raised. The camels were meharis, pale slender-legged creatures, unlike the slow dark-brown pack-camels or jemels, and his horses were thin-headed Arabians with flowing tails that swept the ground—unbelievably swift, and as nearly tireless as anything on four legs can be.

Our visitors had heard that Hamet was to be helped by America, and they wanted to know about this America. Was it as large as Tripoli? They wagged their heads, as at a fairy tale, on being told that it was as large as Egypt, Tripoli, Tunis, Algiers, and Morocco put together, if not larger ; that it was a green country, everywhere green without sand, with houses standing thick along narrow roads, as if the road from Jalo to Tripoli, instead of being unmarked desert, should be a narrow strip edged on both sides with unending fields and trees and wooden houses.

They couldn't understand why houses should be made of wood when any man could scrape together the dirt to make bricks. Nor could they understand why people in America should eat with spoons and forks from small dishes, instead of dipping their hands into a common bowl. It struck them as an idiotic custom, since the spoons and forks, being indestructible, must have entered thousands, thousands, thousands of mouths, perhaps the mouths of eaters of unclean things ! It was better, they said, much better, for all to eat from one bowl with their right hands, as Arabs did. One's hand is one's own hand, they said : a man knows where it has been ; but a fork or a spoon, by the very God, they said, who knows where it has been !

They talked politics endlessly. It was a great affair, they said, enormous, deep, wide, pleasing, by the very God, that Americans were coming to put Hamet back in power in Tripoli ! Under Joseph Kara-manli there were intriguers everywhere, by God, and tax-collectors had to be employed to collect money to pay the intriguers. Intriguers were bad because they had no love for a quiet life ; they wished to be important and wage war, and war increased taxes and raised prices and closed caravan routes and tempted men to be robbers. That was what came of heavy taxes, by God : men stole, stole, stole !

What they wanted to know, was the custom of Americans in regard to keeping their word. If they promised help to Hamet, would they do as they promised ? Among the English, it seemed to be the custom not to keep promises to Arabs, which was wrong. " By God, by the very God, wrong, wrong, wrong ! " exclaimed Ibrahim Bishari.

I told them they needn't worry about that. Joseph Karamanli had insulted America and declared war on her, which was something that Americans could never forgive. Their country's honour was at stake, and because of this they had promised to help Hamet, so they couldn't possibly go back on their word.

Late that night, however, the French Spoliation Claims crawled unbidden from a corner of my brain ; and I perspired, lying there in the dark, at the memory of how Benjamin Franklin had promised American aid to France in return for France's help, how he had signed a treaty guaranteeing that the aid would be forthcoming when needed, and how America had then refused to carry out its part of the agreement. I was glad my Arab friends didn't know about that treaty—I even wished that I had never heard of it myself.

CHAPTER LIII

MESSAGES from Lydia came to us at two-week intervals, as regularly, almost, as the packet boats I used to watch on the Schuylkill when I worked in Bartram's Gardens. Her letters were filled with small things as well as great : an American ketch loaded with explosives and commanded by some of Preble's best men had been sailed into Tripoli harbour in the dead of night, evidently with the idea of setting fire to all the Tripolitan gunboats, and the ketch had exploded prematurely, killing every man aboard her . . . Autumn rains and autumn gales had put an end to Preble's blockade of Tripoli . . . The Bashaw had moved back to the Castle from his country villa . . . The price of seedless fresh dates was rising and they were hard to get, while vegetables cost twice what they had last year, because of the war . . . Some of the American prisoners had turned Moslem to escape being beaten . . . She had persuaded Hamet's wife to allow a story-teller to come to the Castle twice a week and tell stories from the *Thousand and One Nights* to her three pupils, so that they could turn them into English ; but all the women in the Castle had insisted on listening, and the story-teller was obliged to sit inside a sort of tent erected within the room, so that he wouldn't see the women's faces . . . Jewish women every Saturday baked beans exactly as baked in Boston, except for using olive oil in place of pork, and had done so for countless centuries, so that she wondered if baked beans hadn't been borrowed from the Jews by Boston sea captains during their Mediterranean travels . . . Joseph Karamanli's eldest son had married his cousin, aged twelve . . . The French consul in Tripoli hated Americans, and was doing everything he could to fill the American naval officers with misininformation . . . The new American Commodore, Samuel Barron, had arrived in the Mediterranean and would make his headquarters in Malta during the winter. . . .

After the first week in Jalo we had gone to drilling each day, making

long rides into the desert, and adding to our troop whenever and wherever
we could ; and at the end of long days in the saddle, the sweetness that
shone out from every line of Lydia's messages was better than food and
drink.

Sometimes (she wrote once) I hear news that brings you suddenly
into my mind, and then I'm afraid my face may reveal that you're not
dead at all. For instance, I have just learned from one of Bashaw's
wives what happened to the French army that went to Haiti. Toussaint and all the Negro leaders surrendered to the French finally ; but,
because the blacks had fought the French and delayed them and tired
them out, the French caught yellow fever, and forty thousand of them
died of it, including Leclerc himself. Then the English fleet captured
what was left of the French army in Haiti, and the blacks got the
island back. Dessalines made himself Emperor. Oh, Albion : hearing
all this news just wrung my heart ; it brought back Haiti so poignantly
that I must have looked like a ghost ! I recalled how you'd fought
Lear ; and couldn't help thinking what Dessalines might have done to
us if we hadn't been able to get away from Cap François. Truly, our
lot might have been far worse !

King Dick's genius for making money stood us in good stead. Every
caravan that left Jalo carried a venture financed by him, and so profitable
were those ventures that the proceeds supported our entire troop and
kept it well supplied with barley meal, sheep, dates, rice, flour and
ammunition.

We bought them sabres, sabre-files for keeping the sabres sharp,
nine-inch daggers, hammers for hitting enemies between the shoulder
blades, forage nets, wooden water-bottles, fishlines for tying up prisoners,
saddlebags, coils of rope. King Dick had a sabre made for himself—an
enormous one, as long as his Haitian cocomacaque. He handled it as
dexterously as he had handled his cocomacaque, and with it he gave the
troop daily object lessons in the use of the sabre, drilling them in the use
of the point as well as in hacking and slashing. He drilled them, too, in
swinging wounded men up on to their saddles : in leaning over, while
galloping, to snatch up objects dropped by front-rank men.

Not until early January did two express messengers ride in from Cairo
with a message from Leitensdorfer saying that the Great Plan was
actually under way. When we had read the message, King Dick assembled
the troop and told them they had been drilled and trained in order to help
Hamet back to Tripoli, and that when Tripoli was captured they would
receive food and clothes and money—enough money to let each of them
buy two camels and start trading with Timbuktu. From the way they
howled and rolled their eyes, the news was warmly to their liking ; and
soon thereafter horsemen drifted in to Jalo from distant desert villages,
asking to be allowed to ride with us.

Leitensdorfer's letter, dated late in December, came from Cairo.

General Eaton arrived here two weeks ago. Hamet is at Fayoum, supporting himself by fighting in a small war. I put myself at General Eaton's disposal, and he loaned me fifty dollars and made me a colonel, a rank I once held in the Austrain army. Since I speak nearly all languages except Russian and one or two others, he has made me his adjutant. He has told me everything and shown me everything. The American President and chief men have promised him forty thousand dollars to destroy Joseph Karamanli and put Hamet back on the throne. Hamet will be in command of the Arabs, and Eaton will be his field general, in command of all branches. Thus Eaton will make it possible for Hamet to employ a thousand men, perhaps, and caravans to supply them. Also the Americans will give Hamet a thousand stand of arms, ammunition for them, and supplies as well.

American ships will probably carry Eaton and Hamet and Hamet's official family to Derna, and put everyone ashore there, with marines from the American ships, probably a hundred. Then we will go over-land to Bengazi and Tripoli, accompanied by artillery, so that the two places can be hammered from sea and from the land at the same time. This is a great project, my dear friends, and this General Eaton a great man ; a man of understanding and vision, who surmounts every obstacle. His ingenuity and energy are prodigious !

I was confident long ago that his plan, once put in operation, could not fail. Now success is assured ! When we shall be able to start I am not sure. The details of the expedition are many and take time. Be in readiness ; and when I give the word, come to meet us. The first place we shall need your help is Derna. Bring as many men as you can, assuring them that everything they need will be supplied—food for all, ammunition, everything. The general will pay them ; and the rewards, once we have captured Bengazi and Tripoli, and Hamet sits again upon the throne, will be great.

Black Arabs love to play games, and we made something of a game out of the duties at which such a troop as ours could be most useful. We wanted them expert at night patrols—which Arabs don't find pleasing—and at getting intelligence. So we sent small patrols into the desert with instructions to do certain things ; then sent other patrols to steal up on the first and report what they were doing, how they were acting, where they were heading, what their equipment was. We blind-folded a trooper ; then had others try to stalk and touch him without being heard. If one was heard, the blindfolded man clapped his hands and the approacher was theoretically dead. Successful touchers received extra rice rations ; and the troopers wagered heavily on their touching abilities. We took away their muskets and replaced them with pistols—two big ones to each man, each pistol holding nine buckshot—and taught them how to fight with knives, at night and on foot—a manner of fighting most distasteful to white Arabs, but a highly amusing sport to our black Arabs. From time to time King Dick would perform sleight-of-hand tricks for all the troopers ; then press them to tell in detail what he had done. This, he explained to them, was the essence of war : to learn what the enemy was doing and report it, so that he could be forestalled ; to pretend to do something, but in reality do something else.

In the beginning they were baffled by the tricks ; overcome with merriment at the mysterious way he made coins disappear before their eyes, or seemed to extract an egg from a trooper's ear. They no more knew, in the beginning, how such things were done than they knew how the sun rises. Then they learned that King Dick's hands were quicker than their own eyes, and were ashamed. This taught them how to open their eyes and really see what they were looking at.

He lectured them constantly : how the chief duty of cavalry is to act as gatherers of information ; the importance of finding the enemy, and reporting his movements with complete accuracy ; how they must always be ready to fall suddenly on an enemy and throw him into confusion ; how they must never reveal their own intentions to anyone—unless they want to be wounded or killed, in either of which cases they would be useless as cavalry.

They took to it as a duck takes to water, the skirling of the troop's bagpiper (for the black Arabs of Jalo have a Scot's love for that doleful instrument) actually became cheerful as he piped the column to drill each morning.

In the midst of this happy activity, one of our Tripoli couriers came in with a letter from Lydia that filled me with a vague disquiet.

I have learned something that I don't understand ; and since I don't understand it I feel that perhaps I shouldn't mention it. Yet it's information, and any information may prove to be valuable.

I told you long ago that Tobias Lear was our Consul General in Algiers. I cannot tell you why the change has been made, or who is responsible for it, but Lear has a new position—that of Political Commissioner with the Mediterranean Fleet, and he has moved his headquarters to Malta. Of course I know that Eaton has the title of United States Navy Agent in the Mediterranean, but I have no way of finding out whether Eaton holds a higher rank than Lear, or whether Lear's is higher than Eaton's, or whether both of them are supposed to be under Commodore Barron.

" Lear ! " I said to myself. " My God, Lear again ! "

As I put down her letter with a shaking hand, King Dick came in. He looked at me. " Anything wrong, Albion ? " he asked. " Who you talking to ? That voice sounded funny."

"I don't know," I said. "It's probably nothing. Just Tobias Lear again—Lydia says he's in Malta. He's been made some kind of commissioner in the Mediterranean. Do you suppose he could possibly have a finger in this war? What else would a 'commissioner' have to do in the Mediterranean? I don't like it!"

King Dick sat down on the raised, carpeted platform on which I slept and stared at me out of round white eyes. "Hoy!" he said faintly. "Colonel Lear! Mister White-lace Colonel Lear! What he understand about war?"

"Nothing," I said. "Not a damned thing!"

King Dick shook his head. "If ships pound Joseph Karamanli from sea, and Eaton and Hamet and us pound him from land, they no room for white-lace colonels!"

"There's always room for the Lears of this world," I said. "They're always pushing their way into honest men's affairs and making a mess of 'em! You can't get rid of the Lears!"

"What else she say about him?" King Dick asked.

"Nothing," I said. "She doesn't know, but she's worried. Not that she says so, but I can tell. She keeps saying she doesn't understand, but she understands exactly what I do! She understands Lear's a trouble-maker. She understands he can't think the same way as we do about anything on God's earth. Whatever we think, he thinks different, about people and everything else. Why, he was even jealous of Washington! Think of it! Tobias Lear thought he deserved to be as big a man as Washington! That meant he hated Washington in his heart. I'll bet he'd love Bainbridge and hate Preble!"

"No need to get excited yet," King Dick reminded me.

"I don't see it that way," I said. "Considering the things he's tried to do to me in the past, out of either spite or wrongheadedness, I can't bear to see him having anything at all to do with my affairs—and this war with Tripoli is as much my affair as it is anyone's!"

Later, when I'd finished and re-read Lydia's letter, with all its intimacies and glowing warmth, I knew that I had better things to think about than Tobias Lear, whom in all likelihood I'd never see again. He might, I realised, have been sent from Algiers to Malta to investigate some of the consuls who represented the United States so shamefully.

Yet I couldn't get him out of my head. Even when I was numb, physically and mentally, from hours in the saddle, Tobias Lear's benignant, pale, over-beautiful face would rise up in my mind, and I'd remember how he'd taken me to task at Christophe's palace: how he'd used all his powers of persuasion to make Christophe give up without a fight: how he'd insisted that anything was preferable to war—even slavery. At moments it occurred to me that my long and lonely days and nights in Murad Rais's garden, my longing for Lydia, my bitter resentment of the injustices we'd suffered from Joseph Karamanli, Murad Rais, and George Lee—that all these might have made me a little "hipped," as New Englanders say, on the subject of Tobias Lear. I wanted to get him off my mind, but I couldn't do it.

I wrote Leitensdorfer that we had raised a troop of cavalry and were waiting for further word from him ; and two of our Jalo men took the message to Cairo. In the letter I asked what he knew about Tobias Lear, what Lear was doing in Malta, whether he was favourably disposed towards Eaton's expedition or had anything to do with it. To Lydia I said nothing about Lear. I knew she'd tell me whatever she learned, and I didn't want to worry her unnecessarily.

The word we had from Leitensdorfer, written late in February, set us to drilling even harder, as well as to rounding up supplies, and planning day and night. The Egyptian Government, he wrote, had refused to let Hamet go aboard an American ship in order to sail to Derna : consequently Hamet had raised an army of Arabs, an army that was already assembling outside of Alexandria. Eaton and Hamet would march from Alexandria to Derna.

I asked the general about Lear (he wrote). This Lear is not important. He is without influence or authority. He went to Malta because that was headquarters for the Mediterranean squadron. There is no reason to be disturbed over him because he has no choice but to be in accord with Barron and Preble, who have given their approval to the general's plan. He has nothing to do whatever with the expedition, as he is no soldier : merely a hanger-on in Washington who has come to the Mediterranean to satisfy his desire to travel, or to seem important, like so many of these American consuls, or perhaps to become rich.

Unsatisfactory Information . . . Not only was it indefinite : I didn't believe it. But it cheered me a little—enough to let me say " To hell with Tobias Lear " ; not enough, though, to banish the crawling distaste for him that hid in the corners of my brain, flowering like a sea-anemone at intervals, only to slip back into obscurity when I tried to put my finger on it.

In spite of King Dick's advice to me not to get excited over Lear, he too must have had Lear on his mind. I often caught him looking at me worriedly on the long march we took each day while we waited for final word from Leitensdorfer. But while I only worried, he acted, though characteristically he said nothing until he'd done it.

When he did tell me, I felt as if a tremendous dark load had been lifted from my shoulders.

" Look, Albion," he said, " you know these Jalo merchants very smart men : very good at making money with caravans."

" We've got good reason to know it, both of us," I replied.

" Yarse," King Dick went on thoughtfully, " and I had a talk with those two good friends of ours this morning. ' Wherever we send a caravan,' I tell them, ' Kufra, Timbuktu, Siwa, Giarabub, Jaghbub, Cairo, always they make money.'

" And they say, ' Yes, all Majabra merchants make money, same as their papas and grandpapas made it.'

" So I ask them why wouldn't it be good to send one to Tripoli and make money there ?

" They say, No, might be too many Tuaregs on the road, looking for things to pick up before Hamet get back in power. They'll keep on trading with Kufra till things quiet down, they say.

" So I say my friend has a friend in Tripoli, and he's worried ; his friend in Tripoli has sent word to my friend, prices of things to eat and skinless dates and salt have gone up, way way up, in Tripoli because Joseph Karamanli keep making war. I say this friend of my friend is always right. So if they'll send a caravan to Tripoli, my friend and I will invest fifty camel-loads in the venture. I say I can see this a good time to do it, because Hamet will march to Tripoli with the Americans, and when he gets there he will need supplies, and the Americans will give him money to pay for them.

" They say, No, they think they continue to trade with Kufra.

" And I say, ' Would you trade with Tripoli if it make my friend easier in mind, and if he and I agree to send twenty of our black Arabs with caravan as a guard ? '

" And they think about it, and drink tea, and smoke pipes. And Bishari say, ' By God, by my God, by the very God, those words make music, like the song of a nightingale in a garden.' And he say to Hadji ben Idriss, ' If we could camp safely, and be undisturbed by an army helping itself to what it needed, the profits would be twice as large as at Bengazi, because during a war somebody always has more money than he knows what to do with.'

" And I say, ' See here : here is map drawn by that friend of Hamlin Bey's—shows Marabout's village outside walls of Tripoli, where ten caravans could camp and be safe for ever.'

" So they drink more tea and smoke more pipes and look sideways at each other, and they'll do it. They say they'll do it, and so they will ! That make you feel good, Hamlin Bey ? "

It did indeed make me feel good ; and the more I thought about it, the better I felt. If all went well with Eaton and Hamet, that caravan at the Marabout's Tomb would mean supplies ready to hand. It would mean twenty of our own black Arabs, fresh and rested, waiting for us at Tripoli—a great relief for men who have made a long, hard journey from Derna.

All my newly acquired Arab philosophy failed me towards the end of March ; for while we were impatiently awaiting word from Leitensdorfer, a message arrived from Lydia that turned our impatience into apprehension. Neither King Dick nor I could calm ourselves, as Arabs are supposed to do, by muttering " Inshallah ! " or numbingly repeating " God will show the way ! "—and we freely admitted to each other that we were worried lest Eaton and Hamet might be too late.

Lydia's letter, as usual, was in two parts : a purely informative part, and an intimate, personal part, tender and consoling.

Joseph Karamanli (the letter began) has had word that Eaton and Hamet are preparing to march against him, and he is both furious and alarmed. His alarm is increased because there are signs of disloyalty in many parts of the city and among the tribes. He sent his son-in-law into the desert to raise an army of tribesmen to defend the city, but with no success.

Joseph himself has succeeded in raising an army to march on Derna to defend that place in case Eaton and Hamet attack it, but he is so fearful lest his leaders go over to Hamet that he has seized their wives and children, whom he is holding as hostages.

This army will march soon. Though I cannot be sure exactly when, I think it will leave next week, going by way of Misurata and Bengazi, at which places it will renew its supplies. It is under the supreme command of Hassan Bey ; the cavalry is led by Hadji Ismail. There are five hundred cavalry from here ; one hundred more will join at Misurata under the Bey of Misurata ; one hundred more at Bengazi under the Bey of Bengazi. If the army reaches Derna in time, it will be increased by one hundred more cavalry under the Bey of Derna.

In addition to the cavalry, there will be three hundred and sixty mounted tribesmen, and one thousand unmounted tribesmen.

There will be four hundred camels in the caravan. The supplies for the caravan are being loaded by the American prisoners and Jews.

The Spanish and the French consuls are advising Joseph, and doing everything they can to help him outwit Eaton and Hamet. The Spanish consul has given him three hundred muskets.

I hope—oh, how I hope—that nothing will prevent Eaton and Hamet from reaching Derna before this army of Joseph's !

Both of us were, as the saying goes, on tenterhooks as we waited for that final word from Leitensdorfer. Our days were nightmares of hurrying and scurrying—of tarring, inspecting, and filling water-skins, cutting and stitching extra burnooses, mending saddles and camel-bags, making extra shoes, assembling piles of goods and provisions, attending farewell feasts, writing final letters. If we'd dared, we would have started for Derna without hearing from Leitensdorfer ; but we didn't dare for fear Eaton and Hamet would change their plans again : for fear his messenger might miss us.

Not until mid-April did we get the word that made King Dick's wives burst into lugubrious howls, and set us pelting off on the road to Derna. It was in a note from Leitensdorfer, written from the coast, five days north of Siwa.

Hurry to Derna. We will be in vicinity of Bomba. Bring us accurate report on position of Joseph's army.

CHAPTER LIV

We saw Derna first from the top of the escarpment that rises abruptly from the sea all along the coast of Cyrenaica. Behind Derna there are two parallel ranges of barren hills—mountains in appearance to men who have long been in the desert ; and the range nearer the sea drops sharply to form the face of the escarpment : a cliff of abrupt descents, of polished rocks, slippery as glass to a horse's hoofs. The cliff is scored by deep clefts—wadis—worn by the torrents of centuries of rainy seasons.

Derna, to me, seemed a sort of miracle, a piece of Paradise. It was a fan-shaped oasis thrust out into the Mediterranean, green with meadows and cultivated fields, a shining fan of emerald, sapphire blue, and gold, with a little white town spiked to the midst of it by minarets—a town that had streets and sidewalks and bright-green growing things along the roadside, and grape vines creeping over the walls of white houses and often draped across whole streets. There was a market-place with thick trees, and shops with people in them, and gardens and palm groves and baths. Everything was on a small scale, packed into an area not much larger than Bartram's Gardens, but for that very reason all the lovelier. It was as though a fragment of the Garden of Eden had slid out into the sea from under the desert, and left the desert snarling and growling at its loss, but never able to snatch back to its harsh breast this beautiful escaped piece of fertility.

The secret of Derna was water—the freshest, purest, most abundant water in all Cyrenaica. It came from springs far up in the Green Mountains and flowed down the Wadi Derna, a deep ravine that slashes through the escarpment and the fan-shaped town right down to the sea. Derna sits at the mouth of the Wadi, and because of all this water there are fountains everywhere : fountains that trickle and tinkle day and night, so that everyone can have as much water as he likes instead of just a daily quart of salty, muddy liquid. That in itself was sufficient to make Derna seem like Paradise to an Arab.

We found no army camped outside the city, as there would have been if Joseph Karamanli's cavalry, troops, and caravan had arrived ; so we went to work at once to ascertain where they were—no easy task, since there are three caravan routes from Bengazi to Derna, and Joseph's army might be using any one of the three. All of them must therefore be reconnoitered.

So the whole troop gathered in a tight circle around Abdul Rahim and Moraja as they described to us the Bengazi-Derna routes. One—the route along the coast—required the crossing of many wadis, or the following of indentations wearying to men, horses, and camels alike, as well as the constant climbing to and descending from the escarpment. This route, they said, needn't be considered, for it would be followed only by express riders travelling light on fast horses. The second and longest route went straight southward from Derna, as if starting back to Jalo ; then bore westward to Bengazi. The third, lying between the coast road and the extreme inland road, divided into three tracks half-way to Bengazi. It would therefore be necessary to send four patrols to the westward. They talked and talked and talked about those four roads, naming every well, every wadi, every Marabout's tomb, every mountain, every cross-path to Tolmita, Merj, Cyrene, Marsa Susa. Here, they said, are Roman baths ; here, cisterns ; here, Arab cemeteries. They knew where there would be gardens, where large cedars in a valley, or barren olive trees ; where there was a spring, a Roman fort beside a reservoir, remains of ancient vine terraces ; where herds of numerous goats would be found feeding ; where there were fruit trees and good pasture.

It was hard to believe that these men were talking about Africa and the desert, for they mentioned gardens of maize and vines, and large five-acre gardens with fig, almond, and apple trees ; spoke of valley after valley where there would be flocks of sheep, cattle, and camels ; of large areas of low forest ; of heavily turfed hills.

Without having these things set down clearly on a map, I myself could no more have remembered them than I could have recalled a random page out of Hariri. But every one of these black cavalrymen nodded his head and moved his lips and made marks with his forefinger on the palm of his hand, and seemed to drop every word he heard into a different slot in his brain, to be pulled out and used when the need arose. And when Abdul Rahim designated the four patrols who were to go to the westward, they left us with all the assurance of a Portland man setting out from his home to go to the custom-house.

The getting of information as to the whereabouts of Eaton and Hamet was easier ; for there was only one road, the Jalo men agreed, that Eaton and Hamet could take to Derna : the coast road through Sollum and Bomba.

While we awaited the return of our patrols, King Dick and I, two innocent-appearing travellers, made our way down off the escarpment, on to the coast road, and to the main gate of the city. We found it well guarded ; but when the captain of the guard learned that we were from Jalo with a message to Hadji ben Idriss's Derna agent, he sent off a messenger readily enough ; and in half an hour the agent, Sidi Abzell—a foppish gentleman with scented whiskers, a striped silk burnoose, and a flower behind his ear—came out accompanied by three servants loaded down with a roast turkey, a kettle of rice, a skin of date wine, and a teapot.

So we sat down in the shadow of that monstrous great escarpment, on the edge of the deep gash in the green meadow above Derna, that steep-walled ravine into and out of which anyone entering the main part of the town would have to clamber, and looked down contemplatively upon the feathery palms, minarets, and flat roofs of that desired city while we stuffed ourselves with turkey, date wine, and tea.

We first captured Sidi Abzell's interest with talk about the large amount of ivory and feathers that Hadji ben Idriss and Ibrahim Bishari had received from Kufra, thus leading him to think that our sole concern was to find out from him whether it would be more advisable for Hadji ben Idriss to send a caravan to Derna or to Bengazi.

Sidi Abzell swore by the very God that if all this damnable talk of war, and running to and fro of messengers, and threats of violence by sea and by land could be over, he would guarantee a larger profit in Derna than could be guaranteed in Bengazi. He would swear it, by God, and the devil take this Joseph Karamanli and his rotten tax-gatherers, sucking the blood of honest men and reducing their profits to such a point that a man might as well cut his throat as to try to make a profit, since, when one does make a profit, by God, by my God, by the very God, the profit is taken from him by Joseph Karamanli, and he is no better off than he was before. Indeed he is worse off, because he may have invested a little of his profit before discovering that it is no profit—bought himself a slave perhaps ; and as a result he has even less than he started with.

" What do they say in the town ? " we asked Sidi Abzell. " Will Hamet return, do they think ? "

He stroked his scented beard. " God knows," he said. " The city is strong ! Strong, strong, strong ! "

King Dick said it didn't look strong to him : if he stood yonder—and he pointed to the crest of the dark escarpment behind us—he could toss cannon-balls into any part of Derna he wanted to take.

Sidi Abzell smiled. " Cannon-balls ! But to have cannon-balls you must have cannon, and nobody can drag cannon across the desert ! It is here in Derna that there are cannon—oh, many ! In the water battery " —he pointed to a brick-walled fort on the opposite side of the city, close to the water's edge—" there are eight guns ! Oh, big, by the very God ! Then at the corner of the city, where the road comes in from the south, the walls of the buildings are solid, like a fort, with gun-slits in them—a difficult place."

We looked politely amazed ; but I knew as well as King Dick what havoc the batteries of twenty-four pounders in two or three American vessels would wreak on that fort of mud-bricks and on those mud-walled houses, loop-holed though they were.

" How many in the city will fight ? " King Dick asked.

Sidi Abzell shrugged. " If the people could be sure Hamet would pay them for *not* fighting, nobody would fight except the Bey."

He leaned forward and spoke violently. " Nobody in this city except those who govern it, and those who fire guns and receive money for so doing, has any desire to see this place remain under the rule of Joseph Karamanli ! All the rest want Hamet back. All, all, all ! We know him ! He was a good governor, and kind. But if any army of Joseph Bashaw gets into this city, every man in it will be robbed. Our food supplies will be seized. All the crops will be harvested by Joseph's soldiers ; all the flocks and herds you see on these meadows will be seized. Yes, by God, all ! But Hamet, if he should get here first—he would let nothing be touched ! Nothing, nothing, nothing ! You tell Hadji ben Idriss that if Hamet takes this city and becomes Bashaw of Tripoli once more I can obtain prices for Hadji ben Idriss that will be the talk of Jalo—yes, and of Siwa, Kufra, and Giarabub ! "

Encamped on the top of the escarpment, we impatiently waited for reports from the patrols.

Our eastward patrol were back in a day's time with word that they'd sighted Eaton's army from the cedar forest east of Derna, marching rapidly through the cultivated fields near Cape Razatin, cavalry in front, about two hundred, then foot soldiers, then a supply caravan of more than a hundred camels. At the rate they were going, the patrol leader said, they would reach Derna in four days.

If we had tried to sit still while waiting the return of the westward patrols, I think we'd have burst. We scoured the ragged, barren valley between the two ranges of hills until we knew every rock on it, every depression, every zig-zag path down the face of the escarpment, every twist of the great wadi that carried the water of Derna's sparkling springs into the town ; made ourselves familiar, too, with the smaller wadis, until we could have found our way down to Derna on the darkest night.

When an express rider at last came galloping in from the west, we learned that Joseph Karamanli's army had been sighted one day's march out from Bengazi, moving slowly along the middle road ; that it was slow, with two thousand men and a caravan of four hundred slow camels ; and that at the rate at which it was marching it would be seven days in reaching Derna—unless it cut loose from its camels. If it did this and rode at night, it could conceivably arrive in Derna before Eaton got there.

" They won't leave their food and they won't ride by night," King Dick predicted. " Things not that important to Arabs."

But he was climbing into the saddle as he said it. We had to get to Eaton and Hamet, and quickly, in order to let them know they must devise a way to reach Derna in a hurry if they didn't want to fight their way through a force too large for comfort. So, leaving a squad camped above Derna to intercept the patrols who hadn't yet returned, we set off as fast as we could go towards Hamet and Eaton.

East of Derna there's an expanse of mountainous ground, covered with pasture lands and herbage of all sorts growing among large and beautiful red cedars ; and as we came out of the cedar growth on to the cultivated fields beyond, we saw Eaton's army moving towards us up the slope. It was late afternoon of a bright windy day, and the throng approaching us looked more like a helter-skelter caravan than an army.

We lined up our troop in a double rank, and a mighty impressive troop it looked to be, all in grey with black veils, and as level-fronted as though the horses stood with their breasts against an invisible barrier.

That army of Eaton's and Hamet's must have been a mile long, for behind the few blue-clad men on horseback who rode at the head of the line there were two small companies of men in uniforms I didn't recognise, led by a handsome mounted officer with a hooded falcon on his wrist and a long-haired, top-knotted greyhound loping along beside him, almost under his horse's belly. Behind the two companies marched the main body of the army : two sprawling troops of Arab cavalry ; then a mass of foot soldiers, all desert tribesmen with guns as long as pitchforks, in groups that put me in mind of shipworkers leaving the shipyards at the end of a day's work ; then scores on scores of lumbering loaded camels ; and behind all these a long straggling tail of Bedouin men, women, children, dogs, donkeys.

When the foremost blue-clad riders were a pistol-shot away, King Dick nodded to Abdul Rahim, who spoke to Moraja, who let fly with that blue-heron's squawk of his. Our troop's sabres came out raspingly, flashed in a half-circle, and stopped rigid, slanted upward before all those black veils, a beautiful double hedge of steel. As King Dick and I sheathed our own sabres and rode out to meet the oncoming column, the double row of sabres came down against our men's right shoulders, as pretty as a picture.

One of the blue-clad men, accompanied by Leitensdorfer in baggy Arab pantaloons, burnoose, and headcloth, pulled his horse away from the head of the line and came over to us. He had a long, ruddy face, side-whiskers, pale-blue eyes, and—as we saw when he took off his plumed hat—one of the queerest heads I'd ever seen : just above his eyebrows there was a shelf, a recession of almost an inch, and from that shelf his forehead rose to thinning hair.

" These are the gentlemen, General," Leitensdorfer said, and to us he added, " General Eaton."

" Good ! " Eaton said, in a round voice like a preacher's or an actor's. " Colonel Leitensdorfer has kept me informed from time to time. A splendid body of men ! Ah—say a word to the Bashaw, will you, Colonel ? "

Leitensdorfer winked at us delightedly, wheeled his horse, and went

M

scuttling off in Hamet's direction. The blue-clad men, eyeing us curiously, came plodding on. Behind the leaders, among whom was an American lieutenant of marines, were six American marines, headed by a marine sergeant. There was something strange about them, something that eluded me at first, though later I realised that the jackets of all of them lacked buttons.

"God help any man who has to deal with these sons of Sapphira," Eaton said, half-humorously and half-bitterly. "We'll delay formalities till we're camped. Did you find out anything?"

"Yes, sir," I said. "We sent patrols to the westward, and Joseph Karamanli's army's now a couple of days this side of Bengazi : two thousand men."

"I've kept telling 'em," Eaton said. "You can't hurry 'em! I knew damned well we'd have trouble ; but no, by God! At the drop of a hat they'd knock off five days to buy dates ; then talk about going home because Joseph's army's too close!"

"It's moving slowly," I told him. "Our men know their business, and they don't think it can reach Derna for another seven days."

"But it might get there sooner?"

"Yes, sir," I said ; "it could if it made a dash. It might even get there ahead of you if it made a dash."

"It won't," King Dick said.

Eaton's expression was sour. "What these people need," he said, "is a dose of turpentine on their tails! Of all the backers and fillers, of all the yes-ers and no-ers, of all the Oh Gods and By Gods, of all the——"

He broke off as an Arab charged full tilt at us and at the last moment reined his dapple-grey stallion back on its haunches. He was brilliantly handsome. Over his white burnoose he wore a short blue cloak, and his headcloth was blue, bound by a gold cord. His face, so softly rounded that it was saved from prettiness only by a little U-shaped beard that outlined his chin, bore a worried frown.

Eaton saluted him, and said to us, "My friends, this is Hamet Karamanli, rightful Bashaw of Tripoli." To Hamet he said, "Your Highness"—and he spoke in Arabic—"these friends of ours came to Derna from Jalo. They sent out patrols towards Bengazi and sighted Joseph Karamanli's army."

"On which road?" Hamet asked quickly. "How many?"

"Merj road," King Dick answered. "Two thousand men and four hundred camels. If they press ahead without camels, just cavalry alone, then five hundred."

Eaton wagged his finger at Hamet. "There's no ' if ' about it! If they know enough to do it, they can put five hundred cavalrymen in front of Derna in three days! Tell your sheiks, and tell 'em nothing else! If they think we have seven days' leeway, there'll be talk and more talk, and God knows what'll happen! We've got to get to Derna before they get there. That means we have just three days to reach Derna!

They'll whine and they'll squirm and they'll haggle, but there's only one answer : we've got to be in Derna in three days."

Hamet bowed to Eaton, somehow contriving to include the two of us in his bow. " You are my friend and protector," he told Eaton. " You know what they'll say. They'll say there is no way of knowing whether the ships will be there to help us. They'll say there's no way of knowing whether they'll be paid. They'll say——"

" Oh, my God," Eaton cried, " I'm sick of their yap ! I won't listen to another damned word ! I won't even come to talk to 'em to-night ! It's *your* throne ! This is *your* town we've got to take ! We've come five hundred miles, and we're only five hours from our first goal ! If the bastards want to ride off into the desert, let 'em ride ! *I* say we've got to be in Derna in three days, with 'em or without 'em ! "

He turned abruptly to King Dick and me. " Get your men settled and come to my tent." To Leitensdorfer he added, " Stay with 'em and show 'em how we lay out the camp." Then he raked his horse with a spur and went galloping off towards the head of the column, with Hamet close behind him.

CHAPTER LV

WE WENT back with Leitensdorfer to stand at the right of our troop ; and as he named each detachment of the bedraggled army that slouched past us, our double line of troopers raised their sabres in salute. Behind the handful of American marines—six and a sergeant—were a company of forty swarthy men in long baggy trousers, all carrying muskets—Greek soldiers, Leitensdorfer said, who had been shipwrecked in Egypt and gone to soldiering for a living. Behind them were a company of thirty cannoneers without a cannon. The Greeks and the cannoneers did their best to look military when our sabres saluted them, but they made hard going of it—for which I couldn't blame them when Leitensdorfer told us that before they reached Bomba, a week earlier, they had been almost foodless for a month.

Behind the cannoneers were the headquarters troop and Hamet's attendants, nearly a hundred, all mounted ; then a troop of Arab cavalry led by two sheiks who glowered at us and made no move to return our salute—at which Leitensdorfer muttered curses under his breath in half a dozen languages. " Sons of whores ! " he called them. " Servants of Shaitan ! Husbands of one-eyed mules ! Eaters of dirt ! Wash-pots ! Wearers of the horns of he-goats ! Kissers of pigs ! " and other terms even less savoury. Behind the cavalry were Bedouin foot soldiers, a motley rabble that seemed to have no leader ; and far, far behind them stretched the surging and weaving heads of the camel train.

I was willing to stand there saluting until even the camels had passed, but Leitensdorfer protested that we must skirt around the column before darkness fell ; so we went back through the cedar grove and on the far side found Eaton's tent in a fertile valley near a little rivulet that trickled down through a barley field—a rivulet in which scores of men were already splashing.

Eaton had made himself comfortable in yellow Arab slippers, and was scribbling in a diary when we came in, using his saddle for a writing-desk. There was a rug on the ground, and his saddlebags, sword, rifle, and pistols were stacked in a corner. He motioned us to the rug, said, " I'll be with you in a minute—take off those veils so I can see what you look like," and went on writing after he had added to Leitensdorfer, " Keep an eye on that cook, Colonel, and make sure nobody steals the supper. I'm damned near starved."

Leitensdorfer hurried out through the rear of the tent, and I smelled the familiar smell of steaming lamb and barley meal.

When Eaton had finished with his diary, he came to sit cross-legged on the rug and stare at us defiantly with eyes as blue as an April sky. " I know Leitensdorfer's been in touch with you," he told us, " and I've seen some of your reports—good ones, too. I never saw the letters he wrote you and I don't know what he promised ; but I may as well tell you right now, gentlemen, much as I need that troop of yours, I'm not going to be able to do a great deal for you in the line of pay. In fact, I'm not going to be able to do anything—maybe not until we get to Tripoli—and I know enough about Arabs to be sure they'll do nothing unless they're paid for it."

" All of our men are desert guides, General," I said. " They trust us. We told them in the beginning they probably wouldn't get their money until they got to Tripoli."

" Good," Eaton said, " good ! These Egyptian bastards that I've got with me——" He closed his eyes, groaned, and shook his head. " Well, you'll probably see what I mean in the morning. Why, damn their thieving, lying, dodging souls to hell and Halifax ! "

Leitensdorfer came back into the tent. " They're at it already, General," he said. " They're all in Hamet's tent, howling as if they had hedgehogs up their tails."

" Let 'em howl, damn 'em ! " Eaton said. " I wish to God they'd get mad enough to cut each other's throats."

" What the matter with 'em ? " King Dick asked. " We don't have trouble with our Arabs."

" Oh, it isn't the men," Eaton said. " It's these blasted Egyptian Arab sheiks of theirs ! There isn't anything in Egypt that's worth a damn ! They're all the time howling for money. Money, money, money ! That's all they think of ! Every morning they howl for more money and threaten to go back home. They'll do it again to-morrow, by God—you wait and see ! Five hours from Derna they are now, by God, and they'll threaten to go home unless I pay 'em more ! You have to pay 'em off every day, like a lot of stove-wood cutters ! Why, damnation, Hamlin, this expedition has been on the road since March sixth. Forty-nine days, by God, and never a day that one of those two damned sheiks wasn't squalling about something, or threatening to go home, or starting to go home, by God! Actually starting! Steal, lie, kill, cut your throat as quick as a wink—why, damnation, there isn't anything I'd put beyond 'em, buggery or anything else!" He left off abruptly and spread his hands philosophically. "But why should I saddle you with my troubles! Most of them are over money, anyway. If we had the money we needed, we'd probably have less trouble—but my God, they won't let me have it!"

Suddenly he became irascible again, his face fiery red. "I've hardly been able to get one damned thing of what was promised to me, and you can't run an army on promises—not an Arab army! We were plumb out of money and supplies and everything else when we were only half-way to Bomba. I had to borrow every cent that my officers had in their pockets—every damned cent—to keep those Arabs quiet! Six hundred and seventy-three dollars we raked and scraped together for 'em, leaving us without a penny to buy food. I thought, by God, we'd starve! We spent two whole days on our hands and knees, scratching for grass and little sprouts of things to put in our bellies."

At this moment a servant with a towel over his arm came in through the back entrance of the tent, bearing a brass bowl of water. Like good Moslems, we washed our hands, after which the servant brought in a bowl of cous-cous decorated on top with gobbets of lamb, and we gathered round it, dipped into it with our right hands, and stuffed ourselves full, saying nothing, like any four hungry Arabs anywhere. When we had finished and the water-bowl had been passed again, the servant brought mint-scented tea and a water-pipe with a number of tubes running from it. The bowl of the pipe was full of something that looked like tobacco, but when the servant put a coal to it and Eaton sucked at one of the tubes, he groaned. "Damned if I know what they put in it," he said. "First it was half an ounce of tobacco to a pound of dried tea leaves; then they started adding dried camel dung to it; and unless I'm much mistaken, they're now using a good deal of goat-hair—from he-goats, too! I'd give five dollars for a good cigar, and fifty for a bottle of whisky!" He tossed each of us a mouthpiece. "My God, what a country! You know what the women put on their hair to make it glossy?"

"Camel urine," I said.

"Damned if they don't," Eaton said. "Camel piss! Oh, well . . ." Again he spread his hands in that characteristic gesture of false resignation—of pretended acceptance of this strange world in which he found himself. "I was mighty glad to have that news you sent about Tripoli," he went on. "Leitensdorfer told me all about it." At the expression on my face he made an impatient gesture. "Oh, don't worry! I understand perfectly the lady'd be in danger if it were known you got away from the bastard Joseph Karamanli! I haven't discussed it with anyone but Leitensdorfer, and I won't. Have you had anything new from her since you last wrote Leitensdorfer from Jalo ? "

" She sent us the make-up of their army," I said, " but our own information is more accurate. She had the names of the leaders, Hassan Bey and Hadji Ismail. Hassan Bey was in command, and Hadji Ismail was leading the cavalry. She said someone had been sent into the mountains to raise troops for the defence of the city, but hadn't been able to raise any. There are signs of disloyalty everywhere, she said—so many that Joseph Karamanli himself is worried sick. She sent me a map of Tripoli, too, that might come in handy." I took the map from my wallet and gave it to him.

" Ha," he said. " Good ! Just the thing ! Look at that road through the Jewish quarter ! When our ships attack, all we've got to do is to make a diversion at the Castle gate, then put our fieldpieces against the wall, blow a hole in it, and run right down that street ! Once the fleet goes into action, I can take Tripoli with a hundred men."

The orotund, confident voice turned bitter. " That's one of the troubles with these damned fools ! They've never seen one of our ships in action. They don't know what one of our ships can do to mud walls ! It'll be a different story, once we're safely inside Derna ! They'll *have* to give me some marines then, and proper supplies, and enough money to keep 'em paid and satisfied. There won't be any more of this damned starving ! My God, did you see those marines ? They cut all the buttons off their coats and traded 'em to Bedouin women for food. Wear 'em around their necks, the women do. Anyway, that'll be over when we get Derna. We'll get what we need ; and when we take Bengazi we'll be rich. That town's lousy with warehouses, all of 'em full ! Why, we'll walk into Tripoli as easy as walking into the First Congregational Church in Ridgefield, Connecticut. What part of New England you from, Hamlin ? "

I limited myself to saying I was from Portland, whereupon Eaton burst into a rhapsody on northern New England. " Ah," he said, " that rich, lush country ! Those fertile fields ! Those golden beaches and air like wine ! Those stately forests ! Those rolling meadows and billowing groves ! Those foaming torrents and the sighing of the wind in the mighty trees ! I'm a son of Dartmouth, Hamlin, and many's the speckled beauty I've whisked from the turbulent waters of the Connecticut ! Ah, Salvelinus fontinalis ! A glorious country, Hamlin—the exact opposite of this hell-hole ! Sand, rocks, gravel, grit ! Winds so hot you can't open your mouth, while they're blowing, without boiling your tongue ! Any shrub over a foot high is a tree, and a pile of horse manure looms up like a mountain ! Christ, what a country ! "

" It's got possibilities," I reminded him. " I did a little farming in Maine. If you could put an end to some of this erosion and get a little lime and fertiliser on the land, you'd grow crops that would make New England look sick."

"Yes," Eaton said, " I guess you're right. I've had such a hell of a time trying to make these Arab sheiks behave like human beings instead of blue-bottomed baboons that I get disgusted with everything. I'll feel better after we take Derna and get money and supplies." He looked at me sourly and growled " Jesus " by way of expressing the resentment seething within him.

"General," I said, " I don't want to seem inquisitive, but why is it you haven't been getting the supplies and money and help you need ? "

"Oh God," Eaton cried, " its the Navy ! Navy officers spend most of their life cooped up in a cabin, and their livers shred all to pieces from lack of exercise. When anybody not in the Navy needs something and asks Navy officers for it, their livers kick up and make 'em mulish. They always say No to everything ; they don't give a damn *what* it is. Their livers won't let 'em say Yes. Most of these Navy officers, they think an army isn't good for anything anyway, and if you left it to the Navy whether there should be any army at all, they'd all say No, the liverish bastards ! I know 'em ! "

"That isn't true of Preble is it, sir ? " I asked.

"Oh, God, no," Eaton said. " Not Preble ! Preble thinks like a soldier. There's nothing the matter with Preble's liver ! Oh, no : if Preble was in charge of things, I'd have everything I need, and before I needed it ; no skimping, no delay, no trouble at all." He flung his hands apart. " I don't know why I bother you with all these troubles ! Everything's going to be all right as soon as we're in Derna."

"As I said," I went on, " I don't like to seem to press this unnecessarily, but is there a chance that Tobias Lear's in any way responsible for your failure to get the proper supplies ? "

"Oh, no," Eaton said. " No. It's just the way the Navy does things in the Mediterranean—I mean the Navy when Preble isn't the head of things. Oh, I know Lear. No, no ; he couldn't stick his nose into my affairs ! " He shot me a sudden piercing look. " You know Lear ? "

I said I did.

"You do, eh," Eaton said. " Don't like him, do you ? "

"No, sir, I don't."

"Why not ? "

"Well, sir," I said, " I don't like his way of thinking. He's secretive, jealous, ambitious. He'll stop at nothing to further his ambitions."

Eaton nodded. " Yes, I know what you mean. He's a pallid sort of lizard—not much endurance at anything but drinking tea and snuggling up to rich women ! God knows why he was sent here in the first place —probably because the State Department never did anything right in its life ! But Lear couldn't have any sort of control over this expedition. Why, he was in Malta just before I left for Alexandria. The whole expedition was threshed out, then and there. Preble was there, and Barron and Lear. Barron was all in favour of it, just as Preble had always been ; and Lear offered no objections. Everything's all right ;

it's just that the Navy's always jealous of the Army, and the Navy's slow. Its slowness damned near killed us, I can tell you that ! "

" Just what are Lear's duties, sir ? "

" Oh, he's called Political Commissioner," Eaton said. " That means that when we take Tripoli and a treaty has to be signed, he's empowered to sign it for the Government of the United States. You see, if just a naval officer signed it for the United States, it wouldn't take effect till it was ratified in Washington ; whereas if there's a commissioner right on the spot, it can be ratified instantly."

" I see," I said. " Do you happen to know what instructions the Secretary of State gave him ? "

" No," Eaton said, " I don't. He's too secretive to tell anyone what his instructions were. I never saw a man like him for talking and acting mysterious. You'd think he was a real colonel, too ! Why, he doesn't know any more about being a colonel than my grandmother's white mare—and she didn't know how to do anything except break wind ! "

" Well, sir," I said, " if you're sure Lear can't interfere with you in any way, I'm sorry I brought the matter up."

" Of course I'm sure ! " Eaton cried. " As sure as anyone *can* be ! You can't really be sure of anything in this world, of course. But I had a letter from Barron when we reached Bomba last week, and so did Hamet, and everything was all right then. You can see for yourself." He turned to Leitensdorfer. " Colonel, get the copy you made of Commodore Barron's letter to Hamet."

Leitensdorfer went to the general's field desk, opened it, took out a sheet of paper, and handed it to Eaton.

" Here you are," Eaton said. " Dated Malta, March twenty-second. Barron says to Hamet, ' With great satisfaction I have received from Mr. Eaton the intelligence of your junction with him, and of the measures you had adopted to commence your march towards Bomba. No sooner did I receive this intelligence than I made every exertion to collect the succours required in your letter, and I now send my faithful and worthy Captain Hull with the *Argus* brig and a sloop loaded with provisions and stores. I hope Captain Hull will find your excellency and your army in safety and in health, and that your measures may be propitious to our cause.' Then he sends him his ardent wishes for the enterprise in which he's engaged." He gave me a quick look in which I imagined I saw something defensive.

" Do I understand he wrote you at the same time ? " I asked.

" Oh, yes," Eaton said. " A long letter. You know Barron's a sick man. Ordinarily he can say what he has to say in about three lines, but this one looked like a book. It kept repeating that I could depend on getting every support and assistance from him. I must say there was a lot of shilly-shallying in it—he'd picked up the idea somehow that Hamet might have a few faults, or that he won't have the support of the Arabs, so that he may not deserve too much help. But, as I say,

Barron's sick, and sick men imagine all sorts of things. Anyway, the letter was written March twenty-second, when the expedition hadn't got anywhere, and when Barron probably thought we never *would* get anywhere ! When he hears we've taken Derna, things'll be different. One of the points he made in his letter was that I was to tell Captain Hull exactly what I wanted in the line of naval co-operation in the future, so there's no possibility of any hitch. Oh, Barron'll be all right as soon as he finds out we're in Derna ! And God knows I won't have the slightest difficulty with those blasted sheiks if Barron just sends me enough money."

He dismissed the subject with a wave of his hand, picked up Lydia's map of Tripoli, and made pleased noises in his throat. " Perfect ! " he said. " Perfect ! We can break in at the back of the town, go straight through the Jewish section, and catch 'em between two fires before they know what's hit 'em ! "

He handed the map to Leitensdorfer. " Copy this, will you, Colonel, and give it back to Mr. Hamlin in the morning ? " To us he said brusquely, " Have your troop ready to march at six o'clock—and don't think I'm not grateful for men who don't have to be bribed to fight on the side of right against wrong."

As we hunted for our troop of black Arabs among the countless camp-fires, I wondered what was in that letter that Barron had written Eaton—that long and shilly-shallying letter whose promises had apparently been larded with doubts. He'd been willing enough to read us the letter Barron had sent to Hamet, but he certainly had no intention of reading us Barron's letter to himself. Yet I had to admit that if Barron had any qualms about the success of the expedition, they couldn't help vanishing if Eaton captured Derna. All that Eaton said was true ; and yet—and yet I couldn't get Tobias Lear out of my head. He stuck there, a pale cockle-burr of a thought, scratching irritatingly at everything in my mind and refusing to be dislodged.

CHAPTER LVI

WE WERE up before daylight the next morning ; but when the horses had been fed and watered and we ourselves had eaten a few dates for breakfast and got ourselves into the saddle, we found that Eaton's prediction of the evening before had come to pass. Not a Bedouin tent had been struck ; not a camel had been loaded ; and the two troops of Arab cavalry were straggling towards the rear of the camp instead of forward, in the direction of Derna. The six marines, their sergeant, and the officer with them were ready to march ; so were the Greek soldiers and the cannoneers. Eaton's own tent had been struck ; and when I rode over to find out what was happening, Eaton was deep in conversation with the two sheiks who commanded Hamet's cavalry.

One of the two was just an ordinary sheik, with grey whiskers and a proud brown face ; but the other had a dark greenish complexion and a cast in one eye, and there was a peculiar twist to his thin lipped mouth, as if he were on the verge of snarling openly. Both sheiks were listening to Eaton with an air of simple dignity, which means little in Moslem countries, where men have mastered the art of appearing simple and dignified, even when caught in the act of telling the most outrageous falsehoods or stealing a horse.

" But, my God," Eaton was protesting to Hamet, " it's been like this ever since the day we left Arabs' Tower ! Haven't they got any sense of honour ? How can they come this far and threaten to turn back when we're practically there ? "

" For the best of reasons," the cock-eyed sheik said. " Joseph Karamanli's army may strike at any time. Suppose, when it strikes, the general is killed and we are defeated ? What becomes then of the money owing to us ? Not only would we have no money, but our wives and children and camels and slaves in the caravan would be cut off by Joseph Karamanli's soldiers. We have faithfully done as we promised, up to now——"

" Like hell you have ! " Eaton cried. " You've caused us more trouble and delay than if you'd been in Joseph Karamanli's pay ! On the third day of the march you held us up half a day. You held us up on the seventeenth of March because you had to have money ! You held us up the next day, until we raised six hundred and seventy-three dollars for you. On the twentieth I had to stop your rations, because you threatened to go home on the ground that we'd never find the ships at Bomba. On the twenty-seventh you held us up another three days ! On the first of April you started a mutiny, because you claimed you weren't getting enough rations. On the eighth you damned near turned your guns on us—us, who were trying to be your friends and get Hamet's

362

throne back for him ! If you'd behaved yourselves, we'd have been in Derna three weeks ago ! If Joseph Karamanli's army is close to us now, it's your own damned fault and nobody else's ! "

He rounded on Hamet. " My God, man, this is *your* country ! We're your guests in it ! You people make a hell of a noise, howling and yelling about Arab hospitality ! Well, let's see a little of it ! Let's have an end of being left in the lurch—an end of trying to cut my throat and yours ! That may be their idea of hospitality, but it's not mine, by God ! "

Hamet looked worried, but the sheiks remained imperturbable.

" Also," the cock-eyed sheik persisted, " you told us that the three ships would be at Derna to help us capture the city. But some of our men went to Cape Razatin last night and also this morning, and there is no sign of the ships. You have promised us things before and not kept your promise. You promised us rice——"

" Listen," Eaton said, " whatever food we had, we shared equally with you. On top of that, you got every cent of money I and my men had. If you hadn't made us give that to you, we could have bought food ; but no, by God, you had to have the money ! Therefore we all starved together. And what do you expect those ships to do ? Hug the shore with an onshore wind ? If you do, you know as much about sailing as one of your camels—one of your sick ones ! I said the ships will be at Derna, and they'll be at Derna ! "

The sheik was stubborn. " We cannot run the risk. If anything goes wrong, we won't be able to feed our women and our children—or our camels. It takes money to feed camels."

Eaton stared icily at Hamet. " If you have any control whatever over these people, use it ! "

" Under ordinary circumstances," Hamet said, " they would do exactly as I told them. Under ordinary circumstances I'd bargain with them. I'd live up to my part of the bargain, and they'd live up to theirs. But the circumstances in which we find ourselves are *not* ordinary. I told you in the beginning how much would be needed to pay these men ; how much would be needed in the way of supplies. The supplies have never been sufficient, and the pay has often been merely promises ; Arabs believe that you should pay as you go. And there's another reason why they act as they do : they think America is only using us in order to get peace with my brother—that the Americans don't care what happens to the rest of us if only they can bring the war to an end."

" Oh, my God ! " Eaton said. " I never heard anything so ridiculous ! Didn't Barron just write you he was doing everything he could for you ? He's in command of all American ships in the Mediterranean, and if he says he's doing everything he can for you, there's no room for argument. He's given his word to support us, and that's official ! Now I'll tell you what I'll do. After the way these two masters of hospitality and hell-raising have acted—after their willingness to abandon this expedition when we're right on the verge of success—I wouldn't pay 'em in advance if I had all the money in the world ! I'll pay 'em, yes ; but not in advance. If they'll behave themselves, if they'll do what they set out to do—finish the march to Derna and help us take the town—I'll give each of 'em a thousand dollars extra. One thousand dollars, by God ! And that's my last word on the subject."

He wheeled his horse, saw me, and motioned me to go along with him. " That's what you have to struggle with when they don't give you enough money," he said. " You can't fight a war without throwing money all over the place. It's as simple as A B C, but those bastards in Washington are too damned stupid to understand it. You'll see a different proposition when we've taken Derna ! They'll *have* to give us money then ; and if they give me enough of it, I'll steal damned near the whole of Joseph Karamanli's army right out from under his nose and reach Tripoli without ever firing a shot ! "

The Arabs followed us. Five hours later the whole army camped on a hill at the foot of the escarpment, two and a half miles from Derna.

One of the peculiar things about good military leaders is their apparent ability to rise above fatigue. If they're good, they seem to be able to go without sleep for ever, write innumerable orders, march twice as far and twice as fast as anyone else, make endless personal inspections of troops and positions, lead their men into battle, and at the end of the battle keep right on with their inspections, order-writing, and marching.

Eaton was like that. He was all over the encampment like a hound-dog, dividing his force, assigning them to stations, issuing orders. A dozen Arab sheiks rode out from the town, but he kept them waiting until he had talked to King Dick and me.

" I want you to take your troop to the top of the escarpment," he told us. " The second those ships reach us, I'm going to attack. I'll send Hamet and his foot soldiers around to the back of the town, with his cavalry in reserve. There's an old fort up there—you can see it from here—that he says he can seize and hold. That'll give him control of anybody who tries to break out of the city on the rear."

" That Arab cavalry pretty poor reserve," King Dick said. " You better put us in behind 'em. They'll never get away then."

" No," Eaton said. " I've got something else for you and your men to do. And I want you to understand what'll probably happen. When the ships reach us, I'll take the marines and the Greeks and attack that battery down by the water. If we can get it, we can turn the guns on the town and blow the defenders right out through the back wall !

" I want you up on the escarpment for three purposes. From up there you can see the ships sooner than we can. When you see 'em, report what you see. Then there's Joseph Karamanli's army—that's the second thing. Send men out on the road to the westward. Send enough so I can have a report every three hours. Have each man come straight here and report to me. Is that all clear?"

I said it was.

"The third thing is this," he went on. "From the top of that escarpment you can see everything that's happening on all sides of the town. I expect Hamet's cavalry to take care of those that try to escape up the wadi and join Joseph's army. But they won't be able to see the coastal roads. Keep your eyes on those roads, and if anyone tries to escape that way, you're to stop 'em. Get an order from Leitensdorfer for whatever flour, water, and rice you need. Oh, yes, and sugar."

He gave me that sour smile of his. "You look worried. Well, there's nothing to worry over! It'll be just like rolling off a log!"

And so it was—for us. So it is in all wars for most of those who go to make up armies. A measly hundredth part of an army does the work; the other ninety-nine hundredths fatten on the labours of those who do the fighting: spend the rest of their lives posing as soldiers, subtly implying that their bravery sets them apart from the rest of mankind, or that the hardships they endured entitle them to greater benefits than other men enjoy. Those who do the fighting find it harder.

We sighted the first of the American vessels—a brig—at two o'clock the very next afternoon. At dawn of the following day we sighted the other two—a schooner and a sloop—far out on the horizon, and sent a messenger pelting down to Eaton. With him went another of our patrols, just in from the westward, with the news that Joseph Karamanli's army was only two days' off.

There's something strangely unreal about a battle seen from a distance. The mounted men seem to be playing a game; those who are shot down seem to have stumbled; and when they lie where they've fallen it's hard to believe they're dead. Ships look like toy ships puffing out harmless jets of smoke: not like floating forts hurling tons of lead and steel that howl through the air like wildcats.

So much happened on the day we sighted the brig, schooner, and sloop that we followed it with difficulty. The brig sent off a boat with two cannon in it, and we could see Eaton's marines and cannoneers at the water's edge, struggling to haul the cannon up over the rocks. while the entire camp boiled, men running here and there, horses galloping, detachments forming, camels moving to the rear.

The sloop, which had hove-to a mile offshore, moved closer in, and closer, until she seemed almost against the face of the battery at the seaward edge of the town—the battery that Sidi Abzell had told us mounted eight guns.

A bellow of thunder rose towards us from the battery, and from the town itself there was a confusion of banging. The little sloop turned broadside to the town, dropped her anchor and began firing. The brig and the schooner, too, were moving in ; they, too, swung broadside to the town, anchored, and were enveloped in clouds of smoke. How any of those three vessels could escape being blown to bits I couldn't understand. We could see the balls from the battery raising gouts of foam all around them and far beyond, as the balls skipped across the water.

We saw Hamet's foot soldiers scramble down the steep sides of the wadi that lay between them and the meadow land behind the town, and some scrambling up on the other side. We saw the two troops of cavalry skirt around them, higher up on the slope, where the wadi was less of a ravine.

The marines had somehow got one of the fieldpieces to the top of the rocks, and we could see them hitching horses to it and running it along the road, towards the gardens and houses that lay between the battery and the town. With them went the handful of blue-clad marines and the Greeks and the cannoneers—and Eaton, too, I knew, must be with them. They went into the groves and gardens, and vanished amid a tumultuous distant ripping and rattling of musketry-fire that sounded like a dozen boys drawing sticks across the palings of a dozen fences. Spurts of smoke jetted from the blank brown walls of the houses in the main part of the city, which lay across the wadi from the battery and the gardens into which Eaton had disappeared ; and over and under and through the stuttering of distant musketry came the thumping of the big guns of the battery and of the three ships.

The fire from the three ships slackened ; then we saw Eaton's men come out from the gardens and start across the barren glacis of the battery. A few of them fell and lay still ; but the bulk of them reached the battery and vanished through the gun-ports.

A few moments later we saw figures emerging from the farther side, running towards the wadi, scrambling down into it, scrambling up on the other side into the shelter of the brown-walled houses.

The fire from the ships started up again ; puffs of dust rose from the front of the houses ; then, miraculously, balls of smoke bloomed from the empty rear gun-ports of the battery.

" Hoy ! " shouted King Dick. " Turned the guns on the town ; got 'em in a cross-fire. They'll never get away now ! "

Nor did they. We saw figures running out of the rear gates of the town, making for the hills and the escarpment ; saw Hamet's cavalry charge down on them and round them up ; saw Hamet's foot soldiers come out of their ancient fort and march into the town. There was a period of spattering gunfire. Then, a scant two hours after the first American vessel had anchored broadside to the battery, an American flag rose to the top of the flag-pole in the battery, and there was no more firing. Hamet and Eaton had taken Derna.

The trooper who rode in from the direction of Tripoli that same afternoon reported that Joseph Karamanli's army would arrive on the escarpment above Derna on the following afternoon ; and when he came back from carrying that message to Eaton, Leitensdorfer came with him.

" The general wants all of you down below," Leitensdorfer said. " If Joseph's army try to attack us, the general's going to make them climb down those hills and do it."

" How's he feeling ? " I asked.

" Tickled," Leitensdorfer said. " Oh, but tickled ! He was shot through the hand when we attacked the battery, but he pays no attention to it. He is tickled with Hamet, with the Greeks, with everybody ! I tell you, my friends, we fought like lions, isn't it ? "

There was nothing offensive about his boasting, and I knew it was the simple truth : he was just stating what had happened.

" I tell you this, though," Leitensdorfer said. " There was a moment, when the fire from the houses was heavy and we were in the gardens, when those Greeks were of two minds. They lay on the ground behind the garden walls and couldn't get up. I hesitate to say it, my friends, but for a moment they were afraid. Even I was nervous, isn't it ? I was able to recognise it because I was irritable. When I told one of those Greeks to get up and fire, and he just lay there, I gave him a kick in his backsides, which is something I have never permitted myself to do in action. Even then he refused to rise, and I saw others lying there rolling their eyes up at the top of the walls where the bullets were going *psst, psst, psst* and making smacking sounds. After all, I suppose they had reason, because thirteen of them were wounded, and also a marine was wounded and two marines were killed.

" I tell you, my friends, it was a fortunate thing that we had Eaton with us at that moment, for he made up his mind in a twinkling of an eye. He came roaring among us, saying the safest place to be was in that battery. There was something electric and nerve-racking in his shouts that stood those Greeks up on their feet in spite of themselves ; and before any of us knew what had happened, we were all running out from the groves and houses and on to that empty glacis, trying our best to keep up with the general. When a bullet hit his left hand, he dropped his gun. But he pulled out his sword and waved it and howled a terrible great howl—oh, extremely exciting, so we all howled ; and then there we were, under the gun-ports of the battery ! "

" How you get through 'em ? " King Dick asked.

" Ah, I was afraid you'd ask that," Leitensdorfer said. " I have no recollection ! None whatever ! At one moment we were on the outside looking in, and the next minute we were on the inside, howling and pursuing the gunners, who were tumbling out of the gun-ports on the opposite side. Then we were wrestling with the guns. I tell you, gentlemen, I have heard some cursing in my time. I have heard Syrians curse, and Egyptians—all kinds of cursing I have heard ; but never have I heard such tremendous, such earnest cursing as I heard when we wrestled with those eight guns, loosening their breechings and getting them to the rear side of the battery, so we could open fire on the town walls *Ha* ! " He shook his head at the recollection.

" The general went aboard the *Argus* to have his wound bandaged, and when he returns he'll pay the sheiks and all the Arabs who came with us from Alexandria. I tell you, my friends, this is a great day ! After to-day the Arabs will go anywhere with us ! Joseph's army can never do anything against us while the ships are here, and if they'll only give us the money, we can raise an army of ten thousand men to march on Tripoli—if we happen to need them, which we don't."

CHAPTER LVII

I WOULDN'T have believed that one man, and a wounded man at that, could accomplish the things Eaton accomplished in the two days after Derna fell. He established his headquarters in the battery, but he was almost never in it. When he wasn't in the Governor's palace, which Hamet had taken over, conferring interminably with the sheiks who wished to swear allegiance to Hamet, he was being rowed out to the *Argus* to have his wound dressed ; or pelting off to look at the cavalry outpost he had thrown along the base of the escarpment in case Joseph's army should attempt a counter-attack ; or inspecting the inside of the ruined fort that Hamet had first occupied, and spurring on the men he had set to work to repairing its walls ; or marking out trenches, or attending gift-giving ceremonies in various parts of the city, or storming at the sheik who had given refuge to the Governor of Derna and refused to yield him up because Arab hospitality forbade such a thing.

He used our black Arabs as a headquarters troop, stationing us in the gardens of Bu Mansur, the little suburb outside the battery ; and it was there that Lydia's letter reached me in the late afternoon of April twenty-ninth, exactly forty-eight hours after the town had fallen. I'll never forget that day, because Lydia's news, even though I'd vaguely anticipated something of the sort, was a blow that made all the other disasters in my past life fade into insignificance.

If my letter is incoherent, it's because I'm hurrying. Hamet's wife has given me a silver chain to give the messenger so that he'll hurry.

Oh, Albion, if it's possible for General Eaton to hurry too, he must do so ! Something strange is happening in Malta. Joseph has had word from there that Commodore Barron is so weak from the attacks of fever that he no longer has any mind of his own, that he sees Tobias Lear every day, and that he does nothing except by Lear's advice. They have found out that Lear is authorised to negotiate a peace with Joseph, and Hamet's wife says that Joseph is so exercised over Hamet's and Eaton's approach that he is determined to make peace before Hamet can get here. He has already made offers to Lear through the Spanish and the French consuls. Both are doing everything they can to keep Tripoli from falling into American hands—the Spanish consul has even given Joseph three hundred rifles.

If only Eaton and Hamet could be here now, I truly believe that Joseph would surrender without firing a shot. He has only four hundred men to defend the city, two hundred of them worthless.

When Hamet's wife told all this to me, this morning, I couldn't believe it ; but now I know it's true. Lear is still in Malta. They say he is staying there to make sure that the American fleet isn't allowed to attack Tripoli before a peace has been signed. I don't know whether or not this is true. There hasn't been a day this month that an attack couldn't have been made, for the weather has been perfect ; but there are only two American ships off the town, and they do nothing but sail up and down.

When I finished reading that letter my mind was a welter of rage and indignation. I didn't dare to think what such a peace, negotiated by Tobias Lear, might mean to Eaton, to Hamet, to Hamet's wife and children, to Leitensdorfer ; to all the Arabs who'd marched with Eaton across the desert ; to the sheiks who had welcomed Hamet back to Derna ; what it might mean to Lydia and to me, to that handful of marines of ours, two of whom were now dead, to King Dick, to the black Arabs who had followed us so faithfully and well.

I looked up to find King Dick staring at me apprehensively. I gave him the letter without comment. He read it through, moving his lips as he read, and when he finished he gave it back to me and put on his headcloth, which he'd removed for the evening. " No time to lose," he said. " We go see Eaton."

At the battery we learned Eaton was on the *Argus*, having his wound dressed, and when he came back with Leitensdorfer, an hour later, he was as ruddy and cheery as though his left arm weren't trussed up in a sling. " What's the matter ? " he asked us. " You look as if you'd been having Arab trouble ! "

When I held out Lydia's letter, he glanced sharply at King Dick and me, stopped smiling, and sat down before a work-table to read it. I think the look in our eyes must have given him some sort of warning. When he'd read a line or two, he said, " Oh, no ; " and as he read on and on, he kept saying " Oh, no ! Oh, no ! "

When he'd finished, he rubbed his head with his right hand, then stared at it as if he expected to find something strange there. " I don't believe it," he said slowly. " If Lear negotiated a peace with Joseph Karamanli—— But he *couldn't* do that ! We're all in this up to our necks ! If he negotiates a peace with Joseph Karamanli, Joseph will go on being Bashaw. My God, it doesn't bear thinking about ! He'll be in a position to murder every one of these Arabs we've persuaded to help us—murder every one of the sheiks that have come over to Hamet yesterday and to-day ! Oh, no, I won't believe it ! " All his ruddy cheeriness was gone ; he looked suddenly haggard, old, sick.

" General," I reminded him, " the day we joined this expedition you read us a letter that Barron sent to Hamet. You also spoke of a letter that Barron wrote you. You said there was a lot of shilly-shallying in it, but you didn't show it to us. In view of what my wife says, would you be willing to let me see it now ? "

" But that was written before we took Derna. The capture of Derna changes everything. Nobody could have fought better than Hamet and his Arabs did."

" Just the same, I'd like to see that letter," I told him.

Eaton nodded to Leitensdorfer. " All right—show it to him."

Leitensdorfer went to Eaton's field desk, took a thick letter from the correspondence slot, and gave it to me. As Eaton had said on the Cape Razatin meadows, it was more like a book than a letter—page after page, each one closely written. I ran through it hurriedly, and with a heart that sank lower and lower with each sentence. " This isn't a sailor's letter," I told Eaton. " *This* is the way they write in the State Department, and it bears out everything that Lydia says. This isn't Barron talking : it's Tobias Lear."

" You've got to bear in mind," Eaton said, " that it was written long before we took Derna—over a month ago."

" I don't care when it was written," I said. " The man who wrote this letter has made up his mind to conduct this war with Tripoli in his own way, and regardless of anything you may have done."

" He can't," Eaton said. " He says right at the beginning that he's disposed to consider my meeting with Hamet a fair presage of future success, and that he's sending the necessary stores and provisions."

" Yes," I said, " but right away he spoils it : he suggests that, if you run into difficulties, you should refuse to let Hamet have the supplies and the money that he sends. That's the Lear procedure, and always has been ! Promise something—and then don't keep your promise unless it's quite convenient. This sentence is pure Lear. Listen to it : ' It is far from my wish to damp your ardour or that of your companions in arms by laying too great a stress upon the cold maxims of prudence whereby the tide of success is often lost.' "

" Oh, God," Eaton said, " I know it—it's terrible. But that was *before* we took Derna."

" Yes, but it's still Lear," I persisted. " He's squirming like a snake. Squirming out of all the things that have been promised to you. Listen again : ' You must be sensible, Sir, that in giving their sanction to a co-operation with the exiled Bashaw, Government did not contemplate the measure as leading necessarily and absolutely to a reinstatement of that Prince in his rights on the regency of Tripoli.' "

Eaton banged the table with his bandaged arm and grunted with pain. " That's a damned lie ! " he shouted. " That's exactly what the government did contemplate—Jefferson, Madison, Gallatin, and Congress ; and if *they* aren't the government, for God's sake, who *is* ? "

" Tobias Lear is," I said. " Listen to this damned double-faced State Department talk of his : ' These apprehensions may perhaps prove groundless on further representations from you, but under my present impressions I feel it my duty to state explicitly that I must withhold my sanction to any convention or agreement committing the United States or tending to impress upon Hamet Bashaw a conviction that we have bound ourselves to place him on the Throne. The consequences involved in such an engagement cannot but strike you forcibly, & a general view of our situation in relation to the reigning Bashaw & our unfortunate countrymen in Tripoli will be sufficient to mark its inexpediency. I shall consider it my duty, as it certainly is my inclination, to afford you every aid compatible with the authority vested in me & commensurate with the means placed at my disposal, & you may depend upon the most active and vigorous support from the squadron as soon as the season & our arrangements will permit us to appear in force before the enemy's walls, but I wish you to understand that no guarantee or engagements to the exiled prince——' "

" Windbag ! " Eaton shouted.

I went on reading : " ' —whose cause, I repeat it, we are only favouring as the instrument to an attainment & not in itself as an object, must be held to stand in the way of our acquiescence to any honourable & advantageous terms of accommodation which the present Bashaw may be induced to propose. Such terms being once offered & accepted by the representative of Government appointed to treat of peace, our support to Hamet Bashaw must necessarily be withdrawn. You will not however conclude that these considerations, important & necessary as they are, ought to induce us at once to abandon the benefits which the measures you have adopted seem to promise. I consider a perseverance in these by no means incompatible with a total freedom from any trammels with respect to a definite object, which freedom I deem it all-important to preserve, especially when I view the particular situation in which Captain Bainbridge & his fellow sufferers may be placed by his co-operation. If by your energy & exertions, added to the supplies now sent forward, you succeed in getting possession of Derna & Bengazi . . .' Did you ever hear such drivel ! "

Eaton groaned.

" I tell you it's Lear, down to the last ampersand," I said. " He'll help Hamet—only he won't help him. Every support will be given to him—but not if Lear decides he's an unfit subject for further support or cooperation. It's his fixed resolution to give you every support and assistance, is it ? It is not, for it's also his fixed resolution not to give you the hundred marines you want ! He applauds your energy and perseverance, but he hasn't the slightest intention of making use of the advantages your energy and perseverance have achieved ! Every line of that letter *stinks* of Tobias Lear ! "

" He can't do it," Eaton said sourly.

" You wouldn't say that if you knew Lear as I know him," I said.

" He can't do it," Eaton repeated. " I'll write Barron to-night—give him a full report of the taking of the city, and of the way Hamet and his men fought. I'll meet all his objections."

" But they aren't Barron's objections, General. They're Lear's."

" I don't care if they *are* Lear's. No man on earth could be such a fool as to throw away all we've accomplished ! Why, it would be the most disgraceful thing any nation was ever guilty of ! "

We sat there in a sort of nightmare silence, a silence made more nightmarish by the senseless gabbling of the Greek cannoneers in the next room, the derisive chuckle of the water flowing down the wadi, the angry gruntings of camels in the gardens of Bu Mansur.

" Well, Hamlin," Eaton said at length, " your wife's in Tripoli. She stayed there to help me—to help all of us ; and if this expedition continues to Tripoli as it should, we'll all of us owe her a lot. But if you're right about Lear, it's not going to be so pleasant for your wife, is it ? "

" No, sir, it isn't. I don't think of much else."

" I can well believe it," Eaton said. " You've got to do something about her, too ! You can't just let matters drift in a case like that."

" No," I said. " I can't. The trouble is, we're all needed here. If Joseph Karamanli's army attacks you——"

Eaton snorted. " Attack from the top of that escarpment, against the eight long guns and a ten-inch mortar we captured in this battery ? When we've got the *Argus*, *Nautilus*, and *Hornet* right here at our elbows with their guns trained on all the wadis ? When Hamet's fort'll be ready for 'em in two days' time ? Pish ! Let 'em attack ! Why, I could hold this place for ever, against an army three times the size of Joseph Kara-manli's, provided I have the supplies ! What did you have in mind ? "

" Well, sir," I said, " if King Dick and I were free to do as we pleased——"

" Wait ! " Eaton interrupted. " I've got it ! King Dick took you away from Tripoli, and he can go there again whenever he wants. That cavalry captain of yours is perfectly capable of handling your troop himself. King Dick can get in and out of places that nobody else could. That's what he'll do, too ! He'll go to Tripoli to get the lay of the land ! No, no ! Don't interrupt ! He'll get the lay of the land : then you and Leitensdorfer can join him ! I'm going to send the two of you to Malta to carry my dispatches to Barron in person. Leitensdorfer's been with me ever since the beginning, and you were trained in the law. Between the two of you, you'll be able to answer any objection that Lear or anybody else might raise. After that you can go to Tripoli ! How's *that* ! "

When Leitensdorfer also protested that we couldn't be spared, Eaton was sharp with him.

" *Somebody's* got to be spared," he said, " somebody who's been with this army and knows what he's talking about ! *I* can't go, because if I did you know damned well half the Arabs would run away the first night. They'd claim they were being deserted. All I can do is write Barron another letter—a letter that takes it for granted he'll keep on sending us the men, money, and supplies that Jefferson, Madison, Gallatin, and Congress said we could have—a letter that assumes he won't allow a disgraceful peace to be made.

" One thing I've learned in the three years I've been in North Africa is that there's nowhere an American can get worse treatment than in Moslem countries, and nowhere he can be as safe from interference, provided he speaks a little Arabic and knows enough to conform to the customs of the people. Of course anyone who doesn't do that is inviting trouble in any land and any language. Colonel Leitensdorfer's been a dervish and gone twice to Mecca. He can recite the poems of Hafiz. All of you have resourcefulness and endurance. Any one of you can go anywhere in Tripoli that he wants to go—and I think that, after what your wife tried to do for all of us, they'll probably help her in any way they can."

He looked inquiringly at Leitensdorfer and King Dick.

King Dick only smiled.

Leintensdorfer stood smartly at attention. " It is true, General, that the two of us will be able to go wherever we please. I shall be happy to remind this Colonel Lear how you performed a miracle in marching five hundred miles and capturing this city. As for the fifty dollars I borrowed from you in Cairo, isn't it, I have not forgotten and will sign a paper, so that if anything should happen to me——"

" Pah ! " Eaton cried. " You and your paper ! How can I think with you buzzing in my ears like a bumble bee ? How can I get a letter off to Barron with all this squawking and arguing ! Get out, all of you ! Oh—you, Colonel : write the orders to Lieutenant Evans of the *Hornet* for the two of you to proceed to Malta aboard his ship with dispatches for Commodore Barron. Put it in the orders that you're free, after that, to proceed on affairs necessary to the welfare of this expedition in any way you may elect. King Dick doesn't need any orders ; he can write his own. Get back here any way you can as soon as you've found out that no man could possibly be such a fool as you accuse Lear of being ! "

Grumbling to himself, he reached for the water-jar on the end of the table and slopped water on to his bandaged arm ; and even before I closed the door behind us, he had opened his field desk and was wiping the point of a quill on the moistened bandage.

I've thought often of that picture—William Eaton, wounded, sitting alone in the yellow candlelight, intent on the pen with which he must plead to stupid and shortsighted men for help that had been already promised, plead for the help that should have been freely given—help to carry out a plan that he, almost unaided, had brought to the very verge of successful completion. How many times—alas, how many, many times—have great men, all alone, planned wisely for their countries and mankind, only to have their wisdom and their labour destroyed by lesser folk who are never sure of anything except that the wisest course is somehow dangerous.

CHAPTER LVIII

KING DICK started on his way westward with two of his black troopers as soon as I had written a hurried letter to Lydia, but Leitensdorfer and I had to wait until mid-morning of the next day, when Eaton finished his report and his protest to Barron—and bulky documents they were.

The sloop *Hornet*, ten guns, Lieutenant Samuel Evans, was anchored close inshore, under the empty gun-ports of the battery she had helped batter into submission. If I hadn't seen her five-gun broadsides smashing clouds of brown dust from the battery that was now Eaton's headquarters, I'd have thought her as harmless as she was small.

But for all her seventy-one tons and her yacht-like lines, she was stout as a rock when we boarded her ; and the neatness of her port and starboard batteries, her trimly coiled ropes, her lavish display of buckets, rammers, and shot, all shipshape and stowed as neat as a pin, made my mouth water.

We must have looked strange to Lieutenant Evans, for both of us were still wearing our burnooses. We had nothing else to wear, and I was glad of it, for a burnoose is more comfortable than can possibly be imagined by wearers of pantaloons, tight vests, narrow-shouldered coats, and thick neckcloths like hot towels.

Evans was a polite young man, inordinately proud of this little ship of his, which never could be little in his eyes. When we first came over the side he was all sternness and official correctness, and highly formal as he gave us the use of his awning on the quarter-deck ; and when he ordered his ship under way, he was brisk about it, rapping out orders like a commodore.

His formality lasted only half-way through the first cup of coffee that he ordered for us ; it was then he let drop the fact that Captain Rodgers had transferred him from the *Constitution* to his present command only two months before.

" Rodgers ? " I said. " Is that by any chance John Rodgers—curly-haired, stocky, with crinkly side-whiskers and an upper arm as solid as a man's leg ? "

"Why, yes," Evans replied—and when I laughed he took immediate offence. "You'll find Captain Rodgers nothing to laugh at," he added huffily. "Rodgers is a great captain—as great as Preble, as you'll mighty soon learn if ever he gets a free hand."

"But you mistake me," I hastened to explain. "I was laughing because his name brought up memories. He and I were together in Haiti when the French landed and Cap François was burned. There'd have been a lot of dead Americans in Haiti if it hadn't been for Rodgers." I told him a little about the fire and about the things that Rodgers had done, and from that moment Leitensdorfer and I might have been Evans's blood brothers, as is so often the case when a seaman finds that his admiration for another seaman is shared.

He made us laugh, too, with his assumption that Leitensdorfer and I had led interesting and eventful lives by contrast with his own, which he insisted on regarding as dull and uneventful ; and he was like a small boy with Leitensdorfer, perpetually egging him on to tell of his adventures—which I'm bound to say were more fantastic than anything I'd ever heard before.

About his own experiences, Evans was inclined to be reticent, not because he wasn't an easy talker but because he considered them, as he put it, uninteresting.

"When a naval officer is given his own vessel," I said, "it's usually because he has done something that's not exactly 'uninteresting.'"

"Oh," Evans said with a shrug, "it was just routine. The captain had an idea that we might want to go in and capture Tripoli some night, and he didn't like the way the Bashaw's guard boat kept sticking its nose out and looking at us. Besides that, he wanted to find out whether they kept a good watch, and how they fought when you jumped 'em unexpectedly. So he told some of us to take four boats and go in and cut her out. He put me in command of the number one boat, so when this ship was put in commission a month ago he let me have her."

"I see," I said. "You've overlooked one or two details, haven't you?"

"Details ? Oh, we rowed in around midnight. There wasn't much to it. They saw us coming, but they don't shoot any too well. Our men think they use their gun barrels for spits—spit sheep on 'em and roast 'em that way. Something's wrong with 'em, certainly. Anyway, the number two boat covered us when we boarded her, and as soon as we got a toehold on her deck, all the others came up too. So we captured her and rowed her out of the harbour, and from then on we could go in and out of the harbour at night whenever we felt like it."

"Well," I said, "that's not so 'uninteresting,' and neither is what you tell us about Rodgers. You say he had an idea he might need to attack the city some night. Apparently there's no question in his mind that the city will have to be attacked."

"No question ? There certainly is no question ! How can there be any question, when we've already captured Derna ? Tripoli's easier than Derna ! We'll have five frigates by July, and about twenty-six others, counting gunboats. When General Eaton's ready to have it done, we can blow those walls as flat as a goatskin rug."

" I'm mighty glad to hear that," I said. " We'd picked up the idea that the Navy didn't think much of Eaton."

Evans looked doubtful. " That might be," he said. " There's always bound to be a few old women mixed up in everything, even in the United States Navy. Those who understand what Eaton's trying to do are all in favour of him ; and they certainly want to see Tripoli knocked to Hell or Halifax. My God, imagine that stuck-up Bashaw looking out at a fleet of twenty-nine American warcraft and having the gall to ask for tribute from America and ransom for American prisoners ! The only tribute and ransom he'd ever get from me'd be a twenty-four-pound shot exactly midway between wind and water ! "

" And what about the commodore, isn't it ? " Leitensdorfer asked. " We heard he was weary of General Eaton's expedition and the expense of it."

" Weary of it ? Who told you anything like that ? What's expensive about it if we knock the tar out of this blasted Bashaw and put a decent man in his place ? It's not half so expensive as keeping a big fleet in the Mediterranean every year, is it ? "

" But no ! " Leitensdorfer protested. " Yet we have heard it said, isn't it, that Barron has no use for Eaton."

" I don't believe a word of it," Evans said promptly. " Captain Hull took letters from Barron to Eaton just a couple of weeks ago—gave 'em to him at Bomba."

" I well know about those letters," Leitensdorfer said.

" There you are, then ! Barron told Hull to find out what Eaton needed, so we could keep on co-operating with him."

Evans, I saw, knew nothing of any trouble. I wondered how much he knew about Barron. " It's too bad Barron's in the hospital," I said. " I don't suppose you get to see much of him."

Evans made no comment, but his expression was choleric.

" I used to do a lot of thinking," I went on, " about how Preble must have felt when he was relieved of his command, just because there was somebody older than he in the service. That's a splendid way to run an army or navy ! Lose a war rather than let a young man win it ! "

Evans still didn't say anything ; just looked at me.

" So far as anybody knew," I said, " he was being relieved by a man in good health."

" Good health ! " Evans broke in then. " Barron hasn't stirred out of hospital since he reached Malta last September."

" I wonder," I said, " what Preble's feelings would have been if he'd known the Navy Department would reward his magnificent work by putting a sick man in his place—a man too sick to leave the hospital, but unwilling to relinquish his command to Rodgers until—well, until Tripoli can be bought off again."

Evans pressed his lips together and seemed to swell a little, as if the pressure of contempt within him were struggling to erupt. "I'll tell you one thing ! " he said. "Ball thought Preble could have made every one of these three-tailed Bashaws and pint-sized Beys and dirty-drawers Deys get down on their knees and howl for mercy. That's Sir Alexander John Ball, Governor of Malta. He was one of Nelson's captains, and Nelson made him Governor of Malta when the Maltese threw out the French six years ago. You know what Ball wrote to Preble last fall when Preble got his orders to go home ? He wrote him it was a damned shame that anyone so eminently fitted for the highest command should be removed from it."

"Did Eaton know Ball ? " I asked Evans.

"Know him ? " Evans cried. "*Know* him ! Why, Ball gave Eaton letters to every damned soul in Egypt when Eaton went there to get Hamet. Ball's a fighter, and he knows a fighter when he sees one ! "

He got up to squint at the sky, eye the topsail, and sniff at the northwest wind, into which we were making long reaches ; then he came back to look down at the two of us, sitting cross-legged and silent beneath the striped awning. "Preble knew all about Eaton," he resumed. "Preble was aching to see him do exactly what he *is* doing ! Why, good God ! Somebody must have given you the wrong steer ! Not even a doddering old fool of a sick man could be such a damned ass as to foul up Eaton ! "

To a seaman's eye, the Grand Harbour of Malta, with lesser harbours radiating from it, ringed with white stone fortifications and with cyclopean stone buildings rising in giant steps from the water's edge, looks to be the most beautiful harbour in the world, but also the most difficult of approach against the will of its possessors ; and as Evans, Leitensdorfer, and I climbed the steep, stone-paved streets to the hospital, I got the impression that the whole place and everybody in it was as flinty as the grey stone on which we trod.

Evans's uniform was our card of admission, and we accompanied him to the commodore's quarters—three rooms on the third floor : bright, high-ceilinged rooms looking out over an irregular panorama of harbour dotted with so many ships that it might have been the crossroads of the world.

There were two orderlies in the outermost of the three rooms, and though they leaped to attention when Evans entered, they were adamant in their refusal to let us see the commodore. Their orders, they said, were to admit nobody when he was asleep except Colonel Lear. He'd be awake, we were told, at ten o'clock the next day.

When I said we had to be with him when he read the dispatches, both orderlies looked at me queerly, and one said, " Colonel Lear has to read to him."

" What's the reason for that ? " I asked. " Can't he read ? "

" I'll take the letter," was all the orderly said.

" But we've got to see it delivered to him," I insisted. " Those are General Eaton's orders."

" Can't do it, sir."

" Then we'll have to wait."

Evans left us, and Leitensdorfer and I settled ourselves on the floor in the corner, two Arabs to outer view—and probably not so far from it inwardly, since both of us had learned how to sit for hours on end in that state of suspended animation known to Arabs as keyf.

It was late in the afternoon when the door opened softly and Tobias Lear came in, sleepy-eyed, palely smiling, and stepping with the cat-like softness of one who walks on eggs.

He gave us a passing glance, walked towards the orderlies ; then suddenly turned to look at us again. " Bless my soul ! " he said. " I couldn't believe my eyes, but it is ! It's Hamlin again ! "

We got to our feet.

He seemed delighted, gave me his hand, and at the same time looked us up and down in complete bewilderment.

" Sir," I said, " this is Colonel Leitensdorfer, General Eaton's adjutant. We've come here with dispatches from General Eaton to Commodore Barron. We had orders from the general to make certain they reached the commodore's hands."

" The general's adjutant ! " Lear said. " Well, well ! An honour, Colonel ! What progress has the general made ? "

Leitensdorfer clicked his heels together as well as a man can when wearing soft Arab shoes. " Thanks to the assistance of your wonderful Navy, the general attacked and took Derna on April twenty-seventh. He now needs nothing but supplies and money in order to attack and reduce Tripoli in the same way. It is all here, in the general's letters to the commodore."

" Good ! " Lear said. " Good ! A remarkable achievement ! A splendid example of energy and perseverance ! " The news, for all I could tell, was warmly to his liking. He turned a speculative eye on me. " I take it you're with General Eaton, too ; but wasn't your wife with you when you sailed for Cette ? "

" Yes, sir," I said, " but Captain Lee——"

" I warned you about Lee," Lear interrupted.

I knew from sad experience that Lear had a genius for doing the wrong thing, and I'd long ago made up my mind that the less he knew about Lydia's and my experiences in Tripoli the less opportunity he'd have to bring down trouble upon either of us. So all I said was : " I know you did, and we took precautions ; but in spite of that, Lee found a way to get the vessel away from us. Since I was in this part of the world when the general started his march on Tripoli, I naturally wanted to do what I could to help him."

" I see," Lear said doubtfully. " And your wife ? She's well ? "

" Oh, yes. I hear from her often. Colonel Leitensdorfer has seen her more recently than I. His headquarters are in Alexandria." This didn't mean anything, of course, but I figured Lear would think it did.

" Ah, yes ! " he said, and he nodded knowingly. " Well, gentlemen, if you'll be kind enough to join me later at Zia Theresa's, above the Valletta Steps, I'll consider it an honour." He held out his hand to Leitensdorfer. " If you'll let me have the general's dispatches, Colonel——"

Leitensdorfer looked distressed. " I find this most embarrassing, Colonel Lear. My orders specifically stated that I was to deliver these dispatches into the commodore's own hands——"

Colonel Lear smiled indulgently. " I understand perfectly, Colonel, but of course the general didn't know of Commodore Barron's condition. If he had, he'd never have insisted, I'm sure. The commodore is not at all strong. Not at all. So——"

" What's the matter with him ? " Leitensdorfer asked.

Lear's reply was urbane. " Well, the fact is that the commodore tires quickly, and the doctors have prescribed complete quiet for him. To complicate matters, his secretary is suffering from a severe eye complaint. Thus I do duty for all, since the commodore is an old and valued friend. So if you'll favour me with General Eaton's dispatches, Colonel, it's the same as though you handed them to the commodore in person. Of course I'll give you a receipt for them, duly signed by the commodore."

We were utterly helpless ! Yet certain things were as plain as a moose's nose : Barron must be incompetent, just as Lydia had written me ; otherwise Lear would have had no objection to our seeing him. And either Barron was mentally incapable of comprehending that Eaton had captured Derna, or Lear was determined that he shouldn't hear of it. In either case, the control of the Navy and the disposition of Eaton's expedition must have passed out of Barron's hands and into Lear's hands—out of the hands of a naval officer who at one time had seen the innumerable advantages of forcing Tripoli to surrender unconditionally, and into the hands of a colonel who had won his title by writing letters for somebody else, had maintained himself in high places by keeping hold of a President's correspondence to which he had no right, and had already shown in Haiti that he believed in avoiding war at any cost—even when that cost was the loss of a people's freedom.

Still, I couldn't see how we could gain anything by antagonising Lear or by trying to force our way in to see Barron ; and it was barely possible that if Lear fully understood Eaton's case, he *might* influence Barron in the right direction. I was pretty sure he wouldn't, but he *might*, and the possibility had to be considered.

" As Colonel Lear says," I told Leitensdorfer, " the general would unquestionably have modified his orders if he'd known the commodore was dangerously ill."

"Not dangerously, Mr. Hamlin," Lear said.

Leitensdorfer raised his eyebrows. "A man too sick to read or write isn't any too healthy, isn't it?"

When Lear didn't answer, Leitensdorfer took the dispatches from his sash and handed them to him with a little bow.

Lear was all amiability. "I know General Eaton would be the first to understand. At Zia Theresa's, then, gentlemen, in about two hours. Just mention my name when you go there."

He went softly into the inner room, putting down his feet so noiselessly that to my way of thinking the only thing lacking in him was a long tail projecting rigidly above his rump, quivering at the tip with feline confidence and self-satisfaction.

At Zia Theresa's Tavern they were only too glad to give two such dubious-looking Arabs a room to themselves in which to await the coming of M. le Consul Général, and we held a council of war in it, looking down at the ceaseless marine activity of Valletta Steps.

"Beyond a doubt," Leitensdorfer said, "your lady was correctly informed. That man is diplomatique. He avoids, isn't it : speaks without saying anything. Therefore he is hiding Commodore Barron from us—and not only that : he is hiding something else. Now what would he have to hide from us, except something we would dislike to hear? There is nothing we would dislike to hear except something that would spoil all our work. Yes, Hamlin, your lady was right!"

"Well," I said, "I've got an idea—from something Evans said. I suspect that Lear's going to use this news about Derna for his own ends, and with no time lost. Probably we'll know after we've talked to him. If I'm right, we've got to find some way to get to Tripoli before Lear does. We've got to!"

In the legal profession, a man meets many a slippery customer : tricky lawyers representing guilty clients ; men who insist that black is white, and produce witnesses to prove it ; men who are for ever persuading juries that the worse is actually the better reason. I've seen a lot of them, and I expect to see a lot more ; but if I live for ever I'll never see a slippier one than Tobias Lear.

He joined us in two hours, as he had promised—the perfect picture of a punctilious and agreeable diplomat, a hail-fellow-well-met companion, who shared with us a bowl of the infinitesimal fried squid or calamaretti for which Zia Theresa is celebrated throughout the Mediterranean, washing them down with Zia Theresa's white wine.

He was as full of compliments as he was of questions about the attitude of people in Derna and other parts of Tripoli.

"Let me speak about that," Leitensdorfer said. "I have gone up and down that country for years, and I tell you the weariness of war that burns within the inhabitants of Tripoli is a flame—a hot wind ! Under Joseph Karamanli it is fight, fight, fight all the time, isn't it, and for ever pay higher taxes for the fighting. Hamet is a peaceful man, and when Hamet reaches the city of Tripoli, as the commodore has promised to assist him to do, I truly believe all those people will be the happiest people in the world."

Lear raised his eyebrows. " But we have been given to understand by General Eaton himself that he was disappointed in Hamet—that Hamet is neither a strong leader nor a prince who inspires confidence."

" That is not correct," Leitensdorfer said. " Everywhere in Arab lands it is customary to pay for the hire of camels and camelmen, and for all other parts of a caravan, before the caravan starts, isn't it ? In the beginning that was not understood by General Eaton, and he had been given insufficient funds. The camelmen were therefore within their rights in going as far as they'd been paid for, and then stopping. So that Hamet often had to perform the impossible : persuade them to go on even though there was no money for them. It was almost a miracle that he was able to do so. At times, when some of them had turned homeward for lack of pay, he would pursue them for as much as two days and bring them back again—something I have never seen done in all the years I have travelled with Arabs, isn't it ? And, of course, Hamet has been obliged to promise all sorts of things to those who follow him. Occasionally he has felt discouraged and disheartened because of repeated rumours that in spite of all the promises made to him by Americans, the Americans would desert him in the end. This disturbed General Eaton, because he felt that Hamet ought to trust the assurances of General Eaton and Commodore Barron and Commodore Preble and the President of the United States. Since the attack on Derna, in which Hamet led his Arab cavalry brilliantly and bravely, the general's admiration and affection for Hamet are unlimited."

Lear smiled. " Your statements differ strangely from those of two other members of Mr. Eaton's venture—two gentlemen of the highest respectability. The commodore and I have had their sworn testimony that Mr. Eaton is—though I dislike to use the word, gentlemen—a madman ; that his march is doomed to failure. Mr. Eaton was repeatedly heard by them to use the most inflammatory and ungentlemanly language. For no reason whatever he was guilty of making defamatory and profane statements about them, and without cause he brutally discharged them from his employ. Also they saw him drinking in public."

At this we burst into a duo of denials—my own protests being against the charge that Eaton was a madman and his expedition doomed to failure. But Leitensdorfer silenced me.

" Now I know ! " he told Lear. " Those two what-you-call respectable gentlemen must have been Farquhar and Goldsborough. I remember everything quite well ! Before the expedition left Cairo there were two

Farquhars : George, who was an English gentleman, a volunteer like Hamlin, a fine young man, brave and resourceful, a tower of strength : but the other, Robert Farquhar, was entirely different. He was a resident of Malta, a sort of half-breed of Scotland and Damascus, who posed to the general as a man of business. I tell you, sir, that Robert Farquhar was everything that was low and cheap. He was a pimp, a procurer, a man who took money from women, isn't it ? He was a liar. He was a drunkard. He was a thief. He stole thirteen hundred dollars that General Eaton had entrusted to him for the purchase of supplies. He and Goldsborough disgraced every American in Cairo. They got drunk in public, fought with their fists, rolled on the floor before highly placed Arabs and Turks. That Goldsborough, too—he was equally worthless. He was a petty officer from the *Argus*, a man without principle or honour or understanding. He insulted Arab women on the streets, crying epithets after them and lifting up their veils ! He was a danger to all the Americans, who might have been killed because of him, isn't it ?

"The general issued formal charges against the two men, stating exactly what I have just stated to you, and ordered them returned to Malta. I was adjutant and wrote that order—I myself ! They were never a part of our expedition at all. Everything they told you about General Eaton, it was a lie ! He is not mad—he is a brave man, a great leader ! If he is given the help he deserves and has been promised, his name and that of the United States of America will for ever be gratefully remembered by the entire world."

Lear, who had been listening with lowered eyes, looked up at Leitensdorfer with a polite smile—a far too polite smile for my taste. " I'm glad to have your assurance, Colonel. I suspected, of course, that the two gentlemen might be exaggerating, and I'm glad to have my suspicion confirmed."

I knew he was nothing of the sort. He had hated Eaton from the beginning ; he had avidly welcomed Farquhar's and Goldsborough's venomous slanders, and he would continue to believe them no matter what we said. He was just another Judge Chase. No evidence or argument could have made Chase change his twisted ideas or his visionless viewpoint ; and Lear would persist in his own wrongheadedness in exactly the same way.

I knew nothing I could say would have any effect upon him, but I had to try. " Colonel," I said, " I think it's only fair to say we've heard some extremely disquieting rumours—though perhaps 'disquieting' isn't the right word. Actually, they've caused General Eaton profound alarm, and they've distressed the rest of us. We've heard from what we consider trustworthy sources that you're going to ignore all the promises made to Hamet—that you're going to purchase a separate peace with the Bashaw of Tripoli, regardless of General Eaton and of Hamet."

For a moment I thought Lear did not mean to answer me, but evidently he decided that a misleading reply was better than none. " My dear

Hamlin," he said, " how could you hear any such rumour, when I haven't been in Tripoli at all, and have had no direct communication with the Bashaw ? " He laughed. " I think you must have been listening to what the Navy calls scuttlebutt."

" Everyone of us, Colonel, from General Eaton down, hopes that the rumour *is* only that—hopes it with all his heart," I said, with such emphasis that he couldn't miss my meaning.

" How could you consider it anything else," Lear asked, " when there have been no negotiations ? You can't have a peace without negotiations, can you ? "

" No, sir," I said. " But our information was that the Bashaw had made you indirect offers—one through the Spanish consul and one through the French consul."

" My dear Hamlin," Lear said, " any dealings I may have, in my official capacity as Political Commissioner with the Mediterranean Fleet, would hardly be with the Spanish consul or the French consul ! "

At this, I didn't dare look at him—nor even at Leitensdorfer. There it was ! Lear had as good as admitted that Lydia's last letter had told us the exact truth : that he *had* received offers from the Bashaw through the Spanish and French consuls. For if he hadn't he certainly would have said he hadn't, flatly. And if he weren't seriously considering accepting one of these offers, he would have told us, equally flatly, that he'd received them, and had indignantly spurned them. All my fears, all my doubts, every one of the dark forebodings that had buzzed wasp-like in my head since Lydia wrote that Tobias Lear was on his way to Malta—all had been justified.

" Colonel," I said after a moment, " my friend and I have, in a sense, come here under false pretences ; for, as you naturally realise, the dispatches from General Eaton could have been carried as readily by Lieutenant Evans as by the two of us. Our real purpose in coming was to plead a case. General Eaton let us come because he himself couldn't come—not without jeopardising the safety of his expedition, which is on the verge of complete success. He felt the testimony of two of us would carry more assurance than the testimony of just one man, unsupported by witnesses."

Lear turned his profile to us and put on that look of his that he must have thought made him resemble George Washington—though to my way of thinking it made him look like a big white cat obstinately refusing to let itself be pulled out of a tree. " You're implying," he said softly, " that I'm unable to carry out my duties as Political Commissioner without outside assistance ? "

" No, sir," I said, " I'm implying nothing of the sort. I'm only hoping that you'll regard us as two men who have taken an active part in the war against Tripoli, and are anxious to see it brought to an absolutely successful termination in the shortest possible time. I ask you to hear us, just as I'd ask a judge to hear an expert witness. I'd have no thought, in such a situation, of implying that the judge was in any way lacking, and I'm sure he would realise that I only wanted justice done."

I saw that Lear remained stonily hostile, but I was determined not to give up until I had to. " Whatever you demand of Joseph Karamanli, Colonel, you can get from him. Because the man is frightened ! If there's anything in the rumour that he has made peace offers, those offers are inspired by fright alone—and with good reason. Not because of our naval strength—there haven't been any demonstrations before Tripoli this season. No—what has given him a genuine fright is that he has seen General Eaton doing the impossible—has watched Eaton and Hamet march successfully across six hundred miles of desert, hold together an army of twelve hundred Arabs, attack the richest and one of the best fortified towns in North Africa, and capture it in two hours. Joseph Karamanli knows by this time that he's got to try to talk the United States into making peace, because if he doesn't—if Eaton and Hamet march on to Tripoli—*he's finished* ! "

" There's one point you seem to be overlooking," Lear replied, apparently unmoved by this speech. " There are three hundred American sailors in Tripoli. Just what do you imagine would happen to those three hundred Americans if they were in Tripoli when the city was attacked ? "

" Nothing," I said. " Nothing at all ! "

Lear threw up his hands. " But gentlemen——"

" No, no," Leitensdorfer cried. " Hamlin is right ! Nothing at all ! I know Joseph Karamanli as well as I know his brother Hamet, who is a great gentleman. Joseph is as bad as Hamet is good. I tell you he is a rat ; and like all rats, he is ready to leave a sinking ship. If Eaton and Hamet keep on, Joseph's ship is as good as sunk, and Joseph knows it. Already he sees the handwriting on the wall ! We have reached Derna. If we have supplies and money, nothing can keep us from reaching Tripoli. Then Joseph Karamanli will have nothing left but life. If he lets those three hundred American sailors be harmed, he knows what the American Navy would do to him."

He tilted his head, drew his forefinger across his throat, and with his lips made a ripping sound startlingly suggestive of the passage of a knife through a windpipe.

Lear pushed back his chair. " I must say, gentlemen, you're optimistic."

" Not at all," Leitensdorfer said. " Prisoners in all these African countries are excellent property, valuable for getting concessions out of the countries they came from. The potential ransom value of one good prisoner makes him worth fivè camels. You never heard of an Arab killing his camels, Colonel ! And they're the same with prisoners, always —just as they always face east when they pray, and eat with their fingers. They don't change, Colonel Lear."

I knew Lear didn't believe us.

" Colonel," I said, " it's true, isn't it, that General Eaton was

authorised by the President, by the Secretary of the Treasury, by the
Secretary of the Navy, and by Congress to restore Hamet to his rightful
position as ruler of Tripoli ? "

" Not at all," Lear answered.

" But, sir, the President authorised a loan to Hamet of field artillery,
a thousand stand of arms, and forty thousand dollars on condition that
he co-operate with the Navy against the common enemy."

" Ah, but I think you'll find," Lear said, " that General Eaton
misunderstood the intention behind that offer. It was made only on
condition that Hamet supply the necessary assistance."

" He *has* supplied it," I retorted, " and he's ready to supply more."

" My dear Hamlin, I'm sure you mean well, but my official position
prevents me from debating the war against Tripoli with you and your
friend. I have never approved of General Eaton's high-handedness in
embarking on a land expedition without the proper authority."

" But he *did* have the authority, sir ! " I protested. " Colonel
Leitensdorfer has the order that Commodore Barron gave Captain Hull
last December. You have that order, haven't you, Colonel ? "

Leitensdorfer nodded and drew a bundle of papers from his sash.

" Really, gentlemen," Lear said, " I'm quite familiar with all papers
that have any bearing on this situation."

" But you spoke of the general's high-handedness," Leitensdorfer
argued. " See, sir : this is Commodore Barron's authorisation to Captain
Hull to take General Eaton to Alexandria to get Hamet. See, sir, it reads :

" To proceed with Mr. Eaton to Alexandria in search of Hamet
Pasha, the rival brother and legitimate sovereign of the reigning Pasha
of Tripoli, and to convey him and his suite to Derna or such other place
on the coast as may be determined the most proper for co-operating
with the naval force under my command against the common enemy ;
or, if more agreeable to him, to bring him to me before Tripoli."

Lear's voice breathed a patient courtesy. " Exactly, my dear Colonel !
Mr. Eaton was to *convey*, not escort, Hamet to Derna. Nothing could be
clearer. If Hamet had been *conveyed* to Derna, he would have sailed there
in the *Argus*. There would have been no expense and no risk. Instead
of that, Mr. Eaton saw fit to march six hundred miles overland at vast
expense and great risk—a quite unjustified proceeding ! "

I found this petty quibbling purely nauseous ; but before I could
protest Leitensdorfer said, " Let me finish, please." He read on :

" Should Hamet Pasha not be found at Alexandria, you have the
discretion to proceed to any other place for him, where the safety of
you ship can be, in your opinion, relied upon. The Pasha may be
assured of the support of my squadron at Bengazi or Derna, where
you are at liberty to put in, if required, and if it can be done without

N

too great risk. And you may assure him also that I will take the most effectual measures, with the forces under my command, for co-operating with him against the usurper, his brother, and for re-establishing him in the regency of Tripoli. Arrangements to this effect are confided to the discretion with which Mr. Eaton is vested by the Government.

"And so," Leitensdorfer concluded, "General Eaton had all the authority he needed to do whatever was necessary in order to join Commodore Barron in an attack on Tripoli."

Lear raised his shoulders, and his face was a study in determined indifference. "You persist, gentlemen, in thinking that in this situation the prime object of our country is to make war, thus endangering the lives of the three hundred American sailors in Tripoli, rather than to make peace and deliver those prisoners from slavery."

He stood up. "I shall have to ask you gentlemen to excuse me. I have no doubt that you are actuated by the highest motives, but your association with General Eaton has blinded you to the fact that often a given plan must be changed to meet changed conditions. I'll arrange for you to return to Derna in the *Hornet* with Lieutenant Evans."

Smiling frostily, he started to leave the room ; but I was quicker than he and slipped around him to stand with my back against the door.

Lear eyed me coldly. "Kindly stand aside."

"There are still a few things to be said," Leitensdorfer told him. "We have worked hard, fought hard, and performed prodigies, and now we are entitled to be heard. Also, we are much averse to being put in the wrong. We cannot abandon friends without a protest ! "

Lear shrugged his shoulders and reseated himself at the table.

"Colonel Lear," I said, "I hope you won't hold this against us, or against General Eaton, but we can't let you leave this room **until we're** told you what we conceive to be the truth, and the whole truth. The order that Colonel Leitensdorfer just read to you promised Hamet that the commodore would co-operate with him against Joseph Karamanli and re-establish Hamet on the throne of Tripoli. In the same way, General Eaton promised Hamet American help and American money to help him regain the position stolen from him, and the wife and children that Joseph Karamanli is holding as hostages. The reason General Eaton couldn't take him aboard the *Argus* and sail to Derna with him was that the Egyptian Government wouldn't allow it. There was only one way to get him to Derna, and that was to raise an army capable of taking him there and capturing the city. The expenses of that march will be met by Hamet when he's re-established in Tripoli. It's a loan to Hamet —not a waste of money as you've implied.

"Now there it is, Colonel Lear ! Commodore Barron promised American support to Hamet, and so did General Eaton ; and in order to raise the army to get him here, Hamet had to extend those promises to cover everybody in his command. He promised them that the Americans would help them ; that the Americans would never desert them ; that they could depend upon the Americans to help them recapture Tripoli. General Eaton, depending on the President of the United States and the Secretary of State and Commodore Barron, promised Hamet that he would never be deserted."

I waited for Lear to say something, but he just sat there, expressionlessly studying his folded hands.

"Now, Colonel," I went on at last "something—God knows what— has happened in the past few weeks. The commodore's letters to General Eaton have shown a singular doubt, at the very moment when confidence should be highest. It's as though he were trying to imply that nobody'd ever promised Hamet anything at all. The supplies and the money that General Eaton must have in order to march from Derna to Tripoli haven't arrived. What's worse, there's no indication when they *will* arrive, which makes it impossible for the general to mature his plans for proceeding. As I told you, we've heard that the Bashaw has been extending peace offers. I'm speaking for myself, for Colonel Leitensdorfer here, and for every man who undertook to make the expedition with General Eaton, when I say that to our minds the acceptance of any such peace offer would run contrary to honour and justice. To agree to it would be to haul down a victorious American flag before an enemy who has no right to claim a victory and no earthly reason to expect one.

" If any offer from Joseph Karamanli should be accepted, General Eaton would be obliged to abandon Hamet at the very point at which Commodore Barron had originally intended to start helping him. To make peace on any terms at all, before Joseph Karamanli has been soundly thrashed, would subject every man who has worked and fought for Hamet to be harried, hacked, and slaughtered by his brother's hired assassins. At the present moment, Hamet and his Arabs respect and admire America and Americans. If they're abandoned, all their respect and confidence will turn to contempt and hatred—and rightly so ! Look at that letter from Commodore Barron, assuring Hamet that he'll not only co-operate with him, but actually re-establish him in Tripoli ! If a peace is signed with Joseph Karamanli now, then we haven't co-operated with Hamet at all. The only 'co-operation' has been with Joseph Karamanli, our mortal enemy ! Hamet has helped us, fought with us, and fought well. He stands ready to put an end to all tribute-paying and piracy. To abandon him would be murder ! Joseph Karamanli—already an assassin, a man beneath contempt—has declared war on us, held Americans prisoner, beaten and stoned them, and is utterly incapable of living up to the terms of any treaty. To appease this man, to allow him to out-general us at the very moment we've got him whipped, would be horrible !

" If Joseph Karamanli is allowed to blackmail America now, when one more push would topple him into the dirt where he belongs, he'll go on blackmailing America until he *is* kicked into the dirt. We've got him where he has no choice but to surrender unconditionally—*if* General

Eaton is allowed to keep on. Any peace that's made should be on our
own terms. Not one penny should be paid out in ransom. Why pay
ransom to a murderer, when the same amount of money given to Eaton
would for ever put an end to ransom-paying? That national honour of
the United States is vastly more important than shortening the term of
imprisonment of three hundred American sailors ; and any American
ought to understand by now that his country should be above haggling
with a pirate !

"For General Eaton's expedition to end in such a way—with all our
promises broken, all human feelings contemptuously disregarded, the
honour, good faith, and good name of the United States degraded—would
be a tragedy so dark that no decent man, if he had foreseen such an end,
would have taken part in it ! "

I stopped, praying that Lear would say just a word, would show in
some way that he was open to argument. But he wouldn't ; there he
sat, his eyes veiled, staring down at his folded hands, and I knew all
argument was useless.

I looked at Leitensdorfer. He shook his head. When the silence
became insupportable, I asked Leitensdorfer whether he wanted to add
anything to what I'd said.

"I want to remind Colonel Lear," Leitensdorfer said in an icy tone,
"that Hamet's wife and three children are held as hostages by Joseph
Karamanli. They have as much right to be freed as have the American
sailors who are prisoners, isn't it ? "

Lear wouldn't answer.

Again silence filled that small room, a silence broken only by the
clattering of chunky carts on the pavement below and the hoarse cries
of the octopus fishermen slowly poling their blazing flares around the
dark harbour. I knew it was hopeless ; Lear meant to have no further
traffic with us. But I decided to make one more try.

"Sir," I said, "can't we have your word that nothing will be done
about accepting any offers from Joseph Karamanli until after our full
fleet has reached the Mediterranean—until our full striking force has
shown itself before Tripoli ? "

"Mr. Hamlin," Lear replied, "you and I held contrary opinions on a
previous occasion—in Haiti. At that time you recklessly urged Christophe
to oppose the landing of the French army, whereas anyone should have
known that such opposition would result only in needless slaughter. The
French would have won anyway, and they *did* win. All that waste of life
and destruction of property were not necessary, as I pointed out at the
time."

"But they *were* necessary ! " I protested. "Evidently you haven't
heard how that business turned out ! The blacks were fighting for liberty,
and by resolutely persisting in fighting the French invaders they delayed
them, wore them out. The consequence was that thousands of French

caught the yellow fever and died of it ! And in the end the blacks got what they'd fought for—liberty. If they hadn't fought for it, they wouldn't have got it—they'd be slaves to-day, instead of free men under Dessalines ! ''

Although Lear was unmistakably startled by this information, it did nothing to budge him. '' That, Mr. Hamlin, is sheer sophistry, not worthy of a reply. Your procedure and Colonel Leitensdorfer's in compelling me to stay and listen to your personal opinions has been nothing short of effrontery ! General Eaton's letters will be answered in due course by Commodore Barron. I have nothing more to say.''

There was silence for a long minute, as I reflected again that I should never understand the workings of a mind like Lear's. Then I turned to Leitensdorfer. '' Well,'' I said, '' if you can't think of anything else——''

I saw a peculiar look in his eye and knew he *had* thought of something else. Indeed, I'd had the same thought myself. But of course that sort of thing, done anywhere except on a battlefield, is bound to be discovered and punished.

So we left Lear sitting there at the table, looking grim and pale and noble, and got ourselves out of Zia Theresa's to plan our next step as rapidly as possible.

CHAPTER LIX

THE GOVERNOR'S palace at Malta, built by the indefatigable Crusaders who erected the monumental walls and bastions that made this harbour an impregnable stronghold, was guarded from intruders by lantern-lighted sentry-boxes. Before the boxes a British marine walked his post in a military manner, with a deal of arm-swing and brisk about-facing. When Leitensdorfer and I halted before the palace, two other marines came out of the sentry-boxes and eyed us without enthusiasm.

One of them made a jerking movement with his thumb, which I took to mean '' Move along.''

'' Is there any possible way in which we can see the Governor to-night ? '' I asked.

The sentry halted suddenly. '' Lumme ! '' he exclaimed. '' Scared me, that did, like 'earing an 'orse speak Hinglish.''

One of the other marines, holding his rifle at a suggestive angle, came closer to look at us. '' Ten o'clock in the morning's the earliest, except for admirals and suchlike.''

'' Doesn't he ever see anyone at night ? '' I asked.

'' Not 'ceptin' on special occasions.''

'' What does a man have to do in order to be admitted on special occasions ? ''

'' 'Ow ! '' the marine said. '' Mostly 'e 'as a pyper or somethink from the Governor. We tyke it and show it to the leftnunt, and the leftnunt 'e says, ' Let 'em in.' Sometimes 'e just says, ' Tell the blighters the Governor eyen't 'ome. Tell 'em to come rahnd in the morning.' "

" Well," I said, " I know we haven't the proper sort of paper, but we do have orders of a sort. If you'd be kind enough to look at one of them, you might be willing to show it to the lieutenant. I think the Governor may just possibly consent to see us."

" Let's see it," the sentry said.

Leitensdorfer took his packet of papers from his sash and handed one of them to the sentry.

The sentry carried it over to one of the sentry-box lights, held it close to the lantern, and mumbled the order. " ' Colonel Eugene Leitensdorfer, Hadjutant, 'ereby hauthorised proceed to Malta, 'companied by Halbion 'Amlin, volunteer, purpose carryin' despatches to Commodore Sam'l Barron. From Malta hauthorised proceed matters nessry to welfare this hexpedition in hany wye they mye elect. William Heaton, Left-Gen.' "

The marine came back to us and doubtfully eyed Leitensdorfer's burnoose and Arab slippers. " You a colonel ? " he asked.

Leitensdorfer smiled and nodded. " I have that honour."

" We 'eard this General Heaton marched an army 'arfway across Africa and fought a battle somewhere."

" That is correct," Leitensdorfer said. " He attacked Derna on April twenty-seventh—a smart and successful action."

" Cor," the sentry said. " Abaht time ! This volunteer in it, too ? "

" Very much so," Leitensdorfer said. " He led a cavalry troop of black Arabs from Jalo."

The marine stared at us open-mouthed, looked bewildered, suddenly straightened up, clicked his heels together, saluted smartly ; then opened the massive doors of the palace and vanished within. In a matter of minutes he was back again accompanied by a slender, stooped young man in a scarlet monkey-jacket. I thought I'd never seen anyone who looked so wholly helpless and vacuous. He wore a single eyeglass, which seemed to require constant adjusting ; and there was a slack look about his lower lip, as though he were almost too weak to close his mouth.

He took in our burnooses and headcloths and seemed completely bemused by them. " By jove," he said, " I thought there must have been some sort of mistake, but I fancy not ! Quite amazing ! Ah—Colonel Leitensdorfer, I mean to say, eh ? "

Leitensdorfer clicked his heels together and bowed a little from the waist.

The young man thrust out his hand and shook Leitensdorfer's limply. " Custers. Leftnant. Governor's aide, what ? Took Derna, eh ? Well, well, well ! Must have been worth watching ! "

When he came to me, I found that his hand-clasp was less limp than it looked. I told him my name, and he said, " Good, good, I mean to say ! "

He scanned the two of us. "Understand from Stodgill you want to see Sraleck." This, I found, signified Sir Alexander John Ball, the Governor. "May not be able to arrange it, but come in, come in! If the old boy's in bed, I mean to say, I'll try to get him out. Always likes to see Americans since Preble was here. Great old boy, Preble, I mean. Took no nonsense from any of these beastly blighters, and all that! Come in, come in!"

Carstairs his name was, not "Custers" as he had pronounced it; and his appearance was as deceptive as his pronunciation. I've heard Englishmen damned by Americans for rudeness, snobbery, and over-bearing ways, and I've encountered a few who seemed like that at first sight, just as Carstairs gave the impression of being vacuous, silly, even a trifle weak-minded. But in my experience Englishmen are given to examining others from behind a screen of their own making: a screen of stolidity, perhaps, or hautiness, or airiness. If they approve of what they see, the screen is withdrawn, revealing them as ordinary humans with a marked leaning towards decency, justice, and honourable dealings.

Carstairs's screen was airiness. "Did themselves well, these old boys, eh?" he said, speaking of the magnificent building into which he led us. "Grand Masters built it for themselves, I mean. Makes Buckingham look like a jolly old hen-roost, what?"

Once inside, he demonstrated that his pose of helplessness was only a pose, for—having ushered us into the outer waiting-room of the palace —he went droopingly off, but in a few seconds his head reappeared in the doorway through which he had banished. "Caught him!" he said. "'Eaton took Derna,' I told him. 'Got some laddies out here who know all about it,' I told him. Got the old boy all a-twitter to hear about it! Come in, come in!"

We followed him past enormous rooms hung with tapestries, rich with suits of armour, blazing with painted friezes of battles by sea and by land, and into a library of which any king might have been proud. At a carved desk in the midst of all this splendour sat a gentleman who may have been, as Carstairs said, all a-twitter, but who seemed to be concealing it successfully. He was a red-faced little man with sharp blue eyes and pursed lips, and he looked as though he'd just eaten a persimmon—a sweet persimmon, if there is such a thing. He was wearing a shapeless sort of uniform made out of dark blue India silk—a relic, possibly, of his days in the Navy, since the garments hung upon him as loosely as though designed by a sailmaker.

"Happy to hear the news about Eaton," he said, when Carstairs had introduced us. "Jolly good sort, Eaton! Far-seeing! Knew he'd save all of us a lot of trouble if he did as he hoped."

He wanted to know all about it: the size of the Derna shore batteries, the size of the garrison, the number and the names of the vessels that had supported us, the position they had taken before the town, the size of Eaton's attacking force.

Leitensdorfer's answers seemed to please him.

" Never saw a man more confident than Eaton," he said. " He knew he could do it, and that's half the battle. Told me he'd undertake to go anywhere in North Africa if they'd give him enough marines. How many did they give him ? "

" Six," Leitensdorfer said.

The Governor looked at him sharply. " I mean, how many marines made the march with him ? "

" Six, sir," Leitensdorfer said, " with one lieutenant and a sergeant."

" They gave him six marines ? " the Governor said, and his face was a study in disgust. " Good God ! *Six* marines ! What did they give him for supplies ? Half a cup of rice ? "

" We got supplies at Bomba," Leitensdorfer said ; " but for two weeks before that we'd lived on dates—when we could get 'em."

The Governor nodded. " Governments never change, do they ? Never save on anything except the really important things. Bloody damned fools, I mean to say ! Waste a million pounds on garden parties for a lot of stupid asses ; then quibble over spending fifty on powder for a soldier to put in his guns ! " He said " Pah ! " in a contemptuous voice ; then gave us a sharp look. " Well, gentlemen, I don't suppose you came to Malta to tell me about the taking of Derna."

" No, sir," I said, " we didn't. We came here with dispatches for Commodore Barron from General Eaton. We're turning to you for help, though I'm afraid we can't offer anything in return."

" I thought possibly that might be in your minds," the Governor said. " Ah—you've doubtless seen Colonel Lear."

" Yes, sir," I said, " we saw Colonel Lear. The chief reason General Eaton sent us here was to talk to Colonel Lear."

I looked at the Governor, wondering how well he knew Colonel Lear and how far I ought to go. The Governor stared back at me with an icy and unblinking eye.

" Sir," I said, " I think I ought to say that I first met Colonel Lear in Washington some years ago. I had occasion to go to him for information—which he wouldn't give me. Then I ran across him in Haiti, at the time of the French invasion. We had a difference of opinion there, because he thought the Negroes of Haiti should surrender to the French without fighting. I don't like to mention these things, but it's necessary because they taught me that Colonel Lear won't fight to attain an end, *if* it can be attained in any other way."

" Very interesting," the Governor commented, though he looked stupid rather than interested.

" Well, sir," I said, " I never expected to see Colonel Lear again when I left Haiti. I lost track of things for a while, because my wife and I were taken prisoner by a Tripolitan vessel commanded by Murad Rais, a Scotsman who's acting as admiral for the Bashaw."

The Governor's fingers beat a tattoo on his desk. " Your wife, eh ? "

"Yes, sir," I said. "They made us sign a paper promising not to try to escape, and they told us that if either of us tried it the other'd be sold to the first caravan that passed ; so I'll have to ask you to hold this information as confidential. They set me to raising vegetables in Murad Rais's garden, and they made her a governess to Hamet's three children, held as hostages by Joseph Karamanli."

The Governor, reaching under his blue-silk jacket, pulled out a watch the size of a doughnut. Hanging from the end of the fob were several small keys. The Governor handed the watch and the fob to Carstairs. "Get me that bottle of Bulloch Lade, my boy, and a box of those three-sided cigars."

Carstairs obediently used one of the keys to unlock a mahogany cellarette, took from it a decanter and a handful of goblets, and placed them before the Governor.

The Governor neatly filled the glasses and handed them to us. "Prefer it to brandy, personally. Sweeter."

I wasn't surprised that he preferred it to brandy. It was whisky, but smooth as liquid velvet, and fragrant.

The Governor pushed the box of three-sided cigars towards us, cracked the tip of his own ; then nodded at me from behind a cloud of pale blue smoke.

"Well, sir," I said, "I've heard from my wife regularly ever since Colonel Leitensdorfer and King Dick helped me get away——"

"Get away !" the Governor cried. "I thought you said you signed a paper. And who might ' King Dick ' be ? "

"Yes, sir," I said, "an agreement never to ask for help. But I didn't ask for help. As for King Dick, he's a Negro, a good friend—good now, and good from my days in Haiti. Well, he figured out where I was, sent Colonel Leitensdorfer hunting for me, and the colonel found me. Then King Dick came and took me away while Preble was hammering the town for the third time. He arranged for my wife to send us information on what was happening in Tripoli. We knew General Eaton would need all the information he could get when he attacked the city."

"By Jove ! " the Governor said. "But look here, my dear fellow ! Your wife, I mean ! They'd threatened to sell her as a slave if you escaped."

"Yes, sir," I said, "but they didn't *know* I'd escaped. King Dick left a dead body in my place."

"Blew it up with a mortar-load, isn't it ? " Leitensdorfer explained. "I worked it out with him—an excellent way to spoil a body."

Carstairs's monocle fell from his eye, and the Governor leaned back in his chair and blew smoke at the ceiling. "Haiti ! " he murmured. "Murad Rais ! King Dick ! Raised vegetables ! Arranged for information ! Left a spoiled body !—Good God ! Do you understand all this, Carstairs ? I put it to you, because I don't quite seem to follow him."

Carstairs screwed his monocle back into place. " Don't understand a word of it, but it must be all right, eh ? Wouldn't occur to a chap to say such things unless they were true, I mean to say."

" Oh, quite ! " the Governor said. He eyed me with an assumed severity that was somehow heartening. " She sent you information, did she ? Information about what ? "

" Well, sir," I said, " she drew a map for one thing—a map you might possibly like to copy." I took the little packet of Lydia's letters from the case I carried strapped around my waist, from among them took the four sheets on which she had drawn the detail map of Tripoli, and laid them before the Governor.

" H'm," he said. " Lime juice ! Very neat ! " He fitted the sheets together and made humming sounds. " Hundred and fifteen guns, eh ? "

" They can't shoot," I told him.

" So Preble wrote me," the Governor murmured.

" He put the *Constitution* right in under the guns," I said. " I never saw such a sight. She looked as if she were sailing through a forest of waterspouts."

The Governor shot a quick glance at me. " Quite ! We all took a sort of personal pride in Preble. Did you hear how the Pope slapped our faces ? He said, ' Commodore Preble, with a small force and in a short space of time, has done more for the cause of Christianity than the most powerful nations of Christendom have done for ages ! ' "

The Governor's praise of Preble caught unexpectedly at my throat and I must have shown it, for he eyed me oddly. " You don't chance to know Preble, do you ? "

" Yes, sir. I come from the same town he does—Portland, Maine. My uncle got him released from a prison ship during the Revolution. His father's my uncle's closest friend."

The Governor nodded. " Hope Portland appreciates him more than his government does." He turned to Carstairs. " Look here, Carsty ; you'll have to copy this map. Copy it as well as you can. Those Jews' names are worth their weight in gold. Get right at it, I mean." To me he said, " Lear got a copy of this ? "

" No, sir, he hasn't."

" Why not ? "

" Well, sir, here's another thing I don't like to say, and I do so only because I'm going to ask you for help—which entitles you to know all the circumstances. I didn't *dare* give it to Colonel Lear."

" Oh, come now," the Governor protested.

" Sir," I said, " there's no two ways about it. Lear is determined to make peace with Tripoli on his own hook."

" You think so, do you ? "

" I know so ! " I said. " My wife wrote me from Tripoli that he was going to, and she's never wrong."

"Never wrong, eh?" the Governor asked. "Would your wife by any chance have fathomed the reason that would lead the gentleman to do such a damned-fool thing as that?"

"She doesn't know that, sir, any more than I do. We don't pretend to understand Lear's mind. He used to be President Washington's secretary, and a man who knows him told me that sometimes he used to be taken for Washington. So he thought——"

"Who thought?" the Governor asked sharply.

"Lear. Lear thought, according to this man, that he was as great a man as Washington, and resented it if he wasn't considered as important as Washington."

"What's your own opinion, Hamlin?"

"I'm sure of only one thing, sir; Lear always contrives to think wrong, somehow. He's kept hold of Washington's private correspondence for years. If he'd done as he should, he'd have turned it over to the United States Government, to which it rightly belongs. He had access to French Spoliation Claims papers in Washington, but he refused to help me get them for my clients, though he damned well knew I was entitled to have 'em. In Haiti he did everything he could to persuade Toussaint L'Ouverture to surrender to the French without a fight—to sell the whole island back into slavery again. Now he means to settle this war with Tripoli in his own way: he's going to sell out the United States Government; he's going to sell out Eaton; he's going to sell out Hamet. The United States Navy in the Mediterranean isn't commanded by Commodore Barron—it's commanded by Tobias Lear; and Tobias Lear's going to run counter to every decent man's opinion! He's going to cut off the money and the supplies that were promised to Eaton. If Preble were in command of our ships in this ocean, as he ought to be, he and Eaton between 'em would have Joseph Karamanli on his way to exile in a month's time, and Tripoli would be governed by a man who'd guarantee safety and equal rights to the ships of every nation in the world. But that's not how Lear does things! I didn't dare give him that map of mine for fear he'd destroy it—as he certainly would have done if he thought it would interfere with any of his own plans."

The Governor stared up at the gold-tooled volumes on the lofty shelves, shaking his head as though he found the sight displeasing. Then he picked up the decanter and refilled our glasses. "We occasionally pick up a bit of information—no good to anybody, of course—seems to fit in sometimes, though. Suppose you've heard of Bainbridge, captain of the *Philadelphia*?"

"Yes, sir. I saw the *Philadelphia* run on the reef. I think her crew could have fought her. There was only one gunboat anywhere near her, and she floated by herself the day after she struck."

The Governor gave me an odd look. "Hard to judge," he said. "Can't quite imagine Nelson striking his flag to a half-pint Tripolitan gunboat—or to ten of 'em, either—not while he still had a whole ship under him and a set of boarding nettings. Rather blow himself up, I mean to say ! Ah, well——"

He sipped at his whisky ; rolled it over his tongue, and returned to his original thesis. " What I'm getting at is that somebody accidentally saw a letter Bainbridge wrote last November—wrote to an American consul in Tunis. Spoke bitterly about the Eaton proposal to put Hamet back on the throne—oh, bitterly ! "

Leitensdorfer got suddenly to his feet and as suddenly sat down again. " What does this Bainbridge know about Hamet ? " he asked softly. " Bainbridge has been in Tripoli for the past year and a half, conversing only with the retinue and the officers of Joseph Karamanli. What would a man in such a postion learn about Hamet ? And what is so wrong about Hamet, anyway, if I may ask ? "

" You may," the Governor said. " I read the letter a number of times. Interested in it, as Bainbridge didn't seem to care much for Preble, either. In fact, he called Preble a liar in it. I mean to say, I know Preble ! Stout feller, Preble ! Never lied in his life ! " He glared at me, as if I might harbour false ideas about Preble.

" According to Bainbridge," he went on, " this is what's wrong with Hamet : He's effeminate ; he's a coward ; he was never popular in Cyrenaica or Tripoli ; if a Christian joined with him to put him back on the throne, all the Moslems would instantly rise in a holy war ; the very idea of an expedition to help him back to power is extraordinary and impolitic, and no possible benefit could result to the United States from giving him any pecuniary or military assistance."

Leitensdorfer groaned and clasped his head in his hands.

" Bainbridge wrote that ? " I asked heavily.

" He wrote exactly that. He wrote that from Tripoli to the American consul in Tunis, in lime juice, just after Eaton left here last November with the full approval of Preble, Barron, and all other American naval officers in Malta, to co-operate with Hamet in a land attack on Tripoli."

" The whole thing's a damned lie ! " I exclaimed. " It might have been written at the dictation of Joseph Karamanli. Are you sure it wasn't a trick ? Joseph Karamanli might have forced him to write it."

" First thing I asked," the Governor said. " Found out all about it. Written in lime juice, and handed to Nissen, Danish consul in Tripoli, by Bainbridge himself. No possibility of a trick."

" But there's not a grain of truth in it ! Hamet's *not* effeminate—he's a great prince, a magnificent horseman, tireless, a true and reliable friend, simple, fearless—everything that Joseph Karamanli isn't ! What's Bainbridge talking about when he says Eaton's expedition is impolitic —that no possible benefit——"

" I understand ! I understand ! " the Governor said. " You don't need to convince me, my dear fellow ! I wouldn't have written letters for Eaton to carry to everyone in Egypt if I'd had any doubts about him, or about Hamet, or about the feasibility of his plan. The point is this :

if Bainbridge sent such a letter to Davis in Tunis last November, he most certainly sent a similar letter to Lear around the same time—probably a longer and more emphatic one."

"Yes," I said. "I see. You're giving us absolute proof that there's no possibility we're wrong in what we think about Lear and a peace offer."

"Exactly," the Governor agreed. "And I'm also trying to say that I think you're wholly justified in your desire to get to Tripoli, and to get there as rapidly as possible. That *is* your desire? That *is* the reason you came to see me?"

"Yes, sir," I said, "it is."

"Well," the Governor said slowly, "it's a little irregular, but I don't see how anybody could raise any objection if one of your blockading squadron off Tripoli had occasion to stop one of our vessels. You've got only two frigates there now—though God knows why Baron hasn't made a demonstration in force. Those two are the *Constitution* and the *Constellation*. The *Constitution's* the flagship, and I'd better give you a letter to her captain, who's an old friend : John Rodgers." He glanced up just as I smiled involuntarily. "You know him already, perhaps?"

"Yes, sir. I knew him in Haiti. He and I were together in Cap François the night it was burned to keep it out of French hands, and I was recalling how his face looked the last time I saw him, covered with soot."

"Indeed !" Sir Alexander said. "Now I think I understand a little better. From the beginning I felt sure you were going to ask me to send you to Tripoli, but I didn't gather how you expected to proceed when you got there. Now I think I see. Since you know Rodgers, and since you've found a way to get letters from your wife, I fancy you have a few plans of your own."

"Yes, sir. Before we left Jalo to join General Eaton, King Dick took the precaution of having a friend send a caravan to Tripoli ; and later, just before we left Derna, General Eaton sent King Dick back to Tripoli to see whether anything could be done. The caravan must still be there, and some of our black Arabs too, just outside the city walls."

The Governor shook his head. "Black Arabs ! Jalo ! Caravan !"

"On top of that," I added, "King Dick's a Marabout, and Colonel Leitensdorfer's a dervish and muezzin."

"Mean to say he—er—shouts from steeples?"

"Yes, sir. That and card tricks are only a few of his specialities." To Leitensdorfer I said, "Go ahead and show him."

Leitensdorfer obligingly threw back his head and let out a deafening howl : "*There is no God but Allah, and Muhammad is his Prophet !*"

"Good God !" the Governor said. "Carsty, run upstairs and reassure Lady Ball, eh? Tell her I'm having two guests over-night. Yes, and Carsty : ask her for a few more bottles of that Bulloch Lade. Shake a leg, Carsty !"

When I protested that we didn't want to inconvenience him and would be perfectly comfortable wrapped in our burnooses in a corner of his garden, he spoke severely. " Young man, one of my functions here in Malta is to get information for my government. You're asking a favour from me. Very well : I'll send the brig *Hesperides* on a cruise towards Tripoli, bright and early to-morrow morning, and you shall go with her ; but I mean to have one or two favours from you in return. I want information, my boy ! I want information about that wife of yours, who's never wrong. Didn't know any such paragon existed ! I want to know about this friend of yours, King Dick ; and where Jalo is and how you get there. I want to know how Colonel Leitensdorfer got to be a dervish. I want to know more about Eaton's march, and about those black Arabs. I want to know how those nasty Tripoli fellows happened to take you prisoner. Rotten bounders, I mean to say ! Yes—and Haiti ! How you jolly well *got* to Haiti, eh ? I want to know all about everything ! I want to hear about that sneaky white-faced Lear, damn him ! Why, damn his damned ordinary damned stupid interfering damned ignorant officious damned shortsightedness ! "

He puffed out his cheeks as if about to burst with indignation ; then was calm again.

" By the way," he said, " speaking of Haiti, did you ever see Toussaint when you were there ? "

" He helped me save my wife's life," I said. " King Dick was one of his generals. He's a great man, Governor."

" Damn it, don't I know it ? " the Governor said. " He *was* a great man—not *is*. Apparently you've not heard that two years ago the French coaxed him aboard a warship under a flag of truce, chained him up, took him to France, threw him in a mountain dungeon, and froze him to death." He glared at me and repeated the words " Under a flag of truce ! Truce, I mean to say ! "

I was horrified. When I muttered something under my breath about the French, the Governor slapped his desk. " Go ahead ! Say it ! Don't try to bottle it up ! That's what they are, damn 'em ! It's their damned crack-brained character ! Why in God's name has there always got to be some blasted crack-brained nation like the French in the world, to murder the Toussaints ? Always some fool like Lear to disgrace the Prebles and the Eatons ! "

I often hear Americans damn England as a nation of rakes, or of fops, or of tradesmen, or of bullies, or of scheming politicians, or of American-haters—a nation of this-that-or-the-other ; and I seldom protest, since there's no sense in arguing with ignorant men, who consistently cling to their ignorance. But always at such times my thoughts revert to Sir Alexander John Ball, Governor of Malta, who would have done everything in his power to help me and my country at the very moment when Tobias Lear, an American, was doing his utmost to bring dishonour to America, and discredit and disgrace to those who were fighting for her good name. And I know in my heart that Ball was right : there'll always be Lears in America as long as America exists. But I know, too, that in England, as long as she endures, there'll always be men like Sir Alexander John Ball, God bless him and rest his soul.

CHAPTER LX

SIR ALEXANDER accompanied us, the next morning, to His Majesty's gun brig *Hesperides*, Captain the Honourable Algernon Percy Mainwaring Crabbe. Not only had the Governor taken a great fancy to Leitensdorfer, but he was determined to have his instructions until the last possible moment on the pea-and-walnut-shell trick. He had made great progress, and could already pick up the pea, though not so bafflingly as Leitensdorfer could.

He went to Captain Crabbe's cabin with us, introduced us, and warned him that the less said about us the better. " I mean to say," he told him, " we've no business carting Americans all over the Mediterranean, have we, Captain ? Let 'em fight their own wars, eh ? So I'm giving you no orders. Just take 'em along. If the men want to know about 'em, don't under any circumstances say they're Americans. Say they're Arab friends of ours, returning to Morocco from a pilgrimage to Mecca. Say we're passing 'em from hand to hand. If the truth leaked out, it might make trouble for some of those American prisoners in Tripoli. Understand, Captain ? "

" Oh, quite ! " Captain Crabbe said.

To Leitensdorfer Sir Alexander said, " Let me see you pick up that pea again." He handed over the three walnut shells and the pea. Leitensdorfer put them on the captain's table and moved the shells rapidly over the pea. One of the shells seemed to descend upon the pea and cover it ; but when Leitensdorfer turned over his hand, the pea wasn't under the shell at all, but was tucked tight in the crook of his little finger.

" What do you think of that, Captain ? " Sir Alexander demanded. " Have him teach it to you as part payment for the voyage, eh ? Make your fortune on it when you retire, I mean to say." He shook our hands, and said to me, " When you get around to writing letters again, let me hear how you come out. Bring that lady of yours to see me. I'd like to be able to say I've met a lady who's never wrong."

Bellowing mirthfully, he stamped out of the cabin with Captain Crabbe, and we could hear the feeble piping of the bos'n's whistle as he went over the side.

We hardly had time to teach Captain Crabbe the shell-and-pea trick, for we made a quick run and encountered two American frigates even before we raised that familiar stretch of palm trees, minarets, and low white houses that was Tripoli. We saw them first as two little specks ;

then as iceberg-like pyramids, far, far away, shimmery in the Mediter-ranean heat; and finally, as we closed with them, as beautiful black-hulled ships, harmless-looking and shining, sliding effortlessly over a sea of blue silk, dwarfing the distant Castle that held so large a part of my heart and life.

The nearer of the two frigates was the *Constitution*, and she must have seen us before we saw her, for her course was laid to intercept us. I saw her as an old and much-loved friend, thanks to the times I'd watched her from every angle, spouting smoke and flame at the Bashaw's dust-wreathed strongholds.

When Captain Crabbe broke out a string of flags at his main truck as a signal that he wanted to speak her, she came into the wind like a big yacht and backed her topsail.

Captain Crabbe loaded the two of us into his gig and rowed us to the huge ship, whose vastness, at close range, was overpowering. Everything about her—her spars, her shrouds and stays, her guns, her anchors, her ratlins—was enormous; even her dolphin-striker, as we rowed under her tremendous bowsprit, looked the size of a schooner's mast. When the gig lay at the bottom of her sea-ladder, she towered above us like a bulging black cliff, and her mastheads, slowly moving against the sky, seemed to be dimmed by distance. From the open gangway at the head of the sea-ladder, a mystified officer stared down at us.

" I'd like to put these men aboard," Captain Crabbe shouted.

" What for, and who are they ? " the officer asked.

" I don't know, Leftnant. I just picked 'em up."

" Picked 'em up where ? "

" I don't know that either," Captain Crabbe said. " In fact, I don't know anything about 'em. If you'll be kind enough to take em aboard, I'll even forget I ever saw 'em. Perhaps you'd be good enough to ask Captain Rodgers to step to the ladder. Will you please ? "

A moment later the well-remembered face of Captain Rodgers, which I had last seen, soot-smeared like a clown's, peering up at me perplexedly from a rowboat in the harbour of Cap François, stared down at us now with equal perplexity.

" Come aboard, Captain," he said to Crabbe. " Come aboard and have a cup of coffee with me so I can get this straight."

"Sorry, Captain," Crabbe said. " I really have no business being here, and since it's a sort of accident, I'd prefer not to have it logged."

I leaned back in the stern of the *Hesperides'* gig, took off my head-cloth, and looked up at Rodgers.

Rodgers opened his eyes wide and blinked a little ; then scratched his chin. " Oh, that's how it is, is it ? " he said. " All right, Captain Crabbe, send 'em up and we'll try to take care of 'em."

He clasped his hands and shook them at Captain Crabbe in a sort of proxy handshake. Captain Crabbe in return flirted a hand at Rodgers, a most unnaval procedure. Before we were half-way up the ladder,

Crabbe was on his way back to his brig, stiff-backed and uncompromising —a gentleman who'd be happy to testify in any court, if need be, that he'd neither seen nor heard of two men in Arab dress on any May day in 1805, or at any other time for that matter.

When we stepped on to the scrubbed planks of the spar deck, we seemed to be the centre of a thousand cannon, a million American seamen, and all the ropes and cables and hawsers in the world.

Rodgers led us to a companionway amidship, motioned to us to follow him, and popped down the ladder, we after him. The tumult of the gun deck was worse than that of a caravan getting under way. The ceiling was almost against our heads, and the long twenty-fours were packed along both sides. In between the guns the gun-crews played cards, rolled dice, mended clothes, and busied themselves at a score of tasks, each of which required every man engaged in it to shout at the top of his lungs. Almost under the ladder was a stove twenty times the size of our kitchen stove in Gorham ; and in our path, as we followed Rodgers, were three behemoths of barrels labelled " scuttle-butt," " pork," and " grog ; " and around the stoves and barrels seamen pushed and yelled, so that the place was like a madhouse.

Rodgers held open his cabin door for us to enter ; then stepped in and closed it. He lived in luxury. Sliding partitions divided it into two sections. One section, whose three walls were the stern windows, had two bed-places, two bathrooms, and a sitting-room. The other section, in which we stood, was the main room, with a round dining-table, a dozen dining-chairs, and a map-stand. Crowded in with us were the breechings of four long twenty-fours, which stuck out like the backsides of four old women on their knees, peering from windows.

When the lieutenant had closed the door behind us and taken himself off, Rodgers came over and walked completely around us. " Well, I'll be damned ! " he said. " When you took off that headgear of yours, and I saw who it was, it jolted me, just like the powder magazine blowing up that night in Cap François ! "

He poked a long forefinger into my chest, as if to satisfy himself that I was really alive and not an illusion out of a mirage ; then looked at Leitensdorfer. " Who's this gentleman ? "

Leitensdorfer had his orders from Eaton in his hand, and gave them to Rodgers.

" Well, I *will* be damned ! " Rodgers exclaimed when he had read them. He threw himself down at the table, motioned for us to do like-wise, reached for a coffee-pot, and poured each of us a cup. " Eaton's army ! How in God's name did you ever get from Haiti to here ? How in God's name did you ever tie up to Eaton ? "

" There's a reason why I can't tell you everything I'd like to," I said. " I can only say that I've been in Tripoli before, and I'm supposed to be dead—and nobody on earth has a better reason than I for wanting to see the city captured and its rightful ruler back in power. That's how

I happened to get hooked up with Eaton. I wanted to do everything I could to help him."

" We had a message from one of our friends in Tripoli, night before last, saying that Eaton had captured Derna. Anything to it ? "

" There is indeed," I said ; " but that's the end of it, so far as he's concerned—unless Barron turns over the command of this fleet to somebody else, and in a hurry."

" Bah ! " Rodgers cried. " Where'd you pick up such twaddle ? "

" It's the simple truth," I assured him. " I got the first hint of it from somebody in Tripoli. That person found out that our old friend Lear was planning to pay the Bashaw to end the war."

" No," Rodgers said. " I don't believe it ! "

" Neither did Eaton. When I told him, two days after we'd captured Derna, he said it couldn't be true. He said nobody, not even Lear, could be such a fool. That's why he sent us to Malta—so that we could find out whether it was true or not. We saw Lear, and it *is* true."

" Did you see Barron ? " Rodgers asked.

" Nobody can see Barron except Lear. Barron's sick, and Lear's using him. He doesn't have any mind of his own left. Lear's making all decisions for him, and he's decided to make peace."

" I'll have to admit," Rodgers said slowly, " that's Lear's privilege. It's what he was sent here for."

" Maybe so," I said, " but whoever sent him—and it had to be either the President or the Secretary of State—didn't intend to have him *pay* for a peace that couldn't possibly last, and at the very moment when we could have peace for nothing : a peace that would be permanent and would benefit every nation in the world. The official who sent him here surely didn't intend to have him make a peace that would break every promise made to Hamet, and endanger the lives of everyone who's tried to help Eaton destroy these damned pirates for ever."

Rodgers shook his head. " I still think you must be wrong."

" I wish to God I were," I said, " but I'm not—unless you take matters into your own hands and forbid Lear to do it."

" I," Rodgers said, " I, forbid ? I can't *forbid* Lear to do anything. He's the government. I'm only acting head of the fleet. Even if I had Barron's position, I couldn't issue orders to Lear ! "

" If you were in Barron's position, you wouldn't let Lear make a shameful peace, would you ? "

" If the Secretary of State has authorised him to make peace, I have no authority to stop him."

" You might not have the authority," I said, " but you could make him understand, couldn't you, that it's a crime to betray people who were promised the help and the protection of the United States ? Couldn't you persuade him not to open negotiations until the rest of our squadron gets here and lets the Bashaw have a good look at a fleet that could blast his town to rubble ? "

" I don't know whether I could or not," Rodgers said. " When the State Department gives a civilian a commission like Lear's, we have to do as he says. I still think you're mistaken, though."

" I'm *not* mistaken ! Lear's a fool, and his mind's been poisoned. I think Bainbridge did the poisoning. I happen to know Bainbridge hates Eaton : thinks *he's* a damned fool : thinks this expedition of his is the most fantastic piece of nonsense ever conceived. He regards Joseph Karamanli as a wise and good man—Joseph Karamanli, for God's sake ! He's written letters insisting that if Eaton embarks on an expedition with Hamet against Tripoli, it will be an alliance between a Moslem and a Christian, and that every Arab in Tripoli will turn against Hamet for making any such alliance."

" Well," Rodgers said, " these people *are* religious fanatics, you know. Bainbridge might——"

" Bainbridge be damned ! There isn't a word of truth in any of the things I've repeated, but Bainbridge believes 'em ! He's never seen Eaton in action, any more than Lear has. He hasn't seen Hamet in action, any more than Lear has. But he's willing to deliver judgment. He's judging Eaton and Hamet from information he's picked up in Tripoli. Bainbridge calls Eaton a fool, and this expedition of his a senseless one. Eaton's no more a fool than Preble was when Preble supported all of Eaton's plans to take Tripoli. I've seen Eaton put up with disappointments and hardships that Lear and Bainbridge haven't any conception of, keep his temper through everything, win the high respect of every Arab who followed him across the desert, and lead his men against superior forces and superior positions with complete disregard of his own safety. My God, Captain, Bainbridge has no idea what he's talking about when he calls Eaton a fool, or regards this expedition as fantastic nonsense ! What right has *he* got, for God's sake, to criticise a man like Eaton—Bainbridge, who gave up his ship without a fight ? Would *you* have done that ? Would *Preble* ? You would not, nor Preble either ! Imagine John Paul Jones or Nelson doing it ! "

Rodgers, looking uncomfortable, said nothing.

"Another thing, Captain," I went on. " Bainbridge calls Hamet cowardly, effeminate, and useless, and says all the Arabs in Tripoli hate him. This is completely false. If you don't believe me, ask Colonel Leitensdorfer here, who's been acquainted with Hamet for years. As for Bainbridge's claim that all the Arabs would turn against Hamet if he allied himself with Christians to destroy Joseph Karamanli, Leitensdorfer and I have seen with our own eyes that any such claim is utter poppycock. Joseph Karamanli has had to imprison the families of his own leaders to make sure they don't desert to Hamet—and at that there wasn't a day, during the week before we attacked Derna, when armed and mounted Arabs weren't coming in by the tens and fifties and hundreds to join Hamet and Eaton, and to make sure that an end was put to Joseph Karamanli once and for all."

I turned to Leitensdorfer. " Have I exaggerated at all ? "

" No, no ! " Leitensdorfer cried. " This Joseph Karamanli is a monster to be destroyed, like vermin ! As for Hamet, he is wise, good, peaceable —the exact opposite of Joseph Karamanli in every way ! "

" In his fashion," I told Rodgers, " he's just like Dessalines—whereas Hamet's like Lamartinière. You remember him, don't you ? "

Rodgers just nodded.

" What's happened is as plain as the nose on your face," I persisted. " Bainbridge never picked up all that hodge-podge of lies by himself. Somebody dangled it in front of him, and Bainbridge sucked it in. Then, somehow, he passed it on to Lear ; he's all the time writing to Lear. We talked to Lear in Malta. Was he interested in having us testify to Eaton's bravery or Hamet's ability ? He was not ! Was he interested in being reminded of all the promises that Barron and Preble and the United States Government had made to Hamet and Eaton to furnish supplies and co-operation ? He was not ! He'd made up his mind ; he'd condemned Eaton and Hamet without hearing any of the witnesses for the defence, without seeing any of the evidence ! "

" I hope you're wrong," Rodgers said heavily. " I hope you're wrong ! "

For a few minutes the three of us sat there in silence. Through the gun-ports the far-off palm trees, the square white houses, the minarets, the tall hulk of the Castle, looked like painted stage scenery. I wondered what had come over Rodgers, that he could now face, with no sign of disgust or indignation, the prospect of having Lear make a peace that ought to turn every American's face red with shame. I wondered whether in some cases a uniform doesn't clothe a man in a sort of moral timidity a man who can face enemy guns without flinching. For by this time I had to admit to myself that we weren't going to get any help at all from Rodgers.

" Well," I said to him at last, " you and I were good friends in Haiti, and in a short time we went through a lot together. Now, if it's not presuming too much on that friendship, I want you to do at least one thing for me personally."

I took Lydia's map from the pouch at my waist once more and placed it before him.

" Why," Rodgers said as he examined it, " this is better than our maps ! It must have been done by someone who knows the inside of the Castle as well as the town."

" Yes," I said. " You'd better have the information on it transferred to your own maps, because you're going to need it if this peace is made with money instead of with guns."

Rodgers went over to his map-stand and with his own hand made notes on the map fastened to the top. When he looked around at us again, I saw that his expression was less severe, and guessed that our abandonment of the main issue had induced him to look with more favour on the smaller request I had mentioned.

"I think I know what it is you want," he said. "You want to go ashore. I suppose you have some particular place in mind?"

I went to his side and put my finger on the spot on the beach where King Dick and his troop of black Arabs had camped while I was still a slave in Murad Rais's garden. "Right there."

"You know what you're doing?" Rodgers said.

"Yes," I said, "we know exactly."

"In that case," Rodgers said, "it would be best for all of us if I didn't try to put you ashore in one of our own boats. Recently, though, we've picked up a few small boats that seemed to—ah—have lost their way, and I'll turn one of them over to you about eleven o'clock tonight. The wind's made to order for it—north-west—and you'll find it as easy as pie. When you leave her, lash her tiller, close-haul her, and let her run off into the harbour. She'll be five miles away by daybreak, with no way for anybody to connect her with you—or with me either."

I've had plenty of opportunity, since that day, to make up my mind about John Rodgers. He was a great sailor—as great as Preble, almost, when allowed to depend on his own judgment. What he couldn't do, though, and what no navy commander who ever lived could do, was to make a successful stand against the blunders or the shortsightedness of a President, a Secretary of State, and a Tobias Lear, when all of them hold to the belief that peace at any price is justifiable.

CHAPTER LXI

IT WAS strange, dream-like, to come ashore so easily on that beach below Murad Rais's wall—strange because I had no feeling whatever of setting foot on enemy soil, but seemed somehow to be returning to the security of home.

We set the little boat loose as Rodgers had suggested, and when dawn came we had found our way between those well-remembered gardens, gained the caravan road through the Pianura, and were just two tired Arabs, in no way different from scores of other travellers, wrapped in burnooses and resting beneath a date palm on the edge of the Marabout's Village.

I was in an inner state that was close to frenzy until we had located Ibrahim Bishari's and Hadji ben Idriss's caravan and our twenty black Arabs, nor did I feel any less frenzied because of having to pretend to the calm of an Arab after we had found it.

It was exactly where we had asked Hadji ben Idriss to halt it, nearly a hundred camels, both pack-camels and swift meharis, grumbling and groaning, another hundred jackasses, a score of Egyptian mules, forty or so horses, black tents, striped tents, piles of supplies and goods, fires of dried camel dung, and all the screaming, cursing, praying, jostling, singing, and laughing that rise endlessly from a caravan during daylight hours when it's at rest.

The lessons we had drummed into our black Arabs in the long drills in Jalo had been well learned, and when we walked towards Hadji ben Idriss's green tent nobody would have suspected that any one of those black Arabs had ever seen either Leitensdorfer or me before. They never seemed to look in our direction ; but I knew from the manner in which their voices grew more shrill after we had passed that they were glad to see us.

Hadji ben Idriss and Ibrahim Bishari were seated before their big green tent. A basket of dates stood before them, and a pot of tea redolent of mint, and the only sign of recognition that Hadji ben Idriss gave us was a waved indication that we were to sit down and fadhl. " How are you ? " they asked politely ; we told them " Well " and in turn made the proper inquiries. They gave us tea : then just sat there stroking their beards and staring at nothing, like two hound dogs resting on a back porch on a Sunday morning.

" This venture will be profitable," Ibrahim Bishari said at length. " We have traded to good advantage ; thanks to your information."

Hadji ben Idriss stared benevolently at me. " We leave to-night. Three hours after dark."

The man's calmness infuriated me. " Not necessarily," I said. " I've got to send a message ! Where's the messenger ? What arrangements have been made ? Where's King Dick ? "

The tent-flap was pushed to one side and King Dick's round white eyes stared down at me. In his hand he held a bowl and a spoon. When I got to my feet in response to his peremptory beckoning gesture, he stood aside to let me enter the tent, then followed me and pulled a carpet from a heap in one corner. Lying there on the dirt, trussed like a fowl and gagged with a turban, was George Lee.

" Have to empty turban out of him and feed him twice a day," King Dick whispered.

Lee's eyes rolled, and he swallowed convulsively.

This, on top of Hadji ben Idriss's calmness, was more than I could stand. " My God ! " I cried. " What did you want to do this for ? You'll have all Tripoli on the alert ! I told you we couldn't pay him back for what he did to us, not while Lydia's in Tripoli ! Somebody was bound to kill him, sooner or later, and you damned well ought to have let him alone ! I don't like it ! What have you found out ? Where's that messenger to carry a message to Lydia—and carry it quick ! She was right about Lear ! "

King Dick knelt beside Lee and tried to squeeze another foot of turban into his mouth, but it was already as full as it could be. " My goo'ness me my ! " King Dick whispered. " No cause get excetticated.

Nobody going miss old Mr. Captain Loot'n-steal Lee while he got sick-sem yards of muslin inside his teeth." He rearranged the rug over Lee, got to his feet and fumbled in the folds of his burnoose, then handed me a gold chain with a green stone hanging from it. The green stone was the thunderstone that Lydia had given me at Beau-Bouclier, ages ago—the stone I'd worn around my neck until Lee had taken it from me on the day we went into slavery. I recognised the gold chain, too. Joseph Karamanli had given it to Lee the same day Lee had stolen the stone.

I took it, too perturbed to thank him. " There's no time to lose," I said. " We've got to get Lydia out of the city and get back to Eaton ! Lear's going to sign a treaty with Joseph, just as we suspected. What's more, I think he's going to sign it without making any provision for Hamet's wife and children. Lydia wouldn't—— Well, you know how she was about the Autremont boys ! We've got to plan something and do it in a hurry ! "

" Everything all orgulated, Albion," King Dick said. " We go see my wifeses, where we talk comfably." He took me by the arm, led me from the tent, between piles of green boxes, corded bales, goatskin water-bottles, rice and flour bags, and heaps of dates, and so brought me to a striped tent near the centre of the caravan.

The tent-flap was down. He scratched at the flap, and said, " Open, Labuda." Labuda was the name of one of his Jalo wives.

The flap was suddenly drawn aside, and there, outlined against the dimness of the tent's interior, was Lydia. . . .

As I write these words I feel dizzy again with the dizziness that struck me like a thunderbolt. The scent of jasmine comes back, and the strange tangle of unaccustomed garments—vest, sash, endless lengths of striped silk, sleeveless coat, and God-knows-what—that kept me from holding her as closely as I wished. I was vaguely conscious of King Dick's three wives going protestingly from the tent, pushed out by King Dick. My heart pounds again like the heavy drumming of hoofs in the night. I recall my breathless inability to do more than whisper her name, over and over ; and her faint insistence, oft-repeated, that she had known I'd come, that she had been sure, that she had listened for my voice, that she had been afraid—all the unintelligible but necessary nothings that help two lovers, after long separation, to still the churning inner tumult that for a time makes coherent speech and thought impossible.

The grumblings and groanings of the camels, the braying of the donkeys, all the shrill screaming and hoarse shouting of the caravan—these ceased to exist ; they were but the faint susurrus of a distant ocean. When those sounds again became audible and I could once more think and speak intelligibly, I began to comprehend my good fortune—a good fortune outweighing all the bad that had dogged me for so long.

" Albion," said Lydia—and so often had I heard her voice in my dreams that I couldn't believe almost three years had elapsed since I'd actually heard it—" Albion, I've never been afraid before, but I was afraid ! When he got the news of Derna—Joseph Karamanli, I mean— he was in a fury. He tore his clothes ! He broke things ! He knew that it meant he'd lose his throne and his kingdom. He sent for Hamet's sons, and when I went with them to him, he sat and stared at us, patting and petting that loathsome scented beard of his ! Then he said that in return for Hamet's treachery—that's the word he used, Albion : treachery !—Hamet's oldest son, Ismail—a beautiful boy, considerate and a gentleman, but delicate—must go to live in one of the under-ground houses on the Gharian plateau ; and that the other two must be shut up with me in the Castle dungeons, where we would see no one and speak with no one. Oh, Albion——" She stopped, her lips pressed close together.

" I know," I said. " I know."

" Yes ! After three years they seemed almost like my own children. They speak English as well as you do, Albion ! I thought of how, years from now, they'd be governing Tripoli and perhaps all North Africa. I'd taught them *so* much—not only everything I'd learned from you, about land and ploughing and erosion, but all the things that everyone ought to know, but doesn't ! They had learned to understand and value fairness and generosity and justice ! "

I held her close.

" I told Joseph Karamanli some of this—though I don't know how well he took it in ! And I ended by telling him that, if he would give up his dreadful idea, if he would leave the boys together, and with me, and would let me talk to the Americans when they came, I was sure I could persuade them to be generous in their turn."

I stroked her hair and seethed inwardly at Lear. When the Americans came ! My God !

" He was furious, Albion ! He shouted at me, awful things, but I couldn't give up ! I told him a prince, of all persons, must be generous, and that no generous man could fight behind children or women. I told him that a political prisoner is a guest of the state that holds him prisoner, and that the vaunted Arab hospitality is nothing but a lie if prisoners are treated as criminals or chattels.

" Well, Albion, that was the end of it ! He wouldn't listen ! He was furious ! He lashed out at me—said I was a nuisance, had never known my place, had been a trouble-maker ever since I'd been brought to the Castle, that he'd do to me now what he should have done to me in the beginning. Oh, Albion, I never *saw* such an angry man ! Then he bellowed for the captain of the guard and ordered him to take us out. We were led off, and no sooner were we out of the room than the soldiers snatched the three boys from me. Two of the men tied my hands, pushed a rag in my mouth, and threw a veil over my head. Then they put me in a litter and carried me away. At first, of course, I had no idea where I was being taken. But I found out, Albion—I found out ! Joseph

Karamanli had sold me to Captain Lee. *Sold* me ! He put me out of the city, Albion, and sold me to Captain Lee ! "

"I see," I said slowly. "He sold you to Captain Lee ! Yes. . . . As I remember, Lee himself told me that he tried to make advances to you when he first saw you in Cap François. And again on the ship—I suppose he thought I didn't notice, but I did. He was perpetually trying to touch you." I rose to my feet. "I want King Dick. I'll call him. I owe him an apology, and a lot besides."

When King Dick, in response to my signals, left Leitensdorfer and the two sheiks and came back to the tent, he flapped a deprecatory hand at my grateful apologies. "My goo'ness ! That nothing at all, Albion ! Mere evening's division, like opening botto rum."

"Thank God for such diversions," I said. I turned to Lydia. "How did King Dick know you'd been sold to Lee ? "

"A friend in the Castle—the one that brought you my first letter— had carried my letters that your black Arabs brought you. The moment she learned I was in trouble, she hurried to them and told them."

"And they told me, so I went to see," King Dick said simply. "Stood and stood in front of Lee's house. Pretty soon I see a camel with litter on top, led by Bashaw's men. So I howl and sing and march along beside camel, waving flag, very gros Marabout ! "

The Bashaw's men, recognising him as a gros Marabout, had accepted him as a harmless and necessary evil, possibly employed by Lee himself. The guards at Lee's gate, in turn, had accepted him as one of the Bashaw's official holy men.

"The moment I heard him howling," Lydia said, "I knew who it was, and thanked God. In among his howlings he kept repeating the word 'Surinam ! ' "

I too thanked Heaven for King Dick's friendship, as I had so often had occasion to do before.

"That Lee," King Dick said lightly. "He very strumpeted about women, always. I knew I might catch him like that, and I did. When he strumpeted, he believe anything, like people wanting to win on horse-racing or betting they know which shell a pea goes under."

Lee, also thinking that the Marabout had been sent by the Bashaw to escort Lydia, made the mistake of letting him get inside the house, on which King Dick had "wiped" George Lee with such accuracy and violence that when Lee regained consciousness his hands were lashed tight to his sides and his mouth was crammed with the major portion of a muslin turban.

"King Dick said we'd be perfectly safe," Lydia said, "and I never doubted him for a moment. We dressed Lee in women's clothes, veil and all. When it was dark, King Dick gave the guards twenty piasters, together with their master's orders to go to the Neapolitan's in the suk and buy rum to drink the health of the new bride. They all went away running, so we just took Lee by the arms and walked him back

here. Nobody so much as looked at us. We left a note behind. It read :
' You who have known the bliss of a bridegroom, rejoice that love has
taken me on the wings of happiness to the sweet waters of Gharian.'
And we signed it with Lee's name."

"My goo'ness me my ! " King Dick said admiringly. " She very
useful lady ! That note very good staff work ! Wings of happiness !
Hoy ! It be two months before anybody look for that old Loot'n-steal
Lee ! "

Lydia stroked my hand. " King Dick told me about Barron's letters
to Eaton and about your journey to Malta. You weren't successful,
were you ? " She stated it as a fact rather than putting it as a question.

" No," I said, " we weren't. Lear paid no attention to us : none
whatever. His mind's made up."

We were silent then, thinking ; and it was a strange, uncomfortable
silence.

Lydia broke it. " They can't stay if Lear signs a treaty, can they ?
The ships will have to go ; Eaton will have to go ; Leitensdorfer will
have to go . . . won't they ? Even Hamet . . . he'll have to go ! "

We didn't answer her.

" All those men ! " she said. " All those Arabs who helped Eaton ! All
those people in Derna who have helped Hamet ! How can *they* go ? "

Again we didn't answer ; again that thick, oppressive silence weighed
us down ; and again it was Lydia who spoke first. " And you and
King Dick," she asked. She was staring down at her hands, and her
voice was barely audible. " Would you and King Dick go, too ? "

" How could we ? " I asked. " Our men depend on us. How could
we leave them and get away ourselves ? "

She looked up at me with a misty smile, and I had the feeling that
I've had so often : the choking knowledge that if I hadn't had the
heaven-sent fortune to find Lydia, I could never have truly lived.

CHAPTER LXII

MEN CAN DO anything they have to do, within reason, and we had to get back to Derna, to General Eaton's army, and to our own troop of black Arabs before Lear's plans, whatever they might be, could come to a head.

When Lear would reach Tripoli we had no way of knowing, but both King Dick and Leitensdorfer were sure it was only a matter of days—a few days. We were equally uncertain how long it would take him to negotiate with the Bashaw ; but Lydia insisted that such negotiations couldn't possibly be completed in less than three days.

The Bashaw, she said, would spend the first day disagreeing with everything, that being Arab nature. The second day he would spend in thinking how to squirm out of the terms offered him. The third day, probably, he would offer terms of his own, and if the person with whom he was negotiating was a great enough fool, he might just possibly agree to them at the end of the third day. Whatever happened between the Bashaw and Lear would then have to be conveyed to Eaton by one of the American frigates, and the best time that any one of them could make from Tripoli to Derna would be five days.

There was no way out of it : in order to be certain, we had to make that trip in ten days and average sixty miles a day.

So we held a council, admitting the troopers King Dick had picked to make the ride with us, all ten of them having followed the coast road from Tripoli to Derna at least twice : never in ten days, though one had done it in eleven.

But we, King Dick told them, must do it in ten days, because he, being a Marabout with the gift of prophecy, knew that something was going to happen shortly thereafter—in which case he wanted to be on hand to lead the troop. His calm assumption that all would be well if he were leading the troop was as convincing as it was heartening.

So the discussion of the trip was begun. The talk covered every well of sweet water, every ruined Greek and Roman fort and temple, every Marabout's tomb, every marsh, salt-water pool, barley field, olive grove, and pasture land along that winding coast road. The men discussed where it was safe to take short cuts by travelling inland ; where we must hug the coast ; where we could travel both day and night, resting only at noon ; where we couldn't travel at night. They argued about where we could be sure of buying sheep to eat, and where certain tribes would certainly be with their flocks.

The worst part of the trip, they said, would be the first two days. We would find sweet water and corn at Mesurata, and again at Zaffran. Therefore if we could, by riding day and night, make Mesurata at the

411

end of the first day and Zaffran at the end of the second, all the other stages would be shorter, and after we had passed the southern-most curve of the Gulf of Sulphur our way would be through the flowering fields of Cyrenaica.

The caravan route to Jalo branches off from the coastal road at the edge of the oasis of Tripoli. Lee, dressed in an old brown barracan no different from the one Murad Rais had thrown me on my first day in Tripoli, rode thus far in a litter on one of the pack-camels ; but at the junction of the roads, while Hadji ben Idriss and Ibrahim Bishari bade us an affectionate farewell, two of our troopers took Lee from the camel, blacked his face with soot from the bottom of a kettle, put him on one of our horses, and tied his feet together under the horse's belly, so that his hands could be free for riding.

King Dick, disregarding the ferocious howlings of his other two wives, had taken Labuda to be company for Lydia. He intended no discrimination, he explained to them carelessly : all three were equally precious to him : Labuda was merely better bumpeted than the other two : better able to endure the bumpeting of the saddle on forced marches. The howling of these black beauties was beyond all howling : a thousandfold shriller than the screams of excited Tripolitan Jewesses : beside them the execrations of Haitian fish-dispensers were no more than the twitterings of swallows.

So sixteen of us—King Dick, Leitensdorfer, Lydia and I, Labuda, Lee, and our ten black Arabs—with four pack-mules and two spare horses set off on that strange road to the south, while the howlings of King Dick's other wives and the wailings of the Jalo bagpipes slowly faded behind us.

We removed the gag from Lee's mouth at the end of the first night's march, but King Dick never took his eye off him, and at night he was tied with cords that were fastened to the wrists of two black troopers. He never spoke to us, nor we to him ; nor did he ever look directly at Lydia—though he couldn't help being aware of her, riding close beside me. To my eyes, she seemed to radiate an indomitable quality which, for lack of better words, I might call an ever-cheerful watchfulness over the welfare of those she loved. Certainly that quality was apparent to King Dick, Leitensdorfer, Abdul Rahim, and all the men. Not even her mufflings could hide it : she wore a heavy veil as much to prevent embarrassment among the men as to protect her from sun and sand-storms ; and both Labuda and she had slit the skirts of their soft brown wool barracans, front and back, and made them into voluminous overalls, so that they could ride astride. Beneath her overall Lydia also wore a white silk garment, baggy but beautiful.

It is hard to guess how much feeling, how much sensitivity there is in a character like Lee's ; but if there was any of either in the man who had once coveted Lydia, that ride down through Lebda and Mesurata, across the marshes to the sweet water of Zaffran and Busaida, must have been a torment as agonising mentally as it was physically.

The half-way mark of our journey was a place known to our men as Braiga, a collection of ruined Roman forts on the edge of the desolate conglomeration of marsh, rock, sand, salty pools, sulphur deposits, and roaring breakers which lies at the base of that hell-hole, the Gulf of Syrtis or Gulf of Sulphur ; and it was there that we untied George Lee and took his horse from him. He could find shelter of a sort, for there were Roman cisterns hollowed in the rock, with sides cemented up with stones that had crumbled while the cement remained undamaged. Of Arab tents, or flocks, or animals of any sort, there wasn't a trace. The place was an abomination of desolation, carpeted with fragments of pottery and glass, undisturbed through the long years that had passed since the governments of Greece and Rome, ever consistent, had seized and tried to keep the lands of others.

He was a defiant figure, amid those ruins, bare-footed and sooty-faced, in his brown barracan and soiled turban, staring at us with hard and hating eyes. I could see that he expected us to kill him, but there was no weakness in his mien, no crack in his iron hardness. He had never been, would never be, anything but hard all the way through.

King Dick, a fitting judge, passed sentence on him. " You getting off easy," King Dick told him, " only because we can't obittalate others just as deservable—Murad Rais, Joseph Karamanli. Maybe you live on snakes and litto lizards. Hyenas do. If you do, be careful keep out my way : my temper very malice towards you."

Lee just laughed—the same brazen man who had eagerly slept with black women but furiously rebelled at eating with black men : who was contemptuous of everything good, and quick to embrace anything wrong : a consistently bad man, above the law, unable to comprehend honour or decency !

When we rode on and I looked back over my shoulder at him, he was fumbling among the bits of pottery and glass, already vaguely animal-like in appearance ; and I wondered whether George Lee among those Roman ruins, would succeed in clinging long enough to life to bring unhappiness to more women and fury to still more men.

On and on we went, northward into Cyrenaica, past Ghimines and Bengazi, and then around the high coastal shoulder—Teuchaira, Ptolemeta, Cyrene, and Suza.

There is fatigue and endless struggle in travelling under the African sun ; yet it seems the only life, the only true life. Food is poor, water often brackish ; nights are freezing cold and days are furnace-hot ; sleep is fitful ; but contentment seems to envelop those who march in caravans or plod along the sea road, mere specks of humanity crawling on the rim of an enormous world so majestic that it defies description, yet full of innumerable small things—of snipe zig-zagging from beside the path ;

of coveys of quail bursting upward like little bombshells ; of gazelles popping out from behind shrubs too small to shelter a bumble-bee ; of red-headed ducks and brown ducks springing from every reedy pool ; of miles of pasture thick with sheep and goats, among whom lambs and kids skitter and prance in sudden delirium ; of ruins in which men from the armies of Alexander the Great, of Scipio Africanus, once cursed their sergeants and wondered what was going on in Argyrocastro or Aquila. . . . The desert scents are strange and intoxicating. The sunset sky blazes into kaleidoscopic colours. At night, the campfire glow touches the wings of bats soaring overhead and stars come down among them, so close that if I had plucked a million to scatter in Lydia's hair, they'd never have been missed. . . .

I wish I might scimp this part of my tale, as histories have a habit of doing ; but I'm writing the simple truth, and cannot hide behind patriotic misrepresentations and confusing omissions, as can more fortunate souls who set down chains of events with scant knowledge of the people who brought them to pass. Because of such omissions and misrepresentations, the name of Derna has long been held to be an honour to America, and streets in America have been called after the place. But I saw mighty little about it that was honourable ! To me it has always been the very symbol of dishonour.

Late on the third of June we sighted Derna from the shore road, far off and pink in the light of the setting sun ; and when we camped for the night to avoid stumbling into patrols, we had made the journey in four hours less than the ten days we had set for ourselves. We moved forward an hour after dawn on the fourth, and were halted by a patrol of Hamet's cavalrymen at a wadi two miles outside of Derna. All of Joseph's army, they told us, remained on the escarpment, well out of range of the guns of the American vessels ; so at eight o'clock we rode unmolested through the outer gardens that lie between the town and the sea, and again saw, across the wadi, the squat walls of the battery over which Eaton's flag stirred idly in the early morning breeze. We halted in the wadi to empty our canteens and water-bags of the brakish water with which they had last been filled, and to refill them from the ice-cold flood that foamed down from the Green Mountains.

It was a sight for sore eyes, those flat-roofed white houses and minarets dotted with palms ; those flower, lemon, and orange gardens all around us ; the hundreds of women from caravan and town, kneeling on both banks of the wadi to pound with sticks at piles of bright-coloured garments ; the brilliant blue of the sea ; the black hulls and white gun-ports of the *Argus* and the *Hornet* lying just offshore with springs on their cables ; the green meadows behind the town, extending to the foot of the towering escarpment, a mass of browns, greys, pinks, blacks, reds, violets in the morning sun. We could see the white headgear and robes of Hamet's Arabs scattered everywhere on the green meadows ;

and off to the eastward, beyond the wadi and the battery and the gardens of Bu Mansur, were the black tents and the camels of the caravan.

It was a scene of peace, of contentment ; and I, knowing what I knew, sweated with rage that such contentment and such peace should, because of the stubborn folly and lack of understanding of just one infinitesimal insect of a man, be on the verge of destruction.

There were tears in Lydia's eyes as she contemplated all this beauty. "How horrible !" she whispered. "How dreadful to have to be William Eaton ! And how awful that the guiltiest people in this world must always go scot-free ; that only the innocent and the trusting must suffer !"

"Don't think about it," Leitensdorfer told her. "That is how we soldiers and politicians are able to exist, isn't it ? We never think about anything : we only plan—usually wrong."

As we rode up from the wadi and out towards the point on which the battery stood, we saw Eaton on the parapet of the fort, peering through a spy-glass at the top of the escarpment. With him was the officer of marines, Lieutenant O'Bannon, and two other young men in American uniforms. When we were under the walls, Eaton leaned over the parapet and spoke to us. "Glad to have you back, gentlemen. Colonel Leitensdorfer, I've got a lot of work for you. Take your friends into my headquarters, and I'll be with you as soon as I make a few dispositions."

When he joined us, ten minutes later, there was something strikingly different about him. His left arm was still bandaged, so that he wore his coat slung on his back like a hussar's jacket, but the change seemed to be in his face. In spite of the heat in that small room, his face looked drawn and dry, as if from cold, and the flesh around his lips had somehow shrivelled, as a dead man's lips shrink back against his teeth. His manner of speech had changed, too, as if his thoughts unexpectedly wandered a little. I think the man's head was full of arguments that he wanted to remember but couldn't because of their vast number, and I think they constantly recurred to him. Lawyers have the same feeling when they have a multitude of facts to put in a brief, and insufficient space in which to do it.

He went straight to Lydia. "A great relief, ma'am," he told her. "You've been very much on my mind. Yes . . . a great relief ! Things aren't what we expected, are they ? I found myself wondering what could be done in case——" He broke off and stared at her blankly.

"You've been a great deal on our minds, too, General," she said. "I want you to know that I've never before heard so much sympathy expressed for anyone."

"Oh, I haven't given up yet," he said. He shook hands with the rest of us, motioned us to seats, and went to sit behind his desk. "When'd you leave Tripoli ?" he asked Colonel Leitensdorfer.

"On May twenty-fifth, General."

He turned to me. He had a queer look, almost as though he expected to dodge. "According to information I received from the enemy's camp last night, Lear opened peace negotiations with Joseph Karamanli the day after you left. Did you see Lear in Malta ? "

"Yes, sir," I replied. "We saw him. He refused to let us see Barron. He made us give him our dispataches to Barron. There's no question about it : Barron's *non compos*. Lear controls him completely, and Barron does exactly as Lear wants him to do. Lear just puts words in Barron's mouth. The only way we could talk to Lear was to pretend that we accepted him as Barron's spokesman. Even then we had to force him to stay in the room until we'd said our say. I doubt that he listened to what we told him. Nothing we could have said would have made any difference. He's Peace Commissioner to the Barbary States, and he doesn't propose to let anyone else make that peace. It's got to be *his* sort of peace, as he can go down in history as the man who made peace with Tripoli and released the American prisoners. That'll make him a great man, just like George Washington."

"Christ ! " Eaton whispered—then looked guiltily at Lydia. "Sorry, ma'am."

"You needn't apologise to me for anything you wish to say about Colonel Lear or anything else," Lydia said. "I was taught to look at things as they are, rather than as Quaker ladies pretend they are."

Eaton reached down beside his table and brought up a half-filled jug. "Get some glasses, will you, Colonel ? " he asked Leitensdorfer. "You've had a hard trip, all of you, and a drop of lakby won't hurt you." When Leitensdorfer hurried out, he said apologetically, "No matter how hot it is, I can't seem to sweat. Makes me feel as if I might split open. Sometimes a drop of this starts it out on me." He got up from his chair and went to the door to stare up at the top of the escarpment. "You know, I was wrong about that cavalry of Joseph's. They came down and attacked without warning a few days after you left. If it hadn't been for your black Arabs and the guns on the ships, they'd have made things too hot for us."

"Without warning ? " King Dick asked. "No reconnoitring patrols on escarpment ? "

"Not at night. Hamet's cavalry won't ride at night."

King Dick got to his feet. "Ours will," he said. "I rather not have that Joseph's army catch me with trousers slippy-down. I go see our men." He left us hurriedly. I knew how he felt : I wanted to get back to those men myself.

Leitensdorfer came back with coffee cups on a tray, and Eaton poured a cupful of lakby for each of us. He gulped down the contents of his own cup, stared at the ceiling, poured himself another cup and drank it more slowly. Suddenly his forehead and upper lips glistened with perspiration ; he sighed with relief and became expansive.

"I'll be frank with you, Hamlin," he said. "I knew, some days ago, that you hadn't been able to do anything with Barron or Lear."

"Almighty God, Mahomet, and Buddha, all three together, could have done nothing with that Lear," Leitensdorfer put in. "I tell you, Hamlin made it as clear as day to him that he would be, how you say, an idiot of three stages, a *polisson*—I do not know how to say it—a worker of iniquity, isn't it, to make peace with Joseph Karamanli when we are as good as at the gates of Tripoli ! I myself was eloquent, calling a spade a spade, isn't it, so that the man ought to have died of shame rather than make peace ; but I tell you it was like shouting down an Egyptian privy ! Merely the stirring up of a stink ! "

Eaton mopped his oddly stepped-back forehead, on which the perspiration stood in beads. "I still haven't given up hope," he said. "I won't ! I can't ! I had a letter from him, the two-faced illegitimate pettifogging——" He broke off, glanced at Lydia, and resumed more calmly. "Didn't even have the courage to sign it. It was supposed to be written by Barron ; but it was just like that other letter you saw. Words in it like ' adduced ' and ' propitious ' and ' sanguine hopes '—words no sailor could use without belching. Lear wrote it, of course. Said right out that Hamet wouldn't be given another scrap of money, arms, or provisions. What's he expect Hamet's army to live on, for God's sake ? Mud pies ? The letter said right out that Lear was going to Tripoli and meet the peace overtures made by Joseph Karamanli. *Meet* 'em ; not consider 'em ! "

"Have you told Hamet ? " I asked.

"Yes, I told him."

"Poor man ! " Lydia murmured. "Poor man ! "

"What did he say ? " I asked.

"What *was* there to say ? " Eaton demanded. "He said we hadn't been co-operating with him ; we'd been co-operating with Joseph Karamanli ! But he could raise hell on earth without mending matters. He's helpless. He can't tell anyone, because if word got out, his men would probably try to save themselves : then he'd be at the mercy of Joseph's army, which is still holding together." He absentmindedly poured himself another cup of lakby and tossed it off. "Holding together damned badly, though. Think of it ! If I could guarantee to feed 'em, pay 'em, and not abandon 'em, three hundred of Joseph's cavalry would come over to us to-morrow. That word was brought in to me yesterday by two of Joseph's sheiks. With money and two hundred marines, I could utterly destroy that army of Joseph's in two days ! In just exactly two days, if only Lear and Barron would let me have marines. Hull says there are four hundred marines eating their hearts out in the Mediterranean, not doing one damned thing except draw pay and rations, and wishing to God they could get into just one decent fight before they rot from idleness ! But Barron and Lear say No : I can't have 'em, because they're needed on the ships. Needed for what, for God's

O

sake ! There isn't a damned thing for 'em to do but clean up after the ship's cat ! "

Again he got up and went to the door, to study the escarpment.

" We're in a hell of a fix," he went on, when he came back to his seat. " We're supposed to pull out of here. Hull sent word to me this morning. He just got orders from Barron—which means from Lear, of course— that all United States vessels are to leave this coast as soon as necessary arrangements can be made. So Hull notifies me two hours ago that the *Argus* and the *Hornet* are ready for sea, and waiting to take me and the men under my command on board as soon as we're ready to abandon this post. Well, my God, I *can't* abandon it ! What happens if I abandon it, and something delays that bastard Lear in signing a treaty ? We're right where we were before we started ! Joseph Karamanli wouldn't sign anything at all if he knew we'd abandoned it ! And if we abandon it, Joseph's army would come down off that escarpment like a bat out of hell—there'd be no artillery, no ships' guns to hold 'em back—why, my God, it would be murder ! Just plain murder ! What kind of poisoned sawdust do you suppose that man Lear has in his head in place of brains, for Christ's sake ! "

Leitensdorfer made a sound that was half-cough and half-curse, a concentrated expression of disgust, contempt, despair.

" That's not all, either," Eaton said. " Joseph's army has us out-numbered three to one, but it's wasting away—just wasting away. Those Arabs can't stand up to artillery. When they attacked the first time, some of their camels were hit by the *Argus'* long guns. Did you ever see a camel hit by a twelve-pound shot ? "

We told him we hadn't.

" Quite a sight," Eaton said. " The camel kind of explodes. The air's full of legs and a big piece of head and about a thousand odds and ends, and they rain down all over the place. There's nothing much left of the rider, either. I guess it's because a camel has so much water in him. You know how a big wave can bust things to pieces ? I guess a cannon-ball hitting all that water makes it act something like a wave. Anyway, the Arabs aren't enthusiastic about it. This is a big country, full of places where big guns can't get to ; and now that they've seen what happens to a camel, they can't see the sense of sticking to the one place where there *are* big guns."

He picked up the jug of lakby, filled his cup once more, and thumped the jug down on the table. " Help yourself whenever you're so disposed," he offered, and added—inconsequentially, I thought—" I never had any of this trouble about not sweating till I understood that Lear was really as much of a louse as you said he was." He sipped from his cup, closed his eyes and tilted his head back. His face looked like a dripping death-mask.

" You were saying ' That's not all,' General," I reminded him.

" Certainly it isn't," Eaton resumed. " Not by a long shot it isn't all !

If you're in command of an army, and your men are drifting away and drifting away, what are you going to do ? Just let 'em drift ? Hah ! Let enough of 'em drift and what happens to you ? The enemy jumps out at you and hacks you to pieces ! You *can't* let 'em drift ! You've got to do one thing or another. Either you've got to retreat, so the enemy can't catch up with you, or you've got to attack while you've still got men left. Well, if I were in command of that army of Joseph's, I know damned well what *I'd* do ! I'd attack, and attack quick ! I *couldn't* retreat, because I wouldn't have enough food. And that's just exactly what's going to happen here. They're going to attack again ! They've *got* to ! Now how in God's name can I abandon this post before I know exactly what's happened ? I *can't* leave ! Oh, God, why must there be Tobias Lears in this world ! "

Lydia leaned over and put her hand on his.

" Thank you, ma'am," Eaton said. " There's one suggestion I'd like to make. Since Captain Hull and the *Argus* are expecting visitors, I suggest that you let me send you aboard her to-day ; now."

Lydia smiled and shook her head.

" You better think it over, ma'am. We're short of provisions, because that misbegotten quack of a Lear cut off all supplies except to Christians. To *Christians*, for God's sake ! " He eyed her curiously. " Did you ever, in any of your reading, ma'am, come across any mention of a religious test being required to entitle a soldier to his rations ? "

Leitensdorfer groaned.

" General," Lydia asked, " did Mr. Lear or Commodore Barron, in the letter you mention, say anything at all about looking out for the interests of Hamet or of his wife or of his children ? "

The general opened his field desk and took out a letter and a pile of closely written sheets, all crossed out and rewritten. He tossed the sheets to Leitensdorfer. " Put these in shape, will you, Colonel ? I sit here morning, noon, and night, trying to put down all the dastardly results of Lear's and Barron's behaviour. I'm not half-finished, but make a fair copy for me, Colonel, so I can see what I'm about. By God, there's no punishment too severe for what Lear's doing to us ! Poison, hanging, shooting, guillotine, strangling, stabbing—they're all too easy ! " He shook his head, as if to clear it of bitter thoughts ; then spoke to Lydia.

" Yes," he said, " he mentioned Hamet." He turned to the last page of the letter and read from it, making interpolations as he read : " ' It is with Colonel Lear's express sanction . . . (the sanctimonious, slippery hyphenated time-serving son of a—well, ma'am) . . . with Colonel Lear's express sanction that I mention his intention to endeavour at stipulating some conditions for the unfortunate Exile . . . (listen to that dithyrambic State Department Bishop of Artful-Dodging, ma'am ! The unfortunate Exile, for God's sake ! He means Hamet ! But listen to this !) . . . provided this can be done without giving up points that are essential, and without any considerable sacrifice of national advantage on our part.'" He threw the letter on the table. " What do you think of *that* ? "

For the first time since I'd known her, Lydia's face was as white as the silk barracan beneath her outer barracan of soft brown wool.

" I see," she said quietly. " I see. ' Without any considerable sacrifice! ' Mr. Lear is saying that he will do nothing for Hamet—nothing whatever —in spite of all that Hamet has done for you and for America. He will do nothing for Hamet's wife or for Hamet's children. Nothing."

" Yes, ma'am," Eaton said. " That's exactly what Mr. Lear is saying. He'll do nothing ! "

" Tobias Lear ! " Lydia said softly. " Tobias Brute ! Tobias Ingrate ! I'd rather die than be bound by the blind perversity of such a man ! "

CHAPTER LXIII

THOSE NEXT few June days were hot and still, but beneath the stillness there was a perpetual turbulence that gave me the feeling of being in the centre of a simmering, hissing cauldron that was on the verge of coming to a violent boil.

Nothing happened in those few days ; yet each day and night was tumultuous with happening.

We thought we knew what Lear proposed to do : in all likelihood he had already done it ; yet there was the possibility that somehow he might, before taking the final step, awake to its enormity. And there was also the fact that the commanders of Joseph's army must be growing more and more desperate—more and more determined to destroy Hamet and his army before they themselves were destroyed. And there was the knowledge that Barron and Lear, in their incredible stupidity or selfishness or lack of comprehension or jealousy, or whatever anyone wants to call it, had determined to send Eaton no more supplies. We had to be ready for anything—anything at all ; and that means hard work.

We arranged for night patrols and day patrols, the night patrols to move in a wide quarter-circle to the rear of Joseph's army, so we could have word in case of large incoming or outgoing movements. We made daily inspection of troopers not on patrol, even going so far as to have them empty their forage nets each morning, to let us look for broken cords, refill their canteens, draw the charges from their pistols and reload, so that there would be no possibility of misfiring.

We went back to daily sabre drill, swinging weighted sabres in unison, first to the left, then to the right. It was a sight to see, with King Dick out in front of the two ranks, thrusting and flicking with that enormous sabre of his—left, right, left, right—as easily as if it were a feather, while all the sabres in the ranks flickered and flashed in a

Encyclopaedia Britannica
NEW 1957
LONDON EDITION

see over ☞

ENCYCLOPÆDIA BRITANNICA Ltd,

11 Belgrave Road,

LONDON, SW1

sort of fog of light, in time with his own. He worked them, too, at hauling wounded men up and across the pommels of their saddles, and at quick turning.

I had half-forgotten, in the weeks we'd been away, what magnificent horsemen these black Arabs of ours were, and their extraordinary skill with sabres ; and the eager precision with which they responded to King Dick's tireless demands upon them was as heartening as it was beautiful. When they weren't drilling, they worked with the Greek cannoneers and musketmen at digging trenches, for Eaton was bound to defend the battery, even though Joseph's army should succeed in breaking into the town.

With all this work, and with Lydia always at my side (for she insisted on riding with us, saying that in some things she might be more observant than we—and so she was, because she found that the rice we were buying for the men had too many stones in it, and that three shoemakers and four barracan-makers were needed to mend their shoes and barracans), I so far forgot Tobias Lear that I ceased to worry over the possibility of impending disaster.

That's one strange thing about soldiering : you forget that you're as subject to disaster as anyone, and get the feeling that disaster can only overtake the other fellow.

On the morning of the tenth of June, our night patrols and the men who had gone out at daybreak to relieve them came pelting back together. Joseph's entire army, they reported, foot soldiers as well as cavalry, were on the move towards the edge of the escarpment. With them, too, they brought a mounted Arab who had been one of the retainers of Hadji Ismail, cavalry commander of Joseph's army. The night patrol had found him fallen behind a body of mounted men, all moving rapidly away from Joseph's army and into the desert.

The Arab talked freely enough when we questioned him ; Hadji Ismail, he said, had been accused by Joseph's commander-in-chief, Hassan Bey, of dilatory tactics during the attempt to recapture Derna from Eaton early in May. Hadji Ismail's Arab pride had been hurt by this charge, naturally ; and he accordingly made plans to convey his displeasure to Hassan Bey in the most emphatic manner possible. The time had seemed ripe on the preceding day. Hassan Bey's war chest had been left in a tent that was guarded by four cavalrymen, sympathisers of Hadji Ismail ; so while Hassan Bey was occupied with a council of war, Hadji Ismail, with complete undilatoriness, seized the chest, loaded it on a fast mule, summoned all his supporters, and set off hell-bent for the fertile meadows and the sweet waters of Upper Egypt and the Nile. Our informant, however, had not been over-enthusiastic about making this long trip to Upper Egypt, for something told him that since Hadji Ismail had been quick to deprive Hassan Bey of his war chest, he would doubtless be equally ruthless in refusing to share it with his followers.

When we had heard this tale, King Dick got to his feet and pulled his headcloth down firmly on his head. " That Hassan Bey," he said, " he got to fight now, and fight hard. Hoy ! This what we been waiting for, Albion."

He shouted for Abdul Rahim : extra rations for the men—feed 'em and get 'em ready to move ; he sent a messenger flying to Hamet in the fort, giving him the intelligence we'd just received ; bawled for his orderly to bring up our horses.

" Now," he said, " we see Eaton, and then I think we get some exercise." He looked thoughtfully from Lydia to me. " You come along, too," he told her. " Everybody feel better if they know it all right for you to come along and watch."

I never saw such a change in a man in so short a time as I saw in Eaton when Leitensdorfer admitted us to his office in the battery. He couldn't sit still : he kept fingering his bandaged arm with his right hand, picking it up and moving it a little, as if fearing it might stick to the table : he kept crossing and uncrossing his legs, rubbing his chin, scouring the corners of his lips with his tongue, wiping the outer corners of his eyes with his knuckles. He was for ever contracting his brows, as if trying hard to understand something, and his head moved constantly, a slight, never-ending nodding, almost as though he grimly admitted the seriousness of the situation in which he found himself. The flesh under his eyes was dull red, and puckered, which made him look as though he hadn't slept for a month ; and he swallowed repeatedly, as a man does when he's had bad news.

" Took his war chest, did they ? " he said, when we'd given him our intelligence. " I knew damned well they were moving up to attack when I saw 'em peeking down from the escarpment half an hour ago. But I never guessed they'd lose their money. Now they're as desperate as Hamet is."

He looked up at Leitensdorfer. " Send a messenger to the *Argus* and the *Hornet*. Tell Hull to keep his eye on the wadi west of the town. Tell him they'll probably try to sneak down that wadi. He can reach it with his long twelves. I guess he'll be willing to do that much for Hamet. And you might make one more appeal for marines. He won't let us have 'em, of course, now that he's been ordered away from here."

He turned back to us. " I swear to God, gentlemen—I hate to admit it—I'm entirely at a loss ! Never in the history of the world, I do believe, was any military commander ever put in such a position ! " He gnawed at a finger-nail, rubbed the corners of his eyes with a knuckle, drew a deep breath, and looked at us expectantly.

" This is a cavalry matter," King Dick said pleasantly. " Nothing for you to do but keep men here in case something bad happen up there." He jerked his head towards the meadows that lie between Derna and the escarpment.

"Don't I know it!" Eaton cried. "But here it is—the thing we've trained for! They need us, and I can't help 'em. There's no dodging it! 'That damned coward Eaton!' they'll say. I'm caught! If that skunk Lear does what I damned well know he *is* doing, he makes me not only a coward, but a traitor to friends when they need me most."

"He does nothing of the sort," Lydia said. "You're a soldier, and you're under orders. A soldier under orders has no choice except to obey them."

"Oh, my God!" Eaton cried. "I know that as well as *you* do, ma'am! But the blame falls on America! I represent America! My country's being disgraced by that contemptible rat! I've promised help, food, everything! Now I can't give 'em one damned thing—not even help! All the rest of my life every Arab, every Englishman, every Frenchman —even the Italians and the Portuguese—will be saying 'America! Tchah! Eaton! Yah!' Christ, ma'am, I can't sleep at night for the eyes in the dark! They glare down from the ceiling, from the walls, rolling and accusing . . ."

"General," Lydia said, "you're a brave man, caught in a chain of circumstances for which you aren't responsible and which you cannot control. We're all like that, General. We're all somehow unfortunate, usually through no fault of our own—often because stupid men bring misfortune on us. Your misfortunes have been strange and terrible; you've borne them with more fortitude than I'd have believed possible; and you should feel certain that disgrace can never be connected with your name because of your part in this expedition."

There was a knock at the door, and Leitensdorfer opened it.

"All right, Colonel," Eaton said. "Tell Mr. O'Bannon to come in."

Leitensdorfer stood to one side, and O'Bannon, the lieutenant of marines, almost leaped into the room. His face was fiery red, and his light-blue eyes were eager.

"General, they've come out of that wadi three miles west of town, and they're skirmishing with Hamet's pickets. If I can move close up to the wadi with our fieldpiece, I think I can slow 'em up if they keep on coming."

"I'm sorry," Eaton said. "I can't let you go."

"Sir," O'Bannon said, "if they get their full cavalry strength down from the escarpment, there'll be hell to pay and no pitch hot."

"I've sent word to Hull, Mr. O'Bannon," Eaton said. "The *Argus'* long twelves can handle that wadi as well as you could. I need you here. I'm very sorry, my boy."

O'Bannon stared at him, stared at us; then looked suddenly at the floor. I knew why. I felt the same hot pricking at the back of my eye-balls—not because of O'Bannon, but because of Eaton: because of Hamet: because of Lear and every damned bad thing.

Eaton got up from his table, put his unwounded hand under

O'Bannon's arm and led him to the door. He gave the lieutenant a pat
on the back ; then stood there watching him march away.

When he came back to the table he smiled at Lydia—the first time
he'd smiled since we'd been in the room with him. " When you go out,
ma'am," he said, " stop and say a word to O'Bannon. All three of you
stop. He's a fine boy, and he'll feel this—feel it bad. The day before
you got in from Tripoli, O'Bannon turned back a feint on the part of
some of Joseph's cavalry. When he rode through the city afterwards
the people mobbed him, shouting, ' Long live the Americans ! Long
live our friends and protectors ! ' They nearly smothered him with
flowers. If your troop should happen to ride out, and he couldn't go
out himself, and then on top of that—then if Lear—— Well, stop and
speak to him, will you, ma'am ? "

He looked defiantly at King Dick. " I won't order you out. I won't
order out any man under my command when there's a possibility that
this war is already over : when that letter of Hull's might be regarded
as orders to abandon this post."

" If there's any possibility that the war is over," Lydia said, " they
aren't under your command at all, General. They joined you to help
you defeat Tripoli. If that's disposed of, they're under their own command
and free to do what they wish."

Eaton looked surprised " They are ? Why, I believe they are ! Yes,
that's one way of looking at it, I suppose. Why, yes : I can't make you
be in my army if you don't want to be." He made a rasping sound in
his throat, a sound of supreme disgust. " Army ! Orders ! I wish to God
I'd never seen or heard of an army—not if windbag Commissioners or
Presidents or Secretaries of State can write orders for it that read like
riddles, and make it kiss its country's enemies on the—— Oh, well, go
ahead out, gentlemen. Ride through the town : it'll hearten the people
And stop here on your way. I'll send a letter to Hamet—and by God,
I'd rather have a bullet through my hand than write it ! " To Lydia
he added, " I want you to take it to him, ma'am. He's entitled to have
a word with the lady who taught his sons for three years."

Poor Eaton ! Poor, generous, far-seeing, kind-hearted, lonely, disappointed, wasted William Eaton ! And as Lydia implied, there's hardly
a man alive who can't see himself somehow reflected in William Eaton :
who hasn't a Tobias Lear of his own to thwart his ambitions and to
wreck his dreams.

The *Argus* had opened fire with her long guns when King Dick led
our troop across the wadi to pick up Eaton's letter : then continued on
through the town as Eaton had told us to do. With Lydia beside me I
closed the files, partly because King Dick thought it gave the men added
confidence, partly because he wanted the men anchored at both ends in
case they had to open out into ranks.

Hitherto I had seen Derna only from the top of the escarpment, and from the outside, and I was astounded at its spotlessness, its beauty and richness. There were fountains everywhere, and baths, and luxuriant gardens full of orange, lemon, and fig trees ; through the middle of the principal streets ran marble gutters in which clear water flowed perpetually. The houses looked newly washed in pinks and blues and whites, probably because water for whitewashing was ready to every man's hand ; and that miraculous water seemed even to have affected the dress and the character of the people ; for most of those we saw wore barracans of spotless white, or of striped silk in delicate colours. They called eagerly to us as we passed. " Go with God ! " they shouted. " Save us ! Strike for Hamet ! " The roof-tops were thick with brilliantly garbed people, mostly women, all busy peering off towards the meadows behind the town, but not too busy to toss flowers down upon us and scream encouragement in the manner of Arab women—" lu-lu-lu-lu-lu " endlessly repeated.

When we emerged from the city's rear gate and mounted into the meadows, the throng that covered them put me in mind of a country fair, or of a field on which a circus is arriving. Hamet's fort, which had been a crumbling ruin before we captured the town, had been built up, and on either side of it were newly dug trenches, to prevent it from being flanked. The trenches were full of Hamet's foot soldiers, the parapets of the fort were covered with them ; two regiments of cavalry, dismounted, were taking their ease on the far side of the fort ; and some of the cavalrymen were herding a throng of camels, women, children, and laden pack-horses towards the main encampment on the far side of the big wadi. Far away, where the western wadi showed as a dark streak beyond the Derna meadows, white-clad figures moved rapidly into sight over ridges, and vanished again in folds between them. Between the fort and the far-off figures moved solitary horsemen, in all likelihood scouts reporting the progress of the fighting we could scarcely see. All this movement of white-robed figures upon the meadows made the meadows seem to flutter, flag-like, at the recurrent banging of the *Argus'* guns and the aerial rippings of cannon-balls, which in their passing made the sound an anchor-chain makes when it rattles through a distant hawse-hole. This effect of fluttering was increased by the spattering musketry fire that faintly reached us from those remote figures.

We found Hamet and his personal attendants assembled at the top of the slope on which the fort stood, where they could be plainly seen by all the cavalry. Hamet must have found a hidden wardrobe when he occupied the castle in Derna, for both he and his officers were garbed in finery that glittered and gleamed. He and his horse were covered with gold and jewels, and his costume beat anything I ever saw before, or have seen since. How he could even sit a horse in such finery, let alone ride it and fight from it, was beyond me—though I soon found that he could do all three equally well.

His trousers were white muslin, tucked into yellow half-boots ; his burnoose, though woollen, was transparent, so that the colour of everything beneath it could be clearly seen—a short jacket of crimson silk gold-embroidered, a purple velvet caftan, a broad girdle of gold and silver, and an additional caftan of pale-yellow damask, so long that it fell almost to the ground behind his stirrups. On his head was an enormous snowy white turban draped with a purple and gold shawl that was held in place by an emerald crescent the size of a green banana. The ends of the shawl, which were gold, were tossed over his left shoulder. His gold-mounted pistols were fastened to him by gold chains, and the scabbard and the hilt of his sabre were crusted with jewels that shot out glittering sparks at his smallest movement. His horse's chest was covered with a sort of necklace of gold, and his saddle and stirrups were gold-leafed and studded with rubies and emeralds. Grooms beside him led two relay horses hung with crimson velvet covered by heavy gold embroidery.

When King Dick halted the troop and rode forward with Lydia and me to report to that dazzling figure and give him Eaton's message, King Dick murmured, " Hoy, hoy ! I bet that the grossest costiveness any *these* boys ever saw ! " He partly explained Hamet's gorgeousness by whispering, " These Arab people, they fight better for someone not afraid put on all he own ; but my, my ! Too bad he not on other side ! My goo'ness me my ! I fight all-day-all-night to cut off just what he got on one arm ! "

In spite of Hamet's finery, he was the same simple, kindly gentleman we had first seen on the meadows of Cape Razatin just before the attack on Derna. He seemed not to notice Lydia when he thanked us for the information we had sent him about Hadji Ismail's flight with Joseph's war chest ; but when he had read Eaton's letter, he made a strangled sound : his horse stood straight up on his hind legs, then plunged past us and came to a sudden halt. I think Hamet did it to get out of earshot of his attendants, for with a movement of his head he beckoned us to come forward to him.

" I have had messages," he told Lydia. " I longed for the day to come when I could show my gratitude. Now I can show nothing—a full heart——"

" Your sons themselves were my thanks," Lydia said. " They loved you dearly. They, too, longed for the day to come when—when there'd be an end to all the cruelties around them. No man living could recognise cruelties and injustices more readily than they. Every day they said, ' My father would not permit this ! ' ' My father would not allow that to be done.' They were gentlemen—true princes ! I read the Koran with them : they read the Bible with me ! They understood what most Arabs nowadays cannot understand : the need of sacrificing individualism and family pride in order to maintain the leadership of their race. They were proud, *proud* of the achievements of the Arab people—of their great astronomers, algebraists, their accomplishments in poetry, physics, geography, medicine, surgery : their wonderful architects : their mastery of agriculture and irrigation : their chivalry. I—I——" She put her hand to her breast in a fluttering gesture.

Hamet stared impassively towards the distant figures on the far edge of the plain. " The things that are known to my good and brave friend General Eaton : are they also known to you ? "

I think Lydia didn't trust herself to speak, for she only nodded.

" When that happens," Hamet asked, and he called her, in Arabic, " my daughter " as he did so, " do you think my sons—do you think that man—my brother——"

" No ! " Lydia cried. " No, no, no ! He is a tradesman—a huckster ! He will use them, yes, as a threat, a persuasion ; but kill them ! No, never ! "

Hamet looked her in the eyes. " I see," he said slowly. " I understand ! You think I'll never see them."

" Oh," Lydia whispered. " I hope with all my heart you will ! I hope so with all my heart ! "

Hamet glanced down at himself as if what he saw were somehow unsatisfactory. Then he raised his hands to the emerald crescent on the front of his turban, unpinned it, and give it to Lydia. " Take this small remembrance, my daughter," he said. " When you see it, think of my sons, and occasionally recall the gratitude of an unhappy father."

Seeing that Lydia was on the verge of tears, I spoke quickly and somewhat incoherently. " There'll never be a decent American, as long as there's any memory of history in this world, who won't think countless times, and with hot shame, of the Americans who have done what they're doing to you and to General Eaton—to your sons—to all those thousands of men—all those thousands in Derna."

Hamet pushed his horse close to mine, leaned from his saddle, put his arm around my shoulders and kissed me on the cheek. Then he unchained the gold-mounted pistols from his belt, and gave one to me, one to King Dick.

I've said a thousand times—and whenever I get the chance I'll say again—that Hamet was a great and good man who was sacrificed to American mediocrities, American petty politicians, American determination to put self-seekers and time-servers in office and leave them there. After all, William Eaton was an American ; and America theoretically has the right, established by constant usage, to destroy great Americans by ignoring them, or underpaying them, or disappointing them, or scoffing at their abilities, or refusing to reward them for their efforts, or refusing to promote able young men over the heads of doddering incompetents. But Hamet wasn't an American : he was a friend in a far land who trusted America, believed in America, was promised help by America ; and any failure to provide that help should have been rightly resented as a stain upon America's honour. If I had my way, I'd

raise a statue to Hamet and set it on a pedestal before the Department of
State in Washington, with the inscription :

> *Hamet Karamanli*
>
> *a Great Man*
>
> *Led to the Heights by Great Americans*
>
> *and Destroyed by Small Ones*

But after all, I'm not a politician, and therefore not privileged to
have my way ; and besides, nothing like that could possibly be done
because small Americans are seldom willing to admit that there are or
ever have been any small Americans ; so they would argue—quite
properly, from their own point of view—that such a statue with such an
inscription would have no value whatever. And probably they'd be
right. But thanks to American freedom of speech and of the press, I can
say what I think of Hamet and of Tobias Lear's—which is to say America's
—treatment of him ; and that opinion, through the years, has in nowise
changed from what it was on that June morning on the meadows back
of Derna, when Hamet pointed out our station to King Dick and me.

It was a mound at the foot of the escarpment, half a mile from the
fort. " Take your troop there and wait," he said. " Joseph's cavalry are
slowly coming down the wadi, trying to drive in our pickets. I'll reinforce
our pickets twice ; then let them be driven in. Joseph's cavalry will follow
them. When our pickets are out of the line of fire, our footmen will open
on Joseph's cavalry from the fort and the trenches. When they hesitate,
as they must, I attack with my cavalry. When you see my cavalry go
out, be in readiness. When we make contact with Joseph's cavalry, then
you too must attack, striking them half a mile in the rear of my own point
of attack ! " He looked pointedly at Lydia. " You, my daughter, must
remain on the mound. That is my order. I ask you to repeat it."

" I'm to remain on the mound," Lydia said in a low voice.

Hamet turned to King Dick. " Everything is clear ? "

" After we cut through, we re-form ? " King Dick asked.

" You re-form," Hamet said, " and wait. I think we can turn them.
If so, attack again when they are turning and drive them hard. I think
we can capture most of their horses. The horses will never take them down
into the wadi. Tell your men to be careful of those horses. Do not shoot
or cut them, for they'll be needed. If, on the other hand, we don't turn
them, come in on their rear and together we will squeeze them, you in
the rear, I in the front. That, I am sure, will be the end. Allah be with
you ! "

When we saluted him, and King Dick had signalled the troop to move forward, Hamet drew his sabre from its glittering scabbard and swung it four times in flashing arcs—to Lydia, to King Dick, to me, and to the troop.

And *this* was the man Tobias Lear and Commodore Samuel Barron had decided to abandon in order to perpetuate as ruler of Tripoli a murderer, a blackmailer, a despoiler of America and Americans !

CHAPTER LXIV

WAR, whether unavoidable or not, is drudgery, boredom, delay, waste, heartlessness, disappointment, cruelty, stupidity, destruction, death, misery, and everything else that's bad ; and not many of those who are doomed to do the actual fighting can find anything pleasant about it, ever.

For a cavalryman, however, thanks to his horse, war is less of a misery than it is for most soldiers. He has his horse to care for and to keep him company ; to carry him and lend him strength when strength is most needed. His horse buoys him up : there's something comforting about the solid suppleness of the beautiful and obedient animal : and there's a wild exhilaration to cavalry movements and above all to a cavalry charge—a feeling of almost superhuman invincibility—a flowing together of horse and man, as though the man had borrowed the speed and sinews of his steed and in return lavished his own training and skill and determination upon the animal, so that the two are an irresistible instrument of attack before which nothing and nobody can stand.

The chief duty of cavalry is to wait as patiently as possible for the proper time to strike, while others do the fighting ; but no man can help being tense and on edge during such a wait ; and when men are tense they make water constantly. Those men of ours were up and down from their horses so frequently that it worried me, but King Dick said it was an excellent sign. " You take out good dog hound for rabbits," he reminded me, " she stop to wet every tree, sick-sem hundred, getting to rabbit swamp : then run rabbits till they dizzy. Bad hound dog go along to swamp, never stop once to wet : let her loose and she forget rabbits. No wet, no good."

Around noon Hamet's cavalry outposts, their burnooses billowing behind them like wings, came trotting back, driven in by superior forces ; and soon afterwards more and more of Joseph's cavalry came up out of the folds and ridges—hundreds of them and added hundreds, until the whole rough plain beyond the meadows was white with them.

I had heard from King Dick and Leitensdorfer about the manner in which Bedouin cavalry prefers to fight—first with insults, then with feints, then with sudden dashes to sound out an enemy, but almost never as we had trained our Jalo men to fight. Bedouin cavalry strikes once, King Dick had said : then sheers off and sometimes doesn't stop running until it has put twenty miles between itself and those struck ; but I doubted greatly that Joseph's men would fight that way to-day. They couldn't run up the escarpment, because it was impassable. They couldn't successfully run back into the narrow winding wadi down which they'd moved, because they'd be chopped to pieces while trying to crowd into it. As I saw it, they could do only one of two things : either try to cut their way completely through Hamet's cavalry and foot soldiers, and regain the escarpment by the road that Eaton held ; or try to destroy Hamet completely, and retake Derna.

There seemed to be no end to the burnoosed cavalrymen that came up out of that wadi. The meadows were covered with them, moving in irregular groups and clusters towards the fort. There were hundreds on hundreds of them—God knows how many : perhaps as many as two thousand.

King Dick came to stand with Lydia and me and watch this scattered mass of attackers coming nearer and nearer, gradually drawing closer and closer together to form squads and troops. The gunfire from the *Argus* had ceased, probably because Hull could no longer lay his guns without hitting the town.

A detachment of Joseph's cavalry, half again as large as our own, left the straggling ranks to move in our direction, led by a sheik in a scarlet burnoose. His beard was bushy and orange-coloured, and his horse pale lavender, extremely beautiful and graceful.

" They feel us out now," King Dick said. He looked apologetically at Lydia. " You hear some groceries now, ma'am ! They very gross abusers. Make even *me* feel very malice. Maybe you be better off some other place."

Lydia gave him a worried glance. " I've heard a great deal of Arab abuse in the last three years. If you think you'll have difficulty answering, perhaps I could——"

King Dick giggled. " Oh my goo'ness me me me ! " he said. " Nuh, nuh, *nuh* ! I try hard to say what I used to hear my wifeses say—my Galla wifeses, when I live in Timbuktu. Her skin always cool on hot days, and she talk just opposite of her skin." He closed his eyes, shook his head and nostalgically murmured " Hoy ! "

The orange-beared sheik in the scarlet burnoose halted his detachment a hundred yards from us, rode forward another twenty yards with two attendants, and addressed us in a squealing voice. " O abusers of the salt ! Man-sellers ! We spit upon thee ! "

The ranks behind me muttered and grumbled, and their saddles squeaked.

" By the very God ! " King Dick shouted. " An old-woman Turk ! How long have old-woman Turks commanded that army of camel-dung gatherers ? Borrow thy sister's teeth, old woman, that I may hear thee better ! "

The lavender-coloured horse lashed out with his heels, so I think his

rider raked him with spurs. " I hold my nose ! " Orange-beard howled.
" Wipe off thy saddle, emitter of farts ! "

Our black Arabs squawked protestingly.

" Begone to the Eunuchs' Bench, castrated one ! " King Dick cried.
" Go blow thy onion breath on whores in the alleys of Cairo."

Our black Arabs cheered him.

" Son of a dog ! " Orange-beard shouted. " Thou hast the face of a
pork-eater ! If thy heart is not that of a milk-peddler, ride out on that
skeleton, that dog-meat from a Jew's butcher shop ! Let a man hack
open that pig-testicle thou callest a head ! "

The black men behind us gnashed their teeth, rattled their sabres, and
made animal sounds.

" My, my," King Dick said faintly, " that an invitation ! " With both
hands he pulled his headcloth down over his ears. " Brush the fleas from
thy pink whiskers," he roared at Orange-beard. He whipped out that
enormous sword of his, and seemed to lift his horse into a full gallop
by main strength.

The orange-bearded Arab put spurs to his horse at the same time,
laying a course designed to intercept King Dick. From our own men
and from Orange-beard's followers came howls of ululations.

King Dick's horse seemed almost to elongate himself until his belly
touched the meadow, so swiftly did he gallop ; then suddenly his forelegs
stiffened : he slid to a stop in a shower of dirt, turned at a right angle
to his former course, and seemed to flee from Orange-beard.

Our men were silent : the shouts of Orange-beard's men were
triumphant.

Orange-beard wheeled his horse in pursuit of King Dick, and King
Dick bore off in a curve so sharp that his horse leaned at an impossible
angle. Orange-beard's two attendants, suddenly aware of King Dick's
intentions, put spurs to their own horses ; but they were too late. King
Dick, racing behind and between them, flicked first at one, then at the
other—little dabs with that huge sword of his, delicate dabs, such as I
had seen him make in Haiti when he dabbed at flies with his cocomacaque.
The first man hurled his sword from him, clawed ludicrously at nothing,
and pitched sideways from his saddle. One of his feet caught in the
stirrup, and he was dragged bumpingly by his furiously bucking horse.
The second fell stiffly back over his horse's crupper, landed on his head,
and collapsed in a motionless heap.

King Dick wheeled again and charged straight at Orange-beard, who
reined his horse back on its haunches. I had the impression of King
Dick's spreading himself over that orange-bearded Arab and surrounding
him with a flickering light that was his sword ; then the Arab's sword flew
high in the air, slowly turning, came down point first and stood quivering.
King Dick had the Arab by the wrist, the point of his sword at the Arab's
armpit. They remained as they were for a moment, like a group of
statuary ; then King Dick turned to scrutinise the troop that Orange-

beard had commanded. There was movement and tumult in its ranks, and we could hear confused shouting.

"Move back," I said to Lydia. "They're getting ready to attack."

She only caught at my arm.

King Dick had raised his sword to draw the attention of those tumultuous Arabs; gestured with it at Orange-beard's head; then signalled to the troop to move back.

The pantomime was unmistakable: either Orange-beard's troop could be off on other matters, or Orange-beard's head would be off.

With another gesture King Dick gave permission for the removal of the two unhorsed attendants, one of whom showed signs of life. When two men obediently rode out from the ranks to pick them up, and the ranks themselves turned reluctantly away, Orange-beard climbed from his saddle and set off towards us, a dejected grotesque, leading a lavender horse.

King Dick leaned from his saddle to pick up the Arab's sword, then followed Orange-beard back to his rapturous Jalo men. So far as I could tell, he wasn't even breathing hard.

He turned Orange-beard over to Abdul Rahim, with instructions to send him to Hamet; then came to stand with Lydia and me once more. When we spoke admiringly of what he'd done, he made light of his success.

"Those people forget swords got points," he said. "Good thing we taught our men thrust'n'stick, not just chop'n'hack! All we do is wait till they lift their arms high up to chop'n'hack: then nick where they ticklish, Pow!"

He wasn't far wrong.

We sat there on that mound through the hottest part of that long hot afternoon while Joseph Karamanli's generals sent sortie after sortie up into musket range in fruitless efforts to force their way past the fort. When they tried desperately to get between the fort and the city gate, they were galled by fire from fort, trenches, and city walls, and had to draw back out of range when Hamet's cavalry galloped from behind the fort to pour a volley into them. When they tried a circling movement in force, they exposed themselves to Eaton's guns and again had to draw back. After each sortie riderless horses galloped aimlessly across the meadows; white-robed figures hobbled, crawled, dragged themselves to safety, or lay huddled where they fell until solitary riders came out to pick them up and carry them away.

"They never get through," King Dick said, after the fifth sortie. "That Hamet, he's Hamet. If he let 'em through, he have his throat cut: so he never let 'em through! Never! Pretty soon they wake up remembering they be better off somewhere else. Pretty soon now!"

The words were hardly out of his mouth when a troop of horsemen detached themselves from among the rearmost of Joseph's cavalry and set off slowly towards the wadi out of which they'd clambered six hours earlier. They moved slowly because they carried wounded men across their pommels, or led horses to whose saddles dead men were lashed.

I knew what that meant. Every last one of our troopers waiting patiently in line knew what it meant. And I could hear them settling themselves in their saddles and taking a fresh feel of their stirrups, as men do when they've got to ride hard. It meant, of course, that Joseph's generals had realised that there was no way out of that meadow, no way to get back to their camp and their provisions, except by the wadi through which they'd entered. It meant that they had decided to retreat, and that this was the time for Hamet and for us to strike. If we struck hard enough, we could turn that retreat into a rout !

I think the only things Lydia and I hadn't talked about all through that long hot frenzied afternoon were war, and the people and the things we hated. We'd talked of William Bartram ; of the French in Philadelphia ; of Surinam and Cette ; of how we'd build our house out of stone with a small wing on either side ; of how we'd build the barn of larch, which James Anderson's book on agriculture says is the best of all woods for building, and paint it red with paint made of red ochre and milk ; of the book by Moreau de St. Méry that she hoped to translate ; of pea soup and fish chowder and finnan haddie and blueberry pie and cinnamon buns ; of apple toddy and Fish House punch as made in Philadelphia ; of my Aunt Emmy, and how she called my uncle " Mr. Tyng " even after being married to him for twenty years, and whether she called him " Mr. Tyng " when they were in bed together ; of the purple dress she'd worn when Stuart painted her ; of the dress I had seen on Pauline Bonaparte in Cap François, and of how Lydia would have just such a dress to wear on nights when we were alone together ; of Arabs and whether they weren't more sensible than other people in building their houses around a courtyard and refusing to allow public display of their womenfolk ; of the decorative effects obtained from a flower garden limited to zinnias and sweet peas ; of the number of ears of green corn that we would devour of a September evening when we were once again in the land of green corn ; of the stupidity of European people in refusing to plant green corn, and the stupidity of Americans in refusing to plant tomatoes because of considering them poisonous ; of exactly why Lydia seemed to me far more beautiful and infinitely more desirable than Pauline Bonaparte ; of the number of dogs that were allowable on a farm, and whether a boy should be allowed to let his dog sleep at the foot of his bed ; of John Milton and blind men and whether a man just married and then blinded wouldn't for ever see his wife as he had last seen her, and whether a man who truly loves a woman doesn't always see her as being young and beautiful . . . Ah, Lydia . . . But when we saw those cavalrymen moving towards the wadi with their dead and wounded, I spoke to her of war for the first time.

"When we start," I told her, "I want you to make for the rear. Go to the big wadi and work down it to Eaton's battery. Tell Eaton——"

"I'm not going, Albion."

"I want you to go. I don't want you here. It might make me—I might be apprehensive if I saw you standing here, all alone. I won't have you on my mind."

"I won't go," Lydia cried. "I *want* to be on your mind ! You'll ride faster if you know I'm here. I won't be separated from you ! I *won't* ! You mustn't tell me again. I won't listen ! Didn't General Eaton say I could come here ? Didn't Hamet tell me to stay here ? "

I stared at her like a moonstruck fool, wondering how any one woman could look so beautiful in so many different ways. When she was happy, she enchanted me ; yet I was newly enravished by her when she was angry ; and I discovered equally diverse sweetnesses in her when she was pliant and when she was stubborn ; in blazing heat and in bitter cold ; in Arab tents, in palaces, or in farmhouses.

"Do you really want me to go ? " she asked.

"No," I said, " I don't."

She turned her horse and went straight through the silent ranks to stand behind them, out of the way. She never liked saying good-bye. She thought it was a kindness to everybody concerned to make such things as abrupt and as matter-of-fact as possible. She never liked public love-making, either, whether in life or in books. She said it was like making love in broad daylight on a park bench : only cheap people exposed themselves in such ways.

CHAPTER LXV

HAMET'S cavalrymen were pouring out from behind the fort. The soldiers on the ramparts of the fort were firing. The foot soldiers had climbed from the trenches and were racing forward to throw themselves on the ground, fire and reload, then race forward again. More and more of Joseph's cavalry were moving to the rear, in the wake of those who were carrying the dead and wounded. Hamet's cavalry were converging, as if the fort were sprouting horns—horns that would curve together to form two long lines. At the head of one of the horns, recognisable by his towering turban, was Hamet himself.

King Dick trotted up and down before our men, giving them final instructions. He wagged that enormous sword of his as lightly as a teacher toys with a pointer, and with it indicated the exact spot where we must strike . . . Our front rank was to fire one pistol into the enemy cavalry when ten paces off, but hold the fire of the other pistol for emergencies, such as helping a friend out of trouble . . . The second rank was to depend on sabres and not use its pistols at all, except in cases of dire necessity ; but on getting into the clear after we had cut our way through, the second rank was to turn and use both pistols. Then the troop was to re-form immediately and reload.

" Strike only men, my children," King Dick kept reminding them. " Clear their saddles, my little Bosos ! Their horses we need and must have. Keep together. Remember all your lessons. Watch enemies who have fallen, lest they bite ! And let me see no one dismount for booty until I give permission, unless you wish a nose flattened by this ! " He shook an enormous fist in their faces, and they smiled delightedly.

" What you laughing at ? " he demanded. " You stop to pick up an inlaid musket and first thing you know you do your laughing inside a hyena with fleas ! Watch me and obey me, little Bosos, and there will be booty for all ! "

He looked over his shoulder at Hamet's cavalry. The two columns had joined and were moving rapidly forward in two long, wavering ranks. King Dick moved to the right of our own line, flirted his hand towards the restless mass of Joseph Karamanli's cavalry—a horde now, unformed, shapeless, seemingly undecided ; unable to re-form, unwilling to retreat.

Our two grey-burnoosed lines trotted forward and broke into a canter. I looked back at Lydia : already she was a small dim figure, obscured by the dust we'd raised. I heard King Dick shout " Hoy ! " We went into a gallop, and the earth slid smoothly towards us and beneath us : Joseph Karamanli's cavalry, too, seemed to slide towards us, as if drawn by the maelstrom of janglings and clatterings and thunderings in which we moved.

That's a strange thing about a cavalry charge : the object towards which you move seems to come irresistibly to you, not you to it. The world reels towards you with startling rapidity ; there's no time to hear, no time to take precautions, no time to feel, measure, take aim. Yet you have sensations and many of them : you remember the smell of sweaty wool, the staring eyes, the open mouths of the cavalrymen on whom you charge —open mouths that seem to give out no sound. You remember the salty taste of gunpowder when you fire a pistol into those open-mouthed faces, and you hear sounds, too : the grunts of men, slashing and hacking ; waves of howling ; a never-ending clattering and clacking and clashing of accoutrements. But you don't feel much : afterwards you find bruises, enormous black and blue spots on thighs, knees, hips ; sabre-cuts, even ; hacked wrists and knuckles—and you ask yourself, " I wonder how I got that ? " But at the time such things occur you're conscious of nothing but determined and violent exertion, mingled with an exuberant elation impossible to describe. You are vaguely surprised at the ease with which a horse and rider can be swept aside by the lightest of sabre strokes : the unexpected manner in which an enemy, hopelessly out of reach, seems to fall at the mere threat of a thrust, but with chest or throat spouting blood.

At one moment the mass of reeling, whirling, rearing, furious-faced men, the tangle of wild-eyed horses, seemed an unending, impenetrable forest of animals and maddened humans. The next moment we had hacked through them and were in the clear : nothing lay before us but the green meadows, the northern outskirts of Derna, the pale blue Mediterranean, with the masts of the *Argus* and the *Hornet* half obscured by the town. Behind us in a haze of dust were Joseph Karamanli's cavalry, all galloping towards the wadi, riderless horses pursued by dismounted men, men who lay quiet, men who struggled to climb up with mounted comrades. They were running ; they had given up ; they had been beaten in their effort to drive Hamet out of Derna !

King Dick, perched on a knoll, was standing in his stirrups, bawling " Hoy ! " and signalling us to hurry. All around him our black troopers were reloading their pistols, filing nicks from their sabres, tying up wounds, boasting to each other. Each one, to hear him tell it, had slain a great sheik, a giant of a man : each one, in doing so, had split a skull wide open, from turban to throat, each had severed a head from a body, each had slain two men at one blow. I heard Moraja, the sergeant with the blue-heron voice, swearing by the very God that he had sliced off a sword arm ; that the sword had fallen point first into the earth, still clutched by the amputated hand and arm, whereupon the great strength left in the arm had wrenched the sword from the ground and hurled it after Moraja.

Our losses were next to nothing. Two men had gashes on their heads, one had a gashed shoulder, another had lost two fingers : that was all.

King Dick silenced them and lined them up. " Listen closely," he bellowed above the clattering, shooting, and shouting that rose from galloping hundreds behind us. " We must have horses ! You must take the horses from Joseph's men. If they have no horses they cannot make trouble for us. Listen : we ride fast, double file, till we reach the wadi. Then we cut in : then they must let go their horses to get down into the wadi."

That wild ride to the wadi, parallel to the galloping, panic-stricken horsemen of Joseph's army, resulted exactly as King Dick had predicted. When, just short of the wadi, we turned and attacked again, those men of Joseph's were caught in a box, with Hamet attacking in the rear, the escarpment on one side, us on the other, and the wadi before them. They had no choice except to dismount and slide down on foot into the wadi.

How many men Joseph's army lost we never learned. We counted sixty dead men : picked up seventy-two wounded ; but for every dead and wounded man there were four riderless horses. The meadows back of Derna looked like a horse fair. Horses were everywhere, all of them saddled, all equipped with saddlebags, water-skins, and personal belongings. Five hundred and eleven horses were rounded up on those meadows that afternoon. At one stroke Joseph's army had been rendered almost immobile and impotent. And the worst of it was that if Eaton had been able to march to that wadi with the two hundred marines he'd been promised in the beginning, but that Lear and Barron had withheld from him, he could have cut off the only remaining line of retreat and not one of Joseph Karamanli's horses could have escaped. Not one ! Hamet and Eaton could have hacked Joseph's army to pieces at their leisure, and been in Tripoli in three weeks.

I'll never forget Hamet's return to Derna that evening.

For years that city, like Tripoli, had been oppressed by Joseph Karamanli ; all through the day the men and women in it had apprehensively listened to the pounding of the guns, and wondered helplessly what their fate would be if Joseph Karamanli's troops swarmed among them. And now, in the rosy dusk, when the scent of roses and orange blossoms and jasmine was heaviest, Hamet came back to them, a regal figure in flowing robes, brilliant with jewels, mounted on the most beautiful of steeds : Hamet at the head of long columns of desert warriors who had fought a good fight to free the land from oppression, injustice, and the rule of evil men. He must have looked to them like a god, for the streets of Derna were roaring, tumultuous, screaming, adoring, rivers of weeping and grateful humanity. Women threw flowers from the house-tops. Men clung to our stirrups to touch and pat us. Children scrambled to the pommels of our saddles to tie ribbons to our bridles.

We escaped at last from that hysterical multitude and crossed the wadi to Eaton's battery to find the Greek cannoneers on the ramparts, listening to the astounding volume of rejoicing that rose above the palms and the minarets like a sort of audible Aurora Borealis.

I didn't see Eaton on the ramparts, but King Dick and I agreed that he was probably eager to hear what had happened.

" Organise patrols for to-night and to-morrow," King Dick told Abdul Rahim. " We join you as soon as we see the general, but get the patrol moving. Find out where Joseph's men go, what they do."

As the troop moved off, Leitensdorfer came out of the battery, said a word to the sentry, and raised his hand in silent greeting.

" We stopped to see the general," I said. " We thought he'd like a report."

" He knows," Leitensdorfer said. " Hamet sent word to him."

" Did he know we took five hundred and eleven horses ? "

Leitensdorfer just nodded.

" We gave 'em a terrible beating," I said. " Hamet fought a great battle."

" You didn't do badly yourselves, my friends, isn't it ? " Leitensdorfer said. He spoke heavily, and I knew something was wrong.

" Perhaps if you let us see the general," Lydia said, " he'd feel better."

" He's asleep," Leitensdorfer said. " He spent most of the day working on that letter to Barron."

I couldn't bear to think of Eaton sitting in that stuffy, fly-filled room in that sun-baked battery, pleading and explaining and protesting and

urging, arguing against treachery and bad faith. What was worse, I
knew Leitensdorfer wasn't telling the truth. Eaton couldn't be asleep.
He wasn't one to sleep while Hamet was fighting for his life. He'd have
wanted to be the first to question us about every detail of our defeat of
Joseph's cavalry. I didn't want to think about that jug of lakby that he'd
had to use when Lear's wrongheadedness had dried up all the juices
in him. That jug of lakby . . . !

"Poor man," Lydia said. "Poor, poor man ! "

There was nothing more to say. There was nothing for us to do but
move on to our camp outside the gardens of Bu Mansur.

We fought and defeated Joseph Karamanli's army on June tenth ;
and when our night patrols came in on the morning of June eleventh
they reported that Joseph's camp was moving straight back from the
escarpment ; that the howling and wailing over their losses in men and
horses could be heard for miles across the desert.

We had plans to make, and they had to be made in secrecy. Our best
means of escape, as King Dick saw it, was to strike due east, past Cape
Razatin and Bomba, until we reached the main caravan trail bearing
south-west through Bir Hacheim towards Jalo. This trail, our men said,
was thick with water-holes, and was far enough to the eastward to baffle
any part of Joseph's army that might sufficiently recover from its defeat
to think of trying to make trouble for us. From it, too, side trails led off
to the oases of Giarabub and Siwa, and thence to Upper Egypt ; so that
those who rode with us could leave us whenever they wished and make
for any destination that pleased them.

There were supplies to be bought secretly ; every man in the troop
had to repair all equipment damaged in the battle ; so all through the
eleventh we were busy and on the evening of that day the blow fell

We sighted the frigate at five in the afternoon, coming in fast from
the westward ; and at nine that night Leitensdorfer came for us. The
general, he said, had received a letter from Lear and wanted to see us :
wanted to see Mrs. Hamlin, too.

I was surprised at Eaton's appearance when we entered his headquarters in the battery. He seemed actually cheerful, and had lost that
death's-head look. He jumped up to offer Lydia a chair, and was almost
benevolent with King Dick and me.

"I wanted you to have this news first of all," he said. "You'd
anticipated it, and—well, you may be in a position to make use of it." He
picked up an open letter and wagged it at us. "Here's a letter from
Rodgers, written June fifth, saying peace is concluded between the
United States and Joseph Bashaw. No further hostilities. We're to
evacuate and withdraw our forces from Derna according to a treaty
signed by Tobias Lear and Joseph Bashaw. I'm moving out of here on
the *Constellation* to-morrow night. I'm taking Hamet and the Americans

and the Greeks—and you, if you'll come. Of course, that's strictly between us. You know what would happen if word got out."

I said I did.

He picked up another letter. "Here's one from Lear. Mighty and polite. Of course it was all Barron's idea that he should negotiate with Joseph ! And of course he got splendid terms—splendid ! And honourable ! Joseph wanted two hundred thousand dollars, but Lear beat him down to sixty thousand ! Aren't you proud of him, Hamlin ? "

He didn't look at me, and none of us said anything.

"Yes," Eaton went on. " Lear says right out that our heroic bravery here at Derna had made a deep impression on the Bashaw ! And what do you think ! He made every possible effort to develop that delusion in the Bashaw's head ! Yes, sir ! It takes a smooth specimen like Lear to keep Joseph from forgetting that Americans aren't worth a damn ! But when it came to Hamet, Lear, couldn't do much. No, no ! Maybe Hamet can have his wife and children back some day—maybe ! But he's got to get out of the country and stay out : never bother Joseph again. I'll tell you what I think : I think he made a secret agreement with Joseph about Hamet's family. I'll bet anything you want that Hamet never sees his wife and children again, and that Lear's a liar when he says he did all he could for Hamet."

" I wouldn't risk a penny on such a bet," I said.

" Insufferable and horrible ! " Lydia whispered.

"Yes," Eaton said. "Everything about the whole business is so dreadful that you can't single out any one part as being worse than another. I suppose Lear's treachery to Hamet and to me, and his amiability towards a man who has proved himself a practitioner of fratricide, treason, perfidy to treaty, and systematic piracy is as bad as anything can be ; but somehow or other Lear's condescension to soldiers is what turns me completely inside out ! He's even got the gall to put it in writing ! He wants O'Bannon and me and our other brave countrymen to accept his sincere congratulations on an event which our heroic bravery has tended to render so honourable to our country ! So honourable ! My God ! Praise from a jellyfish ! Condescension from a worm ! Military acclaim from a puff-ball colonel ! What was it Shakespeare said ?—' a colonel who never set a squadron in the field, and, like a spinster, thinks a division is a form of minuet.' That's not it, but it's something like it ! "

He dismissed Lear and frowned at me. " If I understood your wife correctly, you don't wish to leave here when I do."

" You understood her correctly, sir," I said. " All our arrangements were made on the same basis as yours with Hamet. The difference is that you were acting for our government, whereas we were acting as private citizens. I know only too well that a government can do things no decent man could stoop to. That's how King Dick sees it, how Lydia sees it, and how I see it. We realise you've got to obey orders, and take

Hamet with you, and of course we know you can't put the Arabs and all our sympathisers in Derna aboard the *Constellation*. I only thank God, sir, that I'm not in *your* boots ! "

" I wish your wife would reconsider," Eaton said.

" It's impossible," Lydia said. " I understand you're thinking only of my best interests, but our black Arabs need King Dick and Albion—and they need me."

" What are your plans ? " Eaton asked.

" Patrols out all day to-morrow," King Dick said. " We'll carry your messages and help out till you leave. Things be pretty rappalated when those Arabs find out they sitting in middle of nowhere. Maybe you need a rear guard."

" Thanks," Eaton said. " I can use twenty of your men to-morrow. And you'll want to know where all ammunition, food supplies, and so on are deposited. I'd set detachments to distributing 'em as soon as we've gone."

" That all tended to," King Dick said.

" Livestock, too ? " Eaton asked. " They better take everything if they want to see it again."

King Dick said " Hoy ! " enigmatically, then added broodingly, as if to himself, " One thing I like to know. Where Hamet keep all those brocadled vests, all those fuffy burnooses, all those velavet jellicks ? "

Eaton nodded understandingly. To Leitensdorfer he said, " Make that your business to-morrow, will you, Colonel ? Hamet can't take 'em with him. Too bad we have to leave completely empty-handed."

It's a pity, with America's passion for noisy holiday, that July thirteenth as well as July fourth can't be celebrated with fireworks in America. After all, people easily forget, as I pointed out in the beginning of this book, the meaning of July fourth ; and the fireworks never seem to help them recall it. Perhaps the evil qualities ascribed to the number 13, together with the shameful deed that the celebration would commemorate, would help them remember the reason for the day better than they remember the reasons behind most holidays, and be of more benefit to them.

July thirteenth would be Derna Day : not the day we captured Derna, but the day America went back on her word of honour and abandoned Derna, abandoned her friends, ignored her sacred promises, dealt with those who had flouted, insulted, and robbed her ! I've never cared whether or not my countrymen celebrated the day on which they threw off the yoke of England, as the politicians like to say ; a man might as well brag about the virtue of his wife, or celebrate his own integrity. But I'd be mightily interested in helping America to remember, with fireworks or anything else, the harm that the weakness, blindness, shortsightedness, selfishness, jealousy, and political rancour of small men in high places can bring upon their country and the world.

No soldier who ever lived could have carried out his orders and withdrawn his men in a more masterly manner than did Eaton—and to those of us who knew what was going on, there was an excitement in that withdrawal that was almost unbearable ; for we never knew at what moment Hamet's troops and his foot soldiers and all those people in Derna would understand what was going on and descend on Eaton and his Americans in an overwhelming flood.

At hourly intervals our patrols came down from the escarpment, and the news they brought was hurried to Eaton : then hurried by him to Hamet—hurried openly, too. Our black Arabs who carried the messages, were instructed to talk ; and talk they did : loudly, and to everyone, so that the whole town knew that Joseph's entire crippled army was falling back, falling back, farther and farther : had fallen back eight miles and was still retreating : had crossed the second range of coastal hills, ten miles back from the escarpment, and was still retreating : had fallen twelve miles back ; was now camping fifteen miles away, a routed army, helpless, without food or communications.

At noon on the twelfth Eaton called King Dick and me to the battery. In spite of the blazing heat he was cool as a cucumber and working like a slave. " I want your next patrol," he said, " to take two women out towards the camp of Joseph's army. Hamet got the women for me. They think our whole army's going to follow up yesterday's victory. They think we're going to climb on top of the escarpment and attack—blow 'em into the middle of next week. They think we've had reinforcements from the *Constellation*—marines, food, money, ammunition, eveything ! "

He shook his head. The corners of his eyes were rheumy with fatigue, and he dug at them with his knuckles. " I wish to Christ they were telling the truth ! That army of Joseph's—what's left of it—would never stop running ! Never ! Well—get those women started. Hamet's providing the horses for 'em. When that's done, send me half the men you have left. I'm going to distribute all our remaining ammunition to Hamet's men. They're entitled to it, anyway ; but when they get it, they'll think we *are* going to attack Joseph's army. I'll need thirty men for distributing ammunition : I'll need another ten for a guard of honour. I'm going to inspect the garrison—go through all the motions—divest 'em of heavy baggage—every man at his post, ready to advance at the word ! . . . My God, Lear ought to be shot for this ! Maybe *I* ought to be, too, but I've got to get Hamet and all the Americans and Greeks safely away ! God damn it, I've *got* to ! "

He glowered at us, licked the corners of his lips, and shook his head as if to clear it. " There can't be any mistake about this ! Everybody in Derna's got to think we're attacking ! Why shouldn't they ? If it weren't for Lear, we *would* be attacking ! If it weren't for the damned unspeakable idiocy of that God-damned he-hen-hussy—— Oh, to hell with it ! Get those men over here in a hurry, will you ? "

Knowing what we did know, that inspection trip of Eaton's was

dreadful beyond words, for wherever he went, he was hailed as a con-
quering hero—a saviour.   The townspeople were hysterical when he
went among them, screaming, " Amairika ! Allah ! Amairika ! Father
and saviour ! " The garrison fired a salute of joy when he rode into the
fort, and screamed themselves hoarse.   Hamet's Arab cavalry whirled
their guns over their heads, racing their horses around him in an ecstasy
of admiration.   It was something I couldn't bear to watch, and yet I had
to watch it.

The last thing Eaton did before he went back to the battery was to
set the marines on guard just outside the town, so as to stop any townsman
from approaching the battery.

We went with him to the battery.   The sun was a deep crimson where
it touched the cliffs between Derna and Cyrene, and the furled sails of
the *Constellation*, anchored as close in as she dared, looked as if they'd
been dipped in blood and washed out.

" Get everything packed up and be back here in an hour," he told
us.   " The boats from all three vessels will move in at dark, and I'll send
the field-piece and the Greeks off first."

We saluted him.   I never felt so sorry for a man in my life.

When the troop, in full field equipment, moved out from Bu Mansur
and lined up in a sort of screen that extended outward from the corner
of the battery, we could barely see the boats crawling in from the ships
to the landing place.

God only knows what was in the minds of those black troopers of
ours as they watched the Greeks, dimly seen in the starlight, lower the
field-piece into a boat and silently embark.   So far as we knew, they
thought King Dick was truly a Marabout, I was a Bey from Afghanistan,
and Lydia was my wife and a true Moslem.   Yet Abdul Rahim must
have suspected something, for he muttered to King Dick that if we should
find it necessary to go, since all our friends were going, he would wish to
know—because the men were in doubt and were unhappy.

King Dick spoke as sharply to him as ever I heard him speak to anyone.
" *All* our friends ?   Say one more word to me like that, and your ears
will smoke.   Say two words and they burst into flame ! "

Lydia added in a low voice, " Remind Abdul Rahim that those who
go are our friends, yes, and they go because they have no choice.   But
he and the others are our brothers.   We stay here ! "

" Be ashamed ! " King Dick told him.   " Hide your face, but before
doing so tell the others.   Doubt is a flea in the bowels."

Abdul Rahim was covered with confusion and full of apologies, but
he drifted away in the darkness and I heard the men's saddles creak as
the word went along the ranks.   There was throat-clearing and hawking,
and little gusts of tittering and sniffling ran among them, so I knew they
were pleased.

From the town we could hear piping and discordant singing from
the public square, occasional howlings that I took to be an exuberant

Marabout, the occasional braying of an annoyed donkey ; but in general there was silence as the Greek foot soldiers moved out from the battery and down to the shore. Leitensdorfer rushed out to say he was helping the general with his last-minute preparations, then rushed back into the battery again.

Along towards midnight our sentries stopped a group of men on foot moving silently down our side of the wadi, and when I went to look, I found Hamet and his suite—Hamet, whom I'd last seen, gorgeous in jewels, silks, velvets, and brocades, victoriously riding into Derna, acclaimed with cheers and happy tears—Hamet now in a dark burnoose and headcloth, on foot and carrying a few belongings under his arm and tied to his back by cords !

He and his retinue went silently past us—as complete a reversal, I truly believe, as was ever seen in so short a time : from proud victory to the depths of wretchedness and beggary !

Leitensdorfer came to us again, shook hands violently with King Dick and Lydia : then reached up to me with a gesture that reminded me of a small boy. When I leaned over to him, he put his arms around me and kissed me.

" I am in this damned army, isn't it ? " he said. There were tears in his eyes, and he wiped his nose on the sleeve of his burnoose. " I am still adjutant and colonel, isn't it ? Otherwise I would be with you. Some day, Albion, we will be together again, isn't it, to hunt gazelles and drink lakby."

" When you get to America," I said, " go to Portland and see my uncle, William Tyng, and my Aunt Emmy. Tell them all about Lydia and me. Tell them I never forget them—never ! Not for a minute ! And I don't want them to think of me as unfortunate at all ! If I'd done what Lear's done—if I'd left these men of ours after all the promises we've made to them—I couldn't have faced my uncle any more than I could have faced myself. My mind would have been troubled, always. Tell him he wouldn't have wanted me to do anything else. Tell him I well remember my attempt to argue him into placing security ahead of doing something that needed doing, and have never forgotten his reply : that the only security, the only happiness, is a tranquil mind : that every man has for ever lost all hope of tranquillity when he permits himself, by so much as the blink of an eye, to condone injustice."

Eaton came out of the darkness. " For God's sake, Colonel," he reminded Leitensdorfer in a hoarse whisper.

Leitensdorfer ran towards the marine outpost.

Eaton reached up to shake hands with us. " Very sorry," he said. " Hope everything'll be all right." He seemed to search for words but failed to find them.

Leitensdorfer and the marines came past us at the double ; and Eaton hurried after them to urge them to greater speed. " Don't let down," he called. " Don't let down a minute, or you may be in trouble." That was the last word I ever heard from William Eaton. There was silence for a moment, and I could imagine him standing there looking and listening, like a man waking in the dark, frightened by a dreadful dream and still fearful that it may be reality.

How the word got around so rapidly at two o'clock in the morning, I have no way of knowing. There may have been somebody watching the marines ; and that somebody, seeing them withdrawn, may have spread the news.

At all events, the sound of Eaton's oars was still faintly audible when a doleful wailing came from the city walls. We lit torches then, and set them in the earth at each end of the troop, and in their flickering light we watched townsfolk spew from the gate and towards the battery. They came on foot at first, roaring like madmen, rushing about like animals. They seemed to know by instinct what had happened : seemed endowed with second sight concerning the whereabouts of booty. They seized the horses left by Eaton's officers, struck the tents of the Greeks and the officers, appropriating every last scrap of baggage and equipment that had been left behind, swarmed into the battery, and emerged laden with loot but still howling. More and more people poured towards the water-front, begging to be carried to safety, screaming imprecations, shaking their fists at the black hulk of the *Constellation*, dimly seen offshore against the stars.

A squad of Hamet's cavalry galloped from the gate to push their horses to the water's edge. I never saw men so furious. The leader was the same cock-eyed sheik who had aroused Eaton's ire the day we first met him. He spurred over to us. His cocked eyes were protuberant, and there were gouts of foam on his wispy beard.

" It's true, by God ! " he squalled at King Dick. " They're gone ! Dogs of Christians ! "

" Be calm," King Dick said in his best Arabic. " They had to go. The war is over. Bismallah ! All is for the best. Joseph Karamanli made peace. The general was ordered to go ; also ordered to take Hamet with him. It is Allah's will ! "

The sheik howled like a wolf. " Hamet ? He left us ? Those Christian dogs took him away ? We're lost ! I knew it ! I said it all the time ! All the time I said they were using us, and would abandon us when we had served their purpose ! " Emotion overcame him and he made a squealing noise like a hungry young pig demanding food.

" Be less noisy," King Dick ordered him. " You waste time and make a spectacle of yourself before my troopers, who are not accustomed to enduring the plaints of old women. Be still or I take you apart, starting with your loud windpipe." He whipped out his enormous sword and whisked it beneath the sheik's nose. We could hear the whistling sound it made.

LYDIA BAILEY 445

"We have nothing !" the sheik bellowed. "All is lost !"

"You've got as much as you ever had," King Dick reminded him. "You're no more lost than you were the day before you got to Derna. You threatened to run all the way back to Egypt that day. Remember? Even then I was tempted to take you apart."

"They will fall upon us," the sheik howled. "We will be put to the sword ! Joseph will kill us all !"

"Not if you act like a man instead of like a hyena with a thorn in his sit-upon," King Dick said. "Didn't you hack Joseph Karamanli's army only yesterday? How can Joseph's army do anything to us if we stick together? Half their horses are gone ! They have less food than we'll have when we've helped ourselves to the rice in the houses."

The sheik stared speculatively at King Dick, then started to wheel his horse. King Dick leaned over and seized his bridle.

"Listen," King Dick said. "Since day before yesterday I have cleaned this sword twelve times. Do not make me soil it again ! I know what you are thinking, but we must all share alike. This entire city must move into the desert, by way of Jaghbub and Giarabub. All must go : men, women, children, horses, camels, donkeys, goats. They must be protected—by you ; by us."

"Who will pay us? Who will feed us ?" the sheik screamed.

"The answer to that is this," King Dick said. "Insist on being fed, and I will remove the necessity ! Do you prefer to have your head taken off with this sabre, or to be broken in two with my hands ? Whichever happens, you will no longer need food. Speak quickly ! All of us have business in the city ! We must remove certain things, so that Joseph Karamanli's men cannot have them when they return : fine caftans and jellicks : gold chains : barracans like gauze."

"Hah !" the sheik said. "I have things of my own that I wish to do."

"Harken, Father of the Wandering Eye," King Dick said. "There must be a head—a leader—of everything. We must stand together or fall together ; and since I have no intention of falling, I have decided that I shall be your leader. I will tell you what to do, and until you have done what I say, you can do nothing. Is that satisfactory to you ? I hope so, for if it is not, we will take your horses away and give them to people who wish to stand rather than fall."

The sheik looked proud and arrogant. "What must be done?"

"Get the cavalry and the mounted men," King Dick said. "Prepare the caravan and the foot soldiers. Spread the word among the people : they're to take all food and animals. Leave the money and ammunition to me. Bring all horses to the shore road beyond Bu Mansur. Distribute all the captured horses—one horse to each family. We must leave there by sunrise at the latest. And listen carefully to the promise I now make : If you fail us : if you sulk again : if you let out one more howl from that hyena-mouth of yours, I will pursue you and throw you down from your horse and draw each tooth from your head with my fingers !"

The cock-eyed sheik seemed offended, but when he spoke, his voice was respectful. " Big words, by the very God ! Big words ! " He shouted to his squad of cavalrymen, and the lot of them went pelting back into the town, which by now was in a clearly audible uproar—an all-pervasive threnody of the abandoned.

A little before sunrise we combed Derna from end to end. With the exception of a scattering of ancient Jews, a few beggars, a sprinkling of old women without the strength to understand what was said to them, the entire population of that oasis was on its way to the eastward, a river of laden figures, flowing up the long, long slope and dwindling in the distance to dark insects, outlined for a moment against the rosy skyline before vanishing into the barren wastes beyond.

We pressed close up behind that column of horses, camels, donkeys, mules. Children dropped back to cling to our stirrups and so surmount the slope more easily. So far as we could see, every family (thanks to our victory over Joseph) had a horse to carry its few belongings, and every family within our range of vision seemed wholly free of regrets ; wholly occupied with the business of living. Never a one looked back at Derna, any more than any nomad looks back at his last camping-place.

Lydia, as always, read my thoughts. " They need no one's pity," she said, " any more than we do. Isn't that the way it always is ? The ones for whom we think we ought to feel sorriest are in reality the happiest : those whose lot we're supposed to envy are always the most unhappy." She turned her eyes to the Constellation, which was still in sight, three miles offshore. " Poor Eaton," she murmured. " But poor, poor, successful, important, victorious Tobias Lear ! " Her eyes met mine and clung, and there was no need for her to put in words what was so clear to both of us.

Boston and Washington, Haiti and Africa, by comparison with the happy tranquillity of Cette, where Lydia and I lived so long and so richly after we parted from our friends in Jalo, seem dim and far away : my mind, busy with our vineyards and our unending experiments for William Bartram, finds all those blunderings and failures difficult to remember, like the confused jumble of a dark fantastic dream.

Yet I can remember them, and I'm grateful for them too ; for without them I could never have found the serenity that life with Lydia has brought me. That life has had few regrets. I wish my uncle could have lived to share it with us ; and I shall never cease to wish that all men could be blessed with the same tranquillity.

Why should Justice Samuel Chase have forced his country to bring impeachment proceedings against him ? Why should Bonaparte have had to imprison Toussaint, starve him, freeze him, and destroy him ; then spend his own last days in an island prison ? Why should William

ton have had to drink himself to death ? Why should Tobias Lear have
to put a bullet through his brain ?

Why must so many men be what they consistently are—condoners
injustice or the victims of it, doomed to soured souls, never-ending
cour, and the needless bitterness and sickening burdens of an un-
telligible world ?

THE END

SOURCES

THE FICTIONAL CHARACTERS in *Lydia Bailey* are composites of men and women who existed during the period covered in the book.

Non-fictional characters are based, as far as possible, on their own letters.

Tobias Lear's letters, not yet published, describe Captain Lee's knavery, Lear's own efforts to persuade Christophe not to oppose the French, Captain Rodgers' heroic exertions during the burning of Cap François.

Prentiss's *Life of Eaton* contains Eaton's journal of his expedition, an account of the astounding career of Eugene Leitensdorfer, and Eaton's correspondence with Lear, Commodore Barron, Commodore Preble, Sir Alexander John Ball, Hamet Keramanli and others.

The Navy Department's *Barbary Wars*, Volumes II through VI, are mines of information concerning every detail, disgraceful as well as heroic, of all the actors in our melodramatic war with Tripoli. They even include all secret letters written by Captain Bainbridge in lime juice.

King Dick is portrayed in Josiah Cobb's *A Green Hand's First Cruise*.

A complete list of authorities would be confusingly long and repetitious, and the following will answer the needs of those wishing further information : Beard's *Life of Toussaint L'Ouverture* ; Burton's *Pilgrimage to Meccah* ; Childs' *French Refugee Life in the U.S.* ; Earnest's *John and William Bartram* ; Hassanein Bey's *Lost Oases* ; Hearn's *Two Years in the French West Indies* ; Herskovits' *Life in a Haitian Valley* ; James's *Black Jacobins* ; Ray's *Horrors of Slavery* ; Rodd's *General William Eaton* ; Rohlfs' *Adventures in Morocco* ; Smith's *First Forty Years of Washington Society* ; St. John's *Hayti or the Black Republic* ; Tully's *Narrative of Ten Years' Residence at Tripoli*.

Ea
ha

of
ra
i

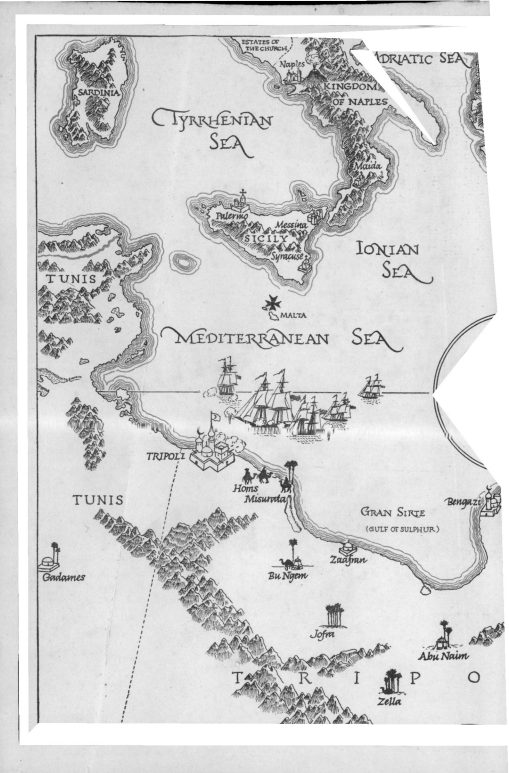